CARTAMANDUA LEGACY

The Lighthouse Duet

CARTAMANDUA LEGACY

The Lighthouse Duet

CAROL BERG

FANTASY

FLESH AND SPIRIT Copyright © 2007 by Carol Berg
   Publication History: Roc mass market paperback, January 2008
BREATH AND BONE Copyright © 2008 by Carol Berg
   Publication History: Roc mass market paperback, January 2009

First SFBC Printing: January 2009

Published by arrangement with
Roc
Published by New American Library, a division of
Penguin Group (USA) Inc., 375 Hudson Street,
New York, New York 10014, USA

Visit the SFBC online at http://www.sfbc.com

ISBN# 978-1-61523-842-2

Printed in the United States of America.

Contents

Cartamandua Legacy: Flesh and Spirit

—◆——————◆—

For Pete and the greatest of all fantasy adventures

Acknowledgments

Best thanks to my ever-attentive muse, Linda, for prodding my thinking. Heaps, mountains, and really awfully luminescent thanks to Susan, Laurey, Glenn, Brian, Catherine, and Curt for refusing to let me slide over those tough details; to Markus, the Fighter Guy, for combat review; and to the doc-on-the-net, Doug Lyle, for a few gory consultations. And, as always, to my readers for the words that get me through the tough days and my family for their forbearance when I go into hermit mode.

The cusp of autumn arrives untimely. Dun haze. Tarnished gold. Leaves . . . glory dulled . . . whipped from their branches. Wolves gather, howling, gnawing the light. No more the culmination of summer, but harbinger of bitter blue days and ever longer nights. The dance is finished, and my heart aches for the waning season. Hollow. Wanting. Dare I sleep?

—Canticle of the Autumn

PART ONE

The Cusp of Autumn

Chapter 1

On my seventh birthday, my father swore, for the first of many times, that I would die face down in a cesspool. On that same occasion, my mother, with all the accompanying mystery and elevated language appropriate for a prominent diviner, turned her cards, screamed delicately, and proclaimed that my doom was written in water and blood and ice. As for me, from about that time and for the twenty years since, I had spat on my middle finger and slapped the rump of every aingerou I noticed, murmuring the sincerest, devoutest prayer that I might prove my parents' predictions wrong. Not so much that I feared the doom itself—doom is just the hind end of living, after all—but to see the two who birthed me confounded.

Sadly, as with so many of my devotions, some to greater gods than those friendly imps carved into the arches and drainpipes of palaces, hovels, latrines, and sop-houses, my fervent petition had come to naught. I'd been bloody for two days now, the rain was quickly turning to sleet, and I seemed to have reached the hind end of everything . . .

"I've no quarrel with ye, Valen, ye know that." The hairy brute stuffed my sweetly chinking leather purse into the folds of his cloak and returned to burrowing in my rucksack. "Ye've been a fine comrade these months. But ye've need of more care than I can give ye, and I've told ye, I can't be hallooing with no monkish folk. If I thought so much as a slavey's hovel lay within thirty quellae, I'd drag ye there."

"And as you're going to abandon me here, well . . . no use wasting good plunder on maggot fodder," I said bitterly, teeth chattering, lips numb. The cold rain sluiced down the neck of my sodden jaque and collected about my knees in the ruts of the ancient road. My elbows quivered as I tried to hold my chest above the muddy water. This damnable goat track had likely not been used since they hauled in stone and wood to build the ghostly abbey tucked into the misty, folded land below us. "I've watched your back for a twelvemonth, you devil. Not a scratch have you suffered since Arin Fay."

One by one Boreas pulled out the remaining carefully wrapped bundles: the onyx jewel case crammed with chains, bracelets, and jeweled brooches, the gold calyx, two daggers with ruby-encrusted hilts—the finest prizes of our infamy. Just one of the daggers could outfit a man with a decent horse, a sword, a thick wool cloak with no holes in it, and a pleasant trimonth of meat, drink, and fair companionship. I'd paid a pretty price in blood and flesh for collecting this bit of plunder, and—Magrog's demons devour this beast I'd foolishly called friend—I wasn't even to profit from it.

He stuffed my goods into his already bulging sack. "None o' this lot'll do ye no good. Wasn't a monk bred won't steal whatever he lays an eye on. And yer in no fit state to argue with them ... or me neither, come to that."

The arrow point embedded deep in my thigh and the fist-sized gouge that had started seeping warm blood on my back again bore ample witness to his verity on the last point. I *did* need help more than I needed my booty, and a wounded man could do far worse than a monastery. These concessions did nothing to ease my mind, however, as I was not yet at the abbey gates and not at all sure anyone would be traveling this particular road with night coming on and a three-year civil war and a sevenday's deluge to keep folk by their own hearths.

I ought to have been angrier with Boreas. But gods knew I'd have done the same were he the one collapsed in the muck, wailing that fire-eyed Magrog himself could not make him take one more step. And I was certainly in no fit state to forcibly reclaim my belongings.

"Just get me down to the gate," I croaked, another wave of chills washing me closer to the grave. "My share ought to pay you for that at least. And leave me one luné for an offering."

"I daren't. The baldpates'll have me swinging ere I kiss ye farewell. No worry, lad. One of 'em'll pass by here and see to ye. And their Karish god teaches 'em to give alms to them with naught, so you're better off with no silver in your pocket."

He shook his head and shrugged his massive shoulders as if the entire mystery of the holy universe was puzzling him at that moment. Then he pulled one last bundle from my rucksack—a flat, squarish parcel, two handspans on a side, wrapped in multiple layers of oiled cloth—and peeled open one flap.

"Have a care; the rain will ruin that," I said, attempting to draw one knee up high enough that I could slide my foot underneath me. If I could just get back to my feet, find a thick branch to lean on, perhaps I could stagger down the hill a little farther on my own.

"Is it plate?" he asked, shaking the bundle and getting no sound. "Heavy enough, but it don't feel right. I don't remember nothing this shape."

My left boot squelched into place under my hip, jarring the festering wound in my thigh, shooting bolts of white-hot fire up and down my leg. "Aagh! It's a book. More valuable than plate. More valuable than those daggers to the right people. And I can send you to the right people if you'll just get me to a leech."

Boreas shifted backward, just out of my reach. "A book! Ye're twinking me, right?"

He poked his dirty fingers into the corner of the parcel, and then glared down at me dumbfounded. "You donkey's ass! Have ye an arrow planted between yer ears as well? All the rich stuff we had to leave behind and ye hauled out a blighting book?"

He threw the parcel and the empty rucksack to the ground and laid his boot into my backside. My shaking elbows collapsed, and I fell forward into the mudhole. Though I twisted enough to avoid a direct hit, I jarred the broken-off arrow shaft protruding from my thigh. Lifting my face from the muck and spewing mud from my mouth, I bellowed like a speared boar.

Unconcerned, Boreas crouched beside me, rifling my clothes. He tossed aside my bracers and the rag I had used to dry my long-lost bow, stuffed my knife into his own belt, and unwrapped the last bite of sour bread I'd hoarded for more than a day and crammed it into his mouth. Fumbling at the waist of my braies, he pulled out a small bag the size of my palm—a scrap of green wool I'd sewn myself and soaked in tallow until it was stiff. "What's this?"

I grabbed for the little bag, but he snatched his hand out of my reach. "By Mother Samele's tits, Boreas, you've got to leave me something."

He yanked it open, sniffed at its contents, and then gaped at me as if I had sprouted three arms of a sudden, shaking his shaggy head until the drips flew off it. "Nivat seeds! But you've no bent to use such stuff . . ."

"Of course not, you clodwit. Would we have scraped and starved this year past if I were some misbegotten spellcaster?"

Lips curled in disgust, he pulled the silver needle and the jagged fragment of mirror glass from the little bag. "By the night lords—"

"The bag was hid in the jewel box." I jumped in quickly to stop his thick head pondering too much. "The nob was surely pureblood. Richer than a prince. And surely Magrog's henchman to practice such perversion." I could stanch my babbling no better than I could stanch the blood from my shoulder.

He dropped the things back into the little green bag and crammed the bag into his pocket. "So you decided to sell the nivat on your own and jupe me out of my share. I thought I knew you, Valen. I thought you were my comrade."

Rain pounded the soggy ground. My gut sent a warning, like a lightning flash beyond the hills. "I thought we could use the seeds to make feast bread come season's turn. Offer it to the Danae. Change our luck. Come, you wouldn't take everything."

"Ye said yerself a man makes his own luck. I'm making mine."

No plea could induce him to leave anything he thought he could sell. Nivat was very expensive, as were the quickened spells worked from it. Only nobles, pureblood sorcerers, or desperate twist-minds without any choice could afford either one.

Boreas straightened up and kicked the book parcel and the ragged rucksack toward my head. "The monks'll heal your hurts if anyone can. Pay 'em with your *valuable* book."

I dragged the rucksack under me, lest the slug-witted ox change his mind.

"You're a coward and a thief, Boreas!" I shouted as he trudged off. "You stink like a pureblood's midden!"

Only moments and he was gone, the heavy footsteps and ponderous breathing that had been a passing comfort at my side for a year's turn swallowed up by the pounding deluge. He couldn't go far. The light was failing. I could scarcely see the slender arches of the abbey church through the sheets of rain. Monks—especially these pious fellows out in the wilderness—put themselves to bed before a meadowlark could sing. Before a whore had her skirts up. Before an owl had its eyes open. Before . . .

Alehouse riddling threatened to squeeze out more useful thoughts. Shaking my head, I stretched out my forearms, dug my elbows into the muck, and dragged myself forward on my side perhaps one quat—the length of a man's knucklebone. Ominous warmth oozed out of the gouge on my back. My leg felt like a molten sword blank awaiting the smith's hammer.

I rested my head on crossed forearms. One moment to catch my breath . . .

Much as I pretended elsewise, even to myself, I *could* shape spells, of course. Mostly destructive things, minor illusions, a child's wickedness. Nothing that could heal a wound. Nothing that could summon help. Nothing useful.

The driving rain splashed mud in my face. Sleet stung the back of my neck. The cold settled deep in my bones until I wasn't even shivering anymore. I hated the cold.

"Magrog take you, Boreas," I mumbled, "and give you boils on your backside and a prick like a feather."

Groaning shamelessly, I jammed my left foot into the rut and rolled onto my back. The dark world spun like soup in a kettle, yet I felt modestly satisfied. I might be doomed to blood and water and ice—madness, too, if breeding held true—but by Iero's holy angels, I would die face *up* in this cesspool.

Rain spattered softly on my cheeks and the ground, on the puddles, the leaves, and a large rock, each surface producing a slight variant of the sound, defining the world on the far side of my eyelids. The scents of rotted leaves and good loam filled my nose . . . my lungs . . . seeped into my pores. My body blemished that vast landscape like a fallen tree, soon to be rotted, dissolved, and completely one with that cold, dark, and very wet place.

Soft padding steps rustled the wet leaves, stirring up smells of grass and moss and sea wrack, everything green or wet in the world. Paused. *Fox? Rabbit? Mmm . . . bigger.* Cold rain and warm blood had long washed away fear. Moments more and I wouldn't care what kind of beast it was. A faint shudder rippled through my depths. *Terrible . . . wonderful . . . to dissolve in the rain . . .*

Creaking wood and iron sent the beast scuttering away. Soft yellow light leaked around my eyelids—a lamp spitting and sprizzling in the rain.

"You heard him at the sanctuary gate? From all the way up here?"

"By Iero's holy name, Brother Sebastian. His cry sounded like the seven torments of the end times. When I poked my head out the shutters and saw none lay at the gate, conscience forbade me to lie down again without a search."

"Never use the One God's name lightly, boy. And in future you must seek Father Prior's permission to go beyond the walls, even when on duty."

A warm weight, smelling of woodsmoke and onions, pressed

lightly on my chest. If I could have moved, I would have wrapped my arms about it. Kissed it even.

The weight lifted. "He breathes. I'd call it a miracle you found him, but now I look, I'm coming to believe you heard the fellow, after all. For certain he's been *through* the seven torments. Here, lend me your hand."

Hands grabbed me behind my left shoulder, where Boreas had extracted a second arrow and a sizable hunk of flesh. I left off any thought of joining the conversation. Breathing seemed enough. Keeping some wit about me. Listening . . .

The two mumbled of Iero and Father Prior and Saint Gillare the Wise, as they laid me on my side on a wooden platform that stank like a pig wallow and then proceeded to tilt it at such an angle that all my painful parts slid together in one wretched lump. The cart bumped forward, causing me to bite my tongue.

"Was he left by highwaymen, do you think, Brother?" The eager young speaker labored somewhere in front of me, expelling short puffs of effort.

"Highwaymen don't leave boots with a man, even boots with soles thin as vellum. No, as his outfit's plain and sturdy underneath the blood, I'd name him a soldier come from battle. Doesn't look as if he's eaten in a twelvemonth, for all he's tall as a spar oak."

"A soldier . . ." The word expressed a wonder that comes only when the speaker can't tell a pike from a poker or a battle from a broomdance. "One of Prince Bayard's men, do you think?"

"He might serve any one of the three, or this mysterious Pretender, or the Emperor of Aurellia himself. Such matters of the world should not concern you. Once Brother Infirmarian sees to the fellow, Father Abbot will question him as to his loyalties and purposes."

Bones of hell . . . one would think an abbey so out of the way as this one might not care which of the three sons of King Eodward juped his brothers out of the throne.

The cart jounced through a pothole. The older man grunted. I sank into mindless misery.

Anyone might have mistaken the cold uncomfortable journey for the everlasting downward path. One of the two fellows—the younger one, I guessed, not the wise Brother Sebastian—chirruped a psalm about running with Iero's children in sunlit fields, a performance so cheery it could serve as proper torment on such a road.

Eventually we jolted to a stop. Above my head arched a stone vault of uncertain height, not an ever-raining sky, though a round-cheeked aingerou carved into a corner spat a little dribble of rainwater onto the wagon bed. The yellow lamplight danced on the pale stone.

"Run for Brother Robierre, boy, and tell him bring a litter."

"But I'm posted sanctuary, so I must give—"

"You've walked me halfway to Elanus. I'll stay right here and give the fellow his blessing."

Elanus. A small market town. South? West? Ought to know. How far did we run? I'd been more than half delirious on the road.

Bells clanged and clamored from the church towers, and out of the night rose the sound of men singing plainsong, clear and strong like a river of music, quickening my blood like a fiery kiss.

"Brother, it's the call to Matins!" said the boy. "You have to go!"

"All right, all right, my hearing's not so bad as that."

Matins—morning at midnight. A perverse custom.

The wind shifted the lantern so that its beams nearly blinded me. I squeezed my eyes shut again. The night's edge seemed sharp as a razor knife. I'd always heard the Ferryman's mortal breath *dulled* the senses.

A dreadful thought shivered my bones: Had the Ferryman himself been breathing at my ear? He'd even smelled of sea wrack. I'd never truly believed . . .

"I'll send Brother Infirmarian," said Brother Sebastian. "When he no longer requires you, hie you to prayers yourself. The good god excuses no green aspirants."

"Of course, Brother."

Footsteps trudged away. A warm hand touched my brow. "By Iero's grace, find safety here, thou who fleest sword or hangman. By the saint's hand, find healing here, thou who sufferest wound or sickness. By gift of holy earth, find strength here, thou who comest parched or weak. And by King Eodward's grant and his servants' labor, find nourishment for thy flesh and spirit. God grant thee ease, traveler."

An interesting prayer . . . gift of holy earth . . . King Eodward's grant . . . all mixed in with the Karish god Iero and one of his saints. For the most part, the Karish dwelt peaceably side by side with the elder gods, but I'd never before heard a joint invocation.

I lifted my head. "Perhaps, if you could just help me out of this corner . . ."

An uncomfortable ricketing tilt of the cart brought a pale, narrow face above me. The lamplight revealed the thickening brows and downy upper lip of oncoming manhood, and such delight and amazement as could only emanate from the same soul that sang cheery psalms while slogging a manure cart down a mountainside in the rain. "You're alive!"

I didn't feel at all sure about that, having come so close as to hear the Ferryman's footsteps. "Not dead. Thank you."

"No need to thank me, sir. It's my duty, you see, assigned me by the prior, who was given the task by the abbot, whose authority is from the hierarch and the One God in Heaven. I sleep above the sanctuary gate, ready to hear the bell and open the gate for any who come. You're the first since I was given the task. You *do* beg sanctuary, don't you?"

His eagerness exhausted me.

"Yes. Certainly."

"Thus you must have broken the law of God or king, or someone believes it so . . ." He tilted his head and drew his brows together. Clearly his excitement at receiving a supplicant was now tempered with consideration of my soul's peril. My offenses were, indeed, countless, and my peril ever present.

"If you could just help me sit up." So long tipped downward in the stinking cart had my belly mightily unsettled, not that there was aught left in it to spew.

The untonsured boy was as diligent with his wiry arms and gentle hands as with his words. By the time a gray-haired monk with dark-ish skin about his eyes, something like a badger's markings, dropped a bundle of long poles on the paving, I sat across the lip of the three-sided cart, my head bent almost to my knees and my lip bloody from biting it.

"Jullian, unfold the litter. Let me examine what we have here. Ooh . . ." A glimpse of the broken, dark-stained shaft protruding from my black and swollen thigh was clearly the most interesting thing the fellow had seen that day.

"I hope you've a sharp knife, Brother," I said, my voice shaking, "and a steady hand."

Then he touched it, and the world slipped out of my grasp.

Chapter 2

"How do you feel this morning, my friend?"

I cocked one eye open. The smudge-eyed monk peered down at me, his arms overflowing with bundled linen and wooden bowls. Plastered walls hung with strips of green-dyed cloth rose up behind him to a timbered roof, and an array of narrow windows, paned with horn, admitted murky light. A smoking rushlight clamped to an iron tripod revealed ten more beds lined up neatly in the long plain room. From my odd vantage—I lay on my left side, some kind of bolster propping me up from the back and legs tipped higher than my head—the beds appeared unoccupied.

"I feel like Iero's wrath," I said. Every particle of my flesh felt battered; my leg throbbed as if the arrow point were grinding its way into the bone. My shoulder might have had rats chewing on it. Damp all over, I shivered helplessly despite a pile of blankets.

I had known better than to pull the damnable arrow out of my thigh when I had no help but Boreas, who was convinced that burying a live cat under an oak at the full moon would cure his crabs, and that spitting over a bridge rampart while wearing a moonbird's feather would speed the healing of his broken hand. I knew little of the body's humors. But one of a man's great veins lay in the thigh, and I'd seen men bleed to death faster than a frog takes a fly while removing an arrow point carelessly from just the same spot as my wound. And we hadn't been able to stop moving. When the Harrower priestess had thrown her legion of madmen against us, the battle had gone completely to the fiery pits, and six thousand other bloodied soldiers who had wagered their fortunes on the wrong side in this cursed war were soon to be right on our heels.

A halfwit would understand what the delay would cost me.

Though I had weighed bleeding to death likely preferable to sepsis and amputation, in my usual way I had postponed the decision, figuring it was better to die tomorrow than today. Now the payment was falling due.

Mustering my courage, I broached the question gnawing at my gut. "You'll take the leg, I know, Brother. But think you I'll live to raise a glass again?"

The monk dropped his bundled linens atop a wide chest pushed against the end wall of the infirmary, then began arranging the wooden bowls on shelves already crowded with ewers and basins, jars and bottles. "If the One God's mercy continues to hold sway, your leg will heal with no ill result. Your fever's broken just this morn. Young Jullian will be certain his prayers are answered. You'd think the boy had delivered you from the gates of hell bearing sword and shield like the Archangel himself."

"But it's putrid, and when you remove the arrow—"

"The nasty bit of iron is two days out, lad, and for certain, you've the constitution of an ox. You're on the mend." The monk was a strapping fellow. Despite his circled eyes and his stubbled cheeks that drooped excess skin about his jaw, his face expressed naught but good cheer. He spread out an array of bundled plants on a long table that stood between the last bed and the stack of shelves. Perching his backside on a backless stool, he began picking leaves from the array. "I'm Brother Robierre, as it happens, by Iero's grace the infirmarian of Gillarine Abbey."

"Oh!" Astonishing how much better I felt straightaway. As if the jagged bits of a shattered mirror had put themselves together again. As if I'd pulled the veil off my contracted bride and found some girl I loved. I dropped my head on the pillow and crowed like a banty rooster. "May the angels scribe your name, Brother! The moment I'm afoot, I'll dance you a jig and carry you to heaven on my back!"

A stoop-shouldered monk with piebald hair and a gray scapular over his cinched black gown scuttered out from behind me, casting a mildly shocked glance my way. The steaming crock he carried past my bed to the table left a scented trail in the air. Chicken—holy mother, could it be?—and onions and carrots and thyme and savory. My stomach rumbled uproariously.

Months had passed since I last tasted meat. In early summer Boreas and I had shot an aged squirrel, three bites apiece and broth from the boiled bones with little more than grass to throw in it. Then and since the Ardran legions had been squatting on land long raided, gleaned, and stripped. We'd had only bread like dried leather made from shriveled peas or even acorns ground into flour. And never enough. No planting or harvest this year in any of western Ardra. The summer campaign had been only one of Prince Perryn's gross miscalculations in pursuing his father's throne. Not even the worst.

"Thank you, Brother Anselm," said Robierre. "I do believe our patient's going to appreciate the soup today. Inform the abbot that our supplicant is awake, if you would."

Piebald Brother Anselm nodded solemnly to the infirmarian and scurried away. To my delight, Brother Robierre put aside his activities and selected a wooden bowl from the shelf. I almost moaned as he filled the bowl from the tureen, acquired a spoon, and dragged a low stool to my bedside.

The good brother insisted I drink some concoction that tasted like boiled scrapings from a stable floor first of all. But after the first spoonful of the soup, I would have knelt to kiss the hairy toes that peeked out from his sandals had he but asked.

"Abbot Luviar has been most concerned about you," he said as I reveled in the savory broth and tiny bits of succulent poultry deemed suitable for an invalid. "He's had prayers said, asked blessings as we sit at table. He'll be in to see you now I've sent word you're awake."

"Mmm," I said, holding the last warm spoonful in my mouth before I let it trickle down my throat. "Iero's holy angels . . . all of you." I was feeling quite devout.

He grinned, an expression distinctly odd for a badger. "I'll get you more."

I had never shared Boreas's horror of monks, but then I had never been fool enough to creep over a priory wall with a bursar's coffer on my back. Boreas had been sentenced to the loss of one hand, a flogging, and a week in pillory, but managed to escape before suffering any of the three. Now he was convinced that every monk and lay brother passed his description about the realm tucked in sleeves or under scapulars, and that every abbot and prior was determined to hang him.

Sadly, my own direst peril had less to do with lawbreaking or sin than with birth and blood, circumstances for which no sanctuary could be granted. But I had no reason to believe that my loathsome family or the Pureblood Registry could find me here or anywhere. I'd shed them both at fifteen and had long since drowned myself in a sea of anonymity. I had no intention of bobbing to the surface. Ever.

Two more bowls of the brothers' heaven-kissed soup and I took even the changing of the dressing on my thigh with good humor. Warm, fed, and clean—indeed someone had washed me head to toe while I slept—and out of the weather, and no one coming after me with arrows, pikes, lances, or hands outstretched for money . . . perhaps the boy Jullian was indeed the archangel who guarded the gates of Paradise. The truest wonder was that he had let me in.

I fell asleep as promptly as a cat in a sunbeam. When my eyes drifted open again sometime later, a long-limbed man of more than middling years sat on the stool at my bedside. A golden solicale dangled from his neck—the sunburst symbol of Iero's glory worked in a pendant so heavy it must surely be an abbot's ensign. Instead of effecting a modest tonsure like the infirmarian's, he had shaved his head entirely clean.

Holding in mind my present comforts, I bowed my head and shaped my greeting in the Karish manner. "In the name of holy Iero and his saints, my humblest gratitude be yours, holy father. Truly the One God led my wayward footsteps to this refuge when the world and all its ways had failed me." I didn't think it too grovelish.

"Iero commands us offer his hand in charity," said the abbot, "and so we have done. It remains to be seen what he has in mind for you." His full-shaven pate, fine arched nose, and narrow, pock-grooved face made his cool gray eyes seem very large.

I squirmed a bit, suddenly feeling even more naked than I already was under my lovely blankets.

A younger monk, full-shaven as well, but with unmarked skin and dark brows that made a solid line above deep-set eyes, stood a few steps behind the abbot, hands tucked piously under his black scapular. Though his expression remained properly sober, his brow lifted slightly and his mouth quickened with amusement as he observed me under the abbot's eye.

"What is your name, my son?" The abbot took no note of his attendant's improper levity.

"Valen, holy father."

"Valen. Nothing else, then?"

"Nay, holy father." No title to mark me as nobility or clergy. No town or profession to mark me as a rooted man even if my father was unimportant. No association with any of the three provinces of Navronne—Ardra, Morian, or Evanore—or with their contentious princes. And certainly no colineal surname to proclaim my family pureblood, and thus my future beyond even an abbot's right to determine. Especially not that. "Just Valen."

"Valen Militius, perhaps?"

Another dangerous topic. The young attendant monk's dark brows lifted slightly. Attentive. At the worktable, Brother Robierre's head was bent over his mortar and pestle, plants and vials, but his hands grew still.

Though I tried to dip my own head farther, being propped on my side made it difficult. "Not a professional soldier, holy father, far from it, nor even a worthy freeman-at-arms. But I once carried a pike for King Eodward, Iero cherish his soul, and stood behind him as he drove the Hansker barbarians back across the sea. He called us his men of light, and so we all felt more than what we were born." All true. And now the test would come . . .

"And what of noble Eodward's sons?" He touched the clean linen that wrapped my shoulder and made a blessing sign upon it. My flesh warmed beneath the bandage. "Which of the three princes owns your fealty? Or do you hope for this ghostly Pretender of current rumor?"

"None of them, holy father. Though the sign of three speaks of heaven, these three sons are so far from worthy of their kingly father that an ignorant lout such as I am cannot choose. And though I reverence any issue of good King Eodward, I fear that naught but tavern gossip has delivered him a fourth son."

Unless I could discover with which prince this man's favor rested, I dared not say more. Perryn of Ardra, whom I *had* chosen as being the most intelligent and least openly brutal of the half brothers, was surely dead by now, or in chains, babbling his plans and the names of his noble supporters to his brother Bayard's torturers. In either case, my oath to him was moot. He had shown himself mean and so stubbornly inept that my loyalty had been ruined much earlier. He certainly was not worth dying for.

I glanced up. The gray eyes held steady, the long, slender bones of the abbot's face unmoved. "So your wounds were not earned in battle, then?"

Well, the battle had been over months before we'd charged Prince Bayard's line at Wroling—in the spring when Bayard of Morian had allied with Sila Diaglou and her Harrowers. But such quibbling wouldn't carry weight with this abbot. Not with a wound in my back, and the admission requiring me to declare not only that I had run away, but which side I had deserted. I needed a better story.

"Nay, holy father, rather my wounds stem from a private dispute with another man regarding property that belonged to me. Though right was with me in the matter, I believed I was going to die and so confessed my sins to a village practor. He sent me on the road with my wounds untended as penance, saying the One God would put me in the way of death or life as was his will."

I held still and listened carefully, fighting the urge to add more words to this collection of nonsense, such as what village I'd come from or why I had suffered the strikes of arrows rather than knife or club. It seemed a very long time until the abbot spoke again.

"Was this, by chance, the disputed property, Valen?"

The dark-browed monk stepped forward, pulled a book out of his black gown, and passed it to the abbot. The abbot laid it on the bed in front of my face, a squarish book some three fingers thick, its brown leather binding tooled in gold with gryphons and dragons, long-limbed angels, roundels, vine leaves, and every flourish of the leather gilder's art. Slightly damp at one corner, but I quickly verified that the dampness had not touched the fine vellum pages enough to damage them or smear the ink.

"If so, and if you have any idea of what you carry and can tell me how you've come by it, then I may believe your story."

I swallowed, puffed out a strong breath, and touched my finger to the golden letters on its cover and the familiar sigil of a gryphon carrying a rolled map in its claws. "Of course, holy father. This is the original volume of *Maps of the Known World*, created by the pure-blood, Janus de Cartamandua-Magistoria, the most famous cartographer in all of Navronne's history." That part was true, of course. My mind raced. "It was given me . . . seven years ago . . . when, with Iero's grace, my service . . . scouting . . . preserved the Mardane Lavorile's troop from capture by the Hansker. Knowing a scout would understand its worth, his lordship said it was fitting recompense for the lives I had saved. One of these wild Harrowers tried to take it. They think to burn all books, you know."

"So you are familiar with the book, studied it no doubt, used its guiding spells when you served the mardane?"

Monks valued books. New initiates often brought them. And the Karish would certainly want this one. Legend said it could lead men to the realm of angels.

"Of course, holy father. I used it often in the mardane's service. I treasure each page." Though my valuing had more to do with the gold coins of pawnbrokers than the gold crowns of angels.

The gray-eyed abbot nodded. "I'll accept this tale for now. Brother Robierre is scowling, for I promised not to tire you. Tell me, Valen, what do you ask of Gillarine Abbey beyond your fortnight of sanctuary?"

This answer was much easier than the previous ones, requiring no instant work of the imagination. "To join your holy fraternity, holy father. To repent my licentious life and serve the god Iero, if I may." That is, to eat and stay warm, dry, and anonymous until I decided where to go and what to do next to revive a fortune that seemed to have reached its nadir. Soldiering, the only work I'd found in two years, had decidedly lost its attractions.

"Granted," said the abbot with astonishing speed. "Brother Sebastian will be your mentor, instructing and guiding you in our rule and custom. Brother Gildas, you will inform Sebastian and Prior Nemesio of our new aspirant."

The dark-browed monk bowed respectfully from the hip.

Once prayers and blessings had ushered the two of them out, Brother Robierre appeared at my side, bearing a clay jar into which I took a grateful piss. He then passed the jar on to the piebald Brother Anselm, who settled at the worktable and began to dip and pour and examine my output as if it were the waters of the heavenly rivers. I recited my stories over and over in my head so I'd not forget them if questioned again.

After a while, the infirmarian provided me with a thick posset, not so savory as the chicken, but sweet, warm, and filling. Setting the empty mug aside, Robierre reached his hand toward the book that still lay on the bed with me. Hesitating. "May I?"

Eyelids heavy, I smiled. "For thou, blessed angel of the infirmary, anything."

He chuckled, lifted the book from the bed, and ran his thick fingers lovingly over the binding. "A Cartamandua book of maps . . . to have such a thing come to Gillarine . . . You will be besieged with pleas to see it. Few of our brothers, even those who labor in the scriptorium, will have glimpsed so rare and precious a work or one so storied. The very book that led the Sinduré and the Hierarch to discover young Eodward in the realm of angels, the book that shows the hidden places of the world. What strange roads it must have traveled. Who would have thought that one like you would possess a sorcerer's finest—? Ah, I'm sorry." His sagging cheeks flushed in kind embarrassment.

"You're not the first, good brother, not the first."

Strange roads indeed! Until five days ago, when I'd discovered the book in a deserted manse I happened to be looting as I ran away from a battle I'd sworn to fight, I'd last touched it eleven years before at a bookshop in Palinur. I'd been desperate for money—a state less familiar then than now. I'd had to settle for less than its full worth because the book pawner refused to believe I'd come by it honestly.

Neither the good Brother Robierre nor the pawner would believe—
nor would I ever tell anyone, could I avoid it—that old Janus de
Cartamandua himself had given it to me, his ill-behaved and
unappreciative grandson, on my tumultuous and unpleasant seventh
birthday. My parents had been furious.

Chapter 3

The bells in the abbey tower fell silent. Brother Robierre had hurried off to the chapter house for the monks' daily meeting, and Brother Anselm had retired to his herb garden, closing the infirmary door softly behind them so as not to wake me. I heaved a deep and pleasurable sigh.

On this second day of trying to sleep away my wounds in Gillarine's infirmary, I had only three complaints of any substance. Firstly, the bells. Bells banged every hour day or night and set off a cacophony whenever the brothers were called to services, which seemed fifty times a day. Second, the shy lay brother Anselm devoutly believed that one window must always be left open in an infirmary to allow ill humors to escape the room, which caused a frigid draft whenever the outside door was opened. And third, endearing as I found Brother Badger, as I called the good infirmarian, a sick man should be exempt from excess praying. Feigning sleep was my only reprieve.

I tugged the blankets over my bare shoulder, luxuriated in the returning warmth from the hearth, and speculated about what delicacy the good brothers would bring from the abbey kitchens to fill my invalid's stomach. I had always been a quick healer, but the brothers didn't need to know that. Life was good.

"Comfortable, are you?"

My eyelids slammed open to reveal the abbot's attendant sitting on the bedside stool. I'd heard not a step or a breath.

"Brother Gildas! How did you—?" Recalling my position as aspiring novice and the tedious duties that were like to involve the moment I was well enough, I checked my tongue and allowed my breath to quaver bravely. "Well, Brother, I'm as comfortable as a man can be with fever shakes and septic blood and holes in his flesh where there should be none. Bless you for asking."

His dark brows lifted, and he pulled a wedge of cheese from under my pillow. "We'll feed you even when you're healed, Valen. And you needn't fear I'll tell the abbot that your devotions are perhaps more directed to his kitchen and his bed than his church at present. Every man here has his own reasons for piety."

"The bounty of the good god is a fit occasion for thanksgiving," I said a bit defensively, tucking the rest of my cache more securely under my head. "And surely he expects us to conserve that bounty for harder days."

Perhaps it was their shaven heads that made this man and the abbot appear so intensely focused, their eyes dominant in their hairless skulls as if they might read a man's very soul. Not that my soul was all that interesting—a man of seven-and-twenty summers who scrabbled from one job to another, doing as he needed to wrest a bit of enjoyment from a world that seemed worse off by the day. But at least this fellow was near enough my own age that he might remember something of a man's needs.

"I do hear Iero's call to the prayerful life quite clearly. But, in truth, Brother Gildas, I am yet a sinful man who enjoys the pleasures of bed and board overmuch. No matter how devoutly my soul yearns to reform, my body forever backslides."

"And yet our abbot, whose eye is infinitely wise, judges you worthy of initiation. I've never known him so precipitate in judgment. He'd have you vowed before Saint Marcillus's Day, scarcely a fortnight hence." His head tilted as if to examine me from various angles, his deep-set eyes unwavering. "Well, neither you nor I may see the right of it, but the god scorns none with a good heart. We must have faith that he will illumine yours as he sees fit. Brother Sebastian has been charged with your guidance and instruction, but Father Prior has dispatched him to Pontia to investigate the rumor of two books brought in by traders. So I was asked to bring you these."

He laid a worn book and a roll of parchment on the bed in front of me. "Your psalter, left by good Brother Horach, who passed to his next life not long ago. And a summary of Saint Ophir's Rule, which you must commit to memory ere you take your novice vows. Brother Sebastian will discuss them with you upon his return."

"A dead man's book?" I said, drawing back from it as far as the heavy bolster allowed.

"He was not diseased, if that's your worry."

"No, no . . ."

I had long abjured the soldiers' maxim that wearing a dead man's boots or cooking in his pot would see your own life forfeit within a year. Books, as it happened, raised other problems.

"It's just that . . . a holy saint's book . . . for my eyes that have looked on so much of the Adversary's wickedness to rest upon such precious pages seems sacrilege. Until I have confessed and labored out the days . . . months . . . of expiation, I doubt I could look upon a holy work without it bursting into eternal flame. And such a waste of a precious book that would be!"

Brother Gildas laughed—a pleasant, resonant sound—and shifted the book and scroll to the bedside table. "We must certainly get you up and working hard to soothe this burdensome conscience of yours. Do you not know that those who cross our threshold for sanctuary are cleansed of past offenses? You are a new man, Valen, whether you like it or not, as pure as a new-dipped babe. The only marks upon your soul will be those you scribe there from this day forward."

The Karish hierarchs pronounced many tenets to admire, but this one—that an unwatered babe could be marked with evil, whereas a failed man of the world who had no intention of repenting his iniquities could be somehow purified by crossing a brick threshold—had always struck me as untenable.

I sighed deeply. "Oh. Well then, when my fever allows my blurred sight to clear, I'll study both book and scroll."

"If Brother Sebastian fails to return by tomorrow, I'll come myself to quiz you on the Rule," he said, rising from his stool. "And, of course, Father Abbot will require the details of your birth. We care naught for high or low, pureblood, noble, or common at Gillarine. But neither bonded men nor natural sons nor purebloods lacking dispensation from their family are permitted to join our order."

"Of course." I had the disconcerting sense that the monk felt my mind racing. "Tell me, Brother Gildas, where is my own book, the book of maps?" After the odd chance of happening onto such a rarity, I'd be a fool to lose track of it.

He smiled in a knowing fashion that I found somewhat annoying. "Safely locked into the abbot's own book press. Father Abbot would not see such a treasure splattered with blood or possets. If you choose to leave before you take vows, of course it will be returned to you."

He offered me a sip of the spicy caudle Brother Badger had left on the stool. I downed it gratefully. My awkward drinking posture left drips enough on my bed linens to make Brother Gildas's point.

I would need to find the book. If this Elanus was a good-sized town, perhaps it had a knowledgeable pawner. A few weeks and

I would suffer for my lack of silver. Of a sudden the beery sweetness of the caudle tasted of brine and bitter. Some of life's unpleasantness could not be so easily evaded as Registry investigators or my family's bloodhounds.

"Thank you, Brother. Iero grant you like mercy." I licked a stray drop from my lips and let my eyelids sag, hoping the soft-spoken Gildas might forgo the prayers sure to accompany his departure. Like flies about raw fish, prayers seemed to cluster about every monkish activity.

But when his soft whisper came in my ear, it bore no pious sentiment. Holy words, nonetheless. "Mutton broth today."

My laughter disrupted all my feigning. He smiled and vanished through the door as quietly as he'd come. I would have to watch my step with Brother Gildas.

With the skill of long experience I banished all thought of the future. Perhaps these good monks would solve all my ills—body and soul together.

My head had scarcely touched the pillow again when a clank of the latch and a damp, chilly whoosh of the draft signaled another arrival. A warm body hovered a handbreadth from my face like a restrained pup awaiting my word to begin licking. This one smelled of rain and mud, onions and innocence . . . and boy.

"Could this be the Archangel Jullian?" I said without opening my eyes. "He of the exquisite hearing and golden tongue, who shall have whatever service he needs of me from this day forward as thanks for preserving my feckless life?"

"Aye, it's Jullian," he said softly. "Are you asleep, then? I shan't stay if you're asleep. But I'm off sanctuary watch and on to kitchen duty as of this day's chapter, so I've more time to see to you. Brother Robierre told me you're healing astonishingly fast and are ready for visitors."

I lifted my heavy eyelids and grinned. "Not asleep. Indeed I'm pleased for cheerful company. As long as you don't make me pay for it by draining my wounds or poking my bruises." Besides, the sooner I knew the ins and outs of Gillarine, the better, whether I chose to stay a season or not.

"I've brought you something to aid your healing. Water from Saint Gillare's holy spring." The boy held out a flask of amber-colored glass as reverently as if it held the saintly woman's tears.

I drew back a little. "Water? Uh . . . I don't . . . not usually . . ." I didn't want to offend the boy, but I'd been leery of that ruinous beverage since my mother's divination when I turned seven. Certainly many a soldier came to grief from it. "So kind. Thank you. But we'd best wait for Brother Bad—Robierre. I'm sure I heard him say my stomach was too weak for water as yet."

He set the flask on the stool, then hiked up his coarse brown tunic and plopped down on the tile floor, leaving his face on a comfortable level with mine. Though the damp, matted hair cut bowl-shaped to his ears could have been any color, the fluff on the boy's full lip and bony chin was red-gold in the lamplight and his skin ruddy. I judged him wholly Ardran. Most Navrons, especially the Moriangi of the riverlands to the north, bore some trace of either the black-haired Aurellian invaders of past centuries—my own ancestors—or the flaxen-haired Hansker who plagued our coast.

"I just wanted— Is there any further service I can offer? Something else I could bring you? A prayer I could offer? Whatever you need." His voice belied his coarsening features and piped clear and boyish, putting him nearer twelve than fourteen to my mind. The ripe stench of less than diligent washing assured me he was entirely human male and no angel in disguise.

I propped my elbow on the bed and supported my head with my fist. "Mmm, I've a wagonload of curiosity. As you may have heard, a penitential pilgrimage led me here, but I was in such a state of sin and remorse that I've no idea what roads I walked or where I ended up."

The battle had begun at Wroling Wood in southwestern Navronne— a damnable, confusing, twisted region of forested gullies more akin to god-cursed Evanore than the fertile hills and vineyards of gentle, golden Ardra. And between my delirium, the impenetrable trees, the wretched weather, and the eerie lack of human habitation along the way, naught had illumined our location since. The desolation was almost enough to make one believe the Harrowers had succeeded in their mad quest to erase all trace of human works from the land. In truth, that our flight had ended near any sanctuary but a bandit's hut, much less by a house so prosperous as to have sheep bones to boil, was enough to make a man a devotee of Serena Fortuna.

Closing my eyes, I offered a quick apology to the divine sister of Sky Lord Kemen for my doubts during those wretched days, promising a libation next time I was blessed with a cup of wine. I thought it prudent to honor all gods and goddesses until someone wiser than me sorted out the contention between Navronne's elder gods and the Karish upstart Iero.

"Gillarine lies eighteen quellae north of Caedmon's Bridge and three quellae south of Elanus, which itself lies one hundred and

seventy-four quellae southwest of Palinur. We sit ninety-three quellae east of Wroling." The boy recited his numbers as if they were an
alchemist's formula.

I gave his information little credence. Boreas and I might have
traveled ninety-three quellae in two days afoot when well rested, with
full stomachs and the wrath of the gods scorching our heels. But we'd
never come so far after months of poor rations and the soldier's flux,
and with my leg threatening to collapse the entire way.

At least it seemed I'd managed to keep us in Ardra. Even ravaged
by war and fiendish weather, my birth province was yet the fairest of
Navronne's three. Morian was flat and ugly, its sprawling ports and
trade cities infested with plague, mosquitoes, woolen mills, and rapacious trade guilds. And our proximity to Evanore, that land of
devils' mountains, yet left me queasy. Evanore's duc, Prince Osriel,
forbade purebloods entry into his lands. I'd been taught that his
border wards would boil a pureblood's brains until they leaked out
his ears.

I grimaced and rubbed my shaggy head.

Jullian hunched his thin shoulders and dropped his voice.
"I've heard a battle was fought at Wroling a sevenday since, Prince
Perryn's army routed by Prince Bayard and the Harrower legions.
Gerard, another aspirant who took up the sanctuary watch after me,
was told to watch for survivors, though Brother Porter said he'd
heard they were all captive or dead, every one."

Disgust at the waste raised my bile. As far as I was concerned, they
could give the cursed throne to the Harrower priestess, Sila Diaglou—
or to this Ardran child Pretender whom no one sober had ever seen.
"Does your abbot favor Prince Perryn, then, to be willing to take in
what's left of his men?"

"The abbot holds Gillarine as a neutral field," said the boy. His
wide blue eyes shone, declaring his faith that a sainted man could
make even such a ridiculous thing be true. "King Eodward built the
abbey years and years ago. On holy ground, the story says. He gave
the Hierarchs of Ardra dominion over it, but only as long as they fulfill the terms of his grant—to preserve and protect all knowledge and
all supplicants—even those who know naught of Iero or his holy
writs. He said the angels themselves, sent forth to journey among
men, would know of this place, and might find their way here in their
need."

I couldn't imagine the warring princes honoring so magnanimous
a legend. But it sounded very nice. Far better than any number of
places Boreas could have abandoned me.

"Holy ground this might be," I said, "but alas, no one will ever mistake me for an angel. Your wise abbot can tell you." Which left open the question Gildas had brought to the fore. Why would a perceptive holy man admit a stranger to his household so readily? Were his stores so plentiful he could afford to take on any vagabond who happened by? Serena Fortuna had ever been kind, but sensible caution had kept me free.

A blast of wind rattled the horn windows, ruffling the parchment and plants on Robierre's worktable and setting his hanging herb bundles swaying. The spring auguries taken by Prince Perryn's pureblood diviners predicted the coming winter would be the worst in living memory. Of course, a blind birdwit could predict that did he but bare his skin to the wind these past days. And the Reaper's Moon had not yet shone.

I scooted a little deeper in the bed. The more I considered a house full of kindly fellows given to charity and good cooking, the better it sounded as a winter haven, prayers and bells notwithstanding. If I'd imagined it so easy to join up with a Karish brotherhood, I might have done so years ago. Best keep the path smooth.

"So, Jullian, clearly you are not some villein boy sent here to be a mere kitchen drudge forever . . . but schooled. An aspirant . . . preparing to take vows yourself when you're old enough. Perchance . . . being a scholarly boy . . . of course, you can read?"

He sat up proudly. "Both Navron and Aurellian, though my Aurellian is not so fine. I read it as well as any in the abbey, but to think out the words to write a new text and set them together with proper variants is very hard. Not that my writing hand is ill. Abbot Luviar says I could scribe for the saint at heaven's gate. He's even allowed me to help in the scriptorium. Not to write, of course, not yet, but to clean the pens and brushes, help mix the inks, and even to rule and prick the pages. With so many books to copy, and new ones coming every month, everyone must help. And I try to read them all. The learning is a wonder." The boy's expression shifted as easily as light in an aspen glade.

"Well then, there is one boon you could grant me."

"Anything."

"My illness clouds my eyes, so that reading makes my head ache and all the letters swim together. Yet I must commit this scroll of your Rule to memory before Brother Gildas tests me, else I'll be thrown out of Gillarine ten days hence to languish again among wolves and sinners to the peril of my soul. So if you could aid me . . ."

One might have thought I had asked Jullian to polish my heavenly crown. He carefully untied the ribbon that bound the scroll and proceeded to recount the fifteen laws of Saint Ophir's Rule. Among the expected admonitions to abjure fornication, gambling, excessive drink, and the lures of worldly wealth, to forgo the practices and use of magic and other earthbound power, to pray the holy Hours and give absolute obedience to the commands of prior, abbot, and hierarch, lay the small requirements that declared a novice must be a free man of sound body and legitimate birth and be schooled so far as to read and do simple sums.

"Am I reading too fast, sir?"

"No, no," I said, swallowing a curse. "I'm just fixing the holy words in my head."

Of necessity, my memory had developed exceedingly keen. The balance of the world had never seemed fair to me—that reading was placed so high in the scheme of virtue while the skill to remember what others read or to make some use of it languished far below.

When he had finished the scroll, he picked up the psalter. "I could read you a psalm, to soothe your tormented humors."

"Truly my head is so weighted down with words, it will not lift from my pillow. My tormented humors must get along as best they can."

He thumbed through the book, paused for a moment, then slapped it down on the stool and snatched his hand away as if it had scorched his fingers. "This is Horach's book."

His anxiety surprised me. Karish held no squeamish notions about unquiet ghosts. "I've heard the fellow has no further need of it. You don't think his spirit minds me using it?"

"It's just . . . whenever I fetch water from the font, I can't help but see . . ." He averted his face.

"See what?" I dragged his chin around again. "Come on, lad. Get it out. It's not healthy to bottle up a story that turns your face the color of sour milk. And you've set up a keening curiosity that needs relieving, else my humors will be more tormented yet."

"He was *murdered*," said the boy in a solemn whisper. "Not a twelveday since, I found him in Saint Gillare's shrine . . . in the font. Someone slashed his skin to threads and left him bound in the water until he bled out every drop in his veins. Brother Robierre said they had pricked his throat so he couldn't scream."

Spiders' feet tickled my spine, and I felt an uncommon urge to ward my soul against Magrog's incursions. I touched the book gingerly—not that I could have said what I was expecting. "Who did such a thing? Not a monk . . . surely!"

"Certainly not!" the boy sputtered indignantly. "Father Abbot questioned every one of us under pain of hell's fire. He even sent to Pontia, and the magistrate brought his pureblood investigator. After three days here, examining us and the abbey grounds and questioning every villager within ten quellae, the sorcerer could say only that a nonbeliever had walked the cloisters. The magistrate said the killer must have borne some tormented grievance against Karish folk and sneaked into the abbey in the night to act it out."

"Such a killing seems more than random grievance. Likely this Horach had made some enemy in his life—before taking vows, of course."

Jullian shook his head vigorously. "Brother Horach was but sixteen, newly vowed, and had lived here since he was five—an aspirant like Gerard and me. Gerard hasn't slept properly since, and he'll not go into the shrine except in company." The boy sat up proudly and straightened the water flask he'd brought me, as if to demonstrate he'd conquered such fears himself.

I nodded in sympathy, but could not shake my disturbance. Common disputes among those who lived in close quarters rarely caused such savagery. And a boy of sixteen . . . Ugly.

To make sure murder was no disease festering in these halls—like mold or pox that clings to old stone—I asked the boy to tell me more of the abbey and its works, and he was soon chattering cheerfully about the scriptorium and library, sheep and barley, and thirty-three holy monks and twenty lay brothers who were all that were left to occupy an abbey built for five times that number.

Before very long Brother Robierre blustered through the infirmary door with a mournful monk named Brother Cadeus, who needed a decoction of rose bark to bathe his filmy eyes. Cadeus, as it happened, was the abbey porter, who sat at the gatehouse in the daylight hours, dispensing alms and regulating entry to the inner and outer courts of the abbey. While Cadeus shared news brought by a starving mason in search of work—of a Harrower riot that left half the city of Montesard in ashes and of a new outbreak of murrain in a sheepfold near Avenus—piebald Brother Anselm arrived with a vat of mutton broth. They propped me up on pillows so I could feed myself.

"This world's in a proper hellish season," I said when Cadeus finished his news. I regaled them with tales I'd heard the previous winter—of Ardrans frozen in their beds, of ice rivers consuming Evanori villages in a day, of Moriangi chopping frozen fish from the rivers and eating them raw as the wood was too cold to burn. ". . . and then in spring I dragged myself half starved down to the Cumbran vale, hoping to hire on for planting, only to wonder at the evil-smelling cloud hung down in the vale. Turns out the crofters had found their seed stock rotted in the bins, and their lord had burned every one of their women as Magrog's whores . . . begging your forgiveness, good brothers, for the unseemly language."

While Jullian drank in every word, eyes as wide as if my reports were hero tales of Grossartius the Revenant, Brother Robierre repeatedly made the sign of Iero's sun-burst on forehead and breast as if the Adversary himself sat on my shoulder. Brother Cadeus nodded as if he had expected nothing else. "The roads are fraught with sorrow. Iero punishes humankind's sinful ways."

"Of course, sorrowful roads can lead to interesting places," I said, swallowing another savory bite. "When the late blizzard hit Cumbra, a shepherd took me in. The snow buried his hut until only a spelled candle he'd got from a witch gave us light. We ate naught but milk and cheese for seven days and taught his favorite goat to walk on her hind legs and play ball games with us. And he taught me twelve new stanzas of 'Caedmon's Lay' . . ."

My tales were not even the worst I'd seen or heard. For eight or ten years now, self-named prophets had roved the length and breadth of Navronne crying out that our spate of cold stormy summers and savage winters foreshadowed the end of the world. Magistrates flogged the doomsayers, which succeeded only in making more folk who spent their days in a frenzy trying to placate the gods. I'd seen a man walking the length of the kingdom naked. I'd seen a cadre of women throwing burnt sheep in the sea. Villeins dangled so many charms and amulets from their wives and children, the whole countryside jingled like a tinker's wagon, and painted their lintels or their foreheads with mule droppings to stave off ill luck.

A man could say what he would of such activities—and I had scoffed at the general foolishness as much as any—but two years had gone since I'd tasted wine from Ardran grapes, though war had never touched the precious vineyards. The vines had now frozen three winters in a row, and folks said they would never recover. Perhaps the bowl of the sky had slipped askew as Sinduri astrologers claimed.

One thing was certain. With grain fields burnt by soldiers or afflicted with smut from the cold damp, with plants unable to thrive in the changing weather, and herds dead or sickly, famine would surely strike again before the new year. And I'd been perilously close to starving three winters running—which unhappy counterpoint with the delectable soup reminded me that I could likely tolerate a few monkish restrictions.

I'd certainly no wealth or earthbound power to give up. Gambling held no allure but for the coin it could provide. And so long a time had passed since I'd experienced the pleasures of excessive drink or fornication that they were easy to bargain away when tucked in a warm bed with a full stomach. Magic was another matter.

I lopped off that consideration faster than a farm wife could wring a chicken's neck. Did I allow thoughts of my worst troubles to take hold, my life would shrink to a hard black knot exactly the shape of a nivat seed.

Once Cadeus had gone, Brother Badger held his hands under his black scapular and peered into my rapidly emptying bowl. "When you've sopped up the remainder of your supper—not long it would appear—it will be time to take a walk. A man with such an appetite as yours must, of necessity, be getting stronger."

"But it's only been—"

"—four days since I took out the fiendish bit of iron. I know. But you've wallowed in your blankets long enough. Damaged sinews need using or they'll knot or wither. You'll thank me."

The infirmarian snatched away my empty bowl and dropped a short brown tunic on my lap. He watched as I eased it over my head and bandaged shoulder and relinquished my lovely blankets. The air felt dreadfully cold on my bare legs. Indeed, as he eased me to my feet, my excessive height left the skimpy tunic excessively short, exposing half my rump and privy parts to Brother Anselm's open window. "You are the Adversary's lackey, Robierre," I mumbled, shivering.

Brother Robierre was a mere half head shorter than I, and built with the sturdy bulk of a smith. Even so he called on Brother Anselm to help propel me up and down the long infirmary. I clutched at their shoulders, scarcely touched my right foot to the ground, and moaned and gasped, only muting my groans when young Jullian looked ready to pound the infirmarian for his cruelty.

"To feel the wound is only to be expected," said the good brother, inspecting my bandages when he at last allowed me to sit again. "See? No fresh blood or drainage." Adding insult to insult, he then insisted I drain Jullian's flask of water from the abbey's spring, swearing that the holy font had been resanctified since Brother Horach's gruesome death.

"You're a proper villain, Brother," I said, wincing as I rolled over and let them prop my leg up again. "I'm not thanking you as yet. This activity has surely stirred up the poisons in my blood. And this drink fit only for dogs and horses, tainted by ill-let blood, will compound them. I could die from it."

"You'll not die today, Valen." Chuckling, Brother Badger tucked me in more gently than my mother had ever done. This was indeed a fine and friendly place.

Chapter 4

"I need to be gone now," said Jullian, scrambling to his feet not long after the bells for the Hour of Compline—night prayers—fell silent. "I've duties."

The door banged behind him. He had been regaling me with descriptions of the various monks, while the infirmarian and his assistant hied off to pray again. Though guileless as a newborn calf, the boy had a wit about him. I felt as if I knew the denizens of Gillarine already.

Left alone, I wormed my way down into the bedclothes, more tired than I ought to be from another day of sleeping and eating and taking Robierre's enforced exercise. Before I could settle, a draft from the door set the rushlights wickering. Another visitor. Boots, this time, curiously enough. Quiet, measured steps.

"Yes, I'm awake," I said over my shoulder, wishing I could lie facing the doorway at least. "And pleased for visitors." The infirmary was beginning to feel more like a public marketplace than a house of healing.

"Good. I've no wish to overtax you."

The quiet boots and low, pleasant voice belonged to a gaunt man soberly dressed in secular garb and a roundbrimmed felt hat. As he came round the bed, he grabbed one of Robierre's stools. Under his other arm, he carried my book of maps.

My welcome froze on my lips, and I set myself ready to muster a host of ailments if the conversation grew dangerous. Jullian's talk of magistrates and pureblood investigators still had me twitching.

"My name is Gram Scriptor," he said, inclining his back and extending his open palm in greeting as southerners do. "My employer is visiting Gillarine and got wind of this magnificent volume. He's an educated man of wide-ranging interests and bids me learn what I can of it while we bide here that I might record the information in his journals. Abbot Luviar graciously permitted us to view the book and suggested I consult you with my questions, if you felt up to it." *Scriptor* . . . a secretary, then, of unnotable family.

"I don't know that I could tell you aught you cannot read from the book itself," I said as he settled himself on the stool.

He was something near my own age, and not a bad-looking fellow, save for an unhealthy gray hue to his complexion. His close-trimmed black hair, beardless chin, and conservative attire—ash gray cape over an unadorned knee-length tunic of dark gray—accentuated the hollows in his cheeks. His eyes sat deep, dark, I thought, though that could just be shadows from his hat.

"If nothing comes of my questions, so be it." A grave, modest smile softened his severe appearance. "At the least I can report to my master that I did as he asked, which is often quite enough to satisfy him once the . . . mmm . . . storm of displeasure . . . is past. Just tell me if I press too much or if you tire."

I had to be careful. To refuse this fellow might offend the abbot. And I'd not wish the abbot—or this man, whoever he was—to conclude I'd stolen the book after all. Likely I knew enough to satisfy a besieged secretary. "Ask what you will. I'll do my best."

"I'm ever grateful." He scooted his stool closer to the bed, so we could view the book together. He leafed through several pages. "Of course I've seen common maps—a few scratched lines and place names and perhaps a landmark or two. But I've no experience of such fine maps—a sorcerer's maps—and so great a variety of them. The written explanations in the book itself are confusing. I thought perhaps that the lord who'd given it to you might have explained what kinds of maps these are and how their magic works."

Gram offered me the book, and I turned a few pages, opening to a leaf displaying four small maps of different kinds. I stared at the page—its lines and symbols evoking far too much of memory. On his random appearances at our house, my grandfather had forced me to sit with him and look at his book, whispering in my ear of its importance, of its perfection, of its cleverness and magic, and how I must learn to use it. His breath had smelled of cloves, onions, and black ale, his body of unwashed skin and horses despite his fine clothes. Disgust rippled through me alongside the recollection. Those sessions had lasted only as long as it took me to spit on his shirt and wriggle out of his grasp. But his lessons had always begun with this page.

"My— Mardane Lavorile told me that every variety of map is represented in this book," I began. "Most, like this one, are fichés." I pointed to the rigorous little rendering of roads, mountains, and rivers—very like the great maps stretched and mounted on the walls of my father's library. "It is accurate in heading, scale, and proportion, so that a lesser distance on the map implies a lesser distance in truth. And the details are as precise as the cartographer can make them . . ."

The secretary listened intently, as I explained about keys and compass roses, and interpreted some of the symbols—for mountains, water features, towns and cities, shrines and temples, and the like. He asked me to clarify a few points, but otherwise did not interrupt.

"This map, on the other hand"—I indicated a fanciful colored drawing of a town with buildings and bridges and roads all mismatched in size—"is of the type known as a grousherre. The streets and structures are drawn with proper connections and relative positions, so that you can know which road leads to which, or which house stands beside which bridge. But the size and proportion of each object is determined by its importance not accurate measure."

"That seems a strange way to make a map." Gram pored over the drawing for a moment, his face drawn up in a puzzle. "Makes me think the maker was an odd sort of fellow."

I grinned. "Exactly my own thought. I've never seen the purpose of them, save for making a page where the cartographer could show off and splash around all his colors of ink."

"So what about these other two? This one looks to be a coastline, but I don't understand the markings." The little map detailed the fanlike outlets of one of Morian's great rivers and the creneled inlets and channels on either side of it. Tiny numbers littered the expanse of land and sea.

"That's a portolan," I said. "A navigation map. The marks are winds and tides and notations for sailors' instruments. I've no skill with ships to be able to tell you more than that. And this last is an example of a *mappa mundi*—a rendering of the wider world as if viewed from Iero's heaven. You can always tell them by their oval shape." My grandfather had included three *mappa mundi* that spanned two pages each. "The one in the very back of the book shows the trade routes to Aurellia and to Pyrrha, the land of volcanoes."

"Now, what of the magic? I've heard tales of Janus de Cartamandua's maps . . ."

"Well . . ." I bit my lower lip, a reminder I often used to watch my mouth. This visitor had set me too much at ease. "I know little of that. I used only a few of the maps, as the mardane needed."

Supposedly, unlike those created by my father or my brother, Max, or any other cartographer in Navronne, my grandfather's maps showed the earth's most secret and holy places—magical pools, sacred groves, the earthly dwellings of spirits and angels, places that no traveler would ever "happen" upon. Places that could be found only by using these maps. So I had been told.

"But the abbot says you used the guide spells that unlock their power. I'm sorry to press. My master is"—he cleared his throat and ducked his head, his gray skin taking on a rosy cast—"excitable. So I beg your indulgence. Whatever you can tell me would be valuable. I'm afraid he's going to ask me to copy one of these before we leave the abbey."

Though I didn't begrudge him the knowledge, I sincerely wished the fellow would stop asking questions. Yet he was gently spoken and seemed a mournful sort. And I knew well of *excitable* masters who asked the impossible.

"You see this oval banner on the larger map," I said. "It's called a cartouche. Look carefully and you'll find the words of the guide spell scribed there, or if the map is too small to have a cartouche, you'll find it buried in the border decorations. But copying won't give you any use of it. The mardane told me that the cartographer's magic is in the *rendering*, not just the words and symbols."

"Ah." He sat up straight and sighed. "Well, that's good news for me, if my lord will believe it. So how would you *invoke* the spell?"

"Speak the words of the spell while tracing your finger along your desired route. With the aid of the spell and a bit of common wisdom, your mind and senses will tell you when you stray from the path. It's useful enough." So I had been told. Endlessly.

"And that's all?"

I sagged back onto my pillows. "If a fellow like me can do it, I've no doubt anyone can."

Gram smiled again as he closed the book and stood to go. "I think you speak yourself an injury, sir. Your explanations were very clear, and you've surely a good head for maps and scouting. Someday perhaps I can return this favor."

I appreciated his effort to be kind. Old resentments about family and books and written words could not but taint my answers. He had no way to know that maps were of no use to me. "Your employer . . . he would like to own such a book as this?"

"In truth, not. He gives all his books to Gillarine." Gram cocked his head to one side, curiosity blossomed like a daylily at dawn. "But I thought you were taking vows. Don't initiates give—?"

"Yes, yes, I am," I said, gathering my wits. "But I wasn't sure what to do with the book . . . or whether the abbot would actually *want* such a valuable one when the price of it could do so much in the way of almsgiving."

Gram nodded and held out his palm again. "Abbot Luviar is very wise. He'll guide you rightly. Heal well, friend, and thank you."

Once he'd gone, I longed for some other visitor to break the evening's quiet. Not right that such a gentlemanly fellow should lance old boils and leave me to suffer the stink.

No one came.

Rain entirely in appropriate to Ardra's driest season drummed on the roof all night, slowing only when the blackness beyond the horned window yielded to gray. I slept fitfully, seeing far too much of both night and dawn. Daylight brought Brother Gildas.

Brother Robierre waved a wooden mallet he used for crushing seeds and pods, as he talked over my head with the dark-browed Gildas. "Ignore his complaining. Any man who can talk and eat as he does is fit enough to take wherever you will for an hour. Keep him moving, and send for me only if he collapses altogether."

"Am I to have no say in this?" I said, spitting out the detritus of hulls and stems that showered from his implement. "My leg—"

"You have applied to take vows, including strict obedience bound by punishments both in this life and the next. If you insist on 'having your say,' perhaps you'd best reconsider your future." Brother Gildas held up a white wool shirt he'd pulled from a black and white bundle in my lap.

"He's not broken his fast as yet this morning," said the infirmarian. He retreated to his worktable, where he dumped a bag of dried seedpods into a large wooden bowl and attacked them with his mallet as if they were a nest of Iero's detractors. "Never saw a man relish our victuals as he does. Point him toward the kitchen, and he'll keep apace."

Shivering in the cold damp, I thrust my head and bare arms into the thick shirt. "There's more folk eating bark soup than mutton broth of late, Brothers," I mumbled. "Must I go barefoot?"

"Wear your own boots today. You'll receive your cowl and sandals on the day you take your novice vows, which we do sincerely hope will be your choice." Brother Gildas smiled as if to soften the sting of his earlier rebuke, while I fumbled with clean white woolen trews and black knee-length hose. When my tight shoulder bandage hampered me, he knelt by the bed like a trained manservant, smoothly tugging the stiff, heavy boots onto my big feet, tucking in the hose, and tightening the laces up my legs.

"Up now," he said, rising and offering me his hand. "Don your gown. Then we'll go walking to stretch your limbs, I'll ask you a few questions for Father Abbot, and we'll find sustenance before you wither."

Ah, the questioning. No one had come to the infirmary on the previous day to test my knowledge of Saint Ophir's Rule. Jullian, who had taken it upon himself to visit me at least three times a day, had reported that Brother Sebastian had not yet returned from Pontia, and Brother Gildas had been closeted with the abbot and "visiting abbey benefactors" all day "except when they went to see the progress on the lighthouse." The presence of a lighthouse here, at least six hundred quellae from Navronne's northern seacoast, struck me as an oddity, even allowing for my usual morning dullness.

The prospect of interrogation damped my already soggy spirits. Awkwardly I wrestled the common black wool gown over my head, not at all sure I could bring myself to take vows here—even for a season. Rules and restrictions and righteous preaching curdled my stomach like vinegar in milk. If I could find a buyer for the book of maps, then perhaps I could find a less restrictive haven, perhaps a lornly widow who needed pleasuring.

The heavy garment enveloped me from neck to ankles, an unlikely happenstance as I had never failed to be the tallest man in any gathering since I had reached my full height at nineteen. But even more extraordinary was the sense of safety that enfolded me with the thick black wool, the same as that worn by every other monk throughout Navronne. Sweet, blessed anonymity.

Most ordinaries viewed pureblood life as god blessed and couldn't imagine why any of us would choose to forgo it. They didn't understand about contracts and protocols, submission rules and breeding laws, all the things that had made me feel as if someone had bound me head to toe with silken cord and locked me blind and deaf in a coffin.

Under the oversight of the Pureblood Registry, pureblood families contracted out their magical services for a great deal of money. As Navronne's nobles, magistrates, and clergy profited handsomely from the magic of our undiluted Aurellian blood, these parties had devised an inviolable compact a century ago, requiring every knight, magistrate, reeve, and sheriff to enforce the Registry's rules. Not even a Karish abbot would dare disobey the fugitive laws. Harboring a common fugitive—a thief or a deserter—past his fourteen days of sanctuary would cost Abbot Luviar disgrace and ten years' income—everything his abbey collected or produced—meaning ten years' groveling to the local magistrates to return enough to allow the brothers to eat. But if the abbot was judged to have knowingly hidden a pureblood renegade—a *recondeur*—those magistrates would burn his abbey and his fields, and then they would hang him.

So they just couldn't know. A *recondeur* with any sense learned quickly to keep his head down, his lies consistent, his past private, and his appearance unremarkable. I smoothed my warm, unremarkable wool layers and felt a grin split my face.

After fumbling briefly in the folds of his own gown, Brother Gildas pressed an alder walking stick into my hand. "A gift from Brother Horatio, our carpenter. Welcome to our brotherhood."

He slipped his shoulder under my right arm, and we stepped through the infirmary door into a chill, watery daylight. The infirmary sat off by itself, separated from the abbey proper by a patch of wet grass and a soggy herb garden. Far across the sea of gray slate roofs and the warm yellow stone of sturdy walls, the vaults of the abbey church soared heavenward.

"We'll visit the cloister garth first," said Gildas, pointing toward the grander structures beyond the infirmary garden. "The abbey's heart."

A flagstone path led us across a rock-lined channel that funneled water under the infirmary and past a squat wooden structure with two massive stone chimneys. Its jumbled wood stacks and the heaven-blessed scent of hot bread proclaimed it a bakehouse.

The place seemed inordinately quiet. Water dripped from roofs and gutters. A fat, cold splatter on my head made me even more grateful for my wool layers. In his unending quest for cleanliness, Brother Anselm had bade me shave my face and trim my tangled hair the previous day.

Once we passed the bakehouse, the infirmary no longer blocked our view to the south. I shook loose of Gildas's arm for a moment and stopped to savor the spectacle. Mists and smokes and occasional pools of pale sunlight drifted over the green, steep-sided valley and the river, a flat band of silver that looped around the abbey precincts. Beyond the sheen of the river, a field of barley rippled gently in the soft rain, as healthy a crop as I'd seen in five years. My throat tightened at the beauty of it, and my eyes filled with more than raindrops, which left me feeling a proper weakling fool. Since I'd left the nursery, I'd never wept but when I was drunk.

"I'm assuming you've seen grain fields, tanneries, mills, and sheep, all those things we'd find in the outer courts and south of the river—the River Kay, this is. If Father Abbot judges your calling that of a lay brother—suitable for manual labor, rather than the more challenging studies of a choir monk—you'll live out your days in those surrounds."

Ranks and privileges—even in a brotherhood. I shouldn't have been surprised. Gildas offered me his shoulder again, but I shook my head and hobbled along beside him.

As we rounded the corner of the garden, the monk walked faster as if to keep up with his thoughts. "The true peace of the monastic life is found in prayer and contemplation, study and scholarship. We don't allow speech in the cloisters, library, or scriptorium, but sign to each other for necessary communication."

"Peace will be welcome," I said, working to keep up with his brisk pace. "There's little enough to be had in this world, and talking never seems to improve matters. Though truly, telling stories of an evening or singing chorus to a bard are fine pleasures . . . holy gifts . . . as well. I'll wager you brothers come from everywhere and have much to share in that way—after all your studying and contemplating, of course." Surely they talked of something besides gods and holy writs. Surely they talked. All this broody silence seemed unnatural.

"Within the framework of our discipline, certainly we converse—some of us more, some less. Brother Infirmarian says you've traveled all over Navronne and are overflowing with curious tales. I'd like to hear of your experiences."

"No denying I've had restless feet . . ." My mind sorted through my spotted history like a washwoman picking through soiled and ragged linen. Sadly, I found little fit for display. Gildas wouldn't be looking for adventures and oddments like those Jullian teased out of me on his daily visits. "I followed King Eodward all the way to the Caurean shores. After he died, I hired out on the docks in Trimori for a while, but the Caurean storms frosted my bones worse than Ardran winter. I think the Adversary's domain is surely ice, Brother Gildas. Not fire at all. Is that false doctrine? The holy writs say the wicked will burn, and I've found that cold burns worse than fire."

"I've not heard that point argued," he said. Though he knit his solid brow, his face was not so sober. "Perhaps Brother Sebastian will pursue the question in your studies. Go on. Tell me more."

"Well, I moved on to Savil and apprenticed to a tanner—honest work, but the stink is poison to a tender stomach such as mine . . ."

At the far end of the walk a plain rectangular building stretched off to our left. On the littered muddy ground behind it, three lay brothers, their gray scapulars tucked up in their belts, wrestled the trunk of a sturdy oak from a donkey dray. Another of the brethren was shifting a pile of new-split logs to the wood stores stacked neatly in the building's undercroft.

"The lay brothers' reach," Brother Gildas said, nodding to the busy fellows when I paused in my babbling. "Their sleeping quarters and refectory, and the food, oil, wool, and wood stores for the abbey. So did you stay in Morian?"

I moved on carefully. "Nay. After the winter in Avenus, cutting stone in the quarries, I heard the call to labor on the hierarch's new cathedral in Palinur. A fine thing to build for Iero's own house . . ."

. . . and excellent pay on a sacred project, intended to proclaim Iero and his Karish church as triumphant over the elder gods and their Sinduri council. I had worked in Palinur only one season, though. The labor had been grueling, the hours long, and the punishments for any lapse in workmanship severe. And indeed, the proximity to my family and the attendant risks of being identified had made the royal city unpalatable. Once I'd padded my purse enough to last a season more, I was off to try something new.

It was not fear of discovery made me move so often. *Recondeurs* were rare, and every one of them was recaptured within half a year, hauled up for public flogging or humiliation, and then vanished from sight and speech, save for horrified whisperings among pureblood families about "close confinement" and "unrestricted contracts." Every sorry soul of them failed in rebellion because the fool could not forgo using the bent to soften the hardships of ordinary life: hunger, cold, hard work, uncertainty. The Registry would never search the places I lived, because they'd never imagine a pureblood forsaking his comforts for a life where he'd not know when he'd eat next. I had refused to learn much of spellworking as a child—as I had refused to learn much of anything they tried to pound into my head—so I'd little to give up.

As it was, I'd just never found any occupation worth the bother of staying in one place. Restless feet, just as I'd told Gildas. Incurably restless feet, in fact. A disease.

The path turned sharply back toward the river. We left it behind and angled right into a brick alley.

"Gillarine seems well constructed," I said, seizing an excuse to divert the conversation from myself. "What building is this to have windows so many and so fine?"

"The monks' refectory," said Brother Gildas. "You'll be happy to hear that novices get meat three times a week and half again the portions of the rest of us. We use all our wiles to lure the worldly into harmony with the god."

As I picked my way across the uneven bricks of the pooled and puddled alley, I caught a merry glint beneath his sober brow. Cheerful humors can redeem even excessive piety. I liked him.

"Gillarine must truly lie on holy ground to produce such bounty," I said. "The patroness of travelers led me here, no doubt of it."

"We've exceptional soil and water here. The font in Saint Gillare's shrine is said to be rooted in a holy spring." All the monks and friars I'd ever met seemed to wear a secret pleasure beneath their holiness, like gamers who carry skewed dice up their sleeves. Gildas was no different.

The brick passage squeezed past a coal store and kitchen building and then widened as we approached a colonnaded walkway that extended right and left and all the way around the broad green garth beyond it. The walkway's tiles had been laid in intricate coiled patterns like those on Aurellian urns and doorposts, with the trilliot, the three-petaled lily of Navronne, tucked into its loops here and there, alongside the golden sunbursts reminding us of the One God's glory.

Gildas laid a finger on his lips. I had not actually noticed the bustle of kitchen and bakehouse, the whacks and grunts of the wood choppers, or the complaints of distant sheep as we walked from the infirmary . . . not until we stepped into the cloisters of Gillarine and all such common sounds dropped away. The place was so quiet, I could almost hear my own blood flowing.

We crossed the cloister walk and paused at the edge of a vast square of healthy green. The garth was bounded on four sides by the slender columns and graceful roof arches of the cloister walks, and dominated by the church's vaulted roof and slender towers, directly across from us. To our left loomed the unadorned bulk of the lay brothers' reach. On our right, a round-domed structure with lancet windows of colored glass and a number of other fine buildings with many windows crowded the cloister walk. And in the center of the garth stood a shrine, its interlocked arches of delicate stonework looking very like a large birdcage.

Few monks were abroad. One sat reading on a narrow bench enclosed on three sides, one of forty or fifty such carrels tucked under the cloister by the church. Another hooded brother halted and bowed before passing into the shrine beneath a stone lintel supported by two lithe stone angels who had somewhere lost their wings. He quickly reappeared, a copper ewer in his hand.

Gildas pointed toward the shrine and stepped onto the cobbled path that led across the grass. I dutifully followed . . .

Darkness engulfed me. I staggered sideways, limbs quivering, joints turned to jelly. Weak . . . sick . . . gasping . . . starved for air and sound, as well as light. *Gods of mercy, what have I done that I should be struck blind?* Guilt and horror, the surety of death and vengeance wrung my neck like a hangman's noose, while remnants of old sins chased each other through my conscience like brightly colored birds, only to be swallowed in the blackness.

And then, as quickly as the night had fallen, all was consumed by light, as if the unsullied sun of summers past shot its beams straight into my eye sockets. As an avenging angel come down from heaven, the light swept away terror and in its place left a bright and sharp-edged tenderness that wrenched my heart. I cried out and stumbled backward.

A sharp crack on my skull brought the world—the green garth, the shrine, the cloister walk, the dull morning light—into focus again. I gulped air into my starved lungs. A cherubic rump protruded from the low arch where I had whacked my head. I spat on my middle finger, slapped the little aingerou, and prayed its friendly spirit to protect me from collapsing or exploding. No battle wound or shock had ever afflicted me so precipitously.

Brother Gildas's gaze flicked from my face, to the serene enclosure, to my hand that now gripped the carved sprite as if seeking only its structural support. I half expected his lip to curl and his mellow voice to denounce me immediately as a heathen blasphemer. But he merely gripped my waist securely and assisted me back into the alley, looking a bit puzzled.

"Perhaps we've overdone," he said when we were outside the cloister bounds again. "And you with an unbroken fast. Can I help?"

The world was so bright. So sharp. I pressed my head to the cool stone of the refectory wall and drew a ragged breath. "A drink of something . . . ale . . . or wine . . . please."

Anything to dull the glare that yet vibrated behind my eyes like a fresh knife wound, to soothe the ache that throbbed in my chest as if I had lost my last friend or heard the last song ever to be sung.

Gildas pried me from the wall and assisted me down the alley, through a wooden gate and a muddy herb garden, and into the steams and smokes of the abbey's kitchen. Two lay brothers, half obscured behind hanging baskets and vermin safes, stood at two long tables, trimming or chopping vegetables—turnips, garlic, carrots, and leeks—while a wizened, stoop-shouldered monk worked alongside them, grinding herbs with mortar and pestle. A slight figure in a layman's hooded cloak of brick red deposited a flat, covered basket on one of the tables and retreated toward a far door.

"Thank you, Squire Corin," called a ruddy-faced, leather-pated monk who stirred an iron vat hung over the great central hearth. "We'll hope poor Gram finds more appetite at supper. Brother Cellarer will send better wine for your master."

"Jerome!" my companion called across the stone-floored vastness.

"What can I do for you, Brother Gildas?" said the ruddy-faced monk as he emptied a wooden bowl of chopped cabbage into his pot. With the efficiency of long practice, he set the cavernous bowl aside, snatched a long-handled spoon from a rack on the soot-blackened wall, and poked at the cabbage that sizzled and spattered in his pot.

"Have you a bit of something mild and sustaining for our newest aspirant?" said Gildas, steadying me as I sank onto a pine bench beside the door. "I fear I've overtaxed him on his first excursion from the infirmary."

Brother Jerome spun around, his wooden spoon raised as if it were a hierarch's crozier, ready to assert his holy authority in this domain. "The supplicant who brought the Cartamandua maps?"

The whole world seemed to stop and stare just then, even the departing layman, who paused in the half-open doorway across the room and lifted his red hood slightly as if to see me better.

"Aye, the same. Still recovering from his injuries and unfed this day. My misjudgment." Gildas returned his sober scrutiny to me. "And I beg forgiveness for that," he said quietly. "Unworthy of me to assume . . . uh . . . that your strength was greater than you showed."

I waved off his concern. My leg and back had contributed naught to my weakness that I could judge. Yet if I told Gildas what I had experienced, surely nothing good would come of it. The monks would call it a sign of Iero's displeasure, pile on penances or rituals to reform me, and likely send me away. If some god or spirit or magical being *did* live within that garth, it must—

The likely truth stung my skull like a pebble from a sling. The shrine . . . the font . . . the murdered Brother Horach! Some people said that spirits loosed in savage torment would linger in the place of death, become revenants. Had I somehow invoked his wrath . . . or his benevolence? The contrary nature of the encounter left it open to myriad interpretations.

The world moved on again. The monks were back to chopping and grinding. The beardless servant vanished through the door. Forgoing fruitless speculation, I breathed deep, pleased to smell the garlic and to feel the steam that hissed from the wilted cabbage as Brother Jerome tossed aside his spoon and emptied a crock of liquid into his pot.

Brother Gildas filled a wooden cup from a nearby barrel. I drained it before his hand had moved away. Lovely ale, new made, not old. "Iero's grace," I said, and he brought me another.

"I've a barley loaf and syfling cheese will suit a fragile constitution," said Brother Jerome, once he had tamed his soup. Thick gray hair fringed his leathery tonsure. He rummaged briskly in the flat basket and extracted a wrapped bundle and a small crock. "Sent back from the guesthouse untouched. Father Prior says Lord Stearc's secretary Gram is a sickly sort and I thought to bolster him, but all the fellow took this morning was Robierre's strengthening tea."

Ah, Gram—the mournful fellow who'd consulted me about the maps. He'd had an unhealthy cast to his skin. A lord's secretary.

The loaf was chewy where it should be and tender everywhere else, and the soft cheese tasted of almonds. Unflinching, I ate every morsel of both and buried my disturbance in the homely comforts of a well-run kitchen. Jerome and his minions, as with all who worked in kitchens and brewhouses, wielded power I understood.

Brother Gildas and I bade the kitchen staff farewell and trudged slowly past the lay brother's reach in a light rain. I felt almost myself again. Likely Brother Gildas's estimate of my collapse had been right, naught but hunger and healing. I'd had little experience of common sickness.

"Gillarine seems a vastly holy place," I said. Healthy grain, plump vegetables, untainted sheep, spirits in its garth . . . I doubted any house in Navronne could boast such bounty.

"Many in our brotherhood have found it so. I have discovered my own destiny here—against every expectation of my life."

His words left an offer hanging in the air, something more generous than tavern friendships. More honest. I was gratified, and a bit astonished, at such trust. But if I probed deeper, he would rightly expect to do the same. And that could not happen. Of all the protections I had built over the years, the surest was to keep my secrets close.

Fumbling about for a new topic, I hobbled across a cart track that led from the lay brothers' reach southward along the Kay. The view of the wide, shallow river and the mist-shrouded valley, bound by forested ridges and the high mountains far to the south, recalled Jullian's odd tidbit. "Tell me, Brother, why would anyone be building a lighthouse so far from the sea?"

Even the broad River Yaronal that separated the kingdom from the brutish herdsmen to the east could be no nearer than two hundred fifty quellae, and likely unnavigable at that nearest point. Indeed, I wasn't certain people *built* lighthouses on rivers, much less in green vales like these.

My inquiry, posed in all innocence, halted Brother Gildas in midstride. "Who spoke to you of a lighthouse?"

One never reveals one's sources when queried with such severity. "Mmm . . . I don't recall. So many people come in and out of the infirmary."

After a moment, he smiled and nudged me onward. "Well, of course, you haven't yet seen the church windows on a day when the sun shines, else you'd grasp the reference. Come now, tell me more of Palinur."

A nice recovery, but I didn't believe him in the slightest.

As we crested a slight rise between the cart track and the infirmary garth, a cloaked horseman barreled up the track through the increasing drizzle, passing just behind us. He vanished in the cluster of buildings behind the lay brothers' reach.

Brother Gildas halted again, glancing after the rider and then to the infirmary, squatting peacefully with its back to the river. "Can you make it the rest of the way on your own, Valen? The hour is Sext, and I've duties before prayers."

"Certainly. The air has done me good. I was beginning to feel like a sheep in a pen, shut up in that infirmary."

With an admonition to inform Brother Badger of my weakness at the cloister garth, Gildas hurried off, not in the straightest path to the church, but in the same direction as the rider, soon lost to sight as well. A departure as enigmatic as his excuse. No bells had rung for the holy Hour. This place seemed to nurture mysteries: lighthouses, savage murders, an intelligent abbot who welcomed vagabonds like me, and a spirit in the cloister garth who did not.

Monastery life moved slowly, so I understood. Though abbots might be required to heed the winds of politics, their flocks of holy brothers sat outside of the stream of time and events, wrapped up in scholarship that spanned centuries and prayer and contemplation that spanned the boundaries of earth and heaven. So why, of a sudden, did I feel as if I were being rushed down a dark alley by a gang of smiling jacklegs who would pick my pockets and plant a shiv in my spleen before dawn? I hobbled quickly toward the infirmary.

Chapter 5

Vesper bells clanged and hammered. The monks were gone to prayers again, the lingering draft from their departure my only company in the quiet infirmary. Robierre had left me a brimming posset, dosed with extra honey in apology for sending me out walking too strenuously.

In truth my leg felt better recovered from the day's adventure than my spirit. I could not shake my thoughts free of the murdered monk. Had this Horach truly made himself known to me? Surely of all residents of this abbey, I knew the least that might ease a tormented soul. But a man left himself open to mortal peril did he ignore the demands of the dead.

My fingers traced the smooth curves of the turned wood mug. The bells fell silent. The monks would go to supper after prayers, which meant near two hours alone here with naught to think of but a youth left in agony to bleed, unable to cry for help.

Before I knew it, I'd thrown my damp gown over my dry shirt, pulled my boots over my bare feet, and retrieved my walking stick. Guided by the church towers and wafting smoke that smelled pleasantly of onion and garlic, I limped across the infirmary garth and through the puddled passage between the kitchen and refectory, retracing our path of the morning. Pigeons' cooing and the fading echoes of plainsong accompanied me into the deserted cloisters. Thick clouds had stolen the early-evening light.

I shivered. Saint Gillare's wingless angels gleamed pure white against the dusk. The chill air, heavy with moisture, clung to skin like mud and smelled of rich earth and green grass. To retreat felt stupid and cowardly, yet now I was here, I couldn't steel myself to step wholly into the garth. My hand squeezed the smoothed knob of the walking stick. There were other ways to approach uncertain ground than just blundering in.

Though I had denied it for years, adamantly avoiding occupation as a scout or guide as if to prove that denial, I *had* inherited the familial bent for route finding and tracking. My Cartamandua bloodlines were well documented, of course, enshrined in the Registry in Palinur before my birth and witnessed on the day I took my first breath. I'd always felt like a prized cow, bred to supply Navronne with the cream of sorcery.

I wandered down the south cloister, past the kitchen wall and around the corner into the walk that fronted the lay brothers' reach. Dared I release magic here? Whether I used it in formulated spellwork or to trigger my family bent, it would leave traces, detectable by a Registry inspector. Or perhaps an abbey sanctified to Iero, its Rule forbidding use of magic, might be warded to prevent spellcasting and give off noises or explosions if I breached its protections. Every instinct said not to risk it, but then again, my instincts were unused to the requests of unquiet spirits.

I tossed some of Robierre's stock of bergamot onto the grass that young Horach might use it for the Ferryman's tally, apologizing that I'd naught better to offer. Then, clutching my walking stick, I eased myself to kneeling. Crouched at the verge of the west cloister, some halfway down its length toward its meeting point with the church, I laid my palms on the cool wet grass, shaped my intent, and released just a spit of magic.

My limited experience of such trials led me to expect an image of the square to resolve itself in my mind: the grass and stones, the shrine, the bounding columns and walkways, the size, shape, and source of the font. Not a visual image, but more of an understanding of structure, composition, direction, and history, and if I was fortunate, a sense of what obstacles, spells, or spirits might lie here. But the sensations confounded all expectations.

The earth pulsed beneath my hands, warm and living, its lifeblood a deep-buried vein of silver, as plainly visible to my eye as the shrine itself. The memory of all who had walked here wove a pattern in the earth, each path sharp edged against the clarity of a long and reverent quiet. The understanding of the garth's composition and direction existed, not as some separate image to be analyzed, but embedded in my flesh as plainly as the skill of walking or speaking. And even beyond these marvels, something more teased at my spirit . . .

I breathed deep and tried to quiet my trepidations, to open my senses and push deeper. Just on the edge of hearing, the sighing notes of a vielle quivered in the stillness, and a woman's clear voice intoned a haunting, wordless melody that swelled my soul with wonder and grief. A memory . . . and yet a presence, too . . . if I could but sort out the music and its meaning—

The unseen bludgeon struck again. *Saints and angels!* I toppled backward, landing hard on my backside. As on my first encounter with this place, the blow slammed me square between my eyes. Dizzy and befuddled, I pressed my fingers to my forehead, sure I'd find a bruise swollen the size of a cat. But, though my wounded thigh complained loudly that it was twisted to the point of tearing Brother Badger's stitches, both brow and temples seemed intact.

If Brother Horach wanted my attention, he had gotten it. But did he want me to see what lay here—something far older than a youthful monk—or was he the one who so forcibly forbade my intrusion? I rubbed my brow and tried vainly to recapture the moments before the blow: the warmth of the earth, the silver thread of an underground spring, the music—so beautiful, so dreadfully sad.

I had long speculated that Iero was just another name for Kemen Sky Lord, Creator of Earth and Heaven. But neither Kemen, nor Iero, nor any god or spirit had ever made himself known to me so forcefully. I didn't like it. My hands trembled and my stomach shifted uneasily.

As I stumbled to my feet and untwisted my gown, a brief burst of plainsong from the church intoned the *perficiimus* that ended every Karish prayer and service. Someone threw open a side door that opened onto the east cloister walk, directly across the garth from me. The monks would soon be filing out on their way to the refectory. Unwilling . . . unable . . . to explain what I had just experienced, I hobbled quickly through an arched passageway that divided the undercrofts just behind me.

The sturdy simplicity of the clustered buildings behind the lay brothers' reach implied design for use rather than devotion. Lingering scents of roasted barley, yeast, and sweetly rotting refuse named the rambling structure with arched doors a brewhouse. The tall, windowless building set on stubby stone piers was likely a granary, its floor raised to discourage vermin and damp. Twilight had already gathered in the warren of wood and stone, and a light drizzle fell from the heavy sky.

The sudden sounds of a slamming door and a horse's whinny, just as I reached the corner of the brewhouse, flattened my back against the stone wall of the deserted alley. No question the evening's events had set me on edge. Heart galloping, I peered around the corner.

A small muddy yard fronted a well-built three-story house with a steep-pitched roof and many fine windows. Soft light from the upper windows and a single torch in a door bracket illumined three saddled horses tethered by the stoop.

A man in a brick-colored cloak darted down the steps and wrestled a leather satchel onto one of the saddles, buckling straps to hold it. But the horse sidestepped nervously, the fellow's arms were too short, and the satchel slid back onto his shoulders, dragging off his red hood. Fine boned and fair, he was younger than I'd guessed from his height. A tight braid bound his thick bronze-colored hair.

Blundering into strangers' urgent business violated my usual practice, so I did not step out to help. In moments, Brother Gildas appeared on the stoop, holding open the heavy door for two other men. These two descended the steps slowly, one supporting the other. The more robust of the pair, a big, hawk-faced man with a narrow beard and meaty shoulders, barked an order at the squire—for the red-cloaked youth was surely Squire Corin from the kitchen. The house must be Gillarine's guest quarters, these strangers the abbey's noble benefactors.

The squire yanked his strap tight and hurried around to help the others lift the weaker man into the saddle. The gaunt, dark-haired fellow, racked with coughing as he gripped the pommel, was none but the gentlemanly secretary Gram. The hawk-faced man's cloak fell back as he shoved his charge into the saddle. The sleeves of a hauberk gleamed from under his holly-green surcoat, and his jewel-hilted great-sword sparkled in the torchlight. A warrior, then, as well as a lord—Gram's "excitable" employer.

Horrid weather to ride out. The faint drizzle had become an insistent shower, pattering on the brewhouse roof and dribbling from the gutters and downspouts. To get back to my dry bed in the infirmary, I had either to return through the cloisters or cross this courtyard, inviting Brother Gildas's perceptive examination. If they would all just go . . .

Relieved, I watched as Brother Gildas gave the squire a hand up to his mount and retreated to the sheltered stoop. The warrior swung his bulky body into the saddle, exposing a device on his surcoat.

I uttered a malediction—under my breath, so I thought, but the lord's head jerked up and twisted in my direction. Snatching my head out of sight, I slammed my back to the wall. Water sluiced down my neck. My skin felt as if swarming with midges.

Once, when I was eleven or twelve and lay in my bed bleeding from an encounter with my father's leather strap, my elder sister,

Thalassa, had chosen to break her long-standing habit and be civil. She told me of *obscuré* spells—certain patterns created in the mind and infused with magic that could cause one to be overlooked. In my usual way I had spat at her, called her a *vyrsté*—a pureblood whose parents had not paid enough attention to breeding lines—and ignored her.

Not for the first time, I regretted that choice. Embroidered in silver thread on the lord's holly-green linen was a howling wolf with a lily under its paw—the device of Evanore and its sovereign duc, Osriel the Bastard.

Lords of the night! Afflicted with a sudden case of the shivers and a raging desire to hide, I hobbled back down the alley and around a corner of the brewhouse, doing my best to keep my stick and my booted feet quiet. Behind me, a man issued a sharp command. In moments, the three horsemen rode right past me.

"Teneamus!" Brother Gildas's call followed them through the alley.

One of the three called an answer, softly enough no one but his companions and I could possibly hear. *"Teneamus!"*

Once the riders had vanished into the rainy gloom, I exhaled and took out as fast as I could down the alley. Though the torch was extinguished, lamps yet shone from within the guesthouse, but I saw no sign of Brother Gildas. As I hobbled across the yard and down the cart track that led through the lay brothers' workyard, inside my sleeves I splayed the three middle fingers of my left hand, and inside my head I recited three saints' names three times each. Whyever would a man of Prince Osriel's party be welcome at a Karish abbey?

Chilled to the marrow, I stripped to the skin before diving gratefully into my bed. By the time Brother Robierre and Brother Anselm returned from supper, bringing me leek soup and hot bread, I had managed to stop shivering. As the two men changed my dressings and fussed about their evening duties, I put my mind to an escape plan should I need to abandon the abbey in a hurry. I would winter in a cave before crossing paths with King Eodward's crippled bastard.

I ought to have had some sympathy with the youngest of Eodward's progeny or at least with his pureblood mother. Though not strictly a *recondeur*—she had not actually run away—Lirene de Armine-Visori had defied her family and the Registry's breeding laws by mating outside the pureblood families, an unforgivable offense, no matter that her lover was a king. Lirene had died when the boy was quite young, and stories named the halfbreed Osriel, raised out of the public eye, twisted in both mind and body.

Veterans who had served in Prince Perryn's ill-fated campaign to wrest Evanore's gold mines from his bastard half brother displayed wicked burn scars from Osriel's mage-fire arrows and told of comrades snatched in the night and returned without balls, tongues, or hands. They described plagues of nightmares that afflicted their encampments, and men and women found wandering the tangled forests naked and mindless, their privy parts blistered from forced breeding with gatzi—creatures from the netherworld, pledged to Magrog's service. And they swore that on every battlefield near Evanore, what dead were left to lie through the night were missing their eyes on the next morning. Which seemed not such a dreadful thing in itself compared to being dead, save that most Navrons believed a man's soul resided in his eyes. Without a soul, a man was left with no hope of an afterlife, for the Ferryman had naught to carry.

It's a soldier's wont to top the next man's tale. For years, I took no more stock in the stories of Prince Osriel's evils than in legends of angelic visitations or of the Danae whose dancing supposedly nurtured fields and forests. Gods knew battle left enough mutilated bodies for every demonic purpose. The pox from unclean whores was a scourge that could flay a man's loins, and drinking raw spirits squeezed from agueroot could scour a mind to blankness for a week. Yet over the summer, as Prince Bayard's march across Ardra drove us toward Evanore, one comrade and then another swore me to find him should he fall in battle, and to pierce his heart before nightfall to ensure he was well and truly dead before Osriel the Bastard came for him. Such stern belief cannot but wear upon a man's mind and take on the likeness of truth.

When the lay brother Anselm had hurried off to bed and the choir monk Robierre to the church for another bout of praying, I prowled through the infirmary stores. Using scraps of twine and linen from Brother Robierre's baskets, I wrapped up small amounts of his powders and herbs—anything he had in plenty that I might sell or need. I discovered an herb knife with a nicked blade shoved to the back of a shelf, and I took that, too, bundling it with the medicines in a rag and stuffing the bundle under my palliasse with the bits of cheese and bread I'd saved from every meal.

As I worked, a lesser puzzle nagged at me. Pureblood families flaunted their unbroken descent from the decadent Aurellians by speaking Aurellian and Navron interchangeably. It was a useless skill that only they and hidebound scholars set store by now Aurellia was reduced from a great empire to a walled city a thousand quellae distant. But such childhood training penetrates very deep. Even after twelve years away from pureblood society, I could not have said in which language I articulated my thoughts. Therefore, I could wonder at the Aurellian farewell that Brother Gildas had exchanged with the Evanori lord. *Teneamus—*we preserve.

The infirmary was dark, a single tall rushlight left burning. After returning from his prayers, the yawning infirmarian had retired gratefully to his own bed in the monks' dorter, declaring me well enough to survive the night with only Iero's angels to watch over me.

The weather had taken a turn for the worse. Sleet clicked on the roof and the stone path outside the open window, threatening to freeze and rot what scanty harvest might have ripened in the disastrously short, cold summer. A month or more remained till Saldon Night, and I ought to be basking in Ardra's golden summer, pleasuring a milkmaid out of her chastity in a haystack instead of shivering in my bed.

Unnerved by the day's events, I was infernally restless. When my breath became visible in the air, I dragged the blankets over my head, abandoning my toes to the cold draft left by the waning flames in the infirmary brazier. My wounds itched and throbbed, more annoying than sore. But deep in my gut sat a small tight knot, cold and quiet for the moment, the threads that linked it to every particle of my being slack.

A disease had gnawed at my gut since I was seven, probably longer if one assumed the rebellious temper and indiscipline that caused my parents to despair of me in the nursery were its first manifestations. Every day of my life I had lived with an unrelenting restlessness. On occasion it would worsen, exploding into a tormenting fire in the blood and a virulent overexcitement of the senses—everything I heard or smelled or looked on exaggerated until my body felt raw. By the time I was ten these attacks had become a regular occurrence, and as I got older, the symptoms grew worse and lasted for days at a time. Even soft candlelight would blind me, whispers set my nerves screaming, and any smell stronger than porridge leave me nauseated. The knot in my gut was ever the precursor of an attack.

I lay wide-eyed, sated with the days of sleep, wishing I had been able to convince Brother Robierre to give me poppy extract again. He hoarded it so carefully. Said their plants were not propagating well in the foul weather. That the abbey had any healthy plants at all was a wonder. Perhaps their god had powers enough to protect his holy place.

Matins came and went, allowing me to forget myself for a while in the beauteous surge of their singing—fifty-three strong male voices honoring their god. What deity could fail to manifest himself with such power at his beck? Yet in the ensuing silence, the warning in my belly grew more insistent, and hot, as if Brother Robierre had made another incision and implanted a burning coal inside me.

I slammed a fist into the thin pillow wadded under my head. *This is far too early. It's scarce been a fortnight.* I buried my face in the pillow, unable to stop the calculation. We had abandoned the battle before its second day and spent two on the road, then I'd lain two days insensible in this infirmary, and four more recovering . . . and I'd last dealt with this a twelveday before the battle. Twenty-one days. Since I'd first chosen to control my disease with magic, I'd never felt its waking sooner than twenty-eight days. The problem, of course, was that the remedy had become its own disease, and I could no longer distinguish one from the other.

So think of something else. The wind whined in the cold and lonely blackness outside the infirmary walls. The blanket wool tickled my nose. Propped up on my elbow, I drained the last of the weak ale Brother Anselm had left me, and then threw the mug across the square red tiles. The clay vessel shattered. No rushes on the infirmary floor. No straw. Brother Anselm thought them unclean. I curled my arms over my head.

This is no battlefield with the stench of death all around. No whorehouse after the women have moved on to other customers. No stinking back street with rats and refuse your only company. Nor even is it that wretched house in Palinur where your existence was an offense to those who birthed you. You're fed and warm and healing. You've friends here already. You don't need this. Let the cursed sickness burn itself out.

But the coal took flame in my gut, its fiery wounding spreading rapidly into my chest and limbs, into my head, my eyes, my dry tongue. I shoved off the blankets and lay there naked and exposed, unbearably hot as I tried to breathe away the pain. The light seared my eyes. The rain drummed like thunder; the wind bellowed like maddened oxen.

Why had I thought of my parents? If ever the gods had played a wicked prank on human folk, it was on the day they quickened my father's seed in my mother's womb to produce me. From the distance of so many years, my parents' hatred seemed wholly out of proportion to my misdeeds—at least in the years before I learned to detest them in equal measure and was old enough to demonstrate it.

A spasm contorted every sinew in my back, as if a giant played knotwork with my spine. Cascading cramps wrenched my shoulder, legs, and belly. *Ignore them. You've been abed too long.*

On a small painted chest near my bedside lay my torn shirt, stained padded jaque, ragged braies, and hose, neatly folded and stacked. The monks had cleaned or brushed them as I lay insensible, and set them alongside my rifled rucksack. They wouldn't have examined the bag too carefully. Surely. I just needed to see.

I grabbed the rucksack, knocking the stack of clothes onto the floor. Every object I touched seared my skin as if it were iron new drawn from a forge. Jerking the scuffed leather bag onto my lap, I prayed that what I needed would be there. I turned the bag inside out and fumbled at the thick seam. Intact. *Blessed be all gods.* Now for a knife . . .

Holding on to the wall, the rucksack looped over my arm, I hobbled across the tiles to Robierre's worktable. I dragged the stinking rushlight close only to find it on the verge of guttering death. Muttering epithets, I snatched another from the stack under the table, set the fresh one aflame from the stub, and clipped it in the iron holder. Then, seated on the brother's stool, I used his well-honed herb knife to rip the long stitches that held the newer layer of leather to the bottom of the rucksack. *Great Kemen Lord of the Sky, Mother Samele, Lord Iero and your angels or Danae or whomever you dispatch to watch over your children be thanked.* The little green bag— the one Boreas had *not* found—fell into my trembling hand. And the craving swept through me as a fire sweeps across a parched grassland.

In the pool of smoky yellow light I set out the shard of mirror glass, the silver needle, and the white linen thread, and spilled the tiny black nivat seeds—all that was left of my emergency store—onto the table. The fragrance of spice, dust, and corruption burst from the nivat as I crushed the seeds with Robierre's knife. I could not rush, could not afford to be careless, yet the first monk who saw what I was about would know me as a cursed twist-mind, Magrog's slave, a gatzé's whore, and boot me over the wall to languish in the darkness with the rest of the Adversary's servants.

A prick of the needle freed three drops of blood from my finger to mix with the aromatic powder, the pain of the bloodletting as exquisitely shrill as a virgin's scream. My sinews cramped and knotted. My hands shook. Sweat beaded my brow, my arms, my back.

Soon . . . hold on . . . Perhaps my injuries had made the disease and the hunger for its remedy come upon me early and so dreadfully fast.

Holding one end of the thread between two fingers, I let the other end dangle into the reeking little mess, using the connection to channel every scrap of magic that lived in me into the patterned spell. Touching the mixture directly with my agonized flesh would sap the spell's strength before it reached full potency—a hard lesson I'd learned when first experimenting with this particular remedy. The black paste heated and bubbled. In the enchanted mirror glass I watched the otherwise invisible vapors rise from the unholy brew. Waiting . . .

A mixed-blood alley witch named Salamonde had given me the glass fragment on my fourteenth birthday. The disease had seared my gut and lacerated my senses with such virulence that day, I'd felt the Ferryman's breath on my neck. For the first and only time in my life, I had swallowed pride and hatred and begged my parents for help with my sickness. My mother, typically, retired to her bedchamber and drank herself senseless. My father tied me to his favorite grate and beat me until I pissed myself, insisting that my malady was naught but my vile nature festered in my soul. He said no remedy existed for it. And so, on that night, for the twentieth time that year, I broke the locks on my room and ran away. By the time they dragged me back home three days later, old Salamonde had introduced me to perversion.

The rushlight flickered. I squinted at the glass. One final wisp of vapor drifted upward, taking the last of the earthy scent. I scooped the dark droplets onto my finger and onto my tongue. The potent liquor spread quickly to my pain-racked extremities . . . the satisfaction of cool ale on a parched tongue . . . the scent of rain after drought . . .

Groaning, I snatched up my rucksack and bit down on the leather strap, for the tasteless paste that was my salvation would not instantly quench the fire. The perverse remedy had first to feed the torment. As did I.

I gripped Brother Badger's grinding stone and slammed it, edge on, into my wounded thigh. Once. Again. Fiery agony swelled to monstrous proportion . . . devouring my organs, my limbs, my senses . . . threatening to completely unhinge my mind . . . until the moment body and spirit teetered on the verge of dissolution, and then . . .

O, elixir of heaven! Rapture! An explosion of exhilaration engulfed every sense, every limb, every part and particle of my flesh and spirit, transforming pain to pleasure as quickly and as absolutely as the ax of a skilled headsman transforms life to death . . .

. . . and then with the same abruptness, it was gone, the convulsion of sensation past. Fire quenched. Cramps dissipated. Throbbing wounds silenced. Every shred of my being quivered with release, the searing heat of my flesh yielding to languid warmth like the aftermath of carnal climax, lacking only joy or merriment. Not oblivion, but assurance that the world was right and ordered exactly as it should be. The rucksack dropped to the floor. My forehead rested on the scratched wood, my dulled mind fallow, my senses throbbing in gratification. The knot in my gut unraveled.

The spell was called the *doulon*. Legend claimed the nasty little enchantment was Magrog's wedding gift to Nemelez when he took his human bride to the netherworld—to ease the pain of their coupling. And more than just the ignorant believed that every invocation of the doulon opened a door to Magrog's kingdom and allowed a demon gatzé to crawl into the earthly plane. Such was no concern of mine.

Some of those enslaved to the doulon burnt or mutilated themselves before they succumbed, for the degree of pleasure in the release always matched the severity of the pain that preceded it. I had not fallen so far out of mind as to do that—not yet, at least. Nor did I use it for ordinary physical discomforts that I could anywise tolerate. I told myself that these practices delayed the inevitable consequence. Every doulon slave went mad eventually, trapped inside a ruined body whose perceptions of pain and pleasure were irretrievably tangled. Unfortunately, between the disease itself and the nivat hunger, the consequences of stopping were equally dreadful. Once in the year just past, I'd had to wait three days until I could get nivat, and I would throw myself off a cliff before doing so again.

Move, fool. Quickly, before losing all sense, I licked the thread clean and purified the needle in the rushlight flame, packed all away in the empty green bag, and stuffed it in the bottom of my rucksack. No time or means to sew the flap shut again.

The bent, the power for spellworking, was the only virtue of my pureblood birth I'd ever seen, and for good or ill, I had chosen to abandon the small magics I had learned as a boy and whatever greater uses I might develop as a man and spend it all on this. I hobbled away from the worktable and threw the rucksack onto the painted chest. Naked and shuddering, I crawled under the blankets and gave myself to dreams of pain and pleasure.

Chapter 6

Between supper and Compline, as the gray light filtering through the infirmary's horn windows faded, I was alternately dozing and perusing the intricate little drawings attached to the margins and headings of my psalter. Though lacking the elaboration and gold leaf one would likely find in the abbey's service books, the little codex had been created with the care always given holy books. Had Brother Horach himself inked the illustrations? The copyist had surely borne a fascination with the natural world, inserting energetic and sometimes fantastical representations of stags, foxes, and racing hounds alongside the angels and vines that graced the prayers and psalms. I speculated as to whether he had suited the beasts' postures to the mood or sense of the prayer, which struck me as a clever idea.

Yawning, feeling lazy and dull-witted as always on the day after the doulon, I traced my fingertips over the letters as I had so often as a child. In those days, believing I might remedy my persistent failure to decipher the mystery of written words, I had allowed magic to roar from my body's center into the confounding shapes on the page—scorching no few books in the endeavor. The fingers are the conduit of magic.

I no longer wasted my resources on that particular exercise. I had come to terms with my incapacity and managed well enough all these years. But if these holy brothers discovered my lack, they would surely pitch me over their lovely wall. That was damnably annoying.

I slammed the book shut and hunched deeper in the bed, warm and dry again after the previous day's unsettling excursions. Jumbled thoughts of murdered monks and abbey benefactors who just happened to serve unsavory princes had plagued me all the boring day—or at least when I could avoid thinking of my empty nivat bag and the difficulty of refilling it. I had trained myself to set that worry aside for a few weeks between necessity, refusing to allow the disease or its unhealthy remedy to set the course of my life. The attack, a full week short of the usual and with so little warning, had profoundly unnerved me.

Under the more direct beams of the rushlight, Brother Anselm worried over his colored chart that detailed astrological influences on the body's humors, certain he would find some correlation with my relapse in the cloister garth. Sooner or later the earnest fellow would approach the bed with his piss jar or his magnifying lens or his well-polished lancet, asking politely to examine my eyeballs or the underside of my tongue or to take some sample of my regenerating bodily fluids.

I was trying to decide whether to give in to sleep and thus keep good Anselm at bay, when a blast of cold air heralded Jullian's appearance in the infirmary doorway. The boy was as pale as an Ardran milkmaid's ass. "Brother Anselm, Brother Robierre summons you immediately with his medicine box and both litters. We've wounded soldiers at the gates!"

"Who?" I said, sitting up straight as Brother Anselm jumped from his stool and dragged litter poles from beneath the vacant beds.

"Ardrans. Fifty of them at the least. Or a hundred . . . bloody . . . torn to pieces . . ."

The boy's peaked complexion and strangled declaration indicated that the evening's events had already profoundly altered his understanding of the world. Exposure to ugly injuries such as mine was one thing, but four or five cadres' worth of battle wounds would be far different. Angels preserve the boy from ever seeing the battlefield itself.

It had required many a tankard to dull the images of my own introduction to the soldiers' mysteries. I had never subscribed to myths of noble purpose or personal glory in battle, but I *had* believed that shoving a spear into a twitching body busily shitting itself could make a man of me. I'd blundered through innumerable bloody days since, as much avoiding other fools' spears and axes as wielding my own.

Brother Anselm wrapped the litter poles in their leather slings, dumped them into the boy's outstretched arms, and threw a stack of linens atop the load. After tossing a few loose items from the shelves into a wooden chest, he slammed the lid, fastened the latch, and hefted it onto his shoulder. Before you could blink, only the chilly draft remained with me in the infirmary.

The laws of sanctuary and the sanctity of abbey walls seemed suddenly flimsy.

Two of the royal brothers, Perryn, Duc of Ardra, and Bayard, Duc of Morian, had maintained a deadly balance for three years. As no one had produced Eodward's authentic writ stating elsewise, Bayard claimed the Navron throne by right and precedent as Eodward's eldest son. But Eodward had granted Prince Perryn regency in Ardra—the ancient seat of Caedmon's line—and Perryn insisted that this demonstrated Eodward's intent to name him king over his poorly educated elder brother.

The third and youngest brother, Osriel the Bastard, regent of Evanore, had taken no active part in the three-year dispute save his grisly reaping on the battlefield. Some said Osriel cared naught for ruling on earth, but aimed to supplant the divine Magrog himself as lord of the netherworld. Others claimed he was waiting only for his brothers to weaken each other so he could sweep them both aside with an army of gatzi.

Only in the winter just past had stories of a fourth brother—this child Pretender—risen, and as sure as dead men stink, before the rumor could gather strength enough to create him a rival, Bayard had made a devil's bargain that looked to win him the day. He had allied with the Harrowers.

The Harrowers denied both the elder gods and the Karish upstart Iero, claiming that Navrons had lost their proper fear of the true Powers who ruled the universe. Their priestess, Sila Diaglou, said that our cities and our plowing had defiled the land and that our false religions had caused us to forget these Powers that she called Gehoum, and that was why the weather had gone sour and the plagues and wars had risen.

For years people had laughed at a woman speaking out as if she were the divine prophet Karus come back again, set on changing the ways of the world. Yet, in the last years of Eodward's reign, when pestilence and storms grew worse and the king could pay no mind to aught but Hansker raiders—Sila Diaglou's direst predictions come true—folk began to listen and nod their heads. More and more wild-eyed rabble, dressed in rags and orange head scarves, heeded her call for burning and destruction to "harrow" the land and appease the Gehoum's wrath. Scorned by priests and nobles, she had grown her ragtag band of lunatics into an army to rival those of Navronne's princes.

Throughout the summer campaign, while Prince Perryn dithered and regrouped farther and farther south, claiming that no rabble could stand against his knights and legions, the Harrowers burnt villages and fields and left us nothing to eat and nothing to defend. And then Prince Bayard and Sila Diaglou had joined forces and swept us up like chaff from a threshing floor.

The abbey bells clanged in an urgent rhythm. Distant shouts, mysterious door bangings, and running footsteps from the infirmary courtyard accompanied the summons. The evening reeked of danger. Unable to lie still, I threw off my blankets and pulled on my wool shirt, trews, and hose.

A brown-clad body burst through the door and pelted down the long room to Brother Robierre's shelves—the other young aspirant, Gerard, a soft, stammering boy of fourteen. He shoved bowls and basins aside, knocking half of them clattering to the floor. Then he whirled about, dark stains on his arms and in his eyes. "B-b-bonesaws. Where does he k-keep them? He said the far end . . ."

I was already on my feet, alder stick in hand. "In that great iron chest down below."

By the time I joined him, the boy's trembling fingers had scarcely got the lid open. Together we lifted out two trays of small, fine instruments—pincers, scalpels, probing tools of thin wire, and the like—laid out between sheets of leather. In the bottom of the chest lay a number of larger, linen-wrapped bundles. The boy dragged out cautery irons, mallets, and strangely shaped implements of unknown purpose. I'd seen enough use of such tools to recognize the wide blade and thin, squared handle of the bonesaw.

"There. That one. That's likely what he wants. And you'd best take the larger iron as well."

The boy looked up at me like a begging pup, raising a small key in his hand. "And p-p-poppy extract. He said you'd know where to find it."

"I'd guess that every wounded man who comes here learns where the good infirmarian keeps Iero's salvation . . ." I limped to the corner of the room where the roof truss lapped over the wall, forming a high shelf, and lifted down the heavy iron casket that likely only Brother Badger and I could reach. ". . . but he chooses not to leave it loose about to tempt boys or weak-minded malingerers like me. It will be a boon to those you've seen, as will the care the brothers give them." Saints and angels, I didn't want the boy to start weeping.

I wheedled the recalcitrant lock open and handed over the precious brown flask. "Anything else?"

The boy shook his head, wiped his nose on his sleeve, and trotted out the door.

I stowed the nicked herb knife and the pilfered herbs and medicines in my rucksack and tied the bag around my waist with a length of linen bandage. Then I pulled my jaque over my woolen shirt, wrestled my boots onto my feet and my damp monk's gown over all.

Caution demanded I bolt. To strike out directly across the River Kay behind the infirmary would get me away from the abbey quickest. But the church would hold valuables—calyxes of gold or silver used for noblemen's offerings, or the offerings themselves—rare oils, coins, gems perhaps, or other gifts from wealthy benefactors and pilgrims. I made Iero's sign on breast and forehead, vowing to take only enough to pay for my book. Stealing from a god's house was a risky practice.

Though twilight lingered in the outer airs, night had already settled in the confines of the inner courts. The wood-splitters' yard was deserted, the wood stacked in the voluminous undercroft, splinters and flakes neatly raked and dropped in weatherworn tinder baskets. The ripe stench of a latrine overlaid the scents of brewhouse and granary. All very natural. Yet I peered over my shoulder fifty times in that short journey, and gripped my alder stick so fiercely I likely put dents in the smooth wood. The guesthouse sat dark. I breathed freely only after I hobbled into the maze of gardens and hedges before the church.

I paused amid the overgrown yews, wondering at the quiet. Perhaps circumstances were not so dire as the fears of naive boys implied. Only a fool would pillage a church and abandon such a comfortable sanctuary without ripe cause. So instead of bearing right into the church, I headed left toward the abbey gates.

Just inside the massive outer wall of the abbey and its twin-towered gatehouse lay the walled enclosure the brothers called the Alms Court. In this pleasant space of fountains and mosaics, where, on ordinary days, Brother Porter dealt with visitors, five dead bodies lay wrapped neatly in linen. A lay brother sponged blood and dirt from a sixth corpse, while a white-haired monk droned prayers over the dead man's battered head. The mournful Porter, Brother Cadeus, filled a pail at a splashing fountain and dashed it over the paving stones as if to expunge the horror.

Save for these few and a trickle of monks hurrying through with blankets, soup crocks, or rolls of gray linen bandages, the courtyard was deserted. I had expected it to be overflowing with wounded.

"Could you take this, Brother?" An overburdened monk thrust

an ale pitcher into my hand. Tucking the heavy pitcher in the crook of my arm, I joined the procession. The gate tunnel itself was quiet, the sharp click of my walking stick and uneven clomp of my heavy boots on the stone paving far louder than the shuffle and swish of passing sandals and cowls. The thick wooden gates halfway along the tunnel had been propped open.

Beyond the vaulted entry lay a scene worthy of the Adversary's domain. The broad sky blazed with orange-edged clouds and swaths of gray and purple. Torches had been mounted on staves, illuminating, not a hundred, but surely sixty or seventy bloodied soldiers sprawled on the puddled apron of grass before the gatehouse. They didn't look to be in any condition to cause much trouble for the monks. I had seen the ravages a defeated army could work upon a town or village. And these men *were* defeated. The wounded huddled quietly, suppressing moans and gasps of pain while mumbling prayers and curses. Other men sat silent, twitching at every noise, each man closed into himself, glaze-eyed with exhaustion and hunger.

Monks moved among the crowd like bees in a clover patch, offering prayers, ale, bread, blankets, and strips of linen men could use to bandage themselves until others could see to them. Fires sprang up here and there as the river damp rolled in with nightfall.

Close by the gate tunnel, an Ardran wearing a ripped tabard and cloak over hauberk and mail chausses fidgeted near a small group of monks. His bearing proclaimed him an officer, as did the sword at his waist and the riding crop in his hand.

The moment the group dispersed, leaving only one stocky, bald-pated brother standing by the gate, the officer pounced. "An hour we've waited, holy father," he said, his tight-lipped sneer more honest than his address. "My lord asks again when the abbot will come and grant his right of sanctuary. Nor have my lord's wounds been attended as yet."

"All in good time," said the monk, his shaven head and the silver solicale that dangled on his breast gleaming in the torchlight. "Abbot Luviar works in our farthest fields today. Though we've rung summoning bells, we've no horses to fetch him. Perhaps you can explain to me: I've granted sanctuary to all comers, but none have entered. They say their officers will not permit—"

"No cowards or gutterwipes will pass this gate before their lord," said the officer through clenched teeth, "and he will *not* share a common blessing given by some underling friar. He will have his proper reception."

"Naturally, protocol must be followed." The monk spread his

hands in helpless resignation. "I'll encourage our infirmarian to attend your lord immediately." One could not mistake a barb of indignation amid the proffered roses.

"See that you do, monk." The officer nodded stiffly and retreated to a knot of men in the very center of the field—a cadre of knights, twelve lances sprouting from them like a stand of needlegrass.

What lord lay there with no horses or banners? Some landless edane, no doubt, who thought himself Iero's chosen for surviving when mardanes, ducs, and princes lay dead or captive. None of the regular soldiers paid him any notice.

Nestled above the tunnel between the twin gate towers was the room where, as Saint Ophir had commanded, one member of the Gillarine fraternity remained ever alert for those in need of sanctuary—certainly to my own benefit. As I weighed the efforts of finding another haven, someone poked his head from the window and yelled, "Hark, Father Prior!"

The stocky monk craned his neck to see the caller. "Must you shout so loud, Brother Cosmos? Even *underling friars* must maintain our wits and decorum." His politeness had shriveled like a currant.

"There are more men on the ridge, Father Prior. Coming this way." Brother Cosmos damped his volume, but he could not mute the quaver of fear that accompanied his report.

"Riders or foot?" said the prior, squinting into the murky evening beyond the firelit field.

"I'm not certain. They seem to move too quickly for foot. Perhaps one with better eyes should take up the watch. If we could just move these men inside—"

The prior sighed deeply. "The soldiers cannot move without their officers' orders, so we must await Father Abbot. The newcomers are likely more sad cases like these."

"But—"

The stocky monk silenced the protest with a warning finger. "Age does not preclude punishment for disobedience, Cosmos. Stay at your post. As the saint taught, good order will carry us through all earthly trials." He folded his arms and surveyed the field, dispatching the monks here and there as they bustled through the gates.

Perhaps innocent men were not primed to expect trouble when dealing with such ugliness as war. Or perhaps the prior was just a fool. I had soldiered on and off since I was seventeen and knew that unexpected company rarely brought any good. The monks needed to get these men behind the abbey walls.

If I were to avoid any ugly encounters, I needed to be on my way as well. But first I'd get a better sense of where these men had come from, lest I blunder into the war I had abandoned. Almost a fortnight had passed since Wroling Wood. Some other noble boil must have been lanced in recent days to spew commoners' blood.

A woodcart rattled through the tunnel. I stuffed the pitcher and my alder stick into the bed, gripped the cart rim for a support, and moved into the field. Once we reached the center of the crowd, I extracted stick and pitcher and wandered off on my own, searching for someone who could tell me what I needed to know. I stayed cautious. Little chance any would know me. But if some of these had fought at Wroling, I'd not want it to get about that I'd arrived at Gillarine so much earlier than they.

"Brother, can you help me?" A scrawny man with one arm bound to his chest was trying to roll a bulky comrade onto his side. The pale, slab-sided soldier was retching and choking, half drowned in his own vomit. The heat of his fever could have baked bread.

"Iero's grace," I said, narrowly avoiding losing my own supper as the poor wretch heaved again, mostly bile and blood. I set my pitcher on the ground and helped prop the fellow on his side. A cold like deep-buried stone weighed my spirit as I touched him. The gore-soaked wad of rags bound to his belly oozed fresh blood.

"Where have you come from?" I said to the other man, snatching my hands away from his friend. "I've heard naught of this battle. Where was it fought?"

The scrawny soldier gaped as if I'd asked him to explain the thoughts of women or the intents of gods. "In the wood."

"The woods close by here? West beyond the ridge? Or more northerly, near Elanus?"

"A fearful dark wood." He could be no more than sixteen. "They kept coming at us. Knights. Halberdiers. And the mad ones . . . screaming like beasts and waving orange rags on their spears." He shuddered and swallowed a little twisting noise. I'd heard that sound before. Felt it. The terror that sat inside your gut and kept trying to climb out. The fellow didn't know any more. He'd likely never left his mother's croft until he was dragged off and told to kill Moriangi.

"Have you a cup or bowl?" I said. "And one for your friend?"

I filled two crude wooden bowls from my ale pitcher. The youth took a grateful sip, and I left him trying to give the bulk of his own portion to his friend. He ought to have drunk both portions himself. The wounded man wouldn't live past midnight. I'd known it when I touched him, known it with the certainty that always gave me the shudders—a hint of my mother's bent, I'd always thought, that showed up at random through the years, never biddable, never revealing matters I could do anything about. Control of death and life were beyond *any* pureblood bent.

On the near side of the field, a blood-slathered Brother Robierre sawed away at a whimpering soldier's thighbone. Young Gerard sat on the man's good leg to help keep the poor sod still, his gawking taking in every gruesome detail. Jullian, pale as a mist-dimmed moon, held the glowing cautery iron in a fire they'd built a few steps away. I gave the wretched proceeding a wide berth.

"Iero's grace." I approached a hollow-cheeked veteran who sat off by himself at the edge of the field, tending his feet. "Tell me, good sir, how close by the abbey was this terrible engagement? And in which direction?"

"Not so close as to threaten holy folk like you. We fought Bayard the Smith himself at Wroling Wood. The whore priestess of the Harrowers rode beside him."

"Wroling! But I thought—" I caught myself before blundering into any confession. "I'd heard rumor of a fight there, but days ago. You must have given Prince Bayard a noble struggle."

He spat and continued blotting his peeling toes with a scrap of dry cloth, pulling off bits of straw he'd used to stuff his boots. "Pssht. Three days' killing and what's left of Ardran honor is scattered to the winds. Unless Kemen Sky Lord brings forth this Pretender, the Prince of Brutes will be king in a fortnight, for all the good it'll do 'im. When the orange-heads finish burning Ardra, they'll burn Morian, too."

He was probably right. But I needed to understand his geography. "Here, if you've a cup, I can ease your thirst. For certain, you've had a long adventure to get here from Wroling. Perhaps you went the long way round and ran into another fight along the way?"

Looking up at last, he wrestled a tin cup from his belt. "Nay, good brother. We'd all be dead if we'd had to face aught since Wroling. If there'd been horses to commandeer, we could have nipped off to these fine walls in three days or less, despite our wounded. But even His Grace and his lordlings lost their mounts there at the end."

"Prince Perryn unhorsed!" Who'd ever believe the cowardly princeling would get close enough to combat to lose his horse? "He's captive, now, I suppose. Or dead."

"Aye, one or the other. At least that's kept the Smith off our backsides. With noble prey ripe for plucking, he needn't bother chasing dregs like us. A few unchartered knights is all they'd have to show for taking this lot."

"But your lord lies just over—" Unreasonably disturbed, I held the pitcher poised above his cup. "Prince Perryn . . . you didn't see him taken, then?"

"Nah. But he's likely squealing in Bayard's dungeons by now. Pompous prickwit." The soldier licked his lips and jerked his cup toward the pitcher.

When I'd heard of Prince Perryn's foiled plot to burn Navronne's fleet—our only defense against Hansker raiders—because his brother Bayard commanded the ships, I was done with the Ardran prince for good. Who of any mind could wish for either the Smith, the Pompous Prickwit, or Osriel the Bastard to wear good Eodward's crown? I feared the tales of a fourth brother, a Pretender, were naught but wishing dreams, wrought to hold off a kingdom's despair.

As I filled the soldier's vessel, my mind toyed with his news. If Prince Bayard had captured his half brother, the throne was indeed likely his, no matter what Eodward's lost writ of succession had to say. In Evanore Prince Osriel squatted on the richest treasure in the kingdom—veins of gold to satisfy an Aurellian emperor's wildest dreams—but most people deemed his sparsely populated domain too small to mount a campaign for the throne.

Over the soldier's head the forested folds of hill and vale were enveloped in gathering gloom. With Perryn taken, Bayard would never chase down sixty wounded men, a few knights, and a minor lord. But if the Duc of Ardra had slipped Bayard's grasp, and some pureblood scout had detected royal blood on this rabble's trail . . . Brother Cosmos had seen riders on the ridge.

I shoved the ale pitcher into the startled soldier's hands. "Riders are coming from the west. Drink up, put on your boots, and set a watch. Remember, you've no sanctuary as long as you're outside the abbey gates. If by some chance a certain unhorsed lord were hiding here among you, and if by some chance the Smith were to get wind of it from one of his pureblood lapdogs . . ."

The soldier stared at me for a moment, and then over his shoulder into the darkness flowing down from the forested ridge and pooling in the valley on every side. "Yo, Tobit, Gerrol!" he called, snatching up his boots.

I sped away as fast as I could hobble. No bed or board was worth involvement in the princes' bloody argument. I'd had my fill of killing. My leg was not up to running, but I needed no stick to propel me across the field toward the river and the cart road south.

Did these monks understand what was going to happen here? Bayard, Duc of Morian, called the Smith for his crude and thuggish manner, would surely slaughter these men to take his rival and might violate the abbey itself. Sanctuary was only effective if the pursuers respected the concepts of mercy and salvation. And in such regards, I had no confidence in either Bayard the Smith or Sila Diaglou.

The stench of charred meat hung over the crowd of wounded surrounding the infirmarian and his assistant. Jullian and Gerard were wiping bloody implements with bloody rags and replacing them in Robierre's wooden chest.

I ought to warn the brothers. Robierre and Anselm would likely not come away from the field. And truly, as I thought of it, I owed them no debt, as their service had naught to do with saving me, but with their own gifts and obligations. But the boys . . . I'd given my word to protect young Jullian, and I didn't break my word.

I pushed through the listless press and crouched down behind the boys. "Father Prior bade me send the two of you into the church," I said quietly.

Gerard gaped at me blankly, as if too horror-sated to make sense of common speech. Jullian, though, snapped his head around. "Valen! What are you doing out here? Your leg—"

"I'm carrying Father Prior's commands. Everyone must help in such a desperate time, even such as me. Come now, leave your task for those more knowledgeable, and get you to the church. You're needed for . . ." My mind juggled to come up with anything that sounded reasonable.

"But we were told to help Brother Infirmarian."

The glassy puddles beside my feet shivered. Horses.

"Well, all that's changed. You're wanted in church . . . for the singing . . . as so many of the brothers are occupied and your voices and hearts are pure . . . and we will need Iero's grace very much with what's to come this night."

In an instant, Jullian's puzzled expression blossomed into the most profound awe. His voice dropped to a whisper. "The dark times . . . the long night . . . come so soon?" He glanced quickly at Gerard, who seemed to comprehend as little as I did of his meaning, and then back at me. Jullian jumped up, dragged the other boy to his feet, and gave him a shove. "Gerard, run for the church! Go! Begin the psalm for the end times!"

Gerard scooted away. Jullian crouched down again, whispering excitedly. "I wasn't sure you knew. This afternoon, Brother Gildas reprimanded me for my loose tongue . . . I mean, I had heard them say that your book could be the key and surely the god had sent you here, and so I assumed you knew of the lighthouse. But for this night to come so soon . . ."

My teeth thrummed with the approaching hoofbeats. Cries of dismay broke out from several sides. "Jullian, I've no idea what you're saying, but you must go into the church with Gerard and say whatever prayers you can think of. Don't come out until Father Abbot himself tells you it's safe. Do you understand?"

Face glowing with more than the ruddy torchlight, eyes pooled with determined innocence, the boy ducked his head and raised his hand. "I understand," he said, and then added softly, so only I could hear, *"Teneamus."*

Chapter 7

I stared after Jullian as he sprinted for the abbey gates. But only for a moment. Matters were deteriorating too rapidly. The first out-riders thundered across the fields toward the abbey, swords raised, cloaks and pennons flying. The little cadre of bristling lances moved slowly from the center of the field toward the gatehouse—*away* from the coming assault, which did naught but affirm what I suspected about the lord they protected.

"Father Prior!" Abbot Luviar himself ran out of the gatehouse tunnel as I picked my way across the uneven ground along the wall away from the gates. "In the name of the Creator, Nemesio, why are they not within?"

"Their officers refused. Their lord insists on you—"

"Run, Nemesio! Get him inside now. By my command as your superior in Iero's service, under pain of your immortal soul, get the lord's party through the gate. Do you understand me? Brother Broun, Fescol . . . ring the bells!"

The prior dashed into the murmuring crowd. As the alarm rippled in from the perimeter, Abbot Luviar strode straight out through the stirring soldiers as well. "Rise up!" he cried, moving from one to another, the golden sunburst on his breast glinting in the torchlight. "You must stand one more time. Rise up and take arms. Support your comrades to stand as well. Navronne needs your strength. Your children and your children's children need your courage. If good is to be made of your suffering, then these riders must not find you asleep." He tugged on weary arms and laid his hand on bent heads. "You are the men of Ardra, Eodward's men of light! Mighty Iero will lift your arms, if you but stand. This fight is bigger than you know. The stakes grander than all of us."

I was astonished. One by one, men who but moments before were ghosts of warriors, drained of blood and spirit, grasped pikes or spears and rose to their feet, drawing their fellows up to stand beside them and face outward. None of them seemed to notice the knights retreating toward the abbey.

I wanted to call after Luviar, "The one you protect is not worthy of more lives; he betrays his men for pride and greed!"

But the abbot was out of my reach. Like a tight eddy in the current of the shaping battle, he spun and touched and cajoled. "Rise up and the archangels will join you with their swords and shields. This cause you serve must not die this day. Show Navronne the strength of your resolve!"

Indeed, the abbot's voice carried across the sea of bloodied faces like an archangel's clarion, almost enough to draw me back into the conflict I had abandoned. Not for the cowardly prince I believed lay hidden behind the screen of his lancers, not for golden Ardra or industrious Morian or mysterious, mountainous Evanore. Yet, perhaps, for good King Eodward who had lived with the angels and dreamed of Navronne, the Heart of the World . . .

Even as I considered grabbing a weapon from one of the men too weak to use it, I shook off the fey notion. I was not ready to die for anyone or anything. To enter a fight at less than full strength was an invitation to the Ferryman.

I climbed the gentle apron slope of the wall and angled away from the gatehouse, resigned to a long and miserable journey. The abbey walls would lead me back to the river. Somewhere the monks would have built a bridge to open the cross-river pastures for grazing. The thick damp of the night resolved into cold spatters on my face. Unvowed, I had no cowl to shield me from the rain.

"Valen!" The call startled me, and I glanced over my shoulder. A pale face lined by dark brows appeared out of the night behind me. "You should get yourself inside the walls immediately, Valen."

Iero's bones, where had the monk come from? "Ah, Brother Gildas," I said, "perhaps you don't recognize the perils of this night."

My gait was slow and clumsy on the uneven ground. Gildas quickly caught up with me, grabbed my arm, and drew me to a halt. "This world is naught but perilous. Nothing is simple. Nothing is innocent. And sometimes, those who think themselves the most worldly are the most innocent of all."

I snorted at the concept of this monk telling me anything of the world. "Sometimes a man must look to his body's safety as well as his soul's. Bayard of Morian is hunting his brother, and any man who gets in his way is a fool. Soon to be a dead fool. Though Abbot Luviar seems to disagree, I doubt Iero would have us throw our lives away for nothing."

Purposeless death was not the only risk in staying. Bayard would surely have pureblood attendants. Any interrogation of Gillarine's inhabitants could be my downfall. Time only increased the Registry's determination to recover a *recondeur*.

I limped past Brother Gildas. He darted in front of me and gently, but insistently, blocked my way. "The god has given your safety into our hands, Valen. Please believe we take that very seriously. You must not leave."

I wanted very much to believe him. The drizzle had yielded to a downpour. My thigh ached. I was already shivering and had no provisions. All that awaited me in the dark and the wet were pestilence, Moriangi swords, and a hungry winter. "But these riders—"

"—will not find the one they seek. I swear to you they'll have no cause to broach our walls. The dangers of this night are outside Gillarine, not in. Come. Hurry. And have faith."

His grip was much stronger than I expected. And perhaps his faith, too. For it was more than the weather and my poor prospects that crumbled my resolve so quickly. Since I'd first taken up soldiering, I had hated the last moments before battle, when it seemed as if the boundaries between earth and body, between past, present, and future, between knowing and experiencing dissolved. But something about this place . . . every moment I stood on this field multiplied those sensations beyond bearing. As a wind blustering my hair and robe, I felt the sweeping onslaught of the Moriangi. As the sea crashing upon my knees, I felt the surging Ardrans step up to meet them. A horse neighed wildly in the distance and a cheer went up among the Ardrans. My soul ached, and I longed for wine . . . for mead . . . for hard spirits or poppy . . . for the doulon . . . anything so I would not feel all this.

As the cold deluge soaked my hair and funneled down my neck, I resentfully allowed Gildas to turn me around. "Answer me one thing, Brother," I said as the monk steadied my steps. "What would it mean if I were to bid you farewell with the Aurellian word meaning *we preserve?*"

Though Gildas did not miss a step, his arm suddenly felt like a post. Moments passed. "Well, of course, preservation of knowledge is our charter here at Gillarine. Many here use *teneamus* as a challenge when our spirits flag. A reminder of duty and service to the god. You never mentioned that you understood Aurellian, Valen.

Most aspirants must learn it from the beginning. What other talents are you hiding?"

My spine froze. I should have known he would turn the question on me. *Stupid tongue-flapping fool. Come on. A story...* "I was schooled early ... a Karish charity school near Ymir ... took to the language. I've a gift with the pronunciations, I'm told, though not the writing of it."

Mumbling curses at my slip and thanking the gods yet again that my curling hair, light complexion, and excess height were so exceptional for pureblood stock, I hobbled back along the wall toward the gatehouse. The sloping apron gave a wide vantage. More riders broached the hardening Ardran perimeter. Arms clashed. Men and horses screamed ...

"They should not shed blood upon that field," I said, shuddering. As the last rays of sunlight pierced the cloud and sculpted the surging sea of bodies with orange and scarlet, the very thought made my veins burn and my stomach heave as they had in the cloister garth. *Holy ground,* Jullian had called Gillarine. Perhaps that was what I felt.

"Shedding blood is a great evil," said Gildas. "Yet some causes demand it. Blood spilled in violence has great power for good."

"Some causes, perhaps." But not this one. I hobbled faster. "King Eodward could not have meant his sons to bring Navronne to ruin."

"So you've no loyalty to any of these princes."

"Loyalty never put blood back in a man's veins."

We reached the gatehouse just as the party of knights entered the arch, moving like a many-legged insect, stepping smartly around dented shields, bloody rags and bundles, and a few sprawled bodies that even the abbot's call had not roused. In the center of the lancers' spiked circle, sheltered from the rain by a cloak held over his head, was a stumbling smudge of silver mail and white-and-purple satin, a tangle of fair hair that ladies called spun gold, a blur of maggot-colored skin, supported on the arms of servants. How like Perryn of Ardra to keep his men in danger while he awaited a triumphal welcome to his last refuge. And now, for the moment, they'd saved him. I'd wager my grandfather's book that he was more drunk than wounded. The cost of the pelisse his knights held over his head could likely have paid for a month's provisions for his legions or a troop of mercenaries to aid us.

"Brother Victor," called Gildas to a diminutive monk who stood in the vaulted entry staring, aghast, at the battle. "Could you please escort Valen back to the infirmary? My duties beckon ..." Gildas planted a brotherly slap on my arm and jogged ahead alongside the lancers.

As Gildas and Prince Perryn's party vanished into the tunnel, the Ardran troops' brief resistance collapsed into a rout. Night and death rode pillion behind the Moriangi horsemen, as their central wedge plunged inward to slice the Ardran force in twain.

Brother Victor, a tight little man whose features seemed on the verge of sliding off his chinless face, wrenched his eyes from the field, took my arm solicitously, and urged me into the gatehouse tunnel. "Brother Valen? Why, you're the supplicant who brought us—"

"Yes, yes, the Cartamandua maps," I said, straining to see over my shoulder. "And you're welcome to view them at any time, if you'll just hold up for a moment."

Halfway along the tunnel, the great oaken gates yet gaped. I drew Brother Victor into the space between the leftmost gate and the wall, where I could peek around and see what was happening here. I dearly wanted to understand it.

The abbot stood at the outer end of the tunnel, outlined against the flares of torches and steel. "Here, brave men, hurry! By Iero's grace, find safety here, thou who fleest sword or hangman. By Saint Gillare's hand, find healing here . . ."

But the Moriangi had encircled the retreating Ardrans and quickly barred the tunnel opening with leveled lances. The snort and snuffles of agitated horses and the chinking of mail and arms could not drown out the shouts of anger and the lingering cries of the wounded.

Through the crush advanced a small party of riders, the foremost being a bull-necked man on a chestnut destrier. Both man and horse were cloaked and furbished in scarlet and blue—not the deep-dyed vermillion and indigo of Aurellian-style finery, but common madder and woad.

Bayard, Duc of Morian, called the Smith, relished his particular ancestry as dearly as any pureblood. He claimed that his Moriangi mother, daughter of a common shipwright, had reinvigorated Caedmon's royal line with uncommon strength. He made a great show of abjuring silks and jewels in favor of coarse woolens and hammered bronze and believed it made him one with his people.

Perhaps. I'd met those who honored Bayard as Eodward's eldest child, and thus, lacking evidence to the contrary, Eodward's rightful heir. Even in the king's lifetime, Bayard's ruthless campaigns against the Hansker were revered by those who lived in the vulnerable riverlands. But I'd met neither man nor woman, common nor other, who professed to love the man.

"Who has passed here, priest?" Prince Bayard's horse was at noses with the abbot. "I would know what men have sought your hospitality this night."

"Your Grace." The abbot inclined his head and spread his palms. "Alas, only the dead have entered our gates this night. I granted all these men holy sanctuary, but they chose to fight instead. How will Iero judge those of us in authority who fail to avert such horrors?"

Hypocrisy among the powerful, even the clergy, did not surprise me. But I was shocked at the abbot's blatant lie, especially in the absolute sincerity of its delivery.

Prince Bayard, of course, was experienced with both lies and hypocrisy. "Prove to me that no one has passed. My men were certain they saw knights at your gate. Surely your holy brothers have not been hiding swords or lances in their trews."

The squires in his party snickered.

The abbot ignored the crude jape and swept an arm in welcome. "Enter as you will, Your Grace, though I must insist you leave your weapons behind. Your noble father's grant specified Gillarine as neutral ground."

Was *that* it? Had the abbot and his prior kept the Ardran soldiers outside the walls apurpose so Luviar could maintain his claim of neutral ground and thus retain King Eodward's grant of this fruitful valley? He'd had an Evanori nobleman ensconced in the abbey guesthouse. But then why hide Perryn?

"Interfering with the capture of a traitor is hardly neutral!" Prince Bayard snapped, voicing my own thought. "All your pious mouthings these past months, bidding me negotiate with this poltroon my father sired . . . Now your true loyalties are revealed. You've set yourself and your holy brothers square in the sapless dandy's camp, and if you've sheltered him, I'll take this house down stone by stone while you hang by your bowels and watch." Bayard's destrier snorted, blew, and sidestepped. The prince drew rein with a heavy hand.

"Iero bids us open our doors in peace to those who request it, and we ask no questions as to past sins or future plans." The abbot yielded no ground, his every syllable precise and clear. "We would welcome either of your royal brothers here as we would welcome your own honored self or the lowliest of your warriors or even yon priestess, your ally, who denies king and god and human soul. I assert that no one has passed this gateway to my inner precincts save those of my own flock and the dead. Leave off your weapons and come see for yourself, or send one of your men. But I would remind you that to violate our precincts lays an interdict upon the soul, unworthy of a man who would be Eodward's heir and awkward for a man who desires the Hierarch of Ardra—my superior—to affirm his crown."

"You presume much, priest." I would not have been Bayard's horse at that moment. Surely the prince's ruthless hand on the reins must shred the poor beast's mouth.

Bayard flicked a gloved finger at those behind him. A man dropped from his mount, bowed to the prince, and strode through the tunnel toward the Alms Court. My heart stuttered when the shifting lamplight revealed his cloak to be the color of claret—the color mandated for a pureblood working among ordinaries. And there was something else . . .

I stared after him as he passed by me. A short, broad-shouldered man with thick black hair and beard, his face half obscured by a silken mask. His walk so like a cat's . . . smooth, confident, a touch of swagger . . . so familiar . . . Once inside the courtyard, he knelt and touched one hand to the earth, then rose and moved out of sight.

My feet shifted as if to follow. Brother Victor jerked hard on my gown. I came to my senses and shrank deeper into our niche behind the gates. Gods, if he saw me . . . I closed my eyes, not daring to so much as think until the firm footsteps passed us by again. Then I peered around the edge of the gate.

"The priest speaks truth, Your Grace." The pureblood's arrogance rang through that tunnel like struck bronze, his words properly blunt and formed entirely without passion. I would recognize Max's voice anywhere. This was business. "The only Ardran soldiers in the courtyard are dead—six of them. I verified their state. Only one set of footprints in the courtyard beyond this tunnel is aught but monks' sandals. That pair of boots walked out the gates, not in. No path beyond the three inner gates showed evidence of either passing soldiers or princes. Your royal brother certainly escaped Wroling with this rabble, but he either abandoned them along the way or is out there with them yet."

Unsubtle, Prince Bayard wheeled his mount and charged back to the field. My brother, Max, swung his compact and brawny bulk onto his horse and rode after him with the rest of the party.

Slowly I relaxed fists and shoulders. It was more difficult to banish the echoes of taunts and mocking laughter that would forever taint the air about my brother like the stink shrouds a midden.

How logical that Max called the Duc of Morian his master. My father was shrewd enough to bind his children into the most prestigious contracts offered, unswayed by sentiment or relative virtue or even hard coin, come to that. Max prided himself on his wit and intellect, and ever ambitious, would have made certain that the contracts offered for his service were to his own taste.

"Come on, then," said Brother Victor, tugging at my sleeve. "No need to watch what they'll do now. We must pray for mercy and for the souls of captors and captives alike."

No. No need to watch the macabre dance of victors and vanquished. Screams followed us into the now deserted Alms Court. I knew what Max had done here: crouched down and touched the stone, then let flow a bit of magic, calling on our family bent for a simple test we had learned as we learned to walk. Whereas roads and portals held the remembrance of all who had traveled them for a very long time—the abbey gates likely would reveal traces of Eodward himself—the lingering footsteps in a paved courtyard would tell the tale only of those who had passed this night.

I dared not read the footprints for myself, even assuming I could draw any magic on the day after a doulon. I dared not work *any* sorcery with Max nearby. My brother, a pureblood with more than ten generations of scouts and cartographers in his lineage, would not miss the residue of pureblood spellworking any more than he would have missed the invisible traces of soldiers' boots or a prince's tread.

So where *were* Prince Perryn and his lancers? As Brother Victor and I crossed the Alms Court and passed through the Porter's Arch, I whipped my head around to look back at the gatehouse and the tiny windows of the sanctuary room, tightly shuttered now. A pulse of satisfaction left me smiling. Of course, the monks would need access to the sanctuary room from inside the gate tunnel, somewhere in the dark nooks and niches along the walls behind the gates, so that the watcher could descend swiftly to open the gates for a supplicant. Brother Gildas would know. And I'd wager my arm that a second stair would lead to the sanctuary room by way of the outer wall walk, so a monk would not need to cross a busy Alms Court to take up his watch.

"Please go on ahead," I said to Brother Victor, slowing my already snaillike trudge. "My leg tires, and I'd like to . . . pray . . . as I walk. I can find my way to the infirmary on my own."

The small monk vacillated. I argued. He yielded. "Well, if you're sure, then. I do have duties. We must prepare to rescue those we can."

As soon as he vanished into the maze of yew hedges, I left the path, squeezed through the thick barrier of hedges, and hurried across the bridle path that led into the outer courts. Sure enough, a few hundred quercae south of the Alms Court, a steep stair led to the walkway atop the abbey's outer wall. Mumbling curses at my overtired thigh and at the cold rain that pelted my face and slickened the narrow steps, I hauled myself up the stair.

I limped northward along the wall overlooking the Alms Court. The walk came to an abrupt end at the south gatehouse tower. And snug in the tower wall sat an iron door, a convenient entry that would allow monks to take up their sanctuary watch or errant princes to slip into the abbey precincts without detection. The rain washed away their muddy footprints.

The wind blustered, flapping my gown about me like a luffing sail and bearing a nerve-scraping screech from the field below. Morbid curiosity drew me to the outer parapet where I could gaze down on the scene before the gates. Dark, still forms lay everywhere. A few shapeless creatures scurried among them on the peripheries where the rain had snuffed the torches—monks, searching for the living or blessing the dead, or perhaps scavengers, drawn from the forest on the trail of a war party like rats following a leaking grain sack.

The majority of Bayard's men, some mounted, some afoot, crowded near a great bonfire not far from the gatehouse. A small mounted party sat slightly apart—Bayard, Max, and a third rider, a slender warrior clad in silver mail and orange cloak, her long pale hair streaming in the swirling wind. The priestess of the Gehoum.

Gehoum were not comfortable gods, not at all like the bickering husband and wife, Kemen and Samele, whose lusty inclinations had peopled the world with lesser deities and whose devotion to the earth had created the guardian Danae to enrich and protect it. Nor were they in the least like the benevolent Iero, the father/brother god of the Karish, who had promised to send angels to carry us all to his heavenly realm did we but forsake our sinful ways. Gehoum were blind immortal powers who cared naught for mortal beings who existed only by their tolerance.

Sila Diaglou, once a temple initiate herself, had traveled the cities and villages of Navronne since she was seventeen, calling for a cleansing of the corrupted temples and a return to blood penalties for those who insulted the gods—beginning with the five members of the Sinduri Council, all Karish, and certain Navrons who had degraded their bodies past redemption, that is, harlots and nivat-crazed twist-minds. When the Sinduri condemned her as apostate, she had staged a public rite of repentance in the temple square in Palinur. Rending her garments and slashing her own face and arms with a knife, she had abjured the elder gods as false and named herself high priestess of the Gehoum. Some people had wept to see Sila

Diaglou's fervent savagery. Some had laughed. No one laughed at her anymore.

Another soul-wrenching scream came from the center of the group. And then another. And another. My fingers gripped the gritty blocks of the wall until the hoarse, burbling cry abruptly ceased. The crowd shifted and surged. Then the screaming began again, but in a different timbre.

The Ardrans didn't know where their prince had gone. They thought him left behind on the field at Wroling Wood. How many would Bayard and the priestess kill before they believed it?

Why did I stay and heed such dreadful doings? I could not aid the poor wretches. I ought to get back to the infirmary. But some stray shred of honor forbade me seek the comfort of bed while men so near were screaming out their last hours on earth.

Nor was I the only observer. A tall, full-shaven monk stood before the Gillarine gatehouse, the gold solicale on his breast glinting in the scalding light. Was Father Abbot pleased with this outcome? Was soldiers' blood the price of his inviolate gates?

A chill shivered my flesh. Beyond the pool of firelight, the night shifted. I peered through the rain until my eyes felt screwed from their sockets. *There!* Another movement, like an inky worm slithering down the hillside. Of a sudden, a horn call pierced the night—no bright trumpet blast, but a low, hollow sound that settled like cold iron in the base of my spine.

The group by the bonfire disintegrated. Moriangi warriors raced to reclaim their mounts and with their leader—Bayard, I thought, from the size and shape of him—reinforced the pickets with a solid defensive line.

A wall of midnight taller than the gate towers swept toward the abbey across the dark plains, no surge of mounted knights or ranked halberdiers, but rumbling, roaring darkness itself. I'd never seen anything like it. Halfway across the plain, giant horses that breathed dark flames took shape and surged out of the cloud wall as if straining to break free of the encompassing dark, drawing it along in their wake. Alongside them strode black-helmeted warriors thrice the height of a man with mailed fists the size of boulders and lances as thick as tree trunks. But these monstrous creatures were but phantasms—an unliving vanguard designed to instill terror and awe, like an Aurellian legion's guide-staff hung with skulls and jangling bells, or the gorgons carved into a Hansker longboat's prow. It was the warriors who rode behind the cloud phantoms that struck my heart cold. Hidden as they were in roiling darkness, I glimpsed only a gray, twisted face here or a blood-streaked arm there. But in that stomach-hollowing, knee-weakening moment before their strike, I tasted a brutal hatred that could grind stone into dust.

The wall of midnight shattered the Moriangi picket line as an ax breaks a dirt clod. Horses reared and screamed. Some riders fell; some slumped in the saddle as their mounts ran wild.

Bayard's defensive line broke and fled, only to be snagged from behind by the swift-moving legion of night. A few escaped by flailing their mounts to a gallop before the wall reached them. Max's wine-colored cloak streamed alongside Prince Bayard's blue and Sila Diaglou's orange, as they rode helter-skelter into the night. Once at the top of a rise beyond the fray, Sila Diaglou drew rein and turned to watch as the monstrous cloud forms lost cohesion and the blackness settled over the battleground, extinguishing the bonfire and remaining torches. But after only a moment, she struck out again and galloped northward after the others.

The black fog enveloped the field, hiding the huddled prisoners, the dead, the injured, and the laggards. Wails of terror rose in chorus. As the wall of night rolled over him, the abbot dropped to his knees, arms extended. "Stay thy hand, O Lord of Night!" he cried. "Have mercy on these that lie before you! Let them pass!"

Suffocating with dread, I pressed my back to the parapet and slid downward to the wet stone walk, my arms flung over my head, praying the holy stones would hide me.

Bells. A clear, measured cadence. Gray light penetrated the dark cave of my arms and dangling sleeves. Dawn—wet, cold, and dismal. I unfolded my stiff, aching limbs and peeled my sodden gown away from my sodden undergarments. Was it possible I had fallen asleep? I remembered vividly where I was and what had made me huddle in a quavering knot at the base of the chest-high parapet. But the wall of night had overtaken the abbey well before midnight, and I could remember nothing since.

The bells changed from simple strikes to a pattern of changes: one-two-three-four, one-two, one-two-three-four, one-two. Prime—the dawn Hour.

Grabbing my stick and the edge of a granite block, I eased upward. My first tentative peek over the parapet propelled me to my feet. One harder look and I hurried down the stair and back toward the gates, ignoring the cold night's ache in my thigh. The dead had moved.

I limped through the gates and into the churned-up ruins of a once-grassy field. Abandoned weapons, packs, ripped blankets, battered pots and cups lay scattered amid blood-tainted puddles and dead horses. Close beside the walls, a muddy, disheveled Brother Robierre sat weeping alongside five other monks, all of them drenched and trembling, several with hands clenched in prayer. Abbot Luviar, seemingly uninjured, moved from one to the other, crouching beside each man to offer words of comfort. But what comfort could there be?

Save for the seven monks, no living man remained upon that field. But neither did the dead men rest where they had fallen. They had been separated into Ardrans and Moriangi, the two groups laid out in orderly rows six wide and stretching across the field. None of this was so dreadful, save when one gazed upon the ranks of fallen warriors and realized that beyond the usual grotesque battle injuries, their eyes had been plucked out, every one of them.

The Karish claimed that stealing the eyes of the dead did *not* remove their souls and forever bar them from the afterlife. Yet of all the battlefields I had walked, many with far more victims than this one, none had so twisted my heart. The gaping bloody emptiness where joy or fear, knavery or kindness, intelligence or dull wit had once lived was worse than any death stare. And the careful placement of the corpses, the cold deliberation of the deed, was far more terrifying than any barbarian battle rite.

At the head of this lifeless array, a lance had been plunged into the muddy earth and an ensign tied to it. The pennon hung limp and heavy, even its color indistinguishable in the gray morning. I stepped forward and lifted its edge. The tight woven fabric was the deep, rich green of holly and fir, and embroidered upon it in silver were the three-petaled trilliot and a howling wolf, the mark of Evanore—the mark of Eodward's third son, Osriel the Bastard, who purportedly had uses for the souls of the dead.

Chapter 8

On the morning after the assault—already referred to as Black Night—we buried ninety-three soldiers and one monk. Every able hand in the abbey, including my own, set to the grisly task. The cold mud weighed my spirits beyond grief, and as we laid the chilled flesh in the earth, I found myself mumbling, "Sorry. Sorry. Forgive." I could not have said why.

I asked Brother Robierre and others who endured that night before the gates what they had seen. Those who could speak of the matter at all agreed on the vanguard of flame-breathing horses and cloud warriors the size of the church. None reported aught else visible in the fog. I did not mention the gray faces I'd seen or the mortal dread that had afflicted me. But I could not let go of the memory.

On that same evening, everyone who could walk was summoned to church for a service of mourning and repentance. Brother Dispenser ladled ysomar, the oil used to anoint the sick and dying, into our clay calyxes—the expensive indulgence signifying the solemnity of the occasion. As we carried our votive gifts forward to empty into Iero's fire, the texts read from the holy writs were all of Judgment Night and the end of the world. The prayers did not sound at all optimistic.

Not allowed in the choir as yet, I stood in the nave with the lay brothers, wishing I could feel the same solace the brothers seemed to find in vague promises of a dull heaven. The music drew me through the hours like a strong current, and the scent of incense and burning ysomar evoked my childhood imaginings of divine mysteries. Candlelight reflected from jewel-colored windows, gleaming stone piers, and gold fittings, until the air in the vaults and domes of the church shimmered as if angels hovered there, the light and gossamer of their wings the evidence of their presence to us mortals below.

So much praying in this place. I'd not spent so much time inside a church on a single day in my life, save perhaps the day of King Eodward's funeral rites. For the first time since escaping my parents' house, I had donned a pureblood's mask and wine-colored cloak— both stolen—and haughty air—inbred. I had lied my way into the half-built cathedral in Palinur and promptly hid in the gallery, lest someone recognize me or attempt to unravel the family connections of an unknown pureblood. Only to honor King Eodward would I have risked discovery. His public glory had been but a part of what he was.

Though I had been presented to the king at three years of age, as were all pureblood progeny, I had met him only once. I was seventeen and feeling slightly giddy, having just survived two fierce days of fighting the Hansker invasion at Cap Diavol. One of my comrades took out a tin whistle and played to lift our spirits. The song moved my feet, and I stepped through a jig, faster by the moment, the surge of life grown wild in me, having been so close to death.

A man crouched by our fire for a moment to warm his hands and watch. When the song was done and I dropped breathless to the ground, drinking in the laughter and cheers of my comrades, I recognized the king. Though I'd heard he often wandered through the camp after a battle, I'd never believed it. But none could mistake the three trilliots blazoned on his breastplate—one lily the scarlet of Morian, one Ardran gold, and one the silver of Evanore. Despite deep creases about his eyes, his hair and beard yet flamed red-gold, scarce touched with gray.

He spoke a few words of thanks and encouragement to each of us seven, all that remained of our cadre of twenty. When my tongue flapped loose, as has always been my worst failing, spewing some foolish comment comparing a soldier's hardships and a king's, he smiled as if my nonsense cheered him in the face of three thousand dead and a worse battle facing us at dawn. And when I chose to take the measure of the only king I was ever like to meet, staring boldly at him rather than dropping my eyes in deference, he did not avert his gaze.

Before or since, I'd never known anyone who left his soul so exposed for another man, a stranger even, to view—and so I witnessed King Eodward's devotion to all who followed him and his grief for the price they must pay for their loyalty. Though I had already decided that the soldier's life was not for me, I vowed right then to serve him until one or the other of us was dead—an easy promise, of course, as he was in his sixtieth year and had few battles left to fight.

As he rose to leave our fire and move on to the next, the king cocked his head at me again, half smiling, half grieving. "Your quick feet and saucy mouth remind me strangely of some I knew in my own youth, lad. If you've happened here from Aeginea, tell them I don't think I'll get back. Tell them . . . *askon geraitz.*" The words, neither Navron nor Aurellian, made no sense to me.

I scrambled to my knees and bowed my head. "Of course, anything you ask, Your Majesty, but I know not this place—"

His hand raised my chin, silencing me. "No matter, then, lad. Just dance."

In the ten years since, I'd asked a number of people where a place called Aeginea might be, but no comrade or acquaintance had ever heard of it. Another of Serena Fortuna's jests—of anyone in the wide world, my grandfather the cartographer would surely know.

Not that I would ever ask the mad old man. He had appeared at our house at random intervals throughout my childhood, pawing at me with ink-stained fingers and babbling meaningless words in my ear, pretending we were allies in the household warfare. Then he'd disappear again without changing anything, abandoning me to my enraged father and hysterical mother. If a bleeding child's curses carried the weight of the gods, as some said, then the old gatzé had long since fallen off a cliff and taken a year to die.

Family. Not a topic to consider in a house devoted to the spirit's health. It was a marvel any of my bodily wounds ever healed with such poison in my blood. Family was long over and done with. I kneaded my scalp and tried again to lose myself in the monks' mournful music. Without result.

Max was the first member of the Cartamandua-Celestine household I'd glimpsed in twelve years. Contracted as Bayard of Morian's hound. Walking straight into my refuge. *Gods . . .* My urge to run blazed like a new-stoked furnace, even as I argued how unlikely he was to return here.

Truly, Abbot Luviar's role in this royal brawl ought to fright me more. Now *there* was a mystery worth the deciphering. If I, a man of thick skull and paltry skills, had come to see that the Duc of Ardra was an arrogant sham who would as soon sell the crown of Eodward as wear it, then why would the Abbot of Gillarine claim that prince's rescue to be the salvation of Navronne? Had Luviar fallen into the same magical stupor as his monks and I had done, or had he watched as the Bastard of Evanore stole the eyes of the dead?

Gillarine's safety seemed more ephemeral than I had hoped.

Though not yet ready to abandon the place, I dared not relax the caution that had kept me free.

"Tell me, Brother Artur, do the Evanori warrior and his sickly secretary yet reside in the guesthouse?" I asked one of Brother Jerome's assistants when he brought supper from the kitchen two days after Black Night. The unsavory thought had crossed my mind that the abbot was brokering some alliance between Perryn and Osriel through this Evanori "benefactor."

"Nay, Thane Stearc and his party departed the day before Black Night," said the grizzled lay brother, uncovering the bowl of carrot and leek chowder he'd brought me.

A thane! Not just some landed knight, but an Evanori warlord—descendant of a family who centuries past, along with the gravs of Morian, had bound their lives and fortunes to Caedmon, King of Ardra, thus creating the kingdom of Navronne. I dropped my voice to a confidential whisper. "It seems a scandal to find Evanori in a holy place. I was taught they served the Adversary in their heathenish fortresses."

The monk's broad brow crumpled. "No, no! The thane's a scholarly man and Gillarine's greatest benefactor since King Eodward passed to heaven. Thane Stearc studied here as a boy and has visited the abbey every month for all these years, bringing us new books and casks of wine, and donating generously to our sustenance."

"But he serves the Bastard Prince . . ."

"Indeed not!" Brother Artur blanched at the suggestion. "Though he wears the wolf of Evanore while in Ardra to proclaim his neutral state, his house is Erasku, which straddles the border. The thane claims both provinces or neither as he chooses."

Convenient, if one could get away with such juggling. The thane must be quite a diplomat or quite a warrior . . . or quite a liar. I hoped these monks were not so naive as to accept the lord's word without solid proof.

The lay brother carried his soup to the other patients—monks wounded on Black Night. I ate slowly, so that when he brought his tray around to gather up my bowl and spoon, he had to wait for me. "So, Brother Artur," I said quietly between bites, "I suppose you must carry a good lot of food to the guesthouse now."

He shook his head, puzzled. "None at all. We've few visitors in the best times. I doubt we'll see another till Lord Stearc returns."

I dropped my bowl on his tray and slumped back in the bed, disappointed and mystified. No infirmary visitor had dropped the least hint of Prince Perryn's presence.

The assault had left the abbey a dreary place. Brother Gildas did not show his face. Jullian spent a great deal of time in the infirmary, doing whatever small tasks the infirmarian assigned him, but scurried away whenever I so much as looked at him. Even genial Brother Badger wore a cloak of grief that lightened only slowly as the sun set and rose and set again, the life of the abbey taking up its plodding rhythm.

Though I had every reason to be satisfied with my prospects, Black Night and my odd experiences in the cloisters had left me on edge. I forever imagined dark shapes lurking in the shadowed corners of the infirmary. One night I broke into a nonsensical sweat when someone paused outside the horn windows with a blue-paned lamp and remained there for an hour.

To distract myself, I took to telling stories and reciting bardic rhymes in the hours between the monks' prayers, though indeed I had to search through my store of experiences and fables for those that would not shock celibate ears. I also began taking regular exercise around the infirmary garth. My leg felt well healed, giving only a bit of soreness and stretching when I took long strides. Though happy to be up and about—activity suited me better than indolence now I'd made up for half a lifetime's missed sleep—I was not yet ready to give up such a perfectly useful circumstance. I made sure to limp and grimace a great deal. I had a better chance of doing as I pleased if no one knew my true condition.

A tarnished silver medicine spoon I'd found in Brother Robierre's chest of instruments and a blood-crusted gold button he'd gouged out of a soldier's chest wound went into the packet under my palliasse—a pitiful lot of nothing. Memories of demon horses and gray-faced warriors left me chary of pilfering valuables from the church. Which meant, should I leave Gillarine, I'd surely need my book.

On one night in the quiet hours between Matins and Lauds, when my companions in the infirmary slept soundly, I tugged on boots and gown and crept through the darkened abbey. Three times I dodged around a corner and peered into the night behind me, imagining I'd catch someone following. But the only sign of life was a flare of light from the church. Someone's lamp illuminated a sapphire outline from one of the colored windows. The wavering light set the blue-limned figure moving. I signed Iero's seal upon my breast and took a long way around the cloister walk, offering a prayer for Brother Horach's spirit.

The small, many-windowed library building nestled in between the domed chapter house and the long, blockish monks' dorter in the east reach of the cloister garth. The scriptorium occupied the ground floor. One reached the actual library by way of an exterior stair.

A rushlight borrowed from the infirmary revealed the upper chamber to be unimposing. The white-plastered walls were unadorned, save for two tiers of deep window niches that overlooked the cloister garth. On the opposite wall, an arched doorway opened onto a passage linking the library with the adjoining chapter house and dorter. Backless stools of dark wood stood alongside five long tables, and deep, sturdy book presses with solid doors and sliding latches lined the side walls.

I opened the cupboard farthest from the door. A locked inner grate of scrolled brasswork revealed shelves crammed with scrolls and books. A careful examination through the grate indicated that the book of maps was not among them. I moved on to the next.

In the third book press, near the bottom of a stack of large volumes, I spied a leather binding of the correct color, quality, and thickness. No gryphon lurked amid the gold elaboration of grape leaves and indecipherable lettering on its spine, but then I'd never actually examined the thing edge on.

In hopes my search had ended, I assembled the spell components for manipulating locks: the feel of old brass tarnished by greasy fingers, the image of the bronze pins and levers that might be inside this type of lock, my intent in the rough shape of a key, ready to be filled with magic and applied to the lock. Then I began to step through the rules for binding these elements together to create an unlocking spell.

With lessons and practice the pureblood bent for sorcery could be used to shape spells that had naught to do with familial talents. Though my childhood indiscipline had prevented me learning the rules for many spells, I'd had a great deal of experience breaking locks as a boy and become fairly accomplished at it. Yet years had gone since I'd done much of any spellworking. Beyond my vow to forgo magic and thus avoid the fatal weakness of most *recondeurs*, I'd needed to hoard my power. Without sufficient time for the well of magic inside me to be replenished, I could find myself lacking enough to empower the doulon, and my nasty habit used almost everything my particular well could produce. But surely I could scrape together enough to break a lock.

I held the spell ready, touched my fingers to the keyhole, and released a dollop of magic. Nothing happened. The brass wasn't even warm to the touch.

I tried again, adjusting my expectation of the inner workings of the lock to something simpler. Feeling the press of time, I applied a much healthier dollop of magic. With a loud snap, blue sparks and bits of brass and bronze shot from the keyhole. The grate hung loose, a severely bent latch dangling from the brass frame.

"Holy Mother!" I waggled my stinging hand. Mumbling curses at my ineptitude, I twisted the latch back into shape the best I could, pulled off the most noticeably broken pieces, and brushed the metal chaff under the edge of the cabinet with my boot. Gingerly, I pulled open the over-heated grate and extracted the book. It was not mine.

I stuffed the book back in the stack and slammed the grate, using a bronze shard to wedge it shut. Once the outer door was latched, I proceeded to the next book press. And the next . . .

So many books. Useless things. Searching those damnable cupboards felt as if I walked down a street of noble houses, where lamplight and singing spilled out the windows, knowing I'd not be allowed through any door. Not that I yearned to read about the world in place of living in it. It just would have been nice to know I could get in if I chose.

With nothing to show for my search so far but a broken lock and a stinging hand, I came to the last cupboard.

"We would be happy to provide you books, Valen, did you but ask." Pale light flared and died behind me.

I dropped my walking stick with a clatter and spun about, backing into a table that immediately began sliding out from under me. "Father Abbot!"

Abbot Luviar glided across the room and rescued the rushlight before I dropped it. "I'm sorry to startle you."

How the devil had he gotten to the far corner of the library without me seeing him? He'd certainly not been lurking there the whole time. I straightened my gown and backed away from him until blocked by the yawning door of the book press. "I was just . . . restless. I've slept so much."

"Understandable." Smiling, he set the rushlight on the nearest table and retrieved my dropped stick. He carried no lamp of his own. "This is a fortuitous encounter. I've been intending to thank you for your service on Black Night and since. Your warning saved lives. Your tales lift hearts. Even the digging—"

"I didn't help. Don't thank me." The last thing in the world I desired was any share of what this man had wrought on Black Night. "Perryn of Ardra should have stood with his men. Died with them."

"Indeed, he should have," said the abbot, using my rushlight to ignite a wall lamp, flooding one study table with pale illumination. "Events demanded otherwise."

"Is he still here?" Anger worked as well as strong mead to embolden my tongue.

Revealing naught but weariness, Luviar propped his backside and his hands on the table. "The prince is safe. I'll not say where."

"I'd have thought holy monks would stay removed from sordid politics," I said.

"Fleshly needs oft intertwine with the spiritual. How can a woman think of heaven while her children starve, or a man contemplate Iero's great love as his vines wither?" His furrowed gaze fixed somewhere in the emptiness between us. "We cannot always see the full span of history as it unfolds. Sometimes I fear that to attempt it is to infringe the role of the One who sees all, past and future. Yet, if the Creator *grants* us sight—"

His hypocrisy forced a choking sound from my throat. He jumped up and offered me his hand. "Here, Valen, are you ill?"

"Must have jarred my wound when I stumbled," I murmured, waving him off. "I'll be all right."

He passed me the rushlight. "You should get back to bed. Rest. Heal. Despite its current troubles, the world is a wondrous place, the earth itself God's holy book. Each man must discover his place in the great story. May you find your place . . . your peace . . . at Gillarine."

I bowed and hobbled toward the door. Behind me, Luviar unlocked one of the brass grates, pulled out a book, and sat down to read. His composure only pricked my fury.

Boreas had been right. Monks were naught but self-righteous thieves. No Cartamandua gryphon marked any binding in that library.

My days of sanctuary expired. As the only way a man of sixteen years or better could stay at the abbey beyond a fortnight was to take vows, that was what I resolved to do—at least until I could put my hands on my book. The monks insisted that my face revealed Iero's joy coursing through my veins. But truly, my good cheer stemmed from imagining the faces of anyone who had ever known me upon hearing of my intent.

"Good morrow, Valen! Iero's grace is full upon you this glorious morn!" Only two days after his return from Pontia, I had already learned that Brother Sebastian was excessively cheerful in the early morning. My mentor, a ruddy-cheeked monk with a round head, a neat fringe of gray hair bordering his tonsure, and an ever-immaculate habit, as might be expected of the son of a ship captain, had just come from chapter to disturb my morning nap.

"Brother." Bleary-eyed, I hauled myself to sitting, keeping the blankets up to my neck as the morning was damp and cold. Five more beds had been claimed by coughing, wheezing monks who had taken chills on Black Night. Jullian crouched by the brazier, stirring a cauldron of boiling herbs.

"What is great, you may ask?" Sebastian's face beamed as he snatched the black gown from the hook on the wall beside my bed. "Brother Robierre and I have decided that you may set sail from your sickbed today."

"But I thought—"

"Sorry to lose your good company, Valen. But you'll be healthier out of here." Brother Robierre pressed a rag across a spindly old monk's mouth as the poor fellow coughed up enough sputum to float a barque. Perhaps he was right.

Truth be said, I was a bit anxious at leaving my simple infirmary life behind for the mysteries of the monks' dorter. As a child in a house devoted to the elder gods, I'd heard outlandish tales of Karish monks who ate children in their secret precincts, of barbed tails grown beneath their gowns, all manly hair plucked out, or even privy parts removed entire. Being older than age ten, and having met a good variety of folk along the years, and having even practiced Karish ways when times made it expedient, I knew such talk as nonsense. Yet missing princes, murdered monks, and their unquiet spirits had left me a bit more wary of Iero and his holy precincts.

As Brother Sebastian exchanged blessings and gossip with the patients, I donned my gown. My little bundle of provisions, medicines, and knife—now well sharpened—went into my rucksack along with my secular clothes. The empty green bag remained safely tucked away at the bottom.

"Until you take your novice vows, they'll send you here to sup, so we'll not lose you entirely," said the infirmarian, grinning as he dispensed one of his potions to another man. "And you must come down here every evening to let me examine your wounds . . ."

". . . and to finish your tale of that tin smuggler in Savil," called Brother Marcus from the bed closest to the door. "You can't leave us not knowing if the fellow got out of the cave."

I laughed. "I've a better one, about the time I fell in with a caravan of—"

"Be off with you, Valen, or I'll chase you out," said Robierre, beckoning Jullian to replenish an earthenware bowl with his steaming decoction. "We've our work to do."

"You've done well by me, Brother Infirmarian," I said, taking a jig step and twirling foolishly into a sweeping bow. "You are Iero's own artist with your lancets and caudles. I do thank you."

Robierre bobbed his head, flushed a little, and went on with his work. Jullian watched intently, a ladleful of his pungent liquid sloshing noisily into the fire. I winked at the boy, grabbed the rucksack and my alder stick, and joined Brother Sebastian at the door.

"I shall strive to do as well by you as Robierre has done," he said.

"You can stick your nose in *his* business, Sebastian," Brother Marcus called after us, "and leave off telling the rest of us when our gowns are untidy or our beds ill made." The red-haired scribe had taken a spear wound next his spine on Black Night and was dreadfully uncomfortable. He lay on his belly all day and all night, sketching odd little drawings on scraps of vellum laid on the floor under his nose. Robierre wasn't sure the man would ever leave his bed.

Brother Sebastian chuckled, held open the door, and waved me out. "Tell me if we set too fast a pace, Valen. Your leg seems to be progressing well."

We strolled past the herb beds and around the bakehouse. "I was thinking that I should go walking in the countryside to strengthen it and cleanse my lungs from the sickly humors of the infirmary . . ." . . . *and scout the possibilities for replenishing my supply of nivat.*

Brother Sebastian halted abruptly. "That would not be at all appropriate. Though yet unvowed, you must draw a sharp separation from the outer world. Once your leg receives Brother Robierre's clearance, you will be assigned outdoor duties more than sufficient to cleanse your lungs."

"But—"

His raised finger ended discussion. We had reached the stair to the monks' dorter, and he was soon busy showing me the rope bed and straw-filled palliasse at the south end of the long, high-ceilinged room where I would sleep.

The empty green pouch in the bottom of my rucksack soon became more worrisome than midnight massacres, eyeless corpses, or monks who explained naught of lighthouses or vanishing royalty no matter what wheedling I did. I had taught myself not to think of nivat or the doulon overmuch. The need could come to affect all a man's dealings, his friends, his choices, until life took shape from it every day and not just the one day in twenty-eight . . . or twenty-one . . . that it devoured him. I swore I'd rather go mad from the lack than let it rule me. But always the hour arrived when my bravado withered.

I had already confirmed that Brother Robierre kept no nivat seeds in the infirmary. An exploration of the bakehouse, while its denizens were at Vespers, had revealed that Brother Baker kept his brick ovens clean, his floor swept, his barrels of flour and salt sealed tight, and his wooden boxes of herbs and seeds labeled neatly, though with no sketch or hint of their contents for any who had difficulty with letters. None of the boxes contained nivat. I would have to go farther afield to replenish my supply.

My hopes of moving in and out of the abbey freely were quickly squelched. Every hour of my day was scheduled: services in the church, meals in the infirmary, washing, and walking. I suffered endless lessons, everything from how to fold my gown and place it in the wooden chest at the foot of my bed, to the signing speech the monks used in the cloisters, to a history of the brotherhood so detailed I could near recite what Saint Ophir had for breakfast every morning of his four-and-eighty years. Even my times of "study and reflection" in the church or the gardens were scrutinized. If I dozed off, one or the other of the brethren would immediately walk by and rap my skull with a bony knuckle.

And so I decided to slip out at night. The monks were abed with the birds, and as the dorter had been built for a hundred and twenty, a wide gap of empty cubicles separated my quarters from those of the thirty-one men who slept at the end nearest the church. And in the main, I was well shielded from their view. Besides the common shoulder-high screen of carved wood that separated one monk's bed, chest, stool, and window alcove from the next man's, a folding screen of woven lath had been set across the central aisle to separate the novices' cubicles from those reserved for the monks. And I was the only novice.

But not only did Brother Sebastian poke his head around my screen twice each night, as the Rule advised, but the very structure of the dorter thwarted me. My cubicle lay between the monks' cubicles and the reredorter. Throughout the night, sleepy monks in need of natural relief made a constant procession down the central aisle, around the lath screen, and past my open cubicle toward the cold wooden seats of the rere.

Worse yet, I was expected to parade down to the church with the monks to pray the nighttime Hours. These interruptions came at such frequent and unholy times—Vespers before supper, Compline at bedtime, Matins at midnight, Lauds at third hour, Prime at sixth—I could not see how I would ever be able to absent myself long enough to acquire what I needed. The anxiety I tried to keep from ruling my life crept inevitably into every hour.

"It's come!" Brother Sebastian hurried down the path from the cloisters waving a rolled parchment. "I worried we might have to lie twixt wind and water for another month."

I slammed the wretched book shut. Excessive meditation was surely ruinous to good health and spirits. While my mentor had attended the chapter meeting that morning, I'd sat on this stone bench in the hedge garden, pretending to study. The characters on the page had tightened into seed shapes. Every scent—of yew, of grass, of smoke from the kitchen—taunted me because it was *not* the earthy fragrance of nivat.

"It's the letter from Palinur. The last impediment to your investiture is removed." Having been informed that I was schooled enough to comprehend Aurellian, Brother Sebastian had blithely deemed no further reading test necessary, and his oral quiz of my mathematical skills had been less taxing than a visit to any Morian trade fair. He had lacked only the proof of my birth.

Sebastian unrolled the parchment under my nose. I furrowed my brow and inspected the page as if I could comprehend it. His chattering implied the cathedral labor rolls had indeed confirmed my status as a freeborn and legitimate son of nobodies.

Neither bastards nor villeins were allowed to labor on holy works. When I'd wandered back to Palinur a few years before in search of work, I had assembled several tavern acquaintances into a poor but devout family, believable enough to testify and get me hired on at the cathedral. I had cheerfully imagined my mother's face if she ever learned she had been mimed by a whore who had serviced Palinur's garrison so often, she could identify the soldiers' pricks blindfolded.

Brother Sebastian's face shone brighter than the hazy sun. "The abbot has given his consent. And, most excellently, it happens that the Hierarch of Ardra himself has arrived for a visitation and will preside at your vesting! Come along with me, lad."

Before I knew it, we had collected my secular clothes from the dorter and a provision bag from the kitchen, and he was bustling me through the doorway of the very guesthouse where I had been certain that the Duc of Ardra was hiding from his royal brother.

"Tomorrow dawn I'll come for you, my son. Open your heart for Iero's guidance." Brother Sebastian pushed a canvas bag into my hands, and for a moment the animation of his round face yielded to a quieter sentiment. "You've a cheerful heart, Valen . . . yes, yes . . . Robierre has seen it as well, as has everyone who's met you. Our brotherhood will benefit greatly from the vigor you bring. But nothing sours a graceful spirit more than taking a path it is not meant to walk, so we would have you be certain of each step along the way." He grinned and retreated down the steps, waving as he disappeared past the granary. Guilt nudged my shoulder, but I quickly dismissed it.

The bag contained bread, cheese, and a traveling flask of ale, provisions for my journey should I decide to abandon the monastic life. An earthenware flask contained a liquid that had no smell. I wrinkled my nose. Water from the blood-tainted abbey spring was to be my only sustenance for my night of meditation. The bag did *not* contain my book. I wasn't sure whether to be insulted that they thought I was so stupid as to abandon my only possession of value, or gratified that they considered me worthy of their company.

I explored the guesthouse, speculating as to where the abbot had installed his royal supplicant if not here. Though its chambers were not elaborately decorated, it was more luxurious than anywhere I'd slept in many years. Plum-colored rugs warmed the bare floors. Brightly woven tapestries blanketed the walls, depicting the events from the life of Karus, the divine mystic from the steppes of far Estigure whose unruly sect had grown into Iero's Karish church.

A magnificent fresco in the dining room illustrated the familiar theme of the *ordo mundi*—the world's proper order. In sweeping bands of blue, yellow, and crimson, the artist illumined the three spheres: the arc of heaven, where the holy saints lived with Iero and Karus; the base foundation of hell, domain of the Adversary and damned souls; and in between, the earthly sphere with its righteous layers of kings and hierarchs, purebloods and peasants, its somber labors and abject wickedness so vividly depicted and its true delights so blatantly ignored. Though Iero extended his hands toward the earthly sphere in invitation, only the winged grace of angels bridged the gaping emptiness between the spheres of heaven and earth. A sad oversight, I'd always thought. In this respect, the Sinduri Council offered a more pleasing view: that every arch, tree, window, grotto, and mud puddle had its pesky aingerou, a messenger to the elder gods. Thus common folk could hold a discussion with our ever-quarreling divine family by raising a glass in an inn or taking a piss in the wood.

It was tempting to build a fire in the hearth, relax on the fine couch, and contemplate this profound and beautifully wrought statement of humankind's place in the scheme of things. But I dared not miss this chance to get out, acquire what I needed, and get back again without prompting uncomfortable questions from my hosts. Unfortunately the guesthouse held no valuables small enough to carry with me.

Though I had been instructed to leave my monk's garb in the dorter for my vigil night, pragmatism had prompted a minor disobedience. Those who prowled the roads of Navronne, whether soldiers, highwaymen, or even the most devout followers of the elder gods, considered it unlucky to touch a wayfaring monk or practor. Interference with traveling clergymen had been a hanging offense since the days of King Caedmon's Peace and the Writ of Balance. The Writ, a declaration of truce between the priests and priestesses of the Sinduri Council and the Karish hierarchs, had been proclaimed at Navronne's birth by King Eodward's great-great-great-grandfather—or his father, if you believed the legend that a beleaguered Caedmon, his beloved kingdom on the verge of annihilation by the Aurellian Empire, had sent his infant son Eodward to live with the angels for a hundred and forty-seven years.

As soon as darkness fell—the time when Brother Cadeus the porter gave up his post at the Alms Court—I downed one more swallow of ale, threw the black gown over my jaque and braies, and slipped out of the guesthouse. From the mouth of the gatehouse tunnel, I skulked northward along the outer wall, avoiding the track across the open field so as not to be observed from the sanctuary room. A wooded hollow near the junction of the track and the main road, where the tricky moonlight shifted shadows, provided a likely vantage for less benevolent observers. Prince Bayard would surely have set a watch on the abbey.

Only when I reached a lonely beech grove did I breathe again. I scoffed at my racing heart. What was wrong with me? These were *monks* after all, and they held no bond upon me. No matter what kind of exit I made, they'd likely take me back come morning if I vouched some saintly vision had changed my heart. This constant prickling of unease was wholly foolish—likely naught but my long-muzzled conscience thrown out of sorts in such a holy place. Laughing at the thought of *myself* shipped off to live in the realm of angels, I shouldered my rucksack again and set out along the mist-shrouded river.

Chapter 9

Aquellé north from the abbey, the River Kay vanished into ripe-smelling boglands. The road, so firm and wide at Gillarine, dwindled into marshy tracks, scarcely distinguishable from the fen in the patchy moonlight. My steps slowed. No bogwight was going to lure me into a muddy death, doomed to take its place until the next unwary traveler set me free in turn! Unfortunately, a careful pace would never get me to Elanus and back in any sensible time, even assuming Jullian's estimate of three quellae was at all accurate.

Thus, I chose to risk using a bit of magic again. If I didn't acquire nivat, no amount of power would save me. As the moon darted behind a wad of clouds, I knelt to lay my palms on the earth and discover my way using my bent. I closed my eyes. The mud was cold and gummy and smelled of rotting timber, moldering leaves, and animal droppings. Softening the boundaries of my mind, I released magic to flow through my fingertips.

Inhale. The scents grew richer . . . stronger. Boot leather and greased axles, cut timber and hay had passed this way. Horses and donkeys. Flocks of sheep and pigs driven to town. *Listen.* Gurgles and trickles spoke of the river, not vanished, but merely hidden beneath and beside and around me, as powerful in its dispersal as in its joined form, just more subtle. I discovered traces of travelers . . . of voices. My youthful ventures in use of my bent had never been so vivid.

I stretched my mind forward and swept from left to right, as a draftsman ties his pen to a string and stretches that string from a fixed point to scribe a perfect arc. Within that arc I could sense the variance of terrain: puddles and gullies, sucking mud pits, submerged trees, plots of firmer ground, the tracks of thirsty deer and bears and skittering mice, and always the road like a band of sturdy cloth, woven of scents and earth and the quivering remnants of those who had trod or ridden or driven over it, talking, braying, singing.

So many sensations all at once . . . and the music . . . A number of singers had traveled this road, leaving behind telltales of their music. One of them . . . ah, what a gift . . . the plucked notes of a harp wound through present and past like a thread of silver, woven into the road for a while and then wandering off into the fens . . . a song to pierce the heart. A prickling crept up my arms, as if I were dissolving into the fens like the river and the road. Beneath my palms the earth swelled, as if a body lay beneath the mud and had begun to breathe. Somewhere eyes were opening . . .

Quickly, I scribed the shape of the land on my mind and yanked my hands away, rinsing the mud off them in a puddle and wiping them on my gown. A glance around the still, moonlit landscape revealed neither man nor beast. But as I set off again, I could not slough off the sense that my eyes were unreliable.

Forests and bogs were favorite haunts of spirits. Though aingerou preferred cities and other man-built habitations, and revenants preferred the places they'd lived or died, tales spoke of older beings who yet walked in the wild—the guardian Danae, whose dancing wove the patterns of the world and who could merge their bodies with ponds or groves, and the demon gatzi, who were but Danae corrupted to Magrog's service. Both were said to whisk folk away from mortal life. I'd never run across any such creatures, so they didn't worry me all that much, but it never hurt to keep one's eyes open.

Holding the thread of path and direction in my head, I hurried down the road, humming the harper's song that still shimmered in my head. The cheerful melody swelled my heart and kept the night's terrors at bay.

The hour was not even Compline when the first glimpse of torchlit roofs and walls, and the first sounds of pipe, tabor, and raucous laughter set up a rampant thirst in me. I stripped off my monk's gown, stuffed it into my rucksack, and trotted the last few hundred quercae up the road and across the ditchwork to the cross-timbered gate. A good-sized town like Elanus should have a fine selection of taverns, sop-houses, pickable pockets, friendly barmaids, and gullible gamblers, not to mention an herbalist or apothecary with nivat seeds to sell. Not to mention a tankard of potent mead to warm away the damp and make a man forget politics, holy men, and conspiracies for an hour or two.

A closer look dampened my optimism. Though the earthwork surrounding the hillside town appeared substantial, the wooden palisade atop it was rotting and the town watch lax and slovenly. My claim that I'd come in search of a secure bed on a journey to visit my brother in Palinur easily satisfied the two half-soused guardsmen who carried but one serious weapon between them—an iron-bladed bill hook that would see its best use as a club. They seemed more interested in my assertion that my brother had a job awaiting me in a Palinur tannery than in the motley bloodstains on my jaque or how I had managed to travel any distance in these perilous times, carrying no weapon but a walking stick.

"Bog iron's failing," said one of the reeking pair as he cracked some aged walnuts with his bill. His blotched skin was peeling. "Half the smelts are cold. Roads too risky to bring in ore, and them as might haul it are fighting or dead. Elanus won't last a year more."

The second guard sneezed and wiped his nose on his sleeve. "Some Harrowers were through here yestereve, preaching. Lot of folk figure the orange-heads have it right. Won't take but another smelt closing down for them to have us all burning for the Gehoum."

"So they've gone now . . . the Harrowers?" I asked, glancing around uneasily, happy I'd taken off the monk's habit. I didn't need any ragtag from Black Night taking out their frights and vengeance on a monk. Harrowers didn't honor the Writ of Balance. "You're sure they weren't soldiers—Moriangi?"

"Nawp. Only orange-heads, but soldierly, especially the woman leading 'em. They're burning farms and outliers these last few days, them they say is offending their holy Gehoum. They burnt Mott's granary, saying his plow was a curse. The watch snagged one of her hags for the pillory. Rest got away."

"Mayhap I'll be on my way sooner as later, then," I said. "Wouldn't want to cause them offense. But I'm for a tankard first." I'd need to be careful leaving. The Harrowers would likely hang about the town to get their woman back. Perhaps theirs was the foreboding presence I'd felt on the road.

The town pillory sat just inside the gates. A frowsy woman, face streaked with ash and blood, yelled at me hoarsely as I hurried past. "The day of terror comes! The Gehoum will have their vengeance!" Her hair was strung up in a greasy wad atop her head and tied with an orange rag. She didn't sound so much crazed as excited.

I sloughed off the worry, waded through a knee-deep gaggle of muddy geese that blocked the town's main street, and happily inhaled the scent of civilization—dung, smoke, and burning fat. Just ahead of me, a ragged donkey boy leveled one whip and manifold curses, trying to get a charcoal-laden dray up the steepening lane.

The people of Elanus seemed a grim and unhealthy lot altogether, just like their town. At the edge of the road bony children dabbled sticks in the puddles, and cripples shook empty cups, bawling for a citré. Everywhere were hollow cheeks and peeling, unhealthy skin, and sunken eyes that would not meet mine. Orange head rags stuck out like bits of bright paint on a wall of gray.

As I strolled past an alley, trying to decide whether to locate a source for the nivat or the means to pay for it first, a burly man with a slack lip and a sinner's nose pawed at my sleeve. "A bed companion this night, traveler? Or an hour's pleasure?"

In the shadowed alley, a squint-eyed young woman opened her threadbare cloak to reveal a tight-laced bodice of ruffled lace. A slim, pretty boy with skin the color of milked tea leaned against the sooty brick, smirking as he shivered in naught but a stained silk tunic and a silver ankle bracelet.

"These two come all the way from Estigure. Blessed is the man who lies with divine Karus's kin. Lay away blessings lest the world's end catch you lornly."

I sighed and let my eyes drink in the sights. "Regrettably I've other holy business must come first."

The man waggled a finger and the girl spun in place, billowing her cloak and a filmy skirt, slit from hither to yon, offering glimpses of long, slim legs. The tasseled string that fastened her lacy bodice swayed most enticingly. My hands twitched as I imagined the smoothness of those long legs and the delights that lay underneath the shabby lace. Serena Fortuna had cursed me with overlong abstinence already, and now proffered the lonely prospect of winter at an abbey. No prayer I'd ever heard could sheathe a man's ache.

With apologies to the goddess Arrosa for refusing her sweet gift, I worked to cool the growing heat in my loins. *Think of battlefields, Valen. Winter. A starving belly. Monks. Nivat seeds. Family.* "Perhaps later."

His pitted, leaking nose twitched, and he licked his sagging lip, revealing stained teeth. "Five citrae will hold the girl for you until midnight. Ten for the boy. I've others as well. Locals. Cheaper, but blessed, all the—"

"I'll come back if Serena Fortuna is kind."

Even if I'd had the price, I wasn't fool enough to give it on a promise. But I bowed to the girl, which brought a lovely flush to her pale cheeks and set her licking lips much finer than the procurer's, and I winked at the youth, which replaced his smirk with a soft and subtle eagerness. Perhaps four years older than Jullian, he stretched an arm behind his head and thrust out one slim hip just enough to make a graceful curve.

I cleared my throat and dragged my eyes away. "Tell me, good-man, where in this sober town might I find good mead and honest dice?"

"Cross-hill toward the smelts, you'll find the Blade. Tell Holur that Tigg sent you for a game and a taste from his cask. He'll see to you." He shrugged and turned his attention back to other passersby.

My stomach rumbled as I meandered down the lane that leveled off westward, "cross-hill," rather than taking the steeper way that climbed the rounded mound of Elanus. A few tight-shuttered houses lurked among others collapsed into weedy ruins. The sweet pale smokes of peat fires laced with pork fat hung over the lane like mist over the bogs. At the far end of the lane, darker billows rose from the charcoal fires of the "smelts," where the folk of Elanus teased work-able iron from treasured pellets dug from the peatlands.

I'd tended a bog-iron smelter one autumn. Hot, smoky, tedious work to keep the fires stoked and burning evenly for days on end. I'd been no good at it. The sheer ugliness of the task could not but set a man's mind wandering.

Just down the lane, a knot of shouting people broke into cheers. Peering over the bobbing heads revealed a squirming, muddy tangle of scrawny limbs and occasional glimpses of bared teeth and blood-ied cheeks and noses. One of the boys, significantly smaller than the other, seemed favored by the crowd, and every twist that gave him a moment's advantage elicited a cheer and a jostle of back-slapping. A stringy man with bulging eyes collected coins from the onlookers. One lad would likely get a meal for his bruises, the other naught but a boot in the backside. I'd earned my share of both. When the pop-eyed man stuck his tin cup in my face, I showed him my empty palms, bellowed an encouragement for each of the boys, and moved on.

A wedge of hammered iron dangling above a lettered signboard announced an establishment blazing with light and bursting with jolly music and fine smells. The Blade. Ah, I did love a friendly tavern, a pocket of warmth and enjoyment amidst all the cold world's ills. My spirits, far too sober with deceptions, politics, abbeys, and damnable diseases, perked up.

The doxy held the law at bay with tit and toe and tongue.
All while the bandit stole away that night before he hung . . .

As ever, the singing snared me like a hook trap. I joined in even before I walked through the door, and as I slammed the splintered plank behind me, a woman draped her arm about my neck and warbled the next chorus right in my ear. Laughing, I grabbed her waist from behind and whirled her about as the song required, while other men tried to pinch her tits or stomp her toe. Spoiling for action and good cheer, I let the music liven my feet to glide and pivot, heel and toe. The rhythm of the tabor took us up and down the room through the clapping crowd as I spun her dizzy and protected her from their gleeful pawing.

Well into the doxy and the bandit's fourth escapade, we collapsed over a table in breathless merriment, and I first glimpsed the woman's face. Beneath a lank cascade of mud-colored hair swelled smooth cheeks of a pleasant pink and naught else worthy of mention. My brother Max would have called her a mirror-bane.

"Two more on my coin, Holur!" she yelled over my shoulder as our pursuers abandoned us in favor of a new ale barrel being hauled in from the back room. "Though my head be swimming, my tongue is dry. And this fellow sings like a carpenter's rasp."

Coins rattled in the piper's basket, and a new dance went on without us. Still laughing, I dragged the woman up and into my arms, my hands finding a sure downward path toward the generous curves beneath her skirt. Max had always been too particular by half. Such yielding firmness demanded further explorations. My feet moved to a more languorous tempo.

She moaned softly deep in her throat, and a pleasant heat rose from her skin and through her layered clothing. I drew her closer.

"La, sir! I can't." Trapping my neck in the crook of one elbow, the woman dragged my head downward until our foreheads touched. Then she grinned wickedly, and with a deft move, stuffed her tongue in my ear, leaving my own lips and tongue poised for naught. Before I could riposte, she slipped my grasp altogether.

She didn't go far, though. A fellow with a dirty apron and skin the color and texture of oak bark held out two foaming mugs. She took one for herself and shoved the other into my empty hands, crashing her mug into mine for a toast. "To my brave defender!" she said with a smile and an ale-sodden belch. "My name's Adrianne, by the by. Though I be loath—sorely loath—to leave so game and manly a partner, my da will beat me purple if I linger one jot more."

"Alas, and I just arrived," I said, discreetly using a sleeve to blot the remains of her sloppy kiss, as I grinned back at her. "Without knowing a soul to ask where I might find the proper seasonings for my Saldon bread."

She giggled and touched my face with a plump finger. "Such a fine handsome fellow as you baking feast bread . . . it's hard to imagine."

"I've baked my own Saldon loaf since I was sixteen, even if I had to do it on a stone in a thistle fire," I said and scooped her finger into my mouth for a lick and a nip. She tasted of garlic and ale and woman. "And as I've come to Elanus in search of work and already heard the bog iron's failing, I'd best not lapse in proper honor to the Danae's feast."

"I saw a Dané once," she said, dropping her head on my chest, either because she didn't want to be heard by our rowdy companions or because she couldn't hold it up any longer. "In the bog when I was late from town and cut across close to Movre's Pool. Tall and beautiful she was. Naked, with her blue marks of magic glowing on her skin. Didn't speak, though her light guided me safe through the bog."

"More likely Iero's angel than a Dané, if your tall, beautiful creature was also kind." More likely yet another tipsy maid waked from a randy romp in a berry thicket. Legend named the Danae spiteful beings who once gave life to forests, lakes, and fields, but hated human folk. Supposedly a furious Mother Samele took the earth from the Danae's charge and gave it to the impish aingerou after Kemen lay with a Danae queen and fathered Deunor Lightbringer. Even the Sinduri Council professed that if the Danae had ever existed, they did no longer.

The girl shook her head vigorously. "Not an angel. She'd no wings. Some say Danae have wings, as they vanish right in front of you, but my grandmere told me they just turn a corner that human eyes can't follow."

"As to my baking needs . . . I've only the clove, ginger, and pennyroyal." I regretted cutting off the discussion, but the girl's time was limited, and such a companionable encounter, a staple of friendly common rooms, should yield *some* fruit.

"Ah," she said and dropped her voice to a liquid whisper. "Down Smelt Alley, third door, you'll find Gorb the seedsman. You needs must bang the door and convince the pinchfist to open his locks and trade with you, but he'll have both hazelnuts and nivat to sell. Mayhap"—she tilted her bleary gaze upward—"I should go with you. I'll bake a Saldon loaf as well and take it to the bog. Da's a smith and not got half the work he used to. Raises his yellow bile, it does.

Folk pray to Iero about the war and the end times coming, or whine to Kemen and Samele about the weather, but naught's offered a pin to the Danae that I know of, asking help to replenish the bog iron here at Elanus. They're most forgotten."

Serena Fortuna's beneficence lay warm on my back. "Well, as you're late home already and risking your da's heavy hand, what if *I* were to visit this seedsman and fetch hazel and nivat for us both? I'll meet you here tomorrow eve, and we'll have a song and share it out. I'll divide my ginger with you, too. This merry meeting will infuse our bread with luck." I brushed my fingers around her cheeks and down her neck to other fetching curves, feeling her desire swell to meet my own. It had always made sense to me that magic flowed through a sorcerer's fingertips. "I'd need your coin, of course, as nivat comes so dear. But better to risk a few lunae with me than your da's bruises on these pretty cheeks, don't you think?"

Her sigh, as I bent over and kissed her on the lips to seal the bargain, came near subverting my wickedness. Willing women with even one attractive feature had the disconcerting habit of making me lose all sense. But the nivat was of first importance. I summoned up chilly thoughts of Gillarine and its confining comforts. As my rousing fever cooled again, I pulled away. Damnable necessity. I might as well be gelded.

Adrianne bade a mooning, ale-sodden farewell to our merry company, leaving me with a mug of ale, a promise of all the dancing I might desire on the following night, and three silver lunae in my pocket. A smith's daughter . . . probably the wealthiest girl in Elanus . . . a more tempting winter's companion than tidy Brother Sebastian. All sorts of schemes flourished in the flush of the moment. I wasn't greedy.

But from the talk I heard from other customers as I finished my ale, the heavy-fisted smith had only enough work to pay his debts and keep Adrianne from Tigg the Procurer's hand until the last of the bog iron was worked. An empty-pocketed son-in-law would do naught for his choler. I'd need to sell my book to make the scheme work, and in that case I could surely do better than Adrianne. Not that I was in the market for a wife. My feet were too restless for shackling.

A rattling from the corner, punctuated by challenges to manhood, prayers to Serena Fortuna, and a caller's flat tones, tempted me to a dice game. Sadly, I had never been able to summon even a glimmer of my mother's bent for divination when it came to gambling. Best not risk Adrianne's offering. Nivat was easily available throughout Navronne, being an essential ingredient for those who observed the elder gods' feasts at the change of seasons. But the native plants—a kind of pepper once grown in Morian—had failed decades ago, and as the only surviving ones were cultured by sorcery, it was always expensive. Even the mead would have to wait. I drained my mug, bade Holur and his jolly piper a mournful farewell, and stepped back into the night. Leaving a tavern for a street, no matter how busy, always put the damp on my spirits.

Chapter 10

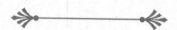

"That should do for whatever purpose you have in mind," said Gorb as he wrapped the nivat seeds in a scrap of cloth and tied the little bundle with a thread. He stretched his tight lips into a smile no wider than the flare of his nose and dragged his dark little eyes up and down my height. "Oh, yes. Saldon Night baking, you said. As night devours the sunlight and spits it out again, you shall be well blessed."

A plaintive tale of my need for Danae help with my witch-cursed prick had induced the seedsman to unlock his door. Truly, the story itself hadn't moved him, but only my invocation of Adrianne as the proposed beneficiary of my reinvigorated better parts.

A wizened little fellow as dry and sharp-edged as his merchandise, Gorb supplied a quantity of black nivat seeds no bigger than my thumb, enough to bake three Saldon loaves or service my unfortunate craving thrice over. And for that he returned only nine citrae out of the three silver coins worth forty each. Iero bless merry Adrianne and blunt her father's fist.

I shook the copper coins in my palm. Spending one of them on hazelnuts might blunt the speculation in Gorb's hard little face. Though I hated wasting the money, nivat was used only for holy offerings like feast bread or for spellworking, and of all the spells that could be worked with nivat, only the doulon required it. I wished no rumors of tall sorcerers with unsavory habits lingering in a town the monks might visit. Fate might lead me to Elanus again.

So . . . a story . . . and how could I help but think of the cursed Boreas, the very one who had caused the need for this journey?

I leaned my head across the table and spoke softly so that Gorb's brisk fingers came to a halt. "I met a man in the wood yestereve, a rough, hairy man near tall as me and twice as broad. He was laid up with the sweats, sick and drooling, pissing himself he hurt so wicked. He showed me plate and jewels he'd stolen from a rich man's house and said if I would bring him nivat seeds, he'd trade me a jeweled dagger that would keep me and Adrianne for ten years or more."

Satisfaction blossomed on Gorb's countenance, and greed sparked his seedlike eyes.

"Iero damns those that steal," I went on as if I hadn't noticed. "But this would not be stealing to my mind, as the guilt of the theft would rest on the one who *first* took the dagger from its rightful owner. If I made the bargain honorably and filled my part as I vowed, no fault would come to me. So I said I'd find him nivat and return tonight at midnight to make the trade."

Nodding slowly, the seedsman dropped his eyes. He shoved the packet across the table and briskly brushed the table's detritus from the flowing sleeves of his green robe. "Twist-minds are an affront to the Powers. You say this depraved fellow lies close by Elanus?"

I straightened up and grinned. "I'm no fool to tell you that, Seedsman Gorb. You've a bigger supply of nivat than I can afford. But once I have my dagger, I'll tell the man where he can buy more, and Serena Fortuna bless you with whatever arrangement you can make with him."

He dipped an iron scoop into his barrel of hazelnuts and slid a few of them into my palm atop the coins. "Good fortune shared always comes back," he said. His sharp chin quivered as if he were on the verge of weeping. Or perhaps laughing.

I paused in the smoky deeps of Smelt Alley and divided my store of nivat. Half went into the green bag, which I restored beneath the false bottom of my rucksack. I tied Gorb's cloth packet, containing the remainder of the nivat, to the waist string of my braies, and tucked eight coppers into my boot. I spun the last coin in the air and caught it, already tasting mead and humming a tune to accompany its sweet fire.

But as I stopped in at the still boisterous Blade, thoughts of perfidious Boreas choked me worse than the smelters' smoke, souring my mood. That pain-racked, drooling wretch I had described would not be *him* deprived of nivat, of course, but me.

Holur's mead cask was empty. But a tankard of his best ale and a bowl of porridge soothed my ill humor, and I bawled every song and galloped the length and breadth of the Blade with every maid and matron that stepped inside—none of whom were Adrianne, all thanks to Serena Fortuna. When I tossed my fifth citré on the barman's counter, ready to buy another round of ale, the lamplight caught the polished copper and flared like a red sunburst . . . which brought to mind solicales . . . and Karish monks . . . and the life waiting for me with the coming dawn. Before Holur could clamp his sticky fingers on the coin, I snatched it back, stuffed it in my boot, and with sober regrets bade him and all the company a good night.

The crier called second hour of the night watch—one hour till midnight—as I headed out for Gillarine. Elanus showed no signs of sleep. No surprise to that. The smelters had to be kept burning through the night. As I strolled past Tigg's alley on my way to the gate, the catamite raised his head and moved a step away from the wall, beckoning me into the alley. He was alone.

I shook my head and raised two open palms in a gesture of peace—or poverty, if one interpreted gestures in marketplace dialect. The message was much the same: I couldn't afford him, but bore him no ill will.

He nodded and slumped back against the bricks.

Though my taste ran usually to women, the youth was, indeed, beautiful. A torch burned in a bracket above his head. His mellow rose-brown skin and acorn-colored hair gleamed in the firelight. The deep blue silk of his scanty tunic rippled enticingly with his movements, and the silver bracelet on his bare ankle sparkled with a gemstone of matching blue . . . a sapphire?

I halted abruptly. That a catamite in the alleys of Elanus would be wearing a sapphire bracelet did not stun me half so much as the fact that I had admired that very bracelet in a noblewoman's jewel box . . . just before I stuffed it in my rucksack and got myself an arrow in the thigh. Boreas!

My blood running hot, I beckoned the youth to the street. Down the alley, Tigg the Procurer was taking a leisurely piss.

The youth summoned a smile from some secret place and lowered his dark lashes in a way that promised to share its source. Well past its days of breaking, his voice wrapped my body like silk. "What's your pleasure, sir? Tigg has a room—"

"Shhh." I laid my arm around the youth's tight shoulders. Though he smelled exotically of cardamom and clove, his accent was directly from the riverlands of Morian, not mystical Estigure. Careful to keep him within sight of his master and myself obscured by the brick corner, I bent my head to his. "No custom from me this night, sorry to say, but I *would* offer you a citré for a question answered."

He raised his heavy lids and buried his secrets again. "One citré buys only a small answer."

"The bracelet on your ankle. I would know where to find the person who sold it to your master. My wife—a harridan the likes of which would drive Sky Lord Kemen himself to the netherworld—would forgive me the worst of my failings if I could but take her such a trinket. And though your beauty is most worthy of much beauty in its turn, I'm thinking this little treasure was not ruinous to buy. Your master seems a . . . thrifty man."

"Your coin?" He stuck out his hand, all languorous invitation vanished.

I dug the copper from my boot and held it above his hand. "And your answer?"

A careless toss of his head threw his silken hair from his face. "Don't think to get *this* bauble. Master covets it. He said I could wear it for the street, but not when I go with aught. Big hairy fellow gave it for a night with me most of a month ago. Said he needed the blessing of lying with Karus's kin, as he was hunting a place to bed for the winter."

"That's all?"

The youth's long lashes fell toward his smooth, empty palm. "We didn't talk so much. He'd been a while without a decent lay."

Disappointed, I brushed my hand across his, releasing the coin. It vanished under the hem of his tunic, and he stepped back so that my arm dropped loose and empty. Even a touch would cost me more. I didn't begrudge him the necessities of his trade.

I eyed his slender form, neither hair nor blemish to be seen anywhere below his scalp. He brought to mind Stearc's squire Corin of the bronze braid and elegant cheekbones . . . fairer yet than this one. I felt a shifting in my braies, which circumstance startled me a bit. I was truly a pitiable case. "Fare you well this winter season, lad, with worthy companions and a light hand from those who profit from you. Indeed, you are almost enough to sway a man who finds his pleasures elsewhere."

His eyes took light from the torch as he shrugged and settled back against the wall, raising one knee to prop his foot on the bricks. "One Mistress Kellna lives out by Graver's Meadow and sells berries and rootstock here in the market. Some say she also buys and sells goods that are . . . outside the common trade. I don't care much for women, but you might find her informative. She come by new stock this month past and made profit enough selling it on to Edane Groult down near Caedmon's Bridge that she bought me two nights running for a new friend come to stay with her."

I grinned. "By Graver's Meadow, you say?"

"Aye. West on the first track outside the gates. Right fork at the old mill."

"Thank you for that," I said.

"Mayhap next time, you'll let me sway your pleasure. You're a leg up on most as come by here." The boy's gaze flicked down the alley, and his face paled. "You won't say who told you?"

"On my soul, not a word." I backed away quickly. When Tigg the Procurer stepped out of the alley and peered up and down the lane, I was well hidden behind a broken chimney.

I pulled the monk's gown from my rucksack and drew it over my head, covering rucksack and all. Then I slipped out of the ruin, clasped my hands to my chin, bowed my head and shoulders as if in prayer, and hurried toward the town gate close behind the ragged donkey boy driving his empty charcoal wagon.

The woman in the pillory spat and yelled as I passed. "Karish perversion mocks the Gehoum. The earth will bleed to cleanse itself. You'll pay, Karish! You'll pay!"

No one paid her any mind, or me, either. Not the gate guards I'd talked to earlier. Not even the short sallow newcomer riding through the gates, wearing a gray silk mask that covered half his face, a claret-colored cloak, and the black-and-yellow badge of an itinerant inspector from the Pureblood Registry. I grinned behind my folded hands, strolled across the stinking ditch, and turned westward onto the track for Graver's Meadow. Though the moon was well past full, its cold light kept me to the path.

Typical of Boreas to hole up for the winter in the first place he came to, a town small enough everyone would learn of him, and then to choose the bed of one who dealt in stolen goods. He'd never been one to think things through. And it was just like the devil to convince his *woman* to buy him a *boy*. I'd never understood what made women fawn on Boreas so—a big, hairy, unwashed brute with a gruff, foolish way about him, who definitely preferred partners with parts between their legs no female could provide. Not that he hated women. Women were his porridge, nourishing and sufficient for every day. Lads were his meat and spice.

As I walked I amused myself planning the encounter. Would it be more pleasurable to slice off the villain's balls with one of our stolen daggers or to tie him up naked in the cold and let him watch me walk away with our booty? Once I'd settled somewhere—Pontia, perhaps, a town large enough to sell one of the daggers and still keep my head down—I'd send an offering to Gillarine to thank them for their hospitality.

The track kicked up sharply. The stream, narrower here, burbled and gurgled, cutting deep into the rocky slope, creating moss-lined nooks and grottos, each with its own watery music. As a child I had imagined such a cool, mysterious nook must be a Danae sianou—the holy place where a Dané gave up its body for a season and became one with the land. Sometimes I would leave feast bread there and pray to be stolen from my family. More often I would yell, stomp the ground, and throw rocks in the water, hoping to wake the sleeping guardian. Neither activity bore fruit.

A cold gust flapped my gown around my ankles as I stepped around fresh horse droppings. And then more. I bent down and passed my hand over a mound. Still warm. Several people had ridden up this path not long before. I swore under my breath, but I'd come too far to turn back. Likely more than Mistress Kellna lived up this way.

After consideration, I removed my monk's gown and stuffed it into my rucksack. A lost monk might walk clear easier than my own self if I encountered ordinary folk, but the talk of Harrowers had unnerved me. And the captive woman had reminded me how they hated Karish.

My thigh was grateful when the path broke over the lip of the rise. The stream lay like a silver necklace across a rocky goat pasture, leading the eye toward a scant woodland and a cottage. A sweet, cozy little hideaway, cupped in the embrace of shallow chalk cliffs, easily defensible.

Unfortunately, the cottage was ablaze. A robust woman sprawled among the grazing goats with an arrow in her back, and somewhere Boreas was bellowing out agonized curses that threatened to crumble the earth beneath my feet. I would recognize his rumbling epithets anywhere.

I ran. Not back toward Elanus, which even a moron's poor sense would demand, but toward the conflagration and the screaming. Boreas had saved my life at the battle of Arin Fay, taking a deep slash on his arm while striking down the halberdier ready to remove my head. We had exchanged the favor a number of times in the long months following, so one could say I owed him nothing—less than nothing since he had abandoned me half dead. But that first time, having seen the Ferryman's hand as clearly as I would until the day I took ship with that grim spirit, I had given Boreas my oath to protect his back. I prided myself that I had never broken my sworn faith.

All too aware that the treacherous moonlight would expose any approach on the meadow track, I circled wide toward the cliffs to come up behind the house, racing as soft-footed as I could manage over the rocky ground. When I plunged gratefully into the clumped beech and oak grown up in the lee of the cliffs, the rush of the nearby flames was already waning. I crept cautiously through the snagging undergrowth of blackthorn and hazel.

The screams—hoarse now, choking grunts, wordless animal cries—did not emanate from the burning house, but from an expanse between the house and the chalk cliffs. Breaking free of the bracken, I sped through a stretch of scattered, pale-trunked beeches and caught myself just before hurtling into the open.

Beyond the bordering trees lay a rolling meadow, dotted with stands of rowan and birch. Nestled in a willow brake, a small, bean-shaped pond shimmered in the cold moonlight, its waters ruffled by the knife-edged breeze. From the pond spilled the stream that gouged the hillside. My soul swelled at the beauty of the place; my skin flushed and quivered as if the angel choirs themselves had come to sing in Gillarine Abbey church.

But my eyes were quickly drawn to a knoll at the heart of the meadow. At the apex of the knoll, five people gathered about a splayed figure, still as death. The angled moonlight stretched their long shadows across the slope.

A howl rose in my throat. Had I a weapon . . . a bow . . . a club . . . a blade longer than my finger, I would have set upon them, never mind the odds. But as in every juncture of my life, I was inadequate. Too late. Unprepared.

A scrawny, tangle-haired man stood at the base of the knoll holding six horses. With a smothered curse at my loose-lipped folly, I recognized him as Gorb the Seedsman. He'd not worn the orange scarf about his neck three hours past.

The five were chanting a pattern of four words, one each, over and over around their circle until I could distinguish the voices—three men and two women—and the Aurellian words: *sanguiera, orongia, vazte, kevrana.* Bleed, suffer, die, purify. With every repetition, the moonlight dimmed and the weight of night and despair descended upon my shoulders like an iron yoke. After the fifth or sixth time around, a tall, pale-haired woman in an orange cloak raised her arms, holding a short staff in her two hands as if to challenge the sky. Her clear voice incised the air like a silver lancet, and every hair on my flesh rose.

> *Powers of Night and Storm and Terror, of Desert and Ice, of Death and Life,*
> *O mighty Gehoum, heed our sacrifice.*

Withhold our doom as we cleanse this land of decadent plea-
sure,
Of all that distracts us mortals from our proper reverence.
May this blood and fire and pain be a sweet odor to fill the long
night of thy passing
And bear upon its vapors our vows renewed to purge the world
of all that stands between us and thy immortal being.

"Heathen witch! Magrog take ye to his everlasting fire!" The raw, choking curse came from the victim at their feet . . . Boreas, no doubt of it, not so dead after all.

"Feel the cleansing fear, mortal man," said the tall woman, lowering her arms and bending over him. "Thou art a blight upon the universe, diseased, depraved, an insult to the Powers who control the world's fate. Of all thy miserable existence, only thy ending will serve a purpose. Suffer and bleed and rejoice in the terror of darkness." She plunged her staff into the ground . . . into the man . . . ripping a cry of agony from his very depths.

Horror rooted my feet as each of the five bent to touch him. Then Sila Diaglou—of course, the pale-haired woman was the priestess I'd seen at Gillarine, the warrior who could rouse people to destroy their own fields and cities in the name of repentance—led her companions down the knoll to Gorb and the horses.

The seedsman gave the priestess a leg up into her saddle. She laid a hand on his head and murmured, as if bestowing a blessing, and then she and her cohorts rode toward me. I hid myself as best I could and still be able to see them as they approached the wood. Using every skill at my command, I etched their features into my memory.

Scarce forty, Sila Diaglou was a handsome woman with a high forehead and intelligent eyes set well below thin brows. The diagonal scar that seamed each cheek tainted her beauty with cruelty. Her hair floated like beaten flax as she rode, yet her wide mouth lacked any hint of generosity or mercy. Her lips, and those of her companions, were painted black with blood.

The smaller woman followed, particolored skirts draping her mount and a fluttering orange scarf wrapped about straight black hair. No more than a doe-eyed girl, eighteen at best, she rode like a queen, soft, copper-hued features devoid of emotion. The three men, too, I memorized as they came: the one with a beardless needle chin and colorless eyes, the one with a malformed ear and oiled black curls tied into a club at his neck, the third with a dog's face, all lumps and crags, with but a fringe of hair about his round chin and a dagged cloak of purple velvet. Weedy Gorb mounted his own beast and rode after the others.

I held still until they had passed out of my hearing. Then I raced to the crest of the knoll.

Spirits of fire and darkness! Stripped to his braies, wrists and ankles stretched and bound to wooden stakes, my old comrade leaked blood from every quat of his length and breadth. Blades had shredded his flesh and punctured his eyes. The priestess had plunged her staff through his middle, not through his heart or his bowel to kill him quickly, but through his side so that every breath, every trembling shudder, tore him apart.

Swallowing my gorge, I knelt beside him and spoke softly. "Ah, Boreas, you god-cursed gatzé, I knew you'd get in trouble without me."

"Who's there?" he croaked. His battered lips scarcely moved. His head rolled side to side, as if he might be able to see, if he but turned his bloody sockets in the proper direction.

Gently I stilled him. "It's Valen, come to help you as I vowed I would."

He gasped, a whooshing stridor that only after a panicked moment did I realize was a laugh. "So I'm dead then. Of all Magrog's servants come to take me at my end, ne'er thought 'twould be you, Valen. And I ne'er thought 'twould hurt so wicked to be dead." His dreadful laughter stretched into a sob.

"Hush now." I bent over so he could feel my breath. "Neither of us is dead. The baldpates saved my leg and my life, so I've you to thank for that. I heard you were up here, and I came to— Well, that doesn't matter. Holy gods, I'm sorry I'm so late."

I could see no way to help him. Pull the stake from his middle and the splintered shaft would draw his entrails, and he'd bleed his life away in agony. Leave it and his every breath would be torment and still he would die. But only after long dreadful hours . . . or days.

"No luck today for neither of us. Threw the last of our loot into the pond, they did. After killing—" A croaking sob. "Ah, Kellna was a merry lay. I never understood when ye said the best girls danced with ye. But Kellna . . . she danced."

"I'll pay her passage, Boreas. I promise." I ripped off my rucksack and scrabbled through the contents of the bundled rag. Nothing in the pilfered medicines would help him. Few did I even know the proper use of. But the little knife . . . "Hold still and I'll get your hands free."

With the pointed, finger-length blade of the stolen herb knife

I split the ropes that bound his wrists and ankles. He could not move his tortured limbs without crying out, so I did it for him, drawing them to his sides. Then I laid my monk's gown over him. His massive body trembled.

"Somehow they knew I'd nivat. Said I was a twist-mind . . . abomination to their Gehoum . . . and I'd be better use to the world bleeding. I tried to tell 'em . . ." Growing agitation had him gasping between words. Blood welled out from around the stake. "They've left me in the dark, Valen. There's naught here. Naught. I'm fallen in a well that has no bottom. Don't leave me this way . . ."

"Hold on." I pressed my hands on his shoulders. "Let me think what we're to do."

Perhaps the stake wasn't all the way through. With one hand on his shoulder to calm him, I touched the wooden shaft. Embedded deep in the earth, the stake did not move . . .

Dread . . . terror . . . suffocation . . . I was drowning in blood. In torment. *Violated.* Soul and mind raped with fire, then immersed in a cold midnight beyond bearing. *Alone.* Sensing a desolation so profound that it seeped into the grass, the earth, the very air.

I snatched my hand away. Lifting my face to the cold air and the moonlight, breathing deep to ease my shaking, I gave guilty thanks for life and light and the broad sky above me. What rite could create this dread that crushed the heart and devoured the soul, that stole the night's glory and blighted this sweet meadow? The thought that I had brought down this vileness on my old comrade appalled me, yet plain sense said I could not have imagined such an outcome. As I could not undo my careless babbling, I saw only one way to make it up to him. No one deserved to suffer so.

"I can't undo this, Boreas. I'm sorry. If I could—"

"Didn't think so." Pain snagged his rasping voice. His forehead felt hot beneath my hand. "Ye ought to leave. Don't let the orange-heads pray over ye. Their prayin' emptied me out, till I can't think of naught but the dark—" Despair edged his words with panic.

"Hush now. You'll not be alone. I swear it. Will you trust me?"

"Ye've never broke yer word."

"Listen . . . you'll not believe my plan for winter . . ."

I told him every detail of my rescue and the abbey. Of Jullian and Sebastian, of Brother Badger and Brother Gildas, of bells and books and prayers and mysteries. Of rich smells and jewel-colored windows and rippling barley. As I talked, I drew out the little green bag and used the mirror to crush the nivat on a rock. Trying not to inhale the scent, lest it trigger my own craving, I pricked my finger and worked my perverse magic.

"Here, now, I've something will ease you a bit. Give it a try." I scooped up the bubbling black paste and poked it in his mouth.

Pain devoured him. Scoured and shook him as would a dragon lion of Syanar. I waited. When, at last, his ravaged body convulsed in ecstasy, I stabbed the sharp little knife—sure and fast and deep—into the hollow at the back of his neck. *Forgive.*

PART TWO

A Gathering of Wolves

Chapter 11

The hierarch's flat feet measured almost the same in their length and width. They pained him when he had to stand on cold hard granite slabs for long periods of time. I knew this because he crunched up his toes and splayed them out again, rocked from toe to heel, and rolled them to the side. He did not wear sandals, for, of course, he was not a vowed brother of any monastic order, but the highest-ranking clergyman in Navronne, a common practor who had achieved a rank on par with a duc. His embroidered slippers were soft purple velvet held on by white silk ribbons that crossed over his thick, stockinged ankles. Every little while he set one foot upon the other to rest it, leaving dusty smudges on the top of his fine shoes.

Feet and their various coverings and the grimy hems of gowns, robes, and other vestments were all I could see of my investiture rites. As I had for the past three hours, I lay prostrate before the high altar of Gillarine Abbey church, the unending prayers and admonitions rolling over me like the billowing incense smokes. My shoulder ached, my leg had stiffened, and my long straight pureblood nose had been rubbed raw by the same cold hard granite slabs that so tormented the hierarch's feet.

Someone sprinkled water on my head and back. Drips rolled down the shaven patch at the crown of my head. *Tonsured . . . great Kemen, Lord of Sky and Storm, what woman will ever lie with me now?* Drips spattered on my black gown, absorbed by the layers of wool. Drips rolled down my bare feet, tickling. I tried not to twitch. My trembling was due more to the marrow-deep chill creeping through me from the floor than awe of my current intimacy with the divine.

I was not wholly irreverent. I honored all gods who professed an interest in human folk, and I respected custom and rituals that evoked the great mysteries of the world: death and birth, forests, ocean, and storms, music, copulation, and fermentation. But I saw no virtue in mere endurance and had never understood why a god would wish to be so long preoccupied with any one event.

Best keep my mind somewhere close to business. News brought by the hierarch's traveling party had only confirmed my decision to stay here—plague had broken out in the Moriangi port of Haverin.

Pestilence, famine, war . . . how many times in the past few days had I heard mention of the end times? *The long night,* Jullian had said, as if it were a lovers' assignation for which he had been awaiting only notice of the time. Before long these doomsayers were going to have me hanging bells on my ears and painting my forehead with dung.

I dared not close my eyes. Brother Sebastian had rousted me as the bells rang for Prime, scolding me roundly for sleeping, for sleeping in the bed, for sleeping too long, and for sleeping naked. *"A monk must always lie down girded in no less than trews, shirt, and hose so he will not be late to pray the night Hours,* so spake Saint Ophir in his Rule." While I reluctantly rolled into the frigid air and drew on the clean underthings he had brought me, my mentor had tightened his lips at some additional transgression. "Are you yet a sapling like these boys who cannot yet control their fleshly dreams? Surely you did not profane your vigil night apurpose!"

It was the bed linens bothering him. I had shaken my head vigorously and shifted the treacherous appendage inside my trews, attempting to look properly humiliated while trying to remember just what had happened on my return from Elanus. Numb, exhausted, I had hidden my green pouch and the packet of knife and medicines in the garden maze outside the church and prayed that the bells I'd heard as I slogged over the last slope and down the road to the gatehouse were Matins and not Lauds.

But "fleshly thoughts" *had* dogged me all the way back through the bogs and woodlands: the taste and feel of Adrianne on my tongue and fingertips and the memory of the dusky-smooth limbs and silken hair of the catamite. Strange and perverse that such images could arouse me after I had murdered a comrade I'd sworn to defend . . . after I'd spent half the night scraping a hole in the soft black dirt of Graver's Meadow and laying Boreas and his woman there, my last coppers on their eyes and some of Brother Badger's herbs in their hands and mouths to pay their tally to the Ferryman. Somehow the simple rites in the darkening meadow had left me at peace, and then the feel of the living earth under my hands as I sought the road back to Gillarine had sent unseemly desires coursing through my flesh. Truly I was a lunatic.

The brothers were singing now. Something different this morning. From each side of the choir, right and left behind me, came a different melody—two songs twined around each other, all the beauty and simplicity of plainsong, but counterposed to make something larger and more wonderful. I had heard them practicing this work, but I hadn't known it was for this occasion. For me. Well, for Iero, of course . . . everything they did, everything they said, was to honor Iero and his saints and prophets. Nonetheless, of all the good comrades I'd encountered through the years, none had ever made a song for me. I felt like an ass, grinning into the floor.

Music infused my bones and sinews, not only my ears and soul. As a child I'd been offered no training in any instrument beyond the minimum necessary for a "cultured man's education"—*that* aborted on the day I smashed my music master's three-hundred-year-old harp into a stone pillar. Alas, my voice *did* sound like a carpenter's rasp, elsewise a bard's life might have suited me most excellently. If only I'd been born to a family of pureblood musicians, perhaps I could have put up with all the rest.

Hands touched my shoulders. "Rise up now, son of Iero and Saint Ophir, and with thy solemn avowal will thy new life begin."

Blessed gods be thanked! I tried not to appear a lumbering ox as I got to my feet.

The hierarch occupied a purple-draped chair between me and the high altar, a regal figure, though his upper lip drew up in the middle like a church spire, and the lower one, full and fleshy, drooped below it like the seedsman's iron scoop, leaving two large yellow teeth on permanent display. In droning solemnity, he intoned, "Swear thou, chosen of the One God . . ."

I knelt before Eligius and a coolly serious Abbot Luviar and swore on my hope of grace and heaven to abide by the particulars of Saint Ophir's Rule. I meant what I said, though, if anyone had listened very closely through the fits of coughing that overtook me at certain crucial moments, he might have noted that I altered a few important words, such as "for the duration of my novice vows" rather than "for the duration of my novice year."

Graver's Meadow had reminded me why I was careful about oath swearing. As the condition of the brothers' hospitality, I would do my best to obey their Rule, but I would not bind myself beyond reason. So as I knelt before the hierarch, I ensured my vows were entirely accurate. They would last only as long as they lasted.

When the swearing was done, Sebastian and Gildas dropped a voluminous garment over my head, shifting it around so that the shortest sewn seam reached halfway down my breast, leaving the black wool cape open the rest of the way down. They adjusted the cowl's soft folds about my neck and shoulders and then lifted its hood over my newly trimmed hair. The abbot himself knelt before me to slip my sandals onto my feet. And then it was done.

From the outside I must appear like these other monks, who rose from the choir stalls and followed the hierarch, abbot, and prior in orderly procession through the nave. But, as far as I could tell, my every failing and regret remained hidden under my cowl, alongside unseemly hatreds, new and old. Too bad. The morning's prayers had promised that I might leave all such burdens behind.

After we washed in the lavatorium—a capacious room in the understory of the monks' dorter where water channeled from the river ran perpetually through a waist-high stone trough—Brother Sebastian led me up the south stair to the monks' refectory for the first time. Most of the monks were already seated at the two long tables along the side walls. Facing the center of the room, backs to the walls, they arranged themselves in order of age, as it appeared, or length of time in the order, which was much the same. At the small head table the abbot and the prior sat on either side of the hierarch. Reminding me with a gesture to keep silent, Brother Sebastian hurried me past the great gap of empty places and delivered me to the table at the lower end of the rectangle. To my surprise Jullian and Gerard squeezed along the wall behind one row of monks and past the long gap of empty seats and took stools on either side of me.

The large room was spare of decoration: no paintings, statues, or carvings, no color but the burnished walnut of the floor and the palest yellow on the walls and between the stone ribs of the high, barreled ceiling. Its truer grandeur was its extravagance of windows on all four walls. Though the chilly room had no hearth, its tall windows, composed of astonishingly clear glass panes, bathed every place, even mine, with light.

Once all were seated, lay brothers carried in bowls of soup and baskets of bread. My stomach was near devouring itself after a long morning's fast on top of my night's adventure. The moment the steaming bowl was set in front of me, I snatched up my spoon and dipped, reaching for the bread basket with the alter hand. The knock of my spoon on the bowl resounded through the cavernous room like a tabor's whack. I looked up. No one else had moved.

I stuffed my hands in my lap and recalled other houses where the protocols were even less comprehensible than these. As a child, I had made an art of hiding under noblemen's tables, tormenting the dogs, tugging on the hanging edges of the table coverings, tweaking startled ladies' toes and wiping my greasy hands on their skirts, and drinking far too much wine from ewers I'd dragged along with me. I smothered a laugh, imagining the poor amusement I'd find under *these* tables.

It was a prayer we awaited, of course, intoned at length by Prior Nemesio. Once the *perficiimus* ended it, the abbot rang a small bell, and Brother Cadeus, the porter, began to read from a book sitting on the lectern. As the monks picked up their spoons and reached for bread, he announced the day's text as the writing of Juridius the Elder, a practor of Agrimo.

Gerard stuffed his mouth and frankly examined my new cowl. Then he stretched his neck and peered around behind me. As I bent over my bowl for my next bite, I tilted my head his way, exposing the bare patch Brother Sebastian's shaving knife had left, which felt roughly the size of a knight's shield. The boy's ready grin appeared around his mouthful of bread. I grinned back at him around my spoon and glanced at Jullian. The Ardran boy's attention held firmly to his bowl, his face pale and solemn. I didn't understand. He had no reason to be angry with me. Had Brother Gildas "reprimanded" him again?

I was no more than halfway through my soup when the hierarch replaced Brother Cadeus at the lectern. "Dearest Brothers, it is our delight to join you for this great occasion," said Hierarch Eligius, spreading his arms so that his wide sleeves and mantle swept in great curved folds like angels' wings. "A soul claimed for Iero's service. A voice added to the chorus that carries our petitions night and day to the halls of heaven. But as your shepherd, I must use this example for instruction as well as celebration, to chastise as well as to commend . . ."

The hierarch preached of the *ordo mundi*—clearly installing himself at the top of the fixed order of the earthly plane and relegating heathenish Harrowers to the bottom. The monks sat motionless, attentive. Gerard's mouth hung open slightly as if poised on the verge of speech. Jullian, though . . . Jullian's eyes remained fixed on his bowl.

"Rather than pronouncing faith in Iero and his anointed clergy,

and fighting to enthrone our rightful king from a proven son of Eodward's body, some servants of despair preach another kind of chaos—
that villeins and practors, scholars and servants must join in some
whimsical preparation for an age of doom and darkness. They pro-
pound a sovereign of rumor, as if Iero might sanction a righteous
claimant to Eodward's crown conjured from peasants' dreams and
tavern gossip. Such deviance invites Iero's wrath and must be purged
from our midst!"

Blessed saints and angels . . . *deviance!* A word to make a man
look to his purse and his neck. So hopes of a Pretender and this talk
of end times were named anathema . . . and poor pale Jullian looked
guilty as a married man caught with his hand under a harlot's skirt.
What had the boy got himself into? No more dangerous enemy exists than a holy man, especially when his writs and precepts get
tangled with royal politics.

The abbot rang his bell. After more prayers, Prior Nemesio led us
from the refectory. My soup remained unfinished, a casualty in a holy
war.

Once down the stair, our orderly processional dissolved into quiet
chaos. Many of the monks squeezed my arm or pressed my hand in
companionable congratulations; others laid one open palm in the
other and gestured as in offering—the monks' signing speech for a
gift of Iero's blessing. As I accepted their good wishes, Brother Sebastian stood at my shoulder as proudly as if I were his own creation.
For certain, the brothers were a friendly lot.

Once most of the brothers had dispersed to their afternoon's activities, a hooded monk tugged at my arm and drew me around and
behind an unlit hearth. "The hierarch will ask you about the book,"
he said, his words penetrating my skull as much by virtue of their ferocity as by my hearing them. "You *will* not reveal its exact title or its
history. You *will* not offer it to him. If you value the boy's safety, see
that it remains here." Before I could respond, he hurried away.

I knew it was Gildas. I recognized the thatch of brown hair on the
back of his hand. And who but Gildas would encourage me to lie to
the authority I had just vowed to obey? He had recognized my lack
of finer scruples early on. Yet it wasn't so much his particular demand
that left me bristling—I'd no wish for Hierarch Eligius to get his
hands on my book. But his reference to Jullian sounded very like a
threat.

People had to get along as they could in this world. Gods knew I'd
done my share of wickedness along the way. But when the account
for a man's deeds fell due, the one to pay should be the man who

made the choice to do them. Never friends . . . and never, ever, children.

"His Excellency wishes to congratulate you," Brother Sebastian said, as he bustled me down the cloister walk toward the scriptorium, where the hierarch was inspecting the monks' work. I was yet grumbling under my breath at Gildas's high-handed manner when we stepped into the cavernous, many-windowed room tucked into the understory of the library.

The place was deliciously warm, though it reeked of sour vitriol and acrid tannin—ink. Amid orderly rows of thick, unadorned columns that sprouted at their crowns into great sprays of vaulting ribs, orderly rows of copyists hunched over sloping desks, writing or painting their pages. A severely stooped monk, wisps of white hair feathering his tonsure, moved from desk to desk with a basket of small flasks, replenishing the ink horns fixed to each desk by metal hoops. Other monks sat at long tables shaving quills or stitching folded pages together. Save for the soft scratch of pens, the whisk of knives, and the rustle of pages, the place was very quiet. Holy silence was kept here as in the cloisters.

"Ah, our new novice." Hierarch Eligius's unmuffled voice resonated like a barrage of stone against a siege wall, causing heads to pop up all over. He closed the small fat book that lay on a copyist's desk, picked it up, and peered at the title. "*A Treatise on the Nature of Evil* written by Jonne of Lidowe. A truly noble work. Have you read it?" He wagged it in the air.

Uncertain whether I was expected to voice my answers or not, I shook my head.

"Do so when this copy is complete." He dropped the little volume on the desk. "Brother Fidelio, you'll see to it?"

The copyist nodded and dipped his pen again.

Brother Sebastian gave me a gentle shove, and I joined the hierarch just as he moved on to the next desk, his elaborate cloak jarring Brother Fidelio's elbow. The monk sighed silently, set down his pen, and scraped at his work with a pumice stone.

Eligius squinted at the second copyist's work. "You've a beautiful hand, Brother. Every character well formed and clear. The history of the Karish in Navronne is an inspiring text. But I would like to see more color and variety in the capitals. You must not starve the glory of presentation in some rush to completion."

The chinless Brother Victor, my diminutive companion of Black Night, seemed to be in charge of the scriptorium activities. He flitted from one desk to another, answering unspoken questions from the copyists, fetching books from the shelves on the end wall, or using naught but his deft fingers to describe corrections to a binder's stitching.

At the next desk, a scrawny, sandy-haired younger monk held his tongue between his lips as his blackened fingers drew tiny characters in long straight lists. The blank parts of the page were marked into columns with lines of light gray.

"A fine presentation, Brother, but this—" The frowning hierarch tapped a white-gloved finger on a tattered scroll held open by lead weights. "*The Tally of Grape Harvests in Central Ardra in the Years of Aurellian Rule*? Surely more uplifting pages wait to be copied—sacred texts, sermons, or noble histories that will turn men's thoughts to Iero or his saints. Who chose this as an exemplar? Come, come, speak up."

"Brother Chancellor gives out the work, Excellency," whispered the sandy-haired monk, "and tasks us with the pages most suited to our skills. Not to set myself high, but both he and Father Abbot say I've a special touch for numbers, so perhaps—"

"I must have a word with the chancellor then, as well as with Abbot Luviar." The hierarch glared across the room at Brother Victor, who leaned over a desk, heads together with a copyist.

The hierarch spoke to each of the copyists, his steepled upper lip rising high and stiff as he named more works frivolous or inappropriate. He condemned anything of mundane use: a scroll on glassmaking, a book on the building of Aurellian roads, an almanac that traced weather patterns in Morian over three centuries.

I was no judge of books and their uses. That a man could learn to make glass from another glassmaker, as I had learned to tan hides, brew ale, and cut stone from those who knew the work, made more sense to me than learning such things from blots on parchment. But then again, I could not see how a book reader would come nearer heaven by reading someone's speculations on Iero's parentage than by reading of the might of storms and sunlight over the river country.

The hierarch moved to a table where a grizzled monk traced his finger over a page in an open book while reading a set of unbound pages. The monk's glance moved from one to the other and back again.

"So, Brother Novice," said the hierarch as he peered over the shoulder of the monk and browsed through stacks that seemed to be awaiting similar examination. "Abbot Luviar has recounted how a journey of penitence brought you to this great conversion. A remarkable story."

I cleared my throat. "A wonder, truly, Excellency. I feel uplifted. Reborn, as to say."

He turned the pages of a small book, the colors of the inked patterns brighter than his ruby ring. "And you truly came upon Gillarine by chance?"

"Indeed, I wandered for days, bleeding and wounded, entirely confused as to my course. Having lived so short a time in the little village of"—I twisted my brain to come up with a name—"Thorn, and diseased with sin and violent behavior as I was, I was unfamiliar with any holy places in the countryside around. Even now, I could not tell you the location of that village or the true course of my wanderings, Excellen—"

Saints and angels! I almost swallowed my tongue. I had not noticed the man who stood stiffly in the shadow of a pillar, his hands clasped behind his back, his eyes dead with boredom. The scarlet surcoat he wore over his gray gown bore the hierarch's gold-broidered blazon of mitral hat and solicale. Of modest stature, with close-trimmed black hair, long nose, and an air of unremitting superiority, he scarcely needed the violet mask that covered half his face to proclaim him pureblood. Protocol forbade an ordinary to so much as notice him without his master's leave.

I dropped my gaze and attempted to shrink inside my cowl. "Truly, Saint . . . uh"—the name escaped me—"that is, the guardian of wanderers must have examined . . . watched . . . over me every moment of that . . . of that—"

"Yes, yes." Eligius's frizzled brown hair bobbed alongside the red cap that had replaced his mitral hat. "You carried a book of maps, did you not? Even that could not aid you?"

I dared not let the name Cartamandua arise in association with me in front of the pureblood. Why had I not thought to take a false name as long as I carried the book? It was not so long a stretch from *Valen* to *Magnus Valentia de Cartamandua-Celestine* to exposure.

"Alas, no, Excellency." *Think, fool.* I spoke slowly, so as not to stammer as I crafted my tale. "Though I valued the book because of its connection to my lord Mardane Lavorile who gave it me, I read no holy places in its maps, which were mostly common drawings of rivercourses and the old Aurellian roads that interlace Morian. Little of Ardra. Little of practical use even when I was scouting for the mardane."

"A frivolous work, then. And what has become of the book? Perhaps it is here being copied?"

"Why, I never thought of it as worthy of copying." I scratched my head, turned about, and gawked as if to review the contents of all the copyist desks. "And none of the brothers took great note of it, save that a poor wanderer had a book at all. It's certainly not one of these. I gave it up, Excellency, along with my secular garb and sinful ways. I've not even seen the thing since I determined to answer Iero's call by taking vows. I can't see how a map would guide a man's soul to heaven."

I dared not glance at the pureblood. Was he listening? Did his bent enable him to detect lies?

The hierarch pursed his odd lips for a moment and then relaxed them into a smile. "Very true. Stay faithful to true teaching, Brother Novice, and your course will be straight."

Sensing dismissal, I bowed, as I had seen the others do, and backed away carefully until my back touched the wall between two stacks of shelves. The pillar blocked my view of the pureblood and his of me. I heaved a sigh, allowing the storm of anxiety to ease.

A lay brother poked the fire and carried a lit taper to the lamps that hung from iron brackets fixed to the pillars. Outside the windows, the haze had thickened into bulging clouds, dimming the sunlight and sapping the room's warmth.

The hierarch summoned Brother Victor with a wave of his jeweled finger. "Chancellor, a word with you before I take leave."

The little monk hurried to the hierarch, his hands tucked under his black scapular, his oddly skewed features sober and attentive.

"All of you, pay heed and bear witness to my judgment of this abbey's great work of writing!" said Eligius. "A member of your fraternity has fallen into grave error . . ." He rebuked Brother Victor at great length, accusing him of supporting the deviant philosophy of those who preached coming doom by his choices of materials to copy. ". . . and so you are to immediately remove all frivolous and mundane materials from this room. Your abbot may keep or dispose of the exemplars as he sees fit. But this—"

He whipped the page of numbers right out from under the young monk's pen and threw it on the floor. A long smear of ink marred the meticulously written page.

"—and this—"

The pages on glassmaking, the Moriangi almanac, meticulous colored drawings of a millworks, and several other part-written pages joined the first one on the floor.

"—and every page copied from a profane work is to be burned in view of all residents of Gillarine as a sign of error and rededication."

Brother Victor's horror-stricken gaze leaped from the crumpled pages to the red-faced hierarch and back again. The other monks looked stunned.

Parchment to be burned? Even *I* knew how appallingly wasteful that was. Though my family's house was a wealthy one, my tutors had scraped and overwritten precious vellum time and time again. And who could measure the time and care these monks had spent on these pages?

"You, Chancellor, are to receive twenty lashes before sunset today and be confined for five days with water as your only sustenance. Set this room in order and your copyists to their tasks, and then accompany *Eqastré* Scrutari-Consil, who will carry out my judgment. He will also question each of you"—his jeweled finger denoted every one of the shocked brothers—"to ensure that you understand your duties to Iero and the *ordo mundi*."

Scrutari-Consil stepped away from the wall and bowed to Eligius, touching his fingers to his forehead. With a limp gesture of blessing, the hierarch swept out of the briskly opened door and into the rainy afternoon.

Chapter 12

"This is outrageous, Broth—"

Brother Victor silenced the sandy-haired monk with a gesture. Other monks left their desks to lay hands on his sleeves or his back, to shake their heads in silent denial, or to offer, with eloquent gestures, comfort or anger or comradeship. The chancellor briskly sent them back to work.

Hands clasped at his back, the pureblood watched impassively as Brother Victor darted about his duties. The man in red and gray needed no word or additional gesture to assert his authority over the room.

Having naught to do, I pressed my back to the wall, attempting to shrivel out of sight. I would have slipped out of the door, but Scrutari-Consil had positioned himself within view of it.

Scrutari-Consil—not a family related to mine, thanks be to all gods. The Scrutaris were known as perceptives. They were often contracted as investigators and inspectors, expected to root out lies and deceptions or to oversee town administrators. His colineal name *Consil* was unfamiliar; I could not recall the lineal bent of every pureblood family. The name's Aurellian root suggested *adjudication*, thus a bent that might lend itself to mediation, untangling puzzles, or rendering judgments. Better for my lies and deceptions if he favored the *Consil* line, though I truly would prefer the man burst into spontaneous flames like a phoenix and not regenerate until I was fifty quellae from Gillarine.

Eligius had addressed Scrutari with the pureblood honorific *eqastré*, an affectation that signified nothing. As a form of address between purebloods, *eqastré* indicated parity in rank. Between pureblood and anyone else in the world, such address had no meaning, for protocol dictated that purebloods were so far exalted by the gods that ordinaries could in no wise be compared with them. The only relationship permitted between an ordinary and a pureblood was that spelled out in a Registry contract. Sweat dribbled past my ears.

Brother Victor's silent hands were busily directing his copyists. Though I had little experience with the monks' signing speech, his instructions were easy to interpret. Those whose work had been halted were to gather their completed pages from the neat stacks on the holding tables and pile them on a long table littered with broken pens, empty ink horns, and less orderly piles of written sheets. They were to collect their exemplars, the original documents being copied, in different piles on the same table.

As each monk turned in his pages, the chancellor passed him a new book or scroll he drew from the cluttered bookshelves. Before the last had been distributed, monks had already spread new vellum on their desks and begun to measure and rule their pages with thin sticks of the same plummet stonemasons used to mark their plans. The pureblood strolled down the rows, examining the titles of the new works.

At first Brother Victor seemed inordinately calm. But as he began sorting the damaged pages and proscribed books, his hands began to shake, knocking over the heaps of pages, books, and scrolls more than once, leaving the table a heaped confusion. When he noticed me watching, a tinge of scarlet touched his pale cheeks. Abruptly, he summoned me to join him. He scooped up the piles of discard pages and dumped them into a large basket underneath the table.

When I reached the chancellor's side, his small, neat hand—steady now—pointed first to the remaining heap of books and papers and then upward. For a moment I had the notion that he was saying something about heaven. But then I realized he merely wanted me to carry the things upstairs to the library. Grateful for the excuse to leave and for the rule of silence that prevented his use of my name, I pressed my palms together in acquiescence.

The rain, now a downpour, had the gutterspouts flowing. Water had pooled in the alley and at the base of the ascending stair outside the door. Moisture spattered across the threshold as I awkwardly tried to draw my cowl over my ungainly armload of books, scrolls, and loose pages. Feeling the pureblood's eyes on my back did not steady my hands. Crinkling his red-rimmed eyes in disapproval, the stoop-shouldered monk set down his ink basket, yanked the heavy wool across the jumble, and stuffed a wad of the cloth into my already over-occupied hand to hold it there.

The open air cooled my incipient fever. The pureblood could not possibly have recognized me.

The stair was not half wide enough to carry such a load. I must either risk tumbling over the open side of the steps or scrape arms and elbows on the wall, thus smearing moss onto my new cowl. At the top of the stair I pawed at the brass latch of the library door, at the same time drawing up my knee to catch some book that was sliding out of my arms. If I took another step, some precious writing was going to drop into the chilly puddle that was seeping into my new sandals around my bare toes. By the time Jullian pulled open the library door, I was crouched in an immovable knot.

The boy gaped as if I were a lunatic. I waggled my brows and my chin toward my laden arms, hoping he or one of the monks in the room would catch my meaning before the growing heat in my thigh burst into flame.

At last understanding dawned. Jullian reached under my dripping cowl and supported the collapsing bundle as I waddled through the doorway. As the monks resumed their studies, the boy rescued the most precariously poised texts. I dumped the rest of the stack on the table beside them.

The boy and I blotted stray droplets from sheets and folios with a kerchief, stacked the books, set aside the scrolls in their cloth or leather cases, and straightened the loose pages. We had reduced the clutter by half, when one brightly colored page caught my notice. As Jullian laid another page on the pile of loose sheets, I gripped his slender wrist and pulled it away, staring at the one atop the stack. The crisply white vellum depicted a detailed diagram of mill cogs, inked in bright red and blue. A square outlined in the text gaped empty, awaiting a second drawing. I shifted several more of the loose pages and found the half-completed list of carefully drawn numbers, a streak of black ink left where the page had been whipped out from under the hand of the copyist.

What had Brother Victor sent out to be burned? Certainly *not* the pages the hierarch had selected. With so many sheets piled on the table, perhaps the chancellor had picked up the wrong ones . . . or perhaps he had assumed that I, a befuddled novice of less than a day who had never worked in his scriptorium—and thus was not subject to questioning at the hierarch's order—wouldn't notice he had switched them.

My suspicions were quickly confirmed. We had just spread out the last few pages, careful of the still damp ink, when Brother Gildas hurried through the library door. He shooed a puzzled Jullian back to his books, wax tablet, and stylus—implements of torture familiar from my own boyhood—then gestured for me to bring the stacked pages. Producing a key from under his scapular, Gildas unlocked the inner grillwork door of the last book press on the south wall and stowed the suspect pages, slipping them between the books along with scraps of vellum he took from a basket to protect the drying ink. One would have to rifle the entire collection to discover the forbidden copies.

As Gildas locked the grate, shut the cupboard's outer door, and shot its bronze bolt back into its catch, I noted the brass solicale affixed on the door—the abbot's sign. So the contraband now lay hidden in the abbot's own book press. Astonishing.

His back to the other three monks, Gildas held a finger to his mouth, laid his clenched fist on his breast, and flicked his eyes toward Jullian. His message was quite clear: *silence, obedience, the boy's safety.* He waited, his dark brow raised in query.

I pressed my palms together and inclined my head. As in the matter of my book, my interests coincided with his demands. I was the least likely man in the abbey to carry tales to the hierarch or his lapdog. Yet only the time and company restrained my anger and resentment.

Vowing to lie in wait for the damnable monk after supper and force an explanation from him, I started out the door to find Brother Sebastian, while Gildas smiled cheerfully, drew up a stool next to Jullian, and began to inspect the boy's work. And then the bells took up clanging. Not a call to the Hours—Nones had rung while I was with the hierarch in the scriptorium, and Vespers would not ring for at least an hour more. These bells stuttered in an unbalanced cadence that summoned the community to lay down whatever duties occupied the moment and gather at the refectory stair.

Everyone rose quickly, gathering their books and tablets and locking them away. But as Gildas and the other monks hurried out the door, I hung back. The bells would ring twice more, allowing time for scattered brethren to stopper their ink, damp cook fires, or round up sheep and goats, and I determined to take advantage of the opportunity. A matter more worrisome than frivolous copying or hidden pages preyed on my mind.

Jullian, scratching one bare, mud-spattered leg with his sandal, held the heavy door open, waiting for me. He blinked in surprise when I dragged him back into the room and pushed the door shut.

"A moment, if you would," I whispered. No finger twiddling would suffice for this. "I need to speak with you, and as you've been avoiding me so purposefully, and my life seems like to get more complicated now I'm vowed, I think this will have to do."

Pressing his back to the doorpost, the boy glanced up at me with the sidewise aspect of a thief caught. This would take some care.

I perched my backside on one of the library tables. "Tell me how you came to live in an abbey so young. Your family, I suppose. Dead, are they?" I'd wager my life on the answer to that one.

It certainly was not the question he expected. He stared for a moment, as if to read my intent. Then he shrugged. "Aye. Mam died birthing when I was six. My da was clerk to a wool factor in Pontia, or, well, he wasn't actually my da, as mine was dead. He said he'd no will left to raise a boy that wasn't his. So he gave me the choice to go on to Cradens Abbey school that's in Pontia or to apprentice to a dyer, as that fee was the best he could afford to pay. I liked schooling, so it was no hard choice. I heard he left the factor not long after that and went off to the fighting. He's likely dead now, too."

He spoke with assurance, not loud, but not whispering either, bold in his secrets and brave in his lonely confession. I knew that not every family was as easy to leave behind as mine. And the story was plausible enough.

"And does Brother Gildas always supervise your schooling?"

"For the most. Brother Fidelio used to tutor me with Gerard, who is great of heart and beloved of Iero as he saw an angel once, but who is slow of eye and head when it comes to reading. We'd work here, and Brother Fidelio would allow me to read whatever I would from the shelves while he taught Gerard. But when Father Abbot found me reading Aurellian plays by Vocaachus and Aerno . . ." His face brightened. "Do you know them?"

I shook my head.

"Well, they are very . . . worldly. Frivolous, the hierarch would call them." A trace of indignation in his posture. "But their words make music in your head and lead you to consider all manner of things. Father Abbot says they are worthy of study, but perhaps not for boys, even ones who read Aurellian fluently." His enthusiasm quickly overruled his resentments. Neither secrecy nor resentment were at all his nature.

"Ah, so you were given a new tutor to oversee your reading."

"Father Abbot said that Brother Gildas could assign my books and lessons as he did for Horach, and I am not complaining, for I am allowed to read and learn all manner of things that—" He glanced up and bit his lip. "We should go down. The bell."

The damnable bell was ringing its second course, but I could not let the moment pass. I bent over and planted my hands on my knees, which put my face something on a level with his. I hated what I would ask him. "Jullian, certain of these monks . . . Brother Gildas, say . . . they don't . . . hurt . . . you, do they? Beat you, or threaten you, or . . . press . . . you in ways you would rather they not?"

"No! Never!" His pale cheeks took on the blush of an Erdru's-month apple. "I am sent to pray without supper or to work extra hours in the pigsties or the stable when I err. No more than that."

"But you've secrets with them . . ."

He stiffened, clamping his mouth shut with the pious stubbornness I had come to recognize.

"I ask because on Black Night you said Brother Gildas had reprimanded you, and you've seemed different these days since. And because when I was not much older than you, I lived rough, and sometimes, so as to eat and stay warm, I would allow men to do things I didn't like. Some in this world, even persons who are greatly respected, will take advantage of a boy, and I would not have such things happen to one so clever as to read Voc . . . cernus and Ern—whoever they are. You are my brave rescuer, and I mislike secrets that damp your spirit."

"But those have naught to do with—" He snapped his mouth shut again and examined my face as if to judge the story of my rough living for himself. After a moment, he blew out a great puff of air and lowered his voice until I had to crane forward to hear him. "The secrets are not of beatings or unwholesome things. Brother Gildas would never! He exhorts Gerard and me to guard our virtue and says everyone should be as pure as we are."

He leaned forward, his forehead almost touching mine. For a moment a fire of excitement and conspiracy pierced his veil of caution. The child was near bursting. "The secrets are of Iero's work, most excellent and righteous that I would tell even my mother did she live and were I given leave to. But you must not *ask* me. I was rightly reprimanded for my loose tongue, and again after Black Night when I took your warning to mean you knew things . . . things you didn't know. Now I've sworn upon my mother's grave that I will *not* speak to you of these matters until Lord Stearc—" He closed his eyes and thumped his head backward against the doorpost.

I was not yet ready to exonerate Gildas. Blackguards could misuse a child's trust in many ways. If Gildas had not posed a personal threat to the boy to compel my obedience, then the danger must lie in these secret matters that linked the boy to my book and the contraband pages. So I caught the strand of Jullian's guileless exuberance and tugged on it again.

"Until Stearc . . . the Thane of Erasku . . . until he does what? Come on, lad. The One God himself arranged our meeting. He likely gave me the book of maps as well and instructed his saints to guide my feet to your abbey gates. Why else would your tongue be so eager to tell me these mysteries? I've seen Prince Osriel's vassal in your guesthouse. I've seen your abbot rally dead men to protect a prince even the sainted Gillare would abhor, and I've seen Brother Gildas cause that prince to vanish so a pureblood could not trace him. I've seen the Hierarch of Ardra nosing around your scriptorium finding *deviance* in almanacs and drawings of mill cogs, and meek brothers subject themselves to water drinking and lashes to hide those same works. And these only begin to touch the mysteries in this place. Truly, I think Iero *intends* you share the burden of your secrets with me." The god had certainly piqued my curiosity beyond common bounds.

The cursed bell ceased its clamor for the moment. Its third summoning would signal punishments for latecomers.

Inside the Ardran boy's soul there ensued such a struggle as to make the mud-soaked wrestling boys in Elanus look like pecking chickens. I thought I'd lost when he stood up straight and said, "Come on."

But he didn't set out for the cloisters. Rather, he led me through the inner doorway and down the passage toward the dorter. Only our footfalls and the spatter of rain sounded in the deserted corridor. Between the library and the monks' dorter, a daystair descended to the cloister garth. Opposite the head of the stair, the passage wall bulged outward in a bay. Each of the five window niches of the bay had its own stone seat, damp from the drizzle that blew through the window port. Jullian stepped up on the seat of the centermost niche, motioned me to crowd in behind him, and pointed a finger out the port.

Most of the world had vanished into the mist. Off to our right lay the river and the low, ghostly structures of the infirmary garth. Directly below us several steep-roofed buildings crowded together, the most prominent of them very like the guesthouse in size and grandeur—the abbot's house, I guessed. At least twenty mounted knights had mustered outside it, along with several pack animals. A liveried servant bore the red, white, and gold banner of the Hierarch of Ardra. I was amazed that no hint of such a large and well-armed escort had penetrated the cloisters when I'd climbed the stair not an hour since.

"Watch," said Jullian quietly. "I cannot tell you secrets I'm sworn to keep. But there's good reason the hierarch departs while everyone is summoned to the cloister."

Riders and servants milled about for a tedious time. The bells rang their third summons.

"His Excellency must be napping," I said. "We'd best go. You'll just have to *tell* me."

But Jullian caught my sleeve and pointed again. I leaned farther forward, allowing the damp stone seat and his muddy sandals to soak my knees so I could peer closer into the gloom.

Two men stepped from the door of the house. The one fellow was thickly draped in red, a broad-brimmed hat shielding hair and face from the rain. As he was handed up to a white palfrey from a carpet quickly spread across the mud, his sartorial splendor denoted him the Hierarch Eligius. The second man, slender and pale-haired, swung himself up with practiced ease to the back of a dappled destrier. His short cape revealed a jeweled sword hilt at his waist, fine tight-fitting boots snugged to his knees, and the purple and gold trilliot of Ardra on his surcoat.

"The hierarch came to fetch him!" I said, wishing I could disbelieve my eyes. I needed no device to identify Perryn, Duc of Ardra. "Your treacherous abbot hid the coward, and the damnable hierarch escorts him back to Palinur. Men of god! Holy men!"

"Shhh!" said Jullian.

But I was unable to keep silent. "This despicable villain dragged good men from their homes, starved them and bled them for months, promising help that never came, and then abandoned them to die. Now he sneaks away under the cloak of a traveling clergyman."

"The abbot would not have him dead," said Jullian. "Gillarine is neutral ground, holy ground. Sometimes duty and faithfulness demand unpleasant things."

The riders, scarcely visible in the rain, wound slowly out of sight behind the ramparts of the church.

"What of the men the abbot kept from sanctuary to save him? What of the men this prince will lead into another slaughter? What have your tutors said of them? Is faithfulness only for the benefit of princes?" It wasn't fair to chastise the boy, who only repeated what he'd been taught. He could not understand the world. "I suppose you pray for them, eh?"

The bells fell silent. "We've got to go now," said the boy, his thin face knotted in concern.

"We'll talk again, Archangel," I said. I yet saw no pattern that linked Jullian's safety, Cartamandua maps, and conspiracies involving abbots and hierarchs and royal dunces.

We raced down the daystair into the east cloister walk. The crack of a whip echoed from the alley between the chapter house and the library. The accompanying groan was muffled as if they'd given the little monk something to bite on. I clenched my fists and wished the man strength for this and the rest of his trial.

Prison cells were not as familiar to me as alleys and bawdy houses, but I'd experienced enough of them. Never for long, thank all gods. So close . . . unable to get out . . . no air to breathe. I'd felt lashes as well, many at the hand of purebloods who could amplify the sting with magic. But in any hour, I'd choose lashes over confinement.

Brother Sebastian glared as Jullian and I slipped into the back row of the monks gathered in the lay brother's workyard. The entire population of Gillarine encircled a bonfire blazing brightly in the afternoon's sodden gloom.

The abbot's voice, calm and precise, pierced the smoke and mist. "The Hierarch of Ardra has chastised us for failure and distraction in our work to preserve humankind's knowledge—the holy charter assigned us by King Eodward and ratified by the hierarch and his predecessors. These pages are the hierarch's evidence of our ill choices. His Excellency has left us much to consider as to the divine ordering of this world, our place in it, and our duties to our god and king. Let us pray to the One God, Creator and Preserver, to guide us onward in the path of His choosing."

A brother emptied the basket of crumpled vellum into the pit. After an initial smoky darkening, the sheets took fire with a thunderous rush, green and blue flames dancing amid the gold, illuminating the faces in the circle as the pages curled and withered. Tears dribbled down the withered cheeks of the stoop-shouldered monk from the scriptorium. No tears scored Brother Gildas's face, though. Only resolve. Jullian stood beside me looking as if he might reach into the flames and drag out the blackened pages with his teeth.

"And now, my brothers," said Luviar, "let a holy fire ignite our souls as we redouble our commitment to the work we have been given. Iero grant us wisdom and give his eternal protection to Navronne's righteous king."

Left unspoken was his opinion of the hierarch's judgment, though I'd come to think the two had concocted this event as a shield for their political chicanery. Then again, perhaps I'd best give the rumor of a Pretender more credence than I'd done before. Nothing gives a rumor foundation so much as a clergyman naming it *deviance*.

The faint honks of geese drew my eyes upward. Long, wavering black wedges arrowed southward, far too early. *Eqastré* Scrutari-Consil stood out of the rain, just inside the shadowed undercroft. He leaned his back against one of the columns, his arms folded across his chest, watching and listening.

Sleep eluded me. Despite my near sleepless vigil night, despite the exhaustion of high emotions and taut nerves—or perhaps because of them—my eyes refused to close in the quiet intervals between the night Hours. An oppressive hostility permeated the deepening night, as if the eyeless shades of Black Night's victims had gathered at my bedside. I could not silence the memory of Boreas's wails, nor of his choked ecstasy as I wrought his murder. Danger. Villainy. By Lauds, I was near sick with it. When I glimpsed Scrutari-Consil observing our procession down the nightstair into the choir, my overstrung nerves snapped.

I could not stay here. Not with a hunting pureblood in residence. No matter my missing book; no matter coming famine. Twelve years I had remained free by moving on when I needed, forgoing attachments that might tempt me to linger past safety. With silent apologies to the monks who had welcomed me so kindly, and to the god Iero who had received so little service from my vows, I slipped out of the dorter into the cold mist and drizzle in the dead hours between Lauds and Prime. By the time I reached Elanus, I'd have daylight.

Life was never so simple, of course. I retrieved my nivat bag and other contraband from the hedge garden and tucked them securely in my rucksack along with my secular clothes and the blanket from my bed. But when I emerged from the abbey gate tunnel, a near impenetrable fog had blanketed the fields. The route through the bogs remained clearly mapped in my head, but just traveling the half quellé from the abbey to the road without getting turned around would be no easy matter. I had no time to waste. Two hours more and I would be missed. And the pureblood would surely hear of it.

Damn all! I ground my walking stick into the mud. Foolish to travel in such conditions. And even the ascetic accommodation of the abbey was a prince's comfort beside what awaited me on the road. But neither argument could persuade me to risk one more day at Gillarine.

I glanced upward to the windows above the gatehouse. I would chance the main track from the gates to the road, rather than going cross-country as I had the previous night. If I was quiet, there'd be no danger of being spotted by the sanctuary watch. I poured the last dram of ale from my vigil night flask onto the path, praying holy Deunor and Saint Gillare to bless this fool's journey. Then I gripped my stick, shouldered my pack, and set out. Fifty paces and I was lost.

The short-lived battle of Black Night had churned the field that fronted the abbey into muck. Without vision beyond my outstretched fingertips, I could not distinguish the well-defined track that had once crossed it. Mumbling curses at the need to spend magic—and on this field of all places in the blasted world—I knelt, marshaled what strength might shield me from the horrors wrought here, and touched the earth.

Spirits of night! how far had I wandered? I lifted my hand, shook my head to clear it, and then touched the cold mud again. The impression was the same. Bloodshed . . . yes. Seething anger . . . grief . . . the death terrors of men and beasts. A hundred quercae to my left, men had screamed out their last moments in focused torment of fire and blade. But as runners of nandia vines and sprouts of fireweed and hearts' ease recapture a blighted field in one season's turn, so had a certain sweetness veined this ground. Not a mask to hide the taint of war, but a balm to soothe its raw wounding, to quiet the din of sobs and screams, to blunt the lingering pain enough to counteract its ruinous poison. No music played here as yet. What heart that perceived such sorrow could sing? But someday . . . perhaps . . . the tread of happier lives could overlay the lingering horror. Seeds slept beneath the cold mud. Living.

Wondering, I turned my mind to business. Year upon year of crossing had created a solid track across the wounded field, easily visible to my talent. Only half a day since the hierarch's party had slunk out of here, and some monk had left traces of his sandals since then. Still wary of Moriangi watchers, I stretched my awareness all the way to the road and swept it across the foggy landscape.

Deunor's fire! Riders lurked in the wooded hollow at the joining of track and road—five . . . ten . . . I could not tell how many. I sat back on my heels and listened. Naught of man or beast scored the night this far away—which likely meant they did not wish to be heard. Wary travelers, perhaps. But the aura of villainy that had plagued me all night of a sudden had focus. Even a small party could spell danger in such times as these. They could be Harrowers. They could be Scrutari-Consil's cohorts—Registry. Before I decided whether to retreat or run, I needed to know.

I touched earth again and sought an approach from the open fields—the direction they'd least expect. Once the route felt sure, I slipped through the pale night, following the guide thread in my head. Fifty times I thought I'd gone wrong; I'd never traveled wholly blind before. But just as the guide thread gave out, my feet felt the sharp rise of the hollow's lip, and I came near breaking my fingers when my extended hands encountered the bark of a young oak.

Lamenting my bulky monk's garb, I crept from tree to tree, now following soft voices and the weak lantern light that gleamed deep in the treed hollow. Somewhere beyond them, horses grazed.

"Dawn approaches. Are you prepared?" The woman's voice, cold and clear as a knife blade, chilled my soul. Only one night removed from her depraved rites, I could not mistake the priestess were a thousand other voices yammering in my ear.

The muffled answer was a man's voice, but I could not decipher his words.

"Witness this noble sacrifice, sister and brothers," said Sila Diaglou, "even as you remain vigilant. May the sweet odor of his suffering serve the Gehoum, drawing out our enemies that we might confound and crush them."

A few of them shifted position in the fog, and I used their footsteps to cover my own as I slipped closer. Embracing one tree and then another, I honed my every sense, so that I would not collide with one of the shadowed forms. Four of them besides the priestess . . . no more. Likely the same I'd seen at Graver's Meadow. Not gathered close as they'd been there. But somewhere in the center would be the priestess and the victim . . .

"*Sanguiera, orongia.* Scream, Monk. The trump of your pain shall open this battle and win the night." *Sanguiera, orongia.* Bleed. Suffer.

A whistling split of the air. A crack, as if a limb of dry oak had snapped. A heart-tearing scream told me they'd stood him upright near one of three trees, some twenty quercae from my position. I gripped the reins of my fury and held still, listening. The next lash told me which tree.

Not again. This *would* not happen again. And certainly *not* to one of the brothers . . .

Blocking out the cries ripped from a man's pain in the name of purity, I touched earth and mapped the grove, recording every tree, every shrub, every rock, stick, trench, or dip that might betray my steps or slow them. I searched out true north and etched the sense of it into my bones so that I could orient myself without thought. It took longer than I wished, knowing that the lash continued to fall, but I also knew they had no intent to be quick about their brutal game.

When my mind held as much as I could reasonably learn of the grove, I crept toward the closest of the four watchers. Only at the last step did he look my way—Boreas's needle-chinned murderer. With every minim of strength I had in me, I slammed my walking stick into the man's throat. Then I darted away. I hoped I'd killed him.

"Who's there?" As a loop snapping into a knot did Sila Diaglou's remaining henchmen gather round her, only to unravel again when one of their company did not arrive. "Radulf?"

Brisk footsteps sought the victim. "Radulf is down, lady!"

"Find the intruder!" The priestess's command slammed my gut like a fist. But I held still and did not flinch. "Falderrene, Malena, all of you, spread out. Do *not* let him escape! Hold, monk. We'll finish with you betimes."

"Quiet!" spat one of the men.

The light wavered, shifted. Another light bloomed, coloring the fog piss yellow. Close enough to hear the gasps of the injured man, the harsh breathing of their captive, and the hiss of whispered orders, I pressed my back to the slender trunk and waited for them to disperse.

The three spiraled outward from the site of their crime. Closing my eyes, I matched their movements with the map imprinted on my mind. Unable to see in the fog, they brushed stalks, snapped branches underfoot, disturbed rocks. As soon as they were spread out from their captive and the cold priestess who guarded him—not so far as I would like—I threaded my way between them. I had little confidence in my fighting ability, but I had a few other skills.

Yanking my abbey blanket from my rucksack, I returned to the downed man. He clutched his throat, wholly preoccupied with choking. I slipped his dagger from its sheath. If he died I would not grieve, but I could not shed his blood on that ground. Instead, I spread the blanket over his body, considered my intent, and constructed the most rudimentary of illusion spells—the only kind I'd ever learned to any effect. Once prepared, I stared, motionless, scarce breathing, toward the ashen cloud whence came the captive's harsh breathing. I stared until I could just make out the priestess's tall figure pacing a short path near the tree. She wielded a short blade.

"You intrude on matters you cannot comprehend, infidel," she cried. "Dare you sully a sacrifice offered to the Gehoum? I am the tool of their wrath."

You bring murder to Iero's holy ground, Harrower, I thought, snarling. *Against his might, you* shall not *prevail.*

Touching the blanket, I fed magic to my working. And waited. As the arm of a siege engine seems to crawl on its skyward journey toward release, so my spell seemed to spend eternity in its binding. My heart near stopped when I felt the blanket shift . . . and then it swelled into the very awkward likeness of a giant monk. Or a giant tent. I didn't care which way she saw it or how crude the work might be. I was already running.

"Infidel!" No coward, Sila Diaglou. She charged out of the fog, crashing through trees and scrub straight at my feeble working. "Falderrene! Morgaut! To me!"

Silently I'd circled wide of her, leaping rocks and pits, dodging saplings and branches and stones, to come up behind the tree. Before she could reach my illusion, I was fumbling at the quivering captive suspended from the thin-boled oak. I could scarce believe my luck—his luck. Two loose, twisted loops of rope were all that held his hands to the limb above his head. I slipped the loops off his wrists, grasped him in my arms, and drew him away from the tree. Though his pale skin ran dark with blood, he expelled only a faint hiss at my handling. He lifted his head—pale, too, shaven as it was, his dark eyes a stain on his white skin . . . *Gildas!*

"Valen?" Even in the wan light, I could feel his shock.

"Do I need to carry you?" I said, grinning, cheered to feel him supporting his own weight.

"No . . . no, not . . . but. . . ." He shook his head. Though his speech stumbled, he gathered up his cowl and gown that had been stripped off his shoulders and left bunched about his waist.

"Then follow me." I grasped his arm and pulled him along.

"I'll bleed you for the Gehoum, infidel!" Sila Diaglou's cry of rage followed us as I led Gildas on the shortest path out of the hollow. I didn't expect her to follow, and she did not. As I supported the stumbling monk across the broken ground, the dwindling thunder of galloping hoofbeats signaled the Harrowers' escape. As soon as I was sure, I halted.

"I think we're safe now," I said, supporting him by his arms, careful not to jar or twist his mangled back. "I'll fetch Robierre . . . the litter."

"No . . . no . . . I'll be all right. Stupid to get caught out. But, Valen"—his gaze was hot—"what, in great Iero's mercy, are you doing out here? How did you—? I don't understand."

"I could ask the same of you, Brother," I said.

"Couldn't sleep," he said, after a moment. "I needed to think, and so I played the fool, wandering about out here in the night. Walked right into their little plot."

"Exactly so," I said. "Only, *I* seem to have lost my blanket as well—hung it up in a tree to distract them. Do you think Brother Sebastian will punish me?"

He laid his blood-streaked hand on my shoulder and flashed his white teeth in a grin. "I'll see what I can do." Despite the smile, his hand quivered like a maid on her virgin night.

When we reached the gatehouse, Gildas refused my offer to accompany him to the infirmary or even to summon Brother Robierre to see to him. "No need for us both to suffer reprimands," he said, pulling his disheveled garments tight. "I'll confess my folly to Father Abbot tonight, so he'll likely not get after you until morning. Not at all, if I can manage it. I'll say only what you've told me, mention nothing of rucksacks, and bless your name eternally in their hearing. But someday, good Valen, we will speak of this night, you and me."

"I'm just happy you're living," I said. "The last fellow I rescued was dead at the end of it." As I slogged back through the hedge garden, I glimpsed Abbot Luviar racing toward the Alms Court, robes billowing. And from the direction of the guesthouse, heading in the same direction, barreled the Thane of Erasku and his secretary Gram. I had not heard that the lord had returned to the abbey. Had I not been ready to collapse as battle fever and tight-held magic drained out of me, I would have gone back to hear what drew them so urgently to the gates. But I could scarce command my feet to carry me.

I slept astonishingly well, until the bells clanged and clamored, waking me to my first day as Gillarine's newest and only novice.

Chapter 13

The fifth day of my novitiate began as had the previous four. In the dark. After the lengthy service of Prime, we washed heads, hands, and feet in the frigid water of the lavatorium, then broke our night's fast with weak ale and bread left from the previous day. As every day, I slogged through these activities half asleep. A night of unbroken sleep had taken its place in the pantheon of unachievable delights, alongside my own private cask of mead and a Pyrrhan courtesan in my bed.

The daily chapter meeting began as usual, too. Abbot Luviar and Prior Nemesio sat beneath the grandest of the lancet windows, the one depicting Kings Eodward and Caedmon worshiping an enthroned Creator. Jullian and Gerard perched on low stools that flanked the door. In between, on crescent-shaped benches that lined the circular walls, sat the remainder of Gillarine's thirty monks, ordered from eldest to youngest. Every size and shape of man.

At my first chapter meeting, Brother Sebastian had led me around the circle to introduce me, as if he were a swineherd and I his prized sow. We had skipped no one, all the way from the eldest—straight-backed Brother Abelard, mostly blind and nearing his ninetieth year—to the youngest—walleyed Brother Simeon, eight years my junior. Birdlike Brother Nunius; the aristocratic Ardran Brother Bolene; the cottar's son Brother Adolfus, whose eyes and throat bulged like a toad's . . . My memory for names and faces had been well exercised.

Sharing this clockwork existence of prayers and work with these men was no bad life by any means. I could surely bear the monotony and excessive piety for a season. It was only when I thought of living this way unchanging until I was the age of Brother Abelard that cold sweat dribbled down my back.

I had scarce settled in my own place at the lowest end of the bench, just next to Jullian's stool and the entry, when every face turned abruptly in our direction. Brother Victor stood in the doorway, looking small and hollow-eyed and unsteady on his feet. Luviar motioned the pale little chancellor to his assigned seat without the least hint of sympathy, apology, or the conspiracy that I believed existed between them. Perhaps that was because the hierarch's pureblood followed Brother Victor into the room.

I fixed my gaze on my hands, clenched in my lap. A frigid draft more appropriate to the Frost Moon than Reaper's Moon funneled up the nightstair, swirled through the open door, and blew straight up my gown.

Scrutari-Consil had remained sequestered in the abbot's house, conducting his interviews. My heart had lurched like a besotted beggar every time a new witness was summoned. Every town of any size and every fighting legion bought pureblood contracts, so it wasn't as if I'd wholly avoided those of my own kind over the years. I told myself I just needed to keep to my usual habits . . . and pray no one spoke my name in his hearing . . . or mentioned my book.

I glanced at Brother Gildas. He appeared soberly attentive as always. To my surprise, I'd never been questioned about our encounter with the Harrowers. Prior Nemesio had cautioned everyone that Gildas had run afoul of them to the peril of his life and that I had chanced upon him and brought him back within our walls. Sometimes I wondered if it had really happened. I had collapsed that morning wrapped in my cowl, but I'd waked with a blanket thrown over me, and my well-brushed cowl hung neatly with my gown.

"Holy Father, a moment's intrusion, if you permit," said Scrutari-Consil without expression, touching his fingers to his forehead.

"Speak as you will," said the abbot coolly.

The pureblood inclined his back to acknowledge the permission. Purebloods *bowed* to no ordinary but their contracted masters and the King of Navronne. "I must commend you on your brothers' piety, Abbot Luviar, and on their . . . ardent . . . personal loyalty to you and your chancellor. My investigations of Gillarine's scribes have revealed no purpose to their work but the One God's glory. As the chancellor's confinement is ended, I deem my work here complete . . . or nearly so."

Luviar said naught.

Scrutari-Consil stepped farther into the room, his cloak billowed by the draft from the doorway. "I understand that some few members of this brotherhood labor in the scriptorium occasionally, although they are not considered scribes. I must question those persons that I may assure Hierarch Eligius I have been thorough in my obligations. And one more small matter . . ."

I tried not to fidget. I would *not* be on that list. He would have no reason to speak to me. Soon he would be gone, and perhaps I would be able to pass an hour without imagining my father's sneer as he devised a method to control me for the rest of my life.

Hands at his back, the pureblood pivoted on one fine boot, as if to take a final appraisal of our faces. ". . . I require a review of your membership list. In my general scrutiny of Gillarine and its residents, I have perceived residue of sorcery. My duty to the kingdom and its law demands that I ensure that any pureblood in your brotherhood has received the proper family dispensation. Much better that I, a Karish observant, take on this review, than a Registry inspector, likely an unbeliever, intrude upon your holy precincts."

Deunor's fire, damnation, and all cursed gatzi! Never *use magic, fool.* Never. *You know it.*

The monks Scrutari had questioned insisted that a man could hide nothing from his magical interrogations. I knew better. To deceive a pureblood perceptive you just had to present plausible, consistent testimony and obliterate any distinction in your mind between the truth and the lie—perhaps a difficult thing for holy monks. For me, the lying was easy. Unfortunately, my history, cobbled up in an instant whilst I suffered from wound fever, was as thin as these monks' finest vellum. And my name was now scribed on the abbey's roster.

"Of course you may inspect our membership roster if you deem it necessary," said the abbot, displaying no emotion the perceiver might probe. "But it would be a waste of your time. Only one of our brotherhood claims pureblood descent. His dispensation is duly recorded, and for more than twenty years he has forsworn the practice of sorcery as our Rule demands. Prior Nemesio can show you this man's credentials immediately after chapter. As for those who assist in the scriptorium, one could say that every man in the abbey does so, whether he be the lay brother who tends the fire or the boy who mixes the ink or the choir monk who petitions blessings for the generous donors of our books. I see no need for you to interview every resident of Gillarine on some arbitrary quest for completeness. The hierarch would perhaps consider it a *frivolous* use of our time and that of his valued pureblood servant."

Scrutari's nostril's flared in disbelief—as did mine, most likely. "Surely, holy fath—"

"Once you have reviewed the record Prior Nemesio will show you, your horse will be ready for your departure. Bear our prayers for good health and Iero's blessings to the hierarch. Now please excuse us. We've business to attend before the bells ring for prayers." The abbot's demeanor stood no more yielding than a granite wall.

Though I applauded his decision, Luviar's refusal made no sense, unless . . . I glanced at the young face beside me. Jullian's eyes were fixed in the vicinity of Brother Nunius's wrinkled neck, and his fingers clenched in a knot tighter than my own. He breathed in shallow fits.

"As you say, Father Abbot. I shall pass your message—and my conclusions—to the hierarch." Stiff as Erdru's prick, the pureblood touched his forehead and withdrew. Were I Abbot Luviar, I would not request any favors from the Scrutari-Consil family before Judgment Night.

An unruffled Prior Nemesio began the day's business. Boring business. He invited Brother Nunius to speak on the fifteenth chapter of Saint Ophir's Rule—that which addressed the management of an abbey's lands and treasury and the apportioning of alms. My attention wandered.

Weak sunbeams shone through the lancet windows behind the abbot's chair, transforming the colored glass into rubies, emeralds, and sapphires. I examined King Eodward's features in the window, searching for some trace of the man I had met. He had been the exemplar of Ardran manhood—big and ruddy, beard and hair as red-gold as summer sunset, his bones sturdy and well formed, his face equally suited to laughter and sober intelligence. I glanced at Jullian—the boy was breathing again—and wondered about a rumored Pretender . . . a child . . . and an abbot who juggled hierarchs and purebloods and princes as if they were oranges. And told myself I was a lunatic.

By the time Brother Nunius's sermon had labored to its conclusion, and the prior began assigning reading tasks for the day's services and mealtimes, my eyelids were drooping. But somewhere between "Brother Aesculpius, Vespers" and "Brother Jerome, Matins," he announced, "Brother Valen, Compline."

Gods' bones! They wanted me to read! Cold dismay wafted up my gown with the draft. My conscience bloomed hotly on my cheeks. Rabbitlike thoughts of escape drew my glance to the door, where I found Jullian staring curiously at *me*.

*   *   *

Except on the coldest or rainiest days, I was supposed to spend the hours between Terce and dinner pursuing my studies in my carrel in the north cloister. Brother Sebastian had selected a dreadfully thick book for me to study over the next months. I didn't even know its name.

I riffled the pages of the book and contemplated the cloister garth and the shrine, mulling the problems of undead spirits and why one of them might have an interest in me, and of how I was to convince Brother Sebastian to read me the text I was supposed to proclaim at Compline.

I had already spent an hour concluding that I couldn't possibly guess which of Saint Ophir's brothers was a pureblood. My own appearance evidenced that "straight of hair, deep of color, short in stature, large in talent" was not an infallible guide to Aurellian heritage, but most purebloods *did* conform to the type. Whoever it was— and a careful recollection of every face in the chapter circle yielded no suspicion—either he was not insightful enough to connect me to the infamous Cartamandua *recondeur* or he had truly shifted his loyalties to the brotherhood and broken contact with the Registry. I was likely safe enough as long as I kept to my usual precautions. I hoped.

Inevitably, as it had all week, my mind returned to the incident in the wood. The more I recalled, the stranger it all was. The Harrowers had not been doing the same to Gildas as they had to Boreas. Sila Diaglou had said they wanted to "draw them out"—referring to her enemies. And Luviar and Thane Stearc had been running to the gates . . .

Ow! I bit my lip to keep from yelling aloud when Brother Sebastian's knucklebone rapped my skull. I stuck my books in my pockets and traipsed after his wagging finger.

Though rigorous in matters of decorum, liturgical observance, and adherence to the Rule, the tidy Sebastian had been undemanding when it came to my studies. He seemed more than willing to believe that my healing shoulder wound restricted any writing tasks and that illness still caused my eyes to tire easily, limiting my reading. In the main, he complained I talked too much, and was forever exhorting me shift my verbal excess from flesh to spirit.

"Fine mornings are too rare of late," he said as we left the cloisters for the maze of yew and hawthorn hedges in front of the church. "Let us discuss the lesson you were to master for today, and, at the same time, give praise for the sunlight. So, Brother Valen, the structure of virtue: Recite for me the seven great virtues and twelve great vices and expound upon their signs and meanings."

If he had known my answers were all guesswork, he might have admired my cleverness at getting almost half of them right. Instead, he cheerfully scolded me as a slackwit, and charged me to obtain a wax tablet from Brother Victor and write out the two lists for the next morning.

"We do not expect every brother to be a scholar of Brother Gildas's level, or even Jullian's, who has as fine a mind as any student we have ever nurtured here. But you *must* master the basic precepts of divine order, be familiar with the holy writs, and the history—" The dinner bell brought a welcome reprieve from his kindly concern.

I'd grown quite fond of mealtimes, beyond the fine and plentiful sustenance. The week had taught me that the light-filled refectory was neither so serious nor so strictly quiet as the cloister or library, save during the actual reading that accompanied every meal. Which circumstance raised my hopes of garnering assistance to break the twin shackles of the Compline reading and my study text. Scrutari-Consil was gone. Gildas had shielded my abortive departure. Truly, excessive worry about the future wasted a man's life.

"Iero's grace, Brother Abelard," I shouted in the ancient monk's ear and took his arm on the refectory stair. "The sun feels a bit more seasonable today, does it not?" The crabbed old fellow frowned and shushed me, and shook off my hold. Horribly deaf, he proposed every morning in chapter to apply the rule of silence everywhere in the abbey.

Undeterred, I dropped back and offered my assistance to another of the elders. "Brother Nunius, someday perhaps you could teach me why we may give alms to ill-reputed women only in famine times. That part of the Rule left me confused." At least I could *speak* of ill-reputed women.

"Indeed, it is a strict provision," said the birdlike monk, graciously accepting my arm. "The fifteenth chapter is more important than most of us credit. Sometimes I believe I am the only one who pays it mind. You were not the only member of our family dozing this morning."

Family! By the god's toes, if I ever thought of the brothers as family, I'd bolt from here for certain. "Tell me, Brother, why does Saint Ophir forbid his brothers magic working? We're taught that pureblood sorcery is a gift of the god"—and thus we pursued *recondeurs* as doubly damned, traitors to the divine, as well as to the king—"so should not our Rule promote its use in holy works?"

"An excellent question! Sorcery is a component of the earthly sphere just as wealth and gaming and pleasures of the flesh," said the old man. "Whilst not evil in themselves, such worldly pursuits leave the soul ripe for the Adversary, who is ever seeking ways to subvert our better natures. Young fellows like you must work diligently to avoid such pitfalls as sorcery."

"And so I shall, good Brother." I laughed and released his arm as we reached the refectory door. "So I shall."

"I need to speak with you, Archangel," I said quietly, when Jullian arrived with the boiled fish and stewed parsnips. "A work of mercy that will ensure your place in the heavenly choir."

He bowed his head for the prayer as the abbot rang the bell. "You should not have lied about your reading," he whispered, his lips scarcely moving. "Lies are the Adversary's tool."

The mealtime reading had begun, so I had no time to question how he had guessed or why such a minor offense caused him to sit there tight as a tabor's skin. No time to remind him that *secrets* are the closest kin to lies.

"You once offered me whatever I needed of you," I said. "Surely the god wishes you to help me become a better man."

He nodded without looking at me. "Meet me in the garden maze just after supper. Tell Brother Sebastian you need to meditate on those you've wronged in preparation for Saint Dian's Day."

His direction sounded a bit pompous coming from a boy of twelve. Of a sudden, my mad whimsy insisted on reviving itself. *An Ardran Pretender . . . here.* If such were true, the danger would be unimaginable. I buried the thought as quickly as it had arrived.

Yet as a drifting cloud grayed the light from the great windows, my spirits chilled. I could not shake the sense of unseen hands propelling me toward an unseen precipice, and even the lovely mound of parsnips touched with thyme could not disperse it.

Every day between Nones and Vespers, I reported to work in the kitchen. Though I could not seem to satisfy the meticulous Brother Jerome with my work—my chopping was uneven, my fish wastefully trimmed, and after the third time I scorched the porridge, he forbade me to come near his precious pots—I enjoyed those hours the most of all my duties. Yet on this day I fidgeted through the time as if I'd buckthorn twigs in my trews, and I came near yanking out what was left of my hair as we dragged through Vespers and supper. I couldn't have said what I was expecting.

Fog had rolled in from the river again, studding the neglected hedges of the garden maze with water droplets. Sprangling branches spattered my face as I hurried down along the graveled path toward the center of the maze and the stone bench that overlooked a green-slimed pond.

"Brother Valen!" Jullian jumped from the bench like a startled cat.

"Are you expecting other oversized supplicants this night, Archangel?" I said with a grin, hoping to put him at ease.

Unsuccessfully, it seemed. He glanced over his shoulder and gripped his arms about his slight body as if gatzi were poised to jump out of the hedges and drag him off to the netherworld. Blue-gray dusk had settled over the abbey. The days were rapidly growing shorter.

"Of course not." He bit his lip and sat on the bench again, curling his bare legs underneath him. His eyes would not meet mine. One would think it was *he* undergoing the humiliation of seeking aid from a child scarce dropped from his mother's womb.

"I thank you for not revealing my problem to the brothers," I said. "They'd pitch me over the wall did they find out. I've nowhere to go." And unholy murderers lurked beyond these walls.

When I tilted my head to glimpse his face and gauge the depth of his worry, he turned away. "I'll help you," he said. "I did say I would. But I'll not lie about it should anyone ask me."

"A fair bargain and a great kindness." I held out my psalter and my lesson book. "All I need is for you to show me which page and to read me whatever I'm supposed to say at Compline, and then to read me the passage about the great virtues and vices from the other book." I could devise some explanation for not writing the lesson.

"How will reading you the passage help you? You're required to proclaim the whole text, and Brother Abelard will complain if you get even a word of it wrong."

"I'll remember. It's just— My eyes—" Of a sudden all my usual excuses felt inadequate. "It's like a blindness in me, Jullian. I see the marks on the page, and I can tell one letter from the other if I work at it hard enough. But when I look at two or more together, they tie themselves into knots that won't unravel no matter what I do. I've tried to learn since I was a boy, but it won't come. I'm just . . . broken . . . somehow." Or lazy-minded, stubborn, demon-touched, god-cursed, soul-damaged, or willfully obtuse—all the things my tutors, parents, and siblings had named me. I must be mad. I had never told anyone what I had just exposed to a child I scarcely knew. "But I'm not stupid. Read it to me exactly, and I can remember it exactly."

Heaving a great quivering sigh, the boy laid the books in his lap and carefully smoothed the worn covers. Some fine friend I was, who had so pompously set myself to ward him from unwanted advances of the flesh, only to subvert his conscience, which he likely valued higher. As for my mad speculations, an hour's contemplation as I worked in the kitchen had already convinced me I was an idiot. Any youthful Pretender of Eodward's loins would be secured in some remote fortress under the protection of pureblood defense works, not scuffing about an abbey in sandals.

"All right, then." Jullian leafed through the psalter until settling on a page bordered with flying geese. "This is tonight's Compline—" His head jerked up at some noise from beyond the hedge.

When his gaze shifted to something over my shoulder, I was still too taken aback to ask what distracted him, for in that moment of surprise, I had glimpsed his face . . . not conscience ridden at all, but keen with excitement and anticipation.

"Brother Valen."

I jumped to my feet, enough blood rushing to my face to feed a cave of bats. "Holy father! I— We—"

Jullian stepped immediately to the abbot's side, halting my stammering with a now-obvious truth. The boy had known he was coming. *Saint Dian's Day . . .* they had conspired to get me here!

"Sit down, Valen," said Luviar. Joining me on the bench, the abbot pressed a finger to his lips and then flicked it in a quick gesture to the boy.

Jullian bowed and melted into the hedges.

"I needed to speak with you in private, Brother Novice. And as you have no doubt learned in these past weeks, privacy is not a condition of monastery life. Not physical privacy, at least, even for the abbot." His brows lifted, widening his gray eyes in an expression I would have called good humor were this anyone but Abbot Luviar.

Annoyed with the boy and the abbot—and even more with my own stupidity—I kept my jaw shut tight and dipped my head in agreement, sure I was now to hear word of my dismissal.

"Hmm. Not so forthcoming as at our first meeting?" Luviar's scrutiny felt bone-deep. "I suppose I must take responsibility for that. Though I am aware that not everything you told me of your journey here is entirely . . . accurate . . . I believe I understand at least something of your reasons for dissembling. Tell me, Brother Valen, were you a more capable pikeman in Ardra's service than you are a cook's helper?"

My skin heated. So he'd guessed that I was a deserter. Best not add more lies, if I could avoid it. "No, holy father."

"Your past loyalties do not concern me so much as your current loyalties, Valen, and I'll not hold you to account for choices made before you were in my charge."

The failing light made it increasingly difficult to read his face, thus I dared not feel relief.

"I've seen and heard enough of you these past weeks to believe that I can entrust you with a task I need of you tonight. Your instincts are ever generous, whether to old or young—or those in peril. You accept what is without complaint, bridling only at matters of justice. And you live your days with relish, no matter their mundanity. You have a certain honesty about you that has little to do with truth or un-truth. I am not a fool. But I'm not sure if *you* trust *me*, and that is im-perative, for I must insist that you keep silent about certain matters that could compromise others' safety. Matters of great importance."

" 'For Navronne'? 'For our children's children'?" Bitterness at this man welled up in me and erased every other consideration, as if the slaughtered Ardrans' blood rose from the ground beneath my san-dals and their empty eye sockets glared at me.

Luviar did not flinch. His face and shaven head gleamed pale in the enveloping night. "Indeed, yes. Now, ask me the one question whose truthful answer might most influence your trust. I'll answer you—truthfully—and then we shall see if we're to proceed."

"Only one, holy father?" Again and always, my imprudent tongue.

He remained cool and sober. "For now, one question. If I cannot satisfy you enough to gain your promise of forbearance, then I must think of some other way."

So many possibilities . . . I was almost drunk with the thought of an-swers. Yet some of Gillarine's mysteries were but simple secrets, and simple facts would explain them. I could ask about Jullian—but a negative answer would leave me more confused than ever, and an affirmative one was so dangerous, I was not sure I wanted to know it. No, the greater challenge to trust was this man's character—which took me right back to the beginning.

"Why did you abandon Ardran soldiers to die—*encourage* them to die—for a prince you surely know is unworthy?"

He nodded, as if my question were exactly the one he expected. "We live in harsh times, Brother Valen, and as a man newly arrived here from the wide world, you know this as well as any. The lack of a righteous king speeds the ruin of our land. I speak not merely of war's grief and devastation, but of the deepest mysteries of earth and heaven, for this conflict is but one piece of a grand and terrible mosaic, with some of the other pieces named Famine, Pestilence, and Storm."

Why was it Luviar could set the hairs on my neck rising with words that would sound pretentious spoken even by a pureblood diviner? His gray eyes warmed with sympathy, as if he understood the unnerving nature of his converse and sought to soothe it even as he made it worse.

"In another age of the world, I would step not one quat in any direction to serve Perryn of Ardra's cause. But as matters stand, neither could I allow Bayard of Morian to take the final step that would assure his ascension to Eodward's throne. Not only because of his own faults, but for this: If Prince Bayard's eye is no longer fixed on his hated rival, and his hammer no longer aimed at valiant Ardra, then his attention—and that of his new allies—will turn to any who dare assert that we must deal with matters more important than the succession. Their hammer will fall on those few who fight to assure Navronne's future beyond one sovereign's reign."

"Assuring the future beyond one . . ." My mind raced, knotting and unknotting the strange events of the past weeks. "You're speaking of this end-times teaching." *The long night*, Jullian had said. *The dark times.* What the hierarch called deviance.

He propped his elbows on his knees and leaned forward to rest his chin on his folded hands, staring at the well-trodden path. "Those Ardran soldiers had pledged their loyalty and service to their prince," he continued. "I, in an arrogance of intellect and conviction, stole that devotion and transferred it to a worthier cause. To Ardra, Morian, and Evanore—to Navronne and to the mysteries that bind our land to the future of Iero's creation. Not to despair, but to hope."

He had shaped his answer with an artist's hand that took bits of colored glass and fit them together to create a portrait of kings and saints. I wondered again if Luviar had the bent—for persuasion, perhaps. For truth-telling, I hoped, for my curiosity was so inflamed, I could not have walked away had he sprouted a gatzé's barbed tail in front of me. I could not say I trusted him, but, gods preserve me, I believed him. "Father Abbot, are *you* the pureblood at Gillarine?"

His head popped up from his meditative posture, and he laughed, a full-throated burst of cheer, as robust as Ardran mead and as unexpected as an honest tinker. "Is that your measure of trust, Valen? You think I am ensorceling you? Not at all what I had hoped to accomplish. But I granted you only one answer, if you remember. More will come only if you vow your silence. If you choose not, then no burden will be held against you, nor will I look further into your past. Now tell me if I should proceed or not. Lives may depend on your declaration."

I scratched my head and tried to bury my qualms about holy men. Who was I to gainsay the abbot, after all? He had all but confessed to me that he supported what his superiors called deviance—high treason in the world of practors and hierarchs. I felt great kinship with all rebellious souls, even if they wore golden solicales. "What is it you want of me, holy father? Not a sevenday since I did swear to obey you in all things. And if you command I trust you and keep secrets, well then, who am I to say it is not holy?"

He sighed and spread his hands in acceptance. "I suppose that will have to do. Your task is simple. I wish you to meet with several others who recognize the enormity of the world's troubles. They need you to demonstrate how to use the Cartamandua maps."

My spirits, tickled with growing excitement, plunged. Of course it would be the book. Though, indeed, he had asked my aid, not for copying, but for use, which raised all manner of questions, such as where his friends wished to travel that no ordinary book of maps could take them. But this book— I was trying to avoid lies. "Father Abbot, I must tell you—"

No. I couldn't tell him I'd never used it. Once I began changing my story, the perceptive abbot would surely unravel the rest of my talespinning. Then he would be forced to choose between his life and my freedom. I trusted no one but myself with that choice. Blood rushed to my skin with the misstep so narrowly avoided.

"The book is certainly magical, holy father, and thus appears differently to any eye that looks upon it. Its usage is likely different for any who attempt it also. I'll share what I can, but in truth, as you've clearly surmised, I've had meager success at anything in my life, thus you'd best not expect too much."

Luviar watched me silently. Waiting for me to confess more lies, I thought. I kept breathing and did not squirm.

At last he nodded. "Very well, then. All we ask is your best effort. At the opening of tonight's Compline I will assign you to keep vigil in the church through the night. When the day's-end bell rings, leave the church and return here. You'll be met. And you will not reveal this plan or what occurs to anyone, on pain of your immortal soul."

"As you say, holy father." I bowed my head, placing a clenched fist upon my breast in their sign of obedience. Then, gritting my teeth, I broached the direst topic. "I am assigned to read at Compline tonight."

"I'll have Nemesio postpone that until tomorrow." He stood and lifted his black hood, so that his body lost definition in the dusk. "Iero's grace be with you, Valen. *Teneamus.*"

"Wait! What does that—?" As he turned his back to my rising question and hurried away, I would have sworn I glimpsed a flicker of teeth that might have been a smile.

Chapter 14

The abbot had failed to mention that the "vigil" he planned to assign me was a penance for dozing in chapter. Because he announced this judgment at the opening of Compline, I was required to prostrate myself throughout the entire service, which left me in no great patience for meeting his friends. Perhaps he thought I would be grateful that he was permitting me to abandon the punishment at the day's end bell, rather than staying in place until Matins. But as the cold, unyielding granite bruised my too-prominent bones, gratitude came nowhere to mind. I could not even rejoice in the postponement of my reading.

Once the monks had snuffed the candles and retired to the dorter, a great chilly silence fell in the church. The vigil lamp gleamed emerald from the high altar. Brother Victor lay on the floor to my right. He had arrived late for Compline and reaped the same penance as mine. The chancellor had a slight whistle in his breathing that prevented any sensible thinking. Had I actually to remain in place for the full span of this vigil, the sound would surely drive me mad long before the bells rang for Matins.

When the bell tolled the day's end, the time for all activities to cease and the monks to take to their beds, I rose from the floor as quietly as I could. Brother Victor did not stir as I padded down the aisle. His presence would not be happenstance. That the chancellor would be part of the abbot's little plot did not surprise me, but it did give me pause. Luviar had not only been willing to sacrifice *strangers* to his "worthier cause," but had yielded his own partisan to lashing, imprisonment, and humiliation. Why did I not heed my own warnings about holy men?

I hurried through the hedge maze and returned to the bench by the neglected pond, vowing to detach myself from this conspiracy as quickly as possible. No good could come from mixing religion and politics. And who could be less equipped than I to get in a fight over books? Did they think to stave off some threat to Navronne with almanacs and treatises on glassmaking? Build a bulwark of books against Hansker raiders, perhaps? That might be a use for the wretched things.

Night birds twittered. The sad little scrap of moon vanished in the west. No one came. I was on the verge of giving up, when light, steady footsteps approached from the direction of the cloisters. Closer. Then heavier, louder steps came running from two other directions at once. I spun like a potter's wheel, but before I could see who was in such a hurry, some cursed villain dropped a sack over my head.

"Gatzé's whore!" I shot up from the bench, pawing at the bag. A hempen drawstring held the rough cloth tight around my neck. I dragged at the rope, but succeeded only in strangling myself. Dust clogged my nostrils. The bag scratched my face and blocked my mouth. *Hot. Close. Choking.* I could not yell. Could not breathe. Terror welled up inside me like molten lava. *No light. No air. Buried . . .*

I flailed my arms and tried to twist away. My right arm slammed into solid flesh, and my left elbow crunched bone hard enough to elicit a curse. Two outsized hands caught my wrists and pinned them hard behind me. "Here now, just be still, monk."

Jerking my shoulders and torso back and forth, I tried to use my size to some advantage, but the harder I struggled, the tighter the rope constricted my neck.

"Stop! Wait! There's no need for force," someone called. Pointlessly. No brutes would heed a man who spoke so softly.

I snarled and dragged them sideways. Feet tangled hopelessly in my gown, I toppled, dragging a heavy body down on top of me. My arms were wrenched back and up.

"Sentinels of the dark, he's broke my foot!"

"Half a madman . . . what's wrong with 'im? Hold on . . ." A heavy someone sat on me.

"Silence, all of you!" The soft voice whispered from somewhere in the spinning darkness. "Don't hurt him, Furz. Get up. What are you thinking?"

"You told us to get him to the camp without him seeing where." This from the brute who was twisting my arms from their sockets while I wriggled like a dying fish in a mudhole. His voice rumbled through my back and aching shoulders. "We heard he might be a danger."

"A danger? He's a monk! Get off him, and don't hurt him any-more. We just need silence."

As the weight rolled off my back, I wrenched one hand loose and tore at the bag. Dug in my knees and scrabbled forward in the muddy grass. Tried to shake free of the hands. At any moment I was going to heave up my guts or die or both. I groaned and writhed.

"What, in all holy—? Iero's grace, just be still, Brother Valen." A new voice penetrated my skull like a bolt from a crossbow. Not loud, but very clear. "We'll take off the bag, if you'll but close your eyes and be silent. This is a terrible mistake. Do you hear me, Brother? Please, just be still, close your eyes, and we'll take it off."

Swallowing my gorge, I nodded and tried to be still. My heart gal-loped like a king's post messenger; blood thundered in my ears. *Just let me breathe.* Were spiders swarming over me, I would have re-mained still on his promise. I squeezed my eyes shut.

"Furz, get it off him," said the newcomer. "Would you, please?"

"They jumped him," said the soft-voiced one in quiet anger. "They weren't supposed to—"

The decisive man interrupted with tested patience. "You should have waited. I told you that Gildas and I would see to this."

I did not hear the response, for the bag was snatched away just then. Cool air bathed my face as I craned my neck upward, gulping great mouthfuls. Soon I was breathing normally, and sensations be-yond suffocation returned. Rocks gouged my belly. My shoulders burned. My chin stung. My left foot, caught in my gown, was bent at an angle the Creator did not intend. I shifted to ease the strain, but the hands only gripped my limbs tighter, and a heavy knee crushed my chest into the ground.

Was every untoward event in all the world linked to Brother Gildas? Perhaps the whispering villain was Jullian, who seemed to be in the thick of these sordid matters as well. Instinct screamed at me to look on my attackers, so I could identify them if I lived or curse them as I died, but this mindless terror of suffocation kept my eyes tight shut and my tongue silent. I lowered my cheek to the muddy grass and inhaled the sweet scent of earth.

What foolish thoughts run through our heads in times of fear and peril. My cowl and gown were heavy with mud, clinging to my skin. Brother Sebastian would scold. I had no spare garments yet, as my height meant they had to be made new. *So rid yourself of this sodden wool and you'll get a full breath*, said my unbidden thoughts. Every-where my bare skin touched earth—face, one knee and thigh—felt free. The earth embraced me, warm and alive and forgiving . . .

"Release him, Furz," said the decisive man, no denizen of heaven or hell, but entirely human and standing over my head. "We'll guide him to the camp ourselves."

"It's taken the two of us to hold him." The thugs growled in concert. "You're a fool to let him go. The blighting monk's got a gatzé in him."

"Did you never consider that a man attacked from behind and smothered with a grain sack might take offense—even a Karish monk? Please, do as I ask."

The weight came off my back, and thick fingers released my wrists. I rolled to my side and curled my arms in front of me, thanking every god for the gifts of air and unbroken bones, promising anew to reform my ways. Slowly I sat up on my heels, unwilling to push my luck by standing up. The two brutes hovered close enough to block the breeze, and this man, though firm and confident, was not their commander. Too much politeness from him, *asking* and saying *please*. And from the brutes mere obedience, no honorifics or respect. Obedience was sufficient, but without respect, I'd not rely on it.

As my heart slowed, my flush of gratitude yielded to the more usual mix of emotions I felt after a fight—embarrassment and anger. For all my height and natural strength, I'd never developed much technique. I'd had no combat training when I was young enough to develop true skill. Pureblood families valued physical prowess like speed and strength, and refinements such as grace and agility, but they had no use for fighting skills. Only barbarians or madmen would dare assault a pureblood. The Registry saw to that.

"We've no wish to harm you, Brother," said the man who had let me breathe, my friend forever. "Somehow these two became confused. They understood that we did not wish you to see where you were being taken and mistook our concern. I would explain why such secrecy is necessary, but that will be clear soon enough, and we need to move quickly. Someone might have heard your shout, and explanations would be awkward. So please understand this binding will be just for your eyes. *Just* your eyes."

When the cloth touched my face, I came near rising bodily off the ground. But before I could lash out, I comprehended what he'd said. Only the eyes. Not nose or mouth.

The blindfold in place, the clear-voiced man clasped arms with me and helped me to my feet. Average in height, perhaps a head shorter than me by the sound and feel of him. "We've a goodly walk ahead of us. Will your leg wound be a hindrance?"

I spat mud, wiped my mouth on my sleeve, and shook my head.

"Please believe me, Brother, we've no ill intent."

Such silliness required a response. I kept my voice as low as his. "Suffocating a fellow and twisting his limbs from their sockets is a poor introduction for those with good intents. Does the abbot know you treat his novices so?"

"Abbot Luviar will be extremely displeased"—as soon as he spoke, I felt his good humor, warm enough to dry my sodden cowl— "and I promise, we shall do our best to remedy our failing. One moment . . ."

Lighter footsteps came up on my left side—the whisperer. Their movements stirred up the faint scent of wintergreen.

"I am going to give your arm to my companion," said my friend. "He will guide you safely to our meeting place, while I dispatch these two oxen back to our camp and make sure nothing like this happens again. I'll join you before you begin."

Smaller hands took a firm hold on my elbow and forearm. "Tell me if I go too fast."

It occurred to me that I could snatch my arm from this one's grip, rip the cursed rag from my face, and run away. I could tell Abbot Luviar that his friends had dreadful manners and I would not put up with them, not even to get my questions answered. But I didn't. Once I could breathe, the whole business was altogether intriguing. Much more interesting than Compline texts or the structure of virtue.

My guide used my crooked arm as a rudder, leading me along the gravel path, northward I guessed, for the breeze which had veered southerly all week was at my back. We turned once, and then again, and the surface under my sandals became paving stone. Scents of incense and ephrain from my right and the bulk of stone told me when we passed the church. We changed direction, veering around it, and when we had gone far enough that the church no longer blocked the breeze from my cheek, the path began to rise. The wind smelled of fish and river wrack, tinged by coming frost. My companion smelled of horses and woodsmoke and something . . .

"Careful, the pavement's broken." And then, "Left."

In the distance behind me, the abbey bell rang. One peal. The first hour past day's end.

"Steps here," said my guide, after a while. "Three downward, then stop for a moment."

Stone steps, not squared paving. Older, then. Out of the way. When I halted, my arm was released. Iron clanked softly—a latch. Oiled hinges. The hands took my arm again and guided me through the gate. We crossed flowing water on a sturdy plank bridge and then took a dirt path. The terrain leveled out, the damp tendrils of fog yielded to a cold dry breeze, and my guide picked up the pace.

Strange to experience the night as a blind man must. Birds flapping away, disturbed from a nest in the grass. Scuttering creatures. Wet grass, stagnant pools. A loon crying out the world's sorrow. The path had been well trod, a narrow trough in the turf, sticky mud in its bottom, its drier, sloping sides little wider than my big feet. So my guide's feet must tread the grass, while I walked the path. Or perhaps . . . I listened. The light footsteps squelched and scuffed much as my own steps did. Ah, a cart track, then, two troughs parallel.

Pleased with that deduction, I turned my attention to the person beside me. Listened more. Felt the hand on my arm shift to get a better hold, one finger now touching the skin of my wrist. I remembered. Inhaled. Considered. Felt my face crease into a grin. "So, Squire Corin, does the Thane of Erasku know you're a girl?"

She halted. Yanked her hands from my arm. Stepped away. Said nothing. If we hadn't already startled the moorhens, the force of her shock might have done it.

"I've not had this tonsure my whole life, you know," I said. "And the world is not kind to girls on their own, so you're not the first I've encountered in youth's attire." The world was little kinder to boys on their own.

She held silent and left me standing in the middle of a stubbled grain field blindfolded, without anything to hold on to. I didn't think I ought to reach for her. She was probably terrified enough already.

"I'll say, you had me mightily confused until today. But cutting your hair off might help. The braid leads a man's eye into thoughts of touching— Uh . . . *my* eye, that is. Perhaps not others." I shut my mouth and held out my arm.

She grasped my wrist and elbow, more firmly than before, and strode out at a faster pace. We'd walked two hundred quercae before she spoke. "You're wearing a blindfold." Her unmuted voice was mellow and richly colored, more like a dulcian than a flute. I'd made a mistake. She was slight, certainly, but a woman grown, not a girl. "How did I give it away?"

I considered the evidence. "Well, you and your friends aren't monks. And after the abbot's talk with me, I didn't think your party belonged to any of our unsavory princes. That meant you were either someone altogether new or the thane's men . . . Well, all right, I guessed. As for you in particular . . . You *whispered* when you truly wanted to yell at those men. That was part of it. And you trusted a monk not to hurt you. Which meant you've clearly not been at the game too long—you mustn't trust *anyone*. And even when I was . . . suffocating . . . whenever you spoke, I thought Jullian was with us, though I knew at the same time he wasn't. You see, in the refectory I sit next to Jullian, whom I'll assume you know, and Gerard, the other lad. You don't—please, forgive me if I offend you—you don't smell at all the same." Excitement would have only worsened the boys' ripe stink.

"I don't smell—" She convulsed with laughter, as alive as the good earth around us. Only a moment; then she closed it all up again. "Sweet Arrosa, save me. Of all things."

"I won't tell anyone. But you should be careful. You'll give yourself away."

"Thane Stearc knows," she said. "And Abbot Luviar and Brother Gildas."

"Ah . . . and the secretary . . . Gram . . . that's who else was back there in the gardens, right? *He* knows." Brutes would care no more for the commands of sickly secretaries than for the commands of pretty youths. And I'd smelled wintergreen, a medicament used for all sorts of ailments.

"He knows," she said. Her voice was well controlled, but she really shouldn't be holding on to people's arms if she wanted to keep secrets. I'd felt far less anger from the brutes pinning my wrists than from her slender fingers touching my sleeve.

"And disapproves, I'd guess," I said.

"I cannot come to the abbey as a maiden. Saint Ophir's Rule permits only vowed celibate women or matrons in company with their husbands to stay in their guesthouse. The abbot dares not except me, lest he be called to account. So I take on this loathsome disguise. If the thane grunts and growls a bit for allowing me to play his squire, so be it. I *won't* be left out. And if Stearc and the abbot agree, the opinions of others do not matter."

I dearly wanted to ask, *Why does his opinion make you so angry, if it does not matter?* And, *Is his grunting and growling the only price the thane exacts from you?* But she was cocked like a crossbow again. Best avoid such personal matters until I knew her better.

"As you can imagine, I am afire with curiosity about what I'm doing in the middle of the night with devious monks and mysterious maidens and people who insist I cannot look upon the lands of my home abbey. But Father Abbot bade me trust him, thus I've little hope of soothing *that* curiosity. So, another question . . ."

Abbot Luviar had declared himself neutral in the royal war. I doubted that, preferring to believe in his "deviant" support of a

Pretender. Yet even if the child Pretender was wholly myth and Abbot Luviar but a skillful liar manipulating me in service of one of the three princes, I could not believe his chosen lord to be Osriel the Bastard. More and more I needed to understand what I had seen and felt in that unnatural assault on Gillarine.

"As you serve the Thane of Erasku, perhaps you could tell me something of Prince Osriel and his powers."

She gasped as if I'd planted my fist in her gut. "Holy gods! How—? Why would you speak of him . . . the vile beast . . . the damned soul? Here in the night . . . when we are unprotected."

She dragged me faster. Before I could ask what *protection* we might need, the path kicked steeply upward, as if a mountain had been roaming the fields and decided to plop itself at our feet like a friendly hound. A gust of wind swirled around us, billowing my damp cowl and flapping the hood in my face. Soon rocks gouged my feet. Roots. Evergreens. Moss. Where the devil were we? I could not imagine we'd come so far as the eastern ridge.

I stumbled, flailing in the dark.

"Careful . . ." She caught me before I fell and steadied me. Then she proceeded a bit slower. "I'm sorry. I wasn't thinking. It's just that Lord Stearc is his own man. My lord bows to no master who sets himself up to rival Magrog in his cruelties."

"I didn't mean to give offense. One of the brothers told me that Lord Stearc holds no allegiance to the Bastard Prince. I just assumed, since Erasku is an Evanori hold, you would know the truth of the cursed land and its sovereign. When he slaughtered the Moriangi at Gillarine, I saw such sights . . . faces in the night . . ."

"Even the land cannot compel loyalty to a monster like Osriel of Evanore." She spat as if the very taste of his name poisoned her. "Everything you hear of him is true. He twists magic into depravity, taints all that is good in the world. I'll not speak of him lest my tongue blacken and rot."

We talked no more for a while. She was bound up in anger and fear and purpose. I was trying not to trip and crack my head on the shin-high rocks that seemed to have sprouted from the hillside like hedge beans.

As the path leveled out, and the air spoke of damp pine, a smoky fire, and horses nearby, my guide halted. She released my arm and reached around my neck, tugging my head downward. "Let me get this off of you. We're almost there."

As she untied the cloth binding my eyes, I inhaled deeply, her hair tickling my nose. No, nothing at all like Jullian. "Thank you," I said most sincerely.

"For what? Allowing our thick-skulled bodyguards to suffocate you? Giving you a laugh at my inept playacting?"

"I had a pleasant walk in the nighttime and an interesting conversation. My head remains intact. And I smelled someone who was not Jullian."

The cloth fell away. I blinked. Her hair shone bronze in the starlight. Her pale lips curved upward. And the eyes that gazed up at me . . . great gods . . . so deep . . . reflections of heaven . . .

"Come, Brother Valen." A slight emphasis on the *Brother*.

The blood rushed from my tonsured head, and no logical thinking prevented it going where it had no place. Blessed goddess of love, what had I done to abjure such a gift, even for a season? I touched her cheek . . . cool, silken . . . and felt the heat rush to meet my finger. "Ah, mistress, you are . . ."

Her breath caught and held one moment, suspending my thought. I bent my head toward hers . . .

A distant bell chimed the half hour. She shuddered and jerked her head away. "Time runs, Brother. You must be back in the church by Matins." Her voice was hoarse. She pulled up her hood and strode away. How had I ever thought her male?

The path led between a stony bank and a forested gully, curving sharply upward. Slightly dizzy, aching with a need far deeper than lust—which great vice had most certainly tainted my soul as well—I watched her move as we walked. Had she led me into a blazing forest or a raging torrent, I would have followed.

Chapter 15

The Thane of Erasku awaited us with the impenetrable solemnity of a standing stone, the smoke of the small campfire curling about his solidity like the telltales of midsummer sacrifice. His thick arms enfolded the solid, leathery bulk of my grandfather's book. Behind him, away from the fire, a gaunt, dark-haired man tethered a horse beside two others—Gram, the lord's sickly secretary. No guards, tents, pots, or baggage were in evidence. No Brother Gildas in evidence, either, which surprised me. Likely he was yet suffering the effects of the Harrower lashes. The bruising always got worse before it got better.

"I thought you would never come." The lord was fair bursting with impatience.

"We were delayed at the abbey, sire," said the woman. "My apologies." She bowed to the thane, and then moved around the fire to join him without acknowledging the secretary.

I remained on the near side of the fire.

"I am Stearc of Erasku, Brother," said the thane. "I presume you know that. You've not endured too taxing a walk? My lad guided you properly?"

I bowed. "Indeed he kept me on the straight-and-narrow path, sir. And I managed not to plague him to distraction with my questions, though they are legion. I was too busy trying to determine where on Iero's good earth we were."

"And were you successful?" No excessive pleasantries here. The intensity that had shivered me to my boots at my first glimpse of him had not diminished. He was every quat a warlord; it was more difficult to imagine him a scholar.

"I am turned hind end first, my lord. In a thorough muddle."

"You *look* a thorough mess. Mud, scrapes. Corin, is the monk's courtesy hiding some mistake of yours? If such simple squire's duties are beyond you, I'll put you back to mucking stalls."

Woe to the man-at-arms who mistook *this* commander's orders. Why would such a man ever permit a *woman*—? Ah! A flash of inspiration struck me. A step to the side, where fire and smoke could not obscure my vision, confirmed that the lord's long braid took on a certain hint of bronze in the firelight. And the arch of their noses was identical. *Sire*, indeed.

The woman lifted her chin as if weathering a familiar gale. "I was unable—"

"My Lord Stearc, we suffered an unpleasant mishap tonight," said Gram, as he joined the other two in the firelight. No mistaking his firm, rich tone. Hard to imagine my decisive savior from the hedge garden to be the frail secretary I had glimpsed being helped onto his horse at the guesthouse. "The two guards who accompanied Corin to fetch Brother Valen set upon him as if to make him a prisoner. Something in their orders charged them wrongly. I've restricted them to camp tonight in your name and will investigate thoroughly tomorrow. Surely this good brother's generous and forgiving nature has brought him here after so rude a meeting."

I pressed a knuckle to my mouth to muffle a snicker. Generosity and forgiveness would never have brought me so far. But curiosity . . . Every moment with this odd troop—all of them angles and edges and raw passion—left me more enamored of their puzzle.

"Is Gram's assessment accurate, Brother?" *Lie at your peril*, Stearc's tone warned.

"It is more Abbot Luviar's influence that induced me to come, my lord," I said. "He intimated that your interests were of great importance to Navronne, which, of course, makes them of great importance to any loyal subject. And these two gentlemen were most sincere in their apologies."

He nodded. Not happy, but immediate fury tamed.

The secretary had a convincing way about him with lords, brutes, and novices alike. As if to cinch my good opinion, Gram offered me a skin of ale he'd brought from his saddlebags.

"Your abbot explained what we need from you?" The thane wasted no time.

I was still relishing the robust ale, wondering if Gram would notice if I drained the skin completely. Reluctantly, I replaced its plug, yielded it to the secretary with a grateful nod, and returned my attention to the lord. "Only that you wished me to demonstrate what

I knew of using the Cartamandua maps, which, as I warned Father Abbot, is little enough. And that I am to keep silent about this company and its interests."

"Good. We need not waste time with discussion. Sit here." Stearc pointed to a fat log rolled near the fire and shoved the book into my arms. "Open to the marked page."

I'd not expected to be treated as a schoolboy. Hackles bristling, I sat on the log and opened the book to a place marked with a scrap of leather. The map filled the broad right leaf of the open book. Its features had been meticulously drawn in red-brown ink and delicately washed with green and rose. The emerald-green-and-black border had an exotic pattern to it.

From the time I'd left the cradle, I had been taught the rudiments of maps: the concepts of distance and proportion, the common symbols, the uses of compass rose, cartouche, and key. I had trailed about Palinur in my father's wake, marking straggling lines on tablets of wax, and pens and brushes had been stuffed in my hands as soon as I could hold them. The shapes and colors of maps had pleased my eye, and I liked to imagine that I could envision the grass and rock, cities and rivers they represented. But never was I taken on a journey of discovery beyond Palinur's walls as my brother and sisters were, because I could not master the most mundane of a cartographer's skills. I could neither write the names and distances, nor read nor write a traveler's notes. Maps spoke with shape and color and symbols, but the key to their wonder was written words. Of which I had none.

"What is it you wish to know, my lord?" I asked, suppressing long-festered bitterness. "I never used this particular map when I served Mardane Lavorile."

The thane stood over me like some oak tree out of Ardra's ancient forests, craggy and thick and overpowering. "If you have used other maps from the book, then you should be able to use this one. We have brought you to a place that appears on this map. *Here.*" He placed a thick finger on an angular mark near the center of the map—a hill. "We wish to discover if you can find your way *here.*" His finger skipped to another spot on the far right-hand side of the page.

I gaped up at him. "Now? At night?"

He lifted his finger to reveal the symbol—a tiny waterfall—my grandfather's common designation for a waterfall, pool, small lake, or any other watery landmark. The name lettered beside the feature would clarify which one it was.

"If you can invoke the guide spell properly, you should have no difficulty, day or night. The distance is not far. Your abbot promised you would make the attempt. So do it, or end this before we waste more time." He crossed his great arms and did not blink, his disdain as odorous as a pigsty.

Could I do what he wanted? Without knowing its bounds and scale, I could not judge distance from this map. Nor could I invoke a spell I could not read nor even discover what kind of water I was looking for without deciphering its name. But I had wits and other skills, and the lord's game posed a challenge interesting enough to overcome my distaste for the family business. For, certainly, this whole evening was a game. These fine conspirators had brought me here blindfolded, assuming I could not judge distance or direction from the abbey, believing that the moonless night would obscure paths and landmarks. I'd wager they had staged the attack, just to throw me out of sense before we began. They expected me to fail.

I touched the skin of my throat, abraded by their drawstring bag. They believed me a thick-skulled vagabond pikeman who had fooled a lord by pretending to use his magic book. Perhaps, with a touch of pureblood instinct and magic, I could do exactly that.

Leaning closer to the blazing firelight, I examined the map—a simple fiché—more closely. Somewhere in its tangled mysteries of words, numbers, and symbols, a fiché would reveal place names and distances, compass headings, landmarks, and obstacles to travel. This particular map detailed a countryside of forested hills, a river and its side streams, one town and three villages, a few cart roads and common walking paths. A solicale designated some Karish landmark. Other symbols I was less sure of. Each mark had a neatly lettered name that could place it in this valley or far Estigure for all I knew. Dangling from the solicale was the impish aingerou my grandfather sketched into every map.

So start with the solicale. It must certainly represent the abbey. We had walked briskly for perhaps an hour to get to this starting point. That gave me an idea of distance and proportion. And we had walked northeastward, in the main, more east than north; I closed my eyes and remembered the wind teasing my right cheek and the shaven patch on my head, a frost wind from the south. Only when we started climbing had we changed heading back and forth a number of times, but no matter, for I had but to follow the path back down to the base of the hill. The night was clear, so I could use Escalor, the guide star, to get my bearing. If the direction from the abbey to this hill was northeast, then the watery spot they wished me to find would be southeast, half again the distance we had come—leaving a conveniently short return to the abbey for a novice who must be prostrate on the church floor by Matins.

"So, can you do it?" Stearc had his hands on his hips.

"I believe I can, my lord. I suppose you would not consider telling me what I'm looking for or why this is so important?"

"You've no need to know more." For certain *this* man had not approved me for the task. Well, let him watch.

Making a great show, I placed my finger on the mark for this hill, drew it downward toward the abbey, and then across the page till I touched a walking path of the sort oxherds used to lead their beast carts to market or villeins might tread to field or woodland. Following the lines of path and road as far as they would take me, southerly through the fields and easterly into the hills of the valley wall, my finger traced a reasonably direct route to the water symbol. I noted the orange flame mark of Deunor along the way—likely a roadside shrine to the Lightbringer. Three short lines marked a dolmen, and near it lay two small arcs that told of burial mounds. That should give me enough. I closed the book.

"Will you not speak the invocation, Brother?" Stearc's skepticism rang clearly.

"When I used the book before, I always read the spell words silently, my lord. I thought to follow the same practice here . . ." I paused, all innocence, as if expecting him to contradict me.

He did not, which confirmed another suspicion. He'd had the book from the abbot—which explained its absence from the library—and he had tried to use it himself without success. Why else would he waste this time on an unlikely prospect such as me?

"We should be off then," I said, placing the book into his hands and suppressing a grin, "unless you wish me to go alone and find my way back here to report."

"No need for you to return. We'll know if you succeed." His great jaw snapped shut. I was dismissed.

I bowed. "My lord. Gentlemen."

As I walked down the path the woman and I had ascended, the three of them stood beside their fire, watching me. I assumed they would follow or ride out to catch me near the end. Or perhaps the thane had his own pureblood or a mage to observe me from a distance or who had set some magical beacon to announce my success. As to what waited at the end, a place no ordinary map could take them, my curiosity outweighed my caution. The abbot did not want me dead.

At the bottom of the hill I sought southeast, keeping the guide star on my left, and holding a balance between winter sunrise and the mountains of Evanore to the south. I knelt as if to relace my sandal. Touching fingertips to the earth, I spilled but a fragment of magic into the simple seeking, hunting a route to a sheep path and a roadside shrine dedicated to Deunor Lightbringer. A spare image resolved in my head, a simple pattern laid upon the landscape.

Once sure of my course, I set out across the open country. Even if someone was watching me, I doubted they could hear, so I sang the fifty verses of "The Doxy and the Bandit" as I walked, imagining clasping Corin's slender waist as I spun her dizzy. Earth's mother, what was her true name? Why hadn't I asked?

Deunor's shrine was little more than a chipped and gouged body, missing one arm, its head, and privy parts. The stones of the altar had been carted away, and the astelas vines that twined every shrine of the elder gods had been dug up. Country folk thought boiled astelas roots made a man virile. I'd no need for that unless this pestilential drought went on too long and my body forgot its dearest pleasures. Near three months had gone since I'd lain with a woman, and here the night air felt like velvet on my skin. Another brief seeking at the split of a path and I angled northerly again toward the dolmen and burial mounds.

The table stones and barrows were only dark outlines against the stars to the north. And just beyond them, the track branched three ways instead of the two marked on the map—assuming I had come to the right place so far. Instinct sent me down the southernmost, the oldest branch, judging by the myriad layers of feet that had trod there. As the map had suggested, the path petered out in the slopes of patchy grass and rock at the base of the craggy ridge east of the valley.

Now came the most difficult part—to find the water source in these trackless hills. A hint as to its nature would have been useful. With no more paths made magic by centuries of feet, and no sure destination, this seeking would require more power.

I scanned the horizon in a full circle. As far as starlight and good eyesight could tell me, no one watched. Kneeling on the rough ground, I closed my eyes and laid my palms on the earth. The wind blustered over and around me, scouring away the barriers of distraction and wariness, allowing my magic to flow freely. *Where is it?*

Images of pools and wells and bubbling springs passed through my mind, but none held for that one moment that proved it true. *A little more . . .*

I laid my forehead on the earth and released another fragment of power, expecting the pattern to resolve as it had earlier. My instincts would tell me the way. But before I knew it, I had pushed up my sleeves, hiked up my gown, and lay prostrate as I had been in the church a few hours earlier, bared arms spread. Instead of masonry and gilding, the dome of stars rose above my head, and beneath me lay the cool damp earth.

As I inhaled the scent of dirt and rotting grass, the boundaries of stars and flesh and earth dissolved. Worms burrowed beneath me, and ground beetles ticked their wings in their holes. A hare breathed anxiously in its den. Clouds drifted across the patterned stars above me, tickling the wool layers on my back. Far below, water trickled . . . deep . . .

Strip off these prisoning garments . . . touch skin to earth and air . . . feel the night's embrace . . . reach through the welcoming earth to find the water . . . Against the urgency of these demands—spoken in the language of mind and flesh and bone—only some remnant thread of present sense kept me clothed. But the rest . . .

Reach . . . feel . . . embrace. Open your mouth . . . taste stone and stars . . . inhale the night . . . listen . . . I plunged my hand deep . . . felt the gritty loam give way . . . dry sand and pebbles graze my knuckles . . . until I touched the sweeter moisture . . . the secret places . . . the pulsing flow of life that told of moving water, deeper yet.

A bell pealed in the distance—a sonorous touch of bronze borne on the breeze. I jerked my head off the ground and rose up on my elbows. What had happened here? My heart raced like a fox at the hunt. I shook my head. Sat back on my heels and examined one bare arm to assure myself that it was not covered with dirt or crawling with beetles and worms from plunging it through the earth. Felt a rush of heat across my skin as I realized I was more than halfway roused in altogether unlikely ways, as had happened on the journey back from Elanus. Fires of heaven . . . chastity was making a madman of me.

I forced my thoughts back to business. The bell signaled another hour gone. How many since day's end? I needed to head northeasterly again, for the water that trickled under this spot fed the abbey spring and its source lay in the ridge ahead of me. Though no overlaid image dwelt in the forefront of my mind, my body understood perfectly which way to go now, in the same way my blood knew which direction to flow in my veins. I scrambled to my feet, hurried across the barren field, and pretended I was not shaking.

The upward path was far too steep for this late of an evening. After so many days of idleness in the abbey, my body protested at the climb. My route had taken me up a treeless jumble of granite that scarred the eastern wall of the valley, a desolate crotch in the otherwise verdant ridge. No direct path. No easy ascent. I scrambled between boulders and across tilted slabs, cursing gowns and cowls and sandals. My sore feet kept skidding out from under me. Every slip meant whacked knees or elbows, abrading the skin through the woolen layers of hose and gown.

A glance over my shoulder for the tenth time in an hour and I yet spied no one following. I climbed.

At least another hour had passed, which meant perhaps one more remained until the brothers filed back into the church for Matins. I could just imagine Prior Nemesio's glee at discovering a novice so ill-behaved as to abandon a penance. Poor Brother Sebastian; my mentor would be beside himself. And even if I broke my word and told them of the evening's events, I would never be able to explain why I had taken on such a fool's errand when the simple truth could have stopped it. The puzzle was just such an intriguing exercise, and Lord Stearc had been so sure I couldn't solve it.

At the top of yet another slab, the rocks formed a wide shelf, backed up to a higher cliff. Behind me the valley of Gillarine, shaped by the sinuous hints of silver that were the looping river, stretched southward toward the mountains of Evanore and northward toward the heart of Ardra, Morian, and the distant sea. The abbey church spires rose out of the gently folded land to the southwest.

I was nearing the end of this journey. Instinct said to go south along the shelf rock and then straight east . . . which would mean directly into the cliff. I moved slowly, examining the rugged wall as I went, searching for cracks or splits or caves.

A short distance away an oddly shaped shadow detached itself from the wall. "Iero's grace, Brother Valen, how was your evening's walk? Not too troubling, I hope, despite its unsettling beginning?"

Fear burgeoned and stilled quickly. No matter that the only light was the dome of stars. I could mistake neither the pale gleam of hairless scalp nor the dark brow line nor the cool presence, spiced and warmed by good humor.

"Brother Gildas, the spider who sits in the web of all Gillarine's mysteries. Of course, you would be here." Would I ever learn to think? Of course, they'd have someone waiting at the end. They were testing me.

"I knew you would enjoy this puzzle," he said cheerfully, "being a man of puzzles as you are."

"You're all right . . . healing?" Only days had passed since his encounter with Sila Diaglou's whip.

"Thanks to you, I live. My scabs and bruises do but remind me—deservedly so—of my shame at falling victim so easily. So, can you finish this?"

I stepped toward him deliberately, continuing my examination of the wall. "Here." A darker line creased the shadowed cliff halfway between us, a seam in the rock wider than first glance showed, a high-walled passage that sliced directly into the cliff.

I led, forcing myself to keep breathing until both the slotlike passage and my search ended. The cliff walls opened into a small grotto—a well of starlight, the circle of sky above it reflected perfectly in a glass-still pool, incised in stone.

As I paused in the doorway where the walls of the notch flared into the encircling stone, a movement atop the cliffs snared my gaze. Something bright. Something blue. But staring until my eyes felt raw revealed naught but stars. Perhaps one had slipped from its place and streaked toward the earth. A warning of evil times, diviners said.

Brother Gildas had joined me and stood at my shoulder. "Powers of night, you've done it," he said softly. Wondering. "Ah, Valen, there is more to you than people think."

He stepped past me and spun in place, scanning walls and cliff tops before walking to the rim of the pool. Even as he knelt and reached out to touch the water, I wanted him to stop. No sensible argument came to my lips, only that this was no common pool to be used in common ways. Something slept here. Power? Spirit? The generous earth itself? "Brother, wait—"

Too late. The rippling rings moved outward, marring its perfection. Gildas downed the water from his cupped hands and looked up at me, smiling. "Come, have a drink. You've earned it."

Foolish. Nothing had happened. Clearly *he* sensed nothing out of the ordinary.

"I don't drink water," I said, trying to keep my voice even. He'd think me mad if I told what I felt here. "Don't trust it. And unless you can dispense me from my penance, I must get back to the church."

In fact, I could not have stepped within that grot were he fallen in the pool and drowning. Smell, taste, hearing, sight . . . my senses, of a sudden, quivered on the brink of explosion. My heart swelled with songs just beyond hearing, with words beyond knowing, with the desolation of a homely street where every door is locked to you or of winter sunset in the wild, when no hearth, no word, no welcome awaits. One step past the doorway and surely I would be flat on the granite, my skull cracked, my heart riven, as if I'd walked into the cloister garth fifty times over. Yet the sorrow that permeated these stones surpassed what a murdered youth of sixteen years could possibly know. This sleeper was not Brother Horach.

Gildas sighed and wiped his hand on his cowl. "I suppose you're right. We've a distance to go yet before we can each put our secrets to rest. But you ought to come see the water. It's so deep. So lovely. So pure."

I dragged my gaze from the pool, shivering as if I'd plunged my whole body into its frigid depths. Oh, yes, I knew that water was cold. I did not have to see the frost crystals that rimed the pool's edge to know. So little sunlight here. The encircling walls so like a prison cell.

"Are you well, Valen?"

Pressing my back and the back of my head against the wall of the passage, I closed my eyes. As if all at once, the activity of the night took its toll: scrapes and bruises, blistered feet, overstretched shoulders. The few quellae back to Gillarine might have been the road to heaven that practors and hierarchs told us was nigh impossible. And something else . . . deep inside my gut . . . a knot of fire. Blessed Deunor, no! With all that had happened . . . this new life . . . I'd scarce given it a thought. A night bird's screech near ripped my ears. "Must get back," I said. "The time . . ."

I fled, scrabbling back down the ridge, bumping, sliding, scraping on the rocks. More was wrong than mystic pools and overzealous bodyguards and wild chases through the night. The scalding in my gut did not cool. How long had it been? Five days since my investiture. Twelve . . . thirteen before that to Black Night, and one more . . . holy gods, nineteen days . . . and the last interval had been twenty-one.

The trek back to the abbey devolved into nightmare, my need quickly overshadowing the mysteries of the night. The garden maze, the green pouch tucked away under the rocks, the fragrant contents . . . *Great Iero, let no one have found it. Let the Matins bell not ring until I am whole again.* I had no idea how I was to manage it, but my growing frenzy to have the blood-spelled nivat in my hand . . . on my tongue . . . in my veins . . . permitted no logic or forethought.

Though as fit as any of the younger monks, Gildas could scarce keep up with me. "What's wrong, Brother? One would think the Adversary dogged your back. Would we all had such long legs as yours to devour a quellé so swiftly."

"I've been too long distracted from my prayers," I said. "And I'd rather not have occasion to visit the prior's prison cell. Though Father

Abbot sent me on this mad venture, I've seen enough to know he'll not shield me from punishment."

I could not speak after that. My cramping legs and back threatened to seize if I slowed. By the time we reached the footbridge and the abbey wall, the threads of fire encompassed every part and portion of my body. The starlight scalded my eyes. I drew my cloak across my face, for the wind felt like a flayer's knife.

Brother Gildas unlatched the iron herdsman's gate, but laid a hand on my arm before I could rush through. It was all I could do not to cry out, for his touch felt like a gatzé's fiery kiss even through the woolen layers. "He'll not punish you, Valen. Tonight's exercise was of great importance—Iero's work. You performed better than any of us could hope. You *will* reap answers to the questions that tease you."

Sadly, his concerned kindness could not soothe me. "I must . . . clean myself . . . before going to the church. Excuse me, Brother." The mere effort of speaking caused spasms in my face and neck. I pulled away and ran across the field, past the church, and into the garden.

Where . . . where . . . ? Beside the statue of Karus as the Shepherd . . . Divine Karus . . . good Iero . . . Kemen, Lord of Sky and Storm, help me. I dropped to my knees and scrabbled in the pile of rocks beside the statue's base, frantic when I found only dirt. I had used my bent to create a void hole to hide my contraband packet here on the night I'd come from Elanus. Had I forgotten so much of magic that I had displaced or vanished them by mistake? I dug deeper until my fingers felt the cloth roll. Using my shoulder to wipe the sweat from my eyes, I rummaged inside the packet and grasped the little bag. I almost wept in thanksgiving.

I shoved dirt and rocks into some semblance of their usual aspect, tucked the green bag into my trews, and raced through the gardens past the lay brothers' reach. Though desperate, I dared not cross the cloister garth, but rather sped down the west cloister and around the south in front of the kitchen and refectory, cursing the waning hour. At every moment I expected to hear the bells.

The trough ran around three sides of the lavatorium, angled slightly so the water would flow left to right. Each of the six shallow bays on each wall formed a semicircular shelf behind the trough, and from the center of each bay protruded a lead conduit that spilled water into the trough. I chose the bay nearest the cloister to take advantage of what little light the night provided. I removed my cowl and laid it on the shelf, as if preparing to clean it. Then I fumbled the green pouch out from under my gown and spilled half my remaining nivat onto the wide outer lip of the trough.

Everything took too long. The seeds were old and tough; I chipped another shard from my precious mirror fragment, using it to crush them on the stone. My fingers were cold and clumsy. I dropped the needle and had to scrabble on the stone floor to find it. It was near impossible to grasp the linen thread, and when at last the mixture of blood and nivat sizzled, I had to fumble with the glass to find an angle where I could see the vapors.

As soon as I released magic into the brew, I knew I hadn't enough. Holy gods, what a fool I'd been. To spend my magic so recklessly on Luviar's game. To lose count of the days. Bent over the trough to hold the mirror and the thread steady, my back, leg, and shoulders cramping until I was near weeping, I squeezed the last magic from my body and let it flow down the linen thread. And still the vapors would not cease their rising and signal the doulon ready.

As if taking voice from my fears, the bell pealed. I held my breath with the first tone, yet my weariness told the lateness of the hour. The next strike came and the next, until the ten measured strikes that signaled the call to services had been completed. The noise threatened to burst my ears, as if I stood in the bell chamber itself. Then rang the triple change, double, and triple that announced the beginning of a new day. The yawning monks would be donning gowns and cowls and sandals and starting their procession through the passage to the nightstair. And still the pungent vapors rose from the boiling nivat. The finished paste should hold no scent.

In the dorter passage above my head, the monks began to sing, tugging at my spirit with their music. *Their* music. Not mine.

I could wait no longer. I scooped the red-black droplets onto my tongue. As I braced my hands on the trough, my head dropped to hang between my shoulders. The first shuddering pain rolled through me . . .

Not enough. Not enough. Sobbing, I slammed my elbow into the stone trough, hoping more pain might jolt the spell into completion. Nothing. Again. Again . . .

As in famine times, when the crust of bread or sip of ale blunts the most acute hunger, but leaves the want and sickness, such was the incomplete doulon. The fire cooled; the cramps eased; the storm of my senses quieted. But I gained no release. No rapture. Every muscle and sinew ached. My veins felt clogged with clay. Only a few days—a fortnight at most—and I would have to do this all again, spend my reserve of nivat because I'd been shamed at my ignorance and determined to prove that I, the most useless of men, could accomplish what some proud lord could not. Now I would pay.

Exhausted and sick, I splashed the cold water onto my face and head, scrubbed at my hands and arms. *Hurry!* I packed away the needle, the mirror, and linen thread and tied the bag's drawstring to the waist string of my trews. Then I threw on my cowl and ran for the church, brushing at the caked mud and dirt as I ran. As the procession descended the nightstair and entered the church, filling the vaults with songs of the Creator's glory, I flew down the aisle and through the choir screen, and threw myself prostrate on the cold marble. Brother Victor had not moved.

Chapter 16

A storm rolled through the valley sometime between Lauds and Prime, bringing sleet and bitter cold—a miserable morning, highly appropriate for a day that had begun so wretchedly and got only worse. A few hours' sleep had healed my bruises and blisters and soothed my torn and battered elbow, but done nothing for the doulon sickness. Plagued by both the indolence the spell always caused and the blood fever it had only dulled, I fell asleep in choir during both morning Hours.

Brother Sebastian pulled me aside after Prime to scold me for inattention, expressing shock at my bedraggled clothes. He dragged me to the lavatorium to clean them as best I could, and then sentenced me to kneel in the center aisle of the dorter clad only in shirt and trews. I was to pray and contemplate Iero's gift of clothing while the rest of the brothers ate their bread and cheese and attended morning services. By the time he permitted me to don my damp gown and cowl for chapter, my blood felt like slush.

Matters worsened. Once my mentor had chastised me in front of the entire brotherhood, Prior Nemesio offered his own scathing reprimand and decided that my punishment should continue until the day's end bell. No church services. No meals. No work or study. No gown or cowl. That this also meant no testing on the great virtues and no Compline reading was scarcely a comfort.

A somber Abbot Luviar approved the sentence. Brother Gildas raised his brows and shrugged ever so slightly. Jullian, sitting on his low stool by the door, would not look at me. I longed to strangle them all, though, in truth, anger was as difficult to muster as anything else.

The hours in the dorter passed in frigid misery. I tried to think, to make some sense of my experiences of the previous day, to sing under my breath, to plan where I would go when spring released me from this tomb. Sleep was impossible, but neither would my blood run anywhere useful like my head or my knees. So much for trust. Perhaps Luviar wanted me dead of frostbite so I could not betray his friends.

How stupid could a man get when his balls ruled his head? Why hadn't I just grabbed the book when it was in my hands and set out for Elanus? But instead I'd had to strut my manhood like a gamecock.

I shifted my knees, wincing with the ache. *Damnable baldpates.* Boreas had been right about them. *Boreas . . . by the dark spirits . . .*

Once the gruesome image of his end took hold of my head, I could not shake it. What kind of woman could do such work? What kind of perverse soul could name it holy? As the memory churned inside my head alongside the night's mad adventure and the bizarre sensations I had experienced at the pool, I could not but recall Brother Horach's equally savage murder. Could a Harrower have decided that innocents should die as well as sinners and sneaked into the abbey to work their deviltry? With orange-heads roaming the neighborhood, it could happen again.

Brother Sebastian visited me at least once an hour to counsel and preach. On the next occasion, I interrupted a sermon on rooting out the vice of carelessness and tried to explain about Boreas and Harrower rites and Brother Horach. I had scarce begun when he stopped me, insisting I must refrain from worldly thoughts for the duration of my penance. As he left me alone again, I damned him and the rest of his fraternity to their fate.

By the time the bells rang Vespers, wind raked and rattled the dorter shutters and raced through the long room. Three more hours. I feared I would be unable to move when day's end came, either from hunger or freezing. On his last visit Brother Sebastian had left a rushlight to hold off the dark. With aching knees and back, and incipient chilblains, I had no gratitude in me.

A quiet rustling at my back did not even prompt me to turn around. Probably Brother Sebastian again to tell me how sorry he was that I needed this kind of lesson. But to my surprise a mug appeared in front of my face, wreathed in steam and cupped in the small dry hand of Brother Victor. "Quickly, Brother Valen, you are wanted elsewhere for a little while."

I would like to have said that, although hell would be a pleasant change, I would prefer to freeze than dance to his abbot's command, but my lips were so numb I was saved from such an indiscretion.

My trembling hands wrapped around the deliciously warm cup, and I drained the thing without taking a breath. "I don't think I can do anything quickly, Brother Chancellor."

He offered me the pile of black wool he carried over one arm. "I would suggest you try. We've only until the end of Vespers."

The still-damp wool felt marvelous. And blessed hose to cover my legs. My numb fingers fumbled with ties and laces. Soon I was following Brother Victor down the passage, shaking out my legs to get the blood flowing.

Our sandals echoed in the deserted library. I could not imagine why we'd come. "Wait here," said Brother Victor, and he disappeared into the corner beyond the last book press. The wind drove sleet against the window mullions. Ardran autumn usually waxed dry and golden. Landlords and villeins alike would be frantic to gather in what crops had ripened in this perverse season. Perhaps the bowl of the sky had slipped farther out of place.

A brief explosion of yellow light, brighter than ten lamps together, assaulted my eyes. A hiss and a snap, and the chancellor stepped into view again, little more than a shadow in my flash blindness. He beckoned me to join him. In the corner where I had ever seen blank walls—the same corner where Abbot Luviar had appeared so suddenly on my first visit—a doorway now opened onto a descending stair. From a hook on the wall, just inside it, the chancellor took a burning lamp. Or rather the implement he held appeared to be a lamp, and it appeared to be burning, though only cream-colored light, no flame, shone through its clear panes. *Blessed saints and angels . . .* Sorcery. In a house where magic working was forbidden. My feet dragged.

"Come on," said the chancellor as I hesitated, beset by visions of dungeons and flaming depths.

"This isn't where the hierarch sent you? To be punished?"

He puzzled for a moment. "Oh. The prison cell? Certainly not. Why would I take you there?"

"To improve my character?" I mumbled.

He didn't smile.

We descended two long flights of steps, which by my reckoning left us deep in the earth under the scriptorium. My throat tightened. I reminded myself of Brother Victor's *only until the end of Vespers* to convince myself that I could breathe in such a confined space. So deep.

Brother Victor halted when we reached a wide door at the bottom of the steps. Intelligent, inscrutable, he peered up at my face.

"Father Abbot says he trusts you. That must certainly be true, as he commanded me to show you this without informing others of our party who have less confidence in your usefulness and character. I take no sides in that dispute as I've so little personal experience of you. I obey my abbot. But I'll warn you that no one will find the doorway or this stair were you to tell of them."

"I understand." Perhaps the opening was hidden by an illusion spell, but I'd wager that an ax applied to the library wall would find the stair.

He pushed open the door and held it to let me enter.

"Blessed saints and angels!" My feet propelled me to the center of a chamber half the size of the church. There I spun like the axis of a wheel, my neck craned so I could view the dome of light above my head. Great ribbed arches of gray stone supported curved wedges of colored mosaic—brilliant, though, as if the bits were glass. Yet I had never seen glass laid in such a shape. And though I stood deep below the earth, the mosaic of light shone as bright as if the sun lay tucked between the dome and the scriptorium floor above it, casting a gentle clarity on the marvels that lay below. For the dome was but the magical capstone on more earthly wonders.

Books, first. The walls of the rectangular chamber, three or four times my height, were lined with shelves, not full, but holding more books and scrolls than I would have believed existed in all the world. Yet this library held much more than books. Ranks of tall cabinets lined the floor with only narrow aisles between. These cabinets, faced with grillwork doors very like the cupboards in the library, held tools—here the needles, spools, thimble, and scissors of a seamstress, there the common hammers, chisels, augers, and gouges of a stonemason. An entire cabinet was filled with a carpenter's tools, another with a physician's instruments. None of the individual items seemed extraordinary. Most appeared well used, though clean or oiled and generally well cared for.

I moved faster through the array, fascinated more by the breadth of the collection than the items themselves. Two doorways opened off the great chamber, one a mere closet, lit by the spilled light of the glass dome. A rope bed, piled with a rolled palliasse and folded blankets, and an old writing desk had been shoved up against stacked barrels and crates.

But the other, much wider doorway opened into a second domed chamber as large and beautiful as the first. By this time I was scarcely surprised to see a plow, a wheel and axle from a cart, millstones, a lathe, a loom, a potter's wheel, and other, larger artifacts standing in neat rows on the floor. On the shelves that lined the walls from floor to ceiling, sat row after row of labeled sacks, earthenware pots, and glass jars. What would they hold? Food? Herbs? Potions?

No . . . the tools were for building and making and creating. The books would be for knowledge and understanding. For remembering. For beginning. The pots would hold seeds.

I turned back. From across the chamber by the outer door, Brother Victor watched with sober interest, his hands loosely folded at his waist.

Some of the pieces came together then. Luviar's grand mosaic of war and famine and storm. The books on glassmaking, and drawings of millworks, and records of vineyards that no longer produced grapes. Were cuttings of grapevines preserved in these bags or jars? Surely those who could create domes of light and a door that opened with magic so powerful it stood my hair on end could preserve a living vine. *Teneamus*—we preserve. For the dark times. For the long night.

I gazed up at the shining dome, majestic in its beauty and magic. A promise of hope. "You call this the lighthouse," I said.

The chancellor dipped his head in acknowledgment.

What was happening to the world? How did they know? What was the connection with my book of maps? I could not even choose where to begin.

"Come. Vespers will be ending soon."

"But I've so much to ask."

"In time, Brother Novice. Should you prove faithful, you'll be told all. For now, I pray you be worthy of Father Abbot's trust."

"Of course. Certainly. I won't say anything. Not to a soul." Who would believe me?

Before I knew it, I was kneeling in the dorter again, shivering in shirt and trews. Save for the taste of leek broth in my mouth and the vision of light in my head, I might have thought the grand library a dream brought on by hunger and cold and a broken doulon. Nothing in my experience or imagination could have conjured such a place.

I dismissed my pique at the monks' annoying discipline and spent the next two hours formulating questions to ask were I given the opportunity. I speculated on how the magic of the lighthouse was done and who in this place might have done it—the mysterious pureblood monk?—and I considered what I would have chosen to preserve were I stocking a magical lighthouse to sustain me beyond the end of the world.

I was almost sorry when the day's end bell rang and good Brother

Sebastian laid a blessing of forgiveness on my head and a blanket on my shoulders. Almost. As I hobbled off to bed, I thought my knees might gleam blue and purple in the dark—as tales described the enchanted sigils of the Danae when they walked the wild places of the world.

"All right, it was *Father Abbot's* little surprise got me near dead from suffocation, not yours. But my skull will surely crack if you don't relieve some of my curiosity."

Jullian and I had met in the hedge garden after supper on the day following my long punishment. Though the maze still had me twitching at every noise, expecting grain sacks to be dropped on my head, it was the only place we could talk for any length of time. My Compline reading had been reset for this night, and gods bless the boy forever, he had fulfilled his promise to read it to me. Now, as we lingered in the gathering dark, I was trying to nudge the boy into some further revelation of Luviar's conspiracy without breaking my promise. My immortal soul could not afford the burden of an abbot's wrath. Sadly, I was having no luck at all.

"I'm sworn, Brother. Please, don't ask me. I can say only that the abbey is neutral ground."

So earnest in his honor. If he knew that I'd spent the time before his arrival stuffing my last supply of nivat into the parcel under Karus's statue, he would run from me like one of these plaguey rabbits. Had these conspirators stored nivat in their lighthouse? The sudden thought cheered me past the point of sense. If I could only ensure a supply, I could stop thinking about this damnable curse altogether. I'd just have to discover how to get into the place.

"Tell me more of Palinur," said Jullian, reverting to his favorite topic of conversation. "I can't imagine such a grand city. Are there truly statues of every one of the Hundred Heroes set before the king's palace? Though I know Grossartius is but legend, because Iero sends our souls to heaven or hell and not back to mortal bodies, he is my favorite of the Hundred. Is he quite large and well muscled? I've always imagined him bigger than Brother Robierre and taller even than you."

A west wind had brushed away the previous day's storm and left the evening astonishingly pleasant. Time yet remained before Compline, and I wasn't ready to go indoors.

"I'd much rather talk of why, in all that's holy, this flock of mad monks and gruff lords shares their secrets with a talkative boy of twelve-almost-thirteen." While babbling freely of his studies and abbey life, the stubborn little donkey would speak nothing of his raising beyond what he'd told me in the library. "It speaks highly of your character. And, of course, Brother Sebastian says you are the brightest scholar ever to study here. You've much to be proud of—"

"You've heard it wrong! I'm not half the scholar Brother Gildas is. And Gerard is far more holy, for I'm so easily distracted when I think of what I've read and the adventure tales you've told us. I *do* talk too much, and I'm wholly untrustworthy, for I've told you more than I should already. The moment I'm sixteen, I'm going to take a vow of silence!"

So soon after our study of the great vices, I should have known better than to use the word *proud*. Truly, if he were Eodward's child, I didn't think he knew it.

I ceased probing and soothed his worries about excess pride and boyish sins with a lurid saga about Grossartius the Revenant's return from the dead to serve King Caedmon. The bells began to strike. He jumped up as if a gatzé's tail poked him from underneath. "We need to go."

I sighed and unfolded myself from the bench. "Indeed. Brother Sebastian will have my skin if I'm late. My knees won't survive more penance."

The boy giggled. "I heard you made a sight, kneeling there in just shirt and trews all day. Brother Jerome said you were as blue as a jay and looked as if you might eat your sandals."

I stuck my foot and its unchewed sandal out before us. "Thanks to holy Iero, no need for that."

My Compline reading went very well, though I realized afterward that I had opened the page for two days previous—the page with the geese—and not the one I was reciting. Fortunately no one looked over my shoulder. Several of the brothers offered congratulations and kind words as we left the church. Brother Gildas stood last in the short line.

"You did very well for your first service reading," he said, as we strolled companionably through the upper passage toward the dorter, anticipating the day's end bell. "A bit stiff, perhaps, but practice should improve you. You are a man of many talents, Valen."

Why did he keep saying that? It bothered me that he might be one of those who had less confidence in my "usefulness and character," as Brother Victor had put it.

"So are you going to tell me what I was punished for?" I said softly enough that no one else could possibly hear. "My knees would very much like to know."

"Soiling your clothes? Sleeping at services?" The good brother grinned cheerfully.

Such a friend could drive a saint to drink. "The grain sack was *your* idea, wasn't it? To get me thoroughly muddled before your test."

"I'm truly sorry for that," he murmured, clasping his hands piously at his breast, looking straight ahead, and picking up the pace. "I had no idea it would distress you so."

"Thus you owe me an apology—a favor." I ducked my head lower and scarcely moved my lips. "And you know what I want: What does that puddle in the hills have to do with preserving knowledge and Evanori warlords and three—or is it *four*—royal princelings?"

"We cannot discuss such things here. Father Abbot warned you. I understand you've been given some *enlightenment*." His mouth shaped the beginnings of a smile.

I wanted to kick him.

"Father Prior will surely assign you more readings after tonight, Brother Valen." He spoke more boldly as we neared the library door. "As you succeed in your assigned tasks, you earn more trust . . . and more tasks. As it happens, Brother Chancellor has received word of a book of Aurellian poetry that might be available to borrow from a lord down near Caedmon's Bridge. Brother Adolfus is to travel there tomorrow. Father Abbot says that, as a man so recently of the world, you might be of use in the negotiation."

Oh, no. No more traveling with the abbot's friends. No more of this conspiracy business. I hated being their ignorant pawn.

"As much as I appreciate our brothers' *trust*, the god teaches me constantly of humility," I said. "I've never been particularly successful at any single occupation, perhaps because my true calling is this quiet, retiring monastery life of simple prayer and simple service. I intend to devote my best efforts to making myself worthy of that calling, avoiding all things grand or mysterious . . . or dangerous . . . or *deviant*. Besides, my leg would never bear me so far."

Surely it would be better to live out the season quietly and escape with my skin intact to enjoy what I could of the world before it ended. The doulon had me in its stranglehold, and were I ever so blessed as to survive its shedding, my diseased senses and explosive restlessness would leave me as mad as my grandfather. Not even such a wonder as the lighthouse would tempt me to use the bent for aught but my own need. Look where such had got me.

Gildas laughed in that way he had, encompassing his entire being. Then he laid an arm around my shoulder and pulled me close, heads together. "Grand and mysterious events have a way of catching up to us even when we have no such course in mind. Someday I will share my own story with you. Good night, Brother. Safe journey."

He was still chuckling as he disappeared through the library door. I walked on toward the dorter, grumbling under my breath, yet unable to be truly angry with him. If only I had displayed my ignorance about the book. One would think I would have outgrown pride after so many years of stumbling so ineptly about the world. Seven-and-twenty years and I'd shed not a single one of the great vices.

The infirmarian had assured Father Abbot that exercise would be good for my healing thigh, thus Brother Adolfus and I were dispatched on our errand as the bells rang for Prime. The west wind's respite had been too brief. Purple-gray clouds hung low over the mountains, threatening a miserable day.

The road cut south through the abbey grain fields, where a few lay brothers were reaping barley that stood astonishingly undamaged despite the storm. Abbot Luviar had charged Brother Adolfus to summon the local villagers along our way. Though bound in service to the abbey, they had not yet come to aid the harvest.

The toad-faced Adolfus made it clear from the beginning that he would likely not speak to me beyond our business. "Journeys are excellent occasions for contemplation of our life's road through the vales of doubt, the fens of sin, and the occasional mountain peak of divine inspiration. Silence will be our guidepost."

As this was the lengthiest statement I had ever heard from the man, I'd borne no great expectation of conversation. But I had hoped he might be one of the "cabal," as Jullian referred to the abbot's little group of conspirators, and thus be willing to enlighten me on our mission. I had no illusion that we were truly off to negotiate use of a poetry book.

Drawing up my hood and tucking my hands up my sleeves against the cold, I wondered how I might divert my "life's road" to some nearby town where there might be a seedsman or herbary. To that end I had brought along the gold button and silver spoon. Though I'd likely not get the trinkets' full worth, I might get enough to buy nivat for a doulon or two. Only enough seeds for one use remained in my pouch, and possessing even a small supplement might soothe this anxiety that dogged me. The disease lurked in my bone and sinews alongside the craving for its remedy, both waiting to take fire.

Shrines dotted the roadside. A patch of wildflowers drooped beside a wooden representation of Karus. Rotting travelers' staves had been stuck in the ground about a painted statue of Saint Gillare.

An older stone figure, half-way devoured by orange and red lichen, represented Erdru bearing his uplifted platter of grapes. A statue of Arrosa, her hand about a naked mortal's member, had toppled over, leaving her poor lover separated from his better parts.

Beyond Gillarine's fields and pastures, the landscape changed abruptly to rolling meadows of yellowed grass and ankle-high briar tangles, dotted with stands of scrawny trees. In one of these meadows, half a quellé past the abbey's boundary fence, stood a ring of aspen trees. Legends called such rings holy to the Danae, who were said to especially love to dance there in autumn when the leaves turned gold. This dreary, precipitous autumn had tainted the leaves black, and they'd fallen before ever they were gold. What if they never gleamed gold again?

Fool, I thought, shoving away the dismal speculation. *These monks will have you believing their end-times nonsense.* Yet such belief as could create the marvelous lighthouse could not be so easily dismissed. The unseasonable cold and gloom seeped into my every pore.

Five quellae past the aspen grove, the cart track rose steeply for a short way, leveled out and traversed a meadow, then rose again, the terrain like a series of giant's steps toward the southern mountains. The river was no longer a lazy looping band of silver, but a younger stream that plunged from the mountains and raced through a gorge off to our left. To our right a gray-green forest of spruce and silver birches mantled the rising hills, occasionally dipping its folds into the sweeping meadows.

We met neither seedsmen nor herb sellers nor indeed any people at all along the way. The first village we came to was well overgrown, red plague circles fading on its crumbling houses. We did not dawdle there. A second settlement showed signs of more recent disaster—tools and carts bearing but early signs of rust, painted sigils of ward and welcome still bright on the lintels. But a heap of decaying sheep fouled the nearby pastureland, and perhaps other creatures lay unburied, as well. We covered our noses with our cowls and hurried past.

As soon as we could breathe, a shocked Brother Adolfus fell to his knees and prayed for the missing villagers of Acceri, who usually worked Gillarine's planting and harvest. Evidently the abbey had received no word of their distress.

He should have waited a quellé more for his prayers. A third village, Vinera, had burned mere days ago. The sharp wind off the mountains shifted a blackened shutter and ruffled a length of frayed, muddy cloth tangled in a smashed loom. No corpses were visible, but I could see what had happened. One of the stone hovels had been made into a charnel furnace.

"Who could commit such sin?" Brother Adolfus's voice shook, as I showed him how the doors and windows had been blocked to prevent escape.

"Harrowers," I said, snatching the fluttering orange rag from a charred post and grinding it under my foot. "They take the folk who'll agree to follow them and send back raiders to slaughter the rest."

We did not linger. Though I pulled my hood lower, so that I could see nothing but the muddy ruts and Brother Adolfus's hem, the odor of burning lingered in my nostrils. Perhaps the world had already ended.

By late morning, we had completely lost sight of the river as we climbed a long series of switchbacks. Horses had traveled this road in the past day. A great rushing noise as of wind or water grew louder as we pushed on.

No gentle meadow awaited us beyond the crest of the climb, but a broad, treeless hillside, creased with a succession of low scarps. Beyond these alternating strips of vertical rock and grassy terraces, the land broke sharply upward into a formidable cap of barren rock. A blocklike fortress perched atop the crags, the grim ramparts more a part of the rock than distinct from it.

The road wound back and forth in deep bends to circumvent the scarps and traverse the broad terraces. Midway across the expanse, a waist-high cairn marked a branching of the track. The left fork arrowed across the slope toward the river gorge. The right snaked westward for half a quellé before beginning the ascent of the breathtakingly steep shelf road to the fortress.

"These mountain lords all think they are eagles," said Brother Adolfus, gawking at the forbidding road we'd yet to climb.

As we slogged toward the cairn, backs bent and heads ducked into the wind that flapped our cowls and gowns, a simple arch of dressed stone came into view in the distance, spanning the gorge. Caedmon's Bridge. Two broken columns marked the bridge approach, and a small mounted party, too distant to make out numbers, waited beside them. One rider galloped in our direction.

"Are these the ones who burned Vinera?" Brother Adolfus sounded ready to charge.

"I'd say not. Were they hostile they'd not be sending only one to greet us."

My eyes did not linger on the bridge or the people, but rather scoured the rugged land beyond the chasm. Caedmon's Bridge marked the boundary of Evanore, the land of trackless forests where the sun never penetrated, of rivers of flowing ice, of forbidden mountains where gods had made it impossible to breathe—the land of Prince Osriel and his terrible warlords and mages who served Magrog, lord of the netherworld. To cross Caedmon's Bridge placed a man's soul in mortal peril, so stories said, and would boil a pureblood's brains.

Though wary of the Bastard Prince and his perverse magics, I had borne no fear of Evanore itself—until I looked upon it. Indeed the land seemed grayer than where we stood, as if the clouds that muted the sun were thicker there. Unreasoning emotion swelled in my blood. Not the sense-blinding assault I'd felt in the cloister garth or at the pool. Not pain or terror at all. More a directionless anger and a sorrow so deep as to make a stone weep. A fearsome thing, that looking upon a landscape could so wrench a man's spirit.

Hoofbeats pounded the track from the bridge. The horseman drew rein at the cairn and waited there, patting the neck of his sidestepping bay as we approached. "Good morning, Brother Adolfus and Brother . . . Valen, is it?"

The dulcian voice erased all thought of the horrors behind us and the brooding land to the south. I yanked off my hood and looked up. She had cut her hair. The wind flicked the chin-length strands of bronze about her eyes and her cheeks, where a smile threatened to break through her sober courtesy.

"Master Corin," I said, bowing to cover my own foolish grin. "A great pleasure to see you again. Brother Adolfus, this gentle youth is the Thane of Erasku's squire."

I tried not to drool or sigh or otherwise make a fool of myself. I even forgave her greeting me from horseback, the beast so close to me I could feel its exquisite temper expelled in hay-scented snorts and blows. The woman's posture astride the beast presented me a full view of a shapely leg clad in scarlet hose—not peg scrawny as with so many of her noble sisters, but rather looking as if she ran and danced and lived with all of herself. Oh, dear goddess Arrosa, what I would not have given to run my hand upward along that red-clad limb.

Harness chinked and jangled in the distance as two other riders approached more slowly, leading a riderless mule. While I gripped my cowl tight against the wind, and my desires against even stronger natural forces, the woman turned to my companion. "Edane Groult is laid up with gout this morning, Brother Adolfus, so he asks if you would be so kind as to attend him in his hall. He has sent down two escorts and a mule to bring you up. Unfortunately, he did not expect two of you. My master was just departing on his way back to his hold and offered my services to greet you and convey the edane's message."

Brother Adolfus was nonplussed. "Of course I will ride up. Brother Valen *could* walk, but his leg is just now healing from a dreadful wound. I don't know . . . to leave a novice behind . . ."

"The edane's men will return for him, Brother. Meanwhile, my own lord is willing to delay his journey and provide Brother Valen company and refreshment for his wait."

"Well then, that will do very nicely." Brother Adolfus's conscience seemed much eased at the thought of me being provisioned. I was less sanguine, seeing now how matters were to work out. No second mule would be sent. Some excuse would be given when I did not appear in the edane's hall, while I would be dispatched on some ghost hunt with the Thane of Erasku. How much finer if I could wait here alone with Corin.

The mule arrived; Brother Adolfus mounted. As the monk and the nobleman's two servants moved away, the woman extended her hand to me, allowing a smile to break through. "Would you accept a ride to the bridge, Brother? Blackmane will certainly carry us both."

"Ah, mistress . . ."

Could she have presented any choice more painful? Saint Ophir had definite opinions on his followers having physical contact with women—a matter I had conveniently failed to recall as she'd led me blindfolded about the valley of Gillarine. I could have conveniently forgotten it again, save the horse appeared much more disturbed by the idea than her kind invitation would attest. He sidled and jinked so anxiously that a determined frown supplanted the woman's smile.

"Alas, I am not permitted." I stepped back to give the demon-cursed animal a bit more room. "And I don't think your beast likes me all that much."

"Nonsense. He's as placid as a cow." She said this with conviction, though, indeed, my distancing might have been a handful of sugar in the devil equine's mouth. "Come along, then. As you answered our first question so well, we've another puzzle for you."

She held to a slow walk, slower than necessary. I did not protest, and walked as close to her as the beast and I could bear. "I don't suppose you might give me a hint about the purpose of these exercises with the book of maps. I've received no reward for my first success but chilblains, bruised knees, and a reputation for slovenliness."

"I'm truly sorry for your trouble. The purposes of the cabal are not mine to reveal, but I vow they are of critical—"

"—importance to Navronne. To our children's children. So I've been told. Lives depend on secrecy, thus a novice's knees and unbridled curiosity are of poor account."

"Many lives. You must believe that. Those who hold this responsibility have yielded everything in their lives to serve this need." Her bitter argument took no heed of my teasing. And surely the horse was not responsible for the hard look she cast toward the bridge. Such an expression did not belong on such a face.

"One answer, then, and I'll pry no more for the moment," I said.

"Good Brother, I cannot—

"I would know your true name, mistress. And don't say 'Mag' or 'Popsy,' for you are no more a villein girl than you are a lad. My mind finds a great void in its constant untanglings and unwindings of these dire mysteries, for I cannot set a proper name to one certain face. Perhaps if I could bound that face with a name and set it in a proper sequence with Thane Stearc the Formidable, Gram the Sickly, and Brother Gildas of the Mysteries, as for labeled jars on a shelf, it would not persist in distracting me from more serious thoughts. Elsewise I must strive to deserve more punishments just to give me more time for contemplating the question, and what would Iero and his saints think of such a sacrilege?"

Ah, Deunor's fire, her laugh resonated in my bones as if I were a harp and she the player filled with passionate music. I would have babbled my nonsense the night through to hear such tunes as she could pluck on me.

"Elene, good Brother. My true name is Elene, but I would advise you not to use it in front of my father. For the time, my own folly has made me none but Corin, his less-than-satisfactory squire." She kicked the bay into a gallop, and they raced through the hazy morning toward the bridge. I could not take my eyes from her.

Elene . . . The name, the flesh, the laugh played out the sweetest harmony of creation.

Chapter 17

"I suppose you wish to rest," said the Thane of Erasku when I joined him, his daughter, and his secretary by the bridge.

"Good morning, my lord," I said. "Indeed my feet are more bruised than a drunkard's liver."

Brother Adolfus's mule had reached only half the distance to the fortress hill. As the goddess of love had produced no chain of circumstances that might leave me alone and naked with a similarly unclothed Elene, I was feeling a bit mulish as well.

"You're most kind to offer to wait with me for Edane Groult's transport, Lord Stearc, but please do not feel it necessary to delay your journey. Surely those clouds will split at any time and beset us with rain. Be on your way and godspeed!"

The three of them stood between the crumbling columns. Shards of white marble, stained and streaked with black, littered the flat muddy ground. What forces had shattered pillars as broad as my armspan? Even broken, they rose to twice my height. Lightning, perhaps, or siege engines, used in some long-ago attempt to destroy Ardra's only link with Evanore for a hundred quellae in either direction.

Elene stood at her father's side, one step behind his massive shoulder. The gray daylight revealed even more likeness between them, if any personage so ferocious and intimidating as Stearc of Erasku could be said to resemble a graceful woman. Their noses were blunt, cheekbones prominent, and jawlines square—hers formed in ivory, his in granite. The air around them seemed to quiver like heat rising from paving stones in deep summer.

The thane snorted. "You're not such a fool as to think this meeting is by chance, are you, monk? We've—"

"Excuse me, my lord." Gram stepped out from behind Stearc, slightly stooped, black hair whipping in the wind. The secretary looked younger in the daylight, though even more wan and weak beside such exuberance of life as this father and daughter. "I've the provisions you required me to pack for the good brother." Head inclined in deference, the gaunt secretary proffered a wineskin and a canvas provision bag. "I'll bring the book, and we can discuss our needs as Brother Valen takes a moment to catch his breath."

"If he can do this at all, he should be able to do it quickly," grumbled Stearc. "He can fill his belly as we wait for sunset—assuming the damnable sun still exists behind these clouds."

Thanks be, Gram's good sense prevailed. I sat on a round of marble and made sure Stearc's impatience did not worsen from waiting for me to devour the barley bread, soft cheese, and good ale. A fire would have been pleasant, but I'd no mind to delay my refreshment until I'd given the lord my answer to today's puzzle. He'd likely throw me from the bridge when I refused to help. I could not waste more magic on their ventures. Only a few days and I'd need everything I could muster.

"My lord, if you've brought me here to question me further about the maps," I said, when I was well through the little feast, "I'm afraid I've no more to tell you. I demonstrated everything I know in your first test. Any man with the knowledge you hold could have done the same."

"Evidently not," snapped Stearc, clasping his broad hands behind his back as if to keep from throttling me. His leather jaque strained with the display of his chest. "Others attempted to use the spell and trace the exact route you took. But they experienced no extraordinary guidance from the map. In hours of searching, they never came nearer the Well than the cliff. What caused your attempt to succeed where others failed?"

He leaned toward me, the pressure of his interest weighing like an iron yoke. Mouth stuffed with bread, I shrugged. But in truth I was not so nonchalant. So the eerie little pool Gildas and I had found . . . the Well, they called it . . . was indeed one of the hidden places that only my grandfather's maps could reveal. The wind poked its chilly fingers under my gown.

I'd not used the guide spell of the map, only my bent and my instincts. What did that mean? I was not familiar enough with the more obscure pureblood arcana to know. My father could not find such places without using the enchantments of my grandfather's maps— one of the matters that embittered him so sorely, I'd always thought.

Max had always been more adept at tracking than at route finding. But then, I had been adept at nothing.

"Perhaps someone told you how to find the Well." Stearc might have been a magistrate. "Or you ran across some mention of it in documents at the abbey."

I came near choking. "No, my lord, I certainly did not read of the place. And I doubt—"

"Show him, Gram."

The secretary sank to the grass just in front of me, sat back on his heels, and opened the book on his knees, searching for the page he wanted.

"Here, Brother." He turned the book to face me.

I wiped my hands on the empty provision bag and tossed it aside, then took the book. The open page contained two small maps. The secretary pointed to a grousherre, painted in bright reds and yellows. The map was too small to have a cartouche. The tiny words embedded in twisting vines and leaves that filled the narrow borders of the little map would hold the spell.

The characters flowed together like a river of ink as soon as I looked on them, of course, but I needed neither cartouche nor border to tell me what this map depicted. The meticulous drawings of fortress, bridge, columns, river, and branching path were enough to identify the very place where we sat. Interesting that the twin columns were shown whole, each of them bearing a capital in the shape of a trilliot. King Caedmon had been the first to order the wild lily of Navronne sewn onto his cape and his banner and emblazoned on his armor.

My gaze swept the grass between us and the gorge. Among the shards of marble tumbled around us might be those very capitals. Such an odd sensation for that moment, as if I lived in both times at once and might soon see Caedmon himself defending the bridge, as his warlords retreated into Evanore to hold its mountains and gold against the invading Aurellians. The black-haired invaders from the east—my ancestors—had turned their acquisitive eyes upon Navronne when they discovered that the minor sorceries they could accomplish in their own land were not only easier to work, but took fire with power here. They called Navronne the Heart of the World.

And then, of a sudden, I envisioned my grandfather, a scrawny, squinting old man, his lean shoulders hunched, his thick hair gone white, beard yellowed around his mouth, sitting alone by a campfire on this hillside, his long fingers like spiders' legs sketching this scene in his worn leather traveling book. Alongside the delicate pen strokes that represented the objects in the map, he would scribe a column of inked letters and numbers, noting the measures and proportions, names, and colors he would use to bring out the message he wanted to convey with this grousherre. He had chosen to show the fortress much smaller than the columns, had decided to depict the thrashing river of less moment than the bridge that crossed it or the overgrown paving stones of the approaches. Grousherres were about relative significance rather than accurate measure.

"Brother?" Gram remained sitting on his heels, facing me across the book.

Fire washed my cheeks. I shook off the cascading visions and the hostility and resentment that inevitably accompanied thoughts of my family. "Sorry. What is it you wish me to find?"

The secretary laid his slender finger on the largest object on the map. "This."

"Oh!" I had assumed the great tree that spread its ghostly branches across the entire page was but part of the book's decoration. Naught but straggling grass grew anywhere on this hillside. Certainly no tree stood where the map suggested, at the cairn where the path from the valley divided into two. "These maps were drawn years ago," I said. "If the tree was ever here, it must have been cut down."

"Perhaps the tree is only hidden," said the secretary, softly encouraging. "Try it."

"Try what?" I said, blank for the moment.

"Invoke the spell of the map!" bellowed Stearc, throwing up his hands. "What do you think? Spirits of night, must we be forever plagued with idiots and fools?"

"Give me a little time with the brother, my lord, and I'll explain what we seek . . . as we agreed."

Gram's quiet insistence held sway. The thane betook himself to the brink of the river chasm. Elene's glance wavered, but after a moment, she followed dutifully after him. They strolled onto the bridge—a fearsome thing to my mind, no more than one horseman wide and lacking parapet or railing. There they sat, legs dangling over the unseen void.

Gram blew out a great puff of air as if he did the same, though his precarious state seemed more related to his testy lord. "Please excuse my master, Brother. He is in a most difficult position, his life forever balanced on a knife edge. Those things he would do to right matters—deeds he has trained for his entire life—slide ever farther out of his reach."

"Because he conspires against his own lord, the Bastard Prince?"

No matter whether Osriel himself came to power—Kemen Sky Lord protect us from such a pass—whichever of the other two brothers became king would need to make alliance with the Bastard Prince to prevent his rival doing the same. Evanori lords who had failed in fealty to Osriel would be safe nowhere.

Gram's gaunt features twisted into a wry mask. "Indeed, that's a part of it."

He tapped the page again. "So, to our problem: We have learned that this particular map will lead us to a location of great importance, a place where we can leave a message. Those who must receive the message live nearby, but we aren't sure exactly where. And we need their help. But we've had no more luck with this map than with the one to Clyste's Well. And so, again we ask your assistance."

"But if they live nearby, surely this Edane Groult—"

"Edane Groult has no dealings with these neighbors," said the secretary dryly. "He would not recognize them were they to sit on his shoes. Or if he did, then his aged heart would stop."

My skin began to creep. How far did Abbot Luviar's arrogance of intellect take him? If he could redirect a man's loyalty to his prince, what could he do with a man's loyalty to his god?

"What neighbors might these be, living so close to the cursed land?" I said, sounding bolder than I felt. "I am pledged to holy Iero's service . . ." . . . and to Kemen's and Samele's and that of all and any gods and goddesses who allowed men to keep their skin and balls and fingernails and enjoy life without excessive torment. Unlike Magrog the Tormentor. The Adversary.

Gram lowered his head for a moment, as if in prayer, then lifted it again and glanced at me, though not so far lifting or so long glancing as to confront me as an honest man. "Good Brother Valen, we propose to deal with neither the Bastard Prince nor the Adversary nor their demonic lackeys, I promise you. Tell me, have you not read the inscription carved above your abbey's gates?"

"When I entered the gates of Gillarine, I was in no state to be *reading* anything, Master Gram," I snapped. I had the sense he was patronizing me behind his quiet manner, so like a monk himself. I didn't like it.

"The inscription says, *The earth is God's holy book.*" He said this softly and with sincere reverence. Without hint of superior laughter.

"I've heard the abbot say that," I said. In point of fact, out of all the prayers and mumblings I'd heard throughout my stay at Gillarine, it had been one phrase that made sense to me. It spoke of worth in common things where others saw naught. And it recalled the words of the sanctuary blessing: *by Iero's grace . . . by gift of earth . . . by King Eodward's grant . . .* And now these men spoke of holy wells. Of hidden trees. Of unseen neighbors whose presence might stop a man's heart. Of my grandfather's maps that could guide men to—

I stared at Gram. His dark head was bent over the book, only a swath of his wide forehead visible. A lock of dark hair had fallen forward, but surely underneath it, his eyes would be wild and fervent. Holy men. Madmen. I fought to keep sober. "By my soul, you're hunting angels!"

He was too intent upon his folly even to blush. "Not precisely. We believe there's been some confusion through the years. Your god may send angel messengers to tend our souls and guard us from temptation, but care of the earth is charged to other beings. Their stories have been told for as long as men have sat around fires under the stars. They live in realms of earth, not heaven, protecting and enriching the land they walk—that *we* walk—yet ordinary men cannot find the way to their dwelling places, save by luck or magic. Somehow, the pureblood cartographer who drew these maps could discover them whenever he chose, using only his pureblood bent. And now, using one of his maps, *you* have opened the way to one of their most hallowed places."

Struggling to keep from laughing at his sincerity, I touched the naked figures that supported the ribbonlike borders at the map's four corners. One was the aingerou my grandfather had stuck into every drawing in the book, claiming he did so because I was so fond of them. But the other three figures, two male, one female, poised on toes, legs stretched and bent as if dancing on the page, were no round-bellied imps, but tall and graceful with perfect bodies and flowing red curls. Angels, one might say, though they had no wings. This all began to make some sort of perverse sense. "You speak of the Danae."

Gram stood up, pulling his billowing cloak tight. "The long-lived have retreated far from humankind. They may be extinct, as reports claim. But a reliable source tells us that if we leave an offering at this tree before the sun reaches the zenith, a Dané will surely come at nightfall to fetch it, if even one yet exists. Then we could present our petition."

A surge of good humor threatened to plaster a grin on my face. I brought my hand up as if to mask a cough. "An offering . . . so you've brought *nivat seeds* to buy a parley." For if the Danae loved feast bread flavored with nivat, lore said they would bargain gems to obtain a quantity of the seeds. Nivat no longer grew in the wild.

"Yes. But first we must find the tree."

I breathed gratitude to Serena Fortuna and controlled my excitement, bending my head over the map again lest he mark my improved humor. "A marvel that would be, Gram, to discover the Danae after so long. I've doubts I can help you, but with Iero's grace, I'll see what I can do."

The wind blustered, snatching at our hair and cloaks and the fine vellum. I smoothed the page and held it to prevent its tearing or wrinkling. My fingers tingled and pricked as I brushed over the inked drawings. Spellcraft, certainly, as much a part of this book as compass roses.

I rotated the book to the left and then to the right, allowing my eyes to travel the lettered border and my lips to move slightly—Gram was watching very closely. Then I laid a finger on the bridge approach and dragged it to the branch point of the path whence the roots of the great tree spread like a spider's web across the painted hillside. All the while my mind was racing, sorting through the magical tricks that pureblood children learn as they learn to breathe and walk. If only I had listened better to my despised tutors.

"I don't think we can find this tree where it is not," I said. "But when I touch the roots on this page . . . perhaps . . ." Leaving the prospect dangling, I shut the book and gave it back to Gram.

I would need a few things to make this work. When I stood up and stepped a few quattae to my left, I made sure Gram could not see what my foot encountered. "Do *you* accompany me this time?"

He bowed in acknowledgment. "One moment, if you would. Lord Stearc would join us as well."

While he hurried off to fetch the thane, I reached down and grabbed the wadded canvas provision bag underneath my foot and stuffed it up my sleeve. Then I began to prepare a small voiding spell, the finest boon for a boy who wished to hide purloined items—wine, coins from his father's purse, his mother's divining cards, his man-smitten sister's love philtres, or his brother's prized knife. Strolling through the clutter of broken marble, I also sought a plant of some kind . . . Ah, there! Tucked up beside a boulder-sized chunk grew a scrabbling astelas vine. Astelas had nice spreading, hairy roots.

The others were returning from the bridge. Cupping my hands to my breast, I dropped to my knees, bent forward, and touched my forehead to the earth. Thanks to the summer's incessant rains, which had left the ground damp and pliable, I was able to pull up the astelas, roots intact. Before rising from my prayerful posture, I stuffed the plant up my sleeve alongside the bag.

At a respectful distance, my companions waited for me to complete my devotions. The first spell structured and waiting, I closed my eyes long enough to prepare a second—this one an inflation, the simplest kind of illusion. When it was ready, I rose and joined the others.

"One thing before we go," I said. "As I prayed Iero to guide our steps, I recalled that each time I've used the book, neither human nor beast has accompanied me. Perhaps that circumstance has somehow contributed to the successful outcome."

"The book says nothing of such a practice," said Gram, "but we can certainly lag behind, if you believe it might help. It's almost midday. If our first attempt should fail, we've no time for another today."

"Exactly my thought," I said, delighted at his practical reasoning.

"Just get on with it," said Stearc. Was the man ever other than angry and snappish? "We can walk. Corin can bring up the horses. We're no womenfolk needing to be coddled."

I refrained from smiling or glancing at Elene, who had drawn up her hood. "All right then."

As I strode briskly across the hillside, I honed my spells, straining to recall the nuances of skills so long unused. I could afford no explosions or sparks this time. I also plucked the leaves and stem from the astelas, scattering the bits and pieces of greenery by dropping them between my cowl and gown so they drifted to the ground as I walked. By the time I reached the cairn, only a thick clump of roots remained of the plant inside my sleeve.

As I knelt beside the pile of stones, I quickly traced an arc on the lichen-covered stone from the earth to a point a handsbreadth above the ground and back down again, allowing magic to flow through my hands into the voiding spell. The substance of the stone retracted—squeezed aside, as to say—to create the void hole, a gap in the side of the cairn. I reached in and scrabbled in the earth, spreading and burying the astelas roots as best I could.

Now the second spell—the inflation. Magic swelled and passed through my tingling fingers into the buried roots. Trusting that I had remembered enough, I unraveled the voiding spell to close the gaping hole. A gamble, this. To use the bent as I'd sworn not to do. To spend power that I would need within days. But to throw such an opportunity back into Serena Fortuna's face was surely more risky yet. I rose and waited for the others to arrive.

"I see no tree," said Stearc, planting his hands on his waist, uncomfortably near his weapons. Gram and Elene flanked him, the secretary paler than ever, the woman flushed and rosy after tethering their horses a few hundred quercae up the hill, then running to rejoin us.

"Though the cairn is not shown on the map, the map spell led me straight to it," I said, feigning puzzlement. "Each step away from it jibes wrong."

"The tree should be here," said Gram, crouching low to examine the cairn. "We should be able to see and touch it as Gildas saw and touched Clyste's Well. The journal speaks of the Sentinel Oak as a meeting place of the two planes."

The cairn bore no markings. The rocks had likely been piled up to mark the path when snows lay deep. The secretary's long thin fingers brushed the stone and earth around the cairn. He looked up. "My lord, come. There's something here . . ."

I stepped back, allowing Stearc a place to kneel beside his secretary. "Take down the stones," he said. "Corin, come. Lay to it."

Elene and the two men dismantled the cairn before I could breathe another prayer. And there, protruding from the ground, was the rough-hewn stump of a modest-sized tree. Its dead roots, a nice thick, woody spread modeled from the astelas roots, poked from the earth here and there. I felt as proud as a father must upon viewing a new-birthed son.

The thane folded his arms and regarded the stump. "It seems smaller than the description of the tree would warrant."

I wanted to mount a defense of my progeny: *Too large and it would have disrupted the cairn. Smaller and you'd not believe. It is so nice and woody, well aged in its appearance. And I've not created so substantial an inflation in twelve years, at the least, so credit me a bit, fearsome lord!* The stump should last a month or more if no one worked a spell of unraveling on it. Unraveling spells—the bane of a boy's illusions—had been as common in my family's house as arguments.

"The map brought you here, Brother Valen?" said Gram, frowning. "You're sure?"

"Nowhere else. The guide thread I feel as I follow the map's course fades even these few steps away." I returned to the secretary's side and knelt beside him. Spits of rain struck my face and pocked the disturbed earth about my lovely stump.

"Nothing for it but to make the attempt," said Stearc. "If the monk is wrong—of which I have little doubt—we've lost nothing but a day already wasted. The morning has almost run."

Gram, still troubled, nodded. He shifted one of the smaller stones left tumbled about from the destroyed cairn and laid it at the base of the stump carefully, as if judging a precise orientation. Elene watched him, and I watched her, wondering at her pinched lips and stormy brow. Some enmity ran deep between these two—both of them people I would be pleased to account my friends.

I kept my preoccupation with Elene's expressive face well hidden beneath the shelter of my hood, shifting my attention only when Gram pulled a small bag from the pocket of his cloak and set it on the stone. A distinctive scent, of pepper and almond, of dust and mushrooms, flooded the air. Blessed Samele, I could have picked the man's pocket twenty times over!

I touched the little bag. Oiled canvas. Common brown. Very like the provision bag hidden in my sleeve. Slightly smaller, closed with a black silk cord instead of a leather tie. Surely enough nivat for a year or more. It was all I could do to refrain from snatching it up and racing the coming storm back the way we'd come, past Gillarine and all the way to Palinur. Sell half the seeds and I would be set for half a year.

But I'd never get away. These three rode horses and carried swords and smoldered with passion about their madness. Deception was a healthier course. Patience. Depending on how the next few hours went, I should be able to take what I wanted with none the wiser.

I withdrew my hand and stood up. "Great Iero, shed your blessings here."

Gram held an open hand out to Elene. "Do you have the box, Corin?"

From the pocket of her jupon, she drew a small tin box that she handed to Gram. He sprinkled some of the contents on the stone and shifted the bag of nivat to cover what he had just put down.

"Salt," he said, as if sensing my question. "To hold the Dané here while we speak."

"Why would you do that?" I said, aghast. No matter that I did not believe anything would come of his offering or his message. Some things were so wrong that it was better not even to mime them. "Fetter a Dané? Bind it? When you've come begging their favor?"

"It's only to stay the sentinel long enough for us to speak. We'd never force them. But we *must* be heard. If we knew another way, we'd use it."

"They'll never forgive you. Of all things, Danae are free." My grandfather's stories came back to me. None could bind the Danae to field or forest or bog. "They choose their own places, Gram. That's why you give them feast bread . . . to induce them to stay. That's why you leave an undisturbed plot when you plow a new field or set aside a wild garden when you build a new house, so the Dané who tends that plot of ground can yet come and go at will. Elsewise he might leave to find another place, or she might be trapped amid the human works and die. Bind them, and you'll lose everything before you speak one word of your message."

"This whole scheme is madness," said Stearc. "We must proceed as we decided. This fool of a monk doesn't know what he's doing. Nor do we. Come, Corin, we need to set up a shelter before this everlasting rain washes us into the river."

"We try as we can, lord," said Gram, more to himself than anyone.

The thane strode off toward the horses, and his daughter followed. Gram shook his head and started up the hill after his master. A few steps and he paused, waiting for me to join him.

The clouds had closed in over the southern mountains, and veils of rain and fog drifted over the river and the bridge. The fortress had vanished into the murk. Confused, unreasonably disturbed, praying their oiled bag would protect the nivat seeds from the wet, I joined the secretary, and we trailed after Stearc and Elene.

Gram walked more slowly than Stearc and his daughter. Though he seemed at the verge of speaking several times, he never did. Perhaps I had offended him with my blunt speech—silly, as I thought about it, to argue over legends. He could do as he liked with his foolery.

"So am I to wait here, too, and help you pursue some other plan should this one fail, or is someone from the fortress truly bringing a mule to fetch me?" I said after a while. "I'd rather see the outcome of this venture. To see a Dané . . . blessed saints, it would be a miracle. But if I'm to go up to the fortress, I'd as soon leave before the rain worsens."

Gram lifted his head, roused from his thoughts. "The edane *will* send his mule for you eventually. We were able to arrange a delay, but only until midafternoon." A few more steps and he stopped to rest. He glanced up at me, a thoughtful expression on his face. "I've already revealed more than Thane Stearc would approve, and he'll not wish you to remain. However, I could argue it with him . . ."

"No, no. He seems a difficult enough master. I'd not put you more in the way of his wrath."

Gram chuckled and glanced out from under the soggy locks of dark hair now dribbling water down his deep-carved cheeks. "That is a kindness, Brother. I could wish you were around us more often. Perhaps we would stay civil. Though our goals are like, our opinions diverge mightily, and to argue with anyone of the house of Erasku is a futile exercise. They are the harder rock from which the mountains of Evanore have sprouted."

Stearc and Elene had moved the horses into the lee of a low scarp that split the hillside. They were already unloading packs and satchels.

"I've sensed that," I said, relishing my view of Elene's delicious body as she went about her work. "And the squire demonstrates as virulent opinions as the lord. At our first meeting, after that unfortunate encounter with a grain sack, I made the mistake of asking Corin about Prince Osriel."

"Indeed?" We plodded uphill again. "And you lived to tell about it? The house of Erasku has no use for the Bastard."

"Corin's vehemence was reassuring. When Prince Osriel attacked the Moriangi at Gillarine—" Of a sudden, the memory laid a blight on my fey mood. "I just wanted to make certain your little test was not enlisting me in the Bastard's legion."

"Ah. I've heard fearful stories of that raid—apparitions, a cloud of midnight, the mutilation of the dead. You do well to keep cautious of the Bastard's poisonous madness. Thane Stearc walks a difficult path, unable to side with any of the three. We had a narrow escape from the abbey that night."

"So who *does* he favor for the throne? Who do you favor, for that matter?"

Gram shook his head in the same hopelessness I felt. "Both Perryn and Bayard have young children. If the brothers maintain a stalemate, Lord Stearc believes we may be forced into some sort of cousinly union and a regency. Not a happy prospect when spring brings Hansker raids."

We had reached a level with Stearc's camp. The secretary rested his back against the scarp, expelling a relieved sigh. He cocked his head. "Tell me, Brother Valen, if we fail tonight—and I am no more sanguine than my master—and we arrive at some new insight that invites your participation, may we call upon you again? I do value your aid . . . and your advice."

"I don't seem to have much choice in the matter. This is all a great mystery, and I'm thinking my head will burst soon with wondering." Indeed my mind was hopelessly jumbled as I tried to link the Danae to the lighthouse and the end times. What interest had Danae in books or looms?

Gram's wry, twisting smile granted a moment's grace to his stark face. "Your abbot must enlighten you further, Brother. Tell him what you've learned this day, and he will likely supply the rest . . . in far more civil terms than Lord Stearc would do. We need men and women of courage, goodwill, and varied gifts. Clearly *you* have a gift where this strange book is concerned."

"Well, we'll discover the truth of that at sunset, I suppose." I returned his smile, regretting the need to deceive the mournful fellow.

Indeed, I felt privileged to be allowed such glimpses of Gram's private self. Servants of volatile lords had to control themselves quite strictly. The secretary had been forthcoming to a degree others had not, and I held no prejudice against madmen. The armies, the alleys, and the finest pureblood houses of Navronne were filled with them.

I offered him my hand. "For now, farewell, sir. I must hike up this monstrous hill before I am soaked through. You'll convey my respects to the thane and his man?"

He nodded graciously and took my hand, showing no surprise at the unclerical gesture. The fingers that circled my wrist were firm, but cold, and his own wrist hammered with a blood pulse that spoke of more excitement than his quiet manner displayed. Or perhaps it was merely the racing heart of an unwell man who had pushed too hard to climb a hill.

I did not take to the fortress road, but hiked only as far as the next scarp that banded the hillside. Though Stearc's party lay hidden behind their own step of rock just below me, the dark ribbon of the cart track was clearly visible down the hill from them. The darker smudge and scattered rocks marked the fine stump where my year's salvation lay waiting. I huddled against the short wall of rock, sinking into its shadow, drawing my cowl and hood close to shield me from the rain. Anyone coming down from the fortress to fetch me would see no one on the road or in the fields. Come dusk, I would put the last step of my plan into action.

The hours passed slowly. Sleep crept over me like the clouds and fog drifting across the gray-green landscape. Yet whenever I started, from grazing my cheek on the rock as I slumped or from the cold drizzle on my hairless patch of scalp when a gust of wind lifted my hood, the light seemed unchanged from my last waking. I was only wetter and colder. I settled deeper against the rock wall. *Pretend you're warm; you've done that often enough. Just stay awake . . .*

Yawning, I played out the plan over and over again. *As soon as the light fades enough to leave shapes and landscape indistinct, slip down toward the stump. Pray the rain continues. They'll never see you. Empower the illusion. Replace the bag of seeds with the empty provision bag that will now appear exactly the same.* To empty the nivat into the provision bag and leave the empty one behind would take too much time. *One last touch of magic . . . a flash of blue light as the night closes in . . . easy, as you creep away unseen. Then the long trudge up the hill to the fortress. I'll think of a story for Brother Adolfus . . . for the edane whose mule driver won't have found me . . . Sympathize with Gram and Elene that their Dané eluded them . . . sympathize tenderly with Elene . . .*

My eyelids weighed like lead . . . and still the game played out . . . over and over . . .

Trigger the spell . . . creep silently . . . careful . . . timing . . . all was timing . . . switch the bags . . . slog upward . . . a story . . . one more lie . . . a flash of spiraling sapphire in the night . . .

I sat bolt upright. Deunor's fire, it was almost dark. The wind had died. The rain had stopped. Banners of fog lay in every hollow and niche, the world now colored with charcoal and ash. I shook off the dregs of sleep, cursing my everlasting carelessness. How long would Stearc wait to scoop up his bag of nivat and yell at Gram to devise him another plan? Impossible . . . unbearable . . . that my scheme or my magic should go to waste. Scooping up a fistful of earth, I recklessly poured magic into seeking a route through the twilight.

Once sure I would not tumble over the scarp into Stearc's lap, I sped downhill. But I had not traveled half the distance when I glimpsed lights of deep and varied blue moving through the fog. A few steps closer, until the scene halted my feet and left me gaping. Exactly as I'd seen in the fog of my dreaming, the light was drawn into long coils and spirals . . . into delicate vines and leaves that hung in the thick air . . . living artworks as bright and rich-hued as the windows of Gillarine Abbey church. They drifted in sinuous unison away from the demolished cairn. Away from the tree—an oak of such a girth its bole could house a family and of such expansive foliage it could shelter a village beneath its limbs.

"Wait!" Gram's cry bounced off the rocks and fell dead in the thick air. "Please! Hear our message . . . for any who dance in Aeginea. We need your help. *Envisia seru, Dané.*"

The blue lights paused and shifted, turning . . . the movement revealing the canvas for the artist's magical pen . . . long bare limbs entwined by sapphire snakes, and flat breasts traced with azure moth wings, half hidden by a cascade of curling red hair . . . a pale cold face upon which a glowing lizard coiled its tail about a fathomless eye, while the reptile's scaled body drawn in the color of lapis stretched across an alabaster cheek. So beautiful . . . so marvelous.

"Human voices are thorns in our ears." The voice of the wind could be no more soulless. She was already moving away.

"Our estrangement shadows our hearts." The speaker's dark shape—Gram's shape—moved between me and the apparition. "Meanwhile, the world suffers, and we seek to understand it. Can we bargain? Will you convey our request to Stian Archon or Kol Stian-son?"

I wanted to scream at Gram to move out of the way so I could see more, yet I could not accomplish even that. My limbs were frozen in place, stricken powerless with wonder. But I smelled her . . . woodrush and willow and the rich mold of old leaves and shaded gullies . . . she came from the fen country.

Everything of my own life—past, present, thought, sense—paled and thinned, having no more substance than smoke alongside the substance of her. I felt starved, fading.

Standing beneath the spreading branches, the Dané paused and cocked her head to one side, raising her brow so that the lizard's tail twitched. "Bargain . . . and forget betrayal? Forget violation and poison? Forget thievery?" She breathed deep of the night air. Her nostrils flared. Her lip curled. "Thou canst not claim ignorance, human, for thy very blood bears the taint of betrayal and thy flesh stinks of thievery. The long-lived do not forget. Offer recompense for betrayal; uncorrupt that which thy poison has corrupted; return what was stolen, and we might consider a hearing."

"Theft? Poison? I know naught of—"

No need for Gram to finish his claims of ignorance. She had vanished in a rush of air, as if she had wings to bear her back to heaven. And no spreading oak stood at the cairn. Only my ugly stump.

Sodden, chilled to the marrow, I sank to my knees and tasted all that remained of the night—charcoal and ash, empty of magic. I pressed my forehead to the cold earth and wept.

Chapter 18

"Brother Valen! Are you injured? We heard a cry."
Bobbing lantern light announced Elene well before she
knelt beside me and brought her face down near my own.
Even without sight I would have known her. She smelled of fennel
soap and horse, damp leather and wet pine smoke, of a warm human
woman, not the woodrush scent of the cold Dané.

"My lord, over here!" she yelled. And then quieter, "Brother?"

"I sprained . . . fell . . . I was on the way . . . the fortress . . ." My
lies limped into nothingness. I inhaled and began again. "I stayed
back to watch. Waited up the hill. Saw her."

That was all I could muster. I could no more explain the fullness
of grief that had overwhelmed me than I could explain my pain in
the cloister garth, my dread at the pool in the hills, or why in the
name of heaven a Dané had come to a tree stump conjured from a
weed. I knew only that when the blue sigils vanished, I felt as if some
great door had opened in the world and all joy had rushed out. Were
the king's own minstrels surrounding me, I could not have sung with
them or danced to their music.

"So it was not just the three of us who saw and heard. Lord Stearc
and I each thought we were dreaming. Gram even spoke to the creature! But you look dreadful, Brother. Are you sure you're not hurt?"
Elene laid a hand on my shoulder, and the sheer kindness of it came
near setting me weeping again.

"I've not been myself of late," I mumbled. "Ill. No sleep. So much
praying. A different life." I tried to sort myself out, dragging a sleeve
across my face as I sat up. How long had I knelt here weeping like a
babe bereft of its mother's tit? My reaction made no sense at all. I

hated feeling so helpless, so at the mercy of emotions without cause. "It's nothing."

I'd wasted the day. Wasted my bent. Of course, the Dané had taken the nivat. She would not have come at all if not for the seeds. So beautiful . . . so strange and majestic and proud . . . such magic . . .

Ah, stars of night, that was what hurt so dreadfully. To look upon such power that dwelt so near us, in tree or pond or meadow, and yet so vastly distant. Never had dirt and ignorance and uselessness weighed on me so. The damp, heavy wool of my drab monk's garb itched and choked me. Stories said the Danae danced to the music of the stars. Easy to see how people might mistake such a being for a messenger of heaven.

"Brother Valen! What are you doing here?" Stearc's sudden presence assaulted my spirit like a cadre of Moriangi foot soldiers.

I shook my head. I was doing well to sit up, trying not to feel anything, terrified that my next move would ignite the fire in my belly. My waste of magic likely meant that the next doulon would be no more successful than the last. And then my nivat supply would be gone. *Ass! Ignorant, blind, rock-headed ass!* I wanted to slam my head on the rocky ground. All the images I kept at bay descended on me at once: the pain-frenzied youth in the Palinur alley, thrashing in his own filth and vomit, the whore in Avenus whose eyes screamed when you touched her hot, rigid limbs, paralyzed with cramps and seizures. Better to slice my own throat than end like that.

"He stayed to watch, sire. He says he's not injured. We should tell him—" After a sharp gesture from her father, Elene bit off whatever else she wanted to say.

"I'll vow I believed you a charlatan, monk," said the thane. "That a nobody, a cowardly hireling bowman with no family of consequence and an arrow wound in his back, could interpret the book when better men could not seemed unrighteous and impossible. But it seems I erred."

I did not even bristle.

The thane crouched beside me, his oiled leather jaque gleaming in the lantern light, his hawkish bearded face flushed with zeal and thirsty with curiosity. "Sword of the archangel, I cannot comprehend what we just saw. I've never believed any of these legends. How did you do it? What key have we missed in this confounded book?"

"I don't know." Luck? Fate? How could anyone believe that I— a man of so little skill that I never had and never would accomplish a single thing of worth in my life, so blindly thick skulled that I could not untangle the meanings of the simplest markings on a page, and so weak of will that I had enslaved myself to the doulon—had done anything to summon such a being? "I did only what I've done before." Exactly nothing. I could not explain it.

Gram arrived shortly after the thane, moving slowly. The secretary was stretched tight. His black cloak and the sharp light on his deep-etched features made him look like death itself.

"We should get back to our blankets," said the thane when he spied Gram. "Foolish to stand here in the cold. Come on."

Before I could resist, Stearc grabbed my elbow and hauled me up as if I were no larger than Elene. No threads of fire shot through my limbs, demanding the doulon's solace. Thank the gods for that.

Stearc grunted an order at Elene, and father and daughter hurried off. Gram and I trailed behind as if drawn along in their wake.

"You removed the salt," I said.

Gram nodded as he muffled a bout of harsh coughing.

"I'm sorry."

"You were right," he said, and absently pushed damp hair from his face. It promptly fell down again. "It wouldn't have made any difference to bind her. She wasn't going to do what we asked in any case."

We found no more to say on the short walk down the hill.

A sullen Elene thrust a blanket into my arms when we reached their camp, and then retreated to a spot well away from us. Stearc removed his swordbelt and tossed it on the ground beside her. Her mouth tight, she rummaged in one of the saddle packs, set out stone, rag, and oil flask, and set to cleaning and polishing his long-sword. Her silence bulged and stretched near bursting.

They had pegged a canvas awning to the stone and supported it with three hinged poles and a tangle of rope. The ground underneath was damp but not soggy. Bundled in cloaks and blankets, Gram and I squatted beside the lantern, as if the weak yellow light might warm us.

The thane pulled out a wineskin, took a few swallows, and tossed it at Gram. "Now we know the nivat works, we should try again. Perhaps a different creature would be more accepting."

Gram took a long pull at the wineskin. "She is a sentinel," he said, rubbing his forehead tiredly. "One charged to watch the boundaries between human and Danae. She would most likely respond to any advance here. Her own sianou is probably somewhere nearby. But after hearing her, I believe that other Danae would reject us as well. Her dislike was not some private matter."

"But it was aimed directly at you." Elene made no attempt to mute her voice or her hostility. "Have you done something without telling the others?"

"Hold your tongue, squire, or be sent home. I warned you." Stearc jerked his head. "Go see that the horses have not pulled their tethers. Now."

Though Elene clenched her jaw in the very image of her father, she slammed the sword back into its sheath, jumped to her feet, and snatched up the lantern.

"Hear me, Corin." Gram rushed into the angry silence as the woman strode into the night. "The only betrayal I know of is Eodward's failure to abide by their terms and return to them. Perhaps they've come to think of that as stealing what 'belonged' to them. Their help. Their care. No theft is mentioned in the journal."

Their family quarrel could not hold my attention this night. The mention of King Eodward's name sparked in me like flint on steel. Eodward who was said to have lived with "angels" for a hundred and forty-seven years. Eodward who had asked a saucy-tongued pikeman to take a message—

"Aeginea." The word spilled from my lips.

"What's that, Brother?" Stearc and Gram said it together, as if they had forgotten I was there.

"When you spoke to the Dané, you mentioned a place called Aeginea. What is it?"

Though I addressed Gram, another bout of coughing rattled the secretary's chest. The answer came from Stearc instead. "Aeginea is the Danae's own name for the lands where their archon holds sway, where they celebrate the turning of the seasons and dance the pattern of the world they call the Canon. Though we don't see the name on any of Cartamandua's maps, we believe it exists both within and apart from our own land."

"It is Navronne," said Gram, hoarse from his cough. "The Heart of the World."

"And King Eodward . . . what does he have to do with all this?" I was half afraid to ask, sensing a tether of obligation reaching out from the past to bind my choices. Somehow doubly bitter after having seen a Dané.

"That is a very long story," said Stearc. He stretched out on the bare ground, wadded a blanket under his head, and pulled his cloak around him. His hand moved out and touched the swordbelt, loosening his knife in its sheath. "Too long for tonight. We should sleep now."

I was as wakeful as if my wastrel drowsing up the hill had been a night's unbroken sleep. Even after the thane began snoring, my thoughts would not keep still.

Though Elene's departure with her lantern left us in the dark, I heard Gram rustling about in the packs, unstoppering a flask, drinking something that seemed to soothe his cough better than the wine had done. He must have sensed my wakefulness, as well, for he began to speak softly, as if not to wake his master.

"Almost seventy years ago, a young Janus de Cartamandua-Magistoria first found his way into Aeginea. I don't know how he accomplished it. Who truly understands pureblood sorcery? But while traveling there, he encountered a human man of some eighteen years. The Danae called the youth *Caedmon-son*, and said his father was a man they honored as a friend of the Danae and the one human who was ever true to his word. History tells us that Caedmon's four elder children were slain as the Aurellians drove through Morian and into Ardra. The Danae told Cartamandua that Caedmon had begged them to foster one remaining child—an infant son. The Danae archon, one named Stian, agreed to take in the child and a tutor sent by Caedmon to see to the boy's education.

"Writings and papers in the tutor's possession, as well as the tutor's testimony, corroborated the story. Though fascinated by Cartamandua and his tales of Navronne's struggles with the Aurellians and the Hansker, the young man had no interest in returning here. Life . . . time . . . runs differently in Aeginea. Though their seasons follow one upon the other at the same pace as ours, their days can seem like a year or an hour—much as a river spans only the distance from Elanus to Palinur, yet meanders faster and slower through straights and eddies on its way. And a human's life spends more slowly there—we calculate seven of our years to every one of theirs."

"Eodward," I said. Of a sudden, dry history took on new life and meaning. Like Stearc, I had never truly believed in the legend, only in the man. One hundred and forty-seven years would translate to one-and-twenty—the age of Eodward when he appeared from nowhere to reclaim Caedmon's throne. "How do you know all this?"

"Lord Stearc has come into possession of a journal relating to those days. Its accuracy is unimpeachable." Clothing rustled in the dark. Gram's hunched silhouette blocked out the stars in the clearing sky. "The Danae insisted Cartamandua swear to keep the secret of Eodward's existence."

"But he didn't." No one in my family would have kept such a secret. Not if the telling could enhance their prestige among the other purebloods.

"For a while, he did. But twenty-one years later, when all realized that Aurellia had become a fragile, decadent shell, Cartamandua told a friend about the young man—Caedmon's living heir. This friend, Sinduré Tobrecan, was the high priest of Kemen, and it happened that Tobrecan's closest boyhood friend Angnecy had just been anointed Hierarch of Ardra, the followers of the elder gods and those of Iero and divine Karus linked by this strange mechanism of fate. Seeing hope for the future in their own friendship and in the miracle of Eodward's life, they convinced Cartamandua to lead them to Aeginea, using his book of maps. There they beseeched Eodward, who had aged little in all that time, to return to Navronne and take up his rightful throne, lest chaos descend upon the kingdom with the fall of Aurellia. The Hansker longships were poised to attack and drive us into barbarism and savagery."

"And this time, he came," I said, wondering. "He was one-and-twenty."

"It was not an easy choice. Eodward loved and honored his Danae family, and considered himself one of them. His Danae mother guided his training, as is their custom, and he rode, danced, and hunted with his Danae father, brother, and sister. But from Cartamandua's first visit, Eodward had dreamed increasingly of Navronne—a land he lived in, but had never really experienced, for as you have noted, the Danae realms are our own realms. We but tread different paths. When Eodward decided to come here, he vowed to return to Aeginea before they danced the Winter Canon thrice more."

"But he didn't," I said, remembering the words he'd spoken to me on that long-ago battle's eve. *Tell them I don't think I'll get back . . .*

"He could not. He had a thriving, glorious kingdom that needed him desperately. The Danae, still bitter at Cartamandua for breaking his vow, and unhappy with Eodward for his leaving, named Eodward's failure to return as betrayal, compounding their own long grievances with humans. After a time, the king began to age as humans do, yet he fully intended to return to Aeginea as soon as his children were strong enough to carry on his work. He died still believing the Danae would forgive him and that he could live out his days among them."

I shook my head. "He knew he would never go back," I said. "His children were never worthy to succeed him."

"Clearly not." Gram sighed and hunched his blanket around his shoulders. "And other things have happened in the years since that caused the Danae additional grievance—perhaps this violation and the thievery she spoke of—and they've forsaken all human contact. Now we need their help again, and I don't know how we're to get it."

"But you won't tell me why. It's this business of the lighthouse and the end times."

"I am but one player in a very large game. You should sleep now, Brother. Tomorrow we'll decide what to do next."

While Gram was speaking, quiet movements in the dark on the far side of the snoring Thane of Erasku told me Elene had returned. "Tell me about Corin," I said on a whim. "I sense a restless spirit there. Is he reliable? Trustworthy?"

"Reliable?" Gram laughed bitterly. "If the world could take shape from one will alone, then it would surely match young Corin's vision of how things ought to be. And it would be a world so just and fair . . . so glorious and compassionate . . . your Karish angels would choose to live here in Navronne instead of heaven. Do not doubt. Should every man of this cabal fail, Corin will carry it ahead alone come heaven or hell, victory or ruin."

I smiled as I pulled up my blankets, a moment's respite from a pervasive despondency. All through that long night, I heard restless movements from two pallets besides my own. Only the Thane of Erasku slept much that night.

"Unable to read while you are walking?" said a disbelieving Brother Sebastian.

I stood before him in the monks' parlor outside the dorter, damp, dirty, and exhausted, more from the night without sleep than the few quellae of the journey. After a predawn breakfast of cold cheese, Stearc had ordered Elene up to Fortress Groult to inform the edane that Brother Valen had wandered into their camp after getting lost in the rain and fog. Brother Adolfus returned with her, as it transpired that the poetry book was one that the abbey had already copied. That fact hardly surprised me. We had arrived at the abbey shortly before midday, and I prayed my mentor's annoyance would not forbid me dinner.

"After vowing to improve your attentiveness, you get yourself lost. And atop this foolery and despite all your promises of obedience, you refuse to honor your elder's wish to join him in your avowed duty of prayer along the route."

"I *am* sorry, Brother. The jarring of walking, especially with my limp, makes the words on the page run together. I'll strive to improve this weakness in the future as the Blessed Gillare heals this lingering mortification of my flesh." Even lies came hard today.

"Clean yourself and fetch your new spare gown and cowl from Brother Tailor," said Brother Sebastian. "Report to Brother Jerome for the rest of the afternoon. After Vespers we shall sit down and work out your reading syllabus and examination schedule for the next month. We must pay more rigorous attention to your studies and deportment."

I bowed and thanked him, dreading the unhappy exposure sure to come very soon now. I would suffer yelling, admonitions, and penances until my hair turned white. But at least I had achieved one of my aims. Luviar would surely not dismiss me after my unlikely successes with the book of maps, whether I could read or not. Somehow, even that small accomplishment could not cheer me. The world felt old. Broken.

Of course, Brother Jerome would be out of sorts that afternoon. He complained of having only barley vinegar to use for his pickling, as the grape harvest had failed, and that salt had grown so dear he had to be a pinchfist with it just when he needed it most. Brother Sebastian must have sent word of my transgressions. Instead of allowing me to sit in the warm kitchen and chop turnips or carrots to go into his crocks of vinegar and salt, Brother Refectorian had sent me to the cold, stinking butcher house to bleed and strip a pig.

As I wrestled the massive carcass in a vat of steaming water to scrub off its hair and buried my hands in its stomach cavity to sever and draw out its entrails, I imagined the scene in the guesthouse. Stearc, Gram, and Elene were likely head to nose with the abbot, the chancellor, and Brother Gildas—probably Jullian, as well—all of them bathed, dry, and drinking hot cider, talking of magical libraries, beings of legend, and the end of the world, while I was rendering a sow.

Sullen and resentful, I sorted all the nasty bits. White, lacy caul fat into the bowl for present use. Bung and rectum onto the waste heap. Emptied guts, destined to hold Brother Jerome's fine sausage, into the brine crock along with the emptied bladder and stomach. My new spare gown was clean no longer, and my sandals and feet were splashed with blood and filth. Brother Sebastian would have no mercy.

The heart and liver had just gone into a bowl for the kitchen, and my sore hands had just plunged another length of gut into the cold running water of the butcher house conduit to scrape it clean, when I glimpsed a brickred cloak in the vicinity of Brother Butcher. The two of them stood outside the doorway of the wooden building.

Though my hands were freezing, my face grew hot enough to cook the damnable pig. Was I to be forever splattered, filthy, or slug-witted in front of Elene? Bad enough that half my skull was bald and I stank worse than Jullian.

"Brother Valen!" Brother Butcher, a lay brother with a neck as wide as his head, also possessed a bellow worthy of his victims. "The squire says you're summoned to the abbot."

Blessed release! "Of course, Brother. I'll stop off at the lavatorium to wash, and then—"

"Not so, Brother Novice. Brother Sebastian has sent out word to all that you're to hop to your duties with no dawdling or digression. They wouldn't have sent for you *now* did they want you to come *later*. So be off with you. I'll take on your pig."

Sighing, I dropped the gut back into the crock, plunged my arms into the conduit flow, and scrubbed at them with my numb fingers. After a handful of icy water to my face and a swipe with the only clean spot on my gown, I hurried through the butcher house, and bowed to the thick-necked lay brother. Though wet and freezing from fingertip to armpit, blood and offal still grimed nails and pores and the cracks in my skin. I grabbed my cowl from the hook by the door and threw it on.

Elene's hood covered her hair, and she did not speak as she marched away. Brother Butcher watched from the doorway as I followed meekly after her.

"Good day, Squire Corin," I whispered from under my own hood as we hurried past sheep pens and pig wallows. "I certainly hope your return to Gillarine was more fragrant than mine."

"The abbot is always welcoming, though we don't come here for the hospitality." Her tone smacked far too much of serious affairs.

"Well, of course, you don't. Though I don't see that purposeful misery will solve any of the world's problems, either. Which leads me to ask . . ."

She tripped briskly up the steps that crossed the low wall dividing the abbey's outer and inner courts, and rather than take the eight steps down, she jumped straight to the ground, as nimble as a cat. I jumped as well, which left me feeling something like a mast with billowing sails, as my gown caught the air. My thigh did not even twinge when I landed.

I paused for a moment and watched her walk ahead toward the lay brothers' yard and the brewhouse, the sight of her an antidote to my dogging melancholy. She moved like a dancer or a juggler, not frail or bony, but well muscled, her back as solid and well formed as her front. A most pleasing view, though truly it seemed very odd to have the luxury of examining a woman in breeches and jupon while I traipsed behind her in skirts.

She peered over her shoulder. Best get my mind back to business. We would soon be in the inner precincts where even quiet conversation could be noticed and overheard. Two full strides and I caught up with her.

". . . which leads me to ask, Is someone ever going to tell me what is coming, so I can decide whether to keep watch upward to see the bolt of fire from heaven or downward to see the ground open underneath me? Will the world end in fire or ice, Squire Corin? Though I have my own guess as to that." I shivered as the damp wind blew off the river, smelling of dead fish.

She slowed just a bit. "I told them they ought to be honest with you. But my father won't hear of it, because—"

"—because he heard I had an arrow wound in the back. He despises me as a coward, and thus believes me incapable of keeping secrets."

"For Abbot Luviar to be dismissed for sheltering a deserter would be disastrous to our cause. But you've proven yourself, so you deserve to hear the truth." She planted herself in front of me, hands on her hips. "The earth itself will not end, only the life we know—cities and towns and villages, plowing and planting. Herds are dying. Famine and disease will bring barbarians, not just Hansker, who will surely come first, but wilder folk from the north and west. Yet they, too, will lose all they have. Summer will vanish, and, in the struggle to survive, men will forget books and tools and art and all the things we've learned in centuries. The Harrowers will get what they want. We will see the end times, but with no blessed ending in heaven."

She believed this quite sincerely. I could tease no further. "How do you know? How do *they* know? Yes, the weather is foul, the war cruel, sickness rampant, yet we survive. Navronne has suffered before. Nobles are always underestimating the strength of common folk. What's different this time?"

"Where are the monks, Brother? Where are the students who once came to Gillarine for schooling—fifty in my father's time, with more hoping to come? How many villages lie ruined like those between here and Caedmon's Bridge? Where are the grapes of Ardra or the summer fruits of the river country or Evanore's wild boar that sustained my ancestors when the Aurellians forced them to live in caves like beasts? People abandon faith and paint their foreheads with dung. We don't know why our downfall will happen. Everyone has a theory. Brother Victor thinks our present cycle of history just happens to be worse than similar ones of the past. Abbot Luviar believes that some dread event has caused a rip in the binding of earth and heaven. But those of the cabal are men and women of intelligence, wisdom, and a vision that is broader than one abbey or one kingdom or one faith. Besides, it has all been seen by a friend of my father's. Now, come. They're waiting for you."

"Thank you for telling me," I said, as I caught up to her. "I won't betray you—any of you. I'm actually quite proficient at keeping secrets."

She didn't respond. As I considered all she'd told me, one word rose from her tale like a youthful blotch on a girl's clear skin.

"Elene . . ."

She picked up the pace through the passage between the granary and the brewhouse, where the cloying smell of roasting barley was so thick it could choke a man.

"Corin . . ."

We strode across the guesthouse yard where I had first glimpsed her face. An exposed place. Three men in green livery approached the guesthouse from the direction of the stables. Anyone could pop out of the door or the five different passages that opened on the yard or could peer out of the myriad windows of the house.

But the blemish had swelled into a boil, and despite the risk of being overheard, I laid a hand on Elene's shoulder as she grasped the brass door handle. "*Seen* . . . you mean *foreseen,* as by a pureblood diviner?"

She dragged the heavy door open and slipped out from under my hand before she answered, else I might not have barged into the columned atrium after her in full view of the group in the guesthouse parlor. By the time she said, "Yes," it was too late.

As Brother Victor passed around a tray of steaming cups, and Gram worked at a writing table, a short, robust woman robed in mauve and blue silk stood talking with Abbot Luviar, Brother Gildas, and Thane Stearc. Her heavy black hair had been twisted and wound into a great loop, fixed to the back of her head with a gold fan, spread like a peacock's tail. The blue, green, and gold sprawl of interlocking beads on her ample breast proclaimed her a Sinduria—a high priestess of the elder gods. The thick stripes of kohl outlining her eyes and the eyes graven on her silver bracelets, set with pupils of opal and lapis, proclaimed her a pureblood diviner. And her shock when she saw me, quickly followed by amusement, quickly followed by triumph and contempt, proclaimed her my elder sister.

She raised her finger and pointed through the parlor doorway straight at me.

"Oh, Deunor's fire, Lassa, don't. Please don't." My voice echoed like frogs rasping in the fine antechamber.

But she was a Cartamandua, and so did my twelve years of freedom end with her one contemptuous word. "*Recondeur.*"

Chapter 19

"Magnus Valentia de Cartamandua-Celestine . . . a Karish monk. What divination could have prepared me for this?" Thalassa's laughter left her breathless. "Have you been driven out of every other house in Navronne in only twelve years, little brother? Or have you conquered every woman's heart with your everlasting charm, so that the only ones left to share your bed are celibate old men and guileless boys? Do these monks know what you are?"

The others had come out of the parlor and now stood in an awkward half circle ten paces from me, gawking.

"I have lived a life of my own choosing," I said, closing my eyes so I could no longer see Elene, clapping a hand to her mouth, or Brother Victor, his odd features so eloquent in condemnation, or Gram, peering at me curiously, as if I were something not quite human. "I have bound myself where I would and walked away when I would—"

"—and great rewards it has brought you. I can see and smell. But I'll not believe you are here because you have chosen a life of purity and service. Even this corrupt and failing world has not changed so much. I'd advise you to check your valuables, Luviar. And look to your daughter, Lord Stearc. Valen bedded every serving girl and lad in Palinur before he was fifteen. Evidently he can breathe on a woman and set her fawning—maybe men, too. We were never able to *prove* he does it with magic."

Thalassa had ever been adept at making her point. Sorcerous seduction was one of the few crimes for which a pureblood could be arrested. As with everything forbidden, I'd tried it. But I left it behind when I learned of pleasuring.

"I knew it," said Stearc, growling. "By rock and stone, a pureblood renegade . . . he endangers us all with every breath. We should kill him—"

"My lord!" said Abbot Luviar, moving slightly to the front of them all, his pock-grooved face unsettlingly flushed. "We do not speak of murder in Iero's house! Whatever his status in the secular world, Brother Valen is a vowed novice of Saint Ophir, my responsibility and my charge."

"Father Abbot," said Brother Victor, "the law is clear. If we do not turn him over and even the remotest hint of his status as *recondeur* becomes known, the consequences could ruin us. We don't know if the lighthouse can survive the destruction of the abbey. Whatever else, *you* and *Gillarine* will be lost to our cause, and the stocking of the lighthouse will surely come to a halt. With the royal succession near settled, our position is precarious enough. Yet, if we give him up, he knows enough to bring us to ruin."

Brother Victor's emotionless logic was far more terrifying than Stearc's outburst. But then again, naught should terrify a dead man, and I *was* dead, no matter whether or not these people allowed me to keep breathing.

"The hierarch will welcome his information about our plans and use it. The lighthouse is compromised, as are the identities of those in this room—"

"Of course," I said. My skin burned. My soul burned. "Because I refuse to live as a slave to my family and the Pureblood Registry—allowing them to tell me whom I may speak to, what profession I must follow, whom I will marry, and what children I will or will not breed, allowing them to sell my life to the highest bidder—then I must necessarily be untrustworthy."

"It is not merely your refusal to submit, Valen," said Thalassa. "It is that your refusal to submit is the key to your nature—wholly and entirely a servant of your own pleasure. I would not trust you with my dog lest you have discovered some amusement in tormenting dogs. I cannot and will not stand idle and allow you to escape the consequences of a lifetime's self-indulgence."

"You know *nothing* of my life," I said.

She broke from the circle and walked slightly behind me, so that I would have to turn away from the others in order to face her. I refused to turn, though I felt her examination taking in my filthy habit and offal-stained feet and the sweating, blood-grimed hands I clenched at my back.

Every bone and sinew demanded I run. But I was not so naive as

I had been at eight, when Thalassa had taunted me into my first break for freedom, only to stand smirking as my father hauled me home by my hair. The liveried men outside would be Thalassa's escort—pureblood warriors with magically tuned senses. She could summon them with a thought.

"You even foul your monk's costume, Valen," she said.

I held my tongue and my position, trapping the familiar hatred inside until my skin stretched with the size of it.

After a moment, she drifted back toward her fellows. Only thirty, she moved with the imperious gravity of a life-long queen. Though her temple position left her exempt from the mask and cloak required of purebloods when mingling with ordinaries, her gown and jewels certainly met the Registry standards of conservative elegance. A Sinduri high priestess, one of the five highest-ranking servants of the elder gods. Our father must be preening.

"Abbot Luviar, I must and will report my brother to the Registry. Our family has endured twelve years of disgrace that will be relieved only when he is returned to our discipline. I am, as ever, wholly committed to our task, but we must find other means to accomplish our goals. Valen is mentally unstable and entirely untrustworthy, and I'll vow that any help he has given you has been purest chicanery. You needn't fear for our secrets. I've ways to ensure his silence before he is remanded into Registry custody."

And *that* chilled me to the marrow. The Sinduri were known to have potions and spells to alter the mind. My bravado crumbled in an instant. "Holy father, please, don't let her—"

Luviar's hand stopped my begging before I completely abased myself. "Sinduria, Lord Stearc, friends and brothers, before we undertake some drastic course, we must proceed with our conclave. Rightly or wrongly, I took it upon myself to bring Valen into our circle. And despite his regrettable lack of . . . candor . . . he has been of great assistance. We cannot separate our needs and his abilities from his fate. So let us sit and consider both issues together."

The abbot swept through the door and into the parlor, Brother Victor on his heels. A seething Thalassa followed. Lord Stearc waved Gram and Elene into the room ahead of him. He himself remained near the door, as if prepared to rush back through and prevent my escape. Only Gildas was left with me.

He shook his head and grinned. "I thought I had guessed your secrets, Brother, but I will say you have confounded me. A pureblood sorcerer. And Janus de Cartamandua's grandson on top of it. I shall surely wake up tomorrow living on the moon."

He took my arm, and we strolled across the atrium as if going into supper in a nobleman's hall. As we stepped onto the plum-colored carpet of the parlor, he leaned close and whispered, "Be patient, friend. We'll not abandon you."

"I'm sorry," I whispered, bolstered by his friendship. "I needed a refuge. I never intended—" But, of course, intention had naught to do with anything. I had knowingly put them at risk. Only now did the callousness of that choice hit home.

Six straight-backed chairs formed a circle next the hearth. Gildas joined the abbot, Brother Victor, Stearc, and Thalassa, who were already in place. Luviar waved me to the last unoccupied chair of the inner circle, between Gildas and Brother Victor. Gram humbly pulled up a stool just behind Thane Stearc. Elene, a proper squire, remained standing beside the door to the atrium, her hands clasped at her back, eyes straight ahead, her face a mask.

"I cannot credit that you would admit Valen to our deliberations, Luviar," said my sister, her bead collar clicking as she shifted in her seat. "He should be confined. He *will* try to run away. It is his lifelong habit. The sooner I blind his knowledge of our secrets the better."

"I appreciate your sentiments, lady," said Luviar. "Yet the tale of our experiments with your grandfather's book might give you a new perspective. Of course, we must evaluate Brother Valen's contributions differently in the light of this new information about his lineage. Gram, would you please report on the events of these past few days?"

The secretary stood, bowed respectfully to the abbot, Lord Stearc, and Thalassa, and began a detailed, well-structured, and as far as he was capable, accurate account of our search for the pool known as Clyste's Well. Nauseated, my throat parched, I slumped in my chair as he recited. The knowledge that Thalassa's accusations were substantially true did not improve my disposition in the least. The room felt unbearably hot. I wished I dared throw off my cowl or open a window.

Gram paused his recitation to ask Brother Gildas to confirm our discovery of the Well. Brother Gildas stated soberly that to his fullest belief, the pool was the one for which they had been searching. ". . . though I saw no evidence of a Dané guardian there."

Before the secretary could move on to the tale of the tree and the encounter with the Dané, Thalassa leaned forward. Her painted eyes, already larger than life, widened into great dark windows. "So you believe that *Valen* read our grandfather's book of maps, recited the guide spell under his breath, and led you unerringly to a Dané sianou?"

The abbot looked puzzled. "Yes."

"Go on. Tell me the rest." Rouged mouth fixed in judgment, she folded her arms and sat back, biding her time, poised like a cat on the brink of a grand leap.

I closed my eyes and sank lower in the chair. I tried to bury my head in my hands, but I could not bear the stink and had to stuff my hands up my sleeves instead. My sister was going to tell them I could not read. Then she would relate how I had made an art form of lies since I was out of the crèche, how I had preferred to steal what I wanted rather than be given the very same thing by people I loathed, how I had destroyed everything of value I had ever touched, that I had spent three-quarters of my life from age five through fifteen besotted with drink, and had broken every rule of civilized society as if it were my sworn duty.

The wretched part was that, once she had told them those truths, they would believe everything she said of me, true or not. I hated that thought more than I had hated anything in a very long while. I hated what I had seen on Elene's face. On Brother Victor's. On Gram's. At least I'd not had to witness Jullian's reaction. *Recondeur*—traitor to family, king, and gods, one who spits on the power to work magic, the greatest gift given to humankind. And the boy already thought he knew the worst of me.

I pondered how I could possibly wrest some shred of dignity from this day. Stripping a pig now sounded like an afternoon's delight. Meanwhile, Gram took up the story from our meeting on the hillside below Fortress Groult, ending with the Dané vanishing into the night.

"You actually saw one of them . . . spoke to a Dané?" For the first time, Thalassa's attention was diverted from scorn and anger, her expression open in sincere astonishment.

"*She* spoke to *us* is more like it," said Stearc. "She certainly did not listen . . ." He assessed the encounter as he had before—wondrous, but accomplishing nothing of substance.

"Have you anything to add, Brother Valen?" asked the abbot, startling me out of my gloom. "Anything that you observed that Gram has left out? Lord Stearc says you seemed . . . caught up . . . in the incident. And we need to know exactly what you did to invoke the power of the map on both occasions. Did you bring some pure-blood sorcery to bear beyond that held in the book?"

They were all staring at me again. Luviar's inquiry had reminded Thalassa of her day's pleasure—righteous duty and personal entertainment entwined. She was near bursting, her heavy loop of hair quivering, her full red lips ready to spew condemnation for years of my petty insults and my not-so-petty offenses against her and the rest of our kin.

Well, nothing for it. I sat up straight.

"I was indeed overcome by the sight of the Dané," I said, feeling lingering echoes of my strange grief even as I spoke of it at such a distance. If I was to attempt honesty for a change, I could not ignore the experience. "I've seen naught in all my life . . . in all my travels . . . in all my dreams . . . so fearsome and, at the same time, so marvelous. I felt this . . . immeasurable grace . . . that they yet live. Someone once told me that the Danae were the living finger of the god in this world. Perhaps that's what I felt . . . that I was unworthy to see such a wonder."

Though I had begun my confession hoping to garner sympathy— any advantage that might help mitigate a dismal future—somehow I had wandered very close to emotions I had never thought to share with anyone, especially one of my family. Profoundly unsettled, I continued. "I cannot tell you how I found the correct place to leave the nivat or even how I was able to locate the Well, except that it was some odd mixture of luck and ordinary experience at finding my way about the world and, yes, inherited talents. But it is impossible that I invoked the power of the maps."

Puzzlement and disbelief had them shifting in their chairs, but I allowed no interruption. If I dared so much as look at them, I'd never go through with this.

"As my sister is yearning to reveal, I am afflicted with a disorder of the mind, a blindness that leaves me incapable of deciphering written words. At a more appropriate time and place, I will beg forgiveness for this and all my deceptions, holy father and good brothers, hoping that you will understand my fear in the face of your great kindness when I came here wounded and desperate. My experience of family is difficult—the details best left unspoken—but I assure you that I professed my vows with sincerity, if not . . . without reservation. As to how my disorder affects my use of my grandfather's book—*my* book, as it happens, not my family's, as he gave it to me on my seventh birthday—it means I cannot read place-names or written spells, and so must rely on my instincts, inborn talents, my knowledge of maps, and my spellmaking skill to interpret the drawings."

I resisted the urge to add more. No need to humiliate myself further. If I was to be shipped off to Palinur to the gentle discipline of my family and the Pureblood Registry, I would get my fill of humiliation.

Stearc mumbled oaths. Brother Gildas masked a grin with curled fingers. Gram looked thoughtful and, for once, did not drop his eyes when they met mine. Unfortunately he was too far away for me to read anything in them—not that I was likely to see anything at all rewarding. Elene remained in the doorway, but now her back was to me. Probably for the best.

"Do *not* allow him to get away with this," said Thalassa, tight as a moneylender's fist. "Were Valen standing at Mother Samele's right hand and suggesting I ascend her holy mount, I would not move one step forward, lest I fall into Magrog's pit. He is a consummate liar—"

"Sinduria, if you please." Gram's quiet insistence drew their attention away from me, for which I was grateful. "Lady, the last time we spoke of Janus de Cartamandua, you indicated that he was very ill. Does he yet live?"

Not shifting her glare one quat, Thalassa jerked her head in the affirmative.

"Impossible!" The old man had been half in his grave before I'd run away—past seventy years old and addled beyond use. And gods knew I'd wished him dead often enough before and since. How could he not be dead?

"Brother Valen, did your grandfather know of your difficulty with reading?" Gram pursued whatever mad line of reasoning he had begun without altering his tone.

"Everyone in the house knew of his willful ignorance," Thalassa snapped before I recovered wit enough to answer. "Valen's only *disorder* is his despicable, intransigent soul. Surely you cannot swallow this playacting?"

"Please, Sinduria, hear me out." Gram raised his hand but not his voice. "The causes of your brother's condition are not relevant here. Only whether Janus de Cartamandua knew of the problem, which you have confirmed that he did. So, Brother Valen, your grandfather gave you the book on your birthday. Do you believe that he intended you to use it? Or was his intent merely to give you something of value to cherish or to sell?"

"To *cherish*? Hardly. Every time Capatronn—my grandfather Janus—returned to that house, he tried to teach me of the book. I hated it. I hated him. I did everything I could think of to be free of his lessons. But he insisted, saying that I must use the book to follow in his footsteps, and that our family would come to be the most powerful in the world. He was crazed with the idea and made me swear over and over, on holy writs, on shrines, on my life, and always, always with my blood, that I would use the book when I was old enough. When I was 'free to do as I pleased,' he put it. He stank—"

Gods, I could still smell his sour body, the stench of urine and ale and his rotting teeth when I saw him last. And I could see him on so many occasions before that, his black eyes bulging as he made me prick my finger yet again and slap the aingerou that supported the mantel over his hearth, leaving a bloody smear.

I reined in my disgust. "He was . . . is . . . mad. It was unpleasant."

Gram nodded as if I had just given a recitation of the great vices and virtues or an accounting of the abbey grain stores. "So I would guess that reading is not essential to your use of the book. That would explain your success. And if you, as a . . . an ill-mannered, rebellious boy . . . refused your grandfather's tutelage, that would explain your uncertainty as to how that success was accomplished."

A nice hypothesis, but I didn't see what difference it made. If I didn't know what I had done, then I could scarcely repeat my "success." But the gaunt secretary had tangled the others in his thread of reasoning. When he leaned forward on his stool, scarcely visible around his lord's thick shoulder, they leaned forward to listen.

"Two matters require we consult the Danae. We must discover if they can shed light on this upheaval in the natural world, and we must present our request with regard to the Scholar. My Lord Stearc sees no hope in further approaches through the Danae sentinels. Danae have ever distrusted humans, and now, it seems, they despise us. Which means we must travel farther into Aeginea and directly approach those among the long-lived who might yet retain some fondness for Eodward. Stian and Kol are our only hope to be heard."

Brother Victor had been rubbing his lip thoughtfully as Gram spoke. Now he dropped his hand to his lap and crinkled his brow even more. "Rightly spoken, Gram, yet the Dané's reference to thievery and violation is worrisome—clearly obstacles in our path, though we've no idea what they mean."

Good to hear of crimes they could not lay at my feet; I had never stolen from the Danae. Though the consideration of how close I'd come to stealing the offering of nivat gave me a sudden shiver. The damnable, cursed doulon.

The chancellor turned to Thalassa. "Lady, have you had any success in learning more of the Danae's withdrawal from human intercourse?"

"No. The old man is confined to his room and speaks nothing of sense to anyone."

"You have mentioned in the past that his ramblings include frequent references to . . . a person you cared not to name. Is it possible . . . ?" Brother Victor was surely a master of diplomacy. His gaze flicked to me, and my sister did not whisk his head off with some priestess's spell.

"Yes," she said, twisting her mouth in distaste. "Valen was ever his favorite. No one could understand it. When he gave that vile, undisciplined child the last extant copy of the most precious book in the world, our parents—"

Thank all gods, she stopped, perhaps realizing that the seamier aspects of the Cartamandua-Celestine household were perhaps not the proper topic for a serious group of monks and lords come to discuss the end of the world. I had arrived at the same conclusion in my own rant.

Gram was standing now, his sober tunic hanging loose on his thin body. "Abbot Luviar, it seems to me that the god has brought us at least a slim hope of answers," he said. Bathed in the smoky light from the tall windows at his back, less stooped, he took on a certain dignity. "Brother Victor is correct. Before we can approach the Danae, we must understand these grievances that have caused them to retreat from human contact. And we must learn how to use the maps to travel in Aeginea beyond the sentinels, for that is where we'll find Stian and Kol if they yet live. Gildas has found no way to move past the Well, yet we know that Eodward visited the Well and walked as far as the 'valley beyond it to the east,' implying that he traveled from the west as from the abbey. So we are clearly missing something. As Brother Valen is the only person who has taken us even so far as this, I believe he holds the key both to these answers and to our interaction with the Danae."

"Pssh!" Stearc regarded me with a look appropriate to rotting meat. "How do you propose for him to discover these answers that even you have failed to unlock? The man cannot even read his own book of maps. I say the danger a *recondeur* poses far outweighs any service he can offer."

I stopped listening. Were they ever going to ask my opinion? Such an odd group of people. The enigmatic abbot. Brother Victor, whose unflappable, relentless reason was more unnerving than Stearc's contempt. The Evanori warlord, himself a cipher—a scholar and warrior, a man who treated his secretary with a remarkably even hand while bullying his own daughter. Stearc seemed genuinely caught up in this mad venture. Worried. They were all worried, even Thalassa. It was easy to imagine my sister had come here solely to bait me, but she was a member of this group. *Intelligence, wisdom, and a vision that is broader than one abbey or one kingdom or one faith*, so Elene had said, referring, among others, to a member of my family. Truly a wonder of wonders.

". . . see your reasoning. You think to have him question his grandfather." Brother Victor's quiet conclusion stung me awake like a stealthy wasp, as if Brother Infirmarian's lancet pricked a mortified wound.

"No!" I yelled, on my feet before his last word had faded. Pain and hatred and crippling memory exploded from that incision like pus and septic blood. "You cannot force me to do that! I have naught to say to any of them. The old man is mad. You heard her say it. I won't."

"Brother Valen . . ." Several of them said it. They were all standing now.

"I cannot," I said, fighting to hold back the onslaught of the past. "You don't understand. Tell them, Thalassa. Tell them what happened every time Capatronn left to go adventuring." The only person my father loathed more than me was Janus de Cartamandua, but pureblood discipline forbade him touching his own father.

I was already halfway to the door . . . shaking . . . furious . . . when I realized I had nowhere to go. Turning my back on them, I retreated toward the window, where I clutched the iron frame and stared into the yard. I tried to recapture my wonder at what I had seen at Caedmon's Bridge—a living magic in the universe. Such a sight should leave all other events trivial. But all I could see, all I could feel, all I could hear were my grandfather's conspiratorial whispers and his robust chortling as he rode away on his great horse, leaving me alone to face my father's strap. Even my hatred for the man who beat me until my bowels released and confined me hungry and bleeding in my spell-darkened room could not match my hatred for the man who kept promising to set me free of it and never did. I had sworn I would never look at my grandfather again. Never speak to him. Never listen to him. He should be dead.

"Destroy my mind with Sinduri magic if you wish," I said through gritted teeth. "Send me back to pureblood slavery if you wish, or throw me in the river with a stone hung round my throat. But do not ask me to sit in a room and have a civilized conversation with my grandfather."

I did not hear their hasty deliberations as I pressed my forehead against the cold glass, raging and swearing—at myself more than anyone else. What use to be so angry over past misery? I had set myself free of that house, and if I had found only fleeting enjoyments and unsavory habits to soothe my restless nature, well then that was unfortunate. But at least I had made my own choices, whether to tan hides or steal a dagger or soldier for a king, whether to bed a woman or winter in an abbey or expend my magic on the doulon. At least I had lived.

When Brother Gildas broke away from Abbot Luviar, took my arm, and led me from the guesthouse and into the garden, I did not speak to him. I would waste no words on them ever again. I would lift not one finger to conspire in their madness.

The evening was still, a pale silver sheen of flagging sunlight behind wads of gray wool clouds. For once, the only storm raged inside me. Back in the guesthouse Thalassa was surely recounting the wicked tales I had so cleverly diverted earlier. Even worse, she could be telling them the whole sordid story of my childhood. Gods, how I hated the thought of that. But I would not waste any more time trying to explain.

Gildas held silent as we strode between the hedges, past the scummy pond, past the statue of Karus and uncountable images of saints put there as reminders of how we ought to live. I soon realized the monk was not leading me anywhere in particular. Thalassa's two guards followed at a discreet distance, ready to pounce should I breathe wrong.

Rabbits sat paralyzed in the center of the path as we approached, darting out of our way just before we stepped on them. Two magpies screeched at us and then at each other and at the squirrels chasing through the hedges. Thunder rumbled from beyond the mountains.

I stared numbly at the path, my steps gradually losing their initial frantic pace. Eventually the bells for Vespers rang, and as the last tones drifted into silence and birdsong, my most acute fury seeped away. Still, Gildas waited.

"Don't you need to be back at the guesthouse deciding what to do with me?" I said at last. "I'm not going to run off—not with those two brawny goslings prancing after me as if I were their dame. They'd have no second thoughts about violating the cloisters to chase me down, if that's what concerns you."

"I belong with the cabalists little more than you," said Gildas. "I've been involved with them only three years. I help where I can, but my primary role is different from that of the others. They've not even told me how to open the lighthouse as yet. Only Victor, Luviar, and Stearc know that."

"They're all mad. Gods . . . Books and plows and Danae. Monks and princes, warlords and my sister the high priestess. An abbot who plays them all like strings on a vielle."

"The ever-sensible Gram has not told you the connection between all these things?"

"It makes no difference. I'll not dance to their music no matter what." I shook my head. "And they're not likely to tell me any more now, are they? Just more of my mind for my sister to obliterate lest I spew my guts to the hierarch and betray you all."

We strolled through the hedge maze, a flock of sparrows twittering as they pecked at the worms the week's rains had washed onto the path. Plainsong wafted faintly from the church, the pure melody twining itself around my anger, soothing my aching head.

"You must confess you are an enigma. What are they to think of you—a pureblood who throws away his position . . . his magic . . . to chop vegetables in a monastery? A man who could vie for power with princes, yet who has not bothered to learn to read?"

"Tell me of *your* vocation, Gildas," I snapped. "Was it your mother's prayers brought you here? *My* mother used predictions of my tormented demise to amuse her friends."

"You don't want to hear of my mother. She forbade us to eat berries on the last day of the week, for all know that the seeds would sprout vines in our bellies to grow out our ears if swallowed on Samele's day. My mother believed that if she left a trail of blood between her door and the town well, a gatzé would come and grant her three wishes. Every child in Pontia would follow her to the well each day, taunting, asking what was her wish. She died with her veins flat from bleeding them. She— Well, you are not the only man with difficult family." He barked a laugh.

I stopped in midstride. Harsh, lonely . . . of a sudden Gildas reminded me of a Pyrrhan exile I'd once met. Pyrrhans believed the world beyond their land's borders existed only in their imaginations, and thus every day spent outside Pyrrha felt askew—outside of time, in the wrong place. A blessed grace that Gildas had found a place he valued so deeply as Gillarine. "Ah, fires of heaven, Gildas . . . I'm sorry."

Flushed from chin to the crown of his shaven head, he averted his face and nudged me forward again. "You'd no way to know, unless thought reading is a Cartamandua bent."

"I've always imagined you at the very least some noble's younger son, done out of inheritance by an elder brother or sister and sent off here unwilling. Perhaps even our rumored Pretender."

His smile tightened. "Not in the remotest instance. My family had nothing. Certainly nothing I wanted. They were not . . . scholarly . . . and my mind hungered for more stimulation than stitching leather to fit other men's feet. Pride of intellect led me astray for many years—until I began to look beyond the material world for answers. Humility is a difficult lesson."

No one had ever shared such a clean and honest piece of himself with me, especially on so private a matter. In my first days at the abbey he had offered me his friendship, and caution had made me refuse him. Too late now. I regretted that as much as any consequence of this wretched day. "At least you've a mind for lessons. Some skulls are too thick."

He grinned and shook his head. "Come now, we have no time to recount our mournful pasts. You need to decide what to do next. Right now they're debating whether to send you to Palinur as a novice of Saint Ophir, as Abbot Luviar wishes, or as a recaptured *recondeur* in the high priestess's custody." He cocked his head in inquiry. "Truly you have a right to know why the abbot wants to keep you on his leash. Shall I tell you?"

"Do as you like."

"Gram could recite it better, I suppose, with his tallyman's mind. But here's what I know . . . Twenty years ago, Brother Victor and Brother Luviar, scholars and visionaries of extraordinary perceptions, came to believe that certain changes they saw in the world were serious enough that they needed to prepare. Their studies and calculations intimated that some twenty-five or thirty years might pass from the depth of crisis until men and women were ready to hear again of books and plows. They recruited a few people to help them build the lighthouse to survive the worst. Being of middle years themselves, they decided they needed a younger man to stand with the lighthouse, a Scholar who knew both the content of the books and how to use the tools they had chosen to preserve. Even in so short a span, much knowledge could be lost. If those who know how to warp a loom are dead, who will prevent others from burning the loom to stay warm?"

I said nothing. I preferred to forget these people and their plotting. They needed no vagabond jackleg to help them.

My lack of response did not deter Gildas. "And what if we were to lose all those who can read? City dwellers are most susceptible to plague. To ravagers. If the cities die, if learning dies, we are sent back to the land, to nights in the wild forest with spirits we can no longer tame with words, to awe of these Gehoum—the Powers who make the sky grow light or dark, whose righteous wrath is fire and storm . . ." His words trailed off.

An icy breath traced my spine, very like the night Sila Diaglou plunged her stake into a bleeding Boreas. I shuddered. "If I didn't know better, I'd say *you* were the diviner in this cabal," I said.

He laughed away the mystical fog that had settled over him like the haze cloaking the river in the night. "I've no magic. I only read the sayings of diviners and heed them." He waved for me to keep walking as he talked. "Luviar and Brother Victor chose one of their finest and most versatile students at Gillarine's school to be their Scholar, a young warlord of Evanore."

"Not Stearc!" I said, not believing it even as I said it.

Gildas nodded, tucked his hands up his sleeves, and rounded a corner between the straggling yews. "Stearc applied himself to read every volume as they stored it away and to learn the working of every tool. But when blight hit the vineyards, and King Eodward had still not named a successor, Luviar and Victor began to believe that the dark time could last longer and lie deeper than they'd thought. The lack of a strong and righteous king makes the coming decline far more severe, you see. Stearc agreed that they needed to prepare someone younger to become the Scholar."

I halted again and stared at his hairless skull and well-hewn face, at the clear, unmarked skin, at the brown eyes never lacking in irony, tucked under the line of his dark brow. "You."

No wonder he forever smelled of sheep or smithing or yeast and barley. No wonder he was forever reading. He was the one chosen to survive and remember and, when the time was right, teach. The keeper of the lighthouse. The memory of a bed crammed up against stacked barrels aroused a dreadful understanding.

"Great holy Iero, they're going to shut you in there, aren't they? Seal you in the lighthouse. So you'll survive the worst. Alone . . . for years . . . alone . . ."

"That was the original intent. Don't look so horrified! I thrive on solitude and silence. It is the only peace we're given in this world. And consider, I would have infinite occupation and no interruptions. However, a few months ago, we received new information that threw our whole plan into doubt."

He moved on. I followed, unable to ignore the story. A rabbit sat chewing in the middle of an intersecting path, scampering away only when we were close enough to step on it.

"Stearc brought your sister into the cabal. He knew and respected her from other dealings with the Sinduri. She worked a grand divination, a whole day of incantations, burning herbs, and magical water basins, a marvel such as those of us raised outside pureblood halls had never seen before. And what she augured confounded the cabal. Two hundred and ten years until the dawn. A very long night indeed. Too much solitude, even for me! Somewhere along the way, Stearc had come by the private journal of Eodward's tutor—a Moriangi monk named Picus, sent by Caedmon to accompany and educate his son in his exile. And so, thoughts turned to the Danae."

Lost in imagining the dreadful destiny they had planned for Gildas, I failed to grasp the connection. "I don't understand."

As joyful evensong floated from the church, Gildas laughed again, not so merrily this time. "It seems we are both condemned to a life we would not choose. Instead of granting me a few decades of peace, solitude, and study, they wish me to go live with beings who despise humans, disdain scholarship, and who fight among themselves over which tree belongs to whom. If it can be arranged, I am to live in Aeginea."

"Live with the Danae? Seven years for one . . . thirty years. So you would be . . . what?"

"According to this fey reasoning, when the madness fades and men realize they need what I can teach, I shall be but nine years past my fiftieth birthday—no older than Abbot Luviar, a hale and vigorous man. And perhaps not even so advanced as that in terms of health and strength, for once back here Eodward remained a man in his prime until well into middle age."

"Deunor's fire!"

And as I contemplated this mad scheme, the most personal of Gillarine's recent mysteries unraveled as well. No more wondering why the abbot had allowed an unsavory vagabond to join his holy brotherhood. He must have thought my grandfather's book a gift from Iero himself. Had I not told him that I had successfully made use of the book, he would likely have kept only the book and sent me away. And I would still be free. After twelve years evading the prison of my birth, my lies had caught me up at last.

"Ah." Gildas halted in midstride and pointed down the path. "It appears as if the decision has been made."

Thalassa's two liveried guards hurried toward us. I imagined shackles tightening about my wrists. My gorge rose.

"Strike me," said Gildas, grasping my shoulders and spinning me about to confront him. Fiery excitement bloomed in his face.

"What?"

"Strike me and run. Through the cloisters to the bridge behind the infirmary. Wait at the dolmen in the grain fields south of the river. I'll tell them a shortcut—misdirect them. As soon as I can, I'll bring food and coin, whatever you need. But wait for me. Promise." He grinned and let his grip slide down my arms, shaking me out of my astonishment. "The cabal will find a road that is not built on the backs of dead men."

"Ah, Brother, you must not—"

"Strike! Go!"

A hopeless scheme. But life's breath to one suffocating.

I drove my fist into his smiling face. His smooth skin broke and the fine bones shifted as I summoned the pent fury of the day to fuel the blow. My aim was not merely to play the necessary part, but to keep him blameless, for his gift was not only the strike, but the suspicion that must inevitably surround it. I knew well which injury could harm him more. Make one worse, and the other might be eased. They'd blame his misdirection on his muddled head.

"Iero's grace, Brother," I said, as he crumpled into the yew hedge. And then I ran.

Chapter 20

"I should just go," I said, as I blotted stray water droplets from my neck.

A storm had blown in soon after I reached the ancient stones of the dolmen, and the broad lintel stone, though something like a roof, did little to shield a man from wind-driven rain. The worst of the storm had passed somewhere between the ringing of Compline and the day's end bell, but by the time Gildas at last popped out of the fog, I was thoroughly soaked and incomparably edgy. I had waited more than four hours, telling myself every moment that I was a madman to do so.

"No! You must not stir from here," said Gildas softly, crouched close enough I could make out his face. Voices carried in the fog. "Your sister insists that you'll run fast and far. They're scouring the countryside, the river, and the woodland tracks. They've alerted the watch in Elanus. They'll never imagine you've remained so near the abbey and in a barley field to boot. Even the purebloods— You're one of them, Valen. Surely you've spells to conceal your path, spells to confuse them."

"I'm not at all good at spellcasting," I said. "*Obscuré* spells are unreliable at best, and I've never made one work. I cannot just sit here."

"Be patient. They'll soon tire of useless searching in the dark. And the moment they decide to wait for dawn, you're free of them."

Gildas's eyes flashed in his pale face, blotched and swollen from encountering my fist. Though breathless from his hurried journey, his voice was tight with excitement. I had been on the run too often for excitement, and I was much too close to the abbey to feel free.

"I'm sorry I had to come here with so little. But I didn't want you to wait any longer without word. I hadn't counted on you putting me in the infirmary!"

"Yet you've brought me Iero's own gift." Upon his arrival, my wet, battered, and bedraggled friend had shoved a fat wineskin into my hands. "And I do thank you for it and for this chance, but I daren't wait longer."

"You need your secular clothes; they'll be watching for the cowl. And if you're going to avoid towns until you're well away, you need food. Give me another hour."

I turned his head so I could see his swollen jaw. "Holy Mother, I *am* sorry for this. You oughtn't be trotting around with a bruised head. You'll get dizzy and fall in the river. And you *must* not be caught helping me. Do you even understand what they'll do to you?" He'd be god-blessed to see daylight ever again.

His teeth flashed in the rainy darkness. "Your sister's purebloods questioned me before Compline and now think I'm asleep. I can get into the dorter and the kitchen without anyone the wiser. But they'll certainly be back to question me, so I'll send one of the boys with your things. The abbey will be in such an uproar, they'll be able to slip in and out easier than any of us. And they admire you so."

"No!" I said, sharper than I intended. "Not the boys. Of course they'd do anything you ask them. But no, please. I'd rather do without."

I had no reason to believe Jullian or Gerard would still "admire" me in any way, assuming they ever had. Even so, I refused to put them in jeopardy. At least Gildas was a man and had some idea of the world and its horrors, but those boys . . . they would die in prison.

"They're very careful and I'm sure they'd not betray you, but if you prefer, I'll come myself during Matins. Promise you'll not leave before that. I'm quite recovered." His hands squeezed my shoulders, solid and reassuring. "You saved me from Sila Diaglou's whip, Valen. Did you think I'd forget?"

I wrestled with fear and need and the desire to be gone. I could likely survive the next few days with no money, no food, no secular clothes. But of course I had a far more urgent lack. Four days gone since my incomplete doulon. Saints and angels, how I hated this. "Brother, if you can . . . I've left a packet hidden in the garden all these months, a few things I'd not like to abandon. A knife. Some extra medicine for my leg."

One look inside the bundle and he would know. By sight or scent, nivat was unmistakable. If Gildas had risked so much to get me this far, then perhaps he could even forgive a bit of perversion.

"I'll bring whatever you like." After I described how to find my bundle, he gripped my shoulders. "An hour. You are in the god's hand, Valen."

"And you, good friend," I said, as he sped through the stubbled field, vanishing almost before I could blink. "Be very careful."

You're a fool to wait, Valen. Better to be caught running than squatting like a toad. It was the same argument I'd had with myself all evening. But for twelve years, doing the unexpected had kept me free. Gildas would do as I asked. A fascination had captured him since the moment he'd learned I was pureblood, driving him to help beyond reasoned friendship. If we were successful, perhaps he'd have a chance to tell me why.

Pulling up my hood, I settled back against the cold stone and took a long pull at the wineskin. Though I expected ale, the essence of grape and oak warmed my gullet. *Oh, friend Gildas, blessed be your name. And mighty Erdru, holy lord of grape and harvest, how could you have so cruelly abandoned your worshipers?* I took a second drink, feeling the wine scald the hollows in my belly. With every swallow, I named Gildas holy.

I ought to sleep. The coming days would be long and difficult, and sleeping bodies were harder to locate with magic. But the events of the past weeks roiled in my head like cream in a churn, and strangeness hung about me like a fever. Through the hours of waiting, I had imagined I was hearing things through the drumming rain . . . sounds like sighs and breathing, like worms gnawing their way through dead flesh, like heartbeats and green shoots struggling to break through the mud and rock. I kept my hands clasped tightly in my lap, remembering the earth breathing under my hand as I searched out the route to Elanus. If I laid my palms down tonight, I felt the eerie certainty that I'd detect a heartbeat.

Holy ground. Of course, the world was infused with divine mystery. Everyone felt such things on occasion—saw faces in the clouds, experienced a day in the midst of winter when it felt as if spring had leaked through the boundaries of seasons, felt prickles when walking through a darkening wood. But I had never thought myself closer to such mystery than the next man. Signs and portents had never shaken me, never driven me to any action beyond kissing the nearest aingerou or pouring a libation for the appropriate deity. But here in this valley . . . in the cloisters, on the road, in the hills. What was happening to me?

Likely what I felt tonight was nothing save these ancient rocks. Simple and stark, dolmens were scattered in the open country

throughout Ardra. No one knew what purposes they had served—
burials, ceremonies, boundaries, markers. Yet anyone with even a
touch of magical sensibility would recognize the power that lingered
about them.

And I had seen a Dané. Only now as the rain spattered on the
stone and showered softly on the barley could I recapture the wonder of it. They lived . . . beings that could dissolve into earth or water
or tree. Beings that could hear the music of the stars and weave life
into the fields with their dancing. Knowing the legends were true . . .
the world could never look the same to me.

A breath of wind swirled the mist, bearing the powerful sweet
scent of rotting grain. I pulled my hood lower, huddled the wineskin
closer, and drank again, closing my eyes. I didn't want to see what
beings might live in a place so ancient. I didn't want to hear the creaking as the stones shifted with the breathing of the earth. I shuddered.
What had Gildas said? *If the cities die, if learning dies, we are sent
back to the land, to nights in the wild forest with spirits we can no
longer tame with words, to awe of these Gehoum . . .*

"Brother Valen?"

The soft voice sent me to my feet with my stomach in my throat.
Giddy with the wine and foolish musings, I imagined all sorts of
things before I associated the voice with the human shape standing
near a mound of musty grain stalks ten paces away. "Mistress
Elene?"

"Yes."

I pressed my back to the stone, peering into the darkness, trying
to glimpse other movement. "Have they sent you to drag me back?
I warn you I won't go other than feet before, and I don't think you're
capable of overpowering me on your own. Or perhaps you've
brought comrades?"

"I'm quite alone." She stepped under the lintel rock, water cascading from her cloak. Her wet hair curled about her face. "I spied
on you and Brother Gildas in the maze and followed you out here,
determined to bring you back. When you stopped so close, I believed
you were having second thoughts. So, like a moonstruck chit, I've
hidden behind that pile of sour barley all this time debating whether
to speak with you or just to pray you would go back on your own."

I did not mistake her reference to "moonstruck chit" for any more
than description. Nor did I tease her about it. Her face, so pale in the
night, was tied into much too sober a knot.

I sank to the ground again, leaning against one upright stone. My
feet and my back reminded me of two exhausting days, a sleepless

night, and a butchered pig. "I'm always glad for company, mistress. But I can't believe your father would approve." Certainly not after Thalassa's jibes.

"He won't." She matched my position against the other upright. "My father would prefer having a son and flies into a rage when I show any independence of mind. Even when he can't find reason to refuse a request, he seeks a way to make his acquiescence unpleasant. If I'm to be chastised anyway, I might as well do as I please now and then."

"Thus your cheerful life as Corin the Squire."

"He calls me Corin even when we're alone."

This confession was couched in such rueful exasperation that I laughed in sympathy and tossed her the wineskin. "So we have both cursed our families with unfulfilled expectations. At least you bear no fault for your father's disappointment, as I'm sure a scholarly man such as Stearc will recognize eventually. My family has no such consolation. I was a dreadful, obstreperous child, who set out from the crèche to turn their well-ordered household bottom side up and who maliciously tormented every unfortunate who stepped within my view. My sister's reports of that are perfectly true."

Elene took a single swallow of wine and slowly replaced the plug. Earning my eternal gratitude, she tossed it back to me. "I think your sister does not know you as you are now."

I took a very long swallow. Perhaps the wine would blunt the whispering seduction of the night. The mist curled around my cheeks and tickled my ears like a woman's tongue. The earth pulsed beneath my legs and backside. The richness of Elene's voice drew soft fingers up my thighs. To keep talking was an effort.

"Nor do you know me, good Corin. If you're feeling guilty for leading me into that little mess this afternoon, don't. I am quite good at embroiling myself in messes on my own." I shifted position, moving close enough to offer the wineskin again.

She shook her head and leaned forward, her knees drawn up, her hands clasped firmly in front of her legs. I could feel her breath on my face. I could smell the barley on her. The layers of damp leather. The woman underneath. Foolish to allow such distraction . . .

"If I'm to feel guilty, then I'd rather more fault than an accidental meeting to justify it." Her voice played like music in the night. "I came here to ask you— No, to plead with you. The cabal needs you, Brother Valen. I'm surprised at Brother Gildas helping you escape. I never judged him a man to care about anyone's personal safety. He is quite single-minded. But he is a fool if he thinks the lighthouse cabal can succeed without your assistance. Your sister has tried everything to glean the information we need from your grandfather with no result. And since the day the gods brought you to Gillarine, each of us has tried to unravel the book of maps and got no farther than a bare cliff and a crossroads cairn."

"And how do you propose I assist you? Do you understand the somewhat limited prospects for a recaptured *recondeur*? Until the day I die I'll not be allowed to piss without three guards watching me. You're all mad anyway." Her choice of conversational topic cooled my rising fever.

"The life of a pureblood . . . I'd always thought it holy. Your people live hidden, so honored, valued, protected, elevated beyond all of us who must struggle with everyday life, as if you spend half your days in heaven, returning only long enough to produce wonders. I thought a *recondeur* must be soul-dead to leave such a noble gift as sorcery behind. Yet I cannot believe that of you."

How could I explain that the favor of kings and a life of luxury, ever shielded from want and war, was not worth the price? What ordinary would ever believe it? Few purebloods besides my own mad self had ever believed it. Everyone who'd ever known me swore that I spoke such heresy to excuse poor skills and willful ignorance, or to service childish whim made stubborn by "unfortunate conflict" with my father. All agreed my nature insupportably perverse. Yet my belief was rooted as deep as any knowledge or understanding I possessed.

The night hid her expression, leaving us a certain intimacy, like comfortable bed partners after the frenzy is past. "Mistress, when your men threw that grain sack over my head, I was convinced I would die from it. No matter that the bag was loosely woven. No matter that your intent to let me live was soon clear, and that the restriction of my sight was part of a well-considered plan. Had the sack been woven of spider's silk wound with gossamer, the cord about my neck softer than angel's wings, and your bodyguards' hands as gentle as your own, it would have made no difference to my horror and dread. I could not breathe. Pureblood life was very like that for me. Now it will be worse."

"Surely, whatever your problems in the past, your family will see you've changed." She was truly naive.

"Ah, lady, you don't know my family." I touched her face, so pale in the fog, cool and damp. And my hand slid around the back of her neck, pulling her gently toward me while stroking the downy hair and soft skin, feeling the strength and pride of her. So alive . . .

Her breath caught, but she yielded, warmth flooding her skin under my fingers. Imminent danger . . . escape . . . caution . . . vows . . . all slipped away, the pulse of the night driving me where I'd no intent to go. It had been so long. The ache within me grew, trapping breath in my lungs, obliterating thought as my lips touched hers . . .

Torches flared from the direction of the abbey. Shouts accompanied them and were answered from the mist on our flanks. Blessed saints and angels, how stupid, how inexcusably weak, lust-blinded, and incautious, could a man get? She *wanted* me taken.

"Magrog have you, woman!"

Elene shot up from the ground in the same moment I did. "Brother Valen, wait! I didn't—"

I didn't dally to hear her excuses, but sped southward into the fog, stumbling blindly until I stopped cursing perfidious women and threw every sense I possessed into the race. *Feel the thicker mist hanging over the river on your left . . . smell the wrack and weed . . . hear the whisper of water in its deep channel. Feel the road on the right . . . the tread of feet . . . of wheels . . . of hooves and paws for a thousand years . . . the restless horses patrolling there . . . waiting for you to stumble. And the earth underfoot . . .*

I stopped and tore at the laces of my sandals. Throwing them off, I ran barefoot, feeling the prickling stubble of the barley field and the cold, sodden earth. Instinct warned me of holes, channels, and rocks and guided me southward, upward, away from the abbey.

The fog swallowed the torchlight and voices, and my bare feet were light, little more than a mouse's tread through the fields. I slowed a bit and controlled my breathing so as not to give away by gasps and gulps what I gained by speed.

A pale line emerged from the fog—a rampart of stone—the abbey boundary, a waist-high rubble wall out here in the fields, not the smooth-dressed ashlar of the abbey's public face. I slapped my hands on the top and leaped over the wall, trying to remember the terrain to the south, the route Brother Adolfus and I had traveled toward Caedmon's Bridge. Broad meadows between the road and the river, broken by swaths of trees, and then the short steep climb toward the higher meadows, the giant's steps toward the mountains.

Chest heaving, I knelt and pressed hands and forehead to the earth. Stretched my mind forward. Swept it across the landscape. *Safety . . . haven . . . guide me . . .* The night shifted a little. *Left. A path limned with moonlight.* I popped up and ran.

The breeze swelled, swirling the fog, thinning it here and there. Patches of stars appeared and were as quickly obscured. *Angle right* and around to avoid a spring and a thicket. Foolish as it was to hope, I began to think I had eluded them. My destination—the refuge—felt near.

Hoofbeats to my right. On the road, much too close. Torches again. Damnable beasts to bring pursuit so fast.

I burst through the edge of the fog. The night was clear; the stars gleamed above a lush meadow, broken only by a ring of trees with smooth white trunks and bright gold leaves. I'd thought these aspens were already bare . . .

"Ho there! Get him!" The hoofbeats dulled when they left the road for the grass of the meadow. Or perhaps my heart thudded so ferociously that it drowned out the sounds of pursuit.

A searing finger touched the back of my neck. Of a sudden my feet felt shod in iron. Stumbling, I dragged them onward, unwilling to concede the race. Another bolt touched my back—no mundane weapon, but sorcery, a brutal binding of limbs and will.

I was so close to the ring of aspens. What safety might lie there when I had already been spotted, I could not imagine. Yet I believed that to reach it must yield victory. Only a little farther . . . a few steps . . .

A third bolt took my knees, and I crumpled a mere ten paces from the rustling trees. The stink of horses and diseased leaves gagged me as I fell.

Until the end of days I would swear that a naked man, a dragon traced in blue fire upon his face and limbs, reached out to me from the grove. But it was too far, and the fourth bolt of fire made the night go black.

They rolled me onto a palliasse thinner than the one in the monks' dorter, and with only hard floor, no sling of ropes underneath it.

"Can he breathe properly? Swallow?"

No, I wanted to say. *He cannot breathe, not if you've put him in a cell.* The place smelled of rusted iron and musty stone, fresh straw and old piss. Prisons were prisons, even in an abbey.

"Indeed, sir abbot, all those things. We are not permitted to injure him." The perfumed man who had hauled me up from the ground and thrown me over his saddle sounded as if he'd a broom up his backside. His scent was cheap; his contract with Thalassa must not pay well. "The spell merely prevents voluntary movement. He is probably awake even now."

Fingers shoved my eyelids open and I stared directly into the yellow glare of a lamp. My eyes blinked and watered. From behind the glare two shadowy faces looked down at me.

"There, you see, sir abbot. He hears us. The *recondeur* seems a bit unhappy at his state."

Trapped within the bonds of my flesh, I struggled to strike . . . to scream . . . to move . . . half crazed already.

A cool hand rested on my forehead. "I regret you could not trust me, Valen," said Luviar. "I would have protected you. Trust breeds faith. And faith, honesty, and compassion are the roots of honor. With your gifts and a smattering of honor, you might have done great good for the world. May Iero transform your intransigent heart."

The blurred faces moved out of view. The lamp was taken away. My skin shrank as the yellow light wavered, latches rattled, and a door was opened, stirring the musty air, causing wild shadows to dance about the low, mold-patched ceiling.

Please don't leave me here!

The door slammed shut. The locks clicked. The darkness and the walls closed in.

Chapter 21

Voices, light, and cheap scent yanked me into full awareness. This event was not a waking. I had not slept. But at sometime in the long frigid night of suffocation and terror, I had clawed open a hole in my mind, a deeper darkness void of thought, a place to huddle and stay sane. Now, unrelieved by sleep's murky unwinding, I could remember exactly the events of day and night that had led to my current position flat on my back, eyes open, in the abbey's prison cell.

Thalassa's kohl-lined eyes and her long straight nose hovered above me. She laid a finger in the center of my forehead, whispered a word, and an invisible whip stroke tore through me from head to toes. A mighty unraveling.

I curled up in a knot and rolled to the side, muting my cry in a fit of coughing, my gritty eyes squeezed shut. My spine stung.

A hand closed over my mouth and pressed tightly, as if to silence my cough, even while another pressed from the back of my head. The hands—Thalassa's, surely—were quickly removed, and I felt a void at my side as she moved away.

"Silos, inform me at once if you sense one scrap of magic from this cell," she commanded. "We'll silkbind his hands at the first hint of it. And tell the monk he may bring something for Valen to drink. But no ale or spirits. And nothing to eat for today. I wish the *recondeur* to remain sober, and a hungry day will remind him of his manners. We leave for Palinur in an hour."

"Yes, Sinduria," said the scented lackey.

Had anyone ever suffered such a sister? Between Thalassa and Elene, I vowed to swear off women altogether. Would Elene have let me take her body just to fulfill her holy purpose?

A swish of silk on stone and the door slammed shut behind Thalassa. I remained huddled on the palliasse, trying to summon the resilience that had sustained me as a child, trying to convince myself that I would not bend to their will just to avoid another night like the one I had just endured. The deepening cold bruised body and spirit, weighing as iron-linked mail on my limbs. I could not stop shaking.

The door opened and closed again. Light danced at the edges of my eyelids. Someone wearing sandals walked the five steps from the door and crouched beside me, smelling of damp wool and the boiling herbs of the infirmary, overlaid with traces of mud and grain fields.

"Sit up, Brother Valen. I've brought you water. You need to drink and change clothes, and then we must pray for your true repentance and a safe journey."

"I don't drink water, Brother Gildas," I said, my voice as rough as if my night's screams had been aloud instead of trapped within my skull.

"They're not going to give you anything else for a while, and if you fail to cooperate, they'll force it down you. You are no longer a child to take petty victories from stubbornness. Now, sit up."

Men of insight. If my childhood had been lived out among ones like these, I might have turned out differently. I rolled onto all fours and sat back on my heels, cramming my frozen hands into my sleeves. Gildas sat cross-legged on the floor in front of me, holding a green pottery flask. Beside him sat a small brass lamp and a pile of clothing that could be none but my own stained jaque, braies, and boots.

"How is it *you* are here?" I wiped my eyes with the back of my hand. "Are you a pris—?"

He pressed a finger to his mouth and jerked his head slightly backward toward the ironclad door at his back. Its upper half was a thick grate. Anyone in the darkness outside the door could see and hear what went on in the cell.

"Father Abbot sent me," he said. "I told him I bore no grudge for the bruises, and assured him that my incompetence could not set you free again. Your guards—*both* of them—are purebloods."

So they did not suspect his complicity in my escape. A touch of resentment cooled my good feelings. I supposed Elene thought Gildas too valuable to their little cabal to reveal his role in the night's fiasco. At least he had tried to help.

"Drink this, and dress yourself in your secular clothing."

I unstoppered the flask he gave me, sniffed at it, and stuffed the stopper back in again, pretending my throat did not feel like gravel.

Water—my foretold doom. My mother might be a wretched parent, but she was a talented diviner. "So my novice year is at an end, is it?"

"For now. The Sinduria and Abbot Luviar have agreed that you will not be permitted to hide behind the cowl as you face the consequences of your transgressions. However, the abbot wishes me to remind you that you are not released from your vows. You remain sworn in obedience to him and to the Rule of Saint Ophir and are not to speak of certain events. Can you tell me which ones?"

I shoved the water flask back into his hand. "Despite what everyone believes, I'm not stupid."

"Come now, tell me. I'm required to hear your recitation."

"I'll not reveal any of his—" My tongue balked at the word *secrets*. I began again. "He assumes I'll tell of the—" I tried to say *lighthouse* but was unable to speak the word.

Again, and then again, I attempted to speak of the abbot and Gillarine and the conspiracy. I pressed my hands to my head as if to trap the words that kept escaping somewhere between my mind and my mouth, but concentration seemed to make no difference. *Danae, lighthouse, conspiracy* . . . I could not voice them.

"What have they done?" I tugged at my hair until my scalp burned. I was awake. In control of my body. Surely I could command my own speech. Surely . . . As I spewed half sentences and fragments, I remembered Thalassa's hands squeezing my mouth and head and began to understand. "Is that why you're here? Did they send you to test her damnable spell?"

Frantically, I sped through thoughts and memories in search of holes or gaps. Nothing of current or past events seemed to be missing, but then, how would I know?

"Valen . . ." Gildas laid his hands on my shoulders, but I knocked him backward.

"Listen to me! Listen!" Gildas got back to his knees and reached for me again. I twisted and shoved him away, but I could not both concentrate on the gaps in my speech and grapple with a man so determined and so surprisingly strong. Eventually he caught my upper arms and squeezed them tight to my body, shaking me until I met his gaze. "Be easy, Brother. This is well done. They've put a simple binder on your tongue with regard to these matters. Nothing more. I promise you. Father Abbot would allow nothing of a permanent nature. Yes, they wished me to test you. As the restriction is now proved, nothing further should be needed."

"Am I to thank Luviar for that?" I said. I thrust my forearms between Gildas's and slammed them outward to break his grip. He winced and rubbed his arms, and I was glad of it.

He did not touch me again but crinkled his brow earnestly. "You ran, Valen. Blame the one responsible"—his face was all apology—"and forgive him. Now we need to move on. They'll be coming for you soon. The Sinduria wishes to leave for Palinur before Prime."

He picked up my old clothes and held them out to me. "Though you must relinquish the cowl and gown, Father Abbot says you may keep the shirt. A biting cold has settled in since the storm."

Stiff with anger at Gildas, at the monks, at myself and everyone else within Gillarine's walls, I made no move to take the stack. What had come over me in this place? I knew better than to trust anyone.

His eyes flicked quite obviously from me to the bundle. And then again. The third time he did so, I held out my hands. As he laid the neatly folded clothing on my open palms, his warm fingers grasped one of my hands and guided it to the middle of the stack. And there I felt a small wad of tallow-stiffened canvas, drawn closed with a leather thong.

I glanced up quickly, my heart galloping.

Raising his thick brows and smiling ruefully, he released the bundle and stood up. "You are a man of many virtues, Valen. Be *very* careful as you don these worldly garments again, lest you be snared from the path of right . . . or reason. There are always choices to be made, even in the life you were born to."

Hot blood flooded my skin until I felt as if I must glow brighter than the lantern. I hated that he knew. What was wrong with me of late, worrying so much about what people thought of me? Gildas was but an overzealous monk. Gram a meek secretary. Jullian a smooth-chinned whelp. I could always find new friends.

Laying the stack beside me on the palliasse, I stripped off my cowl and gown. The stiff jaque bound tight over the thick, loose wool shirt. As I pulled on the braies, I quickly tucked the bag of nivat away and tied it safely to the waist string.

"And now drink the water—yes, you must. Then we'll pray." Gildas held out the flask.

My mouth felt like a nest of thorns. I had to drink something. He observed me closely as I drained the tasteless contents of the flask. *Ugh . . . a drink for cows . . .*

My stomach roiled at the first sip. Then a cramp twisted my gut, and my overheated skin blossomed into a cold sweat, as if my mother's divination had truly come to pass.

"Valen, what do you feel? It's only water." Gildas might have been shouting down a well.

"I don't usually drink—" The word *poison* came to mind as I hurriedly found the rusty pail in the corner of the cell, ripped off its cover, and vomited up every drop of the foul stuff. Even when it seemed everything must be out of me, I could not stop heaving.

Gildas knelt beside me as I huddled over the bucket. His hands felt like ice on my blistering forehead. "Come, lie down. I'll tell Father Abbot and the Sinduria you'd best not travel today. Ah, friend . . . what strange miracles happen in this world. Nothing is out of the realm of possibility."

He half carried, half dragged me to the palliasse, and threw the thin blanket over me, then grabbed his lamp and hurried out the door. Before his footsteps died away, I had fumbled my way back across the floor to the bucket, retching.

The rest of the day flowed together like wet ink on a page. As feeble daylight waxed and waned through a slot high on one cell wall, a string of visitors paraded through my cell—the abbot, Thalassa, Gildas, Thane Stearc, one at a time and then all together, talking and arguing too softly for me to hear. I could pay them no mind anyway. I was on my knees in the corner hunched over the fouled bucket, trying not to vomit up the entire contents of my skin. Brother Robierre questioned me between spasms, examining my tongue and fingernails, eyes and throat.

Even Gram came. He stood in the corner for a while, arms crossed, watching the others as they watched me. After a while he stepped close, laid his hand on my shoulder, and mumbled some incomprehensible sympathy.

As the Compline bell rang, I crawled back to my palliasse. Brother Robierre returned soon after. "The worst seems past," he said, once he had verified that I was alive. "Were you trustworthy, we could have made you more comfortable in the infirmary." I had never heard the kind infirmarian so frosty.

"No matter." My raw throat made everything sound harsh.

He wiped my face with a damp rag and laid yet another blanket over me. "The abbot charged me to inform you of my findings. You were not poisoned. Anselm found naught in your spew or your blood. Your body tells me that you are entirely healthy. So this must be some condition of your blood. Perhaps sorcerers cannot tolerate blessed water. I've not treated your kind . . . purebloods . . . before."

I shook my head and laughed. "Purebloods were never my kind."

He did not see the humor. "Then perhaps it is the soul-poison of a man who would so betray the gifts of the good god and so endanger those who welcomed him as a brother. I will petition Iero to break your sinful spirit, Valen. Here—" With deft hands, he raised my head and emptied a vial of something strong and sweet down my gullet before I could protest. "Now you've settled a bit, this should ease your stomach."

"I'm sorry, Brother," I mumbled, dropping my head to the palliasse, feeling his draft sapping my remaining strength. "But you cannot possibly understand."

He stood to go. "One more thing . . . Young Gerard was supposed to serve in the infirmary this evening, but the lad has not been seen all day. You ever took an interest in the boys, and someone told me you might know where he was off to."

"No . . . sorry. Truly."

The iron door clanged shut behind Robierre.

The day's end bell had rung at least two hours since. That had been the last time I heard movement in the dark stairwell outside the door. Only two pureblood guards, Gildas had told me, and even purebloods had to sleep. Head pounding from holding off the effects of Brother Badger's draft, I crept across the floor and touched my finger to the bottom of the door. Despite the doulon looming ever closer, I could not afford to hoard my magic. Flooding power into the spell, I drew my finger up and around in a sweeping arc on the stone beside the door, and back to the floor again. Then I grabbed my boots and crawled through the void into the stairwell. Still no sound.

The touch of open air on my cheek guided me up one narrow stair. I avoided brushing the wall. Hopes rising, I turned and slipped up the second course, bare feet soundless. One more turn, one more climb. I glimpsed a rectangular opening filled with stars . . . and then a squat silhouette blocked the opening.

"Do you think us fools, *recondeur*?"

I charged upward, barreling into the man, but at least three more bodies flung themselves on top of me as I tried to choke the life out of the one under my chest. It took them little time to wrestle me off their comrade, back down the stair, and into the cell. While two men held me down, two more folded my hands, fingertips interlocked and tucked inward, and bound them with silken cord, effectively precluding any application of magic. By the time they had unraveled my voiding spell and slammed the iron door behind them, the bells rang Matins.

Once I stopped fighting, Brother Robierre's draft drugged me out of thought. The image of a gawky youth with a slow head and a ready grin quickly became tangled with that of riders in wine-colored cloaks and a naked man glowing with blue dragon sigils . . .

When the bells rang for Prime, the two purebloods arrived to release my hands and bring me a cup of small beer. They found me awake already, sitting on my palliasse, attempting to formulate some grand speech to throw at my captors or some scheme to get free. But thoughts of a dutiful boy who was not where he was expected had distracted me. Which made no kind of sense. Gerard had likely had enough of bells and prayers and righteousness.

The window slot yet gleamed gray when Thalassa swept into the cell impeccably coiffed and gowned—today in vermillion that set off her black hair and acorn-colored skin. Gold disks at her temples held back her veil and accented the thick black lines curving about her eyes. She dismissed her men to wait outside and close the door behind them. "Stand up."

Sadly, my morning's meditations had revealed naught to say worth the effort of irritating my throat and naught to do worth the trouble of remaining seated. As a boy I had fought until they forced me—to eat, to dress, to stand, to yield—the forcing far more horrid than whatever submission I had refused. Somehow I had lost that kind of resilience. I could not bear the thought of my sister's pureblood lackeys laying hands on me again. I stood.

"A few rules before we go," she said, nodding in approval at my wordless acquiescence. "No matter how you have abased yourself in these past years, you are pureblood, and you will remember your manners and discipline on this journey. The majority of our escort will be ordinaries, and you will maintain distance and detachment as you were taught. I see no need for you to speak at all, in fact, but I will leave you capable lest you fall ill again. I expect no repetition of your foolish escapade of last night. I would prefer to have left you unrestrained for the journey, but that is clearly impossible. Until you give me your word that you will not attempt escape, and convince me that you mean it, your hands will remain silkbound and your feet shackled."

She paused, chin lifted, as if waiting for me to lash out. But this was not the day to fight. My knees felt like mud. I needed to eat. I closed my eyes, longing for her to vanish.

She didn't, of course. "Punishment and restriction await you in Palinur, as you well know, but your behavior in the next days will influence my recommendations as to their severity and extent.

And despite what you would prefer to believe, my opinion *will* carry weight with both the Registry and Patronn."

"I have no doubt of that, *Sinduria serena.*" I bowed from the hip and touched my forehead with my fingertips, as was proper to a pure-blood of superior rank—which was any one of them at present.

Clearly my intonation of her title and the proper female honorific struck her as insufficiently reverent. When I straightened up again, her full lips were tight, and her dark eyes sparked like struck flint. "You *will* submit, little brother. You have squandered your life and your talents. The time has come for you to focus your attention on something beyond your own pleasure. And we will begin that return to discipline now," she said, and handed me a small piece of embroidered white silk.

I unfolded the fabric and stared at it for a moment, my fingers tingling with the minor magics woven into it. One edge straight and slightly stiffened, the rest irregularly shaped. One oval opening for the eye, its borders elaborately embroidered in white thread. Neatly sewn tucks to shape it around nose, mouth, and chin. A mask, or rather a half mask, for purebloods covered only one side of the face when appearing among ordinaries. The half mask was a symbol of our second self, the sorcerer within us that "ordinary" eyes could not see. The mask set us apart, enhanced our mystery, and gave us a certain anonymity among those we did not care to have know us. Only ones like Thalassa or the Gillarine pureblood, whose positions mandated other facial decoration or required family dispensation, were exempt from the discipline of the mask.

"It won't fit as your own should and will. But Silos had an extra and was willing to loan it until we get to Palinur."

No restraint they would use to bind me would be so loathsome, as she was well aware.

"You believe you know me, Lassa, and in some things"—I flipped the mask between my fingers—"your judgment is correct. But I will *never* be like you or the rest of our kin. I have walked free in this world, and I won't forget it."

But this was not the day to fight. So I lifted the scrap of silk to my face and aligned the stiffened edge down the center of my forehead, nose, and mouth, feeling the spider-thin fabric tighten across my left cheek and brow. Its spelled weaving caused it to adhere along its borders and around my eye and hairline and lips, imperfectly in this case. Silos's face was clearly wider than mine; the thing reached halfway across my left ear. The silk smelled of his cheap perfume.

Thalassa cocked her head to one side as I lowered my hands. "Not comely, especially with your ridiculous hair, but sufficient to remind you of who you are. Perhaps, with a return to discipline and some time for thought, you will come to appreciate your position."

She summoned her two guards, short, sturdy men with the straight black hair and deep skin color typical of purebloods. They wore green half masks trimmed in purple to match their livery and wine-colored cloaks. They silkbound my palms together, fingertips tucked in, as they had in the night. Then they affixed a lightweight shackle to my left ankle, draped the dangling end of the chain over my wrists so I would not trip on it, and led me up the prison stair.

We emerged in the yard between the library and the abbot's house whence Prince Perryn had ridden out with the Hierarch of Ardra. A party of horses and ten leather-clad men-at-arms waited near the front door. What appeared to be the entire complement of the abbey—monks and lay brothers—filled the rest of the yard. Many somber. Most gawking. Neither Stearc nor his daughter nor his secretary was present.

A new storm was upon us. The sharp wind tore the layers of scud that fronted massive gray clouds. Cloaks and gowns flapped like pennons.

Abbot Luviar and Prior Nemesio stepped from the front rank, exchanging farewells with Thalassa. I gathered that my sister's public business at Gillarine had something to do with sheep breeding contracts for her temple's flocks.

Jullian stood alone between the lay brothers and the monks, staring at me in shocked disbelief. His eyes traveled from the mask to my bound hands to the loop of metal about my ankle and the slender chain draped over my wrists. I tried to catch his eye . . . winked at him . . . but it was as if he could not recognize me behind the mask.

The face that had drifted in and out of my troubled dreams all night was nowhere to be seen. Young Gerard, great of heart, but slow of eye and head when it came to reading, was not there.

I turned to the abbot, interrupting the inane formalities. "Is Gerard not found yet?"

Thalassa stiffened and raised a warning finger. "Silence, *recondeur*."

"Please, he is a friend . . . a good boy. Father Abbot—"

"We have a party searching," said Luviar. "You indicated you had not seen him."

"Not since dinner on the day I returned from Caedmon's Bridge. If I could help . . . Lassa . . . *Sinduria serena* . . . perhaps my skills could—"

"You might possess the skills to search for the boy, Valen," said

Thalassa. "But you have long since squandered trust. I cannot permit it."

"But—"

"Silos, see the *recondeur* onto his mount. Bind his wrists to the saddle, his foot to the stirrup, and his horse to mine. Then you may aid Abbot Luviar in his search as we discussed."

The abbot said nothing.

Hatred flooded my veins in that moment. I hated Thalassa and her purebloods and their smug righteousness. I hated the abbot and his single-minded passion. I hated past, present, and future with equal bitterness, and I hated the estrangement I saw in Jullian's eye. I hated that they would not allow me to help one of the few people in the world I'd give a pin for, and I hated that my sister's warning stayed my feet—if I misbehaved again, the future could be even worse. The desire to run was an arrow piercing my lungs. Most of all I hated that after twelve years of running, I could think of nowhere to go but away.

The perfumed man in the green mask and wine-colored cloak took my arm, but I shook off his gloved hands for one moment. For these past weeks, the men of Gillarine had given me a place, and I could not depart without acknowledging their kindness. Touching my bound hands to my forehead, I faced the brothers of Saint Ophir and bowed from the hip. Then I allowed Silos to lead me away.

PART THREE

Bitter Blue Days

Chapter 22

Lukas, the sallow valet, scraped the last hair from my chin and dabbed at my face with a damp rag long gone cold. It was tempting, as always, to poke him in the ribs or let fly a particularly foul obscenity, just to see if he would flinch. He wouldn't. Of years somewhere between forty and fifty, the dried-up little ordinary had likely come into pureblood service when he was twelve. He knew very well that his position and livelihood depended on absolute discretion and perfect deportment in the face of temperamental fits, sorcery, and even forced service to a creature of such reprehensible character as a *recondeur*.

Released from his unwelcome ministrations for the moment, I drifted over to the window, rubbing my head that still felt itchy and odd. Almost three weeks had passed since leaving Gillarine, and my hair was at last the same length all over. Scarcely a knucklebone long, of course. Lukas had trimmed all of it to match my regrowing tonsure. Neat. Seemly. Like my shaven chin, clean, trimmed fingernails, and the plum-colored silk shirt and unadorned pourpoint of sober gray velvet Lukas laid out on my bed. Like my temporary accommodation here in the Registry palace—a small, barren chamber, high above the unhealthy airs of the streets, its window discreetly barred, its door firmly locked, and its walls wrapped in spells that made it impossible I work any of my own. The molds of pureblood custom and protocol were squeezing me back into the shape laid out for me before my birth. No blood, no mess. No breath. No life.

I pressed my forehead to the glass. Snow again today. Frosty Palinur sprawled down the hill toward the river, the unfinished towers of the cathedral protruding like bony arms reaching for heaven's mercy—only too late. The groves and vineyards that blanketed the gentle hills, rolling toward the horizon and beyond, were buried in killing frost. Sky, cloud, and horizon formed one chilling mass of gray, a pure reflection of my spirits.

"Your shirt, *plebeiu*." If such a stick could be said to enjoy anything, Lukas enjoyed addressing me by the low title, reserved for purebloods in disgrace. He assumed I cared.

Lukas dangled the silk shirt from his bony hands, playing another of his games by remaining stolidly beside the bed, so that I must walk over to him to be dressed. If I stood my ground, I would be late. Yet to dress myself in the presence of a servant was a breach of pureblood protocol. Either offense would reap punishment: a meal withheld or reduced to bread alone, an extra hour added to my day's humiliation, or my lamps extinguished an hour early. Every infraction, no matter how small, earned its consequence. Brother Sebastian would approve.

I crossed the room. As I stuck my arms in the soft sleeves of the shirt, the locks on the door snapped open, and a chill draft blew in a thickset man muffled in a claret-hued pelisse. He whipped off his mask, and snowflakes flurried from his hair and shoulders onto the polished wood floor.

"Magrog's prick!" The oath burst out of me like an untimely belch. Though I was working with great diligence at discipline, I was not yet ready to face more of my family than my excessively prim, excessively hostile elder sister. Besides, I had last seen my brother, Max, on Black Night, attending Bayard the Smith. "What the devil are *you* doing in Palinur . . . here?"

Lukas scurried to take Max's things and hang them on the brass wall hooks. With a drawn-out sigh, Max pulled my one chair out of the corner and sat down, raising his thick, bristly eyebrows. "Manners, little brother?"

Blast him to the fiery pits! To abase myself to my brother soured my stomach. But Lukas would relish reporting any lapse in protocol. Gathering up the personal opinions I'd strewn about for public viewing, I clenched my teeth, touched my fingertips to my forehead, and bowed deeply from the hip. Purebloods did not reveal emotions. Purebloods did not develop friendships. Purebloods must remain detached from other people so that their magic, which belonged to their family or contracted masters, would not be tainted. Every human relationship must be rigorously shaped and strictly constrained by manners, protocol, and titles awarded according to rank, gender, and kinship.

"Greetings, *ancieno*. Please forgive my humble welcome after so many years. Alas, I've no refreshment to offer, no gossip to share, and you have already found the only seat in my apartments save the bed. And having no idea of your current title, I can add no more honor to the greeting. Are you as elevated as our sister?"

I chose not to mention I'd seen him with Prince Bayard. I was falling easily into pureblood habits. Secret knowledge was liquor in our veins.

"You tread a bridge of sand with speech like that, *plebeiu*. Did they permit such impertinence in the Karish monk-house?" Max grinned and propped his muddy boots on the bedcovers, just missing the gray velvet garment. "Damn, I wish I'd seen you gowned and shorn! The mere consideration of our wild, truculent Valen all prim and prayerful has me thinking gatzi have turned the world backside before."

"*Willing* submission comes easier, *ancieno*. Would you mind very much if I continued to dress? I am required to be ready at Terce—third watch." He'd likely not know the Karish term that came so naturally to me now.

He waved his hand, weighted heavily with a ruby and sapphire ring. "Wouldn't think of interfering with your duties. Pardon me if I enjoy the sight overmuch. I certainly don't want to be seen out there in the streets gawking at you, but it quite thrills me to watch you brought to heel. You've caused us all inordinate trouble."

I motioned Lukas to continue. He dropped a second shirt of fine wool over my head and then added the pourpoint with its interminable buttons down front and sleeves.

"I arrived in the city late last night and heard the news," Max continued. "The infamous Cartamandua *recondeur* brought to heel at last. Our family disgrace—well, not lifted, but relieved. Nothing can erase what you did. Did you know you cost Patronn his royal appointment? Twelve years he's lived now without a contract of his own. If you thought he detested you before . . . well, you surely know more than I about that. Do you think he still has the strap?"

Clearly my sins had not taxed Max's humor as sorely as they had my elder sister's; he had always enjoyed my punishments and humiliations inordinately. Yet I could not help but feel his excessive good cheer rooted in some circumstance beyond my capture. "You appear to have prospered despite my transgressions. What kind of contract do you serve? Lassa's given me no news of the family."

In fact, my sister had hardly spoken to me in our eight miserable days on the road. And though she had hovered about me like a bee on clover during my two days' testimony before the Registry, taking every opportunity to warn me against demonstrating my tongue-block in front of my questioners, she had not visited me since the judgment.

"I've a respectable contract, though it's paid less than half what a Cartamandua of my skill should command." Max pulled off his gloves one finger at a time. He fondled his grand ring, turning it to catch the light. "At least it's active scouting and advance work, not scrawling maps. Bia's taken the Cartamandua bent as well and is working for Patronn, inking his revisions or some such tedious task. Nilla has entered the eerie realms of divination. Two and two ... so the family balance is left to you. Or do you still resist the call of your blood and the demands of discipline, presuming to some profession beyond the family bent? You've skills in so *many* areas, as I recall. Perhaps you've developed healing powers, or you've chosen to teach fertile young minds to read ..."

As he rattled off a list of scholarly and magical pursuits, I stood mute. Every response that leaped to mind would reap more punishments.

He shoved the jeweled ring onto his thick finger and raised his eyes to meet my own, his smile as gleeful as that of a huntsman who bends his bow at a hobbled buck. "Come, tell me. What are you, Valen? You've surely not taken the bent for divination, else you'd hardly have let yourself be captured. But then again, why would I expect you might be competent at anything?"

His were but a child's barbs, no matter that they stung a nerve grown raw. If I refused to let him see more, perhaps he would win only a child's pleasure from them. So I changed the subject. "I can't imagine the twins grown enough to choose their bent. They were what ... eleven last time I saw them ... twelve? All ribbons and sulks."

Lips pursed in discontent, he settled back in his chair. "Our little sisters have grown up. Nilla is the beauty, as you might guess. Her looks got her a decent match—Luc de Galeno-Mercanti, a physician thrice her age who is contracted to the Duc of Avenus. Her divinations focus on her husband's patients—a bit unsettling for them, I think. Perhaps now you're back under discipline, the Registry will allow her to birth a child before her husband is wholly incapable. Bia's minor rebellions ceased when she saw what happened to you—or perhaps when Matronn locked her in her room for half a year lest she follow your course. Patronn has not yet found a husband for her. Neither girl is happy with you. I'd recommend you stay out of their way. Easier in Nilla's case, off in the damp of Morian as she is. But Bia—"

"I'll watch my back."

Lukas knelt to tie up my hose and lace my boots. I scarcely knew my younger sisters, Petronilla and Phoebia. They had been but wasps in the garden of family. Max and Thalassa had been the snake and the shrew. So what was the snake doing here?

"Who is it holds your leash, Max? Your master must be head-quartered in Palinur. Or has he loosed your golden chains so far as to permit random family visits?"

"My master's business has brought me to the city," said Max. "Business of critical importance to Navronne's future. I've no leave to discuss it—or him—with anyone save family. Yet I doubt such exceptions should be extended to *you*. You might be tempted to use the information to buy your way out of your unhappy lot. Only a sadist or a halfwit is going to consider a contract for a twelve-year *recondeur*. You know nothing of leashes, little brother. Not yet."

My brother rocked the chair back on its rear legs, his bulk overflowing it. From the time I shot past his height at age ten or so, Max had always managed to be sitting when we were together. And he had always enjoyed taunting me with the privileges he earned from being the dutiful elder, while I suffered the consequences of my errant nature. Evidently, nothing had changed.

"Keep your secrets, *ancieno*," I said. "I am, as ever, hopelessly unreliable when it comes to family loyalties."

Having finished with my boots, Lukas picked up a hinged contraption of delicately engraved silver from the small table beside my bed. With perfect patience he waited for me to kneel before him so he could slip it over my head. He could not completely hide his delight in this particular duty.

"You must excuse me from any further conversation," I said, as I dropped to my knees. I thought I had managed the encounter well, but it was impossible to hide bitterness at this point. Not with Max here.

My brother lowered his chair legs to the floor with a jolt, watching goggle-eyed. "Ah, fires of Deunor, they have done you proud, Valen," he whispered. "You, the lad who threw fits when locked in his bedchamber ten times the size of this room."

A delicate silver band three fingers wide encircled my throat. From it graceful silver coils stretched up my neck to support a mask that covered the left half of my face. This mask was not smooth, accommodating silk, but rigid silver that sealed my lips closed, blocked one nostril and one ear, and obscured one eye. Lukas latched the cursed thing at the back of my neck and fastened the thin metal strap that held it over my head. The Registry judge who had insisted on the mask had been most annoyed that in all my tedious accounting of my twelve uncontrolled years, I'd not implicated any ordinary he could hang.

A grin materialized on Max's broad face. "Does it close in on you, little brother? Does the world appear warped, with only one eye to observe it? Can you feel the restraint, the control? Spirits of night, how you must loathe this."

I ignored his baiting as I rose from the floor, fighting the urge to ram my head into the wall, practicing Brother Sebastian's lessons to shift words from tongue to spirit and allow them to float, discorporate, into the ether. Lukas settled a garish yellow cape lined with ermine about my shoulders, adjusted its drape, and pinned it to the left with an amber brooch just as the cathedral bells struck nine.

The key snicked in the door lock again. Two snow-dusted men in wine-colored cloaks and silk half masks entered, carrying deceptively plain bronze staves. Without meeting my brother's eyes, I touched my fingertips to my forehead—half flesh, half metal—and bowed to Max and then to my jailers. The Registry men quickly silkbound my clenched hands—we were all quite experienced at this now—and I followed the two down six flights of stairs and out into the street.

Our boots crunched in the frozen muck. On this, the tenth day of my punishment, our route led to the Stonemasons' District, a familiar haunt from my days working on the cathedral. There I was to spend the hours until sunset exhibited on a public platform, my foot shackled to a loop of iron.

Ten days, ten districts. Two more days to complete the round of the twelve districts of Palinur, and two additional days in the Council District after that. I had reaped the two extra days for a breach of discipline—attempting to throttle my guards the first time they approached me with the silver mask. Since then, I had been a model of submission; the consideration of wearing the silver mask for one extra turn of the glass made me physically ill.

The frost bit at my exposed skin, and I hunched my shoulders, trying to induce the folds of the ugly yellow cape to cover my hands. The cold would be wicked on my immobilized fingers this morning. If only the wind would die down, my layers of fine clothes would keep the rest of me warm enough. Better than most of the poor devils in the streets.

My daily excursions through Palinur—the city I knew best in all the kingdom, a city of culture, beauty, and friendly, expansive people—had shocked me. Filth piled up in the streets. The residents' faces gaunt and frightened. Diseased. Once-prosperous avenues were scarcely more than rubble, wooden houses burnt, stone ones picked apart. At least half of the great statues of the Hundred Heroes that ringed the palace precincts had been toppled and no one had bothered to set them upright. So many stones had been stolen from the low wall that joined the statues that it had the look of a snaggle-toothed jawbone. The richest city in the kingdom was no longer any different from the rest of Navronne.

As we hurried across the expanse of the central market, it seemed even smaller than yesterday. Seedy and grim, the *pocardon* or "little city" of shops and carts took up less than a quarter the area it had when I had first left home. Though a piper's mournful tunes still quickened the air, the denizens of the market, who long ago would snatch an awestruck runaway from the street and lead him in a merry reel through the market stalls for the sheer joy of it, had vanished. And on this morning, the shoppers who had once laughed and made way for those dancers snarled at each other over blighted turnips and tufts of mud-caked wool—or glared at a tall freakish sorcerer in an ermine lined cloak and silver half mask being herded through the lanes by two pureblood guards, and cursed him for squandering privileges they could never aspire to.

On this tenth morning the gaunt face of the royal city had taken on a more immediate tension—beyond the matter of starvation and hopelessness and unseasonable winter. From the moment we left the Registry tower, I had the same eerie sense as in the hours before a battle—the uneasy quiet, the fingers of fear reaching through skin and bone to grip the soul, the blurring of boundaries between earth and sky, between past and future. I could not shake the sense that Palinur, hitherto untouched by the war, was soon to bleed as well as starve.

Above the citadel that crowned the hilltop, Prince Perryn's gold and purple pennant whipped and snapped in the sharp breeze alongside the white trilliot of Navronne. But Max was here on his contracted master's business—the business of our prince's mortal enemy.

The earth itself will not end, only the life we know—cities and towns and villages, plowing and planting. I had not believed in the lighthouse cabal and their talk of end times. But my days in the royal city had given me pause. We were not yet to the solstice—only days past the equinox—and ever-temperate Palinur was buried in snow and ice. The arrow of war was aimed at the heart of Navronne, which was the Heart of the World. What if Luviar was right?

Though it was an ordinary day for working, hardly anyone was abroad amid the mills and tool shops of the Stonemasons' District. Small groups of men huddled together in alleyways, halting their conversations to stare as we passed. Grinding wheels and grimsaws stood idle in the workyards, winches and chains snared in unbroken ice beside piles of old scaffolding, rotted and tangled with dead weeds. Even the crowd of ragged boys who capered alongside us each morning, hurling taunts and frozen mud clots, numbered but twenty or so, less than half the size of the previous days. Only the pigeons seemed lighthearted, making free of the stoops, benches, and rooftops, fluttering upward in great swarms as our little procession marched through the gray morning.

We turned a corner into an open square, where all the streets of the Stonemasons' District came together. Here, as in every district square, Aurellian pipes and conduits fed the district well—this one topped by a pyramid of rose marble. And here, as in every district square, a pillory and flogging post stood on a raised platform. In front of the empty pillory, the Registry had installed a stone block and surrounded it with a ring of iron stanchions linked by silken ropes.

Caphur, one of the pureblood attendants appointed by the Registry to oversee my punishment, jerked his head for me to climb the platform and mount the block. Though a youngish man of modest size, he had inordinately heavy jowls that grew prodigious crops of hair. When I was in place, he attached the shackle about my ankle to the iron loop affixed to the block. Then he and his partner, whose name I didn't know, took their places outside the circle of stanchions.

The two purebloods would prevent curious ordinaries from touching me. As my Registry judges had emphasized so tediously, the purpose of this exercise was not physical harm, but "education by way of unseemly exposure to the common population." That is, a reminder that the "simple" demand of submission to my family and the Registry protected me from such filth, ignorance, and drudgery as existed among ordinaries. That is, shame and humiliation. They had neither understood nor appreciated my laughter at this pomposity.

All in all, this aspect of my punishment could have been far worse. To stand outdoors was cold and uncomfortable, but far less painful than a lashing and, for one with my peculiarities, infinitely preferable to close confinement. A smirking Caphur had told me that the Sinduria had particularly recommended this exhibition as the best way to teach me the lessons I required. I needed to consider that. My sister knew very well of my particular terrors.

Across the square a pyramid-shaped block of granite marked a frowzy lane. Allowing my eyelid to sag, I imagined I could hear Frop the Fiddler sawing on his vielle at the Plug and Feathers, situated halfway down that lane, and feel the music that always set my feet dancing as I downed the taverner's strong mead. A little farther down the lane and around the corner, squeezed between a tool grinder's shed and a smithy, a man could indulge in a hot bath and a friendly whore at the Bucket Knot, my favorite sop-house, a warm and welcoming place.

Smiling to myself, I installed Elene's face and lush figure in my imagining, whirling her to Frop's music and hearing her laugh as she had on that morning at Caedmon's Bridge. Ah, gods, what pleasure to touch her . . . to feel her naked warmth beneath me, her heart racing from the dance . . .

A stinging blow to my frozen flesh shattered my vision. The wind had whipped the hem of my heavy cape into my face. Elene had betrayed me. So no warmth to be had in visions either.

Unlike the first nine days, it took an hour for more than urchins and beggars to gather. But the chance to gape at a pureblood eventually overcame even the mysterious anxieties of the day. The yellow cape announced my offense. Scarred laborers hefting buckets or tool satchels, hollow-cheeked matrons clutching ragged children with haunted eyes, and shopkeepers wearing dirty aprons and furrowed brows drifted into the square like autumn leaves collecting under a maple, speculating aloud as to my identity, my history, my magical talents, and my future, knowing they would never be told such mysteries. They were likely wondering if the silent guards were going to do anything more with me. Likely hoping for something interesting, such as a nice flogging or maiming.

I kept my back straight and my unblocked eye open and focused forward as was required of me. My exposed right cheek stung with the cold. Though the mask shielded the left cheek from the wind, the silver chilled quickly, cooling the sweat that had formed beneath it as we walked. Soon the masked half of my face grew colder than the other, as if encased in ice that penetrated my flesh and froze my bones, as if knives mounted on the inside of the metal half face lacerated my cheek and brow.

As the ragamuffins spat and lobbed mud balls at my back without interference from the masked guards, the people grew bold with their comments: *Soul-dead . . . demon-cursed . . . real silver . . . Has he flesh under the metal, Mam? That fur's no sheep's coat nor rabbit's . . . Don't have to work . . . Don't even have to fight, they don't . . . Everything's given . . . god-given . . . while we starve. Never saw one of 'em so tall. He vomited his gift right back at the Sky Lord's feet . . . their cocks metal, too? Cover a pureblood female and their Registry'll cut off your cock. Spat on the Gehoum . . . Should burn all them as betray the Powers . . . Throw 'im in the river with that mask and he'll sink . . . meet the gods he's cursed . . .* recondeur . . . *traitor . . .* As if I could not hear them. As if I stood somewhere far distant behind a barricade of silver.

Afternoon brought more snow and new waves of muted gossip that rippled through the assembly. Forbidden to turn my head so my exposed ear might hear better, I heard naught of the reports.

As evening approached, my neck and shoulders ached miserably. My fingers felt dead. My nose ran unceasingly, stimulating a subtle panic that I would soon be unable to breathe. Despite my layers, I could not control my shivering. My exposed eye welled with tears from the bitter wind, and no amount of blinking could clear it, threatening my sole occupation. I derived some amusement from observing the odd folk who came to gawk at me, those like the tall, slender man in a sky-blue tunic who stood apart at the back of the crowd, his long hair plaited with green ribbons. He must enjoy spectacles; he had come every day.

A small, purposeful shift in the increasingly restive crowd signaled a new arrival making his way to the front. He soon stood immediately in front of me, a small person cloaked in black. Holy mother . . . I blinked rapidly and risked a reprimand by swiping my upper arm across my eye. The man wore a cowl! He lifted his hood just enough that he could see as high as my face, allowing me to glimpse his own odd features that looked as if they were ready to slide off his chin. Brother Victor.

Great merciful Iero, they'd come to rescue me! Somewhere under his scapular would be an ax to hack the chains away. I strained to see through the flurries and gloom. Perhaps Gildas was here . . . or Stearc. The Evanori warrior could take on Caphur and his friend. Surely . . . My hands trembled in their unyielding wrappings. My blind eye leaked tears unrelated to the cold. *Buck up, you great ox!* Why just now at the verge of freedom did the loathsome horror of this captivity threaten to undo me?

After only a moment, the chancellor dropped his hood and raised his palm, five fingers spread wide in Iero's blessing. But as he lowered his hand, he briefly held it vertically, fingertips heavenward, at his breast—the brothers' signing language for the abbot—and then clenched his fist and pressed it to his heart. *Obedience.* And then . . . nothing. Gods. Nothing.

Anger flooded from my hollow breast to my frost-nipped cheek. How dare they lay their pious obligations on me?

Discipline forbade communication with an onlooker, but surely the little monk must see the flush of fury heating my face. He stood there for a while longer, his small hands folded piously. The milling crowd gradually swallowed him, and I could not judge when it was he left the square.

Gildas had said Luviar would not release me from his tether as long as he had use for me. What did he think I could do for him, trussed up like a string doll forced to perform for laughing children? *Damnable holy men!* I hated them all.

Chapter 23

On the eleventh morning of my exhibition, as we marched into the Temple District, we passed no more than ten people. Though I remained maddeningly unenlightened about events in Palinur, I judged the situation had gotten worse. Five temples faced the great circle—those of Kemen, Samele, Erdru, Deunor, and Arrosa. Throughout the day, liveried servants bore every size and shape of burden up the broad steps of the brightly painted buildings: calyxes and caskets small and large, crates of statuary and rare fruit, wine casks, grain sacks, urns, and caged birds. Someone even led a matched pair of white oxen into Kemen's gold-columned temple. Offerings to placate the gods. The wealthy people of the city were worried. I imagined I could smell the nivat. Some of the boxes surely contained that most favored offering.

Though I tried to banish the thought of nivat as soon as it arose, my mind would not let go of it, and I found myself plotting ridiculous ventures to slough off my bonds and snatch the most likely containers. Whatever would I do when I needed it again?

I had used my last supply on the journey to Palinur. After three days on the road, Thalassa had accepted my word that I would attempt no magic and allowed me to travel with unbound hands—my salvation two nights later when my disease struck and I was forced to pay the price of my incomplete doulon. That her aide Silos—he of the cheap scent and well-aimed firebolts—had eventually detected my spellworking, and that she had angrily bound my hands and shackled my feet for the rest of the journey, did not matter. Neither of them had found the mirror or the needle or discovered the truth. I owned one secret for a while longer, from all but Brother Gildas. The worst part of this whole disgusting mess was that these unpredictable intervals between attacks of my disease had fueled a subtle anxiety that never left me.

Thoughts of Gildas led inevitably to thoughts of Brother Victor and what he could be doing in Palinur. I scanned today's crowd. He wasn't here. Surely he would not have come all this way to deliver one more warning to keep me mute. If the cabal no longer needed my help, then how, in Magrog's fancy, were they planning to contact the Danae? *Bah,* I thought, *let the pious pricks flounder.*

Reminded of the wonders I had seen at Caedmon's Bridge, I let my imagination stray. I imagined the Dané woman dancing in the moonlit fields beyond the abbey, joined by the man with the dragon sigils. The Danae twined the lives of trees and lakes, rocks and stream into their dances, so stories said, joining the elements of the world in a great pattern, so that a vine in Ardra and a river of Morian and a rocky pinnacle of Evanore became part of one great whole. What magic, what vigor, would enliven such a dance. Under my breath I hummed the harper's song I'd heard on the road to Elanus; the Danae would dance to such music as that. I could almost feel them leaping and whirling . . . caught up in the moment as I had been in the Elanus tavern . . . stretching, driving, pounding their feet—

"Attention, *plebeiu*," snapped the voice in my ear. Caphur's fingers dug into my arm and jostled me. "Open your eye and look upon the ugliness of the ordinary world. You are forbidden to escape your punishment in sleep."

The squalor of Temple Square and the gawking crowd scrubbed away the glorious image, and the howling wind deafened me to the music of memory, leaving only a starved ache in my chest. Legends and stories . . . the Danae might live, but no pattern existed in this ugly world. In all my years of running, I had never felt so alone.

As the day waned, the torments of flesh obscured those of spirit. The snow turned to sleet. My face felt stripped raw from peppering ice and the abrasion of freezing metal. The wind drove ice-bladed knives through clothing and flesh and bone. Every part and portion of me was frozen. I could scarcely see, and my clogged nose forced me to breathe through my mouth—the pinched half of it outside the mask. I struggled to remain calm. Only the approach of evening held off despair.

"Harrow! Purify!" A scuffle broke out in the back of the twenty or thirty remaining gawkers—a mix of elaborately gowned temple aides, beggars, and idle drovers, and the tall, odd man in the sky-blue tunic.

I pressed my snow-crusted arm across my eyes, trying to blot the tears and drips. A bony youth, wearing a Harrower's orange rag tied around his head, had pushed to the front ranks, supporting himself on a crutch. Half of one of his legs was missing. He waved a clenched fist at me. "Them as flout the gods cause these evil days. Them as serve the Snake of Ardra or the Bastard of Evanore, them as worship in corrupted temples or Karish halls . . . they bring forth the pestilence. Only Prince Bayard sees the truth. But the drums ye hear be not the valiant Smith's drums but the drums of doom. The Gehoum howl on the wind! The earth cries out for harrowing! Make it level. Make it smooth! Purify!"

He raised his hand . . .

His missile glanced off the silver mask just over my cheekbone. Pain lanced through my skull. Eyes watering, I staggered backward.

Caphur jumped down from the platform and briskly kicked the offender's crutch out from under him. The youth crashed to the pavement, and the masked guard touched his bronze staff to the fallen lad's back. The tip of the staff glowed red. Smoke curled upward from the ragged cloak and burst into flame. The boy wailed . . .

Great Iero's hand! Though the mask trapped my bellowing curses in my throat, I lunged at Caphur, swinging my bound fists at his bristly jowl like a bludgeon. But my shackled ankle brought me up short, and I crashed into an awkward heap, one foot on the platform, the other foot and knee twisted behind me, still on the block. The Registry man dodged my blow without a glance.

The Harrower youth flailed and screamed. A few onlookers rolled him in the snow and beat at him with hands and cloaks to smother the fire. Others ran away. Caphur stepped back and waved his staff, pointing at one and then another of the murmuring crowd until they backed away from the platform.

Caphur's partner dragged me to my feet and motioned me back on the block. I wrenched my shoulders from his grasp. He raised one finger in warning and motioned again.

There's nothing to be done, I thought. *Not today. You'll only make things worse.* Grinding my teeth, I stepped up and dropped my arms, straightening my back and head as was required. My overseers faced the crowd, staves gripped firmly in their hands, prepared to defend me. I could not stop shaking.

A tall woman bundled in ragged cloak and orange scarf pushed to the front and pointed a long finger at the fallen youth. "Heed the work of arrogant princes! Their pet sorcerers, abominations to the Gehoum, can slay us at their will. Noble and pureblood live in corrupted luxury and praise imaginary gods, whilst we burn, our children starve, our grapes fail."

Her voice seared the gloomy afternoon with lightning—blazing far beyond the group in front of me, reaching into alleys and byways, shops and taverns. "Tell your brothers and sisters. Fetch your cousins and uncles and friends to lay hand to the Harrow. Not until the false princes and false teachers have been purified will the Gehoum set the seasons right again."

The last of the temple aides scurried away toward the green-and-red painted temple of Samele. A sudden bluster of wind raised whorls of snow and then died as quickly as it came. As two ragged citizens piled snow on his blistered back, the crippled youth began to whisper between his sobs, "Harrow. Purify."

The woman in the orange scarf took up the chant, tended and nurtured it as if it were a budding flame, moving through the crowd and touching one person and then another on the shoulder. Though only a few in the crowd wore orange rags, many joined her in the chant. More and more, until the words pulsed like a soft heartbeat. "Harrow. Purify . . ."

At the boundaries of the square in every direction, torches winked out of the gloom and flowed toward the center like fiery streamlets emptying into a lake. The Harrowers' chants echoed from the painted facades around the square, the pulse become war drums.

Sleet clicked on my half-metal face. The wind whipped my cloak as if it were tissue. Had the cursed sun not yet set behind the blackening clouds? Shackled to the damnable block, I had no pleasant thoughts about being the center of a riot.

The urchins and beggars scattered like dry leaves in the wind. The remaining drovers ran for their rigs. The man in the sky-blue tunic had vanished. My guards hefted their staves higher, and for once I rejoiced that they were sorcerers. The flood of fire swept toward us.

A shouting arose among the chanters. They pointed toward the golden-domed Temple of Samele, where a short robust woman, wearing the green and gold robes of Samele's priestess, stood on the broad steps between the green and red columns. Torchbearers stood to either side of her, and their light glinted in the gold fan rising from her long black hair. Even from such a distance I could see the dark lines about her eyes like a mask. Thalassa.

The streamlets of fire curved toward the temple, as if they had encountered logjams in their course. When the chanters in front of me hurried off to join their fellows, the rabble-rousing woman hurried away into the dark streets, her evening's work done. The burned youth lay abandoned, already half buried in snow. Melting gobs slid from his blackened flesh.

Two ranks of green-liveried guards poured from the temple and fanned out on either side of Thalassa as she began to exhort the mob. Half deaf as I was, I could not understand her proclamation, but only the hisses and jeers that punctuated it. Flaming torches arced through the night, thrown toward the temple. Thalassa raised her hands and the torches shattered into showers of sparks that fell back on the crowd. Did Mother Samele appreciate the advantages of a pureblood Sinduria?

Mesmerized, I scarcely noticed as Caphur unlocked my ankle. But he tugged at my arm and I half stepped, half stumbled from the block and the platform. As my shepherds marched me away, I twisted my head to see over my shoulder. A green veil of light now hung over the surging throng. The line of temple guards, wielding clubs and staves, had surrounded the mob. Screams and curses rose louder.

The lurid scene was soon lost to view. With grim urgency, the guards rushed me through rapidly darkening streets, winding ever upward toward the Registry tower that sat near the lower walls of the citadel. As we crossed the deserted marketplace, a large troop of horsemen—perhaps seventy men with no visible colors—galloped toward the broad causeway that led to the palace gates. The pennants billowed heavy and listless on the battlements, only half visible in the swirling snow and sleet. I halted in my tracks.

Caphur growled impatiently. "Keep moving."

When I shook my head and raised my bound hands in the direction of the banners, he lowered his staff and stared, as well, touching the shoulder of his partner and pointing where we looked. The trilliot— the white lily of Navronne—still flew on the castle of Caedmon and Eodward, but the purple and gold banner of Perryn of Ardra was nowhere to be seen.

Yet, even as the world shifted, mystery took a stranglehold on my spirit. From across the empty expanse of trampled snow, the tall man in the sky-blue tunic and green ribbons stood watching us. I blinked and squinted. His feet were bare. On such a day. Wondering, I raised my bleary eye, met his gaze, and knew him. He had once reached out to me from an aspen grove, his bare skin glowing with sigils of blue fire.

Caphur snatched my arm and dragged me stumbling from the square.

I paced my tower room in the dark. Though shed of my frozen finery, I was not yet warm. Once free of the hateful mask, I had dared denounce Caphur as an arrogant coward for burning a cripple. That outburst and my violent behavior in the Temple District had cost me food, light, and fire. Lukas had provided me one flask of watered ale for my supper and dressed me in dry layers of cambric and plain, padded wool, but had left my little brazier unlit and taken away my lamp. Tomorrow would likely bring more extensive penalties. I grabbed a blanket from the bed and wrapped it about my shoulders. So be it.

My pacing took me to the window again, back to matters of far more import than impotent *recondeurs* or even scorched madmen. Frost rimed the corners of the panes. After three years of war, could Palinur have been taken without a fight? Certainly Ardra's prince had fallen. The missing banner was no mischance, no oversight. Not in these times. Yet Bayard's banner had not been raised. I saw no evidence of battle in the night and storm beyond the tower, only scattered fires in the lower city. Thank the gods for the snow and damp that would check the spread of flames.

And then there was the matter of the barefoot man. Here in my tower room, it was easy to blame my nonsensical conclusion on cold, hunger, and a yearning to see something of hope in a world disintegrating before my eyes. He'd had no dragon wings scribed on his face or on the bare legs that poked out from under his pale tunic, yet I felt a certainty that stripped of his odd attire he would display the dragon marks. A Dané here in the city. A Dané I had seen before. Stories said Danae died if they remained too long in cities or manmade dwellings.

Locks rattled and the door slammed open. "Magnus Valentia de Cartamandua-Celestine, stand forward."

I spun away from the window and backed into the shadows. Perhaps my penalties had come earlier than expected. A midnight visitation was every prisoner's nightmare.

The lantern dangling from a fleshy hand illuminated a thickset man with a fat black braid and a drooping mustache. He wore his black silk mask in the horizontal fashion, covering only his eyes and brow as some pureblood families prescribed. Caphur and his partner stood behind the newcomer.

Stepping out of the shadow, I dropped the blanket and bowed to my principal Registry overseer, Sestius de Rhom-Magistoria, some colineal relation of my grandfather's family. "*Domé*."

"Prepare to go out."

"Of course, *domé*. If I might inquire—"

"You may not."

Of course he would answer no question of mine. I could imagine the instructions of the Registry judges. *Keep the prisoner ignorant. Keep the prisoner frustrated, isolated, and on edge, not knowing what humiliation will befall him next. Prove to him that he has no control over his life.*

Suppressing pointless fury, I laced up my damp boots, snatched the yellow cloak from the hook, and fastened its clasp at my shoulder. Then I turned to Sestius, the silver mask in my one hand, a silk one in the other, and the inquiry posed on my face.

"Use the silk. We're in a hurry. But bring the other. You are not finished with it yet. More insolence and you will be wearing it for a year."

I bowed and slipped on the silk mask. It felt like a second skin compared to the silver. But I did not escape every discomfort. Caphur brought out his roll of silk cord and bound my hands. Tighter than other days. Showing his teeth, he also made sure that the silver mask came with us. Bristly hair poked through the silk of his own mask around his bulbous chin. Likely his family discipline mandated a clean-shaven face, else Caphur could have grown a beard the size of a hedgehog in three days' time.

They whisked me down the stairs, where a party of two torch boys and eight or ten armed ordinaries waited. Only an extraordinarily dangerous night would occasion purebloods to call in extra escorts.

We hiked briskly through the deserted city, skirting the main streets and marketplaces. Ice coated every blade, twig, gutter, and cornice. I shivered in my ermine-lined cloak and thanked the Lord of Sea and Sky that the wind had abated.

I could not imagine where we were off to so late, until we climbed a long flight of worn steps to a crossing lane that bordered an ancient wall. The otherwise straight bulwark of stone, the remnant of some early defense work, had been designed to circumvent a notched pyramid of native rock. In the notch, water bubbled from moss-lined cracks and dribbled into a pool the size of a wide-brimmed hat. The pool, called the Aingerou's Font, never dried up and never froze, and every spring a different variety of flower grew out of the cracks in the rock. Even lacking the Cartamandua bent, I could have found my way to this lane from the depths of the netherworld. For fifteen wretched years I had resided not half a quellé from the Aingerou's Font.

The tree-shrouded lane followed the ancient bulwark past the Font to a walled stone house built in the grand Aurellian style. Large airy rooms enclosed inner courtyards, the sprawling structure ornamented with pedimented windows, meticulously designed gardens, fluted pillars, and brightly painted arches. A bronze gryphon, grasping a rolled map in its claws, loomed above us from the iron gate. As Sestius rang the bell, my entire being felt as hollow as my growling stomach. I was home.

The gate swung open before the echoes of the bell faded. A man in green livery motioned us into the snow-draped courtyard. Caphur dismissed our escorts, dropping a small pouch in their gawking leader's outstretched hand, while the man in green exchanged a private word with Sestius.

I stood stiffly by, my mind skipping from one thing to another, unwilling to acknowledge the arrival of a moment I had dreaded for so many years. Three lamps hanging from iron posts lit the path to the front door. Lights shone from a few rooms: my father's study to the left of the entry door, the reception room to the right, my mother's bedchamber around the corner on the right. Horses had been here before us. Four or five. They'd been led around to the stables. The hedges had grown tall. The ancient lime tree had lost a limb; it would never survive this kind of cold. The green livery . . . one of Thalassa's men from the temple then . . . Was she here?

Focus, Valen. You must keep your wits. Keep your temper. Control your tongue. Submit. I had to convince them that I was chastened, else I would spend the rest of my life in silken hand bindings and silver masks and ankle shackles.

I gazed longingly through the gate that was closing behind me, back down the lane where the Font bubbled quietly in its niche. Someone now sat in the niche beside the mumbling spring. Startled, I squinted down the dark lane. *Holy gods!*

The gate clanged shut, closing off my view.

"Move along, Magnus Valentia," said Sestius, opening his hand toward the front door in invitation.

The overseer trudged through ankle-deep snow toward the skewed rectangle of light that streamed from the now open door. I followed dutifully behind him. But somewhere deep inside me rose a tickling sensation that quickly spread to my chest and throat and mouth. My cheeks quivered. Droplets pricked my eye. I pressed my lips together, but to no avail. At last I slammed my fists to my mouth, attempting to muzzle the laughter I could not stop. How foolish . . . how wondrous was life.

Sestius halted and narrowed his eyes. He laid a hand on my arm. "What is it, lad?" His testy authority yielded to a gruff sympathy. "No need to be afraid."

No need . . . Another quake of hopeless hilarity shook me and I tried to wipe my eyes with my wrist. Sestius appeared confused.

"What has possessed you, *plebeiu*?"

"Ah, *domé*, pardon . . . please. It's just"—I pressed my wrist hard against my mouth—"no one ever calls me *Magnus Valentia*. Any more than they call my brother *Maximus Goratia*, or my elder sister *Thalassa Minora*, or my younger sisters *Phoebia Terrae* or *Petronilla Terrae*. You see, my father named us all after geographical features, and it was left to us to dig around in them for names that didn't sound ridiculous. And you tell me not to be afraid . . . so kindly . . . and here I am coming home after twelve years away, looking like some gangle-limbed canary and with my hands—"

He did not understand in the least. How could he? He had not seen what I had.

"Please forgive me, *domé*. I am just inexcusably ill-mannered, and lightheaded as I've not eaten since morning and these days have been exhausting, as is only right, of course."

I needed to stop babbling. And I should very likely beg some god or other to remove the grin that would not leave my face. Life was as sublimely absurd as my name—some barren little island off the coast of Aurellia, inhabited entirely by great gawky birds. Why else would I imagine that I had seen the intricate outlines of a brilliant blue dragon coiling down the bare limbs of the man sitting beside the Aingerou's Font? Or that I would swear that he wore green ribbons plaited in his curling red hair and had met my gaze with eyes the color of aspen leaves in autumn? I had not been mistaken. I was being followed by a Dané.

Bowing respectfully to Sestius, in whose word lay the power to extend my unfortunate exhibition in the city, I waved my bundled hands toward the door. He huffed a bit, and looked at me as if I were a lunatic. Which I supposed I was. But perhaps, if the world was going to end sometime soon, it didn't really matter.

We walked down a short brick passage, Caphur and his shadow trailing behind us. I was still smiling when I stepped into a vine-hung courtyard with a giant lily-shaped brazier blazing in the center. My father was waiting.

Chapter 24

The little courtyard had only a latticework roof of scrolled iron, yet the colored flames that danced in the lily-shaped brazier left the enclosure excessively warm. Appropriate, I supposed, as the courtyard was dedicated to Deunor Lightbringer. Lamps hung from iron posts, adding yellowish light to the orange and red firelight.

My first glimpse of my father sobered me quickly, causing a certain constriction in my chest I had experienced since I could remember. In the view of the world and more particularly, the Pureblood Registry, the powerfully compact man standing beside the flaming brazier held my life in his hands.

Oh, he could not kill me without consequence. A pureblood, even a *recondeur*, was too valuable an asset to dispose of without extreme justification. But pureblood heads of family, male or female as lineal customs or contracts dictated, wielded the power of a despot over their offspring by way of the entitlement to negotiate unbreakable contracts for those children's professional services, marriages, and rights of procreation. They could even sell their services to a murderer, as long as that murderer agreed to abide by the terms. Unless one became the head of family or achieved extraordinary rank in the ordinary world, as Thalassa had done, a pureblood never lived other than as a bound servant—a cosseted slave.

My father's appearance had changed very little in twelve years. Though he must be approaching sixty, he was as broad through the shoulders and as tightly built as Max. His wide hands and short thick fingers that could wield pens and brushes with elegance and precision had once choked the life out of three Hansker raiders . . . as he had reminded me on many unpleasant occasions. His long straight hair, gathered into a thick horsetail in the back, remained solidly black, though his forehead, always high, now extended halfway across the top of his head—a tonsure of a kind, to be sure.

I pressed my wrist to my mouth. The fey humor had not deserted me entirely. *Concentrate, Valen. Manners.*

"Patronn." I dropped to one knee on the brick paving and touched my bound hands to my forehead.

Though I knelt to acknowledge my father as head of our family, my resolution to mind my manners did *not* extend to the words of honor and respect a son would normally offer at such a time. He would not believe them anyway. Neither did I wait for his permission to rise. He was not a king.

"It seems the gods have granted you good health," I said, once on my feet again. I kept my tone neutral. "I presume Matronn fares well also."

My father perched half sitting on a stone altar where the household left platters of bread and pots of honey as feast gifts for the god. His dangerous, well-groomed hands were loosely clasped at his firm waist, where a belt of gold shells draped handsomely across a tight-fitting pourpoint of purple and gold brocade. The hands and posture were deceptive. He was not at all relaxed. His dusky complexion, typical of purebloods, had taken on a ruddy cast, and his full lips, so like Thalassa's, formed a thin straight line. No mistaking his state of mind.

"Your mother has no desire to see you."

Not surprising. Seeing me, she might be forced to acknowledge my troublesome existence, a task she had avoided diligently since my earliest memory. "That's unfortunate. Please convey my salutation."

Petty as it was, I could not subdue the satisfaction that coursed through me as I stood before the man I had once named Magrog the Tormentor's twin. I now stood a full quercé—four hands—taller than he. His seed might have grown me, but I liked to think I had taken naught of my parents but the black color of hair and eyes, the straight nose, and the magic of their blood.

A fidgeting Sestius, having removed his mask and retrieved a roll of vellum and the silver mask from Caphur, interrupted this tender reconciliation. "*Eqastré* Cartamandua-Celestine, we must complete the prisoner transfer. I cannot comprehend why the *recondeur*'s punishment has been interrupted . . . and at such an hour . . ."

My father snorted contemptuously. "It was certainly not my doing. Evidently someone in the Registry, higher placed than you, *Eqastré*

Rhom-Magistoria, felt it risky to have any one of us exposed to the rabble during this unsettled time."

He motioned Sestius to the table beside him. As the administrator unrolled his scroll, my father's cold gaze traveled over me. His nostrils flared as his eyes fixed on my silkbound hands. "No surprise to hear that Valen has shown himself insolent and violent," he said to Sestius. "But I'm surprised you found it necessary to curtail his use of magic. He was never competent."

"We've witnesses that he cast spells to aid his escape from the Karish abbey and attempted more on the journey to Palinur. He is completely untrustworthy. Here—" Sestius tapped a spot on one of his pages. "You must acknowledge the transfer of custody, though, as you were informed, we will keep our men here."

"I don't like strangers in my house. My daughter, the Sinduria, has insisted on providing Temple guards as well." My father pressed his thumb on the page, triggering a spell that would identify him to the Registry. I felt very like a hanging goose at the poulterer's.

"Though I am sure the Sinduria's attendants are well qualified, the Registry must supervise the *recondeur*'s restriction until his sentence is completed." Sestius rolled his papers back together so tightly he could have used the roll as a cane. "Your son has three days' punishment to fulfill, at the least. And as he physically assaulted and verbally abused one of his overseers today—a man protecting him from harm from a rapacious mob—I intend to see him flogged before we're done. I advise you keep him on a short leash." Sestius never allowed sympathy to interfere with discipline.

My father brushed his wide fingers over the silver mask that lay on the table. "Valen will not escape his duty again. If I have to pry up every rock in this kingdom, I will secure him a contract with a master who can control him."

Of course, Patronn would wish to remind me. The Registry inserted certain standard clauses into pureblood contracts. Clauses requiring adherence to Registry breeding rules. Clauses requiring recognition of the Registry as arbiter of all contract disputes. And protective clauses ensuring we were maintained in safety, dignity, and luxurious accommodation appropriate to "extraordinary beings of proven magical lineage." In running away, I had forfeited my rights to those protective restrictions. Whatever master he selected for me would be permitted to ensure my faithful service in any way he chose—confinement, whips, isolation, starvation . . .

Sestius took his leave, ordering Caphur to cooperate with Thalassa's temple attendants and to report any conflicts. I remained standing near the brazier, sweating beneath my fur-lined cloak, my face itching beneath the silk mask. My good humor had completely faded.

As the outer door closed behind Sestius, two men in green livery appeared at the inner door. A whiff of cheap perfume identified one of them as Thalassa's temple attendant Silos, the observant fellow whose hands wielded paralyzing firebolts and whose nose sniffed out spellmaking. Worse and worse.

"You may escort the *recondeur* to his quarters," said my father, walking past me as if I did not exist. "I've no need and no wish to see him any more than necessary. He is not to wander the house or grounds unaccompanied. His meals will be taken in his quarters unless I specifically summon him to dine. Work out your guard schedule with these Registry people." He waved at Caphur to join the two in green and then flicked a wrist to dismiss us all.

A hundred retorts popped to mind as my father left the courtyard. At fifteen I would have spat them at his back, sauced them with curses and obscenities, and forced the guards to drag me to my bedchamber. But I held my tongue. I had tasted freedom, and until the day I lay rotting in my grave, I would not give up hope of regaining it. If yielding present satisfaction to lull my captors was the price required, I would pay it.

The east wing was the oldest of the sprawling house, little more than low, musty chambers with small windows huddled along two sides of an overgrown court, on that night draped in snow. The walls were thicker there, and consisted of irregular, alternating layers of brick and rock that gave them a rough appearance. I remembered the rooms as being filled with broken furniture, old carpets, spiderwebs, and beetle husks.

Most of the windows gaped darkly. The low-pitched wavering mewling of a cat in heat came from one dark corner of the square. Silos dispatched his companion to show Caphur his quarters and the facilities of the house and then motioned me toward a section where light gleamed through thick shutters. I had to duck my head to enter.

Despite the rough exterior, a habitable apartment awaited me—two connecting rooms, a bedchamber and a sitting room, cleaned and furnished. Though not the broken sticks I remembered, its accoutrements contrasted starkly with those of the main house. A plaited wool rug on bare stone instead of thick carpets on mosaic and tile floors. An earthenware basin for washing instead of Syan porcelain. A hard chair instead of velvet lounges. A small eating table with two backless stools beside it. A coal scuttle beside the hearth. No hanging maps or exotic artifacts to remind visitors of the Cartamandua talents. No magical cards or bronze water bowls left easily available for Celestine divinations.

Coals blazed in the sitting-room hearth. A kettle hung over the fire, and a bathing tub sat beside it. A shirt of fine linen lay neatly over the chair back. My sour-faced Registry valet stood beside the hearth, eyes unfocused, hands clasped properly behind his back.

"You must be Lukas," said Silos, latching the door behind us. "Assigned for personal service by the Registry."

The valet bowed stiffly.

"As I am sure the Registry overseers have informed you, the Sinduria Cartamandua-Celestine has arranged for me to supervise the *recondeur*'s confinement while in this house," said Silos.

"Yes, *domé.*"

"Overseer Caphur will be taking his orders from me as well."

"I understand, sir. I was told to see to the *plebeiu*'s bathing upon his arrival. Do you approve?" I enjoyed seeing Lukas's face darken and shrivel like an old grape at Silos's assumption of command. My valet clearly did not believe a Registry employee, even an ordinary, should be taking orders from a temple attendant, even a pureblood.

Silos was unfazed. "Proceed with your duties. Unfortunately this wing has no piped water, but you'll find the household staff efficient and accommodating. You've been shown the kitchen?"

The valet nodded, bowed, and departed through the courtyard door. A soft whining and a skin-prickling heat burst infused the room as he passed through the door. They hadn't bothered to mute the door ward, designed to alert my guards that someone had left the room.

Fine as a hot bath sounded, I wasn't sure I could bear another hour with Lukas. At least the rules of household privacy would keep both Registry and temple guards at bay while I bathed.

"I'll take those off now," said Silos softly, pointing at my hands, startling me out of my murky deliberations.

The temple guard had slipped off his mask and hung it over his belt. Large ears poked through his dark straight hair. Though his address was proper as always, his wide face expressed neither gloating nor severity. Perhaps forty, he seemed a bit soft around the edges for a Sinduria's bodyguard. But our confrontations at the abbey and on the journey to Palinur had taught me not to take him lightly, despite the unprepossessing body and his fondness for flowery scent.

"I'd be grateful," I said, extending my arms. "I hope you've less constricting means to ensure my good behavior while I'm here."

As Silos unwrapped the silk-clad lump joining my arms—I could no longer swear the bloodless bundle was hands—one side of his mouth curved upward. "You wouldn't be imagining I'm going to tell you about our precautions, would you? I've not forgot you had the better of me on the road."

"I didn't escape," I said. Happily for me, Silos's skill at spell detection lagged his skill at hurling paralyzing firebolts, else I would be a madman already. On that night of my last doulon, somewhere between Gillarine and Palinur, my spellworking had not waked him. He'd only detected the magical residue in the morning. For the rest of the journey, he had mumbled curses at himself.

"I was too slow picking up on what you were about. That won't happen again." He slipped off the cords and tossed them on the table. Then, kindly, he peeled off my mask and threw it down beside the bindings. "Tell me what spell you worked that night, and I might tell you some of the ways we have to keep you from running away from this house."

"Ach . . ." The cords had left deep grooves in my flesh. I fumbled to unfasten the clasp on my horrid cloak, but my fingers felt like clubs. I shook them vigorously and moved closer to the fire. As my fingers throbbed, I shot him a half-hearted grin. "Tell me what protections you've set up here, and I might tell you what I was doing that night."

He shrugged in mock apology as he unhooked the clasp for me and threw the yellow cape over a chair. "I'll say only this. There's only the one passage out of this courtyard, and you will be sure to meet either me or my partner, Herat, or this Registry man, Caphur, if you should venture it. This door will remain locked—only a formality, as your father requests it—but we will know of any comings or goings. You may walk in the yard in company with one of us. Your needs will be taken care of. The Sinduria sent a personal attendant for you . . . an ordinary . . . but this Registry fellow, Lukas, was here already."

His equitable manner emboldened me. "Can you tell me, good Silos, what news in the realm? I've heard naught of the world since we left the abbey. But Prince Perryn's banner no longer flies above the citadel."

Silos went to one of the windows and ran his fingers along the iron frames—checking the locks, I assumed, or installing wards. Though common wards could prevent spellworking, they could not disrupt a pureblood's bent. Unfortunately, tracking and route finding in this chamber would lead me nowhere but to the door.

"I'm sorry, *plebeiu*," said Silos. "You remain under Registry censure, thus are not privy to news. Your sole task is to attend your own behavior and submission to your family."

Ludicrous. The world was crumbling and I was supposed to be concerned with masks and manners. "Of course, that's true," I said, straining to remain civil. "And you are pureblood and must serve the Registry's wishes, as well as my sister's. But even the Registry does not interfere with a man's duty to the gods. So surely then, as a servant of the goddess Samele and her high priestess, duty-bound to reclaim a soul who has been dabbling with Karish ways, you are permitted to discuss matters of worship . . . of the temple. Such as the rioters today . . . some of them Harrowers . . . so many . . ."

"Once Sila Diaglou declared for Prince Bayard, Prince Perryn gave her Harrowers the run of the city to appease them. But they've no loyalty to buy. Instead they've put themselves on every district council. They run out the magistrates and judges with fearmongering and threats of burning, then name their own to fill the places. And they're doing the same in the temples."

He moved to the door and ran his fingers about the perimeter. "Three months ago, Jemacus, second to the high priest of Erdru, burnt his temple in Trimori and declared himself a Harrower. We've heard he's on his way here and that half the priests in Erdru's temple are his men. Every temple staff is eating itself with suspicions and examinations. Chaos, that's what the Harrowers want. All of us eating roots and cowering in caves. What 'purity' lies in chaos and ruin?"

I shook my head, trying to recapture a memory as fleeting as starfall. Jullian had once said something . . . that someone had told him everyone should be made pure like him and Gerard.

A sudden anxiety stabbed through every other concern. How could I have forgotten? "Silos, did you find Gerard—the boy at the abbey?"

"Is *this* a matter of your soul as well, *plebeiu*?"

"Yes. Well, of course it is. He is my vowed brother."

He raised his eyebrows, but did not argue. "The boy was not within the abbey precincts. We found his footsteps mingled with many others outside the walls, but could discover no definite direction to them. We've no reason to believe he's harmed."

Likely the boy was tucked safely in his own bed back home, having decided that girls were more fun than celibate monks or studious Jullian. Likely. So why couldn't I believe it? Ready to be done with this wretched day, anxious for Silos to depart, I squatted and held my hands closer to the little brazier.

The temple aide brushed the dust from his hands and jupon. "I'm off now. Behave yourself, *plebeiu*. I don't like you twisting words and dealing lightly with the gods to get your way." He remained stiffly by the door, his lips set in a prim line, waiting.

Of course. Manners. I stood up, touched my still-tingling fingers to my forehead, and bowed. Every pureblood was my superior. "Good night, *Domé* Silos."

As soon as he was out the door, I hurried to the bedchamber window. The cold night air took my breath as I yanked the balky casement inward and peered into the night. A quivering energy about the window indicated more magical alarms to warn of my escape. My poor skills gave me no hope of shaping an unraveling spell. Thus, for the moment, I let my eyes adjust to the dark sloping lawn and the thin line of beech trees and low wall that separated this wing of the house from the lane and the Aingerou's Font.

No movement was visible through the leafless branches. No dark blur against the night or the embankment. No blue dragons scribed in light on muscular limbs.

I gripped the casement and stared into the empty night until I was so cold I could scarcely move. *Dealing lightly with the gods . . .* perhaps I had been. A catch in my throat threatened to unleash emotions I had no use for. Somewhere the lonely cat was still wailing.

When Lukas returned to undress me for bath and bed, he snorted and slammed shut the casement. Thank all gods he was not pureblood. They would hang me before I bowed to him.

"I cannot sit in that room all day and pick at my scabs," I said as I strode down the cobbled paths of the knot garden. "My father said I was not to roam unaccompanied, so accompany me or explain it to him, whichever you choose. He very much outranks you, *domé*, and is not happily thwarted."

Caphur, the Registry overseer with the hairy chin and short legs, dodged snow-laden branches and tripped over broken paving, struggling to keep up as I sweated out the frustration of a long night of little sleep and an entire morning of doing nothing. I felt ready to tear down the garden walls with my teeth.

The squalling I had thought was a cat had broken into cackling and screams early that morning. Only one explanation had come to mind: They housed mad cartographers as well as *recondeur*s in the east wing. My grandfather was confined not a hundred quercae from my apartment. By midday, I was half crazed with the racket . . . and the thought of its source. When Lukas arrived with my dinner, I bolted through the door into the open air. Though only one alarm had triggered, not two, prickly Caphur had spotted me instantly and latched on to me like a wasp.

The din from the corner apartment quickly drove me out of the overgrown courtyard, through the brick arch, and around the wash-house. I remembered this garden as the sunniest of the little patches of nature sprinkled about my family's rambling house. Not that there was much sun in evidence this day. Moisture-filled clouds bulged and sagged onto the roof tiles.

The meticulous plantings of the knot garden appeared flat and soggy under the patchy snow, blackened leaves and dead stems instead of colorful swaths that shifted hue and pattern through the year as the various plants bloomed and faded. Silos and the second temple guard posted themselves at the outer wall, lest I take the wild notion to fling myself at the piled stones and skitter over them like the lizards that lived there in true summer. Tempting to try it anyway. Caphur alone, I might challenge. The bristle-faced Registry man was strong, but not particularly quick. Burning the Harrower youth had shown him unimaginative and brutish. But Silos . . . My body well remembered his precise and paralyzing sorcery as I ran from Gillarine.

No, escape would be impossible as long as my guards were so edgy. I had to wait. I had to behave myself, to lull them into belief in my compliance. Stupid to have walked out like this.

When I tired of circling the same half quellé of path and the same gnarled blockage of grievances, I returned to my chambers, bearing some faint hope that Lukas had not disposed of my meal in his haste to report my ill behavior. To my dismay and astonishment, I found my father seated beside my brazier.

"Patronn," I said, genuflecting.

He flicked his hand in a gesture that I interpreted as "continue with what you should be doing, if you can possibly complete it before I get too impatient." So I sat on one of the stools while Lukas, wearing no expression but smug superiority, deftly removed my muddy boots, replaced them with gray slippers, and blotted the damp from my shoulders, back, and head with a soft towel. Unable to stomach the yellow cape, I had worn no outer garment, despite the chill.

Protocol forced my valet to withdraw to the bedchamber and close the door once his sartorial duties were completed. Poor nasty, spying Lukas. I rose and awaited the reprimand to come.

"You didn't run." Less anger than I expected. Suspicious, though, and a bit off-balance. Almost tentative. I had never seen my father this way.

"You did not forbid me to breathe, Patronn. Only to intrude on your sight. I've never seen you in the knot garden." I *would* keep my temper. Or, at the least, I would force him to lose his first. "Did you *wish* me to run? Silos's firebolts are impressive and quite debilitating."

"I've had an inquiry about a contract."

Bravado drained into the region of my great toe. Max had been right; anyone interested in the contract of a *recondeur* was more likely brute than saint. No point in asking the identity of the inquirer. My father would tell me or not at his pleasure. Why had he come here—to watch me tremble? Did he imagine that terror at a perilous future would make me beg him for a lifetime's forgiveness?

"That must be gratifying," I said at last, clasping my hands at my back. At the least, I would give him no leverage.

He leaned forward, his dark eyes blazing of a sudden. "If you had ever shown just one minim of appreciation ... of ... of ... loyalty ..."

"Appreciation? Loyalty? For what?" I gaped at him. What skewed perception had him using such words with me in such aggrieved fashion? "Lord of Sea and Sky, I was your *child*! I never asked to be some weapon of war between you and the cursed gatzé who fathered you."

I would not accept assignment of blame for our difficult past. After twelve years of drowning all serious thoughts in mead and dancing and the requirements of survival, I'd had far too much time to think these past weeks.

"I know not why I am as I am, or why you have loathed me since my earliest memory, but you tried to beat it out of me because you hated *him*. You *made* me, Patronn. You birthed me with your cock, and you formed me with your strap and your hatred. Now, unfortunately for both of us, you must deal with me. So do as you have ever done ... as you damnably well please."

So much for keeping my temper.

Livid and shaking, he shot from the chair, pointing one finger as if to loose lightning at me. "How dare you speak to me in such fashion? You are no child of mine."

His declaration—the foulest, the most dreadful condemnation that could be spoken from a pureblood father to his offspring—fell between us with the impact of an iron gauntlet thudding to the floor. Something—those irretrievable words or the sight of his trembling hand—infused me with inordinate calm. I pulled up to my full height and enjoyed looking down at him. "Then let me go."

"Oh, no," he said, moving to the door, his rage held danger-ously tight. "I have responsibilities to this family—something your unnatural soul will never understand. This contract will remove your face from my sight, your foul speech from my hearing, and the bur-den of your existence from my shoulders. Every pureblood will see the sweetness of this resolution and marvel at the ways of fate. Com-mand your valet to dress you appropriately, Valen. Tonight our fam-ily will celebrate a sealing feast, and by tomorrow the unseemly past will at last be put to rest."

He slammed the door before I could answer. I lifted the chair where he'd sat and threw it at the door. Dust and cushions and splin-ters of wood and stone rained down on the woven rug, but the chair came to rest on its side. Intact.

I bellowed and laughed at the same time, as this rebellion came to the same pitiful ending as every other. Was my life to be the very ar-chetype of futility? Nothing changed. Nothing settled. Nothing ac-complished. Every day I'd lived under his roof I had prayed to hear that I was not Claudio de Cartamandua's child. Now, even if I could believe it true, I knew it made no real difference.

I clamped my hands at the back of my neck and squeezed my head between my forearms, trying to crush the useless rage and nonsensi-cal terror that had set me on this course of madness so many years ago. For it was not just the enmity between me and my father and my grandfather—the anger, spite, and bitterness that had forever plagued this house—that had me ready to slam my head into the stone. The flaw was in me. Somewhere I was broken, not just in my ability to decipher words on paper, but in my ability to live in this world.

One of my childhood tutors, the first and last who had ever both-ered to listen to my rants, had argued that the duties and restrictions of pureblood life were no more demanding than those of any privi-leged family. One had to pay for the position one inhabited in this world, he'd told me, and I should be grateful for what I was given. In a frenzy I had shoved him into a brick wall and ransacked his study, pawning two of his precious books for the money to get myself roy-ally drunk. I was eleven. In the years since, logic nagged that his ar-guments had merit. But my body and spirit yet refused to accept them.

Somewhere in my gut grew this septic knot, this disease that made me lash out in madness at the merest hint of constricting walls, that imbued me with unnamable fears and cravings that tormented my body, savaged my senses, and sent me crawling to the doulon. I had thought I would grow past it, that my disease was an artifact of an unfortunate childhood and that making my own choices would reduce its power. The days at Gillarine had fooled me into thinking I might win. Though I'd known full well that I—an unscholarly man of scattered beliefs and feeble principle—did not belong in Ophir's brotherhood, I had managed to accommodate the abbey's discipline without going mad from it. But now my problem was worse than ever. This sense of entrapment, loss, waste, and emptiness threatened to undo me. I had never felt so hollow, so helpless, or so afraid.

The door to the bedchamber opened softly behind me. A few tiptoed steps. A breath of air as the door to the courtyard opened and closed. Cowardly Lukas. He likely thought I would kill him. He didn't realize that I was no good at that either.

I slept most of the afternoon. Rain hammered on the slate roof and dripped and pooled in the courtyard, making freezing soup of the snow. As the charcoal-colored daylight gave way to darkness, Lukas braved the bedchamber to light the lamps. I felt him creep to my bedside.

"No need to wake me," I said. "And I'll not break your arm. You're not worth the punishment I'd reap."

He jumped back as I swung my feet to the floor and ground the heels of my hands into my eyes. When I at last looked up, he was pouring steaming water from a pitcher into the earthenware basin. Behind him, hanging from hooks on the wall, were such an array of brocades, velvets, and furs as could finance a small army for a year—my assigned costume for the evening.

The signing of a contract outranked any celebration of god or saint in a pureblood household. With the exception of my grandfather, who had not been allowed at table since I was thirteen, everyone would be at the sealing feast: my mother, Thalassa, Max, if he remained in Palinur, Bia or Nilla, whichever of the twins Max had said was still living in this house. It would be unthinkable for them to miss such an occasion, no matter their duties or preferences.

I considered refusing to change out of the rumpled gray pourpoint I'd slept in, but only briefly. Might as well maintain a little dignity. If I behaved, perhaps they would not bind my hands. That one circumstance might yield a sliver of an opening for the flimsy scheme I'd come up with as I had moped and drowsed and toyed with a spider I'd found crawling across my nose.

Might . . . perhaps . . . a sliver . . . The best plan I could come up with was idiocy. But I could not sit placidly and allow them to enslave me. As for the consequence of failure, I could see nothing worse than what I faced already. I'd escaped this house before and had been sure I'd find a way to do so again, given time. But I'd not expected a contract offer so soon.

Two hours later, I was washed, shaved, trimmed, and buttoned and laced into my finery. I wore no jewels; my father would not trust me so far as that. His tailor must have hired half a village to come up with such elaborate garments reasonably fitted to my measure in so short a time. Even so, Lukas had to stitch up my undersleeves of red and gold striped silk to show through the slashed sleeves of the green velvet pourpoint, and take hurried tucks in the rear of my black silk breeches. The tailor must have assumed anyone with so long a leg must also be broad abeam. At least no mask was required. Sealing feasts were not public spectacles; the only ordinaries present would be household servants.

If I was successful in my attempt, perhaps I could draw out the gold thread that picked the borders and seams of my green velvet and sell it for enough to eat. I laughed aloud at the image of my unsewn finery flapping loose as I raced through Palinur's sordid alleyways.

My despairing humor elicited a shocked expression from Lukas, who had spoken not a word since my waking. He pinned the yellow cloak at my shoulder. A ratcheting of the door lock and a blast of winter air brought Silos and Caphur . . . and their ball of gray silk cord.

"By the Creator, *Domé* Silos, am I not to eat or drink at my own sealing feast?" I said, facing the open door squarely as they moved one to either side of me. I clamped my hands tight under my arms, fingering a small porcelain cup I'd kept from breakfast.

"Fold your hands, fingers in, *recondeur*," ordered Caphur.

"*Domé* Cartamandua would not have you run tonight, *plebeiu*," said Silos quietly. "The stakes are greater now, as you well know, and your history speaks against you."

Stupid to run, after all. Thalassa's man had done his work well. The outer walls of my apartments had proved impervious to spells. Guards would surely be standing in the arched passage—the only exit from the courtyard—and every step of the way into the main house would be watched. Only the overgrown wall of the courtyard was left as an escape route. And the voiding spell I had prepared to tunnel through it could not be quickened until I touched the wall—a very long way across the yard.

But when had futility ever slowed me? This house felt like a tomb, the masks and cloaks my grave wraps, this contract the seal that would close the stone behind me. Despite my rage-fed swearing and mindless vows, I did not want to die. So I ran.

The moment I broke the plane of the door, I released the spider I had so carefully nurtured in the little cup, pouring magic into the illusion that would make him seem the size of a cotter's hut. Caphur screamed, which pleased me. Then *I* screamed and pitched forward into the muddy garden, my back burning as if set afire like that of the Harrower youth in the Temple District.

Icy slush seeped around the edges of the yellow cloak and slowly penetrated my layers of silk and velvet. Beneath my face and chest, my voiding spell left a rapidly filling mudhole where daylilies had once grown. I could not move.

"I'm sorry, *plebeiu*. We can't have that. Not tonight." Silos's voice remained quiet and unruffled as his firm, yet not ungentle, hands dragged me up and brushed the dead leaves and crusts of ice from my clothes. The remnants of my spider rained down over the courtyard like flakes of black snow. I had never even touched the wall.

"Magrog's fiends, that's wicked," I croaked. My throat felt scorched. "Where did you learn to do that?"

Silos clapped me on the shoulder, grasped me securely by the arm, and guided me back to my apartments, where a smirking Lukas wiped my face and sponged my velvets. A red-faced Caphur hobbled my ankles with shackles and a very short chain and proceeded to incapacitate my hands. At least the yellow cloak was sodden, filthy, and totally unsuitable. To wear a cloak between the east wing and the main house was a bit excessive anyway. I wasn't even late for the festivities.

Chapter 25

Candlelight splashed over the grand oval table from two long candlebeams of polished ebony, suspended from the coffered ceiling by silver-braided ropes. Reflections of the hundred tiny flames gleamed in silver spoons and sparked and shimmered in gold-rimmed platters, green enameled bowls, and etched glass goblets. The members of my family gleamed and sparkled, too, as they gathered about the knee-high stone table that stood at the heart of any pureblood household—whether or not that household had a heart.

Silos had bade me pause just outside the dining room as he locked an inner door behind us, thus cutting off one possible escape route should some miracle free me from my shackles. So I waited in a small arch, hidden by the shadows that pooled in the corners of the dining room, masking the sideboards and servers' tables. I fervently wished I could remain there unnoticed and unremembered.

My father, resplendent in a stiff pourpoint of red brocade, a heavy pectoral chain banded with rubies and emeralds, and a red mantle worked in gold-embroidered gryphons and lined with white fur, stood at one end of the oval table. He watched with folded arms as Max settled my mother onto her pile of cushions.

My mother's sculpted cheeks looked peaked. The heavy kohl diviner's lines about her eyes appeared more ghastly than I remembered, as her thick black hair was now streaked with white. But her well-filled white bodice glittered with diamonds; her black mantle was lined with the long silvery fur of the Denab fox; and her diamond-ringed fingers still leaked power enough to make the light around her shiver. My mother was a formidable enchantress. And a drunkard. When the doors to the main courtyard opened just behind her, the scent of wine wafted across the vast room to my niche, though the shimmering carafes on the table had not yet been broached.

Thalassa, her green cloak glittering with raindrops and her hood draped gracefully about her neck and shoulders, swept through the gilded doors and hurried toward the outsized hearth. The marble mantel was supported by twin carved gryphons, each taller than two men of my height. There she embraced a thick-waisted young woman in dark blue silk, my younger sister Phoebia.

Bia had grown slightly taller than Lassa, though her body had failed to develop the curves of our robustly female mother and elder sister. Black braids, plaited with pearls and silver cord, wound thick and shining about her head, and her skin had developed a deep coppery hue, which I thought quite pretty, and an immense grace, considering the dreadful bout of girlish pustules that had afflicted her as a child. She had always resented her twin sister's more fortunate complexion. Mine, too, though my pale coloring, so different from other purebloods', had earned me a full measure of her ridicule. Bia looked tight and anxious tonight, her gaze darting about the room until it settled on me.

"Here he is!" Phoebia's exclamation echoed sharply through the room, causing Thalassa to jerk her head around and hushing the quiet talk among the three at the head of the table. "Samele's night, he is so tall!"

Silos motioned me farther into the room. I moved slowly, so that the humiliating clatter of the chains against the floor tiles might sound less like a millworks. We halted at the edge of the thick rugs and the jumble of embroidered seat cushions that bordered the table.

Five pairs of eyes stared at me, seven if you counted the "second eyes" drawn about those of my diviner mother and sister.

"Manners," whispered Silos.

Though tempted to throttle him, I settled for a glare. Who likes to be reminded of irksome duties they are resigned to fulfill?

Taking a knee was, of course, impossible with my ankles hobbled. "Patronn," I said, touching my bound hands to my forehead. "Greetings of evening and feasting." Neither his rigid posture nor unblinking glare relaxed in the slightest. But then again, protocol mandated only some acknowledgment on the part of the superior, not anything of graciousness or welcome. I rose when I spied his fist clench.

A second bow, this to my mother. "Matronn, the years have not dimmed your presence."

A spasm in her shoulders might have been a response. Her painted eyes never left her cup.

And one for Lassa: "*Sinduria serena,* your goddess must be grateful indeed for your courageous defense of her temple yesterday."

I almost added my own thanks. Whether or not she had intended it so, her appearance on the steps of Samele's temple had diverted much ugly attention from me. But then again, I would not have been exposed but for her self-righteous meddling. So, no exceptional greeting for Thalassa. She, at least, opened her palms in my direction, before turning away to speak to my mother.

Though Max was elder, Thalassa's rank trumped his place in the order of greeting. My brother looked dashing in knee-high boots of pale calfskin, studded and buckled with gold, and a handsome topaz-and-copper-colored doublet that set off his dusky skin. The plain gold band about his forehead caught the light, yet his eyes sparked far brighter. His business in Palinur must be going well. He grinned at me as I bowed.

"*Ancieno,* to see you twice in two days after so long away staggers the mind . . ." . . . *and I would quite like to know what causes your smug cheer.*

And finally Bia: "*Serena pauli,* you have grown fairly. I promise not to set your braids afire tonight."

Her lip curled and nostrils flared. I half expected flame and smoke.

I could well imagine my parents' harsh reaction to the least hint that Bia might follow my lead. Any sympathy she may have had for my cause had likely withered under their heavy hands. But as I lowered my wrapped hands from my forehead, I extended them toward her and shrugged in what semblance of humor I could manage on a night when my soul languished in a pit from which it might never emerge.

"*Vyrsté.*"

Bia whispered the nasty word across the table, but my father heard it. Faster than an angel flies to heaven, he stepped around the table to her side and whipped a palm across her cheek. The slap echoed sharply in the silence. "*Never* in my house."

To impugn a sibling's blood purity was to impugn the family's blood purity—an unconscionable slander. My sister glared at me unchastened, the mark of Patronn's hand deepening the rich color of her cheek. What would she say if she'd heard my father's outburst of the afternoon?

I bowed to Bia again, pressing my hands to my breast in sincere apology. How awful that my presence made her willing to suffer

Patronn's wrath. Awful to see that nothing had changed in this house. Awful that her rebellion had not taken her away from it even for a few years. She likely assumed I was mocking her. In truth, my stomach gnawed itself as it ever had when my father struck any of us.

"You may take your accustomed place, Valen," said my father, affable again as he sat on the piled cushions beside my mother. "Despite your lack of apology, I'll not insist you sit at a separate table tonight. As the terms of this contract offer specify a lifetime extent, and I am unlikely to summon you back for any reason, this evening will be the last time your presence or absence at this table need be remarked. The rest of you, be seated so we may begin our celebration."

A hollow welcome, to be sure. The uneasiness that had festered through the afternoon at the abrupt and unlikely offer for my contract flared anew, an unformed anxiety lodged near my breastbone. A lifetime contract—not unheard of. But such an agreement would most often occur after several shorter successful ventures or with exceptional recommendation. What made unskilled magic in an undisciplined package worth gold enough to please my father? I could think of no reassuring aspect of a blind offer for my entire life.

"Are you reciting your Karish prayers, Valen? Take your place." My father's eyes smoldered behind his ungracious humor.

My "accustomed place" was halfway down one side of the table, between Lassa and the empty place that was Nilla's. As her home in Avenus lay too far distant for her to attend on such short notice, her place was marked by a porcelain bowl filled with rosebuds. How had they marked my empty place all these years? A tin plate of thorns?

The ornate gold cup of the head of family sat at the vacant end of the table opposite my parents—a concession to my mad grandfather's continuing existence. My father had assumed the duties of head of family sometime near my fourteenth birthday, after presenting evidence to the Registry of my grandfather's worsening mania and need for confinement. It must gall Patronn sorely that the old gatzé yet lived.

Bia lowered herself to her cushions gracefully. She sneered as my attempt to do the same came near toppling me into the long, shallow libation bowl that adorned the center of the table. Silos caught my elbow and helped me down, preventing the unseemly disaster. After politely assisting Lassa to her cushions as well, he withdrew to the shadowed arch. Max coiled easily into the place between my mother and Bia, kissing our younger sister's hand with a rakish grin and whispers that prompted girlish tittering.

Once we were in place and a steward had poured the wine, my father raised his crystal goblet. A skull-like grimace masqueraded as a smile. "So many of us together again . . . it does my heart good to see it. Though our *recondeur* remains lamentably unchastened, we receive him back into our embrace tonight, while at the same time celebrating an exceptional opportunity for him to do his duty by the family. Amid the vagaries of political change—the rise and fall of princes and kings—the Cartamandua name yet soars. The blood that fills our veins makes even our dregs prized. Let us offer proper reverence to Kemen, Lord of Sea and Sky, to Samele, Lady of Earth and Wind, and to our family's especial patron, Deunor Lightbringer, Lord of Fire and Hearth, for this restoration of our honor."

With each invocation he raised his cup higher. Then he poured half of his wine into the bronze libation bowl and drank the rest in one swallow. The steward had to refill my mother's cup before she could do the same. My father's face flamed scarlet at this slight delay in ceremony. Once my mother had tipped a paltry spoonful of her wine into the bowl and drained the rest, my three siblings poured and drank in their turn.

Truly we were a sorry excuse for a family. No matter the future, the prospect of a curtailed stay in their bosom did not grieve me.

My own crystal cup sat gleaming like a great ruby of temptation, within easy reach for one with usable hands. The smell of the potent vintage came as near anything to driving me into groveling submission. *Ah, gracious Erdru, Lord of Grape and Harvest, if I must be shuffled off to some grim lot, could I not at least be drunk?*

I leaned toward my elder sister. "Will your goddess overlook my failure to join in this pious practice?" I said in a mock whisper. "Perhaps you could hold my cup for me . . ."

Lassa ignored my irreverence. Instead, she raised her refilled glass toward my scowling father. "Patronn, my mistress, divine Samele, surely guided me to the *recondeur*'s hiding place among the Karish. I offer the goddess the entirety of my evening's refreshment and advise the rest of you to do the same. With the realm so unsettled, we must not take our debts to the divine lightly."

My elder sister had never shied from conflict with my father, but was far more diplomatic than I had ever been. She had certainly displeased Patronn by leaving his control for temple service when she was sixteen.

Thalassa proceeded to empty her entire cup of wine into the libation bowl and prevented the steward refilling it. Bia hurriedly did the same. I came near moaning at the scent.

When it became clear that no one else was going to give up their wine to the gods, my father signaled the servants to begin serving the meal. "It matters naught who sits Caedmon's throne," he said. "Our interests will be well served with any outcome."

"Not so, Patronn," said Max, whipping out a jeweled eating knife. "Navronne needs strength on the throne. The Hansker grow bolder every day that Perryn and Osriel refuse to recognize Prince Bayard's legitimate claim. Traders tell us that the Velyar and the Sydonians have sucked all use from their own lands and will be on the rampage by spring, as if they can smell our weakness. Prince Bayard is the only one of the three who knows how to fight barbarians."

"Bayard *is* a barbarian," said Thalassa. "Who else would make a pact with Sila Diaglou? The Harrowers will bring him down in his turn. Did you know they consider purebloods as blasphemous aberrations in need of 'cleansing' the same as Karish priests or Sinduri? At least Perryn could have—"

"Never fear, sister," said Max. "My prince can control a few rag-tag fanatics. Perryn of Ardra is a weakling dandy who tried to cheat his way onto the throne. He couldn't even hire a competent forger. Now that Perryn's cowardly ass is bared for all to see, Osriel will have no choice but to heel as well. He hasn't mages enough or warriors enough to challenge Bayard on his own. Evanore's gold can rebuild whatever these mangy Harrowers tear down better than it was before. Let the storms of purification rage their little while . . . and rid us of a few laggards and slums . . ."

Bia laughed uneasily. My mother drained another cup. Max raised his wine cup with one hand, and with a motion of the other drew from it a burst of colored sparks, swirling the flying particles into a glittering ring that hovered over his head.

". . . and if the fanatics win the day and chaos reigns"—with a quick spread of all five digits, he dispersed his crown into a shower of color that tickled my nose—"then who is more likely to survive than a pureblood, who can terrify the fearful masses with a twiddle of his fingers?"

Fool, I thought. *What do you know of survival?* Unless he had learned to conjure food from grass or wine from bare vines, neither finger tricks nor Cartamandua magic would fill his belly if these end times came to pass. He had seen war, but his royal contract would have assured that he had never gone hungry, never slept but coddled in furs, never lacked for clothes, servants, or gold enough to buy whatever he lacked. I looked around the table at my family, entrenched in this strange world I had so long refused, and of a sudden, felt older than all of them. They had no idea what they faced if the Harrowers had their way.

As if summoned by Max's cheerful bloodthirst, servants descended on us like a plague of silent gnats, carrying platters of roast duck that I knew would have skin like crisp bits of heaven, delicate fish sprinkled with rosemary and nuts, and plump vegetables golden with saffron.

Unable to partake, I closed my eyes and imagined myself away from this table. How fine it would be to be sitting in the light-bathed Gillarine refectory eating stewed parsnips, stolid Brother Cadeus scratching his nose as he droned some interminable lesson at the lectern, Brother Robierre kindly buttering old Abelard's bread, and Jullian and Gerard sitting on either side of me, grinning at each other around their soup spoons. Such a room needed no marble hearth to warm it. I had not thought I would ever miss the abbey so.

Which thoughts, of course, led me back to the nagging worry about Gerard. Had the boy ever been found? He'd not seemed at all a rebellious sort, but always performed his duties cheerfully. What would lure him from the security of Gillarine? Gildas had thought to send him to the dolmen with my provisions, but I'd told him not to. Deunor's fire . . . had he done it anyway? What if the boy had gotten lost or tripped and cracked his head on a stone in the night? No, no. Gildas would say something if he'd sent the boy into danger. And then my thoughts slipped further afield. How much more interesting this dinner would be were the members of the light-house cabal our guests—enigmatic Luviar, incisive Brother Gildas, the scholar-warrior Lord Stearc and his intelligent secretary Gram, and Elene . . . Elene in a woman's gown that clung to her ripe figure . . .

". . . but I was surprised to hear of the Karish hierarch's move. After so many years of loyalty to Perryn, to turn on him so abruptly."

Thalassa's comment snagged my attention. My eyes snapped open.

"The hierarch saw which way the wind was blowing," said Max, gesturing to a serving girl to sauce his meat with fruit conserve from a red enamelware dish. "*Providential* that he would find the long-lost writ so soon after Prince Bayard trounced Perryn at Wroling, don't you think?"

Deunor's fire! Eodward's writ of succession . . .

Thalassa waved away the servant trying to install frosted grapes on her plate. "The Sinduri meet at dawn to discuss the implications. Bayard's debt to this hierarch could alter the balance in favor of the Karish apostates. Though we've tried to remain neutral throughout—"

"You're saying Hierarch Eligius found Eodward's will?" I burst in, unable to withhold longer. All eyes turned to me.

"This Karish priest claims he's found Hierarch Angnecy's copy of the missing writ and that it names Bayard king," said Thalassa, her tone unemotional. "Even if the document is authentic, one wonders at the timing."

Tales said Eodward had made three copies of his will. One he had hidden in some place of safety where it would be revealed at his death. The other two he had entrusted to the two clergymen who had brought him back to Navronne, Sinduré Tobrecan and Hierarch Angnecy. But no verified copy had ever been brought forward. Angnecy had preceded Eodward in death, and his successors as Hierarch of Ardra had long professed ignorance of any such document. Tobrecan had died in Evanore in the same month as Eodward, and his copy had never surfaced. In the early days of the war, Prince Perryn had produced a writ that cited his own name as heir—purportedly Angnecy's copy. But the paper had been declared a forgery by three witnesses out of five. In any case, no one would accept it as valid without the confirmation of either of the other two copies.

Thalassa's ringed eyes, smoky and shadowed, met mine for the first time that evening. I'd have sworn I felt their heat drill through my skull. "As a result of the 'astounding revelations' contained in this newfound writ, Hierarch Eligius has withdrawn his support for Perryn and turned him over to the Smith." Her voice took on a more sober cast. "The implications are profound . . . as even you can well imagine."

I recalled the abbot's warning: Once the succession was settled, Bayard's hammer would fall swiftly on those who had not supported him wholeheartedly. And Thalassa, who had tied herself to conspirators who insisted that the world's survival trumped the rivalries of princes or clergy, sat directly in that hammer's path. By allowing me to hear this news, she had—knowingly and deliberately—laid a weapon in my hand. Were I ever to find a way around her tongue-block, I might sell her secret, perhaps buy myself some consideration in royal circles. Was she so confident in her spellmaking? Or did she believe my new master would assure I had no such opportunity? Or was she telling me something altogether different?

Max brandished a fist-sized portion of duck on his knife. "Are you surprised at your Karish friends' perfidy, Valen?" He grinned at me. "Perhaps your sojourn in the abbey gave you a taste for adult intrigue instead of childish tantrums."

"Valen remains eternally self-absorbed," said Thalassa, reverting to her lighter tone, as if I were not present. "His head is empty, his most important concerns his belly and his male endowments." She nodded to my mother as if to apologize for so indelicate a reference. "I doubt he holds to a single monkish virtue. Even if he knew aught of serious matters of the world, he'd not lift a finger to involve himself."

Why was it that my sister's unrelenting barbs brought to mind the Abbot of Gillarine and his admonitions to obedience, his lessons about honor and the need to divert personal interest and loyalty to higher purpose? Lassa was a member of Luviar's circle—those who had committed their lives to the purpose that gods worth our honoring did not mandate terror or ignorance or unthinking subservience. I watched my elder sister as she picked at her meal and sparred with Max, and confessed that I did not know her as well as I thought I did.

"Never saw anyone so sly as that abbot." Max devoured another bite of duck and distracted me from rethinking Thalassa's motives. "Luviar, is that his name? Prince Bayard was dreadfully unhappy to learn the fellow allowed Perryn to sneak off with the hierarch. The Karish eunuch will pay for that bit of chicanery. I'm not so happy with him either. Sullied my reputation with that little vanishing trick, he did. I'll find out how he hid the simpering snake in that monk-house if I must strip off his holy robes and dangle him over a bonfire to do it. If you know the secret, Valen, I might find it in my heart to pour that cup of wine down your throat! Tell me, little brother, have you ever had such a sober month since you gave up Matronn's tit?"

I shrugged. As Max leaned over and smacked a great kiss on Matronn's hollow cheek, I glanced at Thalassa to see her reaction to Max's talk of the abbot. Even considering Max's penchant for exaggeration, I found his words disturbing. But my sister ignored us all as she spooned honey from a dish and dribbled it on a piece of bread. She handed it across to my mother, who had eaten nothing all evening.

While Max preened and related grand tales of the victory at Wroling, I closed my eyes and tried to plan my next move. Which was, of course, entirely impossible. Every scheme died with the same thought: a lifetime contract with a stranger who could restrain me as he saw fit, who could decree that I would never again see the light of day, who could prevent me ever speaking to another human being if I did not track his enemies or poison his wife or work whatever other magic he required of me. I would live without recourse. Without protection. Bound. *Saints and angels, preserve me.* I dragged my ragged thoughts back to the present before I vomited in my empty plate.

". . . and that was the very same Karish house where Valen was hiding?" said Bia. "What strange fortune!"

"If I'd only known," said Max, cocking his head thoughtfully and narrowing his eyes at me. "I could have dragged him back here weeks ago. Were it anyone but Valen, I might wonder whether he was caught up with Luviar's treasonous games."

"I've heard Bayard will take control of Palinur before morning," said my father. "The Registry has advised us all to strengthen our house wards to fend off this Harrower rabble. Prince Osriel is expected in the city as well." He tore at a dried fig with his teeth. He was relishing this occasion.

Max licked his fingers, smirking. "Did I mention Evanori gold? The Bastard Prince cannot squat atop such treasure any longer, playing his nasty little games and scaring children. He must acknowledge Bayard as his king or prepare to face his wrath."

"Osriel is an abomination," said Thalassa with disgust.

My mother, who had been emptying her wineglass with regularity and trying unsuccessfully to avoid looking at me, shuddered and drew her mantle close. Her dull gaze flicked to me again. "Claudio," she whispered, tilting her head toward my father, her kohl-ringed eyes sunken, her hollow cheeks paler than ever, "I've Seen this Osriel, who steals the souls of the dead. He craves the life of angels, but is forever barred from their realm."

As happened every time my mother spoke the words "I've Seen" in just that way, the room took on a certain tomblike staleness, and the candle flames dimmed as though viewed through smoked glass. Creeping fingers tickled my spine, as they did whenever events recalled the doom of blood and water and ice she had once spoken for me.

Lassa laid down her knife and stared at my mother, as if to glean the wholeness of the vision with her own talent. Max shuddered and tossed another cup of wine down his gullet, averting his eyes.

My father alone remained exempt from the effects of my mother's pronouncements. Dabbing at his mouth with a square of linen, he savored Max's and Thalassa's reactions with the same gusto he chewed his meat. "Let Thalassa worry about the Bastard's soul," he said.

"Think. Osriel surely wishes to examine this purported writ of Eodward's will. Perhaps even challenge it. I've heard he possesses Tobrecan's copy, though he has never produced it. No wonder that, if Bayard's name is cited. It's likely long burned." Patronn smiled with bloodless lips. "If Bayard can persuade Osriel the writ is sound and that alliance is in his best interest, the war is over. We shall all prosper, even—"

"Valen?" The throaty whisper came from the direction of the kitchen door, along with a sneaking giggle. "My boy come home? My good lad grown? Why hast thou kept this news from me, Claudio?"

"Raphus! Petro! Where are you?" bellowed my father, jumping to his feet. "Get the madman out of here!"

My grandfather hobbled quickly across the tile floor, astonishingly spry for a man of more than eighty summers. A green-and-yellow patterned robe flapped over stained tunic and loose trousers. Food was the most pleasant of the likely substances clotting his matted white hair and beard. A fetid stench preceded him.

My mother recoiled and clapped a lace handkerchief across her mouth and nose as he planted a kiss on her cheek. Max wrinkled his nose and sucked at his wine cup when my grandfather grabbed a wad of his hair and jiggled his head affectionately. Bia, rigid, stared down at her plate as if to pretend a madman wasn't patting her coiled braids. But even as he touched the others, his bright mad eyes fixed on me.

"Where hast thou been, boy? Hiding, I think. Good. Good. How old be thou, Valen? How old? Come now, tell me. Thou shouldst be close to the day."

"Seven-and-twenty, Capatronn," I said, bile in my mouth. "And how old are you? Too old to be living, I think. Too wicked to be living, certainly."

He chortled gleefully and clapped his hands as he rounded the end of the table, his bare feet attempting a dance step. I stared at the libation bowl, the etched bronze glinting sharply in the candlelight. I sought the scent of wine instead of my grandfather's reek and tried to imagine it was dulling my senses . . . dulling memory, hatred, and revulsion.

"Wicked certainly. Yes. But I've told no secrets, and they've not found thee, have they, boy?"

My father charged through the door to the kitchen, still shouting for my grandfather's pureblood caretakers. The other servants who cowered in the shadows—ordinaries—were not permitted "adversarial contact" with any pureblood. Thus they could not wrestle my grandfather back to his room. Silos was nowhere to be seen.

Meanwhile my grandfather crept up behind me and whispered in my ear as he had always done, lapsing in and out of Aurellian and Navron. "We'll show them, boy. *Prasima*—how long till thy birthday? Claudio keeps me shut away, so I know not the day or season. Tell me. *Prasima coteré*—how long till thou'rt free forever?"

"You're too late, Capatronn," I said. I did not whisper, but held up my silkbound hands so he could see. "They found me. And I doubt I'll ever be free again." But I would. I would, else I'd be dead or as mad as he was.

"Shhh . . ." He pawed at my shoulders, stroked my arms, and pried at my chin, trying to turn my face toward his. "All grown up now. Tall, aren't thou? Not like these dull fools. I knew it. Tall and beautiful . . . so far above. Stand up and show me. But how long till eight-and-twenty? On that day thou shalt be free of them forever. Tell me." He hammered his fist on my shoulder. "Tell me, Valen. I've kept thee free. Given everything for thee alone. How long?"

Somehow, seeing him in the flesh sapped my fury. However hateful and cruel the old gatzé had once been, he was only mad now, echoing this old nonsense in my ear. His dementia had ever been fixed on my birthdays. "Ten . . . twelve . . . weeks until my birthday, I think."

He wrapped his arms around me from the back as if to heave me up. He was still strong. "Stand up, boy. Stand up and let me see. So cruel . . . so cold . . . they despise any who are not like them in all ways. But they'll never break thee. I saw to it."

"Leave me be, Capatronn," I said in exasperation more than anger. "Live or die as you will, old man, but just leave me be. You never took me away. You never set me free. I had to do it all myself, but I failed."

I shifted around to face him as a tired man instead of a defiant child, so that this once in all my life he might believe what I said. "I don't want your—"

My mouth hung open, paralyzed in the moment. The insult I was poised to throw died unspoken.

My grandfather's face was a landscape of suffering, creased with pain and scarred with madness, his skin rough and tattered like leather left to rot. He had chewed his lips raw. And his eyes . . . Lord of the Sky, I had never looked so close . . . so deep . . . coal black and searingly hot, a damned soul gazing out from the maw of hell, begging for one word of consolation . . . filling with tears even as he bobbed his head like a mummer's puppet.

"Ah, Clyste," he whispered, touching my cheek with a dry trembling finger. "Not even for thee could I allow it."

Two brawny men dragged him away before I could react, before I could ask what he meant or why he invoked that name, a name perched on the edge of memory and mystery.

"Wait!" I said. But the caretakers were already bustling him out the door.

"What was all that?" asked Max. "He wants to throw another party for your birthday?"

"Yes," I said, struggling not to reveal that I was as bewildered as I had ever been in my life. "Perhaps he thinks I'll turn into something useful when my years are eight-and-twenty—the perfection of seven times the magical balance of four."

My livid father straightened his fur-trimmed mantle and stood at his end of the table. "Despite this unseemly interruption, our feast is not yet done," he said, his voice quivering with anger.

It would not have surprised me to see his leather strap appear in his hand. But it was merely a scroll of parchment that he snatched from a silver tray a servant set beside his plate. The scent of hot beeswax drifted on the warm air. "This night we seal the first and last contract of our *recondeur*. When the opportunity arose this morning, I felt Serena Fortuna's blessing enfold our house once more. Valen needs a strong hand, a master who can control his violence and deceit and bend him to his duty. And yet our family will never stoop to unworthy contracts, even to salvage what we may of Valen's honor."

"Perhaps you would like to review the document, Valen?" He brought the scroll around to my place and unrolled it on the table in front of me. "Tell me, do you find any terms you would like to change? I can have pen and ink brought."

Cheeks on fire, I squinted and strained to make out the letters that might hint at whose name was listed on the contract. But of course the sun still rose and set, and the earth still plowed its course through the stars, thus the blotches mixed and mingled on the page like swarming bees, defying my comprehension. Sweat rolled down my neck. I wanted to scream at him to tell me who my master was to be. But without hope of altering his gleeful course, I would not give my father the satisfaction of begging for an answer I would learn soon enough.

"No objection or qualification?" He snatched the page away and returned to his place, pleased with his little joke. "So we can proceed, then."

My mother unsnapped a gold disk from her neck. She turned it over and over in her hand as my father positioned the ends of a red silk ribbon looped through the tail of the page and dripped a puddle of wax from a small pewter ladle onto the joining.

"Who is this master, Patronn?" said Thalassa. "Should we not be told before the papers are sealed? Of course it is entirely your and Matronn's decision, but my position makes certain demands." I was amazed to hear she didn't know.

"No one in the temple will question my choice, Thalassa," said my father, frosty and imperious.

He jerked his head at my mother. My mother pressed her disk to the wax and held it. After a moment, she lifted the slip of gold, threw it on the table, and reached for her wine.

My father affixed his seal beside my mother's. "Who but royalty deserves the service of a Cartamandua-Celestine? The Duc of Evanore will send his man to retrieve Valen tomorrow morning."

My flesh went cold as a widow in winter, and the bottom fell out of my stomach. The Duc of Evanore . . . My father had contracted me to Osriel the Bastard.

"Patronn!" Thalassa jumped to her feet. "What are you thinking? Valen is your son!"

Phoebia gaped at me as if I were already some flesh-eating monster. Max clapped his hands to his head and collapsed backward onto his dinner cushions, roaring with laughter. My mother emptied her glass and waved for more wine.

"Mind your manners, Sinduria," snapped my father. "You are still my daughter, and you sit in my house."

Thalassa snapped her fingers at a servant who scurried away to retrieve her cloak. "Never again, Patronn. Not as your daughter, at the least. You have disdained my path since I first submitted to the temple, and you have scorned my position that brings honor and respect to all purebloods. I do not think the Registry will refuse me independent status. Not after this madness."

In a swirl of silk, my sister crouched beside me. "Forgive me, Valen," she said softly. "I've never understood this bloody war between you and Patronn. I still don't. But I'll do what I can."

I stared up at her, numb, scarcely comprehending what she was saying. What uses would the Bastard have for me? Tracking down corpses and gouging their eyes? Seeking the path to the netherworld? Mapping the realms of the dead? I'd heard that his mages tried to keep a victim living while they took his organs for their dark workings. Perhaps they needed more power. Perhaps I was to hang in their web while they stole my magic . . . my blood.

My sister pressed a cold hand firmly to my forehead for a moment, and then swept from the room, leaving me with naught but a sensation like an arrow piercing my skull and a deadness in my soul.

Bia wailed at my mother, horrified at the thought that the Bastard Prince himself might walk through our door.

My father bellowed at Silos. "Set extra guards about the western walls tonight and lock the courtyard gate. Reinforce the wards on Valen's door. The man who lets him escape will never see daylight again."

Max was still chortling as Caphur and Silos led me out of the noisy brilliance of the dining room and into the quiet night. I hobbled through the ice-skimmed slush, my thoughts as frostbit as the night.

"Your Registry valet has returned to the city, *plebeiu*," said Silos after a while, as we threaded the courtyards and brick passages. "I think he was afraid of you."

The pain in my head dulled. I allowed myself to see nothing, feel nothing. This night's events could not possibly pertain to me. My father could not have bound me to the monster of Evanore for the rest of my life. My grandfather could not be something other than I had always believed. His words . . . the same words he had babbled in my ears for as long as I could remember . . . could not be demanding new interpretation now I was old enough to hear them. And the name he had invoked . . . Clyste. *Clyste's Well*, they had called the walled pool beyond Gillarine's valley, a Danae holy place. I could do nothing about any of it. Osriel . . . holy gods . . . for the rest of my life.

"The bodyservant sent by the Sinduria will attend you tonight," Silos continued, as if I might care.

Even when we stepped into my warm apartments and he began to unbind my hands, my trembling did not cease. Caphur poked up the coals in the brazier and left. Silos bundled the silken cord into a ball and unshackled my ankles. I did not move except to wrap my arms about my churning belly. Probably a good thing I had eaten nothing.

"The Sinduria will do what she can, *plebeiu*." Only as Silos raised his eyebrows and nodded a good night did I heed him. "But do not try to escape again. More than me will be watching the walls tonight, and they'll not hold back as I do." He closed the door softly behind him.

Someone appeared in the doorway of my bedchamber, but I could not be bothered to look. I had to decide what to do. My head felt like porridge. My gut ached.

"I've been sent to attend you, Broth—*plebeiu*." The youthful voice cracked like a donkey's bray.

Purest disbelief spun me about. "Jullian!"

Chapter 26

The boy must have grown three quattae in the weeks since I'd left Gillarine. Whether it was the green temple livery or the grim circumstances, he looked older as well. And though forthcoming with news of Gillarine, he no longer babbled with the tongue of innocence. Resentment and withholding laced his every politeness.

"I'm truly sorry to hear Gerard's not found," I said, forcing my thoughts to focus as we sat close to the little brazier, devouring the cold roast duck and soggy bread he'd brought from the kitchen. "He didn't take anything with him at all? Has he family?"

"Not even his cloak. And he has only his gram in Elanus; she hasn't seen him. Father Abbot fears he is harmed and that's why he brought me away from Gillarine, besides to come here and take your messages and pass on his. I ought to be back there searching for him, not—" He pressed his lips together.

"Not playing servant to a *recondeur*."

His downy cheeks flushed. "The lady—the Sinduria—believes I'll be allowed to stay with you wherever they send you next. She'll set up some way for me to get messages back and forth."

My head swam with heat and fear. Thalassa had sworn to help. Gods, she had asked my forgiveness and threatened to break with my father, and I'd scarcely given her a thought. But she would have sent Jullian before she knew where I was going. "No. You cannot stay. It would be a comfort . . . more than you know . . . but after tomorrow, they won't allow it. *I* won't allow it."

But tonight . . . Somehow Jullian's presence moved me to decision. To action, however useless.

"Who has come with you to Palinur? Brother Victor, I know, and you said the abbot . . ."

"Father Abbot and Brother Victor have been summoned to appear before the hierarch tomorrow at Terce. Brother Gildas and I accompanied them. We're staying at a priory here in the city. When he left Gillarine, Father Abbot spoke to the brothers as if he weren't coming back. He gave the care of the lighthouse to Father Prior—"

"Nemesio? Is he mad?" I threw the bone onto my half-filled plate, the last bites of meat still attached. "Nemesio likely betrayed him to the hierarch!"

"Prior Nemesio helped build the lighthouse with his own hands." Though he kept his voice low, the boy could have cracked nuts in his jaw. "His father and brother are carpenters, villeins of an edane with great landholdings in Morian. We'd not have half the tools and seeds were it not for him. He would never betray the abbot. Never. You don't know us at all."

Clearly not. How easy it was to look backward and see myself as young and stupid and unforgivably self-absorbed. Had *I* aged so much these few weeks? The boy's deepest grievance sat before me as bald as a monk.

"And *you* don't know *me*, either, do you?" I said, wiping my greasy fingers on the table linen. "A traitor to god and king, you think. Not the wounded soul you rescued at the sanctuary gate."

"Aye. I don't know why Father Abbot thinks one like you could help us." He began twiddling his eating knife. "He said I was to obey you on my soul's life."

His chin jutted bravely, but his eyes flicked from his knife to my hands as if hell's fire might come shooting from my fingers. Best he never see Silos's tricks.

I sighed and reached for his wrist, stilling the dangerous play of the knife. If I were to trust him at my back, I preferred him to think me a man and not a monster. "Listen to me, Jullian. Surely some men must come to Gillarine with all sincerity, believing Iero has called them to your life . . . your good and holy life . . . and then chafe at the rules and break them and not understand why. Eventually they realize that they are meant for other things—to marry and have children, perhaps, or to farm their own ground, or to soldier for their king. All good and holy things, too. It just takes them some time and grief to discover the truth of what the god intends. That could happen, could it not? That has happened at Gillarine, I'm sure."

"But you never intended to be our brother—"

I held up my hand to hush him. Why was it this boy demanded

such painful honesty? I had lived my whole life believing what others said of me, while screaming to the world and to myself that I didn't care. Now a half-grown innocent forced me to seek explanations I had never bothered to unravel.

"I'm not speaking of my stay at Gillarine. You're right about that. I was hungry, cold, and wounded, and I needed sanctuary, which you and your kind brothers gave me. But this other matter . . . I did not come to pureblood life of my own choice, but was born to it, and so one could say the god meant me for that life. Yet from my earliest days, before I could even consider such things, I chafed . . . sorely . . . at our rules and did not understand why. For good or ill, I've broken every one of them, much as a failed monk might do while wrestling with his destiny. Many of my deeds are simply my own wickedness, and people are right . . . you are right . . . to condemn me for them. But my choice to be a *recondeur* . . . Jullian, the belief is so strong in me—just as fierce as your belief in the abbot and his lighthouse—that the gods or fate or destiny must surely intend me for other things than this. Likely not the monastery either, to be sure . . . but something . . . and I have to keep searching for it, else I must admit I'm mad as well as sinful and deem my whole life a waste. I am not ready to do that. Not yet." Though the glass was rapidly emptying.

He held quiet and stared at his greasy plate, littered with bones and scraps. Then, abruptly, he jumped up from his stool and vanished into the bedchamber. When he came out again, he carried a large canvas bag.

"Jullian, please don't leave. I need your help to—"

He plopped the heavy bag into my lap. "Are you to ask your grandfather our questions tonight?" he said, still resentful. "Father Abbot said that's what you would do."

The surety of this assertion confounded me, for only as I sat here talking to the boy had I accepted that I must speak to the madman before I left this house. "I wasn't— Not exactly. I—"

"Father Abbot said I was to tell you that he trusts you. Open it."

Skeptical, I drew open the bag. In my lap lay my grandfather's book of maps.

I was dumbfounded. Luviar believed these pages held the key to preserving the knowledge of the world through two centuries of darkness, and he had just entrusted them to the hands of a liar and a thief, a traitor to god and king, a prisoner incapable of escaping his own house.

I felt Luviar's cool gray eyes on me, as if he stood beside Jullian, and I imagined the arch of his brow and the hint of a smile at the corner of his mouth. What kind of magic did a man wield to unravel men's souls and mold them to his bidding? Here at the nadir of fortune, the abbot had granted me a moment of profound grace. In thanks, I would have done whatever he bade me.

Wrestling with time and possibility, I smoothed the leather binding and reshaped my plan. "I must speak with my grandfather before I leave this house tomorrow. If you'll help me get out of this apartment for a little while tonight so I can do that, I'll take this with me. I can't promise. But I'll try to get Father Abbot's answers as well as my own."

Though he did not smile, Jullian jerked his head. His mortal judgment had been stayed, but I was not sure for how long. He put his hands on his slender hips. "So tell me what to do . . ."

Protocol granted even a *recondeur* bound to the Monster of Evanore privacy for anything involving bodily intimacy. Thus, if someone in my father's house took the wild notion to visit a violent renegade in the middle of the night, he or she would hold off long enough for me to finish bathing. Jullian was smaller than Lukas, so it was only natural that it would take him longer than Lukas to haul enough hot water from the kitchen. I would have perhaps an hour.

". . . so if anyone comes, just say I'm unclothed and you'll bring word when you have me dressed again. You must be firm and sure. No wavering. No apology. You must think like a servant of Samele's Temple. Though not a pureblood like my guards, you would consider yourself above the house servants. Can you do that?"

"I think so."

"Be sure, Jullian, for if you're caught . . ."

"The Sinduria told me the consequences if I'm caught helping you. And I told her that I would do whatever was needed for *Iero's* work." His thin shoulders were stiff and square.

I had not thought I had a smile left in me, but the image of this Karish aspirant with a cracking voice and downy lip saying such a thing to a high priestess of Samele could not but make my face twitch. "And my sister truly arranged this . . . approved of your helping me?"

"Aye. She said she wasn't sure you'd be willing to speak to the old man, but I was to tell you that you're the only hope for getting sense out of him. And that she was glad she was there to keep the Harrowers off you. I wasn't sure what that meant."

"Yes . . . well . . . that's another story. But if the occasion should arise . . . when you see her again . . . tell her *I'm* glad of it, too." My sister baffled me.

We pulled the tub from the corner to the rug before the brazier. Then I sent the boy off to the kitchen for the first pail of water, describing how he could take a slightly longer route and verify that no guards were posted at the corner apartment or inside the courtyard.

A purple and black tunic, black breeches, hose, and boots had been laid out in my bedchamber. The silver mask had been laid beside the clothes. I swallowed hard and vowed not to think again of tomorrow, but only of tonight, and how in the name of all gods I might get sensible answers from my grandfather.

I changed out of my fine clothes and into the plainer garb more suited to sneaking about in the night and stuffed the book of maps back into its bag.

The locks rattled, and the door flew open. Jullian lugged in a heavy pail of steaming water. I took it from him and dumped it in the tub. "Only one man inside the courtyard," he said, breathless. "He's standing in the corner at the outer wall, where there are no rooms. It's too dark to see your door from there, but he came running the instant I stepped out. They've closed the archway gate to the rest of the house, and he must unlock its magic to let me through each trip. There's two more fellows in pureblood cloaks posted just beyond the gate, so only a step will bring them into the yard. I heard more voices outside the walls. Lots of them."

"You told the fellow you were coming out again?"

"Aye, but he went back to his post in the corner."

"Good enough. It means they trust my door wards to warn them if I step out. Take a bit more time on your next trip. Tell the kitchen maids the bucket was too heavy, and you'll need to fill it more times with less in it. Tell them I'm demanding the water be hotter. Blame me. They'll understand that."

"Very well."

"If someone seems suspicious, and you think I need to get back here, or if you need me for any reason, drop your pail outside the corner apartment. I'll hear it. But do not—now, listen to me—do *not* lie to the two at the gate or to any other pureblood. You've no experience at lying, and as sure as fleas bite, they will detect it in you. If they ask you if I'm out of my room, tell them the truth. Tell them what you think of me. Tell them I'm a servant of Magrog half again your height and could break you over my knee—which is entirely true, and I'll do it if you try making up stories. Keep your abbot's secrets as you've ever done, but blame me for this whole mess. Do you understand?"

He hesitated.

"Blame me, Jullian. They cannot do worse to me than they've already done, unless it is to hurt you or the brothers of Gillarine. I'll sit right here with this book all night if you don't promise."

"Very well. I won't lie to them if they should ask."

I grabbed the book and a shielded lamp and slipped through the door alongside him, so the ward would be triggered only the once. Flattening myself against the wall, I listened as he met the guard and they walked toward the gate. Then I crept across the courtyard to my grandfather's door.

The windows of the corner apartment were dark. From inside came a soft, low droning, as if a dulcian player had got stuck on one mournful note, and no matter how he wrenched and blew, he could not change it. The absence of charged heat about the locked door meant I had only a lock to break, not magical wards. I dared not use a voiding spell—it was too "loud," too different and would surely be detected by those guarding this courtyard. Rather I touched my fingers to the lock and assembled an unlocking spell, hoping to have better luck than I'd had in Gillarine's library. Trying not to rush, I loosed a bit of magic to flow into the spell and through it into the old bronze pins, shifting them ever so slightly, feeling my way. Such a slow dribble of magic would not be noticeable in the midst of the heavy wards elsewhere in the courtyard. As long as I didn't get impatient . . . or run out of time . . .

By the time the last pin released and I pushed open the door, my teeth were vibrating and Jullian had taken a third trip to the kitchen. At least my eyes had adjusted to the dark. I stepped in, closed the door behind me . . . and almost retreated immediately. The stench was near unbearable—every foulness a confined human could produce.

A couple of low stools and an unlit brazier took form in the shadows. There was little else to be seen in that barren darkness but a clutter of clothes and blankets on the floor. The droning note came from the far left corner of the room, a mournful song of mind-death and despair.

"Capatronn," I said softly. "Are you awake?"

I picked my way through the clutter. Not all clothes on the floor, no . . . parchment . . . pages and pages scattered everywhere. And amid the various stinks hung the familiar mix of tannin and vitriol—ink.

"It's Valen, Capatronn. I've come to talk."

He was huddled in the corner, eyes open, staring into nothing. I set the lamp on the floor, far enough away he could not kick it over, and tilted the cover open slightly. He clutched a wad of vellum sheets, and a string of drool sagged from his mouth and pooled on the crumpled pages. Those who label madness as release from pain and worry have never encountered such a sight. In that moment pain and worry entirely comprised my grandfather's existence.

"Capatronn, can you hear me?"

As if I'd struck him, his head jerked, and his hands flailed wildly, his pages flying everywhere. "Valen! My good boy . . . I feared they'd taken thee!"

"Shhh . . . we must be quiet." I sat down in front of him, leaving the bag containing the book in my lap. To settle him I had to catch his flying hands and hold them tight.

He bobbed his head, chewed his raw lips, and snatched his hands from mine. "Yes, quiet and careful. They're close tonight . . . I feel them close. They *touch* me." He shuddered and tapped his bony fingers on his skull. "Careful, lad. Careful. 'Tis no life for thee."

My skin prickled. "No one's close. I need you to tell me some things I've never understood. Secrets, I think."

He pressed his knuckles to his mouth, his gaze darting anxiously around the dark, filthy room. "Secrets. Bargains. Promises. Contracts. Everything is secrets and contracts. For thee. To be safe. To be free."

I hardly knew where to begin. But the chill beneath my layered clothing and the mystery of the watcher at the Aingerou's Font set my course. "Capatronn, who is Clyste?"

"Cannot tell that. The contract . . . thou canst not know." He gnawed on his bleeding knuckles.

"She's a Dané, isn't she? Her sianou—her place of guarding—is a pool in the south of Ardra, only a few quellae from Caedmon's Bridge near Gillarine Abbey. Clyste's Well, they call it."

"Ahh . . ." He put his hands over his ears. "Thou canst not *know*. Don't say it. He'll think I told thee and put me in the daylight dark."

"Who'll think it? Patronn?" Why would my father care if my grandfather told me one more story about a Dané? And what did pureblood contracts have to do with beings of legend?

"Daylight dark and nighttime dark . . . no light ever. No drawing then. No painting. No scribing. Then I'll go mad!" As if he realized the absurdity of this statement, he planted his hands atop his head and cackled as he let it fall back against the wall. When the manic laughter shifted into shuddering sobs, I came near giving up hope of any sense. But after a moment, he leaned forward, tears glinting on his cheeks, and whispered, "Too late for Clyste anyway . . . too late."

"Why too late?"

"She told them naught of our bargain. So the others locked her away to punish her. Chained her with myrtle and hyssop so she could not take bodily form. Bound her to slow fading. So young . . ."

The others. Other Danae. She was one of them.

I tried to ask more about the Danae, but every question became a knife thrust, wrenching sobs from his bony body. I had to try something else.

"Look, Capatronn, I've brought my book." I pulled it out of its bag and eased around beside him. "I thought you might look at it with me as we did when I was a boy."

His spasms waned as I allowed the weight of it to rest on his knees and opened it, ready to snatch it away if he tried to harm it. But his finger hovered over the title and then glided, not quite touching, over the glorious elaboration of gryphons and angels wrought in emerald green, scarlet, and gold that glinted in the lamplight. "I made this. I. When my head was right. The finest maps ever in the world. Mine."

"Yes, indeed." Madness had clearly not dimmed his self-admiration. "Remember, you gave it to me when I was seven. Patronn was furious."

"Spited Claudio with the giving. He exacted such a price . . . keeping me from thee. Beastly. Shamed me to bargain with my own blood. So it pleased me to spite him. But my mind was forfeit . . . failing . . . and I had to give the book early."

"And I was a wild, horrid child who never appreciated the gift. You made me swear to use—"

"Only after eight-and-twenty!" He snatched my hands away from the book and crushed them in his bony fingers, still incredibly strong. "Go not into their lands until thou art free. Only then. Thou gave me thy promise. Swore on the aingerou with thy blood. Thou must be careful with the book . . . Wait until the time is right and thou canst walk every corner of the world without bond or bowing to any. Thou'lt remain as thou art. Promise, Valen. Promise! I betrayed her so thou couldst be free." His eyes and hands and head twitched.

"I always thought you meant I'd be free of Patronn, free of this house. But you didn't, did you?" I eased my hands from his grip. He clenched his gnarled fingers to his breast and I enfolded them in my palms. "You meant something else altogether."

"Free of *them*. Free of their Law, free of their dread summoning. Thou shalt be the greatest of the Cartamandua line. Our family will be powerful beyond dreaming. Thou shalt map the whirlpools of time, the vales of memory, perhaps even the very bounds of heaven and hell. But I cannot *tell* thee. Forbidden. Punished. Mad . . ." His eyes flared hot and wild in the dim light.

"It's all right, Capatronn. I'm here and safe." I changed course again to soothe his rising agitation, tacking toward answers like a sailing ship against the wind.

I turned a few pages of the book. "Let's look at the maps—tell me again how their magic works so I can use them *after* I turn eight-and-twenty." Time was running, and I had to calm my own frenzy. "Anyone else must read the spell in the cartouche or the border, but I— You knew I could not read words and might never learn. So how could I ever use the maps?"

"Foolish boy. I *taught* thee." He shuffled through the pages to the first map and tapped his finger on a tiny mark at one corner. "I opened this book to thee, who art without words, yet complete. For thee only, every map has one. Feed it magic . . . trace thy path and feed it, too . . . and the land will open its arms to thy skills. Not yet though . . . not yet."

I nudged his dirty finger aside and uncovered a grinning aingerou. He had put one on every page. "So I touch the aingerou and release magic into the page. Then I trace the route, feed it magic as well, and I can find my way without reading. Is that right?"

He clapped his hands and chuckled. "Clever, is it not? And thine own power will take thee farther yet, for thou art of my blood, thy bent incomparably strong."

It was all I could do to hold back my finger from the page, but I dared not work spells here.

"Earth and air and sky are one whole," he said. "At the boundaries of thy knowledge—the boundaries of the world's map—walk and listen and feel the joining of earth, air, and sky, seeking thy desire. Take up thy pen. Thy blood—Cartamandua blood—bears the magic; thy fingers will funnel it through pen to page and the way will be clear. Travel the way thou hast scribed, and begin again."

"But I don't use—" No. No need to confuse him. I had never needed pen or ink to envision a route. When he had enjoined me to "feel the earth" back when I was a child, I hadn't understood that he meant some abstract "sensing" of the universe that would only take shape when marked on paper. I had believed he meant for me to lay hands on the dirt as we did when tracking footsteps.

"Claudio never could do it. He draws only what he sees, for his mind is clay. Thou, lad . . . thou art quicksilver." His trembling fingers turned the leaves, one by one, touching, but not quite touching, the inked features, the bright drawings on the grousherres, the elaborate designs of frames and cartouches. "Thou shalt find the places even I could not."

But unless I could get free of Osriel, I would have no opportunity. Someone other than me would have to lead the cabal into Aeginea. "Tell me, must others use the aingerou as well—before they can use the written spells?"

"No. The book is thine *alone*—not for Claudio, not for Josefina, not Max or the rest. With the gryphon charm canst thou permit others to use it as it was made. *Thy* choice."

The gryphon charm . . . great gods . . . no wonder he'd had me recite that bit of doggerel until my head split. "So I touch the gryphon—this one"—I pointed to the gilded beast on the front cover—"work the charm with a person's name, and that person can use the book. My choice."

He bobbed his head happily. "Thy choice. Thine own book forever."

"Tell me, Capatronn, do any of these maps show a way into Aeginea?"

His fingers paused in their explorations, and he raised his face, stricken. "Go not to this place where I am, Valen . . . to this dark place . . . this mad place."

"No, no. I just want to see the map you used to find Eodward. It must be very fine. Beautiful. Showing the power of your blood, of your art and magic. Then I'll know which map not to follow until I'm eight-and-twenty."

He leafed through more pages until he reached the very heart of the book. The open page displayed a wholly unremarkable fiché, little more than a line drawing without colors or gold leaf or any other elaboration. Very little lettering. One might have thought it a preliminary sketch bound into the book by mistake. The landform outlined so vaguely was certainly Navronne.

"No map can show the way," he said. "Aeginea is everywhere. Nowhere. But this"—his tremulous finger drifted across the page from small notations of a tree and an arch to five rosettes scattered here and there in no particular pattern—"depicts its heart and its mystery."

His chewed and broken nail touched a rosette, causing another symbol to appear beside it like a shadow, only to fade as he moved on to the next. I glimpsed the symbol for a mountain and another for the sea. A third, located beside the rosette at the top of the map,

I didn't know, but the fourth showed the same waterfall symbol he had used for Clyste's Well. If that one did indeed depict the Well, then the tree and the arch must certainly be Caedmon's Bridge and the Sentinel Oak.

"This is the Center," he said, reverently, as he touched the fifth rosette, which was nowhere near to being the accurate center of the other symbols or the page itself. If the arch was Caedmon's Bridge, then it lay well south in Evanore. Its shadow symbol was a bolt of lightning, a notation I had never learned. "Here is where the Chosen dances to bring all life to joining."

His grizzled mouth and chin worked in tight spasms, as he gently smoothed the worn edges of the page. His eyes filled with tears.

"Saved only this one map of them all. Promised Clyste to destroy them, so no human could travel there. The long-lived had grown to despise and fear us. Clyste said I could keep my promises without the maps. But this is my life's greatest work. Our family's glory."

Thus we reached the heart of the matter. "Why, Capatronn? Why do the Danae despise us so?"

He shuddered and jerked, and I was afraid he would retreat again. But he took a quivering breath and gathered his spasming limbs. Summoning control, I thought. Every emotion, every physical expression required constant mastery to prevent it running wild. His head jerked and his eyes squinted and blinked as if someone was striking him.

"We lie," he said at last. "We betray. They cannot grasp our nature and dance it into their patterns. Sometimes our needs make demands of us they cannot understand."

"As with Eodward who did not return to the Danae, though he had promised he would."

My grandfather bobbed his head. "That was but one of so many. They did not blame me for that one. Nor for the Scourge."

"The Scourge?"

"Some humans *want* to drive them away. They foul groves and springs, trees and fields. Sometimes"—he leaned close and dropped his voice—"they damage the Canon itself. The long-lived never speak of it lest we learn the power we have over them. It is their direst secret: that they cannot cross the barriers of tormented spirits. If the guardian is not joined with the tainted sianou when it is poisoned, she cannot return to it. The Canon is corrupted, and the guardian wastes with grieving. If joined, the guardian is trapped—ah, holy ones—trapped inside the sianou. Chained as if with myrtle and hyssop, but chained with poison, and so he does not fade, but dies there. Both land and guardian lost forever. Forgotten. And so is the Canon broken."

"Tormented spirits?" I said, wrestling with the ideas of dancing that could be broken and Danae who could be murdered while outside their bodies.

"Violent death. Corrupt blood." My grandfather's face crumpled. "They did not blame me for those crimes—nor any human save madmen. They could not believe that any reasoning creature would purposely break the Canon. And they knew I loved the dance. Ah"—he clutched his heart—"to see the dancing in Aeginea again. But never will I. Never. I am lost until the last ages of the world. They do not forgive."

As fog lifts from the mountains, revealing snow-draped crags and sunlit pinnacles, so understanding grew in me. Not only about the world and coming chaos, not only about the savage rituals of Harrowers and royal bastards, but about what I saw in front of me. I took his chin and drew his face around so I could look on his pain-racked visage. Every word of sense, every moment of stillness, cost him dear.

"Capatronn, what did you do that the Danae have punished you so terribly? That they have broken their last ties with humans? You must tell me, Grandfather."

"I"—his brow creased; his lips twisted and fought to shape the words—"*stole* from them. A treasure they did not value. I had the right, but they could not forgive the loss of it. And then I failed her. Ahh . . ." He gasped and gripped his head in his hands, drew up his knees, and curled into a knot. The book slipped off his lap.

I laid my hand on his trembling shoulder. "What treasure? What was worth all this?"

His fingers curled and he drew his fists to his head as he began to rock. "Cannot tell. Cannot. Secret . . . secret . . . secret." Though he was trying not to, he moaned . . . louder by the moment.

"Can I help you? I could stay a while."

"Naught." He shook his head wildly, even as he clamped his jaw over a scream, and wrenched his shoulder from my hand. "Naught can be done. Go."

I quickly gathered up the book, stuffed it in the bag, and snuffed the lamp. As I crept through the darkness toward the door, my grandfather began retching violently. The stench of vomit and loosened bowels followed me to the door.

"Go!"

"For the book . . . Grandfather . . . thank you." I pulled the door closed behind me. Breathing deep of the clean, wintry air, I leaned on the thick oak that muffled his rising screams and wished that most futile of all wishes: that I could begin again and weave the knowledge I had just gleaned through the days of my life.

Swallowing hard, I crept silently through the frozen courtyard. I stopped in the rose arbor, brushed the snow from the stone bench, and sat, pulling the book from its bag again. The book must go back to Luviar, and if it was ever to be of any use to the cabal, I had to open it to them. Tonight, for I might never have the chance again. I had to trust that they would use it wisely, accounting for the information I would send them. And so, accompanied by the unholy melody of my grandfather's screams, I touched the golden gryphon and recited the bit of verse he had pounded into me years ago.

> *With mighty sinew, beak and claw,*
> *Feathered wings and eagle's eyes,*
> *The gryphon guards its nest of gold.*
> *Ripping, flaying sinew raw,*
> *Crushing rib and limb and jaw*
> *Of all who seek its agate prize,*
> *Save for the . . . wily . . . hunter . . . Luviar . . . bold.*

I fed magic into the charm, which was supposed to impart whatever virtue you named to whomever you identified as the *hunter bold*. As a boy I had always inserted my own name as the hunter, wishing for strength to fight off my father's next beating or cleverness to elude recapture when I ran away. I had hoped to use the golden nest and agate eggs to pay for my own house or buy my own contract, before I knew such possibilities were as much myth as the gryphon itself. I'd not even known how to quicken a spell in those days.

The golden gryphon pulsed with warmth and light, and I considered whether to give access to anyone else. To leave it with only one seemed risky. So Gildas. He was younger, less prominent, and the Scholar, who needed to find the Danae. And one more? I considered Stearc, but settled on Gram, the secretary, instead. Clearly the conspirators relied on Gram's intelligence. And he understood the Danae better than any of the others.

Once done, I packed the book away and peered around the edge of the arbor to watch for Jullian. When the slight figure trudged down the path from the kitchen, lugging a heavy pail, I followed and slipped through the doorway behind him into the warm and comfortable apartment. The bathing tub was filled to its brim.

The boy about jumped out of his skin when I grabbed the door from his hand and closed it softly behind us. "Did you see him? Did you learn anything about the book? Is he truly mad?"

"Yes to all three. But first, did *you* have any trouble? Any suspicions?"

"The pureblood—not the one in these green clothes, but the other one in black and yellow—stopped me on the last trip and asked if I liked serving you. His hand was on my head as I answered, and I felt . . . unclean." The boy averted his eyes.

"That was Caphur," I said. "An overseer from the Pureblood Registry. Very skilled at his work, and he doesn't like me very much. I hope you told him the truth."

He nodded. I surmised that Caphur had approved his answer. I did not press to hear it.

I sat on the chair and summoned him close, lowering my voice even more. "So tell me, how did the abbot and my sister plan for you to send them information?"

"The false priestess said I should tell the people here that she had thought-summoned me back to her temple," he said. "Or I could ask for Silos and tell him a particular word she gave me, but to do that only if things were very bad. Elsewise, I'm to wait until she sends for me."

I kneaded my scalp. The plan was much too obvious. No one would believe Thalassa summoning the boy in the middle of the night so soon after getting him assigned here. Having grown up with a brother like me, she didn't understand what trouble Jullian would have with lies. And I could not risk his safety by having him sneaking about with secret passwords.

"We're going to do things a bit differently. In a little while, I am going to start yelling at you and throwing some things. I want you to run both to Silos, the fine-scented temple guard, and to Caphur, the one in black and yellow, and tell them that I've frightened you. Tell them you want to return to the temple and that, of course, the Sinduria will allow it. Only that."

"But—"

"You can't take the book. You might be searched. I'll hide it here under my palliasse, and the Sinduria can retrieve it. Here's what you need to report to her . . ."

They weren't going to like what I told them—that my grandfather had stolen some treasure from the Danae but refused to name it, and that they should look to Prince Osriel, who mutilated the dead, or these Harrowers, who sacrificed violated bodies to their Gehoum, as the root of Danae hatred for humans. He had even claimed such rites *broke the Canon.* What did that mean? Was it possible that some ritual dance could determine the fate of the world? Now I had seen a Dané, anything seemed possible.

Perhaps the conspirators could use this new knowledge to strike some bargain with the Danae and find out. And any stolen treasure of my grandfather's was likely to be in this house. If they could persuade the Danae to say what he'd taken, Thalassa could likely find it. Three of the cabal should be able to use the book, at least, leaving them with no need for a Cartamandua to guide them. Whether these things fulfilled their need, I couldn't say. I had no more leisure to think.

"... and lastly, I need you to tell Brother Gildas ... only him, please, no one else, for I am sorely shamed by it ... that I desperately need to see him. Tell him that I am ... beset by my old sins ... and need Iero's grace that only he can bring before I go to my new life. Can you remember all that?"

The boy rolled his eyes, a portrait of pained tolerance.

Despite my guilt at burdening a child and a holy monk with my perversions, I could not restrain a smile. "Well, of course, you can. The brightest scholar ever come to Gillarine. And the bravest. And the kindest. A light worthy of a holy lighthouse. Tell me one thing, lad; you've never— No one's ever said aught to you of your real father, that he was ... special ... in some way?"

He shrugged. "Mam told me he was a scribe who drank so much his liver rotted. She showed me his portrait that his sister drew on a bit of bark, so I could know him. But she said good riddance to him and that my new da was the better man."

So much for legends, rumor, and Valen's clever insights. I squeezed the boy's thin shoulder. "Godspeed, Jullian. You make *me* wish to be a better man."

This time, when I picked up the padded chair and threw it into the wall, two legs broke off. The stools, the upended table, and all the scraps from our dinner splashed into the overfull bathing tub, inundating the rugs. While making silly faces at Jullian to soothe his fear, I yelled and cursed and threw myself at the door until the hinges snapped. As soon as the door crashed into the courtyard, he ran. When Caphur and Silos found me, I was ripping up my fine clothes and dropping the silks, brocades, and fur-lined cloak into the greasy water. A knot burned in my gut.

*   *   *

Thoughts and plans roiled in my head all through that long night as I lay tied to my bed, feeling my disease and my craving devour me and praying for Gildas to come. My grandfather had been trying to protect me, not from my family, but from the Danae. He had violated their trust . . . a man who had traveled their lands for years . . . who had guided a high priest and a hierarch to Eodward and brought them safely back to Navronne. Janus de Cartamandua had turned thief, and in retribution for his crime, the Danae had severed their last ties with untrustworthy humans and threatened the grandson whom, for whatever inexplicable reason, he favored. To shield me from their vengeance he had let them take away his control of his mind and body. Great gods, what had I ever done to deserve such a sacrifice? What secret bargain had he made with this Clyste? And why would one more birthday set me free of the threat?

The Dané at Caedmon's Bridge had confirmed his story, speaking of thievery and treachery, of poison and bargains broken, and she'd said that we must return what was stolen before they would deal with us. What treasure had he stolen that could exact such a dreadful price? A "treasure they did not value," but were determined to have back. Something he believed he had a right to.

The knot in my belly drew tighter, shooting bolts through my limbs, setting off firestorms of cramps in my calves, back, and biceps. Warnings. All my life I had ignored warnings, putting them out of my mind as fast as they were issued, for I believed them but more shackles on my freedom. I could not imagine what significance my grandfather attached to the age of eight-and-twenty. Yet, while lacking weeks until that mystical occasion, I *had* used the book in some fashion to intrude on a Danae holy place and to summon one of them to an unwanted meeting. Now Danae followed me through fields and town. And even before I'd used the book, the earth that was their domain had pulsed under my body as if it were alive, and their holy places—the cloister garth and the pool in the hills—had barraged my senses like siege weapons. What did my grandfather fear might happen to me? Perhaps I had worse things to dread than a lifetime of bound service to Osriel the Bastard.

Amid these fearsome questions rose wonders, too. My sister's help . . . the abbot's faith . . . and one phrase that hung vivid and poignant in the cold night, like the last, lingering tone of plainsong. Unimportant to any but me. My grandfather had altered his book for me . . . *who art without words, yet complete.* What did that mean? Why did those words from a madman soothe a hurt so deep and so raw? Another mystery to occupy my mind in the bleak days to come.

As the hours crawled by, cramps, sweats, and insidious craving claimed one part and then another of my body. Events and words, hopes and beliefs blurred together, impossible to sort. By morning, I could not think at all.

Chapter 27

"**B**rother Valen." The voice sliced through the pain like a steel claw through skin. "I've come to give you counsel."

"Gildas?" I whispered harshly. *Lord of Earth and Sky, let this be Gildas.* I could not open my eyes to confirm it, lest my head fall apart, lest my teeth crack and fall out. The disease had come full upon me in the night. And the hunger.

"Yes. Iero's blessings be upon you this morning, Brother. I understand this fear that sets you trembling. And you are right to seek the Lord Iero's grace before embarking on this voyage of duty. I wish I could change what is, but I've brought at least temporary comfort. You must seek the ultimate solution for yourself."

Praise all saints if *temporary comfort* meant nivat. "Iero's grace, Brother Gildas."

"Sirs, I presume you will leave us some privacy to speak of a man's immortal soul."

A wave of flowery scent had me gagging, and the fingers that tugged at the ropes about my chest and legs might have been a gatzé's flaming tongue. "He looks ill. Perhaps he needs a physician, not a practor."

"Would not the prospect of bondage in Evanore give you pause for your soul's health, sir?" Ever-calm Gildas.

"Bound service, monk, not bondage. Purebloods have duties that ordinaries cannot comprehend." Ever-prim Silos.

Go away, I thought.

"Vowed initiates of Saint Ophir have duties that heathens cannot comprehend. But we shall not argue those things here. I am this man's mentor and confessor, and merest decency demands your tolerance. Please step out whilst I pray with Brother Valen."

Pounding footsteps, crashing doors, slamming shutters. One might think a herd of cattle had stampeded through the cold room. Silos and his scent vanished. Then I felt the scrape of razor knives that was but soft breath on my face. I dragged my eyelids open.

"I don't know precisely what I'm doing here," he said quietly, his eyes remarkably unworried under his dark brow. "To encourage such perversion of the body is a great sin. Brother, you must give up this horror."

"I'm like . . . to give it up in the coming m-months," I said, my teeth clattering with chills, not fear. "It's a sickness drove me to it. Please believe me." Stupid to care what he believed.

"A sickness?"

"Never had a name for it, and now it's so tangled with this cursed spell . . ." The spell that had me yearning for boiling oil to scald my feet or a hook blade to tear my skin. "Please, Brother, I beg you tell me you've brought it."

"I found a bit in the priory kitchen. Not much. I didn't know how much you needed. What must I do?"

To hear that Gildas was willing to help had me sniffling like a maiden. I'd not been able to think beyond the possibility of obtaining the nivat. I'd known naught of how I would manage the using, bound as I was. I tried to concentrate on the task. "At my waist . . . the green bag."

Gildas dug through the layers of blankets and clothing. "The Sinduria said you hold the book of maps. I should take it out when I go."

"You can't. Caphur . . . the Registry man . . . he'll sense its magic. Think you're stealing. He'll take it. Lassa must retrieve it. I can't— Sorry I can't help more. Tell Luviar I would if I could. Willing." I could not examine my growing resolve to aid the cabal, only regret that my damnable weakness and blighted future left me useless to them. Beyond such fleeting concerns lay only pain and need.

"I'm glad to hear you're willing. This devil prince must not have you." I fought not to scream as his fingers fumbled at my waist. "I know people of influence in this city. We'll see you safe with us by midday."

Even as I despaired of its fulfillment, his ferocious declaration warmed me beyond measure.

He drew out the little green bag I had so painstakingly kept hidden through the past weeks. "Now tell me what to do."

"How much did you bring?"

He unwrapped a scrap of cloth and showed me a generous mound of seeds, enough for at least three or four doulons. Amid mumbled prayers and thanksgiving, I told him how to crush the seeds and that he must free two of my fingers so I could work the magic. ". . . only twenty seeds. No more." Only enough to ease my sickness.

As a youth, I'd seen the doulon-mad wallowing in refuse heaps and filthy hovels, scarred, starved, and forever shaking, tongues thick, unable to articulate a clear thought. One old man had scratched his skin off, trying to rid himself of invading "beetles." Even enduring the pain of giving up the doulon would not have healed his broken mind at that late stage. I'd always been careful.

"And the rest of the seeds?"

"Into the green bag."

"Are you sure you don't want me to free your hands entirely?" he said, a few moments later, looking dubiously at the two fingers of my right hand he'd wrestled out of the tight silk bindings. "We could rewrap them after."

"Too slow. Won't take long for Silos to detect spellmaking." I would not have my savior compromised. "Now, p-prick my finger. Draw blood."

He jabbed the silver needle into my fingertip, and I managed not to scream. He had to grip my bundled hands and hold them over the crushed nivat so the blood could drip, as I was too unsteady and too awkwardly positioned to do it.

"D-don't t-touch the stuff," I said, as he squeezed my two trembling fingers together to hold the thread steady. "The instant the fumes stop rising, when the scent fades, help me get it to my mouth. Then get out."

He nodded, his expression curious, but not disgusted as I'd feared.

"Bless you forever, Brother," I whispered, as I released magic to flow through my fingertips and bind the nivat to my blood.

Gildas fixed his gaze to the mirror fragment. I could see neither mirror nor fumes nor even the mound, but only glimpse a distorted reflection of the bubbling mess in his clear eyes. It looked huge and evil. I closed my eyes, ground my wrists against the rope to sharpen the pain, and tried not to vomit into my friend's lap as he crouched beside my bed.

"Now," he said, in what could have only been moments. Or perhaps I merely lost sense in the meantime. "It looks black and thick, as you said. No fumes rising in the reflection. Shall we?"

I nodded, unable to speak. He used my own fingers to scoop up the reeking glob and put it to my mouth.

I convulsed. Howled. Drowned in fens of pain and pleasure . . . of guilt and shame and joyless rapture.

*   *   *

"What have you been up to?" The flower-scented Silos burst through the murk of my perceptions. He tugged at the ropes. Spent an inordinate time checking my hand bindings and fussing over the bloody marks about my wrists.

I raised my leaden eyelids to a glare of cloudy midmorning streaming through the open door. Gildas was nowhere in sight. I hadn't noticed his going. Neither had I felt him tuck my fingers back into their shroud nor seen him pack away the guilty evidence that now poked reassuringly into my hip.

"Nightmares," I said, my tongue thick. Had the world burst into end-times flames before my eyes, I would yet sink into blessed sleep, burying the remnants of my shame. I had never felt so drained. So heavy.

"You work spells in your dreams?" Silos dropped my limp appendages heavily onto my belly. "A good thing *I* came and not Caphur. Your clerical friend did not tuck the extra cord about your fingers. What has he done with you? He looked smug as an adder as he left."

I closed my eyes and smiled. "Brother Gildas cleansed my soul. When the Bastard Prince eats it, he will suffer a flux." As I'd learned on the journey to Palinur, Silos's skills at detection were less impressive than his lightning bolts.

"You are a fool, *plebeiu*. And the Sinduria is a greater one to indulge you. Perhaps when I tell her you're working magic with the Karish, she'll reconsider. Last night she petitioned the Registry for your transfer to her custody, saying this contract your father has arranged is evidence of madness in the Cartamandua line. Her petition was refused." He sniffed the air and poked about the bedcovers.

Shadows chilled my comfortable warmth at his mention of the future. "She's wrong"—my father was not mad, only soul-dead—"but I'll not tell anyone that. Tell her I can keep secrets."

Secrets. Only as I said the word did it penetrate my iron skull that Thalassa had unraveled her tongue-block. I had talked with Jullian and my grandfather of Danae, even speaking the word *lighthouse* to the boy. I dragged my heavy arms across my face and whispered the word into my sleeve just to make sure.

Surely this meant my sister trusted me; Abbot Luviar trusted me. Blessed Jullian had sent Gildas to succor me. And Gildas had promised they'd come to my rescue. Perhaps they *did* need me for their plan. In a wash of unreasoning euphoria, I smiled into my sleeve and mumbled louder, "Need to sleep now."

Silos unknotted the ropes and tossed them aside. I giggled like one of my little sisters.

"Too late, *plebeiu*. Prince Osriel's man has arrived earlier than expected." He shook me again.

Eventually his insistent prodding stole my good feeling. Dully I dragged my cold, heavy body to sitting. As my hands were yet cocooned in silken cords, I persuaded Silos to help me take a piss in the jar. He refused to wipe the crusted drool from my face.

"You should not have frightened off your valets," he said, his mouth curled in distaste. "Though I suppose you'd best learn to groom yourself anyway. I doubt the Bastard Prince will provide you a bodyservant."

Stupid Silos. What did he think I'd been doing for twelve years? Of course, I'd had my hands to use. Perhaps this prince would just cut them off. I pressed my wrist against my mouth to contain my rising gorge. No, no, the Bastard *wanted* my magic. He was paying for it.

Scarcely able to stay upright, I straightened my garments with my elbows and wiped my face with my sleeve . . . three times before I realized the offending substance remaining on my face was merely my skin. The open-necked purple and black tunic hung loose over my wool shirt, and they had provided me no belt.

When Silos held up the silver half mask, I could not summon control enough to disguise my loathing. And pride seemed unutterably foolish at the moment. "Ah, *domé*," I whispered, begging, "not that one. Please, I cannot breathe in it."

"Your new master provided a silk mask for the journey and a standard pureblood cloak," he said apologetically, "but, as you are yet under Registry restriction, you must be delivered wearing this and the *recondeur*'s yellow. Your protocols within Prince Osriel's house will be his choice, of course."

No protections in a *recondeur*'s contract. My master could require that I wear this mask forever. My stomach clenched. Sweat dribbled down my back and sides as the pressure of Silos's hand on my shoulder buckled my wobbling knees. He latched the band about my neck and secured the strip over my head, leaving me half blind, half deaf, and completely muted. Suffocating.

I panicked, trying to clear my clogging nostril, trying to suck enough air through the exposed half of my tight-bound mouth that I would not die. I scraped my arms across my face as if I could dislodge the hateful metal, and when I could not, I slung my bundled fists wildly into Silos, dug my feet into the rug, and lunged forward. My grandfather's whimpers and screams drifted through the open doorway as they did in every hour in that house.

"Settle, *plebeiu*," said Silos. He grasped my flailing arms and shoved me down again. "Settle. You've plenty of air, if you'll just calm down."

His firm assurances eventually slowed my heart, and my gratitude set me weeping. He knelt to shackle my ankles, then hoisted me up and propelled me through the door.

The unending symphony of madness from the corner apartments accompanied our journey through the courtyards and arches. *Poor devil.* I sniffled like a sentimental drunkard. *I'm as mad as you, Capatronn. They'll lock me up in my own filth, too.*

Ssst . . . Silos. My sister beckoned to us from a grape arbor threaded with dead vines. *We're here to save him.*

Silos did not turn his head. I slowed, glancing over my shoulders. Seeing with only one useful eye made everything seem flat and out of proportion.

I bumped Silos's shoulder and nodded toward Thalassa, who now crouched behind a statue of Erdru with his goat's legs. Or were they *her* goat's legs?

The temple guard prodded me to keep walking. I stepped in front of him, forcing him to stop, grunting, jerking my head, and pointing my hands toward my sister. *Look at her. Are you blind?*

Silos paused and spun in a slow circle, stopping only when he faced me again. "Stop playing, *plebeiu*. I don't know what you want."

I whipped my eyes back to the statue. And then to the arbor. Thalassa had vanished. Far behind me, my grandfather cackled. Frenzied, the voice of my fear sealed behind the metal half lips of my mask, I dodged in front of Silos again, pounding my bundled hands on his temple badge and then on my own chest.

"No, *plebeiu*. I cannot take you to the temple."

Grasping my shoulders, he turned me around and gave me a gentle shove toward the main house. Halting again, I tried to show Silos where Abbot Luviar perched beside a crow on a lichen-covered column. Then I pointed out Gildas, grinning from behind a dormant tree.

"What is it, *plebeiu*? What's wrong with you? Move along."

I hobbled forward. Blinked. The garden was empty of all but me and my jailer.

One more glance over my shoulder. The naked man sat cross-legged, tucked into the frost-glazed shrubbery, his gleaming dragon sigils silver in the morning haze. Eyes the crisp gold of autumn aspen observed us. Curious. Disdainful. The world blurred as I turned away, my throat swollen with grief. *Illusions. Visions. Not real.*

We passed through an arched gate and into the house.

Crystal lamps chased the gray morning from the columned reception room. I blotted my damp face on my sleeve and forced myself calm, trying to grasp what was real. I was surrounded by the familiar— the richly colored tapestries that my ancestors had brought from Aurellia, the luminous marble statue of Kemen and his belt of stars, wrought by some Pyrrhan master centuries ago, and the enameled urns and gilt caskets brought from exotic Syanar and set here on pedestals shaped like bundles of reeds. Beneath my feet gleamed the silver and blue mosaic tiles that my grandfather had salvaged from a ruined temple on the isle of Caraskan, shipped to Navronne, and reassembled here to display the order of sun, moon, and earth.

Just beyond the vulgar and exotic display of my family's wealth shone the burnished breastplates of four well-armed warriors who flanked the doorway to the outer courts. The warriors stood at attention, lances at rest, their surcoats the rich, dark green of holly leaves and blazoned with the silver wolf of Evanore, a white trilliot under its paw.

Silos closed and locked the inner door behind me. *Holy gods . . . whoever you are . . . please wake me from this nightmare.* Where were distracting visions when I needed them most?

"This is he?" The words scoured skin and soul like windblown sleet.

The speaker walked in alongside my father. Though the mailed forearms that bulged from his holly-green surcoat were formidable, and his thighs might have been piers for Caedmon's Bridge, it was his face that caused my bowels to seize. Where half of mine was encased in graven silver, half of his was fleshless scars, leathery creases and ruptures surely caused by burning oil or systematic beatings with hot irons that destroyed flesh and sinew and underlying bone. The eye buried within this horror was but a dark slit. The other, fathomless in its emptiness and limitless in its disdain, briskly scoured my sorry turnout.

When Silos prodded my back, I bowed ungracefully to my father and the visitor at once. The planets beneath my feet spun in their paths.

"Magnus Valentia de Cartamandua-Celestine," said my father. "A male pureblood of seven-and-twenty years, his bloodlines registered before birth, witnessed and verified through ten generations. Contracted for unspecified service to His Grace, the Duc of Evanore, for lifetime duration."

Of course, this grotesque man was not the prince. Osriel was the youngest of the three brothers, close to my own age. This man's hair, trimmed close to his skull, was mottled gray.

He clasped his gloved hands behind his back, well away from the sword sheathed at one hip and the Evanori battle-ax ready at the other. "Recalcitrant, you said. Incorrigible. But I did not expect shackles in his family home. Is he violent, mad, or merely undisciplined?" He did not sound as if he cared which.

"Not mad," said my father. "Undisciplined certainly. The hand bindings prevent his triggering any spellworking. The shackles prevent him trying to escape his duty. He has willingly participated in armed combat, so I would put no violence past him. Mardane Voushanti, I clearly spelled out his history when we spoke yesterday."

Unfair! I yelled inside. *To hint at violence to this stranger when I can't defend myself.*

"It is no matter," said Voushanti, returning his gaze from my father to me. "My lord imposes his own discipline. He anticipates training a pureblood to his service, a pleasure he has not yet indulged as he has always found the standard contracts too restrictive. Now if your documents are in order . . . we are in a hurry."

At a small desk of polished rosewood, my father unrolled the scroll he had sealed at dinner. Mardane Voushanti flicked a finger at one of the warriors, who opened the door. A servant carried in an iron casket and deposited it on the desk. The Evanori lord accepted the scroll. He exchanged bows with my father. And thus was I sold like a slab of meat. Silos's iron hand gripped my arm, else I would have run, shackles or no, flaccid limbs or no, madness or no.

An excruciating cramp shot through my arms and shoulders, followed by a wash of heat and a shuddering release—an instant's euphoria before my spirits plunged to the depths, as if an uncrushed nivat seed had only now dissolved to work its perverse magic. One rapturous sensation, swept away in a heartbeat, leaving me dizzy . . . hungry. The doulon, unmistakably. I had never experienced such a momentary burst, more than an hour after the use.

Matters moved quickly. The lord refused wine. They murmured farewells. My father did not speak to me, but watched calmly as the four warriors brushed Silos aside and herded me into the weak and frigid daylight of the outer courtyard.

The warriors unshackled my feet and lifted me onto a horse, binding my wrists to the pommel and feet to the stirrups. A groom sawed at reins and halter as the demon beast thrashed and bucked. Every one of the grooms and warriors cursed and swore until the mardane himself came and laid a hand on the vile equine's head, quieting it for the moment.

Even before we rode away into the midday gloom, the door to the house was shut and the lamps extinguished—as was all light within me. No one had come to my rescue.

The shock of noise and activity as we left the secure walls and wards of my family home was almost enough to banish my waking stupor. Bells clanged in frantic warning from every tower. Panicked citizens mobbed the streets, loading wagons, herding children, geese, and pigs toward the lower city, as if they might escape the coming change, or toward the citadel, as if their missing prince might magically develop a spine and save them. Bayard's hammer was falling.

Voushanti rode in front of me, his snow-dusted back stiff and straight. One Evanori warrior rode to either side and two more behind. Wind blustered and whined through the streets, carrying the scents of ash and offal, stirring up eddies of new snow on stoops and walls, and whipping Navronne's white trilliot that yet flew alone on the heights, two days after Perryn's fall.

Few in the crowds wore Ardran purple. For the first time in three years, Bayard's pikemen roved the city, their scarlet and blue badges spread like a fungus through every square, along the promenades and the grand steps that linked upper and lower city, and at every major street crossing. The orange head scarves of their Harrower allies colored the streets like splashes of sunflowers floating on rivers of brown and gray. Like a plague of locusts, those wearing the rags wrought destruction far beyond their size: smashing windows and doors, toppling carts and statuary, throwing burning torches into gaping shop fronts. Bayard's men, better armed but outnumbered, made no move to stop them. The Harrowers believed cities corrupt. Given a free hand, they would level Palinur.

As we crossed the heart of the Vintners' District, three men wearing orange rags upended a barrel into the public fountain. Acrid steam billowed and hissed. The black water heaved, sluggish, oozing. Three tar barrels lay empty beside the stained stonework.

Twelve districts. Twelve fountains. Valves and conduits bearing the city's lifeblood.

Black smoke billowed from at least three directions. The three men lifted another barrel. No one stopped them. No one attempted to stay the burning.

I wanted to scream at those running away: *They'll not stop with the city! Vineyards. Villages. Aqueducts. Bridges. These lunatics will bring the end times.* But spelled silver sealed my lips. My pleas and warnings bore no more sense than the snarling of a beast.

I clung to the saddle, my head rattling like a tin drum in a hailstorm, every sinew complaining as if I'd fought a ten-day battle. Twice more a rapturous burst took me away from the misery, only to abandon me in the same instant, sicker than ever. Never had I felt so wretched after a doulon. Had I told Gildas to wait until the fumes vanished? Or how many seeds to use? Holy gods, what if he'd used all of them? The desire to touch the green bag, to reassure myself that the supply was intact, soon became a torment. My hands twisted against the implacable silk that held both touch and magic at bay.

"Hold!" Voushanti drew rein sharply as we approached the broad causeway that led from the palace gates into the upper city. Drums rattled in the distance.

My horse balked and whinnied. A warrior grabbed my mount's halter and dragged his head around, while I gripped the pommel with my wrists and forearms until my shoulders burned.

Hoofbeats approached, keeping cadence with the funereal drums. Leather creaked. Harness jangled. Not a hundred quercae in front of us, ranks of Ardran knights rode slowly down the causeway, past the fallen statues that ringed the palace precincts. Swords sheathed, bereft of lance or mace, hundreds of them passed . . . the palace garrison . . . and behind the knights, mounted officers herded the massed men-at-arms, stripped of pikes and halberds, heading for the city gates. For surrender.

Here and there a wail of mourning rose in concert with the whining wind. *Yes, mourn for Ardra,* I thought, besieged with images of fertile vineyards and golden grain fields and the glories of long-ago summers. *Mourn for Navronne. For our children's children to be birthed under the Smith's wreckage.*

Yet what did all this signify if Navronne was returning to the primeval forest . . . if all cities were to end? As the mardane and his warriors led my horse back the way we had come, I hunched forward over the pommel and looked no more upon Ardra's shame.

"By the night lords!" The mardane spat the oath through clenched jaw and reined in again.

A party of Bayard's soldiers, bristling with lances, blocked the end of a narrow lane behind us. I blinked. At the head of the party rode a square-faced knight. At his side rode an iron-visaged woman, wearing light mail and a brown surcoat blazoned with orange.

"Identify yourselves, and declare why you should not stand down and yield your arms," said the leader, his voice young and brash. The single blue band on his scarlet baldric proclaimed his inexperience. When the baldric began to crawl across his breast like a striped snake, I begged it silently to stop.

The few citizens abroad in the lane vanished into the side alleys and doorways. Voushanti rode forward on his own, stopping just short of the Moriangi. "I am Voushanti, Mardane Elestri, commander of His Grace Osriel of Evanore's household guard, escorting my lord's retainers. You've no cause to hinder us, young sir."

"The Bastard does not honor the Gehoum," snapped the woman, before the young knight could respond. "These men must disarm or pay forfeit."

"His Grace of Evanore has maintained neutrality throughout this petty dispute, sir knight," said Voushanti, his words as crystal hard as the icicles dangling from the sagging balconies. "And he expects his officials to move unhindered throughout Navronne as they have since his father's death. Perhaps this . . . warrior . . . at your side does not comprehend the protocols of royalty or that my master's displeasure is not incurred lightly, even by his royal brothers or their favored priestesses."

A faint green luminescence rose from Voushanti's sword and from the shipped lances of his own four warriors. The Moriangi shifted backward, so perhaps more eyes than mine saw it.

"Lord Voushanti, m-my apologies." The young knight held his ground beside the woman, though his teeth rattled like the Ardran drums as he waved his men backward. "Pass, as you will."

"Blasphemous weakling!" The woman hung back as the lancers marched away. Then she wrenched her mount's head around and vanished behind them into the smoke and gloom.

"Quickly! This way," said Voushanti, pointing down an alley scarce wide enough for his warhorse. "She'll set an ambush."

He led us through the maze of broken streets and crumbling arches under the causeway. These remnants of some early incarnation of Palinur had been exposed when the new palace approach was built by the Aurellians. In normal times the narrow, stinking lanes served as a haven for thieves, cutpurses, and very large rats.

We emerged from the ancient warren into the wide boulevards of the Council District, streets of small, elegant palaces favored by the king's household, royal relatives, high-ranking clerics, as well as the foreign embassies that had sat abandoned since Eodward's death. Just ahead of us, a party of six or eight Moriangi troopers rammed a hitchpost into the door of a fine house, bursting it open in a shower of splinters.

A little farther down the street, another party, blazoned with scarlet and blue, dragged a writhing man from a house and threw him onto the pavement next to several mortally still swordsmen. A woman in servants' garb stood watching. Calm. Quiet. The soldiers closed in around the man and laid into him with clubs and feet. As his screams tore the air, the serving woman tied an orange scarf about her head and strolled away. I could not but wonder how many Harrowers served in wealthy houses, silent, deferent, behind the wards that families like mine believed impregnable.

Another turning took us out of the din and into a muddy back lane between gated walls where servants and delivery carts would travel on better days. The only sounds in the dim alley were the breathing of our own beasts and the jingle of harness. At the second or third break in the wall, a tall gate of black iron swung open soundlessly. No grind of gears or squall of hinges accompanied the closing, once we had passed inside it. My clammy skin itched beneath the layers of wool, silk, and fur.

The back of the house stood bleak and unwelcoming. Small windows pocked the tall gray wall, stained with rust and soot about gutters and empty torch brackets. A stone kitchen house lurked dark and shuttered, its chimneys cold. An empty cart had been shoved into a corner of the yard. Dead leaves and dirty snow filled watering troughs. I lowered my eyes, afraid of what phantasms I might see lurking in these shadows.

Mardane Voushanti dropped lightly from his saddle and waved a gloved hand at me. "Get him down."

The warriors released the horse and me from our unhappy partnership. When one of the men knelt to reshackle my ankles, I shook my head frantically and pounded my bundled hands on his shoulders. But for the silver mask that forbade speech, I would have abandoned all pride and begged him not. To face this life . . . this master . . . bound and shackled . . . fear came near choking me. The lock clicked shut. Two of the warriors grabbed my arms and almost carried me down a short flight of steps into a musty corridor. Everyone was in a hurry, and neither my mind nor my feet could keep the pace.

We threaded a maze of empty storerooms, of laundry rooms furnished with rusting tubs and a few stiff rags hung on suspended frames, past coal bins and linen rooms that smelled of moldy herbs.

From the servants' halls, we emerged into a grand foyer, poorly lit and shrouded with cobwebs and dust.

Voushanti halted before a tall door. Every finger's breadth of the dark wood had been carved with beasts and symbols and set with slips of gold and chips of gemstones. Its centerpiece was a snarling wolf with smoldering garnets for its eyes.

"A warning, pureblood." The mardane gripped a strap of the metal mask and pulled my face close to his, forcing me to look into his eyes . . . black, bottomless, one spark of red fire at the center, chilling me to the marrow. No past, no future in those eyes. "His Grace dislikes liars and gaping fools. Remember it." As if I weren't rattled enough already. When he looked away, I almost sobbed in gratitude.

One of the warriors dragged open the door. Another shoved at my back. I stepped through, trying to hold my head high without falling on my face.

The cavernous room was as dark as a well of tar. A few threads of gray sketched tall narrow windows, but heavy draperies barred what modest illumination the overcast morning might provide. Across the room lurked the wolf from the door, grown huge, its fist-sized eyes of garnet pulsing with life. I stepped back, blinking in dismay. But this phantasm was no more than pulsing coals in a cavernous hearth.

No sooner had I exhaled than a streak of blackness darted between my legs. Claws scrabbled on wood. Then, slightly above my head, disembodied in the dark, no wolf, but a cat blinked—its yellow eyes sharp and gleaming like faceted citrine. My sluggish heart thrummed like the Ardran drums. *Saints and angels, fool, take hold of your mind.*

Voushanti's hauberk gleamed in the crimson glow as he tossed a rolled parchment on a table and bowed in the direction of the most profound darkness in all the gloom, the end of the room to our right. "The pureblood, Cartamandua-Celestine, Your Highness. The contract is in order. He is your bound servant until the last breath departs his lungs."

The warmth of the gleaming coals did not touch me outside or in. A lung-frosting chill and a faint medicinal odor pervaded the room. I needed to bow to him. *Curse the damnable doulon.* Why could I not gather my senses? Of all days to have this horrid reaction. Of all hours. I fought my roiling belly, pressed my fingers to my forehead, and concentrated on keeping my knees steady as I inclined my back.

After a suitable interval, I rose again . . . slowly . . . using a glimmer of red on the wood floor as a touchstone to prevent my spinning head losing all orientation.

I could manage this. A thousand times I had passed myself off as sober when muddleheaded with mead.

First, stop the damnable shivering. The silver mask would reveal my tremors even in the minimal light of the dying fire. I could allow him to think me wary and disciplined, or carefree and ill behaved, but he *must* not think me weak or afraid. My future . . . my freedom . . . depended on carving out a position in this household, a position of respect if I could manage it. Yet here I was, near drooling. I inhaled, deep and slow, and forced my body rigid.

"Have you presented his task?" Low. Clear. Large and deep. Larger than the room itself. Rumbles and echoes and nuances beyond hearing. *Not human . . .*

I shook my head sharply, trying to stifle fear with reason. Of course he was human. Somewhere in that unnatural dark were a man's head, body, limbs, eyes. Crippled, so I had heard. Deformed. Surely he was but an ugly sorcerer with ugly habits—like members of my family. His eyes would be watching me. I summoned every discipline I knew. My soul would not go easy into his grasp.

Voushanti clasped his hands at his back in a military rest. "My first concern was getting him here safely, my lord. The streets worsen by the hour. I knew you wished to interview him before his assignment. Perhaps you even wish to give the commands your—"

"Do as I commanded you, Mardane." The voice was a lash.

The mardane bristled, but swiveled to address me. "Your first duty for your new master will be to locate two prisoners in whom he has an interest. The two were taken from their beds earlier today, but are held neither in palace dungeons nor city jails. Tracking a person from a known location should be a minor exercise for one of your bloodline—even one minimally trained, as we understand you to be. Our lord prince will accept no excuses for failure. We shall remove your restraints, of course, and provide you garments less noticeable. Do you comprehend?"

Making sure not to look at Voushanti's dreadful face, I bowed very slightly in acknowledgment. My mind raced—or at least plodded as fast as was possible through knee-deep mud. Freeing prisoners . . . not so bad a task as I'd feared. And I was to be loose in Palinur, my hands unbound. I knew a thousand hiding places . . .

A whipcrack split the murk, a fiery lash encircling my ankles. The shackles shattered into pieces and clattered to the floor. The hobble chain dropped with a loud clank, almost stopping my heart.

The half-faced Evanori stood to one side, inspecting my cooling ankles, his hands clasped in relaxed unconcern behind his back. When his unsettling gaze slid upward, expectant, I squeezed my eyes shut, afraid even to breathe. This whip was not leather, but magic, the hand that wielded it hidden in the darkness.

Another whipcrack. I bit my tongue so as not to cry out. This time the fire encircled my neck and the top of my head, as the metal neck and head straps broke away and the silver mask clattered to the floor. Quickly, I lifted my bound hands and stretched them well away from my belly.

This time the bolt of power flew silently. The air shivered as if a giant sword had whisked by me, its speed and ferocity making it invisible. I blinked. The silken bindings stretched and drooped from my fingers, then frayed into threads of gossamer that floated to the floor. *Free!*

But the mardane quickly gripped my arm and shoulder in such fashion that he could lay me flat should I blink wrongly. My moment's exaltation snapped like a dry twig. The unruined half of his face twisted slightly. "It is certainly as you surmised, my lord. His nature is true. The rebellious spirit does not forsake him."

"Erase any thought of escape from your mind, Magnus Valentia," breathed the voice from the shadows. "Do not think I cannot reconstruct these restraints or provide more . . . restrictive . . . ones should they prove necessary. Though obedience is required by your contract, I know you disdain the rules of your kind, as well as the ordinary courtesies of honorable men."

I tried to reclaim some dignity in word if not posture. "My word, given unreserved, is inviolate, Lord. But I do not honor promises given by others in my name."

"Fair enough. So you will understand why we hold surety for your good behavior."

The door opened, and one of my escorts led in a prisoner. His slender wrists were bound behind him and silk scarves shuttered his eyes and mouth. A tiny sound issued from his throat. Not a sob. Not a wail. Only the choking sound of terror tight reined, of constricted throat and bound heart, of determined courage. Jullian.

"Damnable cowards!" I yelled, rage exploding from my being's core. "What kind of lord . . . what kind of *man* . . . holds a child hostage? How dare you—?"

Voushanti deftly shifted his grip, snaring my right arm in a shoulder lock, bending my neck forward so forcefully I thought it must snap.

"I do only what is necessary to compel your obedience," said the voice from the darkness, cold and deep. "Fulfill your contract, and the lad will survive . . . this day."

I wrenched free of the mardane and dropped to my knees beside the boy. Fear and anger flailed the cotton wool within my skull, so that I could scarcely articulate words. They had brutalized this boy on *my* account. "Jullian, it's Valen here. Have they hurt you?"

The boy shook his head sharply.

"His safety is in your hands, pureblood," said Voushanti, his voice stark as midwinter.

In my hands. Indeed. I gathered the rigid boy close, turning him until his back lay against my chest, laying one hand on his ruddy hair and one hand on his breast. His heart fluttered like a rabbit's throat. "I want him free."

Voushanti snapped, "You have no—"

"Free and healthy as he is right now," I barked into the midnight where the master lurked, ignoring the treacherous servant. "You can throw me in a pit dungeon and lock the trap for a thousand years before I allow him to be your pawn." I could not consider complexities or strategies, but only a certainty that swelled greater than the doulon craving—this outrage could not happen. "Your *word*, Lord Prince, or I do nothing for you *ever* and your contract gold is wasted."

"Free, then, and unharmed, once today's task is done." The voice breathed malice that settled like a cold snake alongside my spine. "But not you, pureblood. Not ever. You claim your given word is inviolable. So swear to me of your own will—without reservation— that you will not run. Prove it this day, and you will have my word in exchange: I will not ever use the boy against you."

Good that I could not hold more than one thought in my head at a time, that I was too dull witted to weigh the balance of this bargain. Yet he was not asking an oath of obedience. Only submission. I spun Jullian around to face me and gripped his narrow shoulders, quickly before I could reconsider.

"I vowed to protect you, Archangel. Do you remember? And so I'll do. My master is noble Eodward's son, thus we must assume he is a man of his word as well. So have courage and say your prayers. While I'm off doing his bidding, you can practice your Aurellian verbs, for I know you have difficulty with them. *Teneo, teneas, teneat . . . teneamus . . .* eh?"

The boy's chin lifted ever so slightly. And then he nodded.

I rose and faced the massive dark in the corner of the room. How does a man yield his lifeblood willing, slit a vein and watch the scarlet flood sap his strength and sentience, silence the music of the world, still his feet? Madness—this foggy mantle the doulon had laid over me that allowed naught of sense, only anger to burn through—that was the only explanation. I bent one knee, inclined my back, and touched my fingertips to my forehead. "You have my word, lord prince. I will not run. Not ever."

"Without reservation?"

"Without reservation."

"Very well, then! Be on your way."

Voushanti bowed to his lord, pulled me to my feet, and hurried me out of the room. "I will outline your morning's task as we go," he said when the door had closed behind us. "Speed is of the essence . . ."

Chapter 28

Blood is unique. Pureblood families insist that each child's blood is identical either to the father's or the mother's, and that the only variance that prevents one of us growing into an exact copy of that parent is malleable "nature." But those purebloods gifted to follow routes and tracks must surely know better—that blood bears the imprint of a singular being who loves and hates and quivers in terror, who sings psalms or grows parsnips or strips pigs— because blood lays down an excellent, unmistakable path to its source.

Though I had no idea whose blood it was, the clotted mess in the sooty, brick-paved courtyard was sufficient to trigger a magical response when I applied my mind to the problem. If only I had more mind.

"Which way?" demanded Voushanti, his voice muffled by the hood that draped his mutilated face. His hand encircled my upper arm with the grip of a pawnbroker holding his last citré. The engravings on his wide gold wristband seemed to writhe in nauseating rhythm with my pulse. "Where were they taken? A month you've squatted here staring at this puddle. We've—"

"—no time. I know that." I pressed the heels of my hands to my eyes, trying to focus on the whereabouts of the unnamed captive whose blood had been so callously shed in this deserted yard. But as quickly as the route to his present location took shape in my mind, the lines and turnings faded again, as if I'd drawn them in breath frost on a window glass. Twice more in the past hour on our way through the chaotic streets of Palinur, I'd felt the shattering explosion of the doulon and the almost simultaneous disintegration of sense. My mind was in tatters. "West, I think. Toward Riie Doloure. There's an old fortress . . ."

Was this a true impression or was it only that talk of missing prisoners recalled a tale I'd once heard about a private jail? Aurellians had inflicted cruel torments on Navron prisoners, not allowing guilt or justice to interfere with retribution, and certain Navron nobles rued the day King Eodward had proscribed such practices. A young thief had once told me of his escape from a grim lockup such men used for torturing "grudge prisoners"—those who bore their especial ire or contempt. Determined to spread word of the dread place before he could be recaptured, the youth had spat out his gruesome story, clutching his burnt, empty wrists to his belly while a fellow vagabond dressed the poor sod's whip-gouged back with goose fat. I'd had no other comfort to offer a lad of fifteen, facing life with no hands.

"Riie Doloure—are you sure?"

I shook my head to clear it and pressed my palms to the pavement beside the dark sticky pool. Icy water dripped on my hands from the cornice that sheltered the unseemly blotch. *Hold the lines this time. Ink them on your senses. The Bastard Prince has Jullian until this task is done.* The traces were so faint. Brick and cobbles did not hold impressions like bare earth. And Palinur bled from every pore this day, confusing me even more. Time crawled by, stretched like a waking cat, and then sagged into a filthy puddle. "Riie Doloure. Yes."

Voushanti dragged me up and shoved me past broken statuary and trampled herb beds toward an elaborate iron gate dangling from one hinge. An aingerou, tucked under the brick arch, spat snowmelt onto the uneven cobbles. I tried to step over the puddle but misjudged the distance and stumbled right into it. Slush seeped into my boot.

"What's wrong with you?" said Voushanti, jerking me through the gate and into the deserted lane. "Your family vouched you were in good health. Said you'd never had so much as a boil on your bum in your life. Are you drunk?"

"No sleep," I said, hurrying alongside him, grateful I was free of shackles and mask at least. "No food. Doesn't promote my best work. I'll not warrant—"

"Sick, starving, or dead, pureblood, you *will* locate these prisoners. Our master has an *interest* in them."

"You should have scraped up the blood and brought it with us, then," I snapped, refusing to meet his glare. I could almost forget his eyes' unnerving lifelessness if I just didn't look at them. "I could sniff it for you like a hound on the scent."

He would not tell me anything—neither the two captives' names nor why Prince Osriel cared about them nor who had dragged them from this house with deadly force. Unfortunately, he understood that names or reasons would not help me locate them. Only a physical link could do that; blood served best.

We hurried round a corner into choking smoke and worsening chaos. A troop of Moriangi men-at-arms entered the square at the same time, and Voushanti retreated a few steps to let them pass. We wore poor men's cloaks that hid my good clothes and his mail shirt.

As we waited for the soldiers to have their fill of shoving and bullying, inspecting bundles by ripping them open and scattering pots, statues, aprons, and blankets in the filthy snow, men's voices rose in plainsong from the courtyard we had just visited. My sluggard mind snagged on the oddity—plainsong here in the city. The melody was familiar, a setting used only at the Hour of Sext—noontide. And then my thoughts drifted back to the blood-splashed yard. The design wrought into the ruined iron gate had been a solicale. A Karish household, then.

The soldiers soon moved on. But as the mardane and I crossed the square and followed the turnings my instincts laid out, an urgency that had naught to do with Voushanti propelled my steps. Our search for these unnamed prisoners had begun at a Karish house where men sang the Hours. And noontide was the hour of execution.

The crumbling square called Riie Doloure had likely inherited its mournful title from the squat, ugly edifice that overshadowed it. Plain round towers pocked with arrow loops marked the four corners of Fortress Torvo and the walls of its blocklike keep. In the style of ancient Ardra, no creneled battlements, but rather steep conical roofs of lead topped the four great towers and two lesser ones that flanked the gatehouse.

On this day *doloure* took on added meaning. Half the squalid houses and shops that lined the cobbled square were smoldering ruins, the other half still burning. Dark smoke billowed in evil clouds, abrading my throat. The snow melted into black slush that soaked my feet and numbed my toes. A jubilant rabble crammed the space before the gray stone walls and gate towers, cheering and shouting over the roar of the flames as ash and embers showered on them like unholy rain.

"The fortress? Inside?" The voice boomed in my ear.

"Yes . . . yes . . . maybe." Clutching the scratchy layers of my cloak over mouth and nose, I closed my eyes and scrabbled through the denser fogs and smokes inside my skull to find the traces. No good.

"Be sure, pureblood. This is no feast-day frolic to venture. Hurry."

I found a patch of unpaved ground, dropped to my knees, and pressed palms into the ash-rimed muck, seeking a stronger link. My fingers squelched in the filth, and I fumbled with the pattern in my head. Awkward. Slow. By the time I grasped the life thread strung from the clotted blood at the Karish house, my skull felt switched wrong way out, raw and throbbing.

"Beyond the wall," I whispered, wiping my hands on my cloak. Beyond the impossible crowd.

My eyes itched and watered. Voushanti hauled me up, and we skirted the surging mob, dodging shattered stonework, trampled grain sacks, and fallen beams that pulsed with dying embers. Snowflakes transformed to raindrops in the heat, then vanished in a hiss when they struck hot ash or stone.

The throng shifted and surged like a living beast, and though only a few orange scarves peppered the crowd, guttural cries for purification pulsed like its heartbeat. "Give us blood to cleanse the filth! Fire and blood! Slay the blasphemers!" Faces shone with mad fervor. Surely naught of Palinur would be left for Bayard to claim. As for the people captive in this wretched place . . . prisoners . . .

"Who are we hunting?" My voice, harsh and strained, could have been a stranger's. "Why won't you tell me?"

Voushanti squeezed forward along the narrow boundary between a ruined shopfront and the mob. "Because the answer should make no difference."

Sila Diaglou stood atop the fortress walls. Not dressed in a warrior's garb today. Her filmy orange robes flared in the wind like more flames, gifting the willowy, pale-haired woman with a majesty and magic that infused the scene with purpose, as if she were the carved prow of a great ship. She raised her spread arms to embrace the scene of smoke and chaos. *"Sanguiera, orongia, vazte, kevrana,"* she cried. "Bleed, suffer, die, purify. Die to the world. Abandon those who cling to your old self, and live henceforth in repentance for as long as the streams of time carry you forward. Harrow the earth, that the Gehoum shall be appeased."

A savage roar rose from the crowd. "Sila! Sila!"

To either side of the priestess, stolid and proud, stood three I'd seen at Graver's Meadow—the doe-eyed girl, the man with the dog's face and dagged purple cloak, and the man with the oiled black curls. Perhaps the needle-chinned man had died of my blow. Other ragged men and women cavorted along the parapet, waving orange rags, garlands, weapons, and other things round and heavy that they tossed into the crowd. Another cheer shook the ground. Glee and greed and an insatiable hunger surged through the pressing bodies like an incoming tide. A certain darkness, the foulest bile, ate at my throat. Heads . . . the round heavy things tossed from the walls were human heads, now passed from hand to hand atop the mob, evoking new waves of cheers.

Great Kemen Sky Lord . . . holy Iero . . . whatever your name . . . guard us from madness. No prayers for Sila's Gehoum, though. I invoked no powers that took pleasure in headless corpses. Evil rioted in that courtyard. If we could save some poor wretch from such a fate, I would league with Magrog himself. Perhaps I had.

"Inner bailey, outer bailey, or belowground?" The Evanori's voice grated in my ear, interrupting my sudden hesitation. "Speak."

"Not belowground. But inner or outer? I don't know." If I could just think . . .

"By Magrog's deeps, man, what *use* are you?"

He scanned the mob. As suddenly as a judge's hammer falls, he grabbed a scrawny man in a ragged coat from the edge of the crowd, bundling him into his massive embrace. "Gert, old friend! Our day has come at last! The earth shall be cleansed. Harrowed!"

He thumped the bewildered fellow on his chest and then shoved him back into the river of people bereft of his orange scarf.

"Tie it on," he said, cramming the damp rag into my hand.

I tied the scarf about my neck, while he absconded with one for himself. We shoved our way through the heart of the press, Voushanti digging his fingers into my flesh, while waving his free hand and chanting the same words as the rest.

The gates stood open, guarded by Moriangi warriors, spears leveled and ready. But the mob was restrained by their own discipline, not the threat of the warriors. Ten men and women, dressed no differently from their shabby fellows, stood in the front rank, hands stretched to the side as if withholding the pressure of the hundreds. Each one of them wore an orange scarf.

When we came up behind these ten, Voushanti grabbed my chin and pulled my ear close to his mouth. "When I give the word, you will follow me. Stay close. Do not slow down. On your life and the boy's, speak no word until I tell you. Do you understand?"

A bellow of agony rose from the fortress and rippled along my spine. Only its beginning timbre identified the victim as a man. I nodded.

Raising the engraved gold band that he had slipped from his left wrist, he clasped his hands in front of his face. "Ready?" he cried. "Now!"

A glare of red brilliance shattered the gray noonday. The whole world paused for that moment; shocked faces turned upward toward the light, shouts and laughter sheared off in midvoicing. I thought I had gone deaf. What in the name of all gods had he done?

The big Evanori sped toward the gate, his gray cloak flapping. I raced after him, agape. Voushanti and I existed between breaths, between swings of the great pendulum that ticked off our lives. No human eye perceived us. No human hand could halt our passage . . . across the short bridge . . . through the tight gatehouse . . . and into the courtyard of hell.

A grim, narrow, smoke-filled slot of a yard squeezed between inner and outer walls of undressed granite. Ruffians armed with pikes and swords stood behind three seated men wearing the red robes and wide-brimmed hats of judges. Flame soared and dark smoke billowed beyond the walls behind them, as would befit Magrog's own tribunes.

Though Voushanti and I existed in profound silence, events inevitably moved forward. A cage of iron poles against one wall bulged with battered men and women, and under the whips of two filthy guards, a stake-cart vomited more human refuse into the cage. Guards dragged a bloodied prisoner from the cage and threw him on his knees in the dirt before the tribunal. Words were exchanged.

We heard none of it. And no one marked us as we dashed across the yard.

A soundless hammer fell, witnesses waved their hands gleefully, and the silently screaming man was hauled toward the blood-slathered gallows that stood in the center of the yard. A bare-legged man and a silk-gowned woman already dangled from the crossarm— the woman crook-necked and very dead, the man in his death throes, his hands scrabbling weakly at the rope choking the life from him. Lashed to a frame at the end of the platform, a second man slumped dead in his bonds, his steaming entrails newly spilled out across the bloody hands of his executioner.

I halted, aghast, not so much at the brutality of this tableau, for such vileness too often passed for justice in this world, but at seeing the faces of the damned. The woman, mercifully, I did not know. But the man in the last agonies of strangulation was Brother Victor, the small scholarly chancellor of Gillarine, and the one whose life lay splattered so casually on this altar of savagery was Abbot Luviar.

O mighty gods! My heart stopped. My gorge rose. My clenched fists slammed my temples as if the blow might jar my sight to look upon a different truth. Luviar, the passionate heart of Gillarine, the one man I had ever met who could make a jaded soul feel worthy of a god's notice, butchered like a beast. Helpless grief and impotent rage stole breath and voice and filled my soul and limbs with lead. And guilt . . . oh, gods of night, if we'd arrived but moments sooner . . . if I'd had a clearer head . . .

Voushanti raced up the steps, motioning me to follow. Surely it was the force of his will that stirred my feet, for I had no will, no strength, no courage to face such ruin. He waved and stomped his foot. He grappled the dangling body and supported Brother Victor's splayed legs, lessening the strain on the slender neck. The little monk spasmed and heaved a violent breath, breaking my paralysis. He lived.

I flew up the gore-slick stair and snatched the blunt, curved blade from the hand of a bull-necked man beside a headsman's block. He gaped, bewildered, at his bare hands. At the limit of my height, I stretched and slashed the rope above Brother Victor's head. The monk slumped into Voushanti's grasp.

Spinning in place, I scoured the yard and the cage, searching for another familiar shaven head and dark brows, sure that he, too, must be a victim of this outrage. "Gildas!" I bellowed.

Noise and confusion fell on my head like a collapsing mountainside. The executioner's bewildered gaze met my own, then blazed with understanding. "Treachery!"

"Useless ass!" Voushanti screamed in fury. "Run! *Now*, or the boy dies!"

Voushanti hefted Brother Victor over his shoulder and raced down the steps, his threat piercing the thunder of astonished outrage that surrounded me.

Spurred more by rage than fear, I leaped from the platform and sped after him, slashing randomly at any hand or blade within my armspan. If Voushanti's own neck fell foul of my blade, I would not weep.

We were most of the way across the yard when the Harrowers on the walls finally grasped what we were about. Sila Diaglou stretched her orange-draped arm over the milling horror and pointed straight at us. "Those three! Seize the blasphemers who dare defy the Gehoum!" she cried, her rich contralto as cold and deep and relentless as the tidal currents in Caurean Sea caves.

Sharp commands rang from the Moriangi troop at inner gate, and a half dozen warriors pushed through the crowd around the gallows. We dashed into the gatehouse tunnel.

"Halt and drop the blade," snapped Voushanti, once we had passed into the dark. "Now."

My hands and feet obeyed the command, whether by his will or magic or my own choice, I could not have said. I saw no possibility of escape without his connivance.

A warm limp weight was thrust into my arms. "Stay close. If you have a hope of life, do as I say."

"Can you work the spell again?" Gildas could easily be the next to have his bowels ripped out.

Red light flared dully from his hand and then faded. "No."

"But the others back there . . ."

From beside me came the unmistakable sound of a sword sliding from its sheath. No doubt the ax he wore strapped to his belt had found its way into his alter hand. "They have no hope of life."

The warriors were on us then, great looming shadows in the dark—distant daylight outlining their bulk. The tight passage restricted Voushanti's opponents to two at once, preventing a quick slaughter. I kept to the deepest shadows behind Voushanti, positioning Brother Victor's slight body across my shoulders while the Evanori efficiently dispatched two, then four, then five pursuers in a blurring flail of sword and ax.

"Now," he gasped as the sixth man fell, "run!"

I bolted. I could have carried two of Brother Victor without slowing, yet we had no route but through the mob. Those outside the walls could not know we were the objects of Sila Diaglou's wrath, and so it was not deliberate opposition that forced us to a standstill, but merely the crush of overexcited bodies.

"Stand aside," shouted Voushanti, over and over, forcing a path through the press, angling toward the side where the crowd was thinner. "Our brother . . . wounded by raiders . . . by Karish infidels . . . Let us through!"

Voushanti's ferocity and our orange scarves gave us passage. But the mardane's cloak had been torn halfway off. We had reached no more than halfway across the square, when a woman noticed the Evanori blazon on his surcoat. "Damn all, he's the Bastard's man!"

Haggard, starving faces, alight with manic fever, closed in, pressing us toward one fiery border of the square, crowding between us and our escape. "Who are you?" yelled a hollow-cheeked man. "What are you about? Who've you got there?"

"The Bastard defies the Gehoum . . . thinks to rival them . . ." The murmurs grew hostile. "Don't trust him."

Voushanti waved them off, spinning a half circle with his fouled ax and the bloody tip of his blade. Yet inevitably they pressed us backward, ever closer to a row of blazing houses. Even through the layers of wool, my back blistered. Brother Victor moaned and shifted in my arms. In moments the mob would devour or shove us into the fire, unless the Moriangi soldiers who had begun slashing a ruthless path through the mob got to us first.

I closed my eyes and imagined my hands penetrating the muck beneath the cobbles, summoning the ruined landscape I had touched with mind and magic: *the fortress like an angry wound on the world . . . the dingy remnants of lives lived solely in its vile shadow . . . the present devastation—half walls, scorched rubble, fallen beams, blazing tenements leaning sideways at precarious angles now that their supporting neighbors had collapsed . . . and the past—ancient stones, broken and buried beneath centuries of filth . . . beneath shifting land and blighted building. Necessity . . . desperation . . . escape . . .* Certainty flooded into my bones.

"This way," I shouted into Voushanti's back. I whipped my heavy cloak over Brother Victor and my own head, leaving only enough of a gap to see my way. Then I turned my back on Voushanti and the mob and dashed straight through the wall of fire.

"Wait, fool!"

Veils of red and orange and blue snapped and roared, engulfing the tall house. To my dismay, we found no sanctuary beyond the dissolving timbers. Flaming debris and flared ash rained down as I clutched the limp body and leaped over a blazing beam. I had no hands free to knock away the embers that singed the back of my hands or set the damp wool of my cloak smoldering. My boots stank of scorched hide, and my feet screamed in agony as I waded through coals and ash. I could not hear for the belching thunder as another wall or bench or barrel exploded into flame, could not think for the suffocating smoke and fear.

Where was the safe, secure stone? I felt it here. Its pattern lived in my mind. Instinct told me we needed to go down. Smoke and garish flames made the patches of darkness too deep to penetrate with watering eyes, yet I dared not slow enough to hunt. To the right the hillside angled sharply upward. To my left a half-timbered wall groaned and sagged as moisture boiled away. Behind me, Voushanti yelped and cursed as an exploding barrel shot burning staves into the air like the brands of Syan fire jugglers. I had to let my feet guide as they would . . . and, in moments, my boot skidded on the brink of emptiness. Littered with charred debris and rills of flame, an ancient stone stair plunged into the earth. Unhesitating, I sped downward.

The stair led into a stone-lined trench. A sewer, I thought at first, so narrow I almost cracked Brother Victor's head on the wall. But as the way angled across the hillside and behind the rows of burning houses, worn steps broke the walls here and there, leading off into jumbles of stone and earth that might once have been far older houses. So perhaps this was an ancient street, its worn base and shoulder-high walls laid with native stone, only this bit of it exposed.

Though fire raged beyond the walls on either side, air flowed gently through the trench, just enough to shift and cool the falling ash without fanning it to flame. The lane widened slightly into a small high-walled courtyard. In its center a stone ring encircled a gnarled apple tree, astonishingly untouched by fire. I hurried past the tree. By the time I thrashed through a snag of dead brush and half-frozen offal and stumbled into an abandoned tanner's yard, all traces of the ancient stone had crumbled into the hillside rubble, and we had left Riie Doloure well behind.

Coughing, gasping, welcoming even the lingering stench of a tanner's vats, I sank to my knees and untangled my cloak. I threw it down on a crusted drift of snow and laid Brother Victor on top of it. His cowl and gown had been stripped away, leaving only his torn and bloody shirt that could neither keep him warm nor cover the vile evidence of his battering. A painful shudder racked his frail body with each wheezing gasp. Broken ribs, like enough, but at least he breathed. His abraded neck had swollen around the arrowed gouge of the noose, but not enough to choke him. One eye socket had been crushed, the eye now little more than pulp.

"We can't stay here," said Voushanti. The warrior was bent over a few steps away, hawking and spitting, one hand planted on his knee. His left arm dangled slack, blood welling from a filthy wound just above the elbow. "Get him up. We have to go."

Brother Victor's hands and body jerked frantically, as if he were trying to defend himself, and his lips moved in a constant soundless stream of words. I bundled the charred edges of my cloak around him. "Easy, Brother," I whispered, wishing I could tell him he was safe. What could Osriel want with a holy monk? "I'll try not to hurt you."

"Valen?" His undamaged eye blinked open—a bruised hollow overflowing with pain. "Iero's grace, you've come."

The spark of hope in his bleak face stung worse, by far, than my seared skin. The implication of his greeting, that his god had somehow ordained me to make things right, choked me with bile. I needed to be designing some strategy, constructing some spellworking to protect him, but the events of the morning floated and churned in my sluggish thoughts like refuse in an oily backwater: Gildas and nivat, blood and fire and Jullian, Bayard's vengeance and Osriel's inscrutable purpose. How could I rescue a man from the Harrowers, only to turn him over to Osriel the Bastard?

A quick glance over my shoulder revealed Voushanti well across the yard, plunging his sword into an ice-crusted drift that still displayed some areas of white through its mantle of soot and ash. His fouled ax lay on the ground beside him. His wounds and heaving exhaustion had eased an unspoken fear that he was something other than human. Perhaps, if I could divert his attention and retrieve the ax before he picked it up . . .

I grabbed a scrap of old hide from the ground and began shaping a divexi—a noisy or frightening illusion designed to ensnare a watcher's attention. But I stumbled through the steps. How did you determine what manner of beast had worn this skin? I could not remember, and without knowing, I could not steal its noise or motion to infuse the spell. I floundered with the interlocking threads of enchantment.

Across the yard, Voushanti pulled the cleaned blade from the snow and wiped it on his cloak, awkward as he favored his injured arm. He sheathed the sword and snapped his head around to look at me, a spark of red piercing the gloom. He raised one hand, and a flare of red light blinded me. I blinked and squinted and turned the scrap over and over in my hand, trying to remember . . .

"Can you lead us out of here, pureblood"—Voushanti squatted beside me, sword sheathed, clean, dry ax snugged in the strap looped over his belt. With one hand and his teeth, he finished tying off the bleeding wound in his arm with the strip of hide that had been in my hand—"and not through a conflagration?"

My stomach heaved at the unnerving gap in my perception. How had he gotten here so quickly? A blast of wind pelted my face with snow. I wrapped my arms tightly about my churning gut. No pain this time. No answering ecstasy. The raw threads of my spell lay in my mind unquickened as I'd left them.

Voushanti tilted his head, watching me, his half-mutilated mouth twisted upward. "Our master waits. Or is your word as valueless as your family insists?"

I gathered the scattered bits of sense enough to speak, not daring to look at his eyes. "I swore I would not run, Mardane, and I will not. But I never said I would drag others into slavery with me. What does your prince want with him?" Osriel, who stole the eyes of the dead.

"This is not the time to discuss our master's intents. Care you so little for your Karish brother that you would abandon him untended or drag him into this battle that rages around us without hope of succor?"

Melting snow under my knees soaked my wool hose as I feverishly discarded one plan after another. My father would not allow me past his house wards; neither would any other pureblood answer a *re-condeur*'s plea. Certainly not on this day. Thalassa would likely help; she knew the little chancellor. But the temples were halfway across the city, and if the sacred precincts were not already burning, they would be overrun with wounded and frightened people. The others I knew in Palinur were tavern keepers, whores, alley rats, many of them kind and generous, yes—I had ever called them friends—but none knew more of me than my name and favorite songs. On a day when every man and woman's survival was in balance, how could I command enough trust to shelter a man snatched from the gallows?

Voushanti scrambled to his feet and extended his hand, the gold wristband gleaming brightly in the murk. Brother Victor lay wrapped in the cocoon of my cloak, struggling to breathe. Of all the facts in this failing universe, one stood clear and invariant. The monk would die if I did not get him help soon.

Cloud and smoke had grayed the midday to little more than dusk. Wind flapped my soot-grimed sleeves, drove flying snow down my collar and up my billowing tunic, and stung the burned patches on my hands and legs and face. Without my cloak, I was already shivering. My mind was numb, my reservoir of schemes barren. "You cannot expect me to believe the Bastard Prince will heal him. He must have some use for him."

Voushanti whipped a knife from his belt. I jumped when he tossed it on the ground in front of me. "I have risked my own survival to preserve this monk's life, which should demonstrate something to a man with limited choices and half a mind. Have you some other plan to save him? If not, then take my knife and one simple thrust will save him from my master's depredations. A second thrust will take care of your own problem." Cold, blunt. He did not care what I chose.

Every tale of Osriel's depravity swirled in my head, yet he had sent me to rescue good men from a terrible fate. Voushanti himself had shown naught but courage in the fight. I could read nothing from his dreadful visage save icy challenge. Perhaps it was weakness or some other consequence of my shameful state, but I trusted his word.

He nodded as if I'd spoken it aloud. "The storm has come early upon us, Magnus Valentia, and much of Palinur has yet to burn. We'd best be moving before we are consumed." The Evanori scooped Brother Victor into his powerful arms, handling him as gently as Brother Robierre would have done. "Now, tell me the way out of here."

Osriel had an interest in Brother Victor's life, and for now my master's will would prevail. As for later . . . we would see. Pressing forehead and palms to the fouled earth, I reached out to find a path through the dying city—through layer upon layer of building and burning, of births and deaths, of commerce and art and piety, of cruelty and war, the footsteps of centuries. A simple route revealed itself. I raised my head and pointed down an alley that would lead us back to the house where the Duc of Evanore waited.

Indeed my course was clear, as nothing had been clear in all my life. The day had scribed two images on my soul, images that demanded I answer for my ill choices: Jullian, quivering in his silent terror, and the wise and passionate abbot of Gillarine splayed and gutted like a beast. Both my fault. Because I could not think. Because I could not act. Because I had clung to mindless pleasure to dull the pain of living. Always I had insisted my perversion harmed no one but myself. Who was there to care if Magnus Valentia de Cartamandua-Celestine, lack-wit *recondeur*, burnt out his senses or locked his useless mind away in a ruined body?

I clenched my fists and wrapped my arms about my eyes and ears, miming that deadness as if to silence conscience for one last time. But Jullian's terrified silence and Abbot Luviar's cry of agony gave my shame a voice I could no longer put aside.

And so, as I stumbled to my feet and followed Voushanti out of the tanners' yard, I left a litter behind in the filthy snow: a fragment of a mirror, a silver needle, a linen thread, and a few black seeds that rapidly vanished into the muck. I threw the empty green bag into a smoldering house. Never again. Ever.

Chapter 29

"You are not forbidden illumination, Cartamandua." The lamplight from the passage set Mardane Voushanti's freshly polished mail gleaming, delineating his bulky shadow in a bronze glow as if he were Deunor Lightbringer himself. The warrior quickly dispelled the illusion by stepping out of the doorway, only to return with one of the passageway lamps, giving me full view of his half-mangled face and worn leather. He displayed no sign of bandages or discomfort from his wounding.

Illumination. Upon our return to Prince Osriel's dismal dwelling, Voushanti had whisked Brother Victor away, declaring the monk would be cared for, while two of Osriel's warriors had deposited me into this fusty little chamber. In the hours since, as the gray daylight faded beyond the slot window, I had sat with muddy boots propped on a dusty clerk's desk, and unshaven chin propped on my curled fingers, seeking illumination. The woolly tangle that had snarled my thoughts and actions throughout the day had at last unraveled, and the mysteries of past and present now surrounded me in stark, immutable stillness like a ring of standing stones: my grandfather, my master, the Danae, Gillarine, the end of the world.

"Unless you've brought me dinner or answers, I would prefer you take your lamp and go," I said, too tired to mask bitterness and self-loathing. I did not expect answers any more than I expected word of Jullian's fate or Brother Victor's health. Everyone I'd met since Boreas had deposited my dying carcass outside Gillarine had excelled at keeping me mystified and on edge. Tonight, though I had defined and bounded these myriad puzzles, I could declare none solved.

"You've not cleaned yourself. Are these breeks not fine enough to cover your pureblood arse?" Voushanti prodded the stack of neatly folded fabrics he'd brought along with a water basin and towel soon after our arrival. A mardane, a landed baron and warrior of more than average skill, both military and magical, serving me like a house-maid—one of the lesser standing stones, but a curiosity, nonetheless. Why was I so sure that deeper investigation would reveal this man had no home, no family, no history or ambition that linked him to anyone but Osriel?

"Tell me, Lord Voushanti, was the spell you worked at Riie Doloure of your own making, or was it Prince Osriel's work?" I believed I had deciphered the answer to this particular puzzle. Quick-ened spells could be attached to objects and keyed with a triggering word, allowing those with no magical talents to use them at will— but only once or twice without a new infusion of magic. Voushanti's limited usage of the spell in Riie Doloure made me doubt he was the originator. And his gold wristband would be a perfect spell carrier.

"Our master will answer questions or not, as he pleases. Just now, he requires your attendance in the proper garb of a royal advisor. So dress yourself or I'll do it for you, and I am no genteel manservant."

Though for once in my life I desired no company but my own, I had to answer this summons. The last doulon interval had been but eighteen days. I bore no illusions about what was to come. Even if I survived the ravages of the doulon hunger long enough to shake free of it, sooner or later the disease that gnarled my gut and flayed my senses, prompting me to seek its comforts, would leave me a drool-ing lunatic. But in the past hour I had vowed to Luviar's shade that for as long as I had wits, I would give what aid I could to those who fought for his cause. For now, my hope of illumination lay with Osriel the Bastard.

Voushanti remained stolidly beside the door as I stripped off my scorched and bloody garb and used my shirt to scrub the soot from face and arms. The water in the cracked basin was long cold. The tiny coal fire in the rusty brazier could not have kept a rabbit warm.

Where was reason and the proper order of the universe? Abbot Luviar, a man of vision and passion, hung from the gallows with blowflies feasting on his bowels, while my worst injury from the day's events, a deep burn on the back of my hand, had already scabbed over. And Brother Victor, a man of intelligence and reason, lay fight-ing for breath, while I was to parade as a royal advisor in a house run by spiders, feral cats, one mutilated mardane, four warriors . . . and, ah, yes, one prince who stole dead men's eyes, brutalized children, and salvaged tortured monks.

Was fortune no gift of a harried goddess, but rather purest chance? Perhaps the Harrowers had guessed the truth, that the universe was naught but chaos, and mankind, fearing the impenetrable, uncaring powers of night and storm, had only imagined these kindly mockeries of ourselves that we called gods.

Luviar would have refused such a hopeless premise. Given voice from the grave, he would argue that a beneficent Creator had instilled in humankind the means to shape our own destiny. In the throes of such guilt as plagued me this night, I desired desperately to believe that. The abbot had given me the grace of his trust, and I had failed him. Now I had to find some way to make amends. My meager vow was all I could devise.

The clean clothes were plain, but fine—a silk shirt of spruce green, a pourpoint of blood-red brocade. I swiped at my hair to remove flakes of ash and splinters.

The mardane handed me the claret-hued cape and mask. So, ordinaries beyond Osriel's household were to be present at this interview. This day had left me beyond surprise.

Voushanti guided me through the winding passages back to Prince Osriel's chamber. Though night had fallen, I could see more of the house than I had in the morning's confusion. Tiered candle rings veiled with cobwebs lit the domed foyer, a circular space cold and bare of any decoration save massive pillars, weighty arches, and a dozen elaborately carved doors. Two Evanori warriors guarded one pair of doors and swung them open immediately upon our arrival.

"His Grace awaits," said Voushanti. "You are on trial here, pureblood."

The mardane pivoted smartly, drew his sword, and took up a guard stance, face outward between the two warriors, leaving me to pass through the open doorway alone. His remarks but confirmed my own conclusions. Jullian's presence, my oath not to run, the hidden identities of our day's quarry—I had been on trial all day. How had Osriel known how to manipulate me so thoroughly? And to what purpose?

Myriad teardrop-shaped lamps of colored glass illuminated Prince Osriel's chamber—a grand hall, hung with thick tapestries of dark reds, greens, and gold. Above the hanging lamps the high, barreled vault hosted lurid depictions of the netherworld—scenes of naked, writhing humans being herded by grinning gatzi toward a lake of fire. In one broad panel a triumphant Magrog, crowned with ram's horns, presided over a charred desolation from his throne of human skulls.

My eyes could not linger on the fantastical paintings above my head. The focus of the great hall was a vaulted alcove to my right, where the impenetrable darkness of the morning had yielded to shifting shadows. In front of a curved screen of wrought gold sat an elaborately carved chair of squared oak, knobbed spires rising from its back. To either side of the chair, fire blazed in great brass bowls. The bowls rested on the backs of gray stone statues depicting chained slaves twice my height. The chair was occupied.

Considering the size of the chair, I estimated its occupant to be a person of a man's moderate stature, though the voluminous folds of a hooded velvet gown, colored the same spruce green as my garb, left sex, size, and demeanor indeterminate. Yet that person's presence was immense. No storm building over the river country, where the turbulent air of the mountains clashed with hot wind from the eastern deserts and the moisture of the Caurean Sea, could have such monumental force pent in its clouds as the power shivering the air about Osriel's throne.

"My Lord Prince," I said, "or at least so I presume."

Even as I made my genuflection, touching my fingers to my forehead, I fought to control my fear. This house and its macabre trappings were designed to intimidate.

A slender, refined hand gestured me up. A man's hand, bearing a single heavy ring of graven gold, almost too large for the finger that bore it.

"See, now, that I am a man of my word, Magnus Valentia." The voice from under the velvet hood hinted at the first stirring vigor of the storm wind. His ringed finger pointed behind me.

I spun in place to discover a goggle-eyed, unscarred Jullian standing roughly in the place I'd left him that morning. He was unbound, his thin shoulders firmly in the grasp of a wary Brother Gildas. Rarely had I felt such a rush of relief and pleasure.

I had feared Gildas lost at Riie Doloure—the lighthouse Scholar, the hope of a kingdom rapidly destroying itself, my friend. The irony struck me that my need for nivat had likely saved him, removing him from the priory before the assault. And Jullian . . .

The boy's anxious eyes searched, taking in my cloak and mask and the looming presence on the dais behind me. Then his clear gaze slid past the eyehole of my mask, met my own eyes, and as a nervous sparrow finds a branch to its liking, stayed a while. His face brightened. I smiled and nodded and breathed a prayer of thanksgiving, wishing he did not have to hear what I had to tell.

Reaffirming my vow to guard the lad and his cause, I turned so that I could both address the prince properly and assure myself that my two friends would not vanish in candle smoke. I crafted my words carefully, estimating what might be expected or permitted in this room, assessing what might be my master's purpose, and cataloguing the news I wished to convey to the remaining members of the lighthouse cabal. "My lord, I appreciate your generosity in permitting me to share this fulfillment of our bargain. Were poor Brother Victor brought in to be released to his brothers as well, with the painful results of his ordeal at Riie Doloure well healed, then I could ask no better return for my submission."

Gildas stiffened, shock and dismay carving their very sigils on his brow. "Victor alive . . . captive . . . here?"

"You must improve your bargaining, Magnus Valentia, and learn to discipline your loose tongue," said the man in the chair, his voice sinuous as an adder, smooth and coiled with danger. "Here I've given you a gift—releasing the boy to his Karish friend, rather than setting him adrift in the sea of Palinur's destruction as your ill-considered pact would have allowed—and you express your gratitude by sharing our private business with a stranger."

Prince Osriel's displeasure settled on my shoulders like an iron yoke. Yet no flaming bolts flew across the room to set me afire. No muting spells were triggered in my silken mask. After the magics of the day, I expected anything. So I pushed farther. A limited future gives a man certain advantages in such a game.

I bowed toward the prince again. "My apologies, lord. Clearly you knew of my association with the monks of Gillarine when you brought these two here. As our venture to rescue their brothers from Sila Diaglou's clutches was so nobly wrought, I assumed that the fate of the two captives, certainly to the summary of one salvaged life and one grievous . . . most grievous . . . death, would not be hidden from them."

Jullian's face drained of blood. Gildas, now holding his emotions close, did not seem to notice, but the chalk-faced boy would surely have dropped to his knees had the monk not maintained such a firm grip on his shoulder.

The swirling shadows darkened, and thunder rumbled just at the edge of hearing. The prince waved one hand at the door. "Brother—Gildas, you called yourself?—please take your young charge and go, bearing with you my sincerest cautions as to the dangers of the streets. Charming as it is to encounter an actual Karish monk, my sorcerer and I have important business to attend, and it seems I must school him beforetime."

Without voiced command, the outer doors swung open. Gildas,

his dark brow knotted, inclined his head to the man in the chair. As he urged the shocked Jullian ahead of him, he glanced over his shoulder, pressed the backs of two fingers to one cheek, and jerked his head at me. The two fingers were the monks' signing speech—an admonition to use thought before speaking. The jerk of his head and the granite set of his mouth were a more universal language—a promise that he would do what he could to set me free. Such a small gesture to put steel in a man's spine. In my deepest heart, I blessed him.

As the doors swung shut, and I was left alone with the still figure in green draperies, all warmth fled that hall. I imagined frost rime spreading on the slave statues and ice spears growing on the corbels and brackets. The shadows deepened, as if their very substance had increased, as if all those who had ever stood in this hall had been sent away empty, their darkest thoughts and fears kept here as the price of their release. By the time my master spoke, I could scarce contain my shivering, though I mustered every shred of control I possessed to stop it. I was *not* afraid of him. Not anymore. What could he do to me that was worse than what I had brought upon myself?

"You tread a crumbling verge, pureblood," he said ever so softly. "Do you think that because my bloodlines are impure, and my body less than perfect, my mind is also flawed?"

I clasped my hands behind my back. "Your Highness, my awe of your talents grows by the moment. To create a cloaking spell such as Mardane Voushanti wielded this morning at Riie Doloure is the work of a skilled sorcerer. To create this aura of terror"—I waved to encompass the hall, feeling proud that my hand did not tremble and my teeth did not chatter—"is the work of a masterful perception."

I strolled to the foot of the dais, striving to prove that fear did not paralyze me—as much to myself as to him. "As I have not observed your physical imperfection for myself, I could not possibly judge it as a source of weakness, though you are clearly not the horned giant of rumor. And as you have surely been told, I take neither pride nor pleasure in my bloodlines, so I could hardly view another man as 'lesser' for not sharing them. If I were ever to sire children of my own, I would as soon throw them to wolves as submit them to the Pureblood Registry. What is it you wish from me, my lord? You seem to know a great deal about me, whereas I know naught of you but tales and the single fact that you dispatched me to save two good men from the gallows." For what? That was the question whose answer was the key to the man in green.

A movement of his hand and the shadows parted, exposing the

bronze-inlaid marble steps in front of him. "A brash mouth you have, Magnus Valentia. More sober-minded than I expected. I was told you were an ignorant buffoon who made jest of all things serious, including your own talents. But then again, this day's events must sober even the most slack mind. Come closer and we'll talk a bit about your friends. And, Magnus"—I shuddered at his particular enunciation of my name, as if he had catalogued every mote of my being and tethered it to his discipline—"always remove your mask when we are alone."

I climbed the few steps to the dais, tugging the silk from my face and tucking it in the glove loop on my belt. Whatever Osriel's game, subtlety played a far greater role than crass brutality.

Moments passed before the prince took up the conversation again. He propped his elbow on the wide arm of his chair and rested his chin on his hand. Relaxed, it appeared. The man seemed as changeable as sunlight in the river country. "Your friend, the Chancellor of Gillarine, fares as well as could be expected of a man who came within a heart's thump of learning the truth of his god. His injuries have prevented my use of him, but they will heal, given time enough."

I could not disguise my astonishment. "My lord, I thank—"

"Do not *thank* me," he snapped, slamming his hand to the chair arm. "You cannot feel gratitude when you suspect I have unsavory motives for snatching the monk from the Ferryman's slip. I prefer honesty from my servants, not mimed groveling, as if I were some simpleton to be swayed with pretense. *Actions* that counter my wishes reap my punishment. Not thoughts."

The colored lamps swayed as if a wind teased them. Weakness raced through my veins and sinews. "Of course, my lord. I only—"

"What would be the pleasure in having bound servants if their thoughts did not resist my own?" Though the prince had not moved, and we were alone, these soft-spoken words emanated from the region of my shoulder, as if the hooded man crouched behind me, his pale lips not a finger's breadth from my ear. "The delight of power is not commanding an army of sycophants, but rather bending one resilient mind beyond its comfortable boundaries."

I suppressed a shudder. Refusing to look over my shoulder, I inclined my head to acknowledge his point—and to compose my expression. I could not allow him to see when his tricks unnerved me. "I appreciate your desire for honesty, my lord. Naturally, I am concerned for Brother Victor's safety and future in the care of a powerful lord I know only from dread rumor. Nevertheless, I *am* grateful to hear news of his state. Accept my thanks or not, as you please."

"Tell me about the lighthouse," said the prince, reversing tone again as if he were two men at once hidden in his robes. This simple request might have been an inquiry about the weather beyond his walls. Yet it startled me out of measure.

That he might have discovered the existence of a collection assembled over so many years was not so unexpected. What other circumstance would send me on a chase for members of the cabal with Jullian held hostage? I did not believe in such weighty accidents of fate. But I did not expect so direct an assault or so prompt. My promise to keep Luviar's secrets left me scrambling for a response. "The lighthouse, Lord Prince?"

The prince's hands hooked on the squared oak arms of his chair and pulled his body slightly forward. The air between us compressed my chest. "We are not here to dice, Cartamandua." Each syllable pronounced precisely. "I know these monks have built a great treasure house, a cache of books and riches gathered from all the known world. I have uses for such things. Only two men have ever known how to open the way into the vault. One of those lies dead; the other lies unspeaking in my guest chamber. Events will not wait on healing salves and poultices. Thus I remember something else I've heard: An initiate of Ophir's order was allowed to visit this treasure house, an initiate with sorcerous powers of his own. A promising development, is it not? If this sorcerer cannot provide me with a monk to open the way, then perhaps he can open it himself."

Damnation! The detail that I had visited the lighthouse was quite recent and quite specific. If he could read thoughts, he'd have no need for my answers. Thus, either he had twisted the juicy tidbit from his captives—Jullian or Brother Victor—or someone else in the cabal was telling tales.

No one had told me the full membership of the cabal. I refused to believe any of those I knew a willing betrayer. The nature and power of their beliefs colored them virtuous in my eyes—even Thalassa, now I looked at her deeds with my childish blinders removed. Then again, if the past few days had taught me anything, it was that I was no good judge of character.

The possibility of an informant gave me little hope of deception; thus I was left with no choice but to test my master's dictum here at the beginning. "Clearly I cannot maintain pretense with you, Lord Prince. I am sworn to silence about the lighthouse and must hope that my promises to you gain credibility from my refusal to break my vow." I rushed onward, hoping to forestall his explosion. "And before you pass judgment, let me also state that neither honor nor intent makes one flyspeck of difference in this case."

His attention threatened to crush both mind and soul. "How so, pureblood? If your intent is disobedience, then it makes a great deal of difference. You'll not enjoy discovering how much so."

I worked to maintain a measured tone, as if on any day I might be found denying the wishes of Magrog's henchman. "Your diligent informants have reported that my undisciplined childhood left me untrained in sorcery. They must also have reported that I lack the basic skills of an educated man. But perhaps the implications were not made clear. I cannot interpret the spells of others. I have no background even to guess what any complex working might be and no trained intuition to know how to go about discovering the answer. I cannot read books of magic, even if any pureblood family would allow a *recondeur* to touch their most prized possessions. So I cannot possibly unravel this spell that opens the brothers' storehouse for you, even if"—I hesitated only briefly before throwing down the gauntlet—"I chose to do so."

Footsteps and voices beyond the doors distracted the prince before his gathering wrath could break upon my head. When the door opened to Voushanti, I found myself able to breathe again.

The mardane hurried across the room, not bothering to bow. His heavy cloak was dusted with snow. "Skay has confirmed that Prince Bayard's men control the city gates this hour. The guards are stretched thin and shitting their trews for fear of the Harrowers. I've transport ready."

"Excellent. Have Saverian see to the monk while I ensure my pureblood's good behavior."

"We'd best be quick, my lord. We caught three Harrowers trying to climb over the wall. Our . . . inquiries . . . revealed they were hunting the little monk." Voushanti bowed and left.

"Alas, we shall have to continue our discussion another time." The prince rose from his chair. Not short, not tall. His voluminous velvets prevented me deducing more of his size or shape. He pointed a finger at one of the blazing bowls atop the slave statues. The fire bloomed scarlet, then vanished, dropping an inky mantle over his left shoulder.

"I believe the time has come to bring my fractious brothers to heel," he said. "Thus I've decided to remove my valuables—including my very expensive pureblood—south to Evanore, far from this precarious city. Until we meet again, you will remain in Mardane Voushanti's sight at all times and obey his commands as if they were my own. You will strictly maintain your pureblood discipline. And you will not discuss this day's business—my business—with *any*one. Now tell me whether or not you *choose* to obey these orders. If you think not, we can just get on with the necessary unpleasantness."

His mild-spoken menace did naught but inflame my curiosity. He had some use for me. To make the best use of my position, to protect my friends and aid their mission, I needed to learn of my new master or, at the least, prevent him interfering with the cabal. "Does not my duty require me to be at your side, lord? I should protect—"

"*Honesty*, Magnus." The second bowl of fire bled and died. My skin felt the flash of heat.

I bowed and touched my forehead. "As you command, Your Grace . . ." Though, *honestly*, I would prefer the freedom to choose my own course.

Chapter 30

We rode out within the hour. In the kitchen courtyard, where Voushanti had first brought me to Osriel that morning, three of Osriel's warriors waited beside a mule-drawn wagon draped in mourning garlands of dried laurel and black ribbon. A stone coffin occupied the wagon bed. *Brother Victor—*

"The little monk sleeps, pureblood," said Voushanti at my mumbled curse. "But not his final sleep."

I gaped at him, unable to contain my horror. "You hid him in a *coffin?*"

"The Moriangi will not inspect Lord Osriel's dead. Now, mount up." He pointed at a beast waiting patiently behind the wagon. "We've found a docile steed for you tonight."

Prince Osriel did not see us off.

Palinur lay eerily quiet as we plodded toward the city gates. Winter held the world fast in its grip. Ice sheathed toppled statues and charred wreckage, and hung in great spikes from gutters and balconies. Churned, filthy snow lay deep in the byways. Hunched figures scuttled into alleyways as we approached and darted out again only after we passed.

No Moriangi gate guard dared so much as glance at Prince Osriel's pureblood or his "fallen knight" in the coffin, not when a warrior of Voushanti's complexion growled hints of the Bastard's retribution should they do so. But neither did anyone want the responsibility of violating Prince Bayard's order that no one breathing was to leave Palinur that night. We were passed from one guard captain to the next—the events a blur of torchlight, waiting, repeated stories, and anxious, stuttering progress. I rejoiced that I was not expected to speak. Exhaustion weighed on my limbs like the burdening ice.

Eventually Voushanti convinced Tiglas Volti, a seedy-eyed senior guard captain, of the mortal risks in insulting Prince Bayard's neutral brother—a brother whose vaults of gold, once opened, would likely dispense their contents as far spread as the Bastard's goodwill . . . even so far as senior guard captains. Eventually, the portcullis slammed shut behind us, and we rolled into the night.

"Get out of the tent or you'll be folded up in it." Voushanti's ugly face poked through the slit in the canvas for the third time since he'd called me out of a dead sleep. The patch of sky behind him was a sunlit blue.

I slipped on my mask and crawled toward him, every bone and sinew complaining, breathing through my mouth to avoid the persistent stench of old sweat, old ale, and old vomit woven into the shelter's fabric. I'd never known a tent that was aught but cramped and stinking. "If you don't give me time to stretch and take a piss before I climb onto that devil horse again, I'll make both sides of your face look equally ugly," I mumbled, as he backed away from the entrance.

I had no idea how far we'd ridden after leaving Palinur behind. I had fallen asleep in the saddle, waked only long enough to break a drover's nose when they threw me into the wagon bed. I'd thought they were going to put me in the coffin. I didn't remember being stuffed into the tent.

Voushanti awaited me in an alder thicket frosted with new snow. Pale sunlight glittered through the crusted branches. "Just beyond these trees lies a party of His Grace's retainers," he said as I unfolded my stiff limbs like some great chick from too small an egg. "We'll be traveling with them. Remember your orders. Keep to your pureblood practices. Once you've relieved yourself, follow me."

"Voushanti!" I called after his departing back. "What of Brother Victor?"

He paused. "My lord yet has hope to extract some return for all our trouble to get him."

I took that as good news. "Where are we going? What does the prince—?"

"South." He vanished into the trees. A flurry of black-birds scattered and circled above the thicket.

I saw no sign of horses, wagon, monk, or coffin in the vicinity of the brown and white tent. But scents of woodsmoke, burnt porridge, and horses wafted through the leafless trees, along with the muted clatter and bustle of an encampment. My most urgent needs met, I followed Voushanti down the well-trod path into the brake.

The busy camp sprawled across a broad clearing. Soldiers moved among the horses, leading them to water, cinching saddle girths, and picking ice and stones from hooves, while servants collapsed tents, rolled blankets, and stuffed packs. One very large tent yet stood in the center of the trampled snow. The green and white colors of Evanore hung limp from its center pole, along with several other pennants of various colors.

Beside the large tent, a group of well-armed men and women encircled Voushanti, their craggy faces contrasting sharply with their jeweled rings and brooches, gold-etched sword hilts, and fur-lined cloaks. Evanori warlords—at least five of them among the small group—each a petty sovereign in his or her own right with bloodlines far older than purebloods, bound by oath to Caedmon's line since the kingdom's founding.

". . . while he attends to his business," the mardane was saying. He might have been a toad addressing a gathering of eagles. "Prince Bayard is not yet seated in Palinur. Our spies report he is paying calls on several noble Ardran houses before announcing his victory, while Harrower raiding parties spring from the brush like grouse before beaters . . ."

The lords seemed attentive, but not deferent. Voushanti was clearly not one of them. Though his manner and accent witnessed to his Evanori blood, his mardane's rank was an Ardran grant, not Evanori inheritance. His authority was strictly Osriel's.

"His Grace will see you at Ygil's Moon. Do *not* disappoint him." Such woe and ruin as Voushanti's tone promised would have sent Magrog running from his throne of skulls.

The proud warlords dispersed slowly, eyes hooded, mumbling among themselves. A round-headed lord in a steel cap and tall boots glared at Voushanti as if to argue, only to think better of it. He tightened his mouth in disgust and turned his back sharply. Perhaps more warlords than Stearc of Erasku viewed Eodward's youngest son as an abomination.

Two of the Evanori turned to intercept the man in the steel cap, thereby facing me straight on, not ten paces distant. A flood of pleasure warmed my veins, and I fought to keep from laughing outright, which was a wholly unreasonable reaction to encountering a warrior who would prefer me dead and his daughter who had betrayed me.

Elene controlled herself well. After one startled blink, she averted her gaze. But little more than a touch of her father's arm drew Thane Stearc's eye my way. The frown lines about his mouth and hawkish brow deepened. He, too, glanced away quickly.

Though a sword hung at her waist, Elene no longer stood as Stearc's squire, but as a woman of Evanore, a descendant of warlords like these. Her wide-legged trousers were suitable for riding, her breasts unbound beneath her copper-colored shirt and fine-linked habergeon, her cropped bronze hair now grown long enough to twist in numerous tiny braids laid flat to her head. I might have been looking on the goddess Mother Samele herself, the exemplar of the earth's health and strength. My hands ached to touch her cheeks, flushed with the cold, and stroke the hips that filled her trousers so delectably . . .

Great gods, I felt like a witless pup, after a month imprisoned, with no hopes to spare for pleasures of mind or body, and before that a novice vowed. Of a sudden my grievances with the woman seemed of no more substance than the frost vapors rising from the sunlit tents. Somehow I found myself willing to believe that she had acted out of devotion to her cause—at least while I stood so near that tantalizing flesh and bright spirit. So much had changed since I'd seen her last.

The man in the steel cap snapped orders to break down the large tent. Elene stood by as her father and Voushanti exchanged stiff courtesies. No love lost between those two men. Stearc's arched nose flared as they spoke. When Voushanti moved on, Stearc began arguing with a bear-like man about whether their party should travel together or take separate, shorter roads to their strongholds. Elene joined in, her cinnamon eyes flashing. No demure maiden she.

As custom and protocol prescribed, no one spoke to me or acknowledged my presence with anything but sidewise glances. Only a pureblood or his contracted master could initiate interaction with ordinaries. Pureblood discipline required me to maintain that distance. After his pointed warnings, the mardane would surely be watching. And these two . . . I could give no one cause to suspect their divided loyalties. No matter their opinions of Osriel, I had no illusions that others of these fearsome folk conspired to preserve books and tools in preference to their duc and his gold mines.

I tore my attention from Elene and wandered through the rapidly dwindling camp, seeking any sign of Brother Victor. Cheered to discover the emptied coffin abandoned in the trees, I drifted toward the three wagons. One was packed with household goods, one with hay and grain sacks. A severe woman in a plain cloak was helping the older servants climb into the third wagon. Before I could sidle close enough to peer inside, the woman looked up—and did not drop her eyes. Her look of scorn near torched my cloak. Donning my own best disdain, I strolled on past her and her charges, hoping she cared more for Karish monks than purebloods. I'd have wagered my prick that poor, battered Brother Victor lay among the bags and bundles in that wagon bed.

I retreated and sat down on a fallen tree. Elene stood listening to a tall woman with iron-gray hair and cheekbones as angular as the crossguard on her sword. Happy for once to be ritually ignored, I stared at Elene and imagined and yearned until her rosy flush expanded to her neck and ears, and she yielded me a sidewise glance. Ah, if only we were back under that dolmen in the rain . . .

A dark-haired man bundled in a thick black cloak hurried out of the great tent, lugging a worn leather satchel. He caught sight of me at once. Of course, Gram would be here, too.

I winked and twiddled a finger at the sober secretary. Gram whipped his glance around the company until his gaze settled on Voushanti's back. He raised his eyebrows and flashed me a grin, then ducked his head and moved on about his business.

I buried my grin in my hands. How fine to discover friends here. I'd no expectation of seeing anyone I knew ever again—save perhaps Brother Victor. Of a sudden I found myself anticipating the coming journey with excitement. Somehow I'd find a way to speak with them.

When Gram strode past her field of view, Elene scowled at his back. No softening of that enmity. For some perverse reason, that consideration cheered me even more.

By the time the cumbersome party moved out, some fifty of us altogether, the rare blue sky had skinned over with clouds, and snowflakes flurried like dandelion fluff. "Stay close, pureblood," said Voushanti, as I tried to find the right combination of knee and hand, curses and cajoling to prevent my beastly mount from shedding me. "I'm charged to keep you healthy."

The mardane moved into the vanguard beside the iron-gray woman, the lord in the steel cap, and Stearc. They scarce looked at him. Someday I would insist someone explain why Voushanti's presence made a man's bowels churn.

Elene rode two ranks behind, alongside two younger men who eyed Voushanti's back with a mix of awe and terror. Over the course of the first hour, I maneuvered my balky mare to her side, close enough we could speak with little risk of being overheard. "May I ask where you are bound, mistress? 'Tis a wretched season to trade hearth fire and good company for a perilous road."

"My father and I have business southward—a Karish school in

which he takes an interest." A glance my way, quickly controlled. "And then, as do all those loyal to the Duc of Evanore, we return home for Lord Osriel's warmoot, the first he has summoned. We're curious to learn if Evanore's position of neutrality in this vile conflict is to change. Perhaps his pureblood advisor could enlighten us?"

I imagined Voushanti's ears straining to hear my disobedience. I kept my eyes on his broad back. "Alas, I've no leave to discuss my master's business. In truth, having been in my lord's service only a single . . . unhappy . . . day, I'm not even sure of our destination, save that it be south—which seems to leave half of Ardra and all of Evanore a possibility."

She bit her lip and bowed her head, which made me believe she knew of Luviar. "My sincerest apologies, sir. I'm not accustomed to pureblood company, or what is proper to ask. So often we can give offense . . . hurt, even . . . when *none* is intended." Her voice shook a little. "I'd suppose you bound for Prince Osriel's great fortress at Angor Nav or, perhaps, his smaller house at Renna."

I nodded with as much hauteur as I could summon. "My life has changed dramatically of late, mistress, and I find life more pleasant when I forget unintended slights. You know, though we've not been formally introduced, you resemble a lad I once knew—a squire of marginal talents, though exceeding fair for a boy. I would not be surprised to see his position vacant."

She kept her eyes on the road, snowflakes dusting her flushed countenance. "Indeed, sir, the portion of your face that I can see resembles that of a man I once knew—a monk of marginal piety and excessive interest in matters he had forsworn. I would not be surprised to see his habit uninhabited."

"Thank all gods that men grow wiser as days pass." I could smell her even in the cold . . . fennel and lavender and leather. But for the snow, one might have imagined us on a pleasure outing in happier times.

Impelled by dreary wisdom, I left Elene and dropped back to ride in the fourth rank for a while, sharing curses of weather and Harrowers with a new-bearded youth who rode as if soul bonded to his mount. The weather worsened by the hour, blowing snow and increasingly cold. We passed several villages burnt to ash. Other cots gaped open to the weather, perhaps one in five showing signs of habitation. In the distance, dark shapes—wolves or wild dogs—loped across the snow-covered fields, which did naught to soothe our unhappy horses.

Gram rode several ranks behind me, his cloak and hood bundled about him. At every stop I tried to draw him aside, hoping he might hint at what use the cabal would make of my grandfather's story, but we were able to exchange only a few empty words. The warlords demanded his attendance. His bottomless well of facts about Navronne's history fueled the lords' never-ending arguments of politics and war. By evening, the rigors of the journey had sapped all conversation.

We sheltered that night in a burnt-out inn, its broken walls blocking the wind. I maneuvered a seat next to Elene as the company shared out hard bread and bean soup. "The boy and the Scholar," I mumbled into my bread. "Safe?"

She bobbed her head over her soup.

"And the book?"

Elene turned to the iron-gray Thanea Zurina, who sat on her right. "No matter how difficult the journey, I'm happy my father chose to leave Palinur," she confided. "When one sees both Temple priestesses and Karish practors deserting the place, one must think the gods themselves have given up on it. With so many clerics, the roads south should be safe enough for children and valuables!"

I smiled and drained my bowl. Thalassa had book, boy, and Scholar and was taking them south.

On the next morning, once we persuaded the horses to move out of their huddle, four of the seven lords split off and headed west on the Ardran high road, taking all the wagons and two-thirds of the soldiers. I had caught nary a glimpse of Brother Victor, but assumed he traveled with them. The rest of us, perhaps twenty in all, continued on the less-traveled way that led south past Gillarine toward Caedmon's Bridge. We kept a slow, steady pace, stopping only to water the horses or pick ice from their hooves. Just after midday, one of our scouts reported a disciplined cadre of orange-blazed Harrowers bearing down on us, he said, like Magrog's chariots of doom. We spurred our mounts and fled.

For a day and a night of driving snow and merciless cold, we forced our way southward across rolling, frost-clad barrens of dead fields and vineyards. Every time we believed we had shaken the pursuit and slowed to ease the strain on our mounts, scouts raced from the rear with the news that they had come up on us again. Fifty Harrowers, the men said, led by a squat, ugly man with a face very like a dog. Voushanti forbade me to go back with the scouts to confirm that he was Sila Diaglou's henchman—one of Boreas's executioners. The warlords were spoiling for a fight, but the lord in the steel cap agreed with Voushanti that Prince Osriel would wish neither his neutrality compromised nor his noble supporters slaughtered in a useless confrontation with lunatics.

The relentless pace and ferocious weather took a toll on all of us, but most especially Gram. The cold flayed him. Skin gray, his features like drawn wire, he rode with back bent and head dropped low to deflect the wind. At noontide on the third day of our flight, when we stopped in a snow-drowned glen and scattered grain for the beasts, he clutched his mount's mane and whispered hoarsely that he'd best remain where he was unless Prince Osriel's pureblood could magically transport him from the saddle and back into it again. Stearc pressed him to drink some medicament from an amber flask, but he waved it away. "I'd rather have my wits," he croaked. "I can hold until we find shelter. All the way home if need be."

We had little prospect of shelter. The towns of Cressius and Braden had refused to open their gates to us. No village had defenses enough to withstand a Harrower assault while we slept. Everyone was exhausted—save perhaps Thanea Zurina—and we'd had three horses pull up lame that morning. I feared for Gram's life if we didn't ease up. And if the Harrowers took Stearc, Elene, and Gram—saints forbid—what would become of the lighthouse cabal or their hopes of appeal to the Danae? Not an hour later, a solution presented itself on the horizon.

"We divide our forces," I said, sketching a map in the snow. "While a few of us lure our pursuers into Mellune Forest, most will remain out of sight at the forest boundary. There's good cover and Lord Voushanti is very skilled at . . . hiding . . . people for short periods of time. Once we've got the Harrowers into the wood, the rest of you can continue on the road south at a more reasonable pace . . . stay alive . . ."

Even Aurellia's imperial road builders had declared Mellune Forest impassable. A snarled swath of beeches, pines, and scrub, inhospitable Mellune traversed a jagged ridge that split Ardra into the wine-growing plateaus of the west and the dry, rock-strewn grazing lands to the east. Its unstable landforms, altered by frequent avalanches and raging floods, provided no reliable markers for guides. Except, perhaps, for a Cartamandua.

Using my bent to devise a route, I could divert and delay our pursuers, keep them on a short leash while getting them thoroughly lost in the wood. After a suitable time, I would abandon them to find their own way out of trackless Mellune, and lead my companions off to rejoin our company for the remainder of our journey to Evanore.

I thought Voushanti would split his hauberk. "You've no leave to go off on your own," he snapped, when I stopped to take a breath. "Prince Osriel—"

"—would not wish Thanea Zurina, Thane Stearc, or Thane Gar'Enov's only son and heir to fall captive to Harrowers," said Gram hoarsely. "Will you tell us that a single pureblood has more value to the Duc of Evanore than three of his warlords? If so, then offer us a better plan. Even if you leave *me* to rot at the roadside as you ought"—scarlet spots stained the poor fellow's pale cheeks— "you'll be but fourteen men and two women against fifty. And the scouts say these are no rabble, but Sila Diaglou's disciplined fighters."

The mardane had no answer. The snow kicked up by the onrushing Harrowers swirled on the stormy horizon. Unwilling to allow me off on my own, Voushanti insisted on accompanying me.

Faster than a frog could take a fly, I was kneeling in the snow, pressing my hands to the frozen earth, and releasing magic through my fingers to seek out the beginnings of our route. When the guide thread took clear shape in my head, I sat back on my heels and looked up at Gram and Voushanti standing over me.

"I don't like this, pureblood," said Voushanti. His wide hands flexed and fisted. The red core of his mutilated eye pulsed like coals. A red crease at the corner of his mouth looked like blood. "Only fools split their forces."

"Complain to Prince Osriel," I said. "I won't see these people— his people—run to ground."

The mardane stomped away toward the gully where Stearc, Elene, and the rest had taken cover. His three warriors awaited Voushanti and me at the forest boundary. Only the secretary lagged behind.

"We'll see you in six days at Gillarine," said Gram. He offered me his hand, feverishly hot, and steadied me as I got to my feet. "Unless . . . Perhaps the gods have sent you this opportunity. With your skills and the weather to hide you, you could take your own road at the end and stay free of the Bastard. Osriel treads perilous paths, Valen. No one knows his plans or the extent of his power."

"I've given my oath not to run," I said. "It was necessary; Gildas can tell you. But my soul has acquired stains enough all these years without my sitting on Magrog's lap. So you can be sure the Bastard will have little good of me. Godspeed, Gram. *Teneamus.*"

"*Teneamus.* I'll not forget this, my friend." He turned his back and trudged slowly toward the gully, his shoulders racked with coughing. Wind and snow and failing light erased his footsteps as if by a sorcerer's hand. I shivered and headed into the trackless wood.

Chapter 31

"Up with you, pureblood. The hounds are baying. No time for sleep." The hand on my shoulder shook me so hard, the blanket slipped off my head. Bitter cold bit my cheeks and plumed my breath as I squinted into the night. Trees. Snow. Unending trees and snow.

"Leave off the bone rattling, Mardane," I said, groaning. "As if a man could sleep with his blood frozen and his backside raw . . ." . . . and his hipbones throbbing from too long astride, and his stomach devouring his liver for want of a meal not eaten on the run, and his mind a roiling backwash of questions, mysteries, and anxieties that neither misery nor exhaustion could quiet. Not the least of which mysteries was how to shake the fiendish Harrowers, now the time had come to leave them behind. We just couldn't seem to move fast enough.

When I had suggested this diversion scheme, I never expected it would mean six god-cursed days of lacerating briar tangles, ice-coated avalanche snarls, unending hours in the saddle, no fire, no sleep, no respite. We'd had to keep our pursuers close, but not too close. If we got so far ahead as to discourage them, or they realized too soon that we had split our party, they might double back on their tracks to escape the forest and hunt down the others. Gram. Elene. Stearc. Every hour I could give them was a boon. But next time I had such an idea, I would stuff a boot in my mouth.

"We can't wait for Nestor." Voushanti's proffered hand hauled me to my feet. "The orange-heads are already coming up the gorge. Maggot-ridden halfwits must have legs like mountain goats. I've sent the last of the horses downslope, but that won't confuse them long. So let's make an end to this. Lead us out of this tangle and onto high ground, where these two and I can take them on, and you can run like hell's own messenger to join the others."

Voushanti's temper sounded far more equitable than my own. The crash of brush, grunt of horses, and shouts of oncoming Harrowers bounced through the darkness from tree to tree from every direction at once, clawing at my already shredded nerves.

Philo, one of our three companions, snatched up my blanket and stowed it in a rucksack before I could wipe the sludge of unsleep from my eyes. The missing Nestor had gone in search of water to re-fill our depleted flasks, as we could not afford a fire to melt the snow. The third warrior, Melkire, stripped weapons and food packets from our abandoned saddlepacks and stuffed them in our belts, rucksacks, and pockets. We'd ridden our horses to frozen, quivering uselessness. Now we were afoot. I could only pray our pursuers fared no better. Deunor's fire, there were so many of them.

I dropped to my knees and scraped away crusted snow until I could touch my palms to the forest floor and heed only the sounds of Mellune: the snap of frost-cracked limbs, the sough of overburdened pine fronds giving up their load of snow, the beating hearts of bur-rowers. Delving deep, I inhaled the faint aroma of the earth warmed by my hands, tasting pine resin and galled oak, dirt and mold on my tongue. As magic flowed from fingers through earth, my mind reached south and west through rotting trees and frozen soil, shear-ing through buried stone and dense thorn thickets, seeking a path to Gillarine's valley and the wide River Kay that fed it. *Tell me the way*, I said as I examined the landscape unfolding in my head. *Reveal your paths.*

Perhaps it was the unaccustomed practice, or the fact that I no longer hoarded magic against the demands of the doulon, but my route finding had grown more assured over the past days. Or per-haps the need to accomplish something of worth in my life had at last forced me to fully accept the bent of my blood, no matter its con-nection to my parents. Or perhaps it was only that Mellune Forest and I had become intimate acquaintances.

The grim woodland straggled straight down the spine of Ardra, grown up in thin, sour land, broken by sills and ridges of limestone, its trails choked with briars and snake-vine since ill weather and dis-ease had all but exterminated its game. Deadfalls, snarls, sinkholes, and gullies had diverted us constantly, making my carefully laid course of southward-spiraling circles resemble the route of a headless chicken. Our purpose was delay and confusion, but for our pursuers, not ourselves. I prayed I could get us out before we starved.

The route took shape in mind and body, a gray pattern of fading game trails, a dry watercourse, a logger's track, long abandoned. High ground, Voushanti wanted. So I shifted the thread slightly here and there, searching for a more elevated way.

Beyond the southern boundaries of Mellune the land opened into the rocky pastures of upper Ardra. A single modest hill, crowned by a scarp, and a few scattered protrusions of dense black rock presented the only defensible positions. The mountain drainages—the upland valleys like the vale of the Kay where Gillarine lay—would give us much better cover, but the inexhaustible Harrowers would be stripping our bones before we made it so far afoot.

"Come on," I said, scrambling to my feet.

Snapping branches and spitting snow, I broke through a wall of snow-laden bracken to find the narrow streambed that would lead us up a seamed ridge, heading the direction my gut named southwest. A chorus of terrified whinnies said the pursuit had discovered our blown horses.

The blizzard had abated on our third day in the forest, which worsened the cold, but lent us more light. Above the canopy of trees the stars shone clear and bitter, providing illumination enough to reflect on open snow and depositing inky shadows under trees and scrub.

An hour along the way, my purposeful spiral took us along the bank of a pond. There we found the signs of a Harrower camp and all that was left of Nestor. The thirsty fool must have walked right into their hands. The Harrowers had shredded his flesh and staked him to the earth as they had Boreas. I blessed all gods I had not eaten that night. Nestor's mouth had been packed with dirt to silence his cries as he bled and died.

"We leave him lie," said Voushanti harshly, snatching up Nestor's waterskins that lay abandoned in a willow thicket. His boots and weapons were missing. "We've no strength to spare and no time. Move out, pureblood."

Closing my eyes, I sought my guide thread, happy I did not need to touch the ground here. "This way," I said and moved westerly.

Philo joined me, whispering the Karish prayers for the dead. Voushanti followed, mumbling curses with the passion of a lover scorned. But Melkire dropped to his knees beside the savaged body. I held up to wait for him, then blurted a malediction as the warrior dipped his thumb in Nestor's blood and marked a spiraled circle on his own forehead.

"What the devil are you doing?" I said, anger and disgust raising my bile. The Harrowers had licked Boreas's blood from their fingers.

"Nestor is a son of Evanore," said Melkire, his eyes hard and fierce in the starlight. "The mark binds my memory, so that I can bring a full account of his deeds and his end to his family."

I walked on. I had to find them a place to make a stand.

"I've not heard an untoward sound for an hour," said Philo, passing Voushanti a waterskin. We had climbed to the brink of a limestone scarp to rest and drink. "We should get away from here and make camp, else we'll not be able to move by morning."

"No," I whispered, plastering myself to the ground and peering over the edge of the scarp into bottomless darkness. The creeping up my back felt like an army of spiders. "They're still coming. I need to understand how they can stay so close on our trail in the night." I had my bent to guide me, but how could the Harrowers determine which crisscrossing trail of churned snow we had trod the most recently?

Voushanti hushed the two young warriors and wormed up beside me. "I sense them, too."

Before very long, yellow light blazed from the wood—a torch, I thought as it moved through the trees. But the wind neither shook nor snuffed it. The silent procession passed below us like wraiths. Perhaps forty men. Fewer horses. They had muted their harness with rags. Only their tread in the snow and the occasional whuffle of a beast marked their passage.

Their leader bore the light—a gleaming ball of piss-yellow brilliance that emanated directly from his hand. And as he walked, he held one hand in front of him, fingers stiffly spread, and he turned his head from side to side, sniffing, his nostrils flared wide like some great hound. Sorcery. *I knew it.* As he vanished into the thicker trees, a gust of wind swept down the scarp to flutter his cloak—worn purple velvet with a dagged hem. The dog-faced man had tasted Boreas's blood, watched the priestess lash Gildas's back, and stood on the fortress walls with Sila Diaglou as Abbot Luviar was gutted. I prayed he would rot in this demon wood.

"Come on," I said through gritted teeth. "We need to move faster. That one might have other skills." He was Sila Diaglou's companion in slaughter, either a pureblood or a mixed-blood mage powerful enough to create light in this overwhelming night.

Though purebloods were unmatched in native talent for sorcery by virtue of their untainted Aurellian descent, any ordinary with a trace of Aurellian blood carried potential for the bent—as did Prince Osriel by virtue of his pureblood mother. Most mixed-bloods became market tricksters, potion sellers, or alley witches, like old Salamonde, who had taught me the doulon spell. Registry breeding laws had assured that little talent remained outside pureblood families, but always a few took their talents seriously, training and testing with others of their kind, calling themselves mages. Purebloods disdained them, of course, and named mageworks trickery. Prince Osriel had already taught me elsewise.

Another day. Another night. The rapacious cold cracked bone and spirit, dulled the mind, and transformed limbs and heart to lead. Using my aching hips and legs to break a trail through thigh-deep snow, laced with broken tree limbs and frozen bracken, became purest misery. Sticks snagged clothes and flesh. Pits or sinkholes beneath the crusted snow left me floundering on my face at every other step. The sweat of my exertions froze beneath my layered garments.

I clung to the gray guide thread in my mind, checked and rechecked it, pouring magic into each test to be sure I followed true. My companions dragged me up when I fell, brushed me off, and trod carefully in my steps. We had to lose these devils, else they would follow us to Gillarine. Stearc's clever choice of a rendezvous now seemed incalculably stupid.

We pushed across a broad meadow. It troubled me to find a clearing where my instincts said none should be, yet I dared not stop to assay another trial of magic, lest I freeze there in the open. It might have been a single hour or ten sunless days that we traversed that meadow.

My head swam with sleepless confusion, my frozen flesh no longer able to feel the pull of north or south. Southwesterly should take us higher, so that we would emerge, a day or so from now, atop Pilcher's Hill where Voushanti could mount a defense. Yet every instinct cried that safety lay downward. And downward did not feel like southwest. Thoroughly muddled, I fell to my knees at the bottom of a long slope and scrabbled in the snow.

"Where are we?" gasped Voushanti, even his leathern toughness on the verge of shredding. "We'll have no feet to stand on or hands to wield a sword, if you don't find us a place to make a fight."

"Just need to find the blasted hill. This terrain is all wrong."

My fingers might have been wooden clubs for all I could feel of them when I touched earth. I poured magic from my core but sensed nothing of the land. *Which way?*

An owl screeched from atop a spindly pine. I rubbed my frozen hands together. Breathed on them. Stuffed them under my arms, trying to warm them enough so they could feel. Another shriek and a spread of dark wings drew my eye to the treetops. And there, shining in yellow-white splendor between the branches, hung Escalor, the guide star. North and south settled into their proper positions in my head.

"Mother Samele's tits!" Sitting back on my heels, I laughed aloud at ignorant fools and their earnest blindness.

"Spirits of night, lunatic, will you be quiet?" Voushanti would have throttled me if he'd not been doubled up by a spreading beech, his lungs wheezing like a smith's bellows. "Never knew a man could move so fast in such cursed weather and still have breath to cackle like a gamecock."

I pressed my wet, filthy sleeve across my mouth to contain the hilarity that simple sense could not. Bound up in pureblood sorcery and earth-borne mystery, it had never crossed my mind to look *up* for guidance. The owl's dark wingspan ruffled against the starry night.

As I pleaded with my aching legs to unbend and bear my weight again, I watched the kindly bird preening. Thus I caught the glimmer of sapphire brilliance in the leafless branches of a giant beech nearby. I held breath and dared not blink. From the snarl of twigs and branches, an arm scribed with blue fire reached out to host the wing-spread owl's claws for a few heartbeats before the bird took flight. My heart came near stopping.

Twice in the past few days I'd believed us irretrievably blocked, facing the choice to be overrun by our pursuers or reverse course and meet them head-on. In both instances escape had come by seeming chance. A falling rock, dislodged by some scuttering animal, had exposed a stairlike descent of an impossibly sheer scarp. A bolting fox had revealed an unlikely passage through an avalanche slide the size of half a mountain. Now I wondered. Chance had never been my ally.

We could not linger. But I touched the earth once more and sent my whispered gratitude into the roots and rock, hoping that the one who aided us would hear. Would he have a dragon scribed on his face? Were his eyes the color of autumn aspen? Was that arm the same that had offered me refuge in an aspen grove as I fled Gillarine? Earth's Mother, how I longed to know.

Of course, the Danae despised humankind. How could they not, when the Harrowers' grotesque rites poisoned them? Yes, they had driven my grandfather mad, but he had stolen something precious from them. Danae were the essence of magic, the gift of beauty and grace below heaven. Even angels brought down the god's righteous fury on sinners.

We ran. Onward. Downward. Slipping and sliding on wooded banks. The owl arrowed southward ahead of us, as if scribing the path across inked vellum, and my fatigued mind gratefully relinquished the guide thread it had gripped for eight unrelenting days.

Soon the trees thinned, and a flat wilderness of mottled white spread out before us. Darker patches marred the starlit landscape as if unseen trees cast shadows on the snow. Clouds burgeoned behind the ridge we'd just descended, hiding Escalor and her companion stars. Wind gusts brought flakes drifting from the heights. We had to hurry. If any of our pursuers were yet mounted, flat ground would be our end.

The owl glided in a circle above our heads, then soared serenely toward the heart of the wilderness. Instinct affirmed that refuge was near, though perhaps not so directly across the flats.

"This way," I said to the three who had just arrived at my elbow heaving and coughing, their collected breath enfolding us in fog. I pointed to the wing-spread owl. "She'll lead us to safety."

I slid down the last few quercae of the steep embankment and struck out across the flats. In our weakened condition, a shorter distance likely outweighed the increased danger of exposure. Voushanti and the others trudged after, well behind me.

Fifty paces into the wilderness, I heard . . . or perhaps only felt . . . an unsettling noise beneath my feet. Instinct screamed warning. I motioned the others to halt so my dulled senses might register the sound, and I cupped my lifeless fingers over my nose and mouth, breathing out my last warmth to thaw my nostrils. Then I inhaled slowly, felt, tasted, and listened, as my father and grandfather had tried to teach me when I was small.

Water. Mud. Rot.

Appalled, I dropped to my knees and speared my hands through the snow and into the cold muck that lay just below. Dead trees. Rotted marsh grass. Burrowed frogs, cold and still. Old droppings and tufts of animal hair caught on buried willows. A harper's distant song . . . Ever so faintly, the sounds, the smells, and the land's retained memory seeped through the winter's blanket. And nowhere did I find my guide thread. *Fool! Blasted mindless idiot!*

Dulled with cold and yearning for finer magic, I had forsaken my own path to follow the owl. And the Danae, who had no use for humankind, had brought us here.

"Stop! Go back!" I shouted hoarsely, peering at the treacherous landscape through the darkening night. I knew exactly where we were. How could my sense of distance be so far askew? It seemed impossible we could be so far south, but I had traveled here before. "Step not one quat outside our tracks. This is bogland."

"What of you?" shouted Voushanti, wind blunting the edges of his words. "We have ropes—"

"I'll be all right. Go around, stay on the side slope, head straight southward . . . that way. Only two quellae to Gillarine. Hurry!"

Thank all gods, the three were in no mind to argue. Voushanti's beard and eyebrows were frosted pure white as if he had aged fifty years in an hour, and Philo and Melkire might have been but four glazed eyes in unfleshed skulls. They were in no state to fight anyone.

I watched until they had made it back to solid ground safely and vanished in the thickening snowfall. Then I shoved magic through my buried fingers and sought a path deeper into the bog. The trickster owl had vanished, leaving me no choice but to twist its vicious cleverness to my own purpose.

The route fixed firmly in my mind, I wiped my frozen, muddy hands, bundled them in my cloak, and set out across the snow-draped fens. The falling snow would blur my footsteps and mask the inadequacies of my spellworking long enough to close the trap—a snare I believed had been set for every human abroad this night, pursuers and pursued.

An irregular mound, well into the heart of the bogland, provided enough substance and variety for my purposes: a leafless willow, a sheep's leg bone, a rotted branch, a charred stick. I structured two spells, one to serve deception, one to serve fear. Then I waited, stomping my sore feet and flapping my aching arms to keep my blood moving. Dawn was near—as much of it as I was like to see with the weather closing in.

As the moments slid by in abject silence, fear nagged that I had miscalculated yet again. I could scarce muster the strength to shake the clinging snow from my cloak. While I became another stupid beast rotting in the bog, the Harrowers would follow Voushanti straight to my friends.

"Aaaagh!" I yelled in inarticulate fury, yanking my hair to force blood to my head. "Come find me! Any of you . . . come do what you will! Show me your face if you dare!"

My grandfather had warned me. Such torment as the Danae had wrought on him displayed a cruelty colder than this cursed winter. So whence came my sentimental folly that because they were beautiful and magical and caused my knees to grow weak with unfounded yearning, they had a benevolent interest in *me*? Perhaps the one writ with dragons had invited me into the aspen grove the better to destroy my mind.

Anger kept me living. I shivered and coughed and honed my spells, determined they would be sufficient to end this wretched journey.

They came in the purple gloom that passed for sunrise. Harrowers flowed over the ridge like a tidal surge, cries hoarse with triumph and fury when they spotted me in the open. I noted with grim satisfaction that they had dropped at least a quarter of their numbers since I'd seen them last. At their head rode the dog-faced man, his orange scarf flying, the glow of his hands like a bilious sun leading their way.

I fell to my knees and fed magic into my mound of sticks and bones, recalling the appearance of my departed companions to shape the illusions of harried travelers, stopped to succor a fallen comrade.

The yowling Harrowers swept onto the flats without pause, and even the shouts of the first to flounder did not slow the rest. When the yellow glow failed—snuffed by mud or fear—their triumph turned to dismay.

Weary and mind-numbed, they did not think to stay calm and press through the muck to seek firmer ground. Rather, weighed down with mail coats and supply sacks and weapons, burdened with legends of bogwights and sucking ponds and trickster Danae, they felt their feet sinking and their clothes waterlogged, and they panicked, as I had gambled they would. I touched the charred stick and set wispy tendrils of flame adrift from my hand until the cold numbed my fingers and I could conjure no more of them. The gloomy landscape was dotted with winking flames, and the men in the bog started screaming.

Half of the Harrowers killed each other, trying to use their comrades for stepping-stones. Others drowned quickly, pulled down by panicked horses or tangled in dead vines and rotted trees swept down from the mountains in long-ago floods. Some wandered, crying for help in the neck-deep mud, climbing on hillocks only to have them sink under their weight. After a while I could only hear them, for the blizzard rose in full fury, and human eyes could not penetrate past the length of my arm. The cold and the mud would finish them. The memory of Luviar butchered, of Nestor and Boreas condemned to slow agony, of tar-clogged wells and villages burned to ash, crushed what glimmers of mercy blossomed in my soul. These gatzi would have ridden my friends to ground.

I huddled on my islet in the center of the bogland, a driftwood club ready should one of the lost find his way to me. Only when my ears assured me that neither man nor beast roamed the upland banks did I press my hands into the muck to seek the path back to firm ground.

I jerked them right out again, then bent double and retched bile until stomach, chest, and throat were raw. The terrors of dying men and beasts permeated the pools and hillocks, and I could not find my way. I sank to the ground, buried my face in my frozen cloak, and begged the earth's forgiveness for the horror I had wrought.

Chapter 32

*V*alen *fiend heart!* The mocking cry stung like a tutor's rod on
cold knuckles. Cold . . . what wasn't cold? The world, all life,
and certainly every part of me was frozen. No one ever
listened when I said how I hated the cold.

I trudged onward. One step. Then a rest. Another step. Hip-high
drifts covered the path that would take me away from the treacherous bog. Perhaps the insulting name, a relic from childhood, etched
itself so vividly in my imagination because I longed so fiercely to
believe that another living person existed in this wintry desolation.

Fiend heart . . . Soon I'd be imagining I heard *iron skull* or *lead wit*
or *gatzi prick,* though the damnable girl would lob that last stone only
outside adults' hearing. I smiled . . . more of a grimace, I imagined, as
I could not feel my face. *Lassa, please be real.*

My sister had once enspelled a connection between her favorite
insults and my ears, so I would never fail to hear them. I'd never
learned the skill, but on one precious occasion, I had managed to reverse her spell and bind one of mine to her. "Toad witch," I mumbled
into the folds of my cloak for the fiftieth time on this dreadful afternoon. If she were within ten quellae, she would hear.

"Magnus! Magnus Valentia!"

"Brother Valen!"

I paused and surveyed the gloomy distance. No one in sight. I
pulled my hood tighter and fretted that these faint voices, too, were
naught but wishing dreams.

Hellish dreams of mud and ice and suffocation had clung to me
like draggle weed as I had crawled out of the bog hours and hours
ago, too tired and too afraid to walk, unable to bear another route
seeking lest I buckle under the weight of guilt and horror. That I

managed to reach solid earth, that I was not drowned or dead, astonished me. I had dug a snow cave to wait out the blizzard and had drifted in and out of sleep, dreaming of long limbs marked with blue sigils embracing me, choking me, setting me afire.

The wind mourned over the frozen fens. Did beasts feel this way after emerging from their winter sleep, as if ice crystals flowed in their veins? I feared the oncoming night. *Find me, someone. Please. I hate the cold.*

Lights moved around the hillside toward me. Torches. Spits of gold against a sky the color of ripe blueberries. I sank to the ground, closed my eyes, and rested my back against a boulder. Let someone else break the path through the drifts. Friend or enemy, wraith or bogwight, I didn't care.

"Gracious Mother, Valen, what have you done this time?" My breathless sister's painted eyes swam huge and worried from her fur-lined hood. "This Voushanti said you were facing fifty Harrowers alone in a bog, and that you'd saved Stearc and Gram and these Evanori lords. But they couldn't find you in the storm. I called and called— No one believed when I claimed to hear you, but I knew. How is it you're not frozen dead, fiend heart?"

"B-been thinking w-warm thoughts of you, *serena* toad witch. Whatever are you doing in the neighborhood? Did you bring them my boo—?"

She hissed, pressed her hot hand on my lips, and jerked her head backward. Several shapeless figures approached from behind her, one leading a donkey.

"Watch your tongue, Valen. And I do mean that. The answer is yes." She glanced over her shoulder. "Listen carefully: I came to continue my negotiations over new sheep pastures for the Temple and was shocked to discover the shambles. Do you understand?"

"Shambles?" I croaked, wretchedly confused.

But she had squeezed her painted eyes shut, and her words kept flowing, so softly no one but I could have heard them. "Who or what is this Voushanti? I See naught but death about him—blood and fire and torment. He says he's taking you to Evanore as soon as the weather breaks. Bound to the Bastard . . . Holy Mother, Valen, I cannot help you more. I must return to Palinur immediately. With Luviar lost, Victor captive, and what's happened here, the lighthouse may depend on my office."

The aura of her divination tickled my spine, as the newcomers joined us, their faces taking recognizable shape in dark wrappings. Indeed, Voushanti brought an ill odor with him everywhere. But I was more confused about her passing hints. "Lassa, I'll be all right, if I c-can just get warm. But what shambles—?"

"Silos!" She snapped, jumping to her feet. "He needs hot wine! And get a mask on him before I report him to the Registry. Good monk, bring your linens. No diviner is needed to see to the pitiful whiner. Lord Voushanti, take up your charge, though even my scoundrel brother is unlikely to run today." Excessive sisterly sentiment would never burden Thalassa.

Voushanti loomed over me like a frost giant, but he said naught as the others ministered to me. A somber Silos took Thalassa's place and offered me a steaming wineskin. My fingers couldn't grasp the leather, so he poured the stuff down my raw throat. *O, great Mother Samele, grant my glorious sister a place at your side!* Silos's masked face drew up in disapproval as I hooked my elbow about his, preventing him from removing the skin until it was half empty. "Careful, *plebeiu.* You cause everyone trouble when you're out of your head. Have you a mask with you?"

He pulled the half mask of purple silk from the pocket I indicated and slipped it on me. Cold, wet . . . it felt like fish skin.

Thalassa threw a blessedly dry cloak about my shoulders as Brother Anselm, the piebald lay brother from the Gillarine infirmary, examined my hands and feet. I despaired of ever being warm, shivering uncontrollably as he marveled that I showed no signs of true frostbite after crawling in the snow for most of a day. Voushanti refused to consider a fire, though I assured him that the dog-faced man and his Harrowers were no longer a threat. I could not bring myself to tell him why.

They insisted I ride Brother Anselm's bony donkey back to the abbey. As the monk led the plodding beast along the embankment, I looked out on the flats—still and silent, the horrors of the morning hidden beneath the mantle of fresh snow. My sister walked alongside me, and her gaze followed mine. "What happened out there, Valen?"

I shook my head and shuddered. "Just don't walk there, Lassa. Don't ever."

"When did they strike?" I said.

Brother Anselm, the donkey, and I slogged up the last slight rise between us and Gillarine. I had dismounted the balky ass. Walking eased my stiffness and kept the blood flowing in my hands and feet. Save for the marrow-deep chill and a general weariness, I'd come out of the day's events astonishingly well. But all relief had fled when the shy assistant infirmarian at last explained Thalassa's references to "shambles."

" 'Twas on Saint Eldred's Night, Brother Valen. You were not a fortnight gone from here. Some hundred or more raiders, both Moriangi and Harrowers, come twixt Matins and Lauds. Their fire arrows and torches took the scriptorium first. Then the church. Then the rest."

"Great Iero's mercy!" We had reached the top of the little rise, and the sight took my breath. The windows of the abbey church, whose brilliance in sun and candlelight had spoken of angels' wings, gaped black as hell's maw; the groins and buttresses mimed the naked ribs of a skeleton. The wooden buildings—infirmary, brewhouse, stables—had vanished, their remains hidden beneath a pall of gray snow. Gillarine Abbey stood broken and dark.

"We were blessed most walls were stone."

But the slate roofs had fallen when the supporting timbers burned—a pureblood firemaster attached to the Moriangi raiders would have seen to that—smashing at least a third of the inner courts to jagged ruin. Only the gatehouse and walls stood unmarred. The damnable cowards had marched straight through the sanctuary gate to wreak their holocaust.

"What of the brothers, Anselm? By the One God . . ." So many good men lived here: the kindly, skilled infirmarian, Robierre; garrulous Cadeus the porter; old Nunius, who reveled in holy minutiae . . .

"Eleven passed to Iero's heaven on Saint Eldred's Night, three succumbed to injuries since then, and five more fell to lung fever— Abelard and Nunius, the eldest and weakest of us who breathed too much smoke or bent to the cold. Dear Brother Robierre died saving poor Marcus from the fire. With the ground so hard frozen and neither hands nor time to spare for digging, we've had to lay them in the cellars."

"Ah, Brother . . ." The physical ruin paled beside such a loss. What words could express sorrow enough? Neither sympathy nor helpless anger could repair this wound or ease the future it boded. The survivors' trials were only begun. They would yet have more than twenty to feed and clothe. "What of your stores? And, blessed saints, what did they do to the orchard?" The trees still standing looked leprous, not burned, bark hanging in rags, trunks gouged and seeping, branches broken. More than half had fallen, bare roots frosted like nests of white snakes.

"The undercrofts were gutted for the most. Naught burns like spilled oil and dry grain. We've a few bales of wool left, though smoked and charred, and Brother Jerome, Iero welcome his cook's soul, fell to a Morian blade defending his last root cellar. But the orchard now"—the lay brother's wide face crumpled like an old rag—"that weren't the soldiers. No man, but only the One God himself sent us that trial. A root rot, Brother Gardener said, that spread through the trees at the same time the murrain come to the sheepfold. It's the sickness in the world, as Father Abbot so often warned of, come to Gillarine at last . . . and now we've heard tidings of his own passing."

Anselm's stolid presence faltered but did not break. His gaitered sandals crunched the snow, and he encouraged the tired donkey with a soft pat and an assertive tug on the lead.

"Prior Nemesio has taken us well in hand. And the good God grants us fortitude. To share the trials of his poorest in this land must surely bring us grace. A blessing we've none with *your* appetite to feed." He chuckled softly, then sighed. "We could use a cheerful story adventure as you're wont to tell, though. We rejoice that our brothers live with the saints, and we know that Iero will give us all we need, do we but ask, but truly we feel a dreadful sadness come upon us with this untimely winter."

Sadness. Yes. More than the failing light and ruined buildings. More than so many good men dead. *Gods grant you peace and care, good Robierre, as you gave so many, and Jerome, may you feast at the god's own table.* A pervasive sorrow held the abbey in its grip, a grieving in the stones and earth that felt as if the sun would never relieve this falling night. The thick dry cloak Thalassa had given me felt thin as gossamer.

As Anselm and I led the donkey across the field toward the gatehouse, the shy lay brother continued his stories of the raid and its aftermath. I'd never heard so many words from the infirmarian's assistant in all the weeks I'd lived at Gillarine. Perhaps trials did bring out new strengths in us.

Behind us, on the road that stretched northward toward Elanus and Palinur, Thalassa, her faithful Silos, and her five temple guards had vanished into the darkening forest, determined to reach Elanus before nightfall. My sister's parting kiss yet burned on my forehead. A kiss from Thalassa. She must believe I was going to die in Evanore. Unfortunately, I could not ease her concern. What use would the Bastard find for a mind-dead former doulon slave?

"Thank you for rescuing me yet again," I'd said after she yanked my head down and planted that unexpected kiss. Then I'd stooped to whisper in her ear, "*Teneamus.*"

I'd never seen her smile like that. Genuine. Pleased. Sad. "Hold on to your soul, little brother," she'd said as she mounted her palfrey. "Be well."

"I'd be happy enough with *warm, Sinduria serena.*"

She'd rolled her eyes and ridden away. I was happy she hadn't told me whether I would ever see her again.

"I'll put old Dob to shelter; then we'll find you a bed and a bite," said Anselm as we slogged through the gatehouse tunnel. A snarl of thick ropes and harness protruded from the drifted snow, and the wooden gates lay twisted from their hinges. "I needs must ask Father Prior if you're to be housed in the dorter—which is now moved to the abbot's house as it's got a roof—or in the guesthouse. That new lord's come today is most forbidding, I'll say." He nodded at Voushanti's retreating back. The mardane had hurried off ahead of us to see where Philo and Melkire were bedded down. "Some folk I knew as a lad would call him marked of the Adversary. You've not renounced your vows, have you, lad, or been dispensed from them?"

"Just taken on new ones, Brother," I said, feeling an unexpected heat in my cheeks. "Lord Voushanti is my new master's proxy."

We trudged through the Porter's Gate and into the trampled gardens in front of the dark church. Anselm frowned. "So you'll to the guesthouse, then. We've a fire laid. And you'll need dry clothes. Secular garb. You take a good rest tonight, and I'll put a flea in Father Prior's ear to ask if Lord Stearc might have left some things would come near fitting you. I'll send a posset as well, to stave off chills and damage from frostbite. Not so excellent as Brother *Badger* would have made for you, of course."

Summoning a smile, I clapped him on the shoulder in thanks.

Once left alone, the sad emptiness of the abbey gripped my spirit sorely. Despite the cold, I lingered in the familiar paths and courts. To rush toward fire and food seemed somehow lacking in respect. So, rather than taking the straighter way to the guesthouse, I wandered past the church into the north cloister walk and looked out on the cloister garth—the abbey's heart.

Rubble littered the square, the angular bulk of fallen cornices and corbels bulging awkwardly beneath the snow, alongside the birdcage shape of Saint Gillare's shrine. Though every building showed damage, the primary target of the raid was obvious. The walls of the abbey library and scriptorium had collapsed completely, crushing the eastern cloister walk. Naught was left but heaps of scorched stones and charred beams. The chapter house on one side and the monks' dorter on the other gaped open on the sides that had adjoined the library. Both structures were gutted shells. Of the jewel-like chapter-house windows, depicting Eodward and Caedmon, only one soot-marked pane remained, bearing the outline of an upraised hand.

So what had become of the magical lighthouse and its tools and books and seeds, gathered to sustain humankind past these dark times? Its creators had surely built it to endure through end-times chaos and destruction. Was this raid Bayard's vengeance for the abbey's sheltering Perryn? Or was this Sila Diaglou's handiwork? The lighthouse would be anathema to her, a promise to undo the chaos she worked for. I thought back to her savage attack on Gildas . . . a ploy to "draw out" her enemies . . . and Luviar and Stearc and Gram running for the gate. Yes, she knew of the lighthouse and its creators.

Firelight flickered in the far corner of the cloister, where the great hearth of the calefactory was required to remain lit until Saint Mathilde's Day. As I rested my back on a slender column, a handbell broke the oppressive silence, ten measured rings calling the monks to the Hours, a thin, strident summoning compared to the sonorous richness of the bronze bells fallen from the belltower. The pattern of two, three, and one, followed—Vespers, the Hour of peace. But I felt no peace and could not shake the sense that more than bodies and buildings had been shattered here.

I believed in the gods and their creatures—whether they were named Kemen or Iero, angels or Danae or gatzi. Even a dolt could see that the universe was no soulless clockwork, but infused with life beyond human understanding—wondrous and mysterious, perilous and exquisite. But as to whether the deities truly listened to our prayers or desired our votive gifts or libations or blood sacrifices, I'd been content to leave that study to wiser heads. And never had I given literal credence to the god stories and myths I'd been told—of Deunor's stolen fire that lit the stars or of the Danae whose dancing nourished the world and held it together. Not until I looked on the ruins of Gillarine and knew in flesh and spirit, breath and bone, that the Canon, the pattern of the world, was truly broken.

Curious, apprehensive, I knelt at the edge of the cloister walk and brushed away a patch of snow. The grass of the garth, so thick and green but a month ago, lay yellow and slimy. I pressed my hands to the earth.

Nothing. No slamming darkness. No piercing light. No music of grief or longing to wrench my soul as it had every time I'd tested this particular patch of earth. I felt only the sickness of the outer world that had intruded here. Plague into the sheepfold. Rot into the orchard. Fire and death into the cloisters.

Wiping my hands on the hem of my cloak, I sat back on my heels. Stories nagged at me. King Eodward had built this abbey on "holy ground." I had almost forgotten the first death. Young Brother Horach had been brutally murdered inside Saint Gillare's shrine, where the holy spring bubbled up into the font. Harrowers poisoned the land's guardians with violated corpses. That was what Sila Diaglou and her cohorts had tried to do with Boreas. I recalled Graver's Meadow, the lush grass and shimmering pond that swelled my spirit as if the angel choirs sang in the abbey's soaring vaults. Easy to believe a guardian had lived there.

What if the legends of Eodward and the angels and Gillarine's holy, fertile ground had given someone to believe the abbey spring a Danae sianou? And what if that someone had tried to poison the guardian Dané with the murdered Horach? The plan would have failed, because the true sianou lay at the spring's source in the hills at Clyste's Well. Clyste would have lived on, locked away for her part in my grandfather's crime, yet still infusing the abbey fields and flocks with her own life and health, a balm to such horrors as Black Night. And then I had opened the way to her holy place . . .

Faces, events, information shifted, twisted, and settled into a new pattern like tiles into a fine mosaic. Gerard had disappeared on the night of my attempted escape, only days after I had led Gildas to Clyste's Well. And only days later, pestilence had come to Gillarine.

I jumped to my feet, horror and certainty wrenching mind and heart. I knew what had happened to Gerard. Tears that had naught to do with the cold blurred my vision. Murdered. Great gods in all heavens, they had murdered the boy to kill the Danae guardian of the abbey lands. I knew it as I knew my own name. And now I understood what crime had been committed, it became clear who had committed it.

I stepped into the cloister garth and spun as I yelled, violating the holy silence and the land's grieving. "Where are you, monk? Gildas, come out here and tell me what you've done!"

Blind and stupid, Valen. Self-absorbed wretch. From the moment I had stepped into this abbey he had played me like a vielle. How had I not seen? Great Iero, he had all but told me outright. *I belong with the cabalists little more than you,* he'd said. And, *If the cities die, if learning dies, we are sent back to the land, to nights in the wild forest with spirits we can no longer tame with words, to awe of these Gehoum—the Powers who make the sky grow light or dark, whose righteous wrath is fire and storm. Righteous* wrath. *Everyone should be pure like you and Gerard,* he had told Jullian. Horach had been his student . . . and an innocent, too.

The part of me that believed I was unworthy of this place, that bore gratitude and affection for Gildas, who had welcomed me with good humor and allowed me to imagine I could be friends with scholars and men of substance, cried out that I was wrong. But I was not. Not this time. Clyste was dead. And so was Gerard.

"God-cursed child murderer!"

Brother Cantor intoned the opening note of Vesper plainsong as if to correct the abrasive timbre of my shouts, and then the voices—so terribly few—joined in the chant. Perfection, continuity, clarity . . . the music swelled as their procession approached the ruined cloisters.

Sila Diaglou's spy had told her of the lighthouse. But he couldn't tell her how to get into it and destroy its contents, because he was not privy to that secret. And a runaway novice had disrupted their ruse to lure Luviar and Stearc into her clutches with a bloody Gildas as bait. No wonder his hands had been left loose that night; he had *offered* himself to his Gehoum—*a noble sacrifice.* So he had waited until Palinur and given her Luviar and Victor. No wonder Gildas had looked dismayed when I told him Brother Victor had survived the gallows—not only because the chancellor was in Osriel's custody, but because the little monk could reveal who had betrayed him and his abbot.

Where are you, betrayer? I tugged at my hair. Gildas would not be at prayers. The worm would lurk in the heart of the cabal—with Gram and Stearc and Elene. I ran for the guesthouse, forced by shattered walls and rubble to circle south of the lay brothers' reach and past the ruined kitchen. Across the yard. Up the stoop.

"Come face me, gatzé! Tell me how clever you are to fool an ignorant pureblood!"

I slammed through doors and kicked aside the toppled furnishings and soot-grimed couches littering the dark rooms of the ground floor. A single rushlight burned in a tripod holder near the stair. I sped up the narrow, winding ascent. Yelling. Heedless.

The middle floor was dark. I raced upward and burst into a firelit chamber that smelled of scorched plaster and spiced cider.

Stocky, pale-skulled Prior Nemesio knelt by the meager fire, a sooty poker in his hand. He was alone. His startled expression quickly smoothed into satisfaction. "Brother Valen! It's Iero's own blessing to see you safe here again."

"Where is Gildas?" I snapped.

"At Vespers, I would think." Worry carved a mask on his big-boned cheeks. "What's wrong? Brother Anselm said you'd had quite an ordeal. I offered to bring his posset so I could tell you—"

"Where are the Evanori—Thane Stearc, his secretary?" I said. Jullian had vouched that Nemesio was one of us. "I must speak with them outside Mardane Voushanti's hearing."

"That's what I've come to tell you. Thane Stearc and his party moved on to Fortress Groult with the rest of the Evanori. When they saw what's happened here, they dared not stay."

Cold dread bound its fingers about my rage. "Did Gildas go with them? Or Jullian?"

"Brother Gildas thought they would do better to remain here. It's entirely unsuitable that an aspirant run about the countryside in the midst of—"

"Father Prior, Gildas murdered both Brother Horach and Gerard." My hands trembled with scarcely held rage. "We must find him. Confine him."

"What slander is this?" Nemesio surged to his feet, his thick neck scarlet. "Gildas is your vowed brother! The lighthouse Scholar!"

"I'd wager my life that Gildas is a Harrower. He took Gerard to Clyste's Well and bled him to death. You *must* send this news to Stearc right away. Don't you see? Gildas betrayed Victor and Luviar to Sila Diaglou. He knows your identities. I'd give much to be wrong, but to be certain, we must secure him tonight."

"I cannot credit this." Prior Nemesio chewed his full lips. "Gildas is a pious man. Holy and generous. Hours ago, when the Sinduria said she'd heard your call for help, both he and Jullian wished to set out with her at once to succor you. Your sister refused, unwilling to risk his safety. The two of them went straight off to the church to pray for your return."

I glanced about the room, dread and helplessness threatening to undo me. "Father Prior, where is the Cartamandua book? Please tell me that Stearc took it to Fortress Groult."

"No." Nemesio looked up. Uncertain. "Gildas kept it. To study, he said—"

I bolted for the stair.

Plainsong floated on the bitter air, along with the mingled odors of charred wood, of broken sewage channels, of incense and peat fires. The monks stood in a circle about the high altar of the ruined church, under vaults now open to the sky, and sang of their god's joy and care. Depleted ranks of lay brothers stood in a small area of the nave that had been cleared of rubble and dirty snow. Only a few heads moved as I sped through the nave yelling Gildas's name and Jullian's.

The boy was nowhere to be seen, and, as always, the monks' hoods were drawn up, hiding their faces. Knowing the search was futile, I snatched a lit candle from the high altar and intruded on their circle, peering at the hands clutching tattered psalters. Gildas's hands, backed by their thatch of wiry brown hair, were not among them.

I replaced the candle and strode out of the church, cursing. Halfway across the trampled garden, hurried footsteps behind me spun me in my tracks.

"Brother Valen? Is that really you?" The hard-breathing monk lowered his hood. The round head and fringe of gray hair identified my novice mentor.

"Yes, Brother Sebastian."

"The mask makes it difficult . . . and no tonsure anymore . . ." Uncertainty snagged his speech.

"I'm happy to see you alive, Brother. But I'm in a great hurry."

"Well, of course, I knew it was you. Not so many purebloods come here, and none so tall. Brother Gildas said this pureblood life"—he fluttered his hand at my mask and my clothing, giving no impression of having heard me—"has changed you. Secular law forbids me to speak to you, but Saint Ophir's Rule says you are yet my charge."

I stepped back, brittle with impatience. "Excuse me, Brother. Unless you can say where Gildas—"

"Brother Gildas is gone off to Elanus. Left something for you, he did. Said you would come looking for him . . . angry . . . saying terrible things. Said he wanted you to have this." From his cowl Brother Sebastian pulled a thumb-sized wooden box, tied with a string. He laid it in my hand. "And he said to tell you that an archangel would be his shield when the last darkness falls. Brother Valen, what did he—?"

"How long?" I said, scarcely able to shape words. My shaking fist threatened to crush the little box. "When did he go?"

Sebastian hesitated, his unsteady gaze not daring to meet my own. He expelled a sharp breath, as if he knew how close he stood to the blood rage threatening to crack my skull. "Just after Sext I encountered him coming out of the chapter-house undercroft, where we've stored what supplies we've salvaged from the fires. Young Jullian was with him. I remarked that they had missed the service—understandable, as they had just ridden in this morning with the Sinduria. But I said that I would expect to see both of them at Vespers. Our vows must not founder on the shoals of trial and sorrow. That's when he told me they had borrowed a horse from the Evanori and would be off to Elanus right away on Father Prior's business. Then he gave me the box and the message for you. The two of them rode out well before Nones."

"Thank you, Brother Sebastian. Please excuse me." Nones rang two hours before Vespers. I gave no credit to the stated destination. Gildas was taking the boy and my book to Sila Diaglou.

"The night drowns us, Valen," Sebastian called after as I hurried away. "Go with Iero's light."

I ran for the guesthouse. Nemesio would know if the Evanori had left horses for Voushanti and his men. If so, I could ride out . . . use my bent to follow Gildas. But before entering the guesthouse, I paused by the stoop and ripped open Gildas's parting gift. One glance and I launched the damnable thing into the night, scattering its contents into the churn of mud and snow. I could not find a curse vile enough for Gildas, and so I cupped my arms over my throbbing head and leaned against the stone wall, screaming out self-hatred and rage. The scent lingered: spicy, earthy, pepper and mushrooms, lighting an ember in my belly, where lurked a diseased knot the size of a fist. Nivat's claws settled into mind and body, ensuring I could not ignore it, could not forget, could not commit what wit I had to any other cause but servicing my hunger.

Smug, Silos had called him that morning in Palinur, and rightly so. Gildas, the scholar who had surely read about herbs and medicines among all his studies, would have known that giving me too much nivat would turn my head to muck and would grow my craving when the need came on me again . . . and again . . . and again. He had abetted my escape before calling down Thalassa's hunters and then so very kindly had fed my perversion. He knew his service would put the weak and gullible fool in his debt, give him a leash to control the ignorant sorcerer. Who in the world had measure for my folly?

I shoved open the guesthouse door. Harsh reality dispensed with my silly imaginings of riding off on my own to retrieve Jullian. Of a sudden every fiber and sinew of my body ached. Exhaustion weighed my limbs with armor of iron. And Voushanti sat on the stair beside the rushlight, paring his fingernails with his knife.

"So, pureblood," he said, without looking up from his task, "I thought perhaps you had gone wandering again. Lost yourself in the bogs and forgotten your oath."

"I do not break my oaths." Though I too often failed in my striving to keep them. As with Boreas. As with Jullian. Gildas would use the boy to manipulate me, as he had used the nivat. His shield. His hostage. *When the last darkness falls* . . .

I kicked a broken chair out of my way and tried to muster some semblance of a plan. Perhaps I could convince the mardane to let me "aid the brothers" in a search for Jullian and Gildas. "Tell me, Lord Voushanti, is our master Sila Diaglou's ally or her rival?"

"You needs must ask him that yourself. I've had word he'll be here tomorrow."

"Tomorrow? Here?" So soon. I'd expected . . . what? I was too tired to imagine.

"Prince Osriel's plans ripen. He needs neutral ground for an important parley, and this place happens to be convenient." He stood and stretched out his shoulders. "We'll likely move fast after tomorrow. I'd advise you to sleep off these past days' trial while you can."

He would never allow me to go out. I shrugged. "Tell me, Mardane, do *you* ever sleep?"

His face twisted in his grotesque mockery of a smile. "When my duties permit. Tonight, I keep watch." He moved aside just enough that I could squeeze past him to reach the stair. No doubt I would find him there in the morning.

The nagging ache of failure filled my boots with lead as I climbed to the upper chamber. A meal had been laid out on a tray—bread, boiled parsnips, dried apples. Anselm's posset sat in a pitcher by the hearth. Too weary to eat, I pulled off my sodden boots and hose, sat cross-legged on a woven hearthrug, and poked up Prior Nemesio's fire.

A cabal that thought to preserve humankind past the end times. A master who stole dead souls. Fanatics who used tormented spirits to slaughter the land's guardians and unravel the fabric of the world. How in the name of all gods had a man who prided himself on keeping his head down stumbled into events of such magnitude? Stumbled . . . had I?

My thoughts wandered back to Wroling Wood, to the day Boreas and I had given up on Perryn of Ardra and deserted his legion. When we spied the tidy manse, sitting unguarded in the forest outside Wroling Town, we thought Serena Fortuna had at last acknowledged our meager libations. Unfortunately, rodents had found the larders before us, and we had to be satisfied with inedible spoils. We stuffed our rucksacks and ran, arguing about whether to head straight for Palinur or to pawn the goods in a lesser town. I had laughed at finding my book after so many years, crowing that an unwelcome gift could pay me twice over.

Just as we dropped from the outer wall to head for the road, the Moriangi outriders attacked. The arrow strikes pitched me into an overgrown ditch, thick with soggy sedge and brambles. Boreas dived in beside me, blackening the air with his curses. Our attackers, caught up in a blood-frenzied pursuit of hundreds like us, failed to stop and ensure we were dead.

We lay in that ditch waiting for nightfall, hearing the pursuit pass over and around us. I bled into the sodden earth throughout a long afternoon, praying that the rain would not turn to ice and seal my foretold doom, longing to be warm and dry and safe, to be free of pain and feel my belly full. And when I at last staggered out of the ditch, half delirious, my gut and heart and blood had led us . . . driven us . . . here. Straight to Gillarine.

I stirred the coals and asked the question that had squatted in the back of my mind since I'd waked in Gillarine's infirmary. How was it possible that I had traveled ninety-three quellae in two days, starving, delirious, and half drained of blood? I could not answer it any more than I could say why my heart ached so sorely in the cloister garth of Gillarine, or why I wept when I looked on a Dané, or how a man who reveled in impiety and scorned all consideration of family had come to think of a Karish abbey as his home. My fists overflowed with shards of mirror glass, but I could not put them together in any way that made sense. I could not see myself anymore.

Perhaps I must have faith that whatever . . . whoever . . . had brought me here would show me the rest of the way. I dragged the tray of Gillarine's bounty close and poured a generous dollop of Brother Anselm's posset into the fire as an offering for Iero, for Kemen, for Serena Fortuna or whichever god or goddess might welcome it. As the sweet liquid sprizzled and scorched, I wolfed down the food and downed the remainder of the posset, pretending it cooled the fire in my gut. I would need my strength in the coming days, whether or not I chose to run. I would need it for Jullian. For my grandfather and his book. For the lighthouse cabal and the treacherous, dangerous Danae, whom we must beg to help us hold the world together. I had no time for weakness.

Cartamandua Legacy: Breath and Bone

For all who dance

Acknowledgments

Again, incalculable thanks to Susan, Laurey, Glenn, Brian, Catherine, and Curt for two years of hard-nosed reading; to Linda for listening; to Markus, the Fighter Guy, for combat review; and to the doc-on-the-net, Doug Lyle, for more gory consultations. No words can express gratitude for my family's support, especially this past year. And last, but certainly not least, to those ever in the hunt for inspiration, my thanks to National Public Radio for a small feature called "The Last Lighthouse" that launched me into these wild and wondrous realms.

PART ONE

Tarnished Gold

Chapter 1

"I don't understand why I must remain locked in this god-cursed chamber all morning, dressed like a ducessa's lapdog," I said, scraping the frost off the window mullion. The distorted view through the thick little pane revealed naught but the snow-crusted ruins of the abbey brewhouse, a sight to make a stout heart weep. "You seem to forget that I'm yet a vowed novice of Saint Ophir's Rule. I should be helping the brothers rebuild their infirmary or salvage their stores if there's aught to be found under the rubble."

Storm, pestilence, civil war . . . the world was falling apart all around us. Abbot Luviar's hope to protect the knowledge of humankind against this growing darkness dangled by the thinnest of threads. A monk I had believed holy . . . and my friend . . . had abducted a child I'd vowed to protect. And I was stuck here in Gillarine Abbey with a guard who never slept, awaiting who knew what. I needed to be doing something useful.

I wrenched the iron casement open and let the snow-riddled wind howl through for long enough to remind me of the dangers abroad. Setting off alone on a mad chase through the worst winter in Navronne's history was a ludicrous idea for anyone, much less a man who was like to lose his mind at any hour.

My unlikely nursemaid, a warrior whose presence turned men's bowels to water even before they glimpsed his mutilated face, blocked the doorway of the abbey guesthouse bedchamber. A pile of velvet and satin garments draped over his arm, and a pair of low-cut doeskin court boots—large enough they might possibly fit my outsized feet—dangled from his thick fingers. He waited until I slammed the casement shut before vouchsafing a comment.

"His Grace wishes you to dress as befits his pureblood adviser.

You must be ready whenever he summons you, so you should do it now." Voushanti twisted the unscarred half of his mouth in his unsettling expression of amusement. "And you're as suited to be a Karish monk as I am to be a pureblood's valet."

Though my dealings with Voushanti were anything but amusing, I could not but laugh at the bald truth stated so clearly. My novice vows had bought me a haven here two months previous, when I'd been a wounded deserter with no prospects of a roof, a meal, or a kind word anywhere. That my attachment to Gillarine Abbey had grown into something more was a virtue of the people here and no reversal of my own contrary nature. Circumstances—the law, my loathsome family, and the contract with which they had bound my life's service to the Bastard Prince of Evanore—had halted my brief clerical career . . . and every other path of my own choosing.

I peered into the wooden mug on the hearth table, discovered yet again that it was empty, and threw it across the chilly room. "Let me dig graves, if naught else, Voushanti. The brothers have not had time to bury their dead since the Harrower assault. Prince Osriel has not yet *arrived* at Gillarine, so he couldn't possibly need me before afternoon. I'll not run away. I gave him my word. Besides, I'm still half frostbit and wholly knob-swattled from the past seven days, so I'm hardly likely to wander off into this damnable weather again."

Were I the same man who had claimed sanctuary at Gillarine two months past, I'd have broken my submission to Osriel the Bastard, bashed Voushanti in the head with a brick, and gone chasing after the villain monk and his captive, be damned my word, the weather, and the consequences. But for once in my seven-and-twenty years, I had tried to think things through. Brother Gildas wanted Jullian for a hostage, a tool to manipulate me; thus he would keep the boy alive. I had already sent word to the lighthouse cabal, people who were far more likely to be able to aid my young friend. And in my own peculiar interpretation of divine workings, I believed that breaking my oath of submission, given to save Jullian's life on another day, would somehow permit the gods to forsake the boy. Two months past, Jullian had saved my life. Perhaps the best service I could do for him was to behave myself for once. *Dear Goddess Mother, please let me be right.*

Voushanti tossed the fine clothes on the bed. "Dress yourself, pureblood. Remain here until you are summoned. You don't want to know how sorely Prince Osriel mislikes disobedient servants."

I pulled off the coarse shirt the monks had lent me and threw it to the floor. Propping my backside on a stool, I began to untie the laces that held up the thick common hose so I could replace them with the fine-woven chausses Prince Osriel expected to see on his bought sorcerer. Deunor's fire, how I detested playing courtier to a royal ghoul who wouldn't even show me his face. Though, in truth, if Osriel's visage was more dreadful than Voushanti's purple scars and puckered flesh, it would likely paralyze any who saw it. His Grace of Evanore had the nasty habit of mutilating the dead, and was reputed to consort regularly with the lord of the underworld.

Argumentative murmurings on the winding stair slowed my fingers and stiffened Voushanti's spine as if someone had shoved a poker up his backside. The prior of Gillarine, a black-robed monk with a neck the same width as his shaven head, swept into the room, laden with drinking vessels and a copper pitcher. A ginger-bearded warrior burst through the doorway on Prior Nemesio's heels.

"I'm sorry, sir," said the frowning warrior, a robust Evanori by the name of Philo. "The monk insists on seeing the pureblood. I know you said to keep everyone away, but to lay hands on a clergyman—"

A second warrior, also wearing my master's silver wolf on his hauberk, joined his fellow. Their drawn swords appeared a bit foolish with none present but one stocky, hairless monk, one gangle-limbed sorcerer wearing naught but an ill-fitting undertunic and one leg of his hose, and their own commander.

"For mercy's sake, Philo, Melkire, sheath your weapons," I said, stuffing arms and head back into the shirt I had just shed. "Father Prior! Iero's grace." Hose drawn back up and laces retied, I jumped to my feet and touched my fingertips to my forehead. "I was shocked to find such devastation here, holy father. If I can do aught to help . . ."

Though protocol ranked any pureblood, even an illiterate, incompetent one like me, above nobles, clerics, or any other ordinary, I prayed my respectful address might prevent Voushanti and his men from hustling Nemesio away. The prior was my only link to my friends of the lighthouse cabal. I hoped for news of Jullian.

Nemesio's nostrils flared as if an ill odor permeated the room. Difficult to imagine this unimaginative and slightly pompous man conspiring with the passionate, aristocratic Abbot Luviar to create the magical cache of books and tools they called the *lighthouse*.

The prior set his copper pitcher on the table and arranged the five cups beside it in a neat row. "Indeed, I have come to request your aid, Brother Valen."

Voushanti rumbled disapproval.

I acted quickly, lest protocol violations end the visit. "You must not address me directly, Father Prior, but only Mardane Voushanti, as he represents my contracted master, Prince Osriel. But I'm sure the prince would hear your petition favorably in appreciation for your hospitality."

I held no such assurance, of course. Though I had served him less than a fortnight and met him only twice, Prince Osriel seemed even less likely than most of his ilk to express gratitude of any sort. But perhaps he liked to *pretend* he was reasonable.

Prior Nemesio's thick shoulders shifted beneath his habit. He clutched the silver solicale that hung about his neck as if the sunburst symbol of his god could protect him from these minions of the Adversary. The dark blots in his wide, pale face spoke of a sleepless night. "Mardane, a few weeks ago, one of our young aspirants disappeared. We have searched, questioned, and expended every resource to find him without success. We fear greatly for his life. Perhaps you remember Gerard, Brother Valen? A good, devout boy, just fourteen."

I nodded, a chill more bitter than Navronne's foul winter shadowing my spirit. Of course, I remembered. This recital was for Voushanti's benefit. Only the previous night had I shared with the prior my new-formed belief that Brother Gildas, scholar and traitor, had not only stolen young Jullian away, but murdered his friend Gerard.

Nemesio straightened his back and spoke boldly. "We of Saint Ophir's brotherhood are Gerard's family. If he lives, then we must locate him and ensure his safety. If he is dead, he must be returned here where we can afford him proper rites. We understand that Brother Valen's pureblood bent involves tracking and route finding, thus request his aid in our search for the boy."

Fool of a monk! I wanted to strangle Nemesio. Gerard's body must be retrieved, and I was more than willing to lend my paltry skills to the task, but Voushanti was Prince Osriel's man and could not be permitted to know of the place I believed the boy lay—or its significance. The Well was secret. Holy. And Voushanti and our master were not. "Father Prior, I couldn't possibly—"

"Cartamandua is not brought here to serve you, monk," Voushanti snapped. "Prince Osriel has chosen this monkhouse as a neutral meeting ground suitable for his royal business. The pureblood is required to attend his master. Nothing else."

Nemesio's hairless skull and wide neck glowed crimson. "Well, then. It was but a thought. We would never wish to distract a man from his duty. Here, I've brought refreshment for you all." He filled the five plain vessels from his pitcher, handing them around first to Voushanti and the two warriors, then to me. "In all the excitement of your arrival yestereve . . . the various comings and goings of so many . . . we lapsed in our sacred rituals of hospitality."

Nemesio raised his cup to each of us. His hands were shaking. "May the waters of Saint Gillare's holy font bring good health and serenity to our guests."

Voushanti shrugged at Philo and Melkire and the three of them raised their cups and drank. I raised my cup in my two hands, but only touched my lips to its rim. Since the day I turned seven, the day my mother the diviner first pronounced that I would meet my doom in water, blood, and ice, only desperation could drive me to water drinking. And were I naught but a withered husk, I could not have touched *this* water. The holy spring that fed the abbey font had its source in the hills east of Gillarine—in the very pool where I believed Gerard's body lay.

A glance across my cup revealed Nemesio glaring at me as if I were defiling a virgin. I had no idea what I'd done, but his shoulders sagged a bit as I lowered my cup. He snatched away the vessel and gathered the emptied cups from the others.

"I'd best leave you gentlemen to your preparations," he said. "The guesthouse is yours for as long as you need, of course. Though we can provide but meager fare since the Harrower burning, we shall send what refreshment we can for His Grace when he arrives. Our coal garth is intact . . ." Nemesio's nervous babbling slowed as Melkire sagged against the doorframe, rubbing his eyes.

I glanced from the prior to the soldiers. Something untoward was going on.

"Mardane Voushant . . . s'wrong . . ." Philo's voice slurred as he dropped to his knees and slumped to the floor. Melkire tumbled on top of him with a soft thud.

"Gracious Iero!" said the prior softly. But he made no move to succor the men.

"What treachery is this?" Voushanti's hand flew to his sword hilt, and the core of his eyes gleamed scarlet. But before he could draw, he blinked, sat heavily on the low bed, and toppled backward.

"Father Prior, what have you done?" I said, my stomach lodged so far in my throat, my voice croaked as if I were a boy of twelve.

Nemesio dropped his vessels on the table. "They'll sleep for a few hours and wake confused, so Brother Anselm told me. We'd best go right away."

I could almost not speak my astonishment. "Nemesio, are you

absolutely mad? These men serve Osriel the Bastard, the same prince who conjured horses and warriors the size of your church from a cloud of midnight, the same who, not two months ago, cut out the eyes of a hundred dead soldiers who lay in your fields. We know neither his capabilities nor his intentions in this war. Great Iero's heart, for all we know *he* may have dispatched the Harrowers to burn you out!"

"I'm well aware. If the Bastard Prince wishes our destruction, then he'll do it. I cannot control that. But *you* have made a grievous charge against Brother Gildas—the lighthouse Scholar—and we cannot know how to proceed until you prove it. As we've only these few hours until Prince Osriel takes you away, and as only you can find this place in the hills, I see no alternative."

"Did you send my message to Stearc and Gram?" Thane Stearc was likely the leader of the cabal now that Abbot Luviar lay dead and Brother Victor lay comatose somewhere in Prince Osriel's captivity. Stearc despised me and would no more believe my charges than Nemesio did, but Gram—Stearc's quiet, pragmatic secretary—was a man of reason. He'd see that a search was mounted for Jullian and Brother Traitor.

"Indeed I sent news of your safe return. I also informed them of your foul accusation and my determination to seek the truth. You claim that you are one of us—sworn to Abbot Luviar's memory to aid us in our mission—and *this* is the service we require of you." Without waiting for my hundred arguments against this lackwit plan, he stepped over the two warriors and vanished down the stair.

Gods preserve me from holy men. It was Abbot Luviar's persuasive passion that had got me caught up in his mad scheme to preserve the entirety of human knowledge in his magical library. Now his splayed and gutted corpse hung from a gallows back in Palinur. Crossing Prince Osriel . . . laying out his men with potions . . . the prior would have us end up the same or worse.

Yet as I pulled on a heavy cloak, I could not deny the virtue of retrieving poor Gerard. Unlike Jullian, a wily, experienced conspirator at age twelve, simple, good-hearted Gerard had been but an unlucky bystander. He should not lie forgotten.

For the fiftieth time since we'd left the abbey, I glanced over my shoulder and saw no one. A frost wind gusted off the mountains to the south, whipping the snow into coils and broomtails that merged with the gray-white clouds, hiding Gillarine's broken towers. Ahead of me the prior, his black cowl billowing, strode eastward across the wind-scoured fields toward the valley's bounding ridge, leading Dob, the abbey's donkey.

Though the calendar marked the season scarce a month past Reaper's Moon, the once-fertile valley of the Kay lay blanketed in snow. The Karish said Navronne's past ten years of increasingly cold summers and bitter winters were caused by the One God Iero's wrath at mankind's sinfulness. The Sinduri Council claimed the elder gods' bickering among themselves had shifted the bowl of the sky. Those of the lighthouse cabal feared the cause lay with the earth's guardians—the mysterious, elusive Danae, who had withdrawn from all contact with humankind. Though I had no sensible arguments to make, my instincts told me that matters were worse than they imagined. Whatever the cause, famine and pestilence had taken on bony reality and crawled into our beds with us.

"We should be hunting the living, not the dead," I said, puffing out great gouts of steam in the cold air. "Don't you understand, Nemesio? Not only does Gildas have Jullian, he has my grandfather's book of maps. And the god's own fool that I am, I *unlocked* the book to him. Given rumor of a Danae holy place . . . given even a guess as to where one might lie . . . he can follow the maps and take the Harrowers there to destroy it. Once Prince Osriel takes me away from here, I'll not be able to help you anymore. And without me or the book, you've no hope to find the Danae and ask for help."

"Brother Gildas has been a member of Saint Ophir's order for nine years." Nemesio's voice quivered with suppressed fury. "With unmatched scholarship, holiness, and devotion, he has devoted himself to work and study that he may carry the world's hope into the future. You, sir, are a liar, a charlatan who has mocked our faith and suborned the weak-minded with your unending prattle, a hedonist and libertine, an illiterate wastrel who has spurned Iero's greatest gift—the magic in your blood—and accomplished nothing of value in your life. Why would anyone accept your word as truth?"

Knowing that his every charge had merit did nothing for my bitter temper. "Have you no fear of walking out alone with such a rogue?"

"Two of our brothers hold missives to be forwarded to Thane Stearc should I fail to return."

"Spirits of night . . ."

Nemesio halted where the land kicked up sharply into the ridge, motioning for me to take the lead. "Abbot Luviar, the most admirable and perceptive of men, insisted that you were more than we could see. Yet he also named Brother Gildas as the Scholar. In which man was he deceived?"

And so was I silenced. I could not argue Gildas's guilt without confessing my own—that my slug-witted reaction to an excess of nivat seeds had prevented me rescuing Luviar from his hideous death. The fact that Gildas himself had abetted my perverse craving could never exonerate me.

Our path twisted upward through gullies and rockfalls, every crevice and shadowed nook treacherous with ice and crusted snow.

"Not far now," I said, as I led Nemesio and the flagging donkey up the last steep climb and onto a shelf of rock that abutted a shallow cliff.

Shivering, uneasy, I gazed back out over the valley of the Kay and the slopes we had traversed, shrouded in snow fog that teased the eye. Drifting clouds mantled the cliff tops above us. I could not shake the certainty that we were being watched. How could I have been so stupid as to come here? Only one day ago I had narrowly escaped a trap set by the trickster Danae down in the bogs of the River Kay. And now we were to intrude on their holy place, an unassuming little hollow that touched on the most profound mysteries of the world.

Chapter 2

Sila Diaglou, priestess of the ragtag Harrowers, wished to send Navronne back to the days before cities and roads and tilled soil, to a time when women hid in caves and men cowered in terror of night and storm. She named all gods false: Iero, the benevolent deity of the Karish, as well as Mother Samele and Kemen Sky Lord and the rest of the elder gods, worshiped in Navronne since time remembered. Harrowers ridiculed belief in Iero's angels, called the impish aingerou naught but fools' wishing dreams, and denied the existence of the Danae, whose dancing defined the Canon—the pattern of the world.

I could not name which gods were real and which but story. Nor could I argue the truth of angels or aingerou, though I spat on my finger and patted the naked rumps of those cherubic messengers carved into drainpipes and archways in hopes my prayers might be carried on to greater deities. But Danae . . . As boy and man I had scoffed at my grandfather's claims to have traveled their realms. But Danae existed. Since I'd come to Gillarine, I had glimpsed at least two of them for myself.

The prior and I trod slowly along the snowy shelf path. Repeated melting and freezing had left small glaciers along the way.

"Are you having second thoughts, pureblood?" asked Nemesio, blowing on his rag-wrapped fingers to warm them. "Why would Brother Gildas choose this particular spot to hide a body when any of these gullies would do? Perhaps you'll tell me this is the wrong location after all."

There was no mistake. "He chose this place because killing Gerard was not his object. He wanted to kill the Danae guardian."

Despite their claims, at least *some* of the Harrowers believed in the Danae. It could be no accident that their savage rites murdered Danae guardians one by one.

Legend said Danae lived both on the earth and in it. Everywhere and nowhere, my mad grandfather said. Most times they took human form to walk their lands—our lands, for the human and Danae realms were both the same and not the same. But for one season of every year a Dané became one with a sianou—the grove, lake, stream, or meadow he or she had chosen to guard. The protection of a Dané infused the sianou and the surrounding land with life and health.

Our destination was such a sianou, a pool I had located at the bidding of Abbot Luviar, before I even understood what kind of place it was. I had brought my friend Brother Gildas there, and in the weeks since that night, Gerard had gone missing, blight had infected Gillarine's orchards and fields, and disease had come to its sheepfolds. When I touched my hands to the earth in the abbey's cloisters, I could no longer feel its living pulse. Harrower raiders had left the abbey buildings in ruins, but I believed the cause of its underlying sickness lay here and that Gildas was responsible.

Snow and ice packed a jutting slab beneath its slight overhang. Dob balked and brayed in protest at the tight corner. As the prior slapped the donkey's rump and hauled on the lead, a horse whinnied anxiously just ahead of us.

Startled, beset with imaginings of lurking Harrowers, I hissed at Nemesio to keep silent.

Footsteps and jostling spoke of one man and one beast. "Easy, girl, it's friendly company on the way. We'll be about our business and be off again to hay and blanket."

The quietly persuasive voice brought a smile to my lips. Gram could convince a cat to play in the ocean.

"How in great Iero's mercy do *you* happen to be here?" I said, abandoning the prior to the donkey while I hurried around the rock and along the shelf toward the slender, dark-haired man stroking a gray mare. "Did you get Nemesio's message about Jullian and Gildas? Well, of course, you must have done. That's why you've come. Gram, you must believe me. Gildas has taken Jullian and the book. He's murdered Gerard . . ."

I wanted to pass on everything I knew: what I had sensed in the abbey's cloisters, the truth about my damnable perversion and how Gildas had thought to use it to bend me to his will. My determination to rescue Jullian—perhaps the only true innocent left in this blasted world—had become a fever in me. Ever-sensible Gram would understand the importance of prompt action. The man spent his days as the calm center of the lighthouse cabal, juggling his testy employer, Thane Stearc, and Stearc's ebullient daughter, Elene. But I'd scarcely begun my tale when Gram raised his gloved hand.

"Hold, friend Valen," he said. "We are already moving. Thane Stearc and his men have spent the night scouring the countryside between here and Elanus for the two of them. Mistress Elene leads another search party between here and Fortress Groult. We told Thanea Zurina that a wayward monk had kidnapped a young friend of yours and asked her to keep an eye out along the roads west as she makes her way home."

The flushed Nemesio joined us, hauling Dob behind him. "What are you doing here, Gram?"

Gram bowed politely. "Good Father Prior, your god's grace be with you this morning. As I was just telling Valen, Thane Stearc has dispatched several parties to search for Jullian and Brother Gildas. As he wished to move swiftly, my lord left me behind at Fortress Groult. So I rode up here, hoping to make myself useful."

The secretary's pale skin took on a hint of scarlet. Though no older than I, Gram was sorely afflicted with ill health.

Prior Nemesio shook his head. "Brother Valen's story is nonsensical. How could a scholarly man such as Gildas give hearing to Harrowers? Even if he be apostate to divine Karus and the One God, which I cannot credit, who but mindless lunatics could imagine that a world without tools or books is what any god intends?"

Sila Diaglou claimed her dark age would be a time of appeasement, a time of cleansing, required because we had forgotten our proper fear of the Gehoum, the elemental Powers who controlled the land and seasons. The bitter wind whined through the crags, as if to answer my skepticism with a reminder of our wildly skewed seasons, and the disease and starvation that howled at Navronne's door like starved wolves.

Gram stroked the mare's neck and fondled her ears. "Men are driven in such varied ways, Father Prior. Brother Gildas relished his task as Last Scholar, destined to be the holder of humankind's accumulated wisdom. Perhaps—and who can say what is in a man's heart?—he does not relish the task of First Teacher."

Nemesio tightened his full lips. "We have only Brother Valen's surmise. I'll not believe ill of Brother Gildas without some proof. So where is this pool, Brother? We must get you back before the demon prince's heathenish servants awaken."

I'd been to the Well only once, in conditions of light and weather so different I didn't trust my memory to recognize the cleft in the wall. So I crouched down, recalled the passage, the grotto, and the pool, and allowed magic to flow through my fingers into the stone beneath my feet. Cold, harsh, its cracks filled with frost crystals, the stone gave up its secrets far more reluctantly than earth. But I stretched my mind forward, swept the path and the cliff, and after a moment, a guiding thread claimed my senses—a surety something like that birds must feel when the days grow short and they streak southward beyond the mountains toward warmer climes. Such was the gift of the Cartamandua bent, the legacy of my father and grandfather's bloodline—a gift I had spurned because of its cost to my freedom. "This way," I said, moving northward along the shelf path.

"You said Prince Osriel himself comes to Gillarine tonight?" said Gram to the prior, as they trudged behind me, leading the beasts and sharing a flask Gram had brought.

"Aye," said the prior. " 'Twas only out of respect for good King Eodward's memory that I could stomach hosting such a visitation. How could a noble king breed such a son?"

Gram downed a long pull from his flask. "Abbot Luviar himself could not explain the ways of the gods sufficient to that question."

Dikes of dense black stone seamed the pale layers of the limestone cliff with vertical bands. Some twenty paces along the cliff, a wide crack split one of these dark bands. "Here," I said. "We'll find him here."

The gray morning dimmed to twilight in the narrow passage. We stepped carefully. A dark glaze of ice sheathed the straight walls and slicked the stone beneath our feet. Ahead of us, beyond a rectangle of gray light, lay the little corrie, centered by a pool worn into the stone.

Clyste's Well, the pool was called, named for the Dané who had last claimed guardianship there. On one of his journeys into the Danae realms, my grandfather had involved Clyste in a mysterious theft that had driven humans and Danae apart. For his part in the crime, the Danae had tormented his mind to madness. For hers, they had locked her away in her sianou, forbidding her to take human form again. She had lived on all the years since, enriching the lands watered by her spring, including Gillarine Abbey. But no more. My every sense insisted she was dead. Murdered.

Heart drumming against my ribs, I bade Nemesio leave the ass where he stood. A few steps more and we reached the entry, the point where the passage walls expanded to encircle the grotto like cupped hands. *Ah, Holy Mother . . .* I clamped my arms about my aching middle. I would have given my two legs to be wrong.

Translucent, blue-white cascades of ice ridged the vertical walls and sheeted the smooth ground. The pool itself lay unfrozen, dark and still, no matter the wind that whipped the heights, showering us with spicules of ice. Gerard floated on the glassy water, naked, bloodless. Rain must have washed his shredded flesh clean of blood and what scraps of his abbey garments the knives had spared. The thorough savagery could have left no blood inside him. Iron spikes had been driven through his outstretched hands, tethering him to the rocky bank like a boat to its mooring. But one hand had torn through as he struggled to escape his fate, and now dangled loose in the water. Harrowers left their ritual victims to suffer and bleed, for it was both their blood and their torment that poisoned the sleeping Danae and the lands they guarded. So my grandfather had told me.

Nemesio choked, and I shoved him ruthlessly back into the passage to empty himself, though it was likely foolish to worry about further desecrating a place so vilely profaned. Gram pressed his back to the cliff wall at the entry, his pale cheeks as stark and drawn as the frozen cascades. "I cannot go here," he whispered. "I'm sorry. I can't help you with this."

"No matter. Rest as you need." I retrieved a worn blanket from the donkey's back and entered the grotto. Kneeling at the brink of the pool, I touched Gerard's tethered hand. *Cold. Great, holy gods . . . so cold.* Darkness enfolded me, threaded my veins and sinews, tightened about my heart and lungs until I felt as if I shared the terrifying, lonely end of this child's short life, and with it, the cold suffocation of the dead guardian. I needed desperately to empty my stomach, too, to cry out my sickness, to run, to be anywhere but this dreadful place. But I could not leave the boy. *Forgive. Please gods and holy earth, forgive us all.*

Stretching out from the brink, I drew him close, then worked awkwardly to wrap the blanket around him. By the time I had pulled his weakened flesh from the remaining spike, an iron-faced Nemesio had rejoined me. Together we used the blanket to lift the boy from the pool, then wrapped him in an outer blanket and carried him into the passage.

As the three of us tied the gray bundle to Dob's back, a movement caught the corner of my eye back in the corrie. A glint of sapphire brilliance quickly vanished in the gray light.

"Go on out," I whispered, still fighting to contain my own sickness. Gram looked ill, and the prior's teeth clattered like a bone rattle. Nemesio and I were both soaked. "I'll be along before you start down the steeps."

Nemesio clucked softly to the donkey. I slipped back down the passage toward the rectangle of light, flattened myself to the icy wall, and peered into the grotto.

A tall, naked man, every quat of his lean flesh ridged with muscle, knelt on one knee beside the pool. Back bent, head bowed, he extended his long arms over the water in a graceful curve as if to embrace the very essence of the pond. Red hair twined with yellow flowers curled over one shoulder. Patterns of blue light scribed his skin—a sapphire heron on his back, vines and flowers the color of mountain sky on his powerful limbs, a spray of reeds drawn in azure and lapis along one thigh and hip.

The Dané lifted his head, and a single anguished cry tore through him—echoing from the ice-clad walls, resonating in my bones. And then, stretching his arms to the heavens, he rose on his bare toes and whipped one leg around so that he spun in place. A quick step and then he spun again . . . and then again, moving around the pool in a blur of flesh and color and woven light, one arm curved before his chest, one above his head. The very rocks wept with his sorrow. I thought my heart might stop with the beauty of it.

When he reached his starting point, I stepped farther into the grotto. He halted in midspin and dropped his hands to his sides. He was not at all surprised to see me. And I recognized him. Three times I had glimpsed this same one of them . . . but never so close. Never in the fullness of his glory.

His eyes glowed the fiery gold of aspen leaves in autumn. On his left cheek the fine-drawn pattern of light scribed a dragon, whose wings spread across brow, shoulder, and chest, and whose long tail wrapped about his left arm. Below the graceful reeds that curved from his hip across his belly, a hatchling dragon coiled about his groin and privy parts. He appeared no more than thirty, but Danae lived for centuries and did not age as humans do.

"I didn't know this would happen," I said. "The man I brought here pretended to be what he was not. The child he slaughtered was an innocent . . . chosen because he was my friend. Never . . . never . . . did I mean to bring this on the one who slept here—this Clyste. My grandfather—" I caught myself before saying more. The Dané wouldn't care to hear that a human wept for her.

"As wolfsbane art thou, Cartamandua-son," he said, speaking fury and grief in the timbre of tuned bronze. "Beauty and poison. Taking life. Giving it back. Speaking the language of land and water, but with words graceless and ignorant. Intruding where thou shouldst not, violating—" He broke off, trembling, and swept his hand to encompass the grotto. "Thou dost lead me here, cleanse the Well so I do not sicken, return it to my memory so I cannot escape knowing what is lost—though I must lose it all over again as I walk away. Is this thy pleasure to taunt those thou dost not know? Dost thou think my love for Clyste can shield thee from the judgment of the long-lived?"

As flint to steel, his indignation sparked my anger, erasing all caution. "I know naught of you, Dané, save that you once offered me a haven in my need, then stood back and observed my captivity as if I were a performing bear chained for your amusement. I know that Danae vengeance has left my grandsire a madman. And I know that you or one of your fellows tricked me and my companions and our enemies into the bogs as if *all* humans were naught but beasts worthy of a slaughterhouse." Naught would ever erase the memory of luring my enemies into the freezing mud to save my companions' lives, of hearing . . . feeling . . . them drown. "I once believed your kind to be the blessed finger of the Creator in this world. But you are no better than we are."

"Pah!" With a snarl of disgust he turned away. Kneeling once again by the pool, he scooped water in his hands and poured it over his head. "*Askon geraitz, Clyste,*" he said, his voice breaking. "Live on in my heart, *asengai*. Let me not forget thee."

"Kol, don't leave. You must— Please hear us!" I had forgotten Gram. The wan secretary stood framed in the dark band of the passage entry, astonished . . . stammering. "Many of us . . . most . . . despise these murderers. The Everlasting is in upheaval, to the ruin of our land, our beasts, and all humankind. Whatever the cause, we desperately need the help of the long-lived to understand it . . . to make it right again. The gard of the dragon names thee Kol, friend and foster brother of Eodward King, brother to shining Clyste, who danced as none before her. In Eodward's name we beg hearing. Please, take us to Stian Archon or to any who might heed our message . . . our need . . ."

The Dané shifted his gold eyes to Gram. Cocking his head, he flared his nostrils and inhaled deeply. His lip curled. "Human speech is briar and nightshade. Human loyalty is that of wild dogs and weasels. Stripped is Stian of his archon's wreath." His finger pointed to the dark pool. "These evils are the gifting of Eodward to those who sheltered him. Begone! Thou dost bear the stink of betrayal and shalt not pass one step into our lands until his debt is paid." He strode toward the ice-clad wall, but before he reached it, he vanished in a ripple of air and light.

Never had I stood in a place so unforgiving, so empty. Gram might have been frozen into the wall. I gave him a nudge, and we abandoned the grotto.

Halfway down the dark passage, a spasm of coughing caused Gram to stumble and skid on the ice. I grabbed his arm and steadied him. "You should come back to the abbey with us, Gram. You look like walking death."

"I might as well be dead. I should have listened better at Caedmon's Bridge, but I didn't want to hear their judgment. I should have believed what you told us about the Harrower rites poisoning sianous."

"My grandfather said it is the Danae's greatest secret. But when I walked into Gillarine yesterday and found it ruined . . . when I touched the earth in the cloisters . . . Gram, I felt the world broken. I know it sounds presumptuous. I've meager skills and a history of lies, but you must believe that every breath, every bone, every drop of my blood tells me that this breaking is cause of the world's upheaval . . . the weather . . . the sickness . . . I'll swear it on whatever you like."

Someday, perhaps, someone might believe what I said without the backing of god-sworn oaths. My myriad swearings had my life tangled upside over and backside front.

"We did not doubt your sincerity, Valen. We just believed that no human action could compromise the Canon itself. We assumed your grandfather's tale was but guilt speaking through madness. And now I've wasted this opportunity. I should have been better prepared. Ah, cursed be this weakness . . . inept . . . ." The racking cough forced him to stop and lean on the wall. He slapped his hands against the stone in frustration, his reserve shattered for the first time since I'd known him.

"If all this is true," he said, when he caught his breath at last, "if the Danae forget a place when it is corrupted and lost to the Canon, then how could Kol be here?"

"He follows me," I said, able to answer that one question, at least. "I saw him the first time on the night I tried to escape from Gillarine. He waited in an aspen grove and offered his hand—tried to rescue me. Then he watched me every day of my punishment exhibition in the streets of Palinur. I even glimpsed him in a courtyard of my family's house. I saw a Dané in Mellune Forest, too, but I'm not sure it was he. I didn't know the one with the dragon on his face was Kol.

Spirits of night, Clyste's brother . . . he likely *was* the one who tried to drown us in the bog. My grandfather warned me that I was in danger from the Danae."

Gram stared at me for a moment in the dim light, then rested his back against the passage wall and averted his eyes. I'd never met a more private man. "That makes no sense," he said, collecting his scattered emotions. "Your grandfather is being punished for his crime and will continue to be until whatever he stole is returned. Thus his debt is being paid. The Danae would never take vengeance on others, even his family, unless they believed those others complicit in Janus's crime. Their law—the Law of the Everlasting—forbids it."

He ran his long fingers through his hair as if to drag ideas from his skull. "Danae justice is quite clear and quite specific. Everything is balance. Bargains. Exchanges. Think of what Kol said and how he said it. Death and life. Violation and restored memory. He clearly did *not* blame you for Clyste's death. He would blame the one who did the murder. Perhaps he was already following you about when it happened. Yet he implied that you've raised the ire of other Danae . . . *the judgment of the long-lived* . . . and with your grandfather's warning . . ." He looked up at me again. "Valen, do you have what Janus stole?"

"No!" I said. "I didn't even know of my grandfather's crime until a fortnight ago. And he refused to tell me what he took. If their 'justice' is so balanced, then why does Eodward's betrayal bar us all from their realms?"

"I don't think he meant all humans." Shivering, Gram bundled his cloak tighter. "I've got to consider all this . . . inform Thane Stearc and see what he makes of it. Our plans may have to change. Come, we'd best get back."

"Brother Valen!" As if in echo of Gram's conclusion, Nemesio's call bounced urgently through the passage. "Get out here now!"

"So you go back to Osriel?" said Gram as we hurried toward the light.

"I would rather do anything else. But I must honor my word or else— Well, I don't know what would happen, but my word is the only thing I've ever held to. I promise you, I'll be no good to him."

He stopped me as we approached the mouth of the passage. "You said something similar back at Mellune. What do you mean?"

No need for him to know what my nivat-starved perversion was like to make of me. I pulled my arm from his hand. "Be well, Gram. Give the thane and his daughter my regards."

"*Teneamus*, Valen," he said.

We preserve—the Aurellian code word of the lighthouse cabal. Gram's invocation of it expressed the sincerity of his concern for me. I had no answer for his kindness. "We'd best go before Nemesio bursts."

It was as well I chose not to further compromise my vow of submission. When Gram and I stepped from the cleft into the open air, Nemesio and the donkey waited with Gram's gray mare. Beside them stood Voushanti.

Chapter 3

No argument of mine could persuade Voushanti that I'd no intent to run. "His Grace will decide your punishment," he said as he bound my hands to the donkey's harness. "And you *will* be there to heed it."

Though pale and quivering, Nemesio bore Voushanti's impossible arrival with a straight spine and unbowed head. I should have warned the prior about Prince Osriel's favored commander. I had seen Voushanti recover from terrible wounds in a matter of hours. I had witnessed his resiliency as we tramped day and night through the winter nightmare of Mellune Forest. More than once I had looked into the red core of his eyes and suspected he did not sleep. What common sleeping draft would affect such a man, if man he was?

At least the mardane showed no interest in exploring the cleft. Whether or not Prince Osriel was Sila Diaglou's rival in the pursuit of chaos, the last thing I wanted to do was teach him a way to interfere with the Danae.

When we reached the flats, Voushanti dismissed Gram with a promise to report his interference both to Thane Stearc and Stearc's liege lord Prince Osriel. The last I saw of the secretary, he was vanishing at a gallop into the frozen haze that had settled in the valley. Voushanti, the prior, the ass, and I slogged toward the abbey afoot.

With no silken cords binding my hands to stay the flow of magic, I could have unlocked the chain that linked my wrists to the donkey even with my limited skills. But in truth I could not summon the wits to work a spell. A storm of blue light filled my head—the image of the Dané as he danced out his grief. I had never imagined such expressive power in mere movement, as if his body formed words and music I could not hear. My own feet dragged like brutish anvils through the snow. My arms felt stiff as posts. Compared to his, my body was no more living than a wall of brick.

Remnants of our exchange swirled in my thoughts like water through a sluice. He'd said that I had cleansed the Well, as if it were some marvel. Yet I'd done naught but remove the dead boy, hardly difficult for a man of his strength.

Kol, the son of the Danae archon who had sheltered King Caedmon's infant son more than a century ago . . . My mind balked at the imagining. My grandfather, a cartographer with a sorcerer's bent, had discovered Caedmon's heir living in the realm of the Danae—the realm of angels, legend called it. Life spent differently in Danae lands, for a century and a half after his royal father's death, Eodward had just been passing from youth to manhood. A Karish hierarch and a high priest of the elder gods had persuaded the young man to return to Navronne and revive the wreckage of his father's kingdom. Though Eodward had promised the Danae to return to them after only a few years, he never had. Navronne had needed her strong and honorable warrior king, who had freed her from the disintegrating Aurellian empire and a succession of invasions from the barbarian Hansker.

Three years ago, good King Eodward had died, abandoning Navronne to his three sons—a blustering brute, an effete coward, and my master, rival to the lord of the netherworld. Between my grandfather's unexplained theft, Eodward's betrayal of his word, and the depredations of the Harrowers, it was no wonder the Danae brooked no dealings with humankind.

Nemesio unlatched the wooden gate in the low eastern wall of the abbey. The prior had been silent on our return journey. Praying, I thought. Mourning. *Deunor's fire, Gerard* . . . an unscholarly boy with a quick smile and an innocent heart. What punishment would be dreadful enough to requite this crime? Gildas . . . the Harrowers . . . Sila Diaglou . . . I *would* see them brought to account for it.

As soon as we left the field path for the abbey walks, the monks began to gather, like blackbirds to a rooftop. Despite their anonymous robes and hoods, I recognized them by their shapes—short, tight Brother Sebastian; willowy Brother Bolene; squat, stooped Brother Adolfus—and by their hands, roughened by cold and hard work or stained indelibly by buckets of ink. These men, who had so kindly welcomed me as a vagabond into their brotherhood, offered no signs of blessing, greeting, or welcome. Why would I expect it? Most of them had last seen me a month past, when my sister had led me from the abbey with shackled feet and silk-bound hands—a disgraced *recondeur*, named traitor to god and king, a liar and thief who had mocked their vows by pretending he could be worthy of their company, even for a season. And now ... chained to the ass that carried Gerard's body ... as if I were responsible ... My skin heated with shame.

"Set me loose," I said to Voushanti through my teeth. "I'll not run. Please. They'll think I did this."

But he wouldn't until we reached the bedraggled garden maze in front of the church. As the brothers lifted the boy gently and carried him toward the lavatorium where they would clean and wrap him properly, Voushanti detached my chain from the ass and led me toward the guesthouse like a troublesome dog.

Philo and Melkire awaited us in the guesthouse bedchamber, dark rings about their eyes and glaring resentment pouring off them like steam from a lathered horse. Voushanti unlocked my manacles and jerked his ugly head to the fine clothes, still strewn on the bed, and a copper washbasin sitting beside the hearth. "Clean and dress yourself."

Days of fear and frustration boiled over despite my best intents. "What, no whips? No dungeon? The abbey has a prison cell, you know. If I'm to be treated as a brainless dog, why not kennel me?"

Voushanti grabbed the laps of my cloak and dragged my head down to his, where I could not ignore the scarlet pits of his eyes. "I would gladly whip sense and respect into you, pureblood. Be sure of it. Your flesh is weak and your mind undisciplined. But our master has charged me to preserve your skin and your mind for *his* pleasure, and his will is our law. Now prepare yourself for his arrival." He shoved me away.

I clamped my hands under my folded arms, fighting to control my anger. Deep in my gut an ember flared in warning. Before very long—a day or two at most—its fire would grow to encompass my whole body, triggering the hunger for blood-spelled nivat seed. Ravaged with guilt on the day Luviar had died, I'd sworn off the doulon—the enchantment that transformed fragrant nivat into an odorless black paste that warped the body's experience of pain and pleasure. I'd thrown away my implements and the last of my nivat supply, so when the hunger came on me next, I had naught to feed it. That's when I would go mad.

"Have we word of His Grace?" Voushanti blocked the narrow doorway.

"Santiso rode in not an hour since," said Melkire. "He says the prince should arrive at any time. The other parties to the parley are expected tonight as well."

As the three of them discussed horses, guard posts, and the best places to billet Osriel's retinue, I stripped off my sodden garments. The water in the copper basin was tepid. A clean linen towel, many times mended, lay beside it. They'd left me no comb, but my hair had not grown much since it was trimmed to match my regrowing tonsure. I dunked my head in the basin and thought fleetingly of not pulling it out again.

I had to put the morning's events aside for now. I needed to use the next hours to the cabal's advantage. Perhaps I could acquire some notion of Osriel's plans in this damnable war or learn the nature of his power. His mother had been pureblood and clearly he had developed his magic far beyond the weak capabilities of other mixed-blood Navrons. But I didn't even know what parley was to happen here.

For three years, Osriel had sat on his gold mines in his mountainous principality of Evanore, weaving devilish enchantments while his half-brothers' war ravaged their own provinces of Ardra and Morian. Theories abounded on why he raided his brothers' battlefields and mutilated the dead—none of them pleasant. I had believed the stories of Osriel's depravities exaggerated until the night when Prince Bayard of Morian had flushed his brother Perryn to Gillarine's gates, slaughtering a hundred of Perryn's Ardran soldiers along the way. Hellish, dreadful visions had descended on the abbey that night, and by morning every corpse lay under Osriel's ensign and stared toward heaven eyeless. The monks had called it Black Night.

As I laced my chausses, Philo raced up the stair, snapped a salute, and reported Prince Osriel's arrival. "The prior has given him his own quarters and offered any building save the church for his use. His Grace sent me to fetch you, Mardane."

Voushanti eyed my half-dressed state. "Inform His Grace that I am unable to yield my charge until he summons his pureblood. I will deliver the sorcerer and my report at the same time."

Philo pressed a clenched fist to his breast and bowed briskly.

I refused to rush my dressing. The clothes were of the sort expected of purebloods: a high-necked shirt of black and green patterned silk, ruched at neck and wrists, a spruce-green satin pourpoint, delicately embroidered in black and seeded with black pearls, and a gold link belt. The doeskin boots felt like gloves. Ludicrous apparel for wartime in a burnt-out abbey. But if my master wished me decked out like a merchants' fair, so be it.

Voushanti's impatience came near scorching my back, but eventually my hundred buttons were fastened and fifty laces tied. I lifted the claret cape and mask and raised my brows. He jerked his head in assent. So other ordinaries were to be present, not just my master and his household.

The lightweight cape of embroidered silk fastened at my right shoulder with a gold-and-ivory brooch, shaped like a wolf's head. The mask, a bit of silk light as ash, slipped onto the left side of my face like another layer of skin and held its place without ties or bands of any kind. Someone had given my exact description to the one who had created and ensorcelled it. Of all pureblood disciplines, I most hated that of the mask.

Then we waited.

Though the great bronze bells had fallen from the church tower, the monks rang handbells to keep to their schedule of devotions and work. I would have preferred to get on with whatever vileness Osriel planned for me. It would save me fretting over the worthwhile tasks I ought to be attempting while I yet had a mind: rescuing Jullian, retrieving the book of maps, discovering where Sila Diaglou hid her supplies and trained her Harrower legions. I wasn't even sure whether or not the lighthouse yet existed after the ruinous assault on Gillarine.

I had believed the magical domed chambers and their astonishing cache existed underground below the abbey library and scriptorium, but I'd seen no evidence of the downward stair in the rubble. Why hadn't I asked Gram what had become of it? If Osriel chose to lock me away in one of his mountain fortresses, I might never learn. My contract with the prince, negotiated by my father and approved by the Registry, lacked the customary protections afforded more tractable pureblood progeny, thus allowing my master to do whatever he wished with me.

I slammed my fists against the window frame, rattling the glass in the iron casement. Voushanti snorted, but said naught.

By the time Philo brought the prince's summons, Vespers had rung through the early dusk. The ginger-bearded soldier led Voushanti and me past the charred hollows of the west-reach undercrofts, where the fires had been so fierce that the entire upper structure of the lay brothers' dorter had collapsed, and around behind the squat stone kitchen building to the refectory stair.

"His Grace will speak to the mardane first," said Philo. "The pureblood is to wait inside the door, where he can be seen." The ginger-haired warrior pulled on his helm, took up a lance propped against the wall, and joined Melkire in a proper alert stance flanking the wide oak door.

We entered the refectory halfway along one side of the long chamber. The barreled vault of the roof stood intact, but the tall windowpanes were broken and the pale yellow walls stained with smoke. The long tables and backless stools had been shoved together at the lower end of the cavernous hall.

The refectory had been my favorite place in the abbey. But no robust ale or steaming bowls of mutton broth sat ready to warm the belly on this eve. No beams of light streamed from the soaring lancet windows to warm the spirit. No grinning boys or teasing monks awaited to warm the heart. I splayed my five fingers and pressed my palm to my breast, praying Iero to welcome Gerard and to comfort Jullian, boys who had honored their god with such cheerful service.

Two braziers provided the only light or heat. They flanked a single plain wood chair set before the delicate stone window tracery that gaped empty at one end. There, robed and hooded as severely as any monk, our master awaited us.

"Stay here until you're called," muttered Voushanti.

An enigma, Voushanti. His touch left me queasy, and his glance induced me to spread my fingers in ward against evil. Yet for all his single-minded ferocity and spine-curling presence, the mardane had never harmed me. Together we had survived the ordeal in Mellune Forest.

He hurried across the worn wood floor and prostrated himself at Osriel's feet—an elaboration more suited to an Aurellian emperor than a Navron prince. The prince motioned Voushanti up, but only as far as his knees. I could not hear what was said, but felt the Bastard's anger stirring the shadows like the first breath of a storm wind.

If Voushanti's presence disturbed my stomach, Prince Osriel's disturbed my soul. My imagination conjured a thousand horrors beneath his hooded robe. Some said the prince was crippled; some said his body had been corrupted by his dealings with the Adversary.

The wind whistled and moaned through the broken windows, swirling the detritus of dust and glass that littered the floor. I twitched and fidgeted, fussed with my cloak, with my belt, with the iron latches of the lower windows. I strained to hear the monks' Vesper singing down in the ruined church, and tried to recall the words of the psalm and the comfort they promised. Deunor's fire . . . what was taking so long? Voushanti must be reciting every detail of the eight days since we had left Prince Osriel in Palinur. I tried not to imagine what punishments Osriel could devise for my morning's misbehavior. My every sense, every nerve, felt stretched to breaking.

The light wavered. For a moment I thought the flames in the braziers had gone out. But rather the shadows were creeping in from the corners and vaults to envelop the prince and his kneeling servant, roiling and thickening until I could scarcely see the two men. Sweat beaded the base of my spine beneath my fine layers, even while the night air pouring through the empty window frames froze my cheeks.

A quick strike of red light fractured the gathered darkness. Voushanti's shoulders jerked, and he could not fully muffle a groan. Twice more, each eliciting a similar cry, and then the mardane bent down as if to kiss Osriel's feet.

The prince, shapeless in his enveloping robes, leaned back in his chair. Voushanti climbed slowly to his feet. Stepping back a few paces, the mardane motioned me to approach.

Wishing myself five thousand quellae from this place, I took a deep breath and crossed the expanse of floor through the swirling dust and snow. Heat radiated from Voushanti's body as if he had swallowed the sun. As he bowed and withdrew, blood trickled from the unscarred corner of his mouth. *Mighty gods...*

Remembering Osriel's instruction from our last meeting, I whisked off my mask and looped it over my belt. My knees felt like porridge, my skin like cold fish.

"My lord prince," I said, touching my fingers to my forehead and bending one knee—the proper pureblood obeisance to his contracted master.

The flames in the two braziers shot into the air in spouts of blue and white flame, pushing back the rippling shadows. Not enough to reveal the prince's face. Only his hands were exposed. Long, slender, pale fingers, one adorned with a heavy gold ring. Their smooth firmness reminded me that Osriel was no older than I. He twitched the ringed finger, and I rose to my feet.

"Magnus Valentia." The harsh whisper came from behind and beside and before me, raising the hair on my arms. "The reports of your behavior puzzle me."

In our previous interview, the prince had expressed a preference for honesty over feigned deference, for boldness over cowering. Swallowing hard, I shoved fear aside, clasped my hands at my back, and hoped he'd meant it.

"How puzzled, my lord? Since leaving your side in Palinur, I have followed Mardane Voushanti's direction, and I've not strayed from his sight save when his sight was clouded with sleep. We traveled companionably. Indeed, we worked together to preserve the lives of your Evanori subjects on our journey from Palinur. Never once, even when Mardane Voushanti and his men were . . . debilitated . . . by the severities of that journey and we were separated by necessity, did I break my submission to you. Nor did I have any intention of doing so this morning when I aided the good prior to retrieve one of his abbey's lost children. Mardane Voushanti had no basis to assume I would run away." The weight of Osriel's attention slowed my words.

"Yet this morning's excursion occurred over his objections, and only after a monkish potion laid him low—he has reaped his proper harvest for *that* slip of attention. I instructed you to obey him as if his word were my own. So tell me, shall I punish *you* for disobedience, or shall I punish this Karish prior for poisoning my servants and abducting my pureblood for his own purposes?"

The questions and accusations nipped at my skin like the claws of demon gatzi. I kneaded my hands at my back, expecting to feel bloody pricks and scratches. *Hold on to your mind, Valen,* I thought. *No supernatural power exists in this room. You have felt the stirrings of true mystery in the Gillarine cloisters, and you have witnessed a living Dané dance his grief.* Whatever Osriel of Evanore might be— and I had no doubts he possessed power unknown to any of my acquaintance—he was neither god nor demon.

"Prior Nemesio believes that my novice vows, made but a few weeks ago, give him a claim on my loyalty. Though my oath to you is more recent, I saw no compromise of your interests in helping him retrieve a dead child."

I stepped closer to the chair and did not squirm. "As for potions and poisons, the unfortunate effect of the abbey's blessed water on Mardane Voushanti and his men is perhaps a reproof from their gods at some failure in their devotions. For surely, my cup was filled from the same pitcher, yet I did not fall asleep. Then, too, Mardane Voushanti arrived at the sad scene of this boy's death not half an hour after I did, thus he could not have been much affected. Were the prior's water poisoned, would not the mardane have suffered its effects longer? Or is there some reason his constitution does not succumb to the effects of potions or poisons?" I braced, expecting red lightning to strike.

But instead, the prince leaned his elbow on the arm of the chair and propped his chin on his hand. "Ah, Magnus, your tongue is as soft and quick as a spring zephyr in the Month of Storms . . . and just as deceitful. Unfortunately I've not the time to test your stamina at this game tonight. But I believe I shall reap great pleasure from our sparring in the deeps of this coming winter. Snug in my house, I shall strip you of your pureblood finery and raise the stakes for untruth."

I bowed, hiding my satisfaction, as well as my face, which his throaty humor had surely left void of color.

"And now we must discuss a few things before my guests arrive."

"Of course, my lord." I straightened my back and forced myself to breathe.

The prince angled his head upward, then waggled his hand toward the floor. "Sit," he said impatiently. "I've no wish to break my neck gaping upward. Is your father or brother so tall as you? Your grandfather, perhaps? Purebloods are of wholly modest stature."

"I am an aberration of pureblood lineage in countless ways, my lord. My own father would gleefully deny my birth had he not scribed it in the Register himself and seen the entry countersigned by two unimpeachable witnesses."

Off balance from his abrupt shift from chilling threat to peckish complaint, I settled on the wood floor and wrapped my arms about my knees. The hairs on the back of my neck prickled. The shadows that reeled and twirled on the refectory walls had no correspondence to the flames in the braziers. Nor did their shapes—heads, limbs, writhing torsos—correspond to those of the prince or my own body.

"An aberration? Yes, I suppose you could be," the prince mumbled.

I did not flinch or turn my head when his next comment seemed to come from behind my left ear. "So tell me who would be considered unimpeachable witnesses to a child's birth? Truth and lies are of infinite interest to me. I might like to interview such a person."

At least this answer was easy, though I could not fathom the intent of the question. "For good or ill, lord, the witnesses to my birth are beyond your inquiries. Indeed, they are more a part of your own history than mine. Two of my grandfather's oldest friends happened to be visiting our house on the day I was born—Sinduré Tobrecan of Evanore and Angnecy, the seventh Hierarch of Ardra, the very two clergymen who brought your father to Navronne from the realm of . . . angels."

"A most interesting coincidence."

Though forced to parrot the facts and validation of my lineage since I could speak, I'd never considered them at all interesting.

The prince settled back in his chair and did not move. Thinking, surely. Watching, too. The velvet hood might mask his own face, but I did not believe it obscured anything he wished to look on. Rather than squirm under his scrutiny, I stared back at him. From this angle

I could glimpse his jaw—fine boned, square, clean shaven—and mouth—generously wide, lips pale but even. Unsettling. *Well, of course,* I thought, after a moment, *he is Eodward's son.* Though I had met the king only once, every coin in the realm bore the imprint of those fine bones. What was so dreadful about Osriel's face that he kept it hidden, when his man Voushanti walked freely with his own ruined flesh bared for all to see?

"Tell me, Magnus, what magics can you work? You've said that you paid no mind to your tutors and that your inability to read prevented your study of pureblood arcana, but Voushanti's report indicates you are not incapable of spellworking. What have I received for my hundredweight of gold?"

No wisdom lay in *under*reporting my paltry skills in some hope that Osriel would set me free of my contract. He might decide my best use was that he made of corpses. *Over*reporting might yield me a better position in his house. My grandfather constantly babbled that I had talent beyond the usual for purebloods. Of course, even before he went mad, my grandfather had an overblown opinion of our family's talents, and I'd never seen evidence of anything extraordinary in myself.

"Honestly, my lord—you see, I remember you are very strict about honesty, even if the honest statement fails to please you—my catalogue of spells is thin. Beyond my family bent of route finding, tracking, identifying footsteps, and the like, I've meager skills in spellworking. Opening locks is perhaps my strongest, and I can accomplish voiding spells—making holes in things." I closed my eyes and wished I had more to report so that I might hold back some small secret advantage for the future. "I can work inflation spells—that is, I can create an illusion by exaggerating an existing object. For example, I once conjured a tree stump from a weed with spreading roots. Creating an illusion from nothing is beyond me . . ." Truly it was a pitiful collection when one considered the vast possibilities of magic.

I was straining to come up with something more to boost my worth, when the refectory door burst open and Voushanti hurried toward us. "My lord prince, your guest has arrived. As you commanded, I informed him that only the two principals and his pureblood would be allowed in your presence. He was not pleased, but neither did he leave."

"Well done, Mardane. You've taken the measure of his desperation, it would seem. Let him cool his heels for a moment, while I instruct my sorcerer."

The visitor had a pureblood in attendance. He was nobility, then, or clergy, or a civic official wealthy enough to purchase a pureblood contract, someone who thought to profit from traveling to this remote site to wait on the Bastard Prince, even as Osriel's eldest brother was ready to declare victory in Navronne. All parties to this war were realigning themselves since Prince Bayard's alliance with Sila Diaglou and the Harrowers had broken three years of stalemate.

Voushanti left as he had come. Once the door had closed behind him, Prince Osriel returned his attention to me. "I require your complete obedience tonight, sorcerer. Without reservation or any of your clever deceptions. You will stand to my right and slightly in front of me, angled where you can see my hands and I can see your face without moving my head. I wish you to listen carefully to all that's spoken and observe all that remains unspoken. You will say *nothing* without my permission. Do you understand? Nothing, even if you are addressed directly. But if I require you to respond or offer an opinion, you will speak in perfect honesty, without subterfuge or withholding. Is this clear or must we argue it? I promise you, I *will* prevail."

Though such threats could not but raise my hackles, innate perversity no longer drove me to pointless rebellion. For the sake of my friends in the cabal, I needed to learn what I could of Evanore's prince and those who came seeking his favor. So I rose and bowed, touching my forehead. "As you command, Your Grace."

If my master thought my presence would lend him some kind of prestige in a lordly negotiation, he had an unhappy lesson coming. By now every pureblood in the kingdom would know of Osriel's contract with the infamous Cartamandua renegade.

Moments after I slipped on my mask, straightened my cloak, and took my position at Prince Osriel's right hand, the great door burst open, and I gaped as if I'd seen a fish walk out of the ocean. Prince Bayard of Morian walked in, followed by his half-brother, Perryn of Ardra, and Bayard's attendant pureblood sorcerer—my own brother, Max.

Chapter 4

Bayard and Max, layered in mail, leather, and fur-lined traveling cloaks, each made a quick survey of the room. The two of them were similar in build, though Max's tight bulk came in a smaller package than the Duc of Morian, called the Smith for his brutal manners. The last I'd seen of Max, he had been chortling at the news of my father contracting his rebellious younger brother to the most feared man in Navronne.

Perryn, Duc of Ardra, remained near the door, shivering in grimed silk and torn lace, his once golden hair greasy and unkempt, his head bent, and his arms wrapped about his middle. His furtive glance took in Osriel and the dancing shadows. Then, as if he had seen enough, he hugged himself tighter and closed his eyes.

Max bowed respectfully to Osriel, touching his forehead with his fingertips. His eyes reflected humorous irony as he pivoted to face me, touching one middle finger to the center of his brow—the proper greeting of one pureblood to another while in the presence of ordinaries.

I made sure to close my mouth, which still hung open in astonishment. Unsure whether my master would consider a returned greeting as speech, I remained motionless, my hands at my back, grateful for the mask that might hide the extent of my surprise. What possible circumstance could bring Bayard supplicant to his despised youngest brother in the very hour of his triumph? Every notion of politics claimed the Smith should be seated on Caedmon's throne at this moment, planting his brutish foot on the necks of groveling Ardran nobles.

"So is this the kind of foolery the terrifying Osriel spends his time on? Playing with shades and gargoyles in a Karish ruin?" Bayard's posture, feet apart, hands resting lightly at his waist, spoke everything of self-assurance. But deep creases in his brow and stretched smudges about his eyes hinted that victory did not rest firmly within his grasp . . . as if his presence at this assignation so far from Palinur was not indication enough.

"Is one fool's occupation to be preferred to another's? My shades leave no one bleeding." Prince Osriel's cool jibe heated his elder brother's cheeks. "You requested this parley, brother. And you said I should choose a neutral venue."

Osriel snapped his fingers. The flames in the twin braziers surged to the height of a man, causing the shadows to lengthen and dance wildly. Two armless wooden chairs took shape out of nothing, positioned to face him. Bayard paled and shifted uneasily.

My master gestured toward the chairs. "Come, brothers, sit. I would not have you stand like servants or courtiers. I've missed our long dinners with Father, talking of history and geography, building and art. Should I send for food and wine? Perhaps we could begin again in his memory." The words pelted the faces of his brothers like hailstones, evoking a cascade of expressions, even as they whetted my own curiosity.

"No need for games, Bastard. You know why I'm here." Bayard snatched one of the chairs, realizing only after he'd sat how awkwardly it suited. It was much too small for his blacksmith's frame. Max moved to Perryn's side, touched his arm, and gestured to the second chair. The blond prince shook his head and huddled deeper into his own embrace. One might have thought him cowed, save for the occasional glance of purest hate that speared Bayard's back.

"I am guessing you've at last seen Father's writ of succession," said Osriel. "And that you are preparing to proclaim to the people of Navronne that it names you heir, just as you've insisted all these years that it would. But we know the truth of that, don't we? As does our frighted brother. Have you found a better forger than his?"

The truth laid out so quietly exploded in my head. My gaze snapped from one to the other. Osriel—Eodward's named successor? I recalled the grand depiction of the *ordo mundi* painted on the walls of the Gillarine guesthouse and imagined it flipped end over end, the denizens of heaven and hell dislodged and poured out to mingle with the tangled creatures of earth's sphere. Horror, wonder, denial, and awe mastered me in rapid succession.

One would think Bayard chewed iron. "You will never wear my father's crown, Bastard. I'll gift it to a Hansker chieftain first."

"So what do you propose to do about this little disappointment?"

Osriel's throaty whisper exuded subtle menace. "Do you think to snatch those few who know the truth and feed them to Sila Diaglou? I hear her executions are most efficient, if a bit gruesome. I quite resent your allowing the bloodthirsty priestess to destroy *my* city and slaughter *my* subjects—even holy monks, I've heard."

All confused bulk and outrage, Bayard spluttered. "Navrons will never accept a crippled, half-mad sorcerer as king. You've no warrior legion and no strength to lead one. That's why you've never pressed a claim. Fires of Magrog, you sneak onto our battlefields and mutilate the dead. You squat on your treasure, waiting for the two of us to kill each other off—"

"You and Perryn chose your own course of fraternal mayhem," snapped Osriel. "I warned you at the beginning I would not play. As for the rest, I have my own purposes. Now, what do you want of me? I will never kneel to you. Put that right out of your thoughts."

Osriel . . . king. Every belief must shift and skew at the imagining.

Bayard burst from his chair, swung around behind it, and gripped the squared oak back, as if wrestling a hurricane into submission. Both face and posture declared he would prefer to open his belly with a dagger than speak what he had come to say. "The woman Sila Diaglou is a demon gatzé. But using her legion of madmen was the only way I could get this sniveling imbecile to heel before he burnt my ships and yards—our only hope to hold off the spring raids from Hansk. I agreed to cede her territory—some wild lands, a few villages, a town or two. She said that with sovereign territory 'properly cleansed,' she could prove to the rest of us the power of her Gehoum. But this lunacy she's wrought in Palinur . . ." He spat his words through the bitter edge of humiliation. "I gave her no mandate for executions. I ordered her to stand down and withdraw her filthy lunatics from the city, but her partisans goad everyone to their own madness. Now the witch has presented me with a list of demands, threatening to raze Palinur and set her madmen on Avenus and other cities if I don't comply. I've squeezed Morian's treasury dry to get this far, believing I'd have Navronne's wealth—mine by right— to control her at the end. But what have I found?"

He strode to Perryn, huddled against the wall, dragged him to Osriel's feet by the neck of his silk tunic, and shoved him sprawling. Perryn threw his arms over his head and lay quivering, and I cursed myself once again for ever believing he was man enough to lead Navronne.

"This parasite," snarled Bayard, "this weak-livered vermin, did not merely exhaust Ardra's patrimony, but Navronne's, as well.

Our father's treasure house sits empty, its gold squandered on oranges from Estigure, on brocades and perfumed oils from Syanar, on follies, jugglers, and lace, on miniature ponies for his whores, on puling spies and legions of mercenaries from Aurellia and Pyrrha who have never set foot in Navronne, if they exist at all. If I am to crush this devil woman, I must have Evanore's gold."

Osriel perched on the edge of his chair, coiled tight as a chokesnake. Bayard bulled ahead without a breath. "You will not have to kneel. You will have autonomy in your own land until the day of your death, and I will recognize you publicly as my sovereign equal in Evanore. Together, we can prevail. Together . . ." Bayard's speech trailed away in the face of his brother's frigid stillness.

"What does she want?" said Osriel, quiet and harsh.

Bayard's beard quivered with pent rage. "It doesn't *matter* what she wants. She's a madwoman. We yield on these demands and she'll come back for more. I see that now."

Osriel leaned forward slightly, and I knew Bayard felt the pressure of his brother's will as I had earlier. "Tell me what she asked for."

Heaving a sigh of suffering patience, Bayard whipped his hand toward Max. "Tell him."

My brother stepped forward and bowed slightly to his master. "First, she demands the province of Evanore, whole and entire. Second, she desires that one of my lord's brothers, either one, be turned over to her as mortal forfeit for the offenses the line of Caedmon has wrought against the Gehoum." My brother cataloged the unthinkable as if the items sat on a shelf like tin pots.

Osriel tented his pale hands, his fingertips just touching his chin. He did not speak.

Max bowed again and flicked a glance at me. "Third, she desires a piece of information—the location of a secret library that she claims is anathema to the Gehoum. It does not appear to exist where she was told. And lastly, she wishes to own the contract of a particular pureblood sorcerer."

"A pureblood?" Prince Osriel dropped his hands abruptly into his lap. "Who? For what reason?"

The public half of Max's face remained perfectly neutral as his position required. But an eye accustomed to looking past a pureblood's mask could not miss the wicked humor behind the sheath of dull blue silk. "She insists on controlling one Magnus Valentia de Cartamandua-Celestine, lately returned to the discipline of the Pureblood Registry. She did not explain why."

Magrog's teeth! My suddenly sweating hands came near slipping out of each other behind my back.

Bayard shoved his chair away so viciously it tipped over and clattered to the floor. "The cheek!" he fumed, striding to the windowed wall only to reverse course and return to kick the toppled chair. "As if I would go scrambling about the city like her pet hound, hunting libraries and purebloods. My own sorcerer's brother, as if that would make her my equal." He paused and glared at me as if Sila Diaglou stood behind me with her hand on my shoulder. "What does she want with you, pureblood, eh? I hear you are a renegade, a liar, and a thief."

Mind reeling, I pinned my gaze on Osriel's hands. They were still, so I kept silent and asked myself the same question. Why would the Harrower priestess want me? Not merely for the Cartamandua blood. Max . . . Phoebia . . . my father had no contract, for the gods' sake. They all displayed the bent of my grandfather's line. Unlike me, they were trained and skilled and intelligent enough to read books and make sense of the world.

"You'd best keep an eye on him, little brother," said Bayard with a sneer. "By the Mother's tits, I'd give her Perryn and offer to gut him myself, save for the damnable impertinence of her insisting on a kill of my own blood. But Evanore . . ."

Perryn had crept to the foot of Osriel's chair and hunched there in a shriveled knot. "You wouldn't let him give me over, brother," he said. "I was ever kind to you. It was Bayard played the bully. He swears he'll do this bargain, and throw you in as well if he can persuade the witch to forgo Evanore's gold."

"Does anyone outside this room know that you two have come to me?" Osriel spoke over Perryn's head as if the fair prince were some whining hound.

Bayard spluttered. "My aides know, of course. My field commanders. I'm not a fool—"

"Tell me the truth, Bayard, or I'll send you back with an ox head instead of your own. Does *anyone* but these two know you've come to Gillarine to meet *me*?"

"No one else knows," said Perryn, emboldened like a lapdog that finds its courage only at its master's feet. "He says we must be secret, else she'll find out he's plotting against her. He near pisses his trews at the thought. She sees everything."

"Good." Osriel pointed to a spot in front of his chair. "Now stand here, the both of you, and listen. Yes, you, too, Perryn. Your 'kindness' fell short back when your pleasure was to lock me into emptied meat casks. Stand like a man and listen to me."

Perryn slouched to his feet, while Bayard stood his ground ten paces back, bristling like an offended boar. My master waited silently. Only when Bayard expelled an exasperated oath and moved to Perryn's side did Osriel speak again.

"You came here seeking my help, brothers. Did you think I would shovel gold into your pockets and allow you to continue sending my people to the slaughter as you've done these three years? You've countenanced crimes that make my activities look tame, and I should rightly take your heads for it."

Reason. Assurance. Command. Of a sudden this mad parley felt grounded in something more than terror.

"I am the rightful High King of Navronne, whether anyone beyond this room ever understands that or not, and you will stand or fall by my will."

"You are a crippled whelp who knows nothing of warfare." Bayard spat the brave words, but held his position in the place his half-brother had indicated. He must be at the end of all recourse.

Osriel raised a hand in warning. "I am allowing myself to believe that the two of you have been stupid and blind these three years, rather than vile and malicious, and that your excesses have been as misreported as my own deeds. Either we work together to salvage this mess you've made, or you can walk out of here this moment. As for the fool who attempts to touch my gold without my consent, I will take his eyes living from his head and hold his soul captive in everlasting torment. Choose, brothers. For Navronne. For our father, who foolishly believed in all of us."

A seething Bayard, his complexion the hue of bloomed poppies, whirled and strode away. I was certain he would broach the door, but instead he circled the refectory. Perryn lifted his chin, sneering as if ready to defy both brothers, but glanced at the ceiling, peopled by writhing shades, shuddered, and dropped his head again. Osriel waited. I held my breath.

Halfway between his brothers and the door, Bayard slowed, growling with resentful fury. "What do you propose? I concede nothing until I've heard your plan."

Osriel flicked his ringed hand toward me. "Magnus, tell me: Is your brother trustworthy? I will send him out if you say."

Max stiffened as if one of Silos's firebolts had fused his spine. Not the least hint of a smirk appeared on either half of his face. For a pureblood adviser to be dismissed in a negotiation accounted him as

useless to his master. If report spread of such a thing, it could ruin
Max.

Past grievance, childish pride, and my every base instinct gloated
in such opportunity. Yet, for some reason surpassing all speculation,
my brother and I stood at a nexus of Navronne's history. My master,
who astonished and mystified me more by the moment, required me
to offer a fair measure of a man I scarcely knew. And I'd begun to
think I'd best heed the Bastard's wishes. Petty vengeance had no
place here.

"My brother is not and has never been my friend, Lord Prince," I
said. "Neither has he been my enemy save in the petty strife of family and as a danger to my freedom in my years away from my family.
I have encountered him only briefly as a man, thus I can say nothing
of his honor or his moral strength. But he has ever supported and
embraced the strictures of pureblood life. Thus I believe he would do
nothing to the detriment of his bound master. In any matter of con-
tractual obligation, I would trust him completely."

"Good enough. He stays." Osriel's brisk assent near sucked the
words from my mouth before I could speak them. He nodded to
Bayard. "Here is what I propose, brother: Send your pureblood back
to Sila Diaglou. Tell her you accept her terms."

"What?" Bayard bellowed.

The green shoots of hope that had sprung up so unexpectedly in
the past hour were sheared off in an instant. The Harrower priestess
had plunged a stake through Boreas's gut, reciting her blasphemous
incantations: *sanguiera, orongia, vazte, kevrana*—bleed, suffer, die,
purify. And then she had licked my old comrade's blood from her fingers. I struggled to hold my position without trembling.

"Great Kemen preserve!" said Perryn, looking as if he would be
sick. The blond prince backed toward the door. "You can't do that,
you twisted, depraved—"

"Have your man say that your brother Perryn is already forfeit
because of his treasonous looting of Navronne's treasury and his forgery of our father's will." Osriel pressed forward, his words harsh,
decisive, shivering the air. "Have him report that your bastard
brother is mad and can be persuaded to yield his land, his pureblood,
and the secret of the library. Set a meeting with the woman and use
it to haggle with her over the gold and apportioning of Evanore—
she will never believe you would concede it all. Let her think she is
going to win, while you control the damage as you can. At the last,
settle for the best deal you can make, with the stipulation that her
legions enter Evanore at Caedmon's Bridge and attack my hold at

Renna on the winter solstice. Tell her that I submit myself to Magrog at Dashon Ra each year at midnight on the winter solstice; thus my magic will be at an ebb."

"And then?" Bayard growled in contempt and snatched Perryn's sleeve, before the cowering prince could run away.

"Either the joined might of Eodward's sons defeats her, or the world we know will end."

The simplicity of this declaration left Bayard speechless. My head spun; my stomach lurched at the speed of events. Even Max's mouth hung open.

"Osriel, you *are* mad," said Bayard, recovering his wits sooner than my brother or I. "And I must be mad to listen to you. Yet Father's writ claims— Tell me this, Bastard. What do you do with dead men's eyes?"

The challenge echoed from the vaults as if the hideous beings dancing there had joined in the question. I wanted to cry out in chorus, "Yes, yes, tell us."

"Ask first of Sila Diaglou how long she plans to let you rule," said Osriel with such quiet menace as to raise the hair on my arms. "Bring me her truthful answer, and I'll give mine."

Osriel uncurled one slender hand to reveal a white ball of light, pursed his lips, and blew on it. A shivering lance of power split the air between Max and Bayard, causing Perryn to yelp and crouch into a ball at Bayard's feet. "This will keep our brother quiet for the nonce. Lock him up safely, where no one can harm him. I'll send a messenger to your headquarters in Palinur on the anniversary of Father's coronation. At that time, you can inform me of the outcome of your negotiations, and I'll notify you of any change in plan."

Perryn pawed at his mouth and tongue in a wordless, animal frenzy I recognized. Poor, stupid wretch. How many words did his tongue-block forbid?

Bayard folded his arms and stared boldly at the man in the green hood, reclaiming something of the pride he had brought into the hall, but little of the arrogance. "You wear Father's ring. I assumed this sniveling twit had stolen it from his dead finger, then feared to wear it publicly."

Osriel's slim fingers caressed the gold band. "Father gave it to me the night he died. Believe that or not as you choose. Perhaps I stole it. Perhaps my devilish magic twisted his mind."

Testing. All of this was testing. Would Bayard believe? Would he accept what was offered or balk in arrogance, in self-deception, in fear? Would I? For I could not shake the notion that all of this was my test as well. Osriel had no need of me in this confrontation. I brought no power, no prestige, no insight that such a perceptive mind could not have come up with on its own. Yet a man of such well-considered purposes would not have me here without specific intent. Perhaps it was only to witness a kind of power I had known but twice in my life: in an abbey garden when an abbot had peered into my soul and found it worthy of his trust, and long ago beside a battlefield cook fire, when these princes' father had shared his love of Navronne with a youthful pikeman.

After a moment, Bayard shook his head. "Father's writ purports to explain why he chose you over me. Reading it, I heard his voice as clear as if he spoke to me aloud. 'Twas the Ardran hierarch showed me the thing, and I destroyed his chamber after. Had the Karish peacock shitting his robes, I did, naming him a cheat and a forger, as mad as you to believe our father wrote such lies about a crippled weakling."

"Father valued you, Bayard. If you read the entire writ, then you know he named you Defender of Navronne and your sons after you, believing that your strong arm and stubborn temper should hold the righteous sword that mine cannot." It was the nearest thing to an apology I ever thought to hear from royalty. A gift offered without coercion, without demand for reciprocation, with humbling generosity.

I thought Bayard would pounce on Osriel and grind him in his jaws. "Why didn't he *tell* us? He knew what I believed. What everyone in this kingdom believed. Every day of my life I trained to be king, and he never told me elsewise." Pain, not anger, drove his fury—a familiar anguish, rooted in family, in a child's expectation and betrayal.

"You trained to be a warrior, Bayard, not a king. Father made his decision only after I turned one-and-twenty and showed some prospect of living for more than a moon's turning. He told me first. Then Perryn. But you were off pursuing Hansker again, and he would not have you hear such news from any lips but his. Nor would he shame you by telling another soul before you. But you spent more time on your ships than in Navronne those last few years. How many times did he summon you home? He risked everything to save your pride and lost the gamble." A gentle reproof, taking its power from unbending strength.

"I could not abandon my men halfway between Hansk and Morian just so I could play courtier. Let up the pressure, and barbarians lose all respect. I saved Navronne. I—"

Bayard cut off his own protest. Even he could hear how foolish it sounded now after three years of war and thirty thousand Navrons dead. He spat on the floor. "You'll never rule; you know that. A bastard. The evil stories told of you. Clerics of either stripe won't accept it. The people won't. Not when there's a strong, legitimate elder son. The hierarch's paper is ensorcelled so it cannot be destroyed, sad to say, but without a valid second copy no one will believe it."

Osriel did not accept the gauntlet Bayard threw, but rather slipped it back on his brother's hand. Only time would tell whether he had left a spider in its folds. "We will preserve this kingdom first, brother, and then turn our minds to its ruling. I'd recommend you not go setting any crowns on your head before the solstice."

Bayard jerked his head in assent. "I'll see you on the solstice, then. Betweentimes . . . I'd recommend you look to your back, little Bastard. I think you're the only thing in this world the mad priestess fears."

Bayard grabbed Perryn's collar and shoved the moaning princeling toward the door. Max hurried ahead and held open the door, casting me a long, curious gaze before following his master from the room.

As soon as the door had closed behind Max, the flames in the braziers faded. The shadows flowed together, pooling in corners, settling over the monks' tables and stools. The man in green slumped backward in his chair and leaned his head tiredly on his fist.

My mind, numbed with wonder and shock at what had just unfolded, slowly began to function again. Should I kneel to my king or should I topple his chair through the gaping windows and protect Navronne from a madman, a honey-tongued servant of Magrog who had convinced me that even the evils he acknowledged would admit to rational explanation?

Before I could choose any course, he swiveled his head my way, still resting his temple on his pale fingers. His eyes remained shielded behind his green velvet hood, but I felt their scrutiny. "So advise me on my plan, Magnus Valentia. Perhaps I should allow this bargain with the priestess to stand. The land is mine. The pureblood is mine. I know the whereabouts of the lighthouse. My brother Perryn has fallen to ruin in defeat and is useless to anyone. Bayard has too many dead Navrons on his conscience to be trustworthy. I could throw him into the bargain and allow Sila Diaglou to take care of all my problems."

Slowly, deliberately, I removed my mask and tucked it into my belt. A hundred responses darted through my head. I could not be easy, not with my fate bandied about as a bargaining chip of less worth than a slip of gold from Evanore's mines. Yet neither fear nor resentment shaped my answer. "You wish me to be honest, my lord. So I must confess, I am very confused."

Confused was too simple a word. I could not shake a growing admiration for this man—the same villain who had bound Jullian in terror to manipulate me, who claimed pleasure in bending minds to his will and refused to deny he stole the eyes of the dead. In the space of an hour I had both learned the unthinkable truth that the Bastard of Evanore was the rightful king of Navronne, and heard enough to suspect that choice not so unthinkable. Even as he quipped of betrayal and surrender, the echo of his charge to Bayard fed a mad and greening hope. Beyond shadows and sparring, nothing this man did was a lie—which frightened me to the marrow. Yet . . .

He laughed, deep and convincing. And familiar. Was I again recalling his father who had smiled as he watched me dance away the horrors of battle so long ago?

"I, too, sit confused," he said, "for I know why Sila Diaglou wants the lighthouse. She wishes to destroy it so there will be no healing or recovery from the ravaging she plans. And I know—"

"Iero's everlasting grace!" The shattering explosion of truth set my mind reeling. *Healing . . . recovery . . .* spoken like good Eodward's chosen heir . . . a prince who hid wisdom and reason behind a gargoyle's mask . . . who had sent his newly acquired pureblood out to rescue two holy men that a villain had no reason to aid. No discretion, no forethought, no tactic could keep my discovery from my lips. "You're Luviar's man!"

Chapter 5

"My princely pride prefers to think Luviar was *my* man. You understand, pureblood, that your tongue will blacken and rot before I allow you to speak those words outside this room." A red glow suffused two fingers of Prince Osriel's left hand as he made a slight circular gesture.

I clamped the back of my hand to my mouth, battling a sudden nausea as my tongue grew hot and swelled to half again its normal size. The taste of decay . . . of rotten meat . . . flooded my mouth. *Spirits of night!*

At the very moment I believed I must choke on my own vomit, the sensations vanished. I took a shuddering breath. "Not a word to anyone, lord. Not a word."

"Only five living persons—and now you as a sixth—know that Luviar de Savilia was my first tutor. He remained so until I was ten, when my father built Gillarine and installed him as its abbot. He would have schooled me here, but . . . circumstances prevented it."

My mind raced. Who else would be privy to such a secret? Brother Victor, of course; if Luviar had been one face of a coin, Victor was its obverse. And Stearc, who was himself a student of Gillarine, and the first to bear the title of lighthouse Scholar, would surely know. But Elene had been horrified . . . disgusted . . . when I asked her about Osriel, so perhaps Gram, not Stearc's daughter, was a third. Yet Gram was wary of this prince.

I must be wary, too. Perhaps this was but a ploy to pry names from me. "Lord, these other five . . . they must be Luviar's people as well."

"Some are. Some are not. If you are attempting to discover whether I know that Thane Stearc and his daughter and his secretary have plotted with Brother Victor, Prior Nemesio, your sister the

Sinduria, and even young Jullian to salvage what they can of learning before Sila Diaglou remakes the world, the answer is yes. If you are asking me to tell you which of those conspirators might know of my involvement with the lighthouse cabal, I will not, for you are not to speak of it with *anyone*."

I licked my dry lips. No need to remind me of that. "But *Brother Gildas* did not know?"

"Ah. Indeed that is perhaps the one favorable circumstance of this betrayal."

"So you know that Brother Gildas . . ."

". . . has taken the boy and the book of maps. Yes. And we must assume he is taking them to Sila Diaglou. Which means we must wonder if her demands of my brother will change once she knows what she has." He held up four fingers and ticked off one and then a second. "It is obvious why the priestess wants the lighthouse. Its treasures thwart her aims of an ignorant, helpless populace. As for why she desires one of Caedmon's line to go under her knife: My family is consecrated to Navronne—I will be displeased if you laugh too openly at that consideration after such close viewing of us three together—and she has long held that our blood will be all the more potent for these purification rites she works, releasing a great deal of power at the same time."

He wagged his third finger, offering me no opening to respond. "As for Evanore . . . she hungers for it. Not solely for its gold, for which she has little use, but because my land is the true heart of Navronne, which is the Heart of the World. You have not seen such magic as can be worked in Evanore."

The prince wriggled his remaining finger. "But you, Magnus Valentia de Cartamandua-Celestine . . . why did she ask for *you* instead of your grandfather's book? You have already unlocked the maps to her man Gildas. To seek out Danae holy places so that she can work her abominations, all she needs is the book and time enough to use it. You've no more insight than the monk as to *which* places in the book are significant—perhaps less—and a book is far easier to manage than an obstreperous pureblood. Certainly purebloods have skills in magic—most of them superior to yours, it seems—but Sila considers your kind a disease akin to royalty and practors, an affront to the Gehoum, and she vows to dispossess purebloods of their favored place in the world. Did you not know that? So lay your mind to the question. Why does she want you?"

The wind moaned through the jagged glass. A quick review of everything I had learned and experienced over the past weeks, most especially my grandfather's fractured testimony, brought me only one conclusion. "I suppose because I can take her past the boundaries of the maps. Gildas can lead her to any location on the maps, but to travel deeper into the realms of the Danae, they'd need my grandfather or me. My grandfather told me that my bent could take me anywhere . . . even to places he had not mapped . . . even to the boundaries of heaven or hell. Silly to think . . . No one would believe such a thing."

The prince settled back in his chair. "The boundaries of hell . . . I doubt you'd care for that."

My skin crept. He spoke as if he'd visited there.

Dread encircled and choked me like smoke from the braziers. "I've told the others, and so, I suppose you know that these murderous rites the Harrowers perform destroy the Danae guardians and corrupt the Canon. If Sila Diaglou were to lead her Harrower legions into their land . . . My lord, what better way to accomplish her ambitions than to destroy them all?"

He fell into a deadly stillness. Then he rose from his chair and grasped the back of it for a moment, as if to steady himself. "Well then, we certainly can't allow you to fall into her hands."

He turned away and moved in measured steps, not toward the outer door, but toward the kitchen stair. His shapeless green robes hinted at a slender man slightly more than average height.

This could not be the end of the subject. Luviar's passion . . . the certainty of the darkness to come . . . only in these past few days had the urgency penetrated my understanding: the end of the Danae . . . the death of Navronne . . . the long night, the end of the world we knew become a reality as palpable as the wood beneath my feet.

"My lord, protecting *me* is not enough," I said to his back. "What if they've other ways to make the attempt? What if they abduct my grandfather? The danger—"

"Your sister has secured your grandfather and hidden him somewhere not even I can find." He paused at the edge of the pool of light cast by the braziers. "You've tested well, Magnus. Better than the first reports led me to expect. That morning in Palinur . . . Voushanti doubted your mind's clarity."

"My lord, what use do *you* think to make of me?" Even as the essential question took shape in my head, I was not sure I could bear the answer. Such a deep-buried longing gripped my heart, far deeper and more profound than the doulon hunger, I thought my chest must burst.

"I think you have just answered that question," said Osriel, as if plucking thoughts from my head. "The Danae dance on the solstice; did you know that? Whatever magic exists in the world is renewed on that night. The music of the universe reaches its crescendo, so they say, and without magic we will not prevail. That's why I chose that day for our confrontation with Sila Diaglou. The assistance we need from the Danae must be arranged before they dance. And someone must warn them of the priestess and her plot."

The treacherous, trickster Danae. Blue fire spun in my head . . . dragons and herons and long muscled limbs. Glimmers of light and shadow shifted and leaped on the burnished wood floor. I stared unblinking, as if these things might form some pattern I could comprehend.

"Good night, friend Valen."

Startled, I glanced up to see his pale lips graced with quiet amusement. And for the first time that evening, he spoke without whisper or throaty harshness. So familiar.

Words rushed out of me. "Your Grace, this night has left my curiosity pricked beyond all reason. Excuse my impertinence, but you are not at all the person I expected. And I have a fancy . . . foolish, I know . . . that we are not strangers. I would look upon your face, lord, that I might know my rightful king."

"You're not afraid? Even my eldest brother, who regularly dropped me down the sewage sluice at our father's house in Avenus, fears me. And rightly so." His gold ring gleamed in the dying light, defining his hand against his shapeless robes.

"I do fear you, lord. Reason demands it. Instinct insists upon it. Yet I do not find myself afraid."

"I've planned to force your service blind," he said. "How can I trust you—a proven, skillful liar? I've been given reason to believe you involved in the matter of this murdered boy. And you could easily have betrayed Luviar and Victor, hoping to buy yourself a more comfortable future."

"No, my lord! I never—" Guilt aborted my protest. For certain he must feel the heat of my shame about Luviar's death. Yet some circumstance had gained me his favor. "The mission to rescue Abbot Luviar and Brother Victor . . . you were testing me."

"Luviar, may his Creator cherish his great soul, trusted you. That—and desperation—bought you that morning's chance. I *do* regret I had to use Jullian in such vile fashion, but I had no time to argue or explain or devise a better trial." He raised a hand and the flames in the braziers flared, bathing us both in yellow light. "I suspect Luviar was right. He said you were but lost and searching for your place. Perhaps that place is at my side . . . for as long as I can survive." His smile widened, and he lifted his hood.

I gawked like a crofter's child brought to a palace. Then a pleasured warmth suffused both flesh and spirit. Reclaiming sense, I sank to one knee and touched fingers to forehead, making proper obeisance to my bound master and sovereign lord . . . to the Thane of Erasku's intelligent and persuasive secretary, Gram.

"My Lord Voushanti!" The urgent voice and pelting footsteps from the bottom of the guesthouse stair halted my ascent and spun Voushanti halfway round.

The mardane was escorting me to my bedchamber. No matter that for me the sun had shifted in its course, Voushanti's zeal to ensure my security and compliance with our master's wishes had not.

"We've trouble!" Philo, chest heaving, cheeks ruddy, beard and leathers dusted with snow, appeared at the bottom of the stair carrying a lantern. "Harrowers accosted Ervid and Skay on the road to Elanus. When the orange-heads found the prince's safe passage letter on Skay, they tore into him. Left him for dead. Ervid fought free, but instead of pushing on with his dispatches, the fool bided and brought Skay back here."

"Has he lost his mind?"

"They're lovers, lord. He could not—"

"Were they followed?" Voushanti's question punctured Philo's excuses like a bodkin.

"He believes not, sir. Skay lies in the monks' kitchen. His life ebbs quickly, lord. If the prince—" The warrior's voice quavered and halted. Fear for a friend's life? Fear of Osriel's wrath?

Of course, Philo would not be privy to Gram's secret. This facade of horror . . . the gruesome stories . . . had been spread to shield a frail man with too few warriors to hold his own in war. And he had devised this masquerade to allow him to move freely through the kingdom, for his brothers' supporters would have no qualms at removing the inconvenient bastard from the reckoning of power.

"Post Havor's men about the abbey's inner walls," snapped Voushanti. "I'll inform His Grace."

I'd wager my life that Voushanti—the loyal bodyguard, messenger, nursemaid—was one of those few who knew Osriel's secret. Yet the mardane was not a true member of the cabal. He served Osriel only.

Philo pressed a fist to his breast and vanished into the gloom below. Voushanti motioned me up the stair. "Get to your bed and sleep, pureblood. We'll likely be traveling tomorrow. And I'll advise you: Do not wander. It's a dangerous night to be abroad."

In the depths of his black eyes the warning gleamed like molten iron. This was a dangerous *season* to be abroad.

"Will your duties permit you sleep tonight, Mardane?"

Amusement lifted the unscarred corner of his mouth. "Matters do not seem promising."

As he galloped down the steps, I slogged upward again. Sleep . . . after such a day. My body felt as if the clouds had opened and rained stones on me. Yet how could my mind ever still itself enough to sleep? The prince had not lingered in his hall after his revelation, but assured me that we would talk more in the morning when Stearc and his daughter would join us. If they did not have Jullian and Gildas in safekeeping, we would set out in search of them by midday. The prince . . . Osriel . . . Gram.

No mystery now how the cabal had come by the journal of Eodward's tutor. Or why Stearc offered his secretary such deference and care. Perhaps Elene had been near panic when I inquired about Osriel, not from distressed sensibility at her lord's depravity, but fear that somehow I had guessed a perilous secret. Eodward's chosen heir . . . I had witnessed Gram's intelligence, reason, judgment, his calm strength that had naught to do with arms. Aye, but therein lay the peril. How could a man with no legions hold a fortress, much less win a kingdom?

I rounded the last spiral of the stair carefully, wishing I carried a torch. Only a faint wash of a rushlight in the upper passage touched the steps, leaving most of them dark as spilt ink. I grabbed the rushlight from its bracket and carried it with me. The coals in my bedchamber hearth were carefully banked, but I let them lie for morning. Instead I threw off my cloak and attacked my legions of buttons, hoping Gram would not require such grandiose attire too often.

Great gods . . . Gram . . . Every time I thought I had accepted what had just happened, a wave of excitement washed over me. I'd never felt like this before . . . a part of something so important, something that felt so right. Of course, not even the most foolhardy gambler would risk his coin on our chance to put Gram on Caedmon's throne, much less to hold off the plagues and famine that augured the coming years of trial. Even if Bayard kept to this truce of necessity, the prince must confront Sila Diaglou on the winter solstice, some two months hence. A night of magic, perhaps, but even devout Karish folk believed the longest night of the year to be the apex of the

Adversary's strength, when he set in place his schemes to ensnare the innocent, while the angel legions sang in holy chorus and formed up ranks to face him.

The choice of that particular night for Gram's first step was perhaps the finest irony of this whole tangled story. For I had been born at midnight on the winter solstice, so the family tale had always run— the ill-famed winter's child of bardic rhymes, the get of gatzi, conceived when Magrog's demonic servants infiltrated the bawdy rites of spring. And on this birthday would I turn my grandfather's mysterious eight-and-twenty. My ears itched with his whispering: *Thou shalt be the greatest of the Cartamandua line. Thou art of my blood, incomparably strong in magic.* I, the least gifted of men. Grinning like a fool, I shed the satin pourpoint, wondering if it was too late to learn a bit of spellworking.

And then, from out of nowhere, an invisible ax shattered my skull. Knives . . . lacerating . . . my flesh bathed in fire. Paralyzed with dread . . . awash in pain . . . drowning in blood . . .

Choking, gasping, I dropped to my knees. The weak glimmer of the rushlight seared my eyes with the glare of a thousand suns. Gray, transparent faces, twisted with hate, hovered above me, striking . . . cutting . . . I felt my bones shatter. Blade-rent, beaten, my body reported every color of pain, and my mind every nuance of grief, of rage, of regret, of unfounded horror and hatred.

Even as I experienced the agony of such wounding and felt a frigid numbness creep upward from my toes, I knew my limbs whole and unmarked, my palms resting on cold, solid stone. No one stood beside me.

The physical pain ceased as abruptly as it had begun. The emotional tumult dwindled more slowly into a directionless anger. Then that, too, faded until I was empty of all but my own terror. I lay curled on the floor, trembling, my arms wrapped about my knees, afraid to move lest I trigger another assault.

My disease, surely. Yet this was not the familiar ground of doulon perversion. The pain . . . the searing dread and anger . . . never in all my years had I experienced such a ravaging, as if my sickness had itself become some live thing inhabiting my body, wreaking purposeful vengeance now I'd sworn I'd no longer service it with nivat seed.

After a time I sat up. Slowly. My blood started flowing again, and reason crept out from hiding, dragging with it a dismal conviction. I had to tell the prince. Tonight, while this pain remained fresh, reminding me of the madness to come. The hopes raised in the past few hours could not overshadow that inevitable result. Nor could they shake my certainty that one more use of nivat would destroy both soul and body. Life's last great joke. I had found a master I was willing to serve, but my irredeemable folly had ensured my service would be cut short. I could not allow Osriel to imagine he could rely on my help.

I pulled on the heavy cloak I'd worn in the morning and hurried down the stair. One might have thought the world had already ended. The abbey ruins lay burnt and frozen, dark and silent. One faint gleam shone from the kitchen building in the south cloister, where the prince had been summoned to succor his fallen messenger.

The night air frosted my lungs, and I clutched my cloak around me. The world felt askew, as if my body were besotted with mead.

The grimed windows of the kitchen flickered with odd light of purple-streaked scarlet. I shoved open the plank door and stepped into a dark vestibule. Wet heat slapped my face, and with it the sweet, ripe alchemy of human dying—sweat, piss, emptied bowels, and the overwhelming iron taint of blood. A young man in padded leathers stood off to one side, his one arm held tight across his breast, clenched fist at his heart, the planes of his face eroded with grief. Voushanti's wide hands gripped the young man's shoulder and pressed him against the bricks of poor Brother Jerome's beloved hearth. But it was the tableau in the center of the room that turned my blood to sand.

The kitchen worktables had been shoved aside to clear the stone floor. Fire blazed—a broad ring of tall flames, scarlet and purple and the deepest blue of midnight, of storms, of bruises and pain. No fuel fed the flames; no hearth contained them. Within the fiery ring a stocky warrior lay dead, his body hacked and battered, the top of his skull caved in. Far worse than those mortal wounds were the fresh bloody holes that gaped where his eyes had once looked upon the world.

Prince Osriel—the gaunt, dark-haired man I knew as quiet, persuasive Gram—knelt beside the body, his velvet robes stained dark. Gore adorned the prince's face, not random splatter, but precisely marked patterns of circles and lines on brow, temples, cheeks, and chin. The blood signs burned with a power of their own that thrummed in my head as music—songs of pain and bondage, of striking whips and cries of despair. The prince's cupped hands, bloody to the wrist, held a calyx of carved stone—a shallow offering vessel as Iero's worshipers used to carry fragrant oils to his altar. Wisps of gray smoke trailed from the vessel.

". . . come weal, come woe, bound to my will and word until

world's end. *Perficiimus.*" Osriel's chant rang clean and hard and sure.

As he lowered the bowl, I backed away, cracked open the door, and slipped unseen into the bitter night. A haze of smoke and freezing fog obscured the stars. Somewhere soldiers softly called the watch.

Pressing my back to the stone wall, I tried to erase what I had seen, to silence the truth articulated by that sonorous incantation. Holy gods, how many times had he done this? What use did he have for souls withheld from whatever peace lay beyond this life? The wall of midnight that had smothered the fields of Gillarine remained etched in my memory—behind the fire-breathing horses and monstrous cloud warriors, I had seen gray, transparent faces in the blackness, hungry . . . lost . . . angry. And now I understood what I had experienced this hour past.

Life or death. In alleyways, on battlefields, in taverns and hovels and fine houses, I had always been able to determine whether a wounded man was like to live or die, no matter if the last breath had left him. But never before without my hand touching his body. And never before had I lived the actual rending of the victim's flesh and spirit. Somehow Osriel's dread enchantment had opened a door, and my talent had taken me through it to a place I had no wish to go. Navronne's rightful king, the world's hope, my bound master . . . Holy Iero, preserve us all.

For better or worse, my stomach was long empty, thus I left little trace of my retching in the snow. Had matters been different, I might have spent the night in the open air trying to purge the odor of unclean magic that clung to my spirit. But cold and exhaustion drove me back to the guesthouse, along with a vague sense that the prince must not know I'd glimpsed what he was about. I was certainly not as ready as I'd thought to bare my own weaknesses to my master.

Every bone and sinew demanded that I bolt like Deunor's fiery chariot from what I had just seen. It was one thing to accept Osriel's admission of unsavory practices, and wholly another to feel their blight upon my own soul. Could I, who prated of free choices, serve a man who enslaved the dead?

Abbot Luviar had taught me that I could not sit out this war. And if I were to take a battle stance at Caedmon's Bridge on *this* night, I would yet choose Osriel and his lighthouse over Sila Diaglou and the world's ruin. But obedience . . . the loyalty I had been so ready to hand over not an hour since . . . that would be another matter.

Once back in the guesthouse bedchamber, I stripped and rolled up in the coarse wool blankets. But I did not sleep. Instead I traveled the boundaries of hell in the company of savaged corpses with bloodied eye sockets, of a master whose face was marked with blood signs, of a whirling Dané who spat gall. The agonies of a dying soldier wrote themselves over and over again in my soul, and a diseased knot burned in my gut, fiercer with each passing hour.

Chapter 6

The day birthed as gray and forbidding as my spirits. Voushanti did naught to improve matters. When I inquired what had become of the wounded messenger, he said only that Skay had succumbed to his injuries, and that Ervid had lapsed into a forgetfulness, so that he could not even remember how his lover had died. I wanted to be sick.

The scent of spiced cider, mingled with woodsmoke and the abbey's ever-present residue of charred wool, wafted up the stair as I followed Voushanti down to the second floor of the guesthouse to meet the new arrivals. The mardane motioned me toward an open doorway to the left of the landing, then slipped down the stair before he could be seen.

Voushanti had reminded me forcefully that the prince's disguise must be strictly maintained unless Osriel himself signaled otherwise, even with members of the cabal. Never had a man's character confused me so. I had taken to Gram's kind, morbidly cheerful ways in our first dealings, admired his intelligence, humility, and equable humor in the face of his employer's irascible nature. I had believed him my friend and the only honest member of the lighthouse cabal. The absurdity near choked me as I pulled on the silken half mask and stepped into the room.

The sound of friendly argument welcomed me to the modest retiring chamber. Prior Nemesio was conversing energetically with a big man with a narrow beard, a beak-like nose, and the scuffed leathers and jewel-hilted sword of a noble warrior—Stearc, Thane of Erasku.

The talk ceased abruptly at my appearance. Rapidly melting snow dripped from the cloaks flung over chairs drawn close to a blazing fire.

"Cartamandua," said Stearc, sounding wholly unsurprised. He finished removing his gloves and tossed them onto the drying cloaks. "So Prior Nemesio was right that Mardane Voushanti has left you here alone this morning?"

At Stearc's right hand stood his daughter, Elene. Her close-woven braids gleamed the same bronze hue as her father's hair, and her rugged garb and weaponry reflected the same martial seriousness. I hated that I could not give full attention to her blooming loveliness. But Osriel . . . Gram . . . sat bundled in blankets beside the fire.

"Prince Osriel and his main force departed in the night," said the prior before I could answer. "Voushanti rode out to Elanus before dawn in search of fresh horses. I was something surprised the vile fellow would leave Brother Valen unguarded after yesterday's unpleasantness, but he told me he did not wish the pureblood to be seen in town."

I was grateful that Nemesio's eager report prevented me having to affirm this nonsense.

"Fortunate for us," said Gram. "Valen, we could use your talents to aid us in the search for Jullian and Gildas. Neither Lord Stearc nor Mistress Elene has found any trace of them."

"You may have whatever you need of me," I said, trying not to imagine his sober, pleasant face marked with unholy blood. "I just want to find the boy."

"It is nonsensical to go chasing off into the wild until we receive the reports from the Sinduria's spies," said Elene sharply, clenching her fists as if to extract some sense from the air. "We've no idea where Sila Diaglou might be, and we're all more tired than we'll admit. Each of us would give his heart's blood to see Jullian safe, but we need *everyone* fit, so perhaps, for once, insufferable pride and infernal stubbornness won't trump reason and planning. Our purposes are ill served if one of us falls off his horse and must be scraped up and put back on again."

Gram threw his blanket aside and rose from his chair, his lean frame straight and confident beneath his sober garb. The heat of the fire had painted his gaunt cheeks scarlet. "Mistress, you know how many days must pass until we can gather reliable reports. If Valen's talents can give us direction, we should use them. If it is *my* infirmities that concern you, let me ease your mind. I've not been floundering in weakness all morning, but rather trying to give some thought to strategy. May I speak freely, Lord Stearc?"

Stearc nodded. Elene folded her arms across her breast and shot Gram a murderous glance. The little chamber shimmered with heat.

I retreated to the window niche in search of the colder air that leaked through the iron seams of the casement. Urgency pulsed in my blood like battle fever. The doulon fire was rising in my gut.

Gram shoved a renegade lock of hair from his eyes. "Firstly, our overarching goal remains the preservation of the lighthouse, and as the lady suggests, we cannot lose sight of that in our fears for Jullian. As Gildas has the book of maps as well as our young friend, we must pursue him and hope we can retrieve both at once. Meanwhile, Prior Nemesio must find us a new Scholar. Whether he is selected from the survivors here at Gillarine or from elsewhere in Navronne, that one must be brought here as quickly as possible to study and prepare."

The prior sagged onto a couch, his round face stunned, his gaze flicking uncertainly at the man he believed little more than a lord's scribe. "But I am no Luviar, Gram. I've no wisdom to bring to such a task. How can I—?"

"None of us can replace Luviar," said Gram, clasping his hands behind his back. "We must do with our own talents. He chose you to run his abbey, Father Prior, to care for his brothers whom he loved. Thus he had clear faith in your judgment. If Valen's accusations are correct, then Gildas deceived even the abbot. Perhaps a more practical man will make a better choice."

Though his manner was entirely calm and logical Gram, Prince Osriel's eyes had taken on the character of iron when fire, hammer, and coal have had their way. No wonder he kept his gaze shuttered as he played this role. No meek secretary had such eyes.

A cramp tightened my left calf. I propped the toe of my boot on a stone facing and stretched out the muscle. *It's nothing. Nothing.*

Prior Nemesio kneaded his chin, staring at the patterned rug. "Luviar had a great respect for Jon Hinelle, a merchant's son in Pontia who once studied here," he murmured, "and for Vilno, a self-taught practor who once traveled as far as Pyrrha. Hinelle, I think—he's younger, more practical, if not quite so powerful a mind. With the abbey library in ashes, the new Scholar will need access to the lighthouse. And he'll need protection."

Over Nemesio's head, the prince lifted his eyebrows at Stearc and flicked his gaze from the bemused prior to the door. Stearc nodded brusquely.

"We shall open the lighthouse the moment the new Scholar is in place, Father Prior," said Stearc. With a firm hand, the thane dislodged Nemesio from the couch and drew him to the door. "And I'll leave a small garrison here at your disposal for the new man's retrieval and protection. Fedrol is a capable commander and will ask no awkward questions. I'd advise you heed his recommendations . . ."

As their voices faded down the stair, the prince poured himself a cup of cider from the pot on the polished table, lost in his own thoughts as he sipped. I kneaded my aching left forearm and breathed away a sharp spasm that pierced my rib cage.

Elene graced me with a rueful smile. "It is the gods' own gift to see you safe, Brother Valen." Her voice sounded as rich and potent as fine mead, warming even my cold spirit.

I mustered a smile and bowed, pulling off my mask and looping it on my belt. "Just Valen, mistress. I make no further pretense to holy orders."

"Two days ago, when we saw what the Harrowers had done to the abbey, and then Voushanti straggled in, saying you had stayed behind to face our pursuers alone, we feared your brave heart lost. So when your message came to Fortress Groult—" Her red-gold skin took on a deeper shade. "While we could not rejoice at your conclusions, we did rejoice that you were alive to make them. And now"— she jerked her head at the prince—"we've no need to hide certain facts from you. For better or worse."

"For better or worse," I said softly. So she knew Osriel's secret. "Mistress, do you know—? Last night, I—" The prince looked up from his cup, expressionless, and I dared not speak what I had seen, lest he overhear. "Lady, I am unsure of whom I serve." Perhaps I had found the source of her bitter enmity for Gram. I could not imagine a woman so devoted to justice and right, herself so rich with exuberant life, countenancing practices so abhorrent.

"We are an inharmonious collection of comrades, to be sure."

The clamor of boots on the stair signaled Stearc's return, accompanied by a blast of cold air—and Voushanti. Elene promptly moved away from me, poured a cup of cider, and plopped onto the dusty couch.

Welcoming the fresh air, I pressed even closer to the window. The stifling heat was near choking me. Another cramp wrenched my back. I blamed the overbuilt hearth fire and the previous day's climbing. *Please, gods . . .*

"We should inform the prior of your identity, Your Grace," said Stearc, squatting by the fire and rubbing his hands together briskly. "If he is to be an effective ally, he should know all."

The prince shook his head. "Too many secrets have escaped our grasp of late. Nemesio is stalwart and intelligent, but unimaginative in deceit and poor at conspiracy. That Gildas cannot expose me is one slim consolation amid Valen's ill tidings."

"I don't understand why you believe all this about Gildas. The boy's body is proof that he was murdered, not that Gildas did it. We've a far more likely candidate right here." Stearc glared at me with undisguised contempt. "Did your own guilt catch up with you, pureblood? Did you realize you'd be found out, and so turn on the very one who compromised himself to aid you? Perhaps you didn't know that Gildas confessed how he'd induced you to strike him and run. How he sent Gerard after you with supplies for your escape. The monk's testimony shook even Luviar. Now you say some magical *insight* has shown you the boy's resting place? I don't accept it. You were half crazed that night. I say you struck down the boy so he couldn't give you up to the purebloods."

Voushanti shifted his position slightly, intruding between Stearc and me. "You should listen to the pureblood, Thane. Whatever else, he's no coward. Eight days ago I was ordered to kill him did he step wrong, but I found reason enough to leave him walking. Save for his diverting the Harrowers, you, your daughter, Prince Osriel, and the rest of us would lie dead on the Palinur road."

This casual confirmation of how close I had come to dying by Voushanti's hand did naught to cool my burgeoning anger. I'd given Elene the benefit of the doubt, but this . . . Damn the woman; she had been there. She had allowed these lies to fester.

"I am certainly no innocent," I snapped. "But bring me the man or woman who says I have ever used a child ill, and I will show you a liar. As it happens, I've a witness that Gildas himself brought me supplies the night of my escape, that I forbade him send the boys, and that I had no contact with either boy before I was slammed senseless near the aspen grove. As that witness has not come forward to speak for me, perhaps the coward prefers I stand guilty of the crime."

Osriel looked surprised. "A witness?"

Stearc snorted. "I don't believe—"

"You planned to *kill* Valen?" Elene rose from the couch, her face crimson. Had Osriel spouted blood from her glare, it could not have surprised anyone. "You told me you would question him and seek the truth about that night. I never thought— Are we no better than the murderous madmen we fight?"

The prince's face hardened like mortared stone. "We did as we thought best."

"Your secrets blight your life far worse than any illness, *Gram* of

Evanore. Twisted pride and a corrupt soul will be the death of you, not Sila Diaglou or your wretched royal brothers."

"Daughter!" snapped Stearc. "Mind your vixen's tongue!"

Wrenching her glare from Osriel, Elene crossed her arms, touching opposite shoulders, and bowed to me. "I beg your forgiveness, Master Valen. I had reasons for my silence that seemed compelling at the time but were clearly selfish, foolish, and inexcusable. Please believe, if I had imagined such murderous folly, I would never have left the matter in doubt."

She turned back to the others. Though her arms remained in the penitent's gesture across her breast, her fists tightened as if to contain a fury that matched my own. "Papa, Mardane Voushanti, my lord prince, I indeed followed Brother Valen out to the dolmen that night. He did not leave my sight until the purebloods gave chase through the fields. All is as he has said. Only Gildas came. Not Gerard. I heard Brother Valen adamantly refuse to involve the boys in any way. He could not possibly have seen anyone that evening without my knowledge."

"You returned at dawn, girl!" bellowed Stearc, his cheeks burning. "You said you'd been with some ailing pilgrim woman in the Alms Court all night. What were you doing with Cartamandua? And where were you after he was taken?"

"That has no bearing on Valen or Gildas, so I'll not waste our time just now, Papa," said Elene, acid on her tongue. "But I *will* tell you. What misdirected loyalties induced my silence are now moot."

I had no wits to sort out what she might be talking about, save that it surely had to do with Osriel.

"I am satisfied that Valen is innocent of these crimes, Stearc," said the prince, putting a sharp end to the matter. "After yesterday's encounter with Kol, I fear our hopes of aid are even flimsier than before. Yet before we can consider how to approach the Danae, we must attempt to retrieve the boy and the book . . . and Gildas. We ride within the hour."

Voushanti had passed around cups of cider, and now stood across the room, observing me curiously. Every time I blinked, the world seemed to waver. I gulped the cider and set the cup aside before the mardane could notice how my hand shook.

Stearc jerked his head at Elene and snatched up his cloak. "Let's be off, then."

"Not you, Thane. You are to remain here." The prince pivoted on his heel. "You and Fedrol will detail your men as you see fit for the prior's needs and for the security of the lighthouse and the brothers."

Stearc flushed and glared at me. "My lord, if this is punishment for my accusations—"

"This is not punishment," said the prince sharply. "We've no time for petty guilts and reprisals. Believe me when I say I would prefer to have your strong arm at my side. But Luviar has fallen. As the only living lighthouse ward-holder, your personal safety is paramount, and we've no time to transfer your charge to another. Thus, if you perceive the least threat to your person in these next weeks, you will entertain no foolish ideas of brave antics, but will run and hide, no matter the brothers' safety or your daughter's or mine. Do you understand me?"

"Aye, Your Grace. Of course." Stearc gritted his teeth and bowed.

The prince shifted his attention to Elene, who looked as near jumping out of her skin as I felt. "Mistress, though it grieves me to say it, you cannot go with us either."

"I thought we had no time for petty reprisals!" she snapped. "I have not faltered in my duty to this cabal, no matter our personal disagreements. I have not hesitated."

"I would not think of underestimating your determination," said the prince, as frosty as the windowpanes. "My only hesitation is for the dangers I must ask you to venture instead. Thanks to a few brave souls, Brother Victor lies safely at Renna. To move him was a risk, but not so much as leaving him in Palinur. Saverian will keep him alive if any physician in the world can manage it. Mistress Elene, I would ask you to meet Victor at Renna and take on the burden he and Luviar kept safe from Sila Diaglou. Saverian can work the necessary rite. We cannot leave your father the only ward-holder. Are you willing?"

"You wish me to be a lighthouse warder?" Astonishment wiped Elene's fine-drawn features clean of anger and outrage. "Of course . . . of course I will."

"Good." The prince turned briskly to Voushanti while Elene was yet stammering. "Dispatch Philo and Melkire to safeguard Mistress Elene on her travels, Mardane. They're our best, and if they remained with us . . . Well, I'd not wish them to confuse Thane Stearc's secretary with their prince just yet."

Voushanti nodded, as did Elene, only a rosy flush remaining of her surprise.

"I believe we have some time, if we take care," said Osriel to all of us. "Sila Diaglou has some use for Valen beyond his grandfather's book. As long as her attention is distracted with her own plans and she is left guessing as to mine, a small, fast party should be able to move unnoticed to intercept Gildas."

"Gildas knows I'll come after Jullian," I said. I wished I shared Elene's determined composure. My knees squished like mud and my bowels churned like a millrace.

"But you are Osriel the Bastard's bound servant, and Osriel's cruel games would never permit you such freedom," said the prince. "Secrets and deceptions grant us opportunities that fate denies."

No one could have missed this reproof of Elene. But I could read the prince's expression no better than any other time. His cool sobriety revealed no hostility.

"Now that Gildas holds the book," he continued, "Valen is our only hope to warn the Danae and enlist their help. As his safety is critical, and I've still some notion of ruling my father's kingdom, Voushanti must keep the both of us alive through this venture."

Voushanti bowed. "How many men?"

"Only us three."

"My lord, no!" Voushanti and Stearc erupted in unison. "Impossible . . ."

Stearc argued himself hoarse about Osriel's foolishness in taking a single bodyguard "no matter his exceptional talents." Osriel allowed him to rant, but altered the plan not a whit. As Stearc moved from sputtering at Osriel to showering Elene with warnings and advice, the prince took up pen and paper to set his plan into motion.

Osriel took Gildas's threat too lightly in my opinion. The monk might believe me the Bastard's bound servant, but he also knew how I felt about villains who abused children. Worse yet, he knew my weakness; he'd left a box of nivat seeds to taunt me. I'd destroyed the box and yet clung to the belief that I could manage a few more hours of sanity—long enough to set Osriel on the right path. I could not abandon the boy. I had sworn to protect him.

Voushanti charged off to see to horses and supplies, and conversation shifted to a brisk discussion of message drops and rendezvous and other details that needed no input from me. As the moments slipped by, the knot in my belly launched a thousand threads of fire to snarl my flesh and bones. My companions and their concerns and, indeed, the entire world outside my skin began to recede, until they seemed no more than players and a flimsy stage. My time had run out.

"My lord," I whispered from my place by the window. It was all the voice I could muster from a throat that felt scorched. "I need to tell you . . ."

No one heard me. Elene held Osriel's sealed orders for his garrison at Renna and for this Saverian, his physician and house mage. Voushanti returned and hoisted the leather pack that contained the prince's medicines. Osriel donned his heavy cloak and tossed his extra blanket to Voushanti, telling him to pack it. "A dainty flower such as I cannot afford to leave extra petals behind."

My body burned. I tried to unfasten my cloak and padded tunic, but my hands would not stop shaking.

Soon Osriel and Stearc were laughing. They embraced fiercely. Elene clasped her father's hands, biting her lip as she mouthed sentiments I could not hear.

I fumbled with the iron window latch and shoved the casement open far enough I could gulp a breath of frigid air to cool my fever.

"Magnus, it's time to go."

"Magnus Valentia!"

The calls came as from ten quellae distant. I lifted my anvil of a head, sweat dribbling down my temples. The four of them stared at me.

"What's wrong, Valen?" said the prince.

"I can't," I said, pressing one arm to my belly as a vicious cramp tied my gut in a knot. "It's too late. Gildas knew—" But I could not blame Gildas for this betrayal. He had merely taken advantage of my own sin; the excess nivat he'd given me in Palinur had but sped up what was going to happen anyway. "I'm afraid I'm no good to you after all."

"Are you ill, pureblood?" Voushanti dropped the satchel. "You should have spoken earlier."

I shook my head, as waves of insects with barbed feet swarmed my skin. "You'd best go now. Retrieve the book, or you'll have to discover another way to the Danae."

The prince appeared in front of me. Though his years numbered only six-and-twenty, fine lines crisscrossed his brow and the skin about his eyes. Concern settled in the creases as in a familiar place. "You seemed well enough yesterday. Have you some hidden injury? We can fetch Brother Anselm."

When he touched my chin, I jerked away. But trapped in the window niche, I could not evade him. I closed my eyes, though behind my eyelids lay naught but flame. "No, my lord. A disease."

"But not a new one." I felt his gaze penetrate my fever like a spear of ice.

My molten gut churned. "It comes on me from time to time."

"Have you medicines for it? How long will it hinder you? A day?

A week?" Spoken with the understanding of a man who had dealt with illness every day of his life. Did his remedies skew his mind until he could think of naught else, until they became indistinguishable from the disease? Did his salves and potions leave him muddle-headed so that he killed the people he was trying to help? I doubted they tempted him to slash his flesh or scald his feet just to make the healing more pleasurable.

"You're our best hope to reach the Danae, Valen. We'll get you what you need. Just tell me."

There it was. The temptation I feared most.

The doulon hunger sat inside my head like the Adversary himself, whispering its seductions. *One spell and you can hold together for a few days . . . help them rescue Jullian . . . retrieve the book. Then they won't need you anymore, and you'll have kept your vow as best you could. Too bad you threw the enchanted mirror away—so easy to do when your gut is not on fire—but this devil prince can surely enspell another. And he'll have a supply of nivat as a gift for the Danae. Surely . . .*

The fiery agony was my disease. For all these years, no matter its torment, no matter how I rued my folly, cursed the stars, or told myself otherwise, deep inside the darkest core that held a man's un-spoken sins, I had welcomed its pain in aid of its remedy. My chest clenched with hunger. My loins ached with need no woman could sat-isfy. Saliva flooded my mouth. No amount of washing had removed the scent of nivat that clung to my skin, to my fingers that had opened the little box Gildas had left me. So enticing . . .

"Valen?"

Luviar had died an unspeakable death because the doulon had left me slow-witted and confused. Brother Victor lay half dead and Jul-lian was captive because servicing my need demanded my first and clearest stratagems, and every other matter must yield to whatever the doulon made of me. Nivat gave me an illusion of control, but I knew better. A cramp wrenched my back like an iron hook.

"You cannot help me. You *must* not." *Saints and angels, make him believe it, for you'll never be able to repeat these words.* My darkest core prayed he would not listen.

"Look at me, Valen." His icy fingers shook my chin. "Open your eyes. I am your lord and your bound master. I command you tell me what's wrong."

Best let him see the raging hunger. Best see his reaction in turn, to crush hope and understand my fate. I allowed his clear gray gaze to capture mine, then spoke so that only he could hear. "The doulon."

"Ah."

He dropped his hand but not his eyes, his expression such a strange compounding of comprehension, curiosity, and calculation, I could not read it. But at least I saw no judgment. Perhaps a man who enslaved souls saw no perversion in teaching the body to crave pain in order to release one moment's ecstasy and gain a few weeks' comfort.

"You are full of surprises, friend Valen." His voice was soft. Puzzled. Kind. Almost as if he were Gram alone and not the other. "But this one—"

He turned away abruptly, leaving me slumped against the window, where I tried to inhale enough cold air I would not erupt in flames. I was relieved to hear him dispatching the others about their duties, telling them he would set out after Gildas as planned. Good. Maudlin sympathy was no better an asset for a worthy king than self-righteous judgment. Somehow it made my shame easier to bear that he was proceeding with the kingdom's business.

Eyes closed again, stomach heaving, I slid slowly down the wall, trying to decide what to do with myself once these four were dispersed on their missions. I could not remain in the guesthouse. Stearc would not be so matter-of-fact about this betrayal as his prince was. Horrid to think of the thane filling my last hours of reason with bullheaded insults. But I also hated the thought of burdening the brothers . . .

"Come, come, you're not going to get off so easy." A firm hand caught me under the arm and halted my downward slide. "Stand up, Valen. Gather what's left of your wits and come with me. We must find our young friend and your book and this villain who thinks to use them."

"Your Grace, if I could—please believe me—I would. Do you have any idea—?" I lowered my voice so the others would not hear. "Doulon hunger destroys mind and body. I'll be of no use to you."

"I have a *very* good idea. I was born with saccheria."

Saccheria! No wonder reports named him a cripple. Joint fever, a rare and brutal rogue of a disease, could crack a man's limbs or bend them into knots. Even if the first bone-twisting onslaught of fever didn't kill you, you were never free of it. It would attack again and again, vanishing abruptly for weeks or months at a time before the next assault, manifesting itself in a hundred cruel variants—one time as grotesque skin lesions, the next as mind-destroying fever, a lung-stripping cough, or a palsy that transformed a robust warrior into a bed-ridden infant who fouled his sheets. Always lurking . . . always unexpected . . . always, always painful.

He released me as soon as I was standing again. "One cannot live as I have without learning every remedy the world provides for pain. And the first and most difficult thing you learn is that there exists no remedy without cost. I was fortunate that my father forbade me try nivat or poppy until I was old enough to understand their price. I won't give you either one." His calm assurance eased even so blunt a condemnation. "Unfortunately for you, I also know you're not going to die in the next few days."

"I'll want to," I said. And even if I shed the doulon hunger, I would have to face the disease itself.

He pulled my cloak around my shoulders and tugged it straight. "So you will. But I won't allow it, and perhaps you will have accomplished something useful before you expire."

Chapter 7

"I can't eat this," I yelled, knocking away the spoon, spilling hot soup over my clothes, my blanket, and my unfortunate companion. "Tastes like drunkard's piss." I rolled to one side and drew my knees to my chest, the sound of my own croaking voice threatening to burst my eyeballs. I was shivering so violently I could not catch hold of the blanket to draw it over me, and so lay exposed to the frigid evening.

One of my tormentors threw the blanket over me—over my head, so that every breath was tainted with the stench of horse, smoke, vomit, and my unclean body. Moaning, I clawed at the damp wool to get it off my face before I could not breathe at all.

"Just stick a knife in me," I said between gulps of the frosty air that froze the slime leaking from my nose. "It's quicker than poisoning or suffocation." Quicker than devouring oneself from the inside out.

"I give you no leave to die. You vowed without reservation that you would not run away from me. Remember?"

My chief tormentor was no more than a shadowed outline between me and the fire. I closed my eyes and clung to his voice. Calm. Cruel. Kind. The fragile thread of reason that held my body and mind together. Days . . . blessed angels, how many days since I could think, since I could move without screaming, since I could sleep? And now it was almost night again, and we lay on a bleak hillside in a forest of charred trunks, all that remained of a spruce and aspen forest. I had tracked Gildas and Jullian into this desolation somewhere west of Gillarine, but I could not have said where.

"Tell me, Valen, what is it you do when you put your hands on the earth? Do you work a spell to find the way? Or do you ask . . .

someone . . . something . . . to show you . . . as with a prayer? Or is it something else altogether?" Gram . . . Osriel. Of course I knew the one who held me on his leash. It was just difficult to remember the two were the same man. "Answer me, Valen."

"Don't know. I feel. I see. It hurts." I swiped at my face with my trembling hand, only to sneeze again—a great wet gobbet of a sneeze. Samele's tits, I was disgusting. I hunched tighter as the sneezing set off another barrage of cramps. Chokesnakes writhed in my belly, clamping their wirelike bodies about my stomach, liver, and gut. The two swallows of piss soup I'd got down came ravaging back up my gullet, as did everything my companions tried to shove down me.

When I was done with the latest bout of retching, a warm wet rag wiped my face. "I've seen that the seeking pains you, as does everything just now. But Voushanti says it didn't seem to distress you in Palinur or Mellune Forest. So perhaps when you are yourself again, it will be painless again."

The prince's patient baritone never changed. If I could find a blade, I might slip it between his ribs just to see if the next time he said, "Tell me, Valen," it might sound something different. But my eyes watered so profusely, the world and its contents were never in the places I expected them, and my two companions hid their weapons from me.

"Please let me sleep," I whispered, rolling tighter, clutching my blanket to my chest, trying to hold still so the cramps would ease. "Have mercy."

"I'll not give you what you want. I told you that. Sleep will come when it will. Perhaps later tonight. Now it's time to search for Jullian again. You told us this afternoon that we were close. You made me promise to force you to this again when we reached higher ground."

No . . . no . . . no! Impossible when rats fed on my brain, when my parched soul shriveled, when marvelous, glorious life had shrunk to this frozen, wretched, burning hell.

"Come, Valen, will you try?" Ever and always patient.

"Aye, lord. Just help me move."

The two of them unfolded me, supported me as I knelt beside a patch of cleared earth, and then gently unclenched my fists and laid my shaking palms on the cold ground.

"Find the boy, Valen. You are gifted beyond any man I know. You've kept us close these four days, though we've traveled in entirely unlikely directions. This child, your young brother, stolen by a traitor who would use him to destroy you . . ."

Somewhere in the ragged, hollow shell of my being, where the shreds of reason, talent, and sense had collapsed like the walls of Gillarine, anger smoldered. When my tormentor's voice touched that ember, I could grasp my anger, use it to steady my shattered nerves, which in turn gave life to my magic.

Where are you, Archangel? I promised to protect you. Where?

My will drew my mind into the earth, and I sought through soil and roots, frozen now, the cold penetrating deeper than these lands had known since before men walked the earth. The roots tore at my mind's fingers like metal thorns, the dirt and rocks scraped like ground glass, leaving my soul raw and my gut bleeding. But anger held me together, and I swept my inner vision across and through the landscape, seeking the footsteps of the traitor and the boy . . . and discovered they had diverged. *Where are you, boy?* Saints and angels, if I but had a drop of his blood to link a path . . .

I poured my soul into the seeking, existed as worm, as beetle, as root, listening and smelling and feeling the cold grit as I groped for some hint of human footsteps. Gildas had led us on a lunatic's path. This high, rocky wasteland had welcomed few humans, but hosted every kind of wild goat, squirrel, and rock pig for generation upon generation. Most of them dead now. A sickness festered in this desolation.

Cold . . . frigid, searing, mind-numbing cold . . . a thread of ice . . . suffocating . . . drowning . . .

I snatched my hands from the ground and clamped them under my arms, rocking my body to soothe the urge to vomit. "Water!" I gasped. "Gildas has left him in the water. A spring or a seep. Holy gods, in this cold. Hurry . . . hurry . . . no time." I flapped and floundered, struggling to rise. What if Gildas had left him bleeding as he had the hapless Brother Horach, as he had poor Gerard, attempting to poison another Danae guardian? Jullian's brilliant mind and noble heart, his determined courage that had stood up to mad sorcerers and powerful priestesses, laid waste by knives and despair . . . the imagining drove me wild.

"Wait!" Osriel crouched in front of me and clamped his hands on the sides of my head, demanding I look him in the eye. His features swam in the light of the crescent moon that shone bright and heavy in the west. "Be clear, Valen. Jullian is abandoned? Where is Gildas himself?"

I blinked and squinted in the moonlight, trying to connect the wavering landscape with the images in my head. We crouched just below the summit of a rocky bluff, a vantage where the prince and Voushanti could survey the steep-sided, narrow gorge.

"Northwest," I mumbled, shaking my head to clear it. "Over that ridge at the end of the gorge and into the earth. Moving fast as if he knows this country."

"That makes no kind of sense," said Voushanti from behind me. "This is bandit country, riddled with hiding places, true enough, but what purpose for a scholarly monk? Into the earth . . . a cave, then? Does he think to be a hermit like the wild holies in Estigure?"

The two of them had speculated endlessly on why Gildas traveled so far from the impoverished Moriangi villages and failing Ardran freeholds where Sila Diaglou enlisted most of her support, and so far from the estates of Grav Hurd and Edane Falderrene, the two nobles who trained her legions.

The prince's attention did not waver though he had to squeeze his questions between bouts of coughing. His saccheria had flared up a day out of Gillarine. "How far, Valen? Can we reach Gildas before you lose your sense of him?"

"If we stay high . . . traverse the ridge. But Jullian is down. Straight west and down. This side of the ridge." To get down these icy slopes to fetch Jullian and then back up again and over the ridge to catch Gildas would be impossible. And I would lose the monk's track long before we could travel the long way around out of the gorge and up the easier slopes to the ridge. Tears and mucus ran down my face unchecked. "The boy will die down there in the water. Die alone. We can't leave him . . . not fair . . . not right . . . an innocent . . . ."

"We should go after the book," said Voushanti. "The monk believes us weak. He's planned to make us choose. The boy is likely dead already."

"Not yet," I said, holding tight to my anger so I could think. "I'd know."

"I'll not build our future on one more dead child," said the prince hoarsely. The saccheria had left thorns in his breathing. He moved carefully, as if his joints grated upon one another. "If we cannot protect our own, then how can we protect the rest of the kingdom? Valen and I will fetch the boy. You can go after—"

"No," said Voushanti flatly. "I am here to protect you and your pureblood. You have bound me with that duty, and no whim—even yours, lord—will sway me from it."

"You—are—my—*servant*." A flash of red lanced from the prince's fist to the bottomless black of Voushanti's eyes . . . and held.

Muffling a groan, the mardane dropped to his knees. Even in his submission, he struggled and writhed, his body seeming to bulge and swell until he twisted his thick neck sharply, wrenching his eyes from

Osriel's lock. In that same moment the red lance broke and vanished. The mardane yanked his sword from its scabbard, laid it crosswise on his upturned palms, and thrust it at our master. "Do with this as you choose, lord, as is your right and privilege," he said, curling his half-ruined mouth into a demonic leer, "but I will not leave you."

I wiped my eyes with the back of my hand and confirmed that the sword's crimson glow was not some artifact of blurred vision.

"By the mighty Everlasting!" Osriel's upraised fists shook and spat white sparks that showered down on Voushanti's dreadful face.

Surely Magrog's own presence would not taint the night with such a stench—death and brimstone and scarcely bridled violence. The earth shivered at Osriel's wrath, or so it seemed to me, who would gladly have exchanged my body for that of one of the cold worms I had touched. I laid my head on the ground and shrank as small as I could manage.

"You will pay for this, Voushanti. When your day of trial comes next, you *will* pay."

The dispute was quenched as quickly as it had flared. The night became only night once more, rather than the vestibule of hell. Before I could sort reality from nivat-starved illusion, the two of them had tied me to the back of a horse and we were descending the slope into the darkening gorge. I could not fathom why Voushanti yet lived. In what kind of bondage did *he* serve?

The nervous animal's hooves slipped more than once. Voushanti cajoled the beast to stay afoot and me to balance my weight back to help keep it so. But every jogging movement set off my cramps, and before we'd descended halfway to the bottom of the vale, I had stopped worrying about Osriel's scarce-contained furies and was begging Voushanti to throw me from a cliff.

"Tell me which way to the boy, Valen," said the prince, laying his hand on my knee as he walked beside me. Fifty times he had said it, between his hacking coughs. Even through my layered chausses I felt the heat of his fever.

"Water," I said, my chin bouncing on my chest, lips numb, drool freezing to my chin. "Find the water. Down."

The beast beneath me jolted forward. I muzzled my screams in the crook of my arm. Gildas must not hear us.

The night's black seemed washed with silver. Details of the land crept out of the dark—scrubby trees, snow, crooked slabs of ice-slicked rock. Could it be morning already? *Please, holy Iero, no.* After a night in freezing water, the boy would be dead.

No, this light was something else. Not moon. Moon and stars were

lost in cloud. Yet I could see . . . there, the guide thread itself laid out
on the landscape, a gray pattern that sparked and shimmered of its
own light, scribed atop the landscape, like the sigils of the Danae that
shone from within and yet apart from their bare flesh. I dared not
ask if my companions could see it, too.

"Bear left," I croaked. Red sand hardened into stone and twisted
by wind and water had formed a narrow rift. Thistles and scrub
sprouted between its thin layers. "It's narrow. Choked with boulders." Beyond the boulder field a wall rose like the facade of a
temple, an oddly flat face in this rugged wilderness.

We halted, and before I comprehended he had gone, Voushanti
returned from a scout. "It's as he says, my lord. Great slabs fallen
everywhere. Dead trees. No sign of anyone, boy or man. But the
place has an odd feel. We'd best leave the horses and the pureblood
out here. Neither will manage the boulders."

They untied my hands and feet and helped me to the ground.
Propped my back against a rock. Bundled blankets around me and
gave me a sip of ale.

"Are we in Evanore, lord?" I mumbled, my speech vibrating
through my skull.

"No, Valen. Why would you think that?" Gram's endless patience
at my shoulder. Profound weariness. Perhaps the netherworld I had
witnessed in his eyes had been but my own madness.

"Brains boiling."

Soft laughter fell about my head and shoulders like autumn leaves.
"Should we ever travel to my wondrous land, I'll shield your poor
brains, Valen. Now tell me: Is the boy close? We can't take the horses
any farther."

I clutched my belly and rolled to the side, onto my knees, pressing
forehead and hands to the churned snow and dirt. All I could sense
was the blistering heat of my skin. "I can't feel, lord."

"Do we need to warm your hands? We daren't make a fire."

"Can't raise my magic." I could not even remember why I
searched.

"Heed me, pureblood." The presence swelled and darkened just
behind me, close to my ear, sending thrills of terror up my spine.
"Your father and grandfather used you to fuel their war with each
other. Do you think I do not understand why a child's pain touches
your soul so deeply? Stop playing at this and find the boy, or I will
break you."

The boy . . . The ember yet burned. I grasped it and dived into earth. And from the deep crevices between the rocks came the faint trickle of water and a rhythmic tapping.

"Holy Mother, he's trapped in the boulders," I mumbled, hands clawed into the frozen mud, pebbles digging into my forehead. "In the crevices between. Look down. Seek the water."

"Hold on just a little longer, Valen. Not a sound as we fetch him."

"Careful on the ice." Voushanti's parting whisper carried through the night air as clearly as Gillarine's bell.

My every sense stretched to fevered refinement. The crunch of their boots sounded like the tread of a retreating army. The horses snorted and tore at the dead grasses that poked through the snow, their mundane noises the cacophony of the world's end. The hot stink of their droppings choked me.

I shivered and a spasm raked me from belly to lungs like a lightning bolt, near rending the bones from my flesh. "Archangel," I mumbled into my knees. "Jullian! Where are you, boy?"

My agitated mind would not stay still, and I reached farther into the boulder-filled rift . . . into the earthen banks beyond the boulders, past the stone wall . . . where something breathed . . . men, unmoving, waiting, ready in a great hollow. Gildas was *there*, gone *through* the rocks, not over them. And a woman beside him . . . pale-haired, cold, deadly . . . roused with unholy lust to serve her fearsome Gehoum. Great gods . . . a whole citadel buried behind these steep banks. Sentries . . . watchers . . . ahead and to either side of us. Trap.

I clawed at the boulder behind me, willing my useless body upward. Stumbling into the rift, I dodged fallen slabs until the piled ice, stone, and rubble wholly filled the narrow gorge. I scrabbled up the boulder pile, at every touch reaching for their footsteps . . . Voushanti the devil, Gram my friend . . . Navronne's king . . . *Must be silent.* Though I could hear my skin ripping on the sharp rocks. Though I could feel the blood leaking out of me.

There . . . ahead of me . . . Voushanti's dark bulk, and ahead of him a muffled cough that sounded like a wild dog's bark. "Who's there?"

They heard me. Saw me. Caught me as my foot slipped on an icy slab.

"Trap," I sobbed, pain lancing every sinew like hot pokers. "Ambush. At least twenty of them ahead. Sentries on the cliff tops to either side. And beyond them—gods have mercy—a fortress. Hundreds of them. We can't—"

"Do they know we've come? Answer me, Valen. Do they know someone's here?"

They held me tight, and I reached out with my tormented senses and felt the night . . . the watchers . . . listening . . . a shifting alertness . . . stiffening . . . ready. "Aye. They know."

Gram held my jaw in his hot hands. His face was distorted . . . swollen to ugliness with the scaly red signature of saccheria . . . a gatzé's face with dark, burning pits for eyes. "We're going to control this. Voushanti is going to get you out of these rocks and then you're going to scream a warning to *Gram* and his companion *Hoyl* that this is a trap. You must be silent until Voushanti tells you. When you shout, you will think of me only as Gram, and Voushanti only as Hoyl. Do you understand? You *must* do this, no matter how it pains you."

"Aye," I said, though whips of fire curled about my limbs. Though I had no idea why he wished me to do it.

Big hands grabbed me and hefted me across a broad shoulder. Jostling, bumping, slipping, every jolt an agony. I bit my arm to muffle my cries, until at last he threw me across a saddle and bound me tight. I took shallow breaths. Somewhere in the braided silence a hunting bird screeched, and the man with red eyes whispered a count from one to two hundred. Then he snapped, "*Now*, pureblood. Warn Gram and Hoyl of the trap."

Somehow I understood how important it was to do this right. The listeners mustn't know I'd learned about the fortress. They mustn't know I'd brought Osriel and Voushanti here. So I lifted my head and bellowed like a bull elk until I was sure my skull must shatter. "Gram! Hoyl! It's a trap! Come back! Four . . . five of them waiting! Run!"

My shouts set off a riot of noise—shouts from right and left, clanking weapons, drawn bows. But before one arrow could loose, a thunder of moving earth raised screams beyond my own. Voushanti cursed and mumbled until pelting footsteps joined us. "Ride!"

We rode as if Magrog's hellhounds licked our beasts' flesh with their acid-laced tongues. I wept and babbled of Sila Diaglou and the fortress I'd discovered hidden behind the stone, and I swore I had not caused the earth to move and kill the sentries, though I feared I had done so. I cried out the anguish of my flesh until we stopped and Gram tied rags across my mouth. "We'll find the boy again, Valen. On my father's soul and honor, I promise you, we'll save him."

That was the last thing I heard before my brains leaked out my ears.

"Magrog devour me before ever I touch nivat seeds!" Words took shape as if they sat in the bottom of a well. "Are you sure he should travel, my lord? The brothers would gladly keep him here at the abbey. It's astonishing; they still consider him one of themselves—even Nemesio."

The cold air that brushed my face stank of manure and mold and mud. Mind and body were raw, gaping wounds.

"Ah, Stearc, I don't think traveling could make things worse. He'll be safer at Renna while he endures this siege. If he has a mind left by the end, Saverian will find it. Right, Valen?" The muffled voice of my tormentor moved closer to my ear. "My physician's skills are exceptional, complemented and honed with a mage's talents. You will marvel."

I could not answer. My mind was long dissolved, my tongue thick and slow. They had tied rags over my eyes and plugged my ears with wool as I screamed. Light, sound, touch tortured my senses like lashes of hot wire.

"As you're the only one can draw sense out of him, Lord Prince, it's good he'll be with you. And if it makes *you* ride in the cart and keeps you out of the wind until this cough is eased, that's a double blessing."

"I'll survive. Brother Anselm has refilled all my bottles and salve jars. It's still more than a month until the solstice. Valen is the concern for now. I need him well. It was *I* that Kol forbade from entering Danae territory, not Valen. Unless I can think of some gift to placate them, it will be left to Valen to warn the Danae of Sila Diaglou's plot to exterminate them."

"But if the pureblood's vision was true, and we've actually found Sila Diaglou's hiding place . . . that's more promising than any of this Danae foolishness. Fedrol has already set up a discreet watchpost on the hill."

"Carefully, Stearc. I'm still debating whether I was mad to set off the landslide, minute though it was. The priestess must not suspect that Valen recognized the place as more than a convenient site for an ambush. Was Gildas a fool to lead us there or are we the fools to believe we've gained a slight advantage?"

"We are certainly fools. Godspeed, Your Grace. Tell my daughter I will see her at the warmoot."

"I doubt she'll hear any greetings out of *my* mouth, but I'll do my best."

When the world jolted into movement, I screamed. They had bundled me in blankets and cushions and moldy wool, but to little avail. My bones felt like to shatter.

*　　*　　*

For hour upon hour, aeon upon aeon, I existed in darkness, in company with Boreas as he sobbed out his torment, with Luviar as he cried out mortal agony, and with Gerard, alone and freezing, as he fought so desperately to live that he tore his hand from an iron spike. I felt my own hand rip and my own belly tear, spilling my bowels into the cold to be set afire. I screamed until I could scream no more. Tears leaked from beneath my aching eyelids. Life shrank until I felt trapped like a chick in an egg.

Only the one voice could penetrate my mad dreams, and I clung to it as a barnacle to a ship's sturdy keel. I tried to croak in answer, just to prove to myself I yet lived.

"We *must* travel to the Danae, Valen," he said one mad hour. "Luviar believed that the world's sickness derives from their weakness. Everything I know confirms that. Our estrangement from them surely exacerbates it. But, tell me, should we walk or ride as we approach them? My father said the Danae ride wild horses when they please, but most prefer to walk, to feel the earth beneath their feet. Perhaps it would show our goodwill to walk into their lands."

"I hate horses," I croaked, "and they hate me."

He laughed at that and I hated him. Gram was Osriel; Osriel was a gatzé, Magrog's rival.

We traveled onward . . . and the voice touched me again and again. I cherished it like sanity itself and loathed it like the cruelest Registry overseer.

"Tell me about your grandfather, Valen," he said. "What did he steal from the Danae? They wear clothes only when they wish to hide among us or when the whim takes them. They carry nothing from place to place save perhaps a harp or pipe and would as soon leave it and make another as carry it. What do you steal from such folk? Tell me, Valen."

Everything hurt—my hair, my eyebrows, my fingernails. He could stop it, but he wouldn't, and anger enabled me to muster moisture enough to spit in the direction of his voice. "Their eyes, perhaps. Their souls."

In the ensuing silence, pain came ravaging, and I wept and pleaded. "I'm sorry. So sorry. Please speak to me, my lord. The silence hurts."

His breath scraped my face like hot knives. "Do not speak of matters you do not understand, Magnus Valentia. I am your master and your lord. My purposes are not yours to judge."

As the flood of misery swept me along, my tormentor spoke less and less, and I sank deeper into chaotic dreams. I drowned in fear and pain, suffocated in madness, too weak to claw my way out. Though I feared him above all men, only my master could grant me breath.

"Here, taste this. It's very sweet—makes Voushanti heave. But your sister told me you had a special love for mead."

"Bless you, lord," I whispered as the wagon jolted onward. "Bless you." I licked what he dabbed on my lips and mourned because it tasted like pitch instead of mead. But I did not tell him so, because I was afraid he would abandon me to the dark and the visions. "Please speak to me, lord."

"I'm sorry for my reticence, Valen. I've naught of cheer to report. So if you'd have me speak, then you must excuse my mentioning serious matters when you are so sick. Every hour brings us closer to the solstice, and I am in desperate need of a plan. How do I find the Danae? How do I persuade them to trust me? If you don't get well— of course, you will—but if you don't, I'll be in a pretty mess."

"Likely I'll be sicker on the solstice," I mumbled into the moldy wool. "Even if I survive this."

"And why would you be sick on the solstice? I expect you to have your head clear of this cursed craving long before then. From what your sister told me, you're never really sick."

"Solstice is my birthday." The effort of conversation made my head spin. "Always sick."

"Indeed? You must have been a horrid child. Did you make yourself sick on your birthday? Too many sweets? Too much wine?"

This birthday . . . what was it? I had thought of something . . . before sickness and mania took me. Something nagged, like dirt left in a wound. Mustering every scrap of control I had left, I dug through the detritus of memory. *Seven.* The mystery of seven. My grandfather had confirmed it.

"On some birthdays, my disease got worse. On my seventh birthday, I set fire to my bed and ran away. On my fourteenth, I hurt so wicked, I took nivat the first time. Twenty-first, thought my prick would fall off. Almost killed a whore . . ." The wagon lurched and bumped. I clutched the blankets, shivering, and fought to keep talking. The dark waters of madness lapped at my mind. If I sank below the waves, I would never rise. "Gods, I am a lunatic. Always have been. But Janus says I'll be *free* on this birthday—twenty-eighth. Dead, more like. Every seven years, I go mad."

He was so quiet for so long, I panicked, flailing my arms in the darkness. "Please, don't leave me, lord. Please!"

"I'm here, Valen." He caught my arms and laid them gently at my side. I welcomed the searing torment as he laid a firm hand on my head. "That's an extraordinary tale . . . seven, fourteen, twenty-one . . . and now twenty-eight. It reminds me of something in Picus's journal. Picus was my father's tutor, himself a monk as well as a sturdy warrior, sent to protect Father as he grew up in Danae fostering, and to ensure he learned of his own people. Picus wrote endlessly of numbers and their significance, especially seven and four. He it was who calculated the sevenfold difference in the spending of life in Aeginea. The Danae themselves pay no heed to numbers past four—the completion of the seasons that they call the *gyre* and their four *remasti*, or bodily changes: separation, exploration, regeneration, maturity . . ."

Moments seeped past in the dark. The horses whinnied. The cart jostled. The hand on my head quivered. My master's voice shook when he took up again, though he had dropped it near a whisper. "You have always been rebellious . . . out of place . . . never sick, save for this peculiar disease festering in your bones. Your grandfather favored you above all his progeny . . . the same man who stole a treasure from the Danae . . . to which he claimed a right. Janus de Cartamandua, by coincidence the very same man who provided unimpeachable witnesses to your pureblood birth—his own two boyhood friends."

Of a sudden, hands gripped my shoulder like jaws of iron.

"How blind I have been," he said, "I, who have read Picus's journals since I was a child. Think, Valen. Of *course* you can't read. Of *course* confinement and suffocation madden you . . . make you feel as if you're dying. Confinement within the works of man kills them. But *you* don't die from it. Remember on the day your sister was to take you from Gillarine, Gildas gave you water—I'd swear on my father's heart it was from the Well, already tainted with Gerard's murder—and it poisoned you. But, again, you did not die, only got wretchedly sick, because you are *both* and *neither*. By all that lives in heaven or hell, Valen . . ."

And the truth lay before my crumbling mind, as gleaming and perfect as the golden key of paradise, as solid and irrefutable as the standing stones of my long questioning now shifted into a pattern that explained my father's loathing and my mother's drunken aversion and every mystery of my broken childhood. My father's damning curse hung above it all like a new-birthed star in the firmament: *You are no child of mine.*

Indeed, my blood was no purer than Osriel the Bastard's, at most only half Aurellian—and that half given me by *Janus* de

Cartamandua, not Claudio. But unlike that of my rightful king, the taint that sullied my pure Aurellian heritage was not the royal blood of Navronne, but that of a pale-skinned race whose members were exceptionally tall, had curling hair, and could not read. *Thou, who art without words, yet complete.*

". . . you are Danae."

The cart bucked once more, and I lost my feeble hold on reason. The tides of pain, fire, and madness engulfed me, and I heard myself wailing as from a vast and lonely distance.

PART TWO

The Waning Season

Chapter 8

The angel sponged my chest with warm water and chamomile. I scarcely dared breathe lest she realize I was awake—or as much awake as I ever seemed to get amid my cascading visits to hell and heaven. The sponge moved lower. A pleasurable languor settled in my belly and spread to my knees and elbows. This moment was surely wrought in heaven. But who would ever have expected heaven to smell like chamomile?

She lifted the sponge, sloshed it in a metal basin, and squeezed it, the sound of dribbling water setting my mouth watering as well. Her washing was always quite thorough, the water deliciously warm, her fingers . . . ah, Holy Mother . . . her fingers strong and sure. Her hands were not the tender silk of a courtesan's, nor were they rough and calloused like those of a dairymaid or seamstress, but firm and capable. Tough, but unscarred. Her voice named her female, but when she leaned across me to reach my sprawled arm, her body smelled of clean linen hung out in the sun to dry. An angel, then, not a woman. But her hands . . .

"I think you are beginning to enjoy this too much, Magnus Valentia." The angel's breath scalded my ear. "Either you are feigning sleep or your dreams have broached the bounds of propriety. Know this, sirrah: I would as soon tongue a goat as indulge a man's pleasure— no matter the marvels of his birth."

The warm sponge touched my groin . . . I groaned as gatzi drove me back into hell.

Magnus Valentia. The name attached itself to me in some vague fashion throughout my ensuing visit to the netherworld. As familiar spiders crept through my bowels with barbed feet, breeding their myriad children, who then flooded out of my nose and mouth and other bodily orifices, and as gatzi strung me up on a cliff of ice and lashed me with whips of fire, I examined the appellation carefully. Shoving aside pain and madness—what use to heed the twin keystones of my universe?—I turned it over and over in my ragged mind: *Magnus Valentia.* It wasn't quite right. Not a lie, but not truth either. The few bits of truth I experienced—the angel's sure hands, clean smell, and astringent tongue, the clean cold air that blasted my overheated face from time to time, an occasional taste of pungent wine, the plucked notes of a harp—had a certain rarefied quality about them, a hard-edged luminescence that distinguished them from mania.

The uncertainty of name and birth dogged me until I next came to my senses—or at least what portion of them I could claim. A flurry of hands rolled me over in the soft bed and restrained my wrists and ankles with ties of silk. I could not fathom why my caretakers bothered with such. The only movement I seemed able to command was licking my parched lips.

A hand on my forehead brought the world beyond my eyelids into sharper focus. I smelled . . . everything . . . dust and stone, the faint residue of burning pennyroyal, rosemary, oil of wintergreen, medicines and possets, old boots and dried manure, cinnamon and ale, evergreen branches, chamomile, and soap. But unlike the usual case of late, the varied scents did not corrode my flesh. Hell's minions had been using my senses as instruments of torture.

"The spell seems to be taking hold," said the woman—the angel. Her voice crackled like glass crushed under a boot. "His last seizure spanned only an hour, and each seems milder than the one before. He no longer tries to injure himself. His body now responds to pleasure as well as pain. As Your Grace has rejoined us, perhaps he'll open his eyes. He reacts to your presence as to none other. And not entirely with terror. Does that annoy you, lord?"

Someone drew up a sheet of soft linen to cover my naked shoulders and the touch of its fine-woven threads did not make me scream. I almost forgot to listen as I contemplated this odd experience.

"Will he have a mind left after all this? I need him capable. This very hour would be none too soon." The man's voice slid into my thoughts like a sharpened stake into soft earth, rousing a frantic need for sense and strength. Despite his intriguing language of sanity and reason, instinct screamed that to lie here bound and muddleheaded in his presence was dangerous.

Filled with eager dread, I fought to open my eyes, but succeeded only in stirring up remnants of madness. Just punishment. I had broken vows . . . indulged perversion . . . done murder . . . soiled my bed . . . and now I had to pay. Dancing shadows swirled in the landscape of my head, parting to reveal scarlet light glaring from the empty eye sockets of sprawled corpses, a brawny man pinned to the earth with wooden stakes, skeletal fingers drawing me into the snow-blanketed bog, pulling me down and down into the icy mud. Drowning . . . suffocating . . . freezing . . . yet never, ever dead. Seven times seven times seven years was I condemned to live and die, buried in the ice. A wail rose from my hollow chest.

The angel's hand on my back silenced my cry before it reached my throat. Her sere voice swept away the nightmares as if they were no more than ash, drifting like black snow about my bed. "I cannot even venture a guess as to his state."

She moved away. A clank of iron, various rustlings and thumps, and a mumbled "*flagro*" produced a rush of sound and a moment's blistering heat behind me, surging to attack the legions of winter.

"Yet indeed the fellow's constitution is extraordinary," she continued. "A *fortunate* man—that is, one who did not die gnawing his own appendages—would experience the most acute nivat sickness for six weeks after quitting the doulon. Certain effects—nausea, high-strung nerves, tremors, and sweats—would then linger for nigh on a year, and susceptibility to the craving for the rest of his life. This man, or whatever you think he is, is emerging from the acute illness after only a fortnight. Perhaps your theory as to his birth explains why. Whatever the source of his resistance to nivat's worst effects, each succeeding hour convinces me that this sensory disorder that remains is, indeed, fundamental to his body's humors. Yet I see no more evidence of immortality or inhuman strength in him than I see of wings or halos or blue sigils glowing from his skin. Look at the scars on his thigh and shoulder. He's been wounded a number of times, and he's been enslaved to the most virulent of all enchantments for near half his life. No physician could tell you more of his nature than that. Consult priests or talespinners, if you insist on more."

"I've not yet confirmed the details of his birth," said the man. "And we've no idea the implications of dual bloodlines—such bloodlines. Of course, he would be neither immortal nor invulnerable. You've not mentioned this to anyone else?"

"Certainly not. I'd sooner spread plague than dose idiots with more superstitions. It's wretched enough to see their response when I confess that my employer is Magrog the Tormentor's rival, while I am forbidden to reveal that he's naught but a disease-ridden celibate with a diabolical bent for magic and an overgrown opinion of himself."

"Someday, mistress, you truly will overstep." Frost edged the man's words, so bitter that my tattered soul curled into a ball and hid, certain I was fallen to hell again.

But my astringent angel laughed, her fearless merriment a silver sword banishing the demon gatzi that tried to take shape behind my eyelids. Pillows lay soft beneath my cheek; tendrils of warmth wafted from her hearth. Even the silken ties that bound my wrists and wrapped each finger made me feel safe and protected in her presence.

Receding footsteps crossed my muted chamber, then clicked on tile as they passed into a place of echoes. Behind my eyelids I envisioned a long, wide passage of clean white stone, bordered by arches hung with brightly woven curtains. The lamps that hung from the high ceiling shone, not with burning oil or lit fingers of wax and braided wick, but with the pure blue fire of daylight, held captive within their glass panes. The image held the same hard-edged truth as the angel's hands and stray moonbeams.

Whence came such certainty? I could not have *seen*. I'd been a raving lunatic since well before they brought me here, my eyes covered, my ears and nose stopped to tame the agony of my senses.

"Someone's coming to sit with him? I don't begrudge you rest after this long siege, but I'd not have him left alone." The man's voice echoed faintly down the passage.

"The fellow must have some charm about him," she said, sere as the uplands of Ardra. "Everyone seems eager to take a turn to help—even your little heart's bane. I've made a schedule . . ."

Gatzi surged out of the corners of my mind, pricked at my skin, and drew me downward into the frozen bog. Mud and water filled my lungs, so I could only choke and gurgle, not scream.

"There, can you feel it, Brother? A marvel as we've not seen since we left Palinur. Awkward as this might be for us were you sensible, Saverian said that to expose your skin might do more good than harm, so . . ."

Hands drew stale linens away, tugging gently where they snarled my tucked limbs, carefully settling the scant weight about my hips. The touch of air on skin set off a defensive tremor deep within me where some primitive function kept my heart beating and lungs pumping. Yet it was merely sharp-edged heat that bathed my flesh.

Every nerve burst awake in that moment, not in the overstretched agonies of madness, but in a fevered baptism of delight. My lungs filled with light. My ears rang with its brazen song. I tasted its tart and searing flavor. And as heat filled my veins, I groaned and uncurled, stretching to gather more of it before hell's minions snatched it away.

"Dear Brother, I'm sorry if this hurts you!"

My eyes flew open to dazzling brilliance, and a sweetly curved form shimmering red against the haloed light—my angel. The memory of her strong hands tending my naked flesh sent the liquid sunlight in my veins surging toward my groin and possessed me of such aching desire, I dared reach for her wrist, even as I breathed fire. "O blessed one . . ."

"Brother Valen, the Mother be praised! What are you—?"

I drew her close and kissed her—gently, for angels are but cloud and music and divine light, thus bruise easily. Her lips were as sweet and rich as heaven's cream. Her silken gown flowed as water on my skin. And underneath that fabric . . . As my left hand fingered her bronze corona of soft hair, my right released her wrist and smoothed the gauzy robe from her shoulder. *Great gods of earth and sky, what gift of mortal substance have you granted your holy messenger?* My mouth followed my hand's guidance, as it unmasked the tender hollow below her shoulder and the firm swell of her breast . . . skin so like silk . . .

"Brother, what magic do you wield? Ah, Holy Mother . . . your hands are unbound. I've never felt such. We ought not . . ."

I kissed her lips to quiet her. Suffused in exquisite radiance, she yielded to my embrace, only a sighing breath as my hands slipped away her layered raiment, until she lay entwined with me, her skin cool against my fever, no sexless divinity, but full and ripe and enduringly female.

Hands cupping her firm backside, I drew her sweet center against my swollen need and buried a groan in her neck. Gods, I had been ready for an eternity. I tumbled her over, released her to the pillows, and straddled her. She lay beneath me in the brilliance of winter sunlight, arms flung over her head. Her eyes were closed, long lashes delicate on her cheek, lips full and slightly parted, golden skin flushed. Ready, too. I inhaled deeply.

As if a finger had snatched a blindfold from my eyes, her scent snapped me awake. *Fennel soap. Thyme and leeks. Woman. Elene.*

I hesitated, quivering with the difficulty of restraint, trying not to let thought or fear intrude where they had no place. Naught had changed but my perceptions. I touched two fingers to her lips and drew them down the fine line of her jaw and her neck, across her breast, and down to her belly. She shivered deliciously.

I smoothed my palm across her belly . . . and a certainty intruded on my overcharged senses, one of those spine-rippling moments of prescience I'd experienced throughout my life. I must not lie with her. Some heated core within her insisted I had no right.

Shaking with pent desire, I snatched my hand away.

"Lady . . ." I drew a wavering breath and shifted to the side, making sure not to touch her again. Then I spread the fallen red silk over her, gathered the tangled bedclothes into my lap, and turned my face away as if I had not looked on her abandon. Assuredly this was not her first time to lie with a man. Was it my own past sin that burned my conscience and stayed my hand? Fire-god Deunor, what had I done?

"Forgive me, lady." My voice sounded coarse and strange, scarcely audible. "My madness has drawn you in. Or some magic of the sunlight. Unable to control— By the Goddess Mother, I would not take you unconsenting. By magic. Even mad, I can't believe I would."

She stiffened and drew away, the catch in her throat no longer healthy lust, but shock. *My* body's demands were not so speedily dismissed. *Great gods* . . . I clawed the bright-woven blanket and clamped it in my lap. Perhaps I'd best keep babbling.

"Your kindness seems to have brought me back to life," I said, as hurried fumbling took her clear of the bed. "My head so muddled . . . a lunatic . . . I thought you an—"

Tell her I'd believed her an angel, and she'd be sure I was mad and have me bound again. I could scarce argue with such a judgment. I had no idea of year or season, of where we were or what had brought us here. Only now were life and memory settling into some explanation of this eternity of pain and nightmare. Nivat. The doulon. Disease.

"You've cared for me all these wretched days . . . Iero's hand of mercy . . . and I so disgusting in my perversions. I'd no idea that I had . . . I don't know what to say."

She didn't run away. Scarce controlling my urge to wrestle her back into my arms, I could not but shove the wadded bedclothes tighter into my treacherous parts and shut my foolish mouth. A warrior woman of Evanore. She likely had a knife to hand—though where hidden in that gown I dared not imagine. What business had she in red silk instead of her habergeon? Yet truly, mail as sturdy as her father's might not have resisted my urgency this day. Her father . . . Now there was a remembrance made my shaft begin to shrink.

The silence stretched long enough, I ventured a glimpse to make certain she was no stray illusion after all. She stood at the wide window, where the unexpected brilliance of sunlight split by mullioned panes had set off my befuddled misbehavior. Red gown in disarray, bronze hair tousled, she folded her arms and pressed one hand against her lips as her shoulders shook.

Just as I, shamed and regretful, returned my attention to the rumpled sheets, muzzled laughter burst that fine barrier and brightened the room even as the sunlight. "Dear Brother Valen," she said, when her first spasms had eased, "when you wake, you *wake.* Though I must appreciate, and approve, your gracious conscience, I don't know if I will ever, *ever,* forgive you for stepping back. I've imagined this occasion since I first took you walking out of Gillarine. Were I living in my grandmother's day, I might have carted you off to my fastness that very night! Somehow you cause a woman to lose her mind and forgo all other . . . yearnings. Indeed your fingers carry magic."

Unable to keep my gaze from her, I gaped, uncomprehending.

She shook her head in mimed rue. "What's more, honesty requires me to confess that this is the first time I have visited you this tenday of your stay at Renna. Other tasks have occupied my time. It is Renna's physician, Saverian, you must thank for your care. Though I'll warn you: Play your finger tricks on her, and she'll have you a eunuch before you can sneeze."

The astringent angel. How could I ever have believed that sexless messenger of the heavenly sphere to be Elene, who was abundant earth itself? I felt ridiculous . . . and marvelous . . . and then, of a sudden, weak as a plucked chicken, as the sunlight faded into flat gray.

Elene produced a comb from her pocket and began to tame her hair. Chilled and chastened under my rumpled sheets and blankets, I curled up around my regrets and considered the mysterious certainty that had halted so fine a pursuit. I was no diviner. The only thing I'd ever predicted with accuracy was whether a sick or wounded man was like to live or die.

Life or death . . . I closed my eyes and recalled that core of heat beneath Elene's silken skin . . . that core of life . . . My eyes popped open again. "Oh, good lady!"

My face as hot as the color of her garments, I motioned her near. What I had discerned might be more dangerous than any magical indiscretion. She approached my bedside, brows raised in amused speculation, her face at a level with mine. Not even the spider on the windowsill could have heard my whisper. "Mistress Elene, do you know you are with child?"

Clearly not. For a second time the sun vanished behind burgeoning clouds, and I existed once more entirely within the bounds of disastrous winter.

"You're wrong! No god would be so cruel . . . so foul . . . the Mother would not permit it!" She spun in place, her arms flailing in helpless frenzy, until her bloodless fists gripped a warming iron and she smashed it onto the bed not a tenquat from my head. "Damnable, accursed madman! How could you know?"

I didn't take the warming iron so much for a personal assault, as for a measure of shocked desperation. Her earlier confessions affirmed the child was not mine, begotten in some lunatic frenzy I could not remember. I kept a wary eye out for a second strike. "I've always had this instinct—"

I began to say it was a scrap of talent inherited from my mother, the diviner. But returning memory swept through me as a spring wind through an open door, swirling away dead beliefs like dried leaves. My hands trembled, no longer from frustrated lust, but from evidence revisited and truth laid bare. Josefina de Cartamandua-Celestine, drunken diviner, wife of Claudio, was not my mother.

"Valen, are you ill? Did I strike you? Holy Mother, I'm sorry. You've been so— I didn't mean— Let me find Saverian."

The warming iron clanked onto the floor, the noise making me wince. Elene streaked out of the room in a blaze of scarlet, while I flung off the bedclothes and examined my naked flesh. What did I expect to see? Blue dragons tearing through my skin? Surely the doulon sickness had unstrung my reason.

But my mad grandfather's words popped into my head as clearly as I'd heard them that last night at my family's home. *Everything is secrets and contracts . . . I stole from them. A treasure they did not value. I had the right, but they could not forgive the loss of it . . .* Only, Janus de Cartamandua-Magistoria was not my grandfather. He was my father.

I stumbled to my feet and strode the length of the chamber, an expansive room of whitewashed stone walls, of clean curves and arches and broad paned windows. Swelling anger gave strength to limbs too long cramped and idle. My skin buzzed as if I'd been buried in a barrel of flies.

Thou canst not know! He'll think I told thee . . . Claudio exacted such a price . . . keeping me from thee. His babbling made sense now. I could reconstruct the history: Janus de Cartamandua, whose pureblood wife was long dead, had brought home an infant, a child of his own body, and struck a bargain with his son, Claudio. *Raise this child as your own*, Janus would have said, *and I'll not announce to the world that the Cartamandua bloodline is corrupted. I will even supply unimpeachable birth witnesses for the Registry.*

Claudio, furious, filled with hate for the man who put him in such a position, would have agreed in a heart's pulse . . . on condition that Janus stay away . . . never tell the child the truth . . . never interfere. For seven-and-twenty years Claudio had pretended to the world that the loathsome child, whose very existence promised ruin to the family, was his own pureblood offspring. And all the anger he dared not show for his own father, he had expended on the child he despised—the son of Janus de Cartamandua and a Dané named Clyste.

"Spirits of night . . ." Truth pierced my heart like a sword of fire, as painful as any remnant of my madness: I had heard my true mother's voice. Beyond a barrier of mystery in Gillarine's cloister garth, I had felt the pulse of her lingering life . . . experienced her grief and wordless tenderness, heard her music that had touched places within me that I didn't know existed. But I'd not known it was she, imprisoned for Janus's crime . . . trapped, condemned to slow fading. So he had described her fate. Now she was dead, and I could never know her. And I . . .

I propped my hands on a long bare table of scraped pine, my whole body shaking.

"Return to your bed, and I can keep the others away from you for a while longer."

In an arched doorway stood a tall whip of a woman, dressed in riding leathers. Though her height spoke contrariwise, her nose, as long and straight as my own, her skin, the hue of hazelnuts, and her hair, straight, black, and heavy, tightly bound in a thick braid, testified unmistakably to Aurellian descent. Pureblood or very near. Tangled as I was in the unraveling of long deception and a loneliness that threatened to unman me, I had no capacity to guess who she might be.

"On the other hand, if you roam the halls of Renna, I'll take no responsibility for the consequences, especially if you insist on wearing naught but your skin. The housemaids rarely see such sights. Evanori are a modest people."

The prospect of visitors and questioning nauseated me. "I thank you for the offer, lady, but I doubt Kemen Sky Lord himself could keep Prince Osriel away once he hears a report of my state." Once he knew his captive half Dané could speak.

"What state would that be?" Decisive footsteps brought her up behind me, and her leather gloves skittered onto the table. "As a physician, I propose *dead* as your most likely condition and that what I see before me must perforce be an apparition. Surely no human body could withstand what you have gone through this tenday and stand here speaking as if he'd a modicum of sense."

"Physician?" I whipped my head around. She stood three or four paces away, her brows raised. "You're Saverian . . ." The astringent angel.

"Please don't bother me with 'What an odd name for a woman,' or 'How could such a *young* woman possibly know enough to be a physician?' or 'You must mean hedge-witch, do you not?' or 'How could a *modest* woman bear to mess about with such nastiness as physicians must?' So, Magnus Valentia, are you human or apparition or . . . something else?"

I averted my face, propped my backside on the table, and rubbed my aching head. Someone had trimmed my hair short again, disguising its telltale curl—so unnatural for a pureblood. "I don't know what I am."

To my discomfiture, the woman briskly installed herself in front of me and held out one open palm as if to demonstrate it held no weapon. Then she touched me with it—raised my chin, felt my forehead, and lifted my eyelids, peering inside me as if I were a vat of odd-smelling stew.

"For one, you are a doulon slave," she said, as she retrieved my hand from my groin where it was attempting to maintain a bit of dignity before a stranger. She attended the beat in my wrist veins as dispassionately as ever Brother Robierre the infirmarian had done at Gillarine. "No matter how remarkably fast you have sloughed them off this time, nivat's chains will ever bind you. I would be remiss if I did not say that here at the beginning. A fool should know what his stupidity has cost him."

I examined her face, all unrelieved planes and angles. A small mouth and ungenerous lips. The pureblood nose narrow and sharp. Small creases between her dark brows, and crinkled lines clustered at the outer corners of her eyes, as if she spent a goodly time at her books, though the smoothness of her dusky skin testified that she could not yet have seen thirty summers. Naught of warmth or passion in that face. Naught of disgust either, which spoke decently of her philosophy as a physician.

Using both hands now and spitting a few unintelligible epithets under her breath, she explored my neck, strong fingers poking and prodding in search of who knew what. Yet the annoying agitation of my skin dulled, even as she produced a silver lancet and glass vial from out of nowhere and nicked and milked the vein in my left arm.

"What does that mean?" I said, watching her stopper the vial containing my blood and slip it into her pocket. "About the doulon. I'd not dared hope—"

"It means you'd best put nivat seeds right out of your head. To touch or even to smell them risks waking your craving again. And it means that you must find some other way to deal with this." She blew on her fingers and touched my ears.

The world exploded in sound. Bleating, crunching, crackling, drumming ... the noise trapped inside my skull felt as if it were bulging my eyes from the inside out.

Birds scrabbled on the roof. Pots rattled in a distant kitchen. Two women argued. A sick man moaned and mumbled in drugged sleep. A rhythmic crashing could only be someone raking hay. Horses chomped ... mice scuttered ... this very structure—a house of wood, not stone—creaked as the wind pushed on it. My heart rumbled like an avalanche beside the woman's steady drumbeat.

I cringed and clapped my hands over my ears. "Blessed Deunor!"

Saverian's warm hands covered mine and, at her muttered word, mercifully damped the clamor. Strong, capable hands. I would never mistake them.

"Thank you," I whispered as the din in my head subsided. To my relief, my voice remained a whisper and not the onslaught of a whirlwind. "For *all* your kindness these days."

"Kindness had nothing to do with it," she said, dry as the desert winds of Estigure. "Prince Osriel insists that he needs your functioning mind as soon as may be. Yet each one of your senses seems to suffer this same incontinence. This muting enchantment is a somewhat brutish remedy, but the only way I see to solve a problem I've been given no leisure to investigate. It is far from a permanent solution to your excess sensitivity, as it fades quite rapidly. Perhaps if you could tell me more about the progress of the disease. Do these symptoms vary?"

"When I was seven, attacks came every month or two, and lasted a few days at a time. Over time, they became more frequent, more severe, and lasted longer, but still coming and going. By fourteen ... well, I started the doulon at fourteen, and after that ..."

"... everything was a muddle. Yes. I would imagine." She gestured insistently toward the rumpled bed and offered me her arm. "Elene indicated that the sunlight roused your member. Is that true? Is there some connection?"

Since I'd first discovered the merry art, I'd never understood why so many shrouded it with shame. But her brazen questioning made it sound as if one could set down a recipe for desire as Brother Jerome had seasoned stewing parsnips. Disconcerted, I refused her assistance and set out for the bed on my own. "I don't— Perhaps. The light fed whatever— I've never noticed a connection."

By the time I'd gone half the length of the chamber, I decided I should have kept her beside me instead of leaving her behind to observe my naked rump. Of a sudden I could not get myself back under the bedclothes soon enough. I certainly had no mind to tell her that it was the memory of her hands had done the rousing.

I sank to the low bed—a boxlike wooden platform, built right into the floor—dragged a blanket from the tangle, and bundled it around my shoulders. I was shaking again, this time from the cold. The sun had lost itself in the gray and white world beyond the window glass.

Saverian knelt by the hearth, threw three logs onto a heap of glowing ash, and snapped her fingers. The ash glowed brighter, but the logs remained inert. "*Flagro*, you misbegotten twigs!" she shouted with a certain cheerful virulence. Bright blue flames as high as my knee burst from the logs with a throaty roar before settling into a tidy, robust blaze.

"You'll find clothes in the chest and cider by your bed. I'll have food brought. Though you may yet experience nausea or poor appetite, you should eat and drink. Someone will sit with you until we're sure my conjuring can sustain you, but by heaven and earth, keep your appendages to yourself! If someone had found you with Thane Stearc's only child . . . You'd not like thinking on what meager bits of you would be left for me to study." The woman retrieved her gloves from the table and moved briskly to the doorway. She paused, thoughtful. "You don't fancy *men*, do you? Should I warn them as well?"

An abortive laugh burst through my heavy spirit. "Not in that way. At least, not recently." Then again, one heard so many different tales of Danae. Who knew what was true? Some tales said Danae mated with the wind or the sea or with animals or kin. My stomach lurched unpleasantly.

"Osriel has told me your history, and of his theory as to your birth. I must tell you that I'm skeptical. Even if there exist beings who live for centuries and can conjoin themselves with trees or mud, I doubt you're one of them. These past days . . . if you could have escaped the consequences of this unforgivable injury you've worked on an otherwise healthy body, you'd have done it."

"Perhaps I just don't know how."

"Pssh." She leaked skepticism.

As her departing footsteps echoed in the passage, I tried to imagine what it might be like to yield my soul and body to a tree and be confined by its immovable bark and leaf or to find myself locked into the barren stone and blue-white ice of Clyste's Well. I lurched from the bed to the night jar, threw off the copper lid, and heaved up bile from my empty belly.

Chapter 9

I held the spell fragments—the essence of the turned wood cup, the image of the large wooden bowl I desired, the linkages of power, the rearrangement of perception, the connecting threads of what *was* to what would be—and then, carefully, slowly, I unleashed the flow of magic. Nothing happened. I closed my eyes, focused on my fingers and on the warm center somewhere amid lungs and heart and spine whence I drew magic, and tried again, this time with less caution. Failed again.

A stupid test. But my question had been answered. Either the doulon sickness had drained me of magic or Osriel had somehow precluded my use of it. And without working magic, I could not begin to understand what the nonhuman part of me might bring to it.

I tossed the cup on the bed and ran my fingers about the window frame, searching in vain for the faint prickles that would indicate a barrier to sorcery. My fears that the *power of Evanore* might explode my small illusion or bloat my cup into a house now seemed absurd. Evanore . . . the haunted realm.

The view beyond my window was stunning—a sprawl of blue-white mountain peaks and plunging chasms, shrouded in wind-whipped cloud. Nearer, dominating a tortuous slope, a small, solid fortress backed up to a low bluff, the two appearing to have sprouted together from the stone core of the mountains. Scattered about the lower slopes, colorful tents billowed like the sails of a Moriangi fleet. Riders streamed from the encampment and the lower valley toward the fortress gates, banners fluttering, squires, servants, and soldiers trudging alongside.

More than the barren, windswept slope separated this house—where I was kept—from the fortress. These clean open arches, the finely carved ceilings, polished woods, and expansive windows were altogether unlikely for an Evanori war lair.

Of course, Osriel himself made no more sense than this house. It would have been easy to dismiss him as a cynical and unprincipled sorcerer, the most skilled manipulator of men I had ever encountered, able to convince abbots and nobles that he held the interests of Navronne preeminent, while using cruelty and torment to ingratiate himself with the lord of hell. Yet I knew the answer to his mystery was not so simple. He had risked his own life on our last venture, not just to retake Gildas and the book, but for Jullian, whom wise men would name the least of our cabal. And some quality in the prince had reached me through pain and madness and kept me from losing my mind. No matter how much I wished to distance myself from his red lightning and blood-marked rituals, I owed him a debt.

I snatched up the green sash and knotted it about my waist. I'd found it along with a knee-length tunic and wool leggings in the carved clothes chest at the foot of the bed. True to her promise, Saverian had sent a serving man with a wooden dish heaped with bread, cheese, and dried apples. I had made it through one rubbery slice of apple before my rebellious stomach halted further attempts. She had come herself an hour later. Inspected my tongue and eyes, taken more blood, sat at the table to write extensive notes in a worn book. She had refused to say when I could travel or whether anyone was out searching for a captive child.

Gods . . . Jullian. The thought of him held by Harrowers tore at my heart. Unfortunately this past hour had left me no nearer choosing a course of action. I had sworn not to run. Yet, did a man's oath bind when the one who'd sworn it discovered he was something altogether different than he believed? Not entirely human. I kept staring out the window half hoping, half terrified to see a Dané with a dragon on his face. My uncle. Holy Mother . . .

"Hsst! Valen! Over here." The whisper came from the corner beyond the empty table and a yellow painted washing stand stacked with towels.

My heart's stuttering calmed when Elene poked her head through a heavy curtain woven in colorful stripes. Against the rich greens and blues, her complexion took on the color of whitewash. She beckoned me to join her. Not at all a difficult summons to obey. Truly the woman was more addictive than nivat, especially as I now had a true memory of her unclothed, instead of mere imaginings. The truth outshone the image as an angel outshines a frog.

"Great gods be thanked," she said softly, inspecting me from head to toe, her very presence lifting my spirits. "Saverian told me I'd not harmed you, but I kept imagining a great charred dent in your skull."

I spread my arms and twirled about, then ducked my head so she might view its integrity. "Your weapon never touched me. Rather, it's I who must apol—"

"Valen, you *must* not tell anyone what you told me. Please, promise me. I beg you."

I could not help but smile at this ferocious reversal of her earlier indignation. Glancing about to ensure no weapon was at hand, I spoke softly. "So it's true, then?"

"By the Mother, promise me! On your word—the same oath you gave Osriel!"

Though I could foresee no circumstance that would make me betray such a confidence, the prospect of one more binding oath filled me with misgiving. I was already hamstrung by my submission to Osriel. Yet I did need a friend in this house, and I could well understand her desperation. An unexpected pregnancy was no happy news for an unwed girl of any parentage. So I raised my hand.

"I could never be such a madman as to betray the confidence of a daughter of Evanore. But if it eases one worry, mistress, then by the Mother I swear you my silence without reservation. And perhaps in return you'll be kind enough not to mention my . . . indiscretion . . . of this morning to any who might take offense." I didn't need irate warlords drawing practice targets on my hide.

She rolled her eyes. "I'm hardly likely to speak of it. Remember *you* are the lunatic, not I. Well . . . clearly I am, as well . . . but you can be sure my tongue is mute. I told Saverian you'd made an advance. In the confusion of your illness, of course. I had to report your . . . condition. For your sake. You can be sure the frost witch will bait us with it, but she'll not tell anyone else. Though she's wholly Osriel's creature, it suits her to keep her patients' counsel. She'd not have them withhold information she needs to succeed in her work."

This barren bluntness belied any assumption of a womanly confederacy.

"So, what of you, lady? Will the man be upright about all this? What will you do?" Though I was ferociously curious, I chose not to risk Elene's wrath by asking who had begotten the child. She lived in a world of men. One glance from her and she could have her pick. Her fury had not implied an unconsenting liaison, which precluded any temptation for noble reprisal on my part. But jealousy could easily lock my fingers around the damnable oaf's neck. Better not to know.

"I should have some time before anyone will guess—except perhaps Saverian. And I'll just stay out of her way. Whatever must be done, be sure no *man* will decide for me."

She beckoned me to duck my head again and startled me with a ferocious kiss planted square atop my head. "You've a good heart, Valen. The Mother shield you from your master's vile works."

Brisk footsteps echoed from the main passage. Elene paled. Stung by her warning, I caught her shoulder before she could duck beyond the striped drapery. "The prince . . . Voushanti . . . all these warnings . . . I feel as if I'm running blind down the road to hell. Someone needs to explain what I should fear, and you're the only person I trust to be honest with me."

Her brown eyes flamed amber. Resolution stamped her face. "You're right. But later tonight . . . during the warmoot. This last night is mostly ceremony. The main gates of the fortress face westerly. When the lords start singing, get you to the rock gate behind the east end of the hall, and I'll show you what to fear. Now, please . . ."

I released her, and she vanished. Snatching up a towel from the painted stand, as if I'd been washing, I spun in place and greeted my master as he hurried into the chamber. Garbed in an ash-gray tunic and black leggings no finer than my own, his hair tied back by a purple ribbon, he appeared more servant than prince. His pleasure as his first glance assessed me reflected that part of him I would ever name Gram.

I sank to one knee and touched fingers to forehead. "My lord."

"Will you never cease to astonish me, friend Valen?" he said, cocking his head to one side as he gazed down at me. A smile played over his fine countenance—noble Eodward's handsome features writ on a darker, frailer, sterner canvas. "I expected to find you weak and woolly on your waking day."

I dared not meet his eyes. Had our king known what his favored son played at? "I am both of those things, lord."

He touched my shoulder. "Come, get up. I won't keep you long. I've a hundred warlords in my hall, drinking my ale and spoiling for battle. Do you feel up to a walk?"

I held out my incapable fingers. "As long as you don't expect me to seek out our route."

He laughed quite genuinely and motioned me toward the passage. "That's Saverian's doing. She found silkbinding your hands tiresome and dodging your nightmares dangerous. You'll learn, as have we all, to avoid annoying Saverian. Thus you must tell me promptly if we need to get you back to bed. I doubt I could carry you, even under-fed as you are."

Despite his claim of warlords waiting, we strolled down the passage—the very one I had envisioned so clearly in my madness, even to the patterns and colors of the woven hangings. Above every arch hung a shield of beaten gold, each shaped as an animal—a fox, a lion, a boar, even fanciful beasts such as a dragon, phoenix, or centaur. One was a gryphon, its feathered wings spread from its lion's body, as on the Cartamandua family crest.

Bearing left around a corner, we arrived at a long gallery where weavings no longer blocked the arches. On one side of the gallery, the openings held paned windows that overlooked the descending slope, the grim fortress, and the grand mountain landscape; on the other, the openings stood unblocked, accessing a courtyard garden almost as large as Gillarine's cloister garth. Trees, shrubbery, and flowers grew in healthy profusion in air that held the warmth of late spring rather than winter's bite.

The notion struck me that I'd mistaken Elene's reference to my stay at Renna as a mere tenday. But when I looked to the sky to verify the season, I gasped in wonder. A dome of faceted glass separated us from the gray sky. Snowflakes flurried and danced, melting when they touched the intricately patterned glass.

"It's very like the domes in the lighthouse," I said, recalling the twin mosaic vaults of colored brilliance that had imbued the store-house of books and tools with magic and majesty.

"This was an early experiment," said the prince. "It told me that what I wanted to do was possible. Luviar and Victor had created the underground chambers early on—did you know that Victor is a pure-blood stonemason?—but his design was very . . . monkish. We had no time to cache works of art, but I felt our lighthouse ought to include something of no worth beyond its beauty. We'd not want humankind to forget something of such importance."

Once I would have marked this unsentimental declaration as the wisdom of ever-sensible Gram, and reveled at the new knowledge he'd let slip. Now I worried at his purpose, sure his every utterance hid meanings within meanings. And, too, a knife of guilt twisted in my heart at the reminder of my forgetfulness.

"Brother Victor . . . how fares he?" I'd heard a sick man struggling to breathe and wondered if it was the little monk. "I'd like to visit him. And Jullian . . . have we word of his fate? Plans for his rescue?"

His expression grave, Osriel clasped his hands behind his back. "We've had no further word of Jullian, and no word on the negotiations between my brother and Sila Diaglou. Be assured I remain committed to getting the boy back safely. As for Brother Victor . . . he improves daily, but his injuries were dreadful. Saverian has kept him asleep as she works to repair them. We hope he'll wake again when they've healed enough to cause him less pain. Best leave him in peace for now."

I was hardly surprised at his putting off my visit to the chancellor. "Later, then. As soon as he's able. I would never have guessed Victor pureblood."

"A humble man is a rarity among purebloods."

"True," I said, glancing at the magnificence above us. "For certain, I am no judge of men."

I longed to pour out my myriad questions to my friend Gram, but I dared not expose my ignorance to Osriel. Which was a wholly foolish sentiment. After weeks of raving mania, what part of me could be left private?

We ambled down one of the paved walkways that interlaced the garden, pausing when we came upon a fountain tucked into a grove of elders. Water bubbled from the feet of a statue depicting a tall, nude woman with an eagle taking flight from her upraised hand. Beside her, a sculpted man bent one knee and stretched the other leg behind him in a straight line with his muscled back. His fingers touched the center of his forehead in a gesture of respect, as his stony eyes gazed on a small tree bursting from the earth just beyond his bent knee. My skin slithered over my bones when I noted the fine whorls and images carved into the figures' marble flesh.

The prince stood at my shoulder. "My obstinate physician declines to reveal what the two of you discussed this morning. So I must ask if you remember our last conversation?"

I stared at the statues and forced my voice steady, as if on every day I spoke the unthinkable. "Janus de Cartamandua-Magistoria sired me. The Dané named Clyste was my mother."

"It explains a great deal, don't you think?" he said. "So you believe it's true?"

"Yes." Though questions piled upon questions, like a flock of sheep at a narrow gate, each pushing to get through. "I wonder . . . did they lock her away in the earth for lying with a human or for allowing a human to steal me away?"

I stole a treasure they did not value, but could not forgive the loss of, so Janus had said. I could not yet think of the old man as my father.

"Almost certainly the latter," said the prince. "My father and the monk Picus left Aeginea well before you were born. But I have Picus's journals, where he recorded all he learned of the Danae. He wrote that once past the third change—the passage of regeneration—a Dané is capable of mating and can choose his or her partners at will. As long as a joining is consensual, none may gainsay it. Certainly for Clyste to conceive a child could have been no accident. Danae females are fertile on the four days of season's change and no other. No matter that her family, the archon, and every other Dané would disapprove her choice, we must assume she chose Janus, and she chose to make a child with him."

They'll never have thee. I saw to it. The mad old man's words hung in my memory like stars in the firmament, sharpening the familiar aching void in my chest. Of a sudden, no caution could restrain my questions. Half my life had been denied me, the other half twisted out of all recognition, and this prince held some answers at least. "Then why would she let him take me? Everything he said leads me to believe she consented."

"Danae dislike halfbreeds"—he squatted beside the fountain and ran his fingers over the marble branches of the new-birthed tree—"but they believe no one else has any business raising one of their blood. Unlike Aurellian purebloods." He flashed a grin up at me. "Once *our* blood is proved tainted, the Registry cares naught what becomes of us. Perhaps you'd like to send the Registry a notice of your changed status?"

I had already considered that. "They'd only believe it another of my lies."

"Mmm . . . likely so." He removed a stone cup from a niche beside the fountain, scooped water from the font, and drank it down. I declined his offer of the cup, and he replaced it in its niche.

"So Clyste's child vanished," he continued. "The Danae believed the child belonged with them and punished her. But as to Clyste's purpose . . . A Danae mother is responsible for her child's education, including preparation for the remasti. She selects the child's vayar—the dance master. This preparation is the most serious and sacred duty among the long-lived. Perhaps she meant for Janus to bring you back at some time."

I hadn't even known the right questions to ask that night in Palinur, and my grandfather's ragged mind had skipped from one thing to another. But there had been something . . . "He said she bade him destroy his maps to keep other humans away from the Danae lands, because he could 'keep his promises' without them. And he said he'd failed her. But that could mean a thousand things." It was all very well to explore past intents, but the future concerned me more. "Why did he say I would be *free* when I turned eight-and-twenty? What happens then?"

"Four times in their lives—at the ages we would name seven, fourteen, one-and-twenty, eight-and-twenty—Danae undergo these bodily changes they call remasti or holy passages. We know little about the passages, save that each results in new gards—their skin markings. They consider the whole thing very private. Most of what Picus learned of them came from the confidences of one disaffected Dané female—a halfbreed girl named Ronila who left Aeginea before making her fourth change. He knew only the results of the fourth: The newly matured Danae are bound to a sianou and allowed to dance in the Canon itself for the first time, and from that day they are free to walk the world as they choose, subject to no person, law, or duty save the Law of the Everlasting as interpreted by their archon."

"But Janus had no intention of me living as a Dané. He wanted me to stay clear of them until I passed my birthday." *'Tis no life for thee,* he had told me. "Perhaps that was it. He had promised Clyste that he would send me back and then changed his mind."

Osriel nodded as he picked dead blooms from the violets massed about the fountain. "Therein, too, lies freedom of a sort. Picus wrote that those Danae who choose not to undergo the fourth remasti, or are forbidden to do so, or are incapable of it, lose the power to become one with a sianou. They revert to an ordinary life span—longer than humans live, but far short of the centuries a mature Dané would expect. It sounds as if you will become wholly human on your birthday. That must be what Janus wished."

"There must be something more," I said. "He told me I would be the greatest of the Cartamandua line. He said our family would be powerful beyond dreaming." Dawning understanding knotted my hands and heated my cheeks. For a lifetime I had hated Janus de Cartamandua with every scrap of my strength. But he had given up his mind to the Danae, and in the throes of despair and weak-minded sentiment, I had come to believe he'd done it to protect *me* from harm. But now matters became clear. It was never for me—child or man. All was for the Cartamandua bloodline. "He must have thought staying free would strengthen my bent or change it in some way. He thought I would make our family 'magnificent.' "

"Would that we could question Picus. But not long after he and my father returned to Navronne, the monk vanished without a word to anyone. Come along." The prince motioned for me to walk with him. "What happens or does not happen on your birthday is not the only mystery to unravel. Would you like to hear what I know of your mother?"

"Very much." I needed to move, to walk if I could not run.

"Clyste was my father's foster sister, making you and me cousins of a sort. I hope that does not disturb you too awfully." We walked out of the garden, through the airy passages, and into a series of shuttered rooms. "She was daughter of the Danae archon Stian and beloved of every Danae for her joyful spirit and for the skill and glory of her dancing. When Clyste came into her season for her fourth change, the powerful Dané who had guarded the Well for time unremembered announced that he was tired and ready to yield his sianou to a younger guardian. All believed that the Well, a place revered among the Danae, had chosen Clyste. Kol told Picus that she brought an intelligence and a perfection to the Canon that the long-lived had rarely seen."

"Until Janus corrupted her," I said, near spitting gall. Anger burrowed under my skin and throbbed like a septic wound, poisoning the hard peace I had made with the old man on that last night in Palinur.

Osriel shrugged and strolled through a chamber littered with old paint splashes and stacks of canvas into a room hung with every size and shape of willow birdcages—all of them vacant. Someone of wide-ranging interests had lived in this house. But no longer.

"My father's failure to return to the Danae caused much anger and grief, and as years passed, visits with Clyste and Kol and my father's other friends among the Danae grew rare. But on one night not long after I was born, Kol barged into my father's bedchamber. Bitter and furious, Kol told him that Clyste had been bound to her sianou with myrtle and hyssop, forbidden to take bodily form again. He left with no further explanation, and my father neither saw nor spoke to another Dané before he died."

I held back a curtain, and we passed into what must once have been a gracious library, its dusty shelves now holding only a few scattered volumes. I guessed that the rest now sat in the magical lighthouse.

"Clearly there is even more to the story than we know," the prince continued, "for one must ask: If the Danae knew Janus de Cartamandua had stolen you and punished him for it, why did they never claim you? It would have been no great leap of intelligence to see that the infant who appeared in the Cartamandua house at the very time of the theft must be the half-Danae child."

I caught his meaning. "Yet if they had known I was half Danae, they would never have tried to drown me in the bog along with everyone else."

"Exactly so. I believe that, of all the Danae, only Kol knows who and what you are. Clyste never told them that *Janus* had fathered her child."

Which meant that Kol alone had driven my grandfather mad and that it was unlikely that Kol had launched the owl to drown us in the bog. If he had wanted me dead, he'd already had ample opportunities.

"Had I known all this before Mellune Forest, I might have run into the wild and begged the Danae to make me one of them," I said, "assuming such a thing is even possible. But whatever their reasons might have been, to trick fifty people into drowning—without judgment, without mercy, guilty and innocent alike—is as despicable as the Harrowers clogging wells with tar in Palinur. To protect my friends, I had to become complicit in their evil. I won't do that again."

Perhaps it was my imagination that Osriel's complexion darkened. A perceptive man as he was would surely understand it was not only of *Danae* evils that I spoke.

I moved swiftly to make my intent clear. "I will uphold my oath of submission to you, lord—I'll not run—but I intend to stay out of their way until my birthday." I had no desire to live as a stone or a tree.

Our meandering path had led us back to the passage of shields and curtained doors. "Your position makes sense," he said as we neared its end. "But you have also sworn to serve the lighthouse cabal. As there seems to be no immediate danger to you from Kol, I must call upon your oath and bid you guide me to a place where I can try once more to speak to him. We must discover if the Danae know the cause of the world's sickness, and we must warn them of Sila Diaglou."

Bonds of oath and obligation, now made all the more repugnant by this deeper loathing, settled about my limbs. "But, my lord—"

"You'll not have to face him yourself. In the hour I stand in Danae lands—beside the Sentinel Oak at Caedmon's Bridge—I shall deem your present obligation to me and to the cabal complete, and you may choose your own course to face your past and future. Saverian will maintain her remedy for your sickness as long as you require it. You will be welcome to reside here or come and go as your health allows." His face—Gram's face—expressed his particular earnest sincerity that could persuade a hen to lay its neck beneath the ax blade. "After the solstice, the world and our place in it will be changed for good or ill. At that time we will renegotiate the terms of your service. So, are you willing?"

Free to choose my own course . . . how sweet those words, offering the one thing I'd ever begged of the gods. He was right. If Kol meant to hand me over to the Danae or drive me mad, he could have taken me at Clyste's Well or fifty different times back in Palinur. And the deed should be possible; I had seen the great oak where only a crude illusion should have existed, where nothing grew in the human plane. I could take Osriel there, then be on my way . . . search for Jullian. Once the boy walked free and Gildas had paid a price for Gerard's murder, all my oaths would be fulfilled. Free to choose . . . "My lord, yes. Of course I'll take you."

"Good. I'll have done with my thirsty warlords tonight. If you feel in anywise fit enough, we'll leave for Aeginea tomorrow. Time presses us sorely."

"I'll be ready."

I pulled aside the blue and yellow curtain and waited for the prince to enter my bedchamber, but he motioned me to go ahead alone, bidding me to rest well.

A wolf of hammered gold adorned the wall above the archway. Its garnet eyes gleamed fierce in the lamplight. Kindness, understanding, generosity . . . how easily Osriel induced me to forget my doubts. No matter my chosen course, this time I must not avert my eyes.

I took a knee and touched my forehead in proper obeisance, and rose at his nod. "Tell me, my lord," I said, as he turned to go, "if Brother Victor dies, will you take his eyes?"

The gaze he cast over his shoulder could have frosted a volcano's heart. "Yes."

I wanted Osriel to be worthy of his inheritance and worthy of my trust, but as the Duc of Evanore vanished down the passage, it felt as if he dragged my entrails with him. I needed to learn what Elene would tell me.

Chapter 10

Restlessness drew me out of my bedchamber before Osriel's footsteps had faded, and I paced the sprawling house as if paid to measure its myriad dimensions. In hopes of finding Brother Victor, I bypassed the domed garden, the painter's room, the scavenged library, and the other places I'd walked with the prince. Wisdom advised me to seek a confidant who did not transform my loins to fire and my mind to jam as Elene did. Loyalty bade me warn the monk of his peril. I could not believe he knew of Osriel's unsavory practices. I was already chastising myself for agreeing to my master's plan. Why did I trust him? He didn't even bother to mask his infamy.

Though dusty and deserted, the house was finely proportioned and lavishly ornamented with windows and murals, painted ceilings and rich hangings. Yet the farther I walked, the worse the stench: latrines, rotting meat, male sweat, candles, incense, and wood ash, mouse piss, boiling herbs. I'd always thought Moriangi houses the nastiest in the kingdom.

By the time I rounded a new corner only to find a corridor I had traversed three times already, I suspected some magical boundary kept me separate from the ailing monk. I touched the smooth tiles of the passage floor, seeking some trace of him, but as before my bent failed to answer my summons. Confessing defeat, I chose to retreat.

I could not find my bedchamber. My footsteps thudded on the tiles. The mice scuttling in the walls were surely the size of houses. Anxiety grew like dark mold in my lungs and heart.

Increasingly confused, I burst through a door I'd not yet broached. Tables jammed with neglected plants crowded the long room, and the glare of the westering sun through its three walls and roof of glass near blinded me. Eyes blurred, nauseated by the stink, I stumbled sideways.

An explosion of pain in my skull sent me crashing to the floor. I crawled into a corner and huddled quivering, arms wrapped about my head.

Running footsteps hammered the passage floor like the thousand drums of Iero's Judgment Night. With a hiss of disapproval, the newcomer wrenched my arms aside, pried my chin upward, and slapped something cold and round onto the center of my forehead. As worms burrowing into my flesh, magic flowed outward from the disk, gnawing skin, muscle, and bone, quieting whatever it touched before squiggling onward . . . deeper . . . farther . . .

When the disgusting sensation faded, the world felt dull and distant, as if my entire body had been sheathed in silken hand bindings. "Could you not make this enchantment feel more like your fingers and less like maggots?" I said.

"My apologies, O Magical Being!" Saverian grabbed my hands and hauled me to a sitting position. The world spun only slightly. "What a fool I was to design this spell for your relief and not your pleasure."

"Mistress, I didn't mean—"

"Of course, had you remained where you were told, I could have renewed your shield at the proper time, and you would not have experienced the spell's less pleasant aspects so acutely. But then, the parts between your legs do resemble those of mortal males, so I shouldn't expect too much in the way of common wisdom." Her complaints were issued with the same ironical humor she had used to address the uncooperative logs in my bedchamber hearth. "And I dislike being labeled as anyone's mistress. My name is Saverian."

I rubbed at the crusted mess on my eyelids, hoping to regain my faculties now she had withdrawn her hand. Water sloshed and dribbled. She whispered, "*Igneo,*" and not long afterward, a hot damp cloth scalded my eyelids.

"Ouch!"

"*Must* you forever complain?"

Her blotting was indeed more satisfactory than rubbing away the grit of sweat and tears . . . and blood, I noticed when she paused to rinse the cloth. My collision with the brick wall had split my head in more than my perception. But the sharp sting served as pleasing evidence that my senses now functioned in a somewhat normal fashion.

The physician had changed from her riding leathers into a skirt and shapeless tunic of dull green. A slim leather belt settled about her hips, more for the purpose of attaching a knife sheath and two leather pockets than any decorative enhancement of her spare figure.

"I was hoping to visit Brother Victor," I said. "He is a friend . . . mentor . . ."

". . . and the prince told you, 'Not yet.' It might soothe your conscience to see the monk, but it would do *him* no good at all. His health improves. His injuries have challenged me, but will yield in the end."

She dropped a jingling something into one of her pockets and tightened the drawstring with a snap. Her insistent grip on my hand hauled me to my feet with astonishing ease. As I concentrated on remaining upright, she surveyed me head to toe and sighed heavily.

"Come along. Our doughty prince insists that you remain out of sight while he plays Evanori chieftain in his hall. He fears your presence would be a distraction. Nothing sets Evanori warlords slavering more than a tall, scrawny pureblood."

Untwisting my trews, I padded after her through another garden room and into the chilly corridor. My head throbbed, but only with bruising, not madness. "I'm no more pureblood than he is—or you are."

Saverian raised one instructive finger. "Ah, but Caedmon's holy blood flows in Osriel's veins, which means they will forgive him anything, and despite being a woman who prefers books to battle-axes, I can at least claim half an Evanori birthright. Were I in your place, I would certainly not attempt to explain to a hundred warlords come to the last night of a warmoot that, despite my Registry listing, I was not an Aurellian pureblood because my mother was an angel . . . or a water sprite . . . or whatever it is you claim. Of course, *I* say you can be damned and do as you wish, save that our lord has commanded me to see you obey him. And I *will* see to it. You must have peeved him something dreadful to put him in such a vile temper."

Her heavy black braid had been knotted at the back of her long neck and fixed in place with an ivory skewer. Easy to imagine that skewer stretching all the way down her spine. Half Evanori, half Aurellian—that likely explained her odd nature. Evanori hated Aurellians—and thus purebloods—with a passion wrought of gold, starvation, and survival.

After Ardra and Morian had fallen to the Aurellian Empire, and Caedmon had sent his infant son to the Danae for protection, the king and the remnants of his legions had retreated into the wilds of Evanore. Raiding, running, hiding in caves and corries, freezing and starving alongside his men, Caedmon taught the warlords to fight as one and helped them build impregnable strongholds to hold off the invaders and their cruel emperor, who lusted for Evanore's gold. When Caedmon fell at last, having earned their eternal loyalty, the Evanori held out a century more. Had they yielded their region's treasure, Aurellia would likely yet stand, and Navronne would yet be subject to an empire that built its strength on magic, slavery, and brutality.

Though feeling mostly myself again in body, my spirit remained tight wound. If Osriel meant what he said about my choosing my own course, I'd no mind to put off our coming journey into the Danae realm, no matter the state of my recovery. Thus, to learn what secrets Elene could teach, I had to see her that night. Which meant I had to find a way into the fortress. As a prison guard Saverian did not elicit the same unnerving fears as Voushanti, but she had shown power enough to make me wary, nonetheless.

"You seem excessively compliant for one who speaks of our master so slightingly," I said as she marched into the familiar passage. The hammered gold wolf with garnet eyes glared from the far end, guarding my bedchamber door. "Is it to benefit the lighthouse you do all this?"

She snorted. "I am Renna's physician and house mage, not a member of Osriel's band of merry monks."

"Your privileged position must shield you from his wrath. You don't seem to fear him as the rest of us do."

She waved me through the blue and yellow door hanging. "If you assume my familiarity with the prince buys me leniency from his strictures, I'd recommend you actually *use* these senses I'm protecting for you. Bear in mind, I've known him from infancy and have learned in what matters I dare cross him and in what matters I dare not."

I made as if to enter the bedchamber, but instead blocked the doorway. "Prince Osriel wishes me out of sight—fair enough. But might there be some hidden vantage from which I could observe tonight's events? I've no experience of Evanori customs, so I'm greatly curious. And, by every god in heaven, if I am left alone to parse my birth, my body, or my future for one more moment, not even your magics will keep me sane." This last came out sounding a bit more desperate than I liked.

She tipped her head to one side and pursed her thin lips into an unflattering knot. Her brow ridges were angled slightly downward from midforehead, giving her a forever-quizzical expression. After a breathless moment, she shrugged. "Why not? Let it never be said I granted Osriel of Evanore exactly what he desired on any occasion whatsoever."

I didn't think I'd ever met a person so unattached to human feelings. All the world seemed subject to her disdain. Recalcitrant logs or foolish sorcerers could cause her transitory annoyance, but I couldn't imagine what it might take to truly frighten her, or to please her, for that matter. At least she had no red sparks centering her pupils.

Saverian sat in my room for several hours that afternoon, writing in her journal, reading from several books, annoyed when I tried to talk or ask questions.

"Sleep, if you can't think of anything better to do," she said, after one ill-timed query. "I'm not here to entertain you. You've taken enough of my time over the past few weeks."

But my skin itched and my insides felt like a nest of ants. I could no more sleep than I could read her books. "What do you do with your time when not nursing twist-minds or demon princes? I've never seen anyone save monks or schoolmasters sit so long with a book."

"Books don't prattle. Books don't make demands. Yet they give you everything they possess. It's a very satisfying partnership."

I considered that for a while, as I watched her read. Annoyance vanished as the words absorbed her attention, replaced by a fluid mix of interest, curiosity, and serious consideration. Her brow would furrow; then she would write something in her journal. Once the thought was recorded, the furrow smoothed, and she went back to reading. Books supplied companionship, perhaps, but I doubted any words on a page could do what her hands had done for me as I lay in the doulon madness. "*Satisfying* doesn't sound like much to aim for."

"Enough!" With a spit of exasperation, she scooped all her belongings into an untidy armload and headed for the door. "I'll fetch you in time for the warmoot."

I spent the next few hours berating myself as an idiot. I hadn't meant to voice my musings aloud. At least she had given me something to look at beyond four walls and a bed.

One of her books had fallen to the floor beneath the table. I thumbed through it, picking out one or two letters that I knew, then watching them melt and flow into the ones next to them. *Gods, useless.* I threw the book across the room and went to sleep.

True to her word, Saverian returned just after a bristle-bearded serving man had lit the lamps. As I snatched a long black cloak from the clothes chest, I felt warmly satisfied that, for the first time in forever, I was both reasonably clearheaded and taking some action on my own behalf.

"You need to eat more than one bite of meat and a dried plum," said the physician after inspecting the food tray that had arrived an hour earlier. She stuffed a slice of oily cheese into my hand. "Eat this as we walk, and I won't find a reason to abort this venture."

I could make no plans until we reached the fortress, but if I were to shake free of Saverian and find Elene, I would likely need magic more than nourishment. I obediently took a bite of cheese, then held out my fingers. "Can you unlock these, good physician? I feel a cripple without my bent even to know north from south."

Her dark heavy cloak made her look taller and more than ever like a stick. She shrugged. "You assign me more skill than my due. It's not your fingers, but only this house I've sealed against your magic—and that only possible because it is a peculiar house with a number of in-built protections already. I assumed you would be more in control of yourself by the time we took you out walking. Please tell me that's true."

"I promise I'm in possession of all the reason I was born with." I grinned and took another bite of cheese to please her. "Honestly, I do appreciate your care."

She blew a derisive breath and hefted a stout leather bag over one shoulder, the bag of the sort that Voushanti used to carry Prince Osriel's medicines. The outer doors waited in a pleasant vaulted alcove I'd not glimpsed in all my wanderings. The four broad panels of the twin doors had been painted to depict the seasons, the rich hues and intricate drawing giving the depth of truth to the design. Though stunningly beautiful, the paintings left a hollow in my breast. Each panel showed a pair of dancers, their pale flesh twined with designs of azure and lapis. We pulled open the doors and stepped into the winter night.

The cold snatched my breath away. Fine, sharp grains of snow stung the skin, the particles more a part of the air itself than anything that would pile or drift on the barren ground. Across the windswept slope, bonfires and torches lit the fortress gates and walls, orange flames writhing alongside a hundred or more whipping banners that flew from the battlements.

As we trudged down the path, thick darkness crowded the light-pooled fortress and the soft-lit windows of the house we had just abandoned, as if the mountains had drawn closer under cover of the starless, moonless night. I drew my cloak tight, grateful for

Saverian's enchantment that tamed my senses. It must be that Evanore's violent history remained raw enough to taint the night with the anguish of its dying warriors and the wails of its starving children, for the wind bore grief and despair and anger on its back as surely as it carried shouts of greeting or the smells of horses and smoke. A harsh, dry land was Evanore. I would no more touch my fingers to this earth than spit on a grave.

From the battlements sounded the low, heavy tones of a sonnivar, the hooked horn that stretched taller than me when stood on end and that rang so deep and so true its call could be heard for vast distances through the mountains and vales, guiding Evanore's warriors home. Evanori claimed the timbre of each warlord's sonnivar unique, so that a fog-blind warrior could identify which fortress he approached from the sonnivar greeting alone.

A party of horsemen rode over the steep crest of the valley road and cantered up the gentler slope to the gates. Gruff voices carried across the dark hillside, shouting challenges and orders until the portcullis clanked and rumbled open and the party rode through.

"Pull up your hood," said Saverian softly, as if fearing that we, too, might be heard from afar. "And carry this." She shoved her leather bag into my hands. I hefted the heavy little bag onto my back, as our path joined the trampled roadway to the gates.

"The password, Saverian," said a slab-sided warrior standing to one side of the sizable detachment manning the gate tower and portcullis. "Even for you this night. And identify your friend."

"Pustules," said the physician. She stepped up close to him, as the sonnivar boomed again from above our heads. "Is your wife pleased with your renewed affections, Dreogan? Perhaps I need to reexamine your little—"

"Pass!" bellowed the guard. A snickering youth waited behind an iron wicket set into the tower wall. At the guard's signal, the youth unlocked the little gate, let us through, and locked it again behind us.

"You're on report, Dreogan!" Saverian called over her shoulder. "This is no night to be slack."

"Deunor's fire," I said, "has every man in the universe got crossways with you?"

"You've not seen me crossways, sirrah. Dreogan would kiss my feet did I but ask. More fool he."

More fool the man who imagined my companion a feeling woman.

The burly warrior's curses followed us as we hurried through a passage so low I had to duck and so narrow we could not walk abreast. The close quarters set my teeth on edge. Once through, we passed without challenge across the barren outer bailey and through the inner gates into the bustling main courtyard. Thick smoke rose from torches and warming fires, as squires and men-at-arms groomed horses, honed weapons, greeted friends, and shared out provisions. A burst of cheers and oaths pinpointed a dice game on our left, and whoops rose from the milling crowd when servants rolled three carts loaded with ale casks into the yard. We kept to the quiet perimeter, dodging several sighing fellows who'd come to the shadowed wall to piss or satisfy a lonely soldier's fleshly urges.

Naught fazed Saverian. She headed briskly for the northwest corner of the yard, where a tight stair spiraled up one of the fortress's barrel-like towers. The thick tower walls damped the noise of the courtyard until we emerged on a parapet walk. On one side we overlooked the noisy throng of waiting warriors, on the other a close, dark well yard. Two heavily armed guards, their heads wreathed in steaming breath, halted Saverian at a thick door of banded oak that led into the blocklike heart of the fortress. She complained of a sore elbow from riding and named me her servant, brought along to carry her medicine bag.

"I'm sure I needn't remind you to stay quiet and out of sight," said the woman under her breath once the guards passed us through the low doorway. "A warmoot is a sacred meeting between the warlords, their heirs, and their sovereign. It is closed to other Evanori no matter how favored, even wives or husbands, and most certainly closed to outsiders."

"But a half-Evanori physician is admitted?"

"Only if I remain out of sight and hearing. It is an ongoing argument between His Grace and me. He wishes no public reminders of his difficult health, yet he knows saccheria can flare without warning, so he tolerates my presence. Few know the truth of his condition: you, your fellow madmen in this monkish conspiracy, and those few who have served in Renna Syne—the 'window palace' where you're housed—since he was small. Even his royal brothers have it wrong. The cretins think he shapeshifts to disguise a crippled back."

"Does he?"

Her glance could have withered heaven's lilies.

Of a sudden the fine, graceful house set apart from the fortress made sense. Osriel had grown up here. Eodward had housed his pureblood mistress in Evanore, away from the Registry's interference, and he had named their child the province's duc, so that Lirene would own the bound loyalty of the Evanori, if not their love.

The house protections used to damp my magic would be those of any pureblood home where the children had not yet learned to control their sorcerers' bent.

More anxious than ever to make sense of Osriel, I leaned in close and touched the physician's hand, hoping to soften her in the way I'd had most success throughout the years. "I'll confess, mistress, Prince Osriel leaves me not knowing which ear to listen with. If you could but tell—"

"I am not your mistress, Cartamandua," she said with long-suffering patience. "I am a servant, as are you, and Renna's servants do *not* gossip about Prince Osriel. Best learn that." She removed my hand from her arm with a grip worthy of her warlord ancestors. Foolish to imagine my . . . natural skills . . . could lure *her* into anything she had no mind to.

Beyond a short vestibule, we came onto a gallery that overlooked a smoky feasting hall. Below us an elderly woman decried the depredations of a Harrower raid. Prince Osriel and a hundred or more warriors sat listening.

Saverian frowned speculatively when a grin broke over my face. The hall's arrangement reminded me of nothing so much as the refectory at Gillarine, with the monks seated according to seniority at long tables along the side walls, the abbot and prior at their head, listening to the day's reading of the holy writs.

Of course, rather than a splendid window overlooking the cloisters and the abbey church, a solid wall of war banners rose behind Osriel's great wood chair. And rather than the tall glass windows of the refectory, only arrow slits penetrated the thick side and entry walls. Every other quat of wall space from floor to wood-beamed roof was given to a vast collection of war trophies: shields, weapons, bits of armor, several long oars and a carved wooden figurehead with snaky hair and peeling paint—evidence of Hansker longboats. A few dried, hairy lumps looked disconcertingly like long-dead squirrels . . . or scalps.

"No question where Evanori hearts find pleasure," I murmured.

Saverian folded her arms and gazed down on the panoply. "Indeed, the most welcomed entertainment at this gathering would be a Harrower raiding party storming the doors. What a collection of idiots. And the women are as bad as the men."

At least we agreed on one matter.

Despite the smoky heat, both men and women wore heavy fur cloaks over thick leathers, mail, and weapons. The only concession to ornament were the fine-wrought clasps, earrings, chains, rings, and bracelets—all gold—that adorned every head, neck, and limb. A gold band set with garnets circled Osriel's brow atop a soft hood that obscured his face.

Evidently Osriel had allowed Stearc to venture from Gillarine for this gathering. Elene sat just behind him on a bench against the wall, along with the other warlords-in-waiting, some young and blooming as she was, some older and as battle-worn as their sires and dams.

I examined our immediate surroundings for some way to slip the bonds of Saverian's custody. The featureless gallery where we stood stretched the entire length of the hall. I could imagine bowmen poised at the iron rail. Or musicians with harps and vielles—if Evanori subscribed to any display of the gentler arts. About halfway along the outer wall, I noted a narrow gap.

Leaving Saverian in the vestibule, I ambled down the gallery. A sidewise glimpse confirmed the gap was a downward stair. I squatted just across from it and peered through the iron railing, as if trying to watch the events below without being noticed. Clutching the medicine bag, I considered what excuse I might devise for a venture down the stair.

One after the other, the warlords took their place in the center of the room, gripped a staff topped with a wolf's head of wrought gold, and recited the incursions of Ardran or Moriangi raiders who scoured the countryside for food stores, or the vile deeds of Harrower burning parties who ravaged isolated villages and farmsteads on both sides of the border. I gathered this was the third night in a row they had recounted these same grievances, determined to implant them in one another's memory as if the offenses had been dealt against them all. When Thane Stearc took the staff, he told of the dog-faced man who led the Harrower pursuit on our journey from Palinur and how the pursuit had been thwarted only when his pureblood guide had tricked the Harrowers into a bog and drowned them all.

As always, reminders of events in the bog left me nauseated and uneasy. Reflexively, I glanced over my shoulder. Saverian was staring at me, her nose flared in disgust. Perhaps she had never heard the story, or had only now connected it with me.

During each report, the rowdy onlookers shouted confirmations or approvals, curses or reprimands for the speaker's tale. When a young thanea, sized like a brick hearth and clad in scarred mail, reported that she had dreamed of shadow legions overrunning Evanore, I expected derisive hoots and laughter, but the lords thumped fists on the tables and shouted that the time had come for Evanore's legions to take the field.

Prince Osriel listened to all without comment. Once the staff had passed through every lord's hand, the company fell silent. The elderly woman returned to the center of the room and began reciting. As her voice rose and fell in the fashion of talespinners, the torchlight dimmed.

The old woman spoke of Aurellian ships come to the river country in the north and Aurellian legions crossing the broad Yaronal from the east after discovering that the small magics they worked in their distant homeland took fire with power in the lands of Navronne. But they found this favored land ruled by a stubborn king . . .

It was Caedmon's story she told, tracing his lineage into the deeps of history and telling of his rise and fall. Her tale recalled the great window in the Gillarine Abbey chapter house. In jeweled glass it had depicted the sad and honorable king who had first united the gravs of Morian and the warlords of Evanore with his own kingdom of Ardra. He had made the disparate realms into something greater than the sum of its parts, only to see his beloved Navronne brought to heel by the predatory Aurellians. The storyteller painted her portrait with words, not glass, depicting the king leading the tattered remnants of his legions to the great bridge he'd built to link Ardra and Evanore.

Deep shadows enveloped the gallery. Saverian could not have seen my hand rummaging in her medicine bag. I snatched out a few items and stuffed them in my pockets.

When the old woman's tale was done, the lords began to sing. I stood up, fumbling the bag until I dropped it, spilling the loose contents on the gallery floor. *That* Saverian noticed. And came running.

"What have you done, fool?" she whispered, snatching up vials, packets, and tight-wrapped bundles of linen and wool. I held the bag open as she put the things away, sensing her itemizing each article, as I'd guessed she would. She patted the floor around us and hissed, "Three packets and two small jars are missing. Holy Mother . . ."

One of the lords took up another song— "The Lay of Groshug," an interminable recounting of a bloody boar hunt that I enjoyed only when I was roaring drunk. They'd be bawling it for an hour at the least. Saverian would not dare risk a scene. And I gambled that she'd not dare leave her post. Her first duty was to Osriel's health.

"I fear things dropped through the railing," I whispered. "I'm sorry . . . I'll fetch them." And before she could protest, I shoved the bag into her hands and darted down the stair.

The stair dumped me into a dark vestibule, crowded with two big tables, piled with empty tankards and dirty serving platters. A wide door led back into the hall. A narrower door led outside, where an arcade fronted the long side of the building. Accompanied by the lords' robust rendering of the chorus to "The Lay of Groshug," I sped eastward through the arcade in search of the *rock gate* Elene had mentioned.

The geometries of such a fortress were fairly simple. A cross wall joined a long barracks building to the Great Hall. The arcade tunneled through the wall and ended abruptly in an alley at the far end of the hall. Follow the alley to the left, and you would end up in a paved yard surrounded by kitchens and bakehouses and storage buildings. Go right ten paces along the east end of the Great Hall, and you ran straight into the mountainside.

No gate was visible where the blocklike hall merged with the rocky buttress, but I guessed that the perilously steep set of steps cut into the mottled gray and red rock would lead me there. As I half climbed, half crawled up the interminable stair, I blessed Saverian for clearing my head. With only the diffuse light from the hall's arrow slits to illuminate the rock, I needed all the acuity I could muster. My feet were bigger than the altogether too-slanted steps.

Elene awaited me atop the stair, like a warrior angel on a church spire. "I didn't think you'd come, not a day out of your bed and bound by Saverian's spellcraft."

"To meet with you, lady, I would even climb this god-cursed stair again," I said, gasping. "But by the Mother, do Evanori not approve of air?"

I bent over and propped my hands on my knees, coughing as the cold dry air rasped my heaving chest. I prayed I was not so sorely out of health as to be flattened by a hundred steps. But a squirrel could have toppled me.

"Renna is higher than Erasku. It's even higher than Angor Nav—the duc's official seat. Even I notice the sparse air here." Her face was only a pale blur in the night, but her pinched voice hinted at high emotion reined tight. "Osriel told my father you were taking him to the Danae tomorrow. Is that true?"

"That's what he wants," I said. "We've less than a month until the solstice."

"Come."

By the time I accumulated enough breath to ask where, she had pivoted sharply and marched into the night. I followed carefully. The stair had brought us onto a steeply ascending apron of rock that skirted a bulge in the massive ridge. I hugged the rock wall on my left, for on my right, tiny, winking blots of torchlight and bonfires in a gaping darkness marked the heart-stopping drop to the fortress. The irregular path canted outward, and my boots hinted that ice lurked in its cracks and crevices.

"I had decided to send you back to your bed," said Elene, little more than a formless darkness ahead of me. "To show you this betrays an oath I swore on my mother's memory, a villainous oath that should condemn me to the netherworld for the making, not just for the breaking. *He* chose it. Not I—stupid, mooning cow that I am to be so led into godless folly."

"What oath?" I caught up with her just as the path ended abruptly at an iron gate. The tall gate, anchored in the rock, blocked entry to a shallow breach in the ramparts of the ridge. "What folly?"

The gate rattled with Elene's violent application of her boot. "Papa refuses to come here with me or listen to what I say, because my showing him would break my oath and because the secret's owner is holy Caedmon's heir. I'd hoped one of the monks might listen, but I was never allowed to be alone with them. And I could never tell anyone outside the cabal. All I want is to stop this wickedness. And so this morning, seeing how you sensed his evil already—rightly so— and I was so angry, I said I'd bring you. Yet I would send you away ignorant even now if he'd not told me he was going to the Danae right away. He means to do this . . . to use their magic . . ."

She grasped the iron hasp, touched it with a gold ring that shot sparks like fireflies into the dark, and spoke a word I could not decipher for the half growl, half sob that accompanied it.

"Mistress, you must excuse my confusion. Who is going to do what? Osriel?"

Indeed, I thought my acuity must be impaired again, so little sense could I make of all this. The most daunting news I'd gleaned from her avalanche of words was that her fear outstripped her anger.

The breach in the rocks proved to be but a crumbling wash the width of my armspan. It rose at a shallow pitch, which my lungs approved, and wound between huge boulders that were easy to spot— a good thing, as the sky was as dark as tar. I wasn't sure how Elene could show me anything. Yet when we emerged from the gully atop the ridge, a livid haze lit the night before us, illuminating a scene of desolation.

For as far as I could see, the ridge top had been hacked away, gouged and broken into a shallow bowl a quellé wide, at least, seamed with trenches and pocked with dark holes. Broken troughs and sluices, iron wheels, and snarls of ancient rope rotted or rusted amid heaps of crushed rock. Chiseled slabs lay tilted and broken beside a monstrous quern and a cracked mortar broader than my armspan.

But it was not the ugly spoil heaps or grinding stones that colored my soul the same bruised gray as the unnatural haze and made me want to run far from this place. All the grief of Evanore lay here. All the anger. The pent emotions I had felt on the wind, and those I had sensed when first I looked upon Osriel's land, were but goosedown to the leaden weight of sorrow and fury that settled on my spirit. I could scarce breathe.

"What gold could be dug from Dashon Ra has been long carted away," said Elene, standing at my shoulder. "But he says the veins yet thread the earth like a web and extend throughout Evanore. He says they are like ring mail that strengthens our land, holding a power that fires magic. Come on."

She marched down the sloping side of the abandoned mine, hopped across a deep, narrow trench, and skirted the corner of a rubble wall—all that remained of a shed. The haze thickened, coiling violet tendrils about Elene's boots. I followed, wishing I had never asked her to show me this. Making Deunor's sign upon my brow and drawing Iero's holy seal upon my breast, I prayed that Saverian's spell would not fail me. This land held terrible secrets.

Down and down. Our boots slipped and slid on the loose tailings and patches of ice. Nearing the bottom of the slope, we ducked under an ancient leat, solid and unbroken, though only grit and gravel remained where water had once flowed. Beyond us lay the lowermost levels of the mine, a rectangular pit of iron-laced rock the size of Renna's Great Hall, cracked and scarred by weather and men's work. Piles of rubble littered its floor. And across every handsbreadth of the rock walls, every protrusion, knob, or broken shelf held a vessel of carved stone, votive vessels as you would find in Deunor's temple or Iero's cathedral—hundreds of them, some the size of bread loaves or tabors, some smaller, palm-sized like oil lamps, like the calyx I had seen in Osriel's bloody hands in the abbey kitchen.

The bruised haze hung above the vessels as does the stench above a midden. Dread rose in my soul like fever. "This is where he brings them . . . the eyes of the dead."

"He seals each vessel with his own blood. When he brings it here, he unseals it and empties it into the earth. That dark blotch at the center is a bottomless shaft. Though the vessels are no longer needed, he names them sacred because of what they carried, so he leaves them here."

"Not sacred," I said, revulsion clogging my throat. "This is no holy place. No temple. It is a prison." As my gaze roamed the desolation, I clamped my hands under my arms as if some accident might make them touch this violated earth. I didn't want to hear those trapped here. I didn't want to feel their fury and confusion and hatred more clearly than I did already. Madness had owned me for too many days.

Elene scooped up a handful of crushed stone and dirt, then allowed it to rain through her fingers onto the dry earth. "He plans to work some terrible magic here. When he brought me here three years ago to show me—to end what we had begun in happier times— he said he hoped with all his being that he would never have to set his plan in motion, for it would be such a sin as would end his last hope of heaven. Truly, Brother Valen, it is not for his own glory, but for Navronne he strives, yet he does not listen that hope cannot be bought with sin."

The bilious light sapped all color from her warm skin. The tears rolled down her cheeks like gray pearls, and her palms pressed flat across her belly as if to shield the child that grew inside her. "I put *my* hope in Luviar and his noble lighthouse to show him the way of right. For one blessed hour on that same night you escaped from Gillarine, I thought his loneliness had led him back to love. And though that hope proved false, I believed my dearest prayers answered when he told us of the Harrower hiding place you'd found, and that his brothers had agreed to join him to oppose Sila Diaglou. But a tenday ago, while you lay ill, reports came that Sila Diaglou had abandoned her hidden fortress and, at the same time, raised her own banner in Palinur alongside his brother's. A light went out of him that day. Within hours he left Renna with only Voushanti accompanying him. And since he's come back, he has not spoken to me, not looked at me, not told anyone where he went. I've begged him, yelled at him, pleaded with him to explain to the cabal what he plans next, but he refuses."

She waved her hand at the bleak scene before us. "Three years ago, he told me that his own power might not be enough to accomplish what he wants, and that the more certain way would be to ask the Danae's help to join their magic to his. And now you are to take him to the Danae. Whatever this is . . . he's decided to go through with it. By the Holy Mother, Valen, you're a sorcerer and his friend— the only one not blinded by fealty or awe or fear. Only you can stop him . . . save him."

I wanted to laugh at the idea of me stopping Osriel the Bastard, the rightful King of Navronne, the sorcerer who called up red lightning and performed rites that reeked of brimstone, from doing anything he chose. But Elene's grief and fear for the prince tempered my answer with sobriety, at least. "Lady, I cannot even begin to imagine what spells might be worked with . . . whatever lies in this place. And indeed the prince has good reasons to go to the Danae, the same he has stated all along. We must know what they can tell us of the world's sickness and its remedy. If he gives them warning of Sila Diaglou and Gildas, perhaps they will shelter our Scholar and give light to his lighthouse. It is his right and his duty to speak to them for us. But I promise you I'll do what I can to discover his plans and persuade him to some alternative."

I had no faith in my promise. Nor did she, though she thanked me and pretended it so. I took her in my arms as she wept, wishing naught but to offer comfort. For indeed the least significant, yet most painful discovery on this night of dread revelation was that I would willingly suffer any danger to serve Elene, though her heart was not—and had never been—mine to win. No wonder at her agonies if that ebullient heart—and the child she had conceived—belonged to the Duc of Evanore. And no matter the course of past or future, a love already tested by the trials of grim necessity, of denial and sacrifice, of illness, war, and unholy sorcery, was unlikely to be swayed by the fingers of a feckless vagabond, whatever the marvels of his birth.

Chapter 11

Down, down, interminably down. The steep descent from Renna to the borderlands of Evanore in the driving blizzard was unrelenting misery. *Hold your seat. Keep your back straight. Legs forward. Trust the beast.* The distance was not so far, so I was told. Two days, three in such weather. But my backside was already hot and raw, and every other part of me was frozen, save two fiery strips on my fingers where the leather cinch straps, made into knife edges by the cold, had sliced my flesh. My back and shoulders ached . . . as did my spirit, weighed to breaking with the memory of those thousand empty vessels.

I had spent the dreary hours speculating on how I could possibly accomplish what I had promised Elene. To set myself as intermediary between Osriel and Stearc's daughter was only slightly less witless than setting myself between my friend Gram and his dangerous royal self. What in the name of heaven did he think to do with Danae magic and thousands of imprisoned souls? And how could I possibly stop it? Elene had sorely misjudged my capabilities.

Stearc rode point, the dark expanse of his shoulders our guide staff through the world of white. Five of his own warriors rode alongside him. They were to escort him back to Gillarine and relieve the troop he'd left there, while Osriel and I hunted the Danae.

The prince and I followed close behind the thane. In the presence of Stearc's men, Osriel rode as Gram. He had insisted I wear my pureblood garb and return to pureblood disciplines, playing Prince Osriel's contracted servant sent upon a private mission. The mask and cloak felt odd, as if they belonged to someone else.

Voushanti guarded our rear, along with his trusted warriors Philo and Melkire. Just ahead of them rode Saverian, brought along to tend Osriel's health. She had been furious at the prince's insistence that she accompany us and had taken her vengeance by calling hourly halts and forcing him to drink her potions. Saverian reminded me of thyme or savory—useful in small amounts, but like to gag you in too great a quantity.

I'd no more questions about how to rattle her temper. On the previous night, when I had come round the end of Renna's Great Hall from the rock gate stair after bidding farewell to Elene, Saverian had pounced like a starved wolverine.

"Are you entirely without intelligence?" Clearly the question was not meant to be answered. She grabbed my cloak and dragged me past the doorway that returned to the hall, where Osriel's warlords were cheering. "Do you think me blind or just some thick-witted troll? What a striking coincidence that you dropped my things— which I had damned well better get back, by the bye—at exactly the same time the heiress of Erasku slipped out of the hall. I'm truly surprised not to find you naked again! Ah, yes, I forget: a Dané dances naked and reportedly can seduce a brick wall does he but sigh. So it is but your inborn nature to put the moon-mad little warrior at risk of a flaying from her father, and surely the annoying physician can fend for herself when the guards alert Prince Osriel because the woman's servant has gone missing at a warmoot!" Astonishing how she could raise such a lather in a voice that none could have heard five steps away from us.

We had returned straight on to Renna Syne. The walk seemed to cool her temper slightly, but upon our arrival, she made clear that I had exhausted what meager stock of forbearance she had vouched me as her patient. "I don't wish to be friends with you. I don't care to join monkish conspiracies to change the world. All I ask is civilized behavior—which means, among other things, that you do not put me at risk of losing my employment or my life."

When she had me sit on the bed and proceeded to drop a thin chain about my neck, I'd feared she'd decided to strangle me. But the fat little coin that dangled from the chain and weighed so heavily on my chest was, in fact, the gold medallion she used to tame my disease.

"When you feel your senses compromised, hold the medallion in the center of your forehead, infuse it with power until the world quiets, and do not beg me for any favors when it's no longer sufficient to the task."

With the remedy for my disease in my possession, I'd felt well rid of Saverian's attentions and gleefully anticipated setting out on my own business once my obligations to Osriel and Elene were concluded. But a night awash in sweat, plagued with doulon dreams and fits of the shakes, had stolen all the pleasure from my prospective independence. Eventually, I had squeezed enough use from the woman's medallion to soothe my night's ills, but I had sorely missed her hands.

Fingering the gold disk, I glanced over my shoulder. The prince was unrecognizable in thick layers of wool. Somehow I'd thought it might be easier to draw him into conversation with him traveling as Gram, but my every attempt had fallen to naught. In truth he had not spoken to anyone since we'd ridden out of Renna's gates at dawn, leaving Elene behind to tend Brother Victor in Saverian's absence. His visage reflected more of the hammered gold wolf with garnet eyes above my bedchamber door than my friend Gram.

Stearc's back vanished around a steep bank. The billowing curtains of snow had thinned, so that as we followed the thane around the prominence, the rugged borderlands opened to every side. Rival claims, blood feuds, and banditry had ever festered in this harsh land. A few Ardran manses, where villeins worked their lords' wheat fields, lay nose to jowl with Evanori fortresses and freeholds, where crofters kept flocks of rangy goats or coaxed rye and oats from the thin soil under the protection of their warlords.

A little past midday, the air grew thick with black smoke. Voushanti dispatched Philo to scout the road ahead and drew the little troop close around us. Swords were loosed in their scabbards. A flurry of powdery snow announced the warrior's return.

"Raiders burnt out Edane Godsear's villeins at sunrise this morning," said the ginger-bearded warrior. "Harrowers, not bandits. The village is ash. The women say their men were called to the manse, as it's burning as well, and they've seen smoke rising from both north and west."

"Is the manse still under attack?" asked Voushanti, who had come up to the front beside Stearc.

"No, lord," said Philo.

Voushanti and Saverian were of a mind to turn back. Had I not been accustomed to the monks' signing speech, I might have missed Osriel's gesture; as he adjusted his grip on his reins, one gloved finger broke out from his curled hand to point decisively forward.

"We've business west," said Stearc. "No rabble with torches and billhooks will hinder us."

We rode on. The Ardran village had comprised no more than eight or ten dwellings, huddled near the crossing of road and a stream.

Naught but a clay baker's oven was left standing. Women stood paralyzed beside the smoldering ruins, children clutching their skirts. Plumes of smoke and billowing snow could not hide their smudged cheeks or the dull eyes that stared hopelessly as we rode past.

"Lord Stearc," said the prince softly, urging his mount up beside the thane. "We cannot just pass them by."

"We can do nothing for them, Gram. Godsear will see to their welfare. It's too dangerous to linger where raiders can hide so easily."

"They're stronger than we are and accustomed to hardship," said Saverian. "If they've no help for themselves, an hour's attention from us is not going to change their fate."

The prince bowed his head in deference. "You heard Philo's report, mistress. The manse itself is burned. We *must* stop."

And so, of course, we did. Osriel was the first off his horse. He engaged himself with one person, then the next, prodding each to move and think. "Goodwife, have you a place to shelter? Family? You must get out of this weather. Gammy, have you a root cellar here? Or root crops under the snow? Boy, use that fence pole to shove the embers together to make a fire. Then get your sister and bring the unburned beams to build a windbreak. Help your mam stay warm through the night. Have you menfolk?"

Most of the women were lone—their husbands already dead or gone with their lord to fight for the feckless Perryn, which they believed the same as dead. And rightly so. The men called to the manse to help fight the fire had been graybeards or cripples or boys under fifteen.

Saverian dressed burns and tended injuries, moving briskly from one to the next. Our warriors offered packets of bread or cheese, sympathetic ears, and strong arms to build shelters. The people gawked at me, wondering, as if I might perform some magic to rebuild their lives. But of course, they didn't know I was the most useless of sorcerers. I managed only to uncover their well with a minor voiding spell, but I had no confidence they could survive the frigid night.

"The new year will bring a new king," Gram told one trembling goodwife. "Survive until then. Greet him with your needs and sorrows. Those who have done this deed are not messengers of great powers, but vile ravagers, and your king will call them to account for this crime. Gods do not begrudge you a roof."

After an hour, we rode on. Though our escort remained alert, we encountered no Harrowers, only the path of destruction they had crafted. Every manse, croft, village, and sheep shed we passed by lay in ruins, some already cold ashes, some still blazing. We stopped wherever we found people, whether Evanori or Ardran, whether villeins, noblewomen bundled in charred furs, frightened boys, or grizzled crofters with burnt hands. Some mumbled fearfully of the blind immortal Gehoum, afraid even to help themselves. But more picked themselves up and set about their own survival once they heard that a new king would bring them aid with the new year.

As we rode past a ragged Evanori procession on their way from their charred hillside to a warlord's hold, I moved to Osriel's side. "Why, lord?" I said softly so that the soldiers could not hear. "Why do you not reveal yourself to these people? Not that you are Eodward's heir . . . I understand that. But how much more would their spirits lift if they knew the one sharing his bread and blankets to be their own duc? And how eagerly would they rally to his cause when he *did* step forward to claim his father's throne?"

"Fear has ever been the Bastard's staunchest ally," he said, hunching his shoulders against the bitter wind. "Hope must stand aside and do its work softly until the day is won." He kicked his mount ahead of mine and said no more.

Seeing the steadied shoulders, the firmer grasps, the clearer eyes that Gram's care effected, I could not but remember Luviar's talk of the mystical bond between Navronne and its sovereign. *The lack of a righteous king speeds the ruin of the land.* And so, perhaps, was the reverse true; the ascension of a righteous sovereign might have consequences deeper than law or politics. I wanted Osriel to be that king. I believed he could be. But the poisoned fury of the dead that infused this land and hung like battlefield smoke inside my skull made me fear that he was not.

For three days we pushed hard, fearing that a new storm might leave the roads impassable. Late on the third day we descended a steep pass between two spiny ridges only to see a grand prospect opened before us, washed in the indigo light of snowy evening. From west to east the dark, jagged gorge of the River Kay sliced the frosted landscape of treeless terraces. Just below us the river plunged down a great falls and veered northward through broken foothills, where, freed from the confining rock, its character altered into the lazy sweeping flow that fed the fertile valley where Gillarine lay.

Bridging the gorge a quellé west of the falls was Caedmon's arch, its broken entry pillars on the Ardran side resembling thick ice spears. And just north of the pillars lay the crossroads where I had first glimpsed a Dané and a tree that did not grow in the human plane. My stomach tightened.

"Lord Stearc," I said, coaxing my balky horse up beside the thane as the road wound downward onto the flatter approaches to the bridge. "Call a halt as soon as we're across. I'll lead from there."

He jerked his head in assent. Before very long, Stearc passed over the bridge and between the broken pillars. He raised his hand.

"Saints and spirits," I mumbled, as I reined in beside him, gulping great lungfuls of Ardran winter. *Blessed Ardra.* The clouds seemed thinner this side of the bridge, the air clearer . . . cleaner. Only my own anxieties thrummed my veins, not the muted violence and suffering that had tainted my every breath in Evanore. I felt as if a mountain had rolled off my back.

"Are you ill, Magnus? It's been only a few hours since you renewed the damping spell." Saverian slipped from her saddle, squinting at me as if I were a two-headed cow. She'd not spoken three words to me all day. Only diseases piqued her interest.

"On the contrary," I said, wishing she weren't watching as I lifted my mangled bum from the saddle and dropped to the ground. I winced, but managed not to groan aloud. "Both health and spirits seem much improved now we're this side of the river."

"Except for the posterior." Her slanted brows mocked a frown and her small mouth quirked, as she cupped her hand beside her mouth and whispered, "However will you ride naked?"

Gods . . . A number of entirely crude retorts came to mind, but they would likely only encourage the creature. I vowed to ignore her and her odd humor.

Leaving the horses with Voushanti and the soldiers, we joined Osriel and Stearc beside Caedmon's pillars. Thane and prince were arguing quietly. ". . . But you have too few men to protect you, lord."

"Have the past three days taught you nothing?" snapped the prince. "You need to be out of sight. You carry the lighthouse ward. Remain at Gillarine until I give you leave to do elsewise."

The thane stalked away, threw himself into the saddle, and barked a command. He and his five men mounted up and soon vanished into the valley of the Kay.

"Are you ready to proceed, my lord, or do you wish to wait for morning?" I said, removing my mask now Stearc's men were gone. Voushanti, Philo, and Melkire had dismounted and were sharing a skin of ale with Saverian. The prince sat on a stained block of marble fallen from the shattered columns.

"We go now. I'd rather not push our luck with the weather."

"All I know to do is try to find the Sentinel Oak and seek a way to take us past it. I gather we've brought no nivat?" Though my voice remained determinedly neutral, conscience and resolution battled the guilty hope that he would contradict me. Would he dare tell me if they had it?

"No nivat." The prince rubbed his neck as if to ease the stiffness. "What need to lure the Danae into our lands, when your talents can take us into theirs? I trust we'll have no inflated illusions today."

Relieved, yes, truly relieved, I told myself, I sought some trace of good humor in this reference to my artful past. But none of Gram's wry humor or controlled excitement leaked from under Osriel's thick cloak and hood. He manifested only this passionless determination I'd seen throughout this journey.

Voushanti commanded Philo, Melkire, and Saverian to remain with the horses, while he, Gram, and I ventured onward. A few hundred quercae from the bridge, I halted. Time to keep my promise to Elene.

"My lord, perhaps we should discuss how we're to approach the Danae. If I could but understand the terms of your discussion, what exactly we are seeking from them, what's to happen on the solstice . . ."

"That is not your concern. The time for discussion has passed." And that was that.

I could have refused to take him farther, but I had no means to weigh the world's need against Elene's fears. If I postponed my leaving, stayed close if and when this meeting took place, then perhaps I could glean Osriel's purpose.

"It *is* my concern, lord, as your contracted adviser and as a fellow member of the lighthouse cabal. Eventually we must and will discuss it. For now, for the Danae's safety and our need for understanding, I'll fulfill our bargain."

I knelt and touched my hands to earth. At first I sensed nothing beyond the scrape of snow crystals on my wrists and cold grit under my palms. A momentary panic struck me that Saverian's medallion had left my bent useless. But she had insisted that it should not, and as distasteful as her arrogance might be, she had convinced me of her competence.

I closed my eyes and filled my lungs with the cold air, imagining its pungent clarity sweeping aside all worries of Elene and Osriel, of lost souls and abducted children, of familial lies, gravid warnings, and looming birthdays. My fingers prickled and warmed, and I swept my mind across the frozen ground.

Beneath the wind-crusted snow lay a mat of yellowed grass and dormant roots, clotted with damp soil and stones. Sheep had grazed here along with deer, elk, and horned goats come down from the mountains. The beasts left a threadwork of trails down to the willow brakes and fens of the Kay. Human hunters, trappers, and other travelers had beaten two paths across the meadow—one leading down the valley toward villages, abbeys, and cities, the other up the bald rocky prominence to the thick-walled castle men named Fortress Groult. At the conjunction of these paths lingered the faint warm residue of sorcery.

Not much magical structure remained of my illusion—a knotty stump magically inflated from an astelas vine, meant to convince Gram and Stearc that I could read my grandfather's book of maps. Yet two months ago that cheat's ploy had spanned the barrier between true life and myth, between the realm of men and Aeginea. On a meadow with naught growing taller than my knee, I had glimpsed an oak tree with a trunk the breadth of my armspan and a canopy that could shelter a small village, and my companions and I had encountered a Dané female with moth wings on her breasts. I had yet to understand how I'd managed such a feat, but I hoped to repeat it.

My magic enveloped the spot of warmth. Recalling the great tree's particular shape and the wonder I had felt upon seeing it, I sought some trace of a Danae presence upon the land, some evidence of the juncture of two planes that existed here.

The frozen world, the whickering horses, my companions, and my fears receded, and my mind filled with an abundance of the familiar and mundane—the paths of ancient sledges drawn up the hill to build the fortress, the remnants of siege engines and destroying raids, the blood and pain humans left everywhere they walked. Sounds, smells, tastes echoed the richness of the land and its history. Trees had once populated these terraced meadows: maples and oaks, spruce and fir, white-trunked birch. I concentrated, stretched, delved deeper . . .

. . . and came near drowning in music. A legion of musicians must have walked here, leaving behind songs in varied voices . . . a pipe, a harp, a vielle, some instruments unknown to me . . . everywhere random snips of melody that on another day would fascinate and delight. But on this day the pervasive music distracted me, and I pushed past it . . . deeper yet . . . until I felt the weight of the land, the slow-moving rivers of the deeps, the impenetrable roots of the mountains.

Puzzled and anxious, I reminded myself to breathe amid such ponderous life. Yet I sensed more in the deeps: heat . . . circling movement . . . stone dissolved in eternal fire . . .

I backed away quickly. No beings left traces so deep as this. No presence I'd a mind to encounter. I retreated to the veils of music, each melody as rich and holy as plainsong, of marvelous variety, yet not intruding one upon the other, as if designed—

Understanding blossomed like an unfolding lily. Brother Sebastian had taught me that plainsong was a medium of prayer—bearing the petitions we would submit to the gods—and also a mode of prayer—a state of mind that exalted the soul and opened our thoughts to heaven. I focused my inner eyes and ears upon the music as if squinting to see differently or angling my head to pick up fainter sounds, and I began to see and hear and feel what I had previously gleaned in random glimpses and snippets. As blue sigils upon smooth flesh, traces more numerous than the paths of deer had been drawn on the land's music, circling, dividing, rejoining. The earth's music served as the favored medium of the earth's guardians—their paint and canvas, their clay—opening the mind and senses to the deepest truths of the world. Danae shaped paths of music, imposing harmony . . . patterns . . . where they walked. No single thread laid across the landscape, but many silver threads that joined and divided and crossed one another. And now the path lay before me, I, Janus de Cartamandua's son, could surely walk it.

I jumped to my feet. "Follow me."

Mesmerized, I strode across the snow-clad meadow toward a spreading oak that had not yet shed its russet leaves. When at last I touched its bark, I marveled that the great bole's rugged solidity did not waver or vanish. Laughing as would a man freed from the gallows, I pressed my back to the trunk and peered at the hazy blue sky beyond the spreading canopy—no longer winter evening, but autumn afternoon. The chill that nipped my skin tasted of fruit and wine. Then was my attention captured by the prospect beyond the shaded circle.

Earth's Holy Mistress . . . Bathed in the steep-angled sunlight, the land fell away in the familiar giant's steps to the river valley far below. But here, the grass was not crushed with early snow. Rather it rippled in golden, ankle-high luxuriance. The great forests of the Kay, thicker, taller, stretched well beyond the boundaries I knew, so that swaths of red-leaved maples, of deep green spruce and fir and russet oak lapped even these upland slopes and spilled onto these grassy meads. A kite screeched and dived from the deepening sky, only to soar upward in an arc of such exultant grace as to bring a lump to my chest.

No evidence of the human travelers' road scarred the autumn

landscape. No warriors' refuge had been hacked from the rocky pinnacle where Fortress Groult had loomed only moments before. I spun in my tracks. No human work existed anywhere within my sight, nor did any prince, warrior, physician, or beast.

"Lord Prince!" I called, hurriedly retracing my path toward the gorge, out from under the tree . . . back from golden afternoon to indigo evening and snow. When Osriel and Voushanti came back into view, standing not twenty paces from the barren crossroads, I grinned and beckoned, shouting as the wind billowed my cloak. "You'd best stay close!"

Osriel's eyes gleamed as hard as garnet. The deep twilight left Saverian, the soldiers, and the horses as anonymous smudges by the broken pillars of the bridge approach. "You've found your way, then? We lost sight of you."

"Ah, lord, it is a wonder . . ." Osriel's somber visage stilled my desire to babble of music and sunlight. As did Elene, I feared his soul already lay beyond the rock gate without hope of heaven.

Reversing course toward the oak, I walked more slowly this time, relishing the passage, feeling the land and light shift all around me. I sensed a strip of woodland to my left before I could see it, smelled the intoxicating air of Aeginea while human paths yet lay beneath my feet. Voushanti's mumbling told me he saw the tree well after it had come into my view.

When we reached the tree, Osriel touched the craggy bark, and his gaze explored the spreading canopy. It grieved me that I could read no wonder in him.

"I would venture the opinion that we stand in Danae lands, Lord Prince," I said softly, as the dry leaves rustled in the breeze, a few drifting from the branches above us, "and that the meeting you have sought is at hand." For indeed another marvel awaited us.

Striding upslope from the valley were five Danae, their elongated shadows gliding across the rippling grass as if they flew. A big, well-muscled male led the party, his ageless face reflecting unbounded hauteur. A wreath of autumn leaves rested on a cascade of rust-colored hair that fell below his slender waist. A female walked alongside him. Though taller than most human women, she appeared but a wisp beside his imposing height and sculpted sinews. The skin beneath her blue sigils glowed the softest hue of sunrise, and a cap of scarlet curls framed her delicately pointed face. Her lean body spoke of naught but strength.

Slightly behind these two, almost as tall as the male, walked the disdainful female we had met here two months ago—she whose angular face was scribed with a coiled lizard, her flat breasts with intricately drawn moth wings. The Sentinel, Gram had named her. Woodrush and willow, mold and damp—did I truly catch her scent at such a distance or was it but memory?

These creatures value human life less than that of grass or sticks, I reminded myself, summoning disdain and repugnance, lest the empty yearning of that magical night overwhelm me again.

Two other males trailed behind. They seemed younger, less . . . developed . . . than their leader. Or perhaps that was only my assumption as they had no sigils marked on their unsmiling faces. They carried bundles in their arms.

"Let us walk out, Valen. Best let them see us." The prince's command startled me, and my feet obeyed without consulting my head for a reason not. Osriel and I stepped beyond the oak canopy together, Voushanti so close behind I could feel his breath on my neck.

The five Danae halted ten paces away, wholly unsurprised, as if they had come here purposefully to meet us. The hair on my arms prickled, as my true father's warning crept into my memory: *Go not into their lands 'til thou art free . . . not until eight-and-twenty.* My belief that Danae other than Kol did not know me dulled with the fast-failing sunlight, for it could not be mere imagining that five pairs of aspen-gold eyes had fixed on me.

"*Envisia seru, ongai . . . engai.*" Prince Osriel inclined his head to the two in front.

"My lord," I said softly. "What is—?"

"So a human knows of manners . . . and how to keep a bargain," interrupted the small female as if I did not exist. The breeze wafted the sweetness of white pond lilies. "Awe embraces me. But I cannot return thy offered greeting. The sight of thee doth *not* delight my eye, Betrayer-son."

"As ever, the long-lived honor their word," said the prince, nodding coldly to the Sentinel. "Thus I presume it is Tuari Archon"— he acknowledged the male—"and his consort, Nysse"—and the female—"who honor me with their hearing. I regret that my presence offends. My sire reverenced the long-lived and their ways, and rued the division that grew between him and thee. As do I. As thine eyes attest, and the call of thy blood will surely affirm, I have brought thee that which was stolen." His slender hand pointed at me.

No heat, no fire, no explosion of astonishment ignited my soul. Rather a deadly cold crept upward from my toes as floodwaters swamp a drowning man. This quiet betrayal should no more surprise me than should the sharp bite of Voushanti's dagger now threatening to pierce my spine. Would I never learn? *Ignorant, gullible, damnable simpleton.* My family . . . my true parents . . . Luviar . . . Elene . . . Gildas . . . Osriel . . . they were all the same. Only a sentimental fool could have imagined that Osriel the Bastard, master of secrets, might possess some trace of honor and friendship and set me free as he had promised. A prince who had used an innocent boy to gain my oath of submission would not flinch at using me to gain—what?

"What is my blood-price, Lord Osriel?" I snapped before they could complete their inspection of me. "Now you've had your use of me, you might as well explain. At the least may it be some magic to avert the world's end, for of a sudden I've lost all confidence that you are capable of illuminating your lighthouse for any Scholar. And I'd surely not wish my life to feed the evil that lies beyond Renna's rock gate."

He did not flinch. Neither did he offer me further assurances that my life was not at risk. "You will not be alone in your sacrifice," he said.

The two younger Danae had glided to either side of us, cutting off what escape paths did not lie through the Danae or Voushanti's knife. They laid aside what they carried—loops of braided rope tangled with some thick articles of wood—and stood alert. Watching me. Yet for that moment, as I met my master's hard gaze, bitterness out-flanked fear. "Perhaps those who have no sorry history as liars and renegades will be given a choice as to their sacrifice—along with the grace of their lord's trust. Despite your dark mysteries . . . I would have served you willing, Prince, had you but asked."

At that, a tinge of color did touch his cheeks. But he did not waver. "Life is pain," he said. "Only movement—purpose—can make it bearable. As your life's path has now brought you here, I'd recommend you summon what resources you possess to meet your fate. You are not helpless."

He turned his back on me, opening his palms to the Danae in invitation. "Shall we proceed with our exchange? The day wanes. The world wanes. Our people suffer—both yours and mine. Our alliance promises hope for all of them."

Tuari opened his palm in acceptance. "Let us walk, Betrayer-son. You bargained news of the Scourge."

"There is a woman named Sila Diaglou," said Osriel, moving to Tuari's side. "She and her followers wish to return humankind to a primitive chaos . . ."

Heads together, the archon, his consort, and Osriel strolled into the evening meadow. Voushanti and the Sentinel trailed after them at a respectful distance. An owl soared through the air and settled on Moth's shoulder—an owl just like the one that had tricked me and my companions into the bogs.

The two young Danae stepped toward me. At once Janus's warnings took on a firm and terrifying reality. I'd come to Aeginea before turning eight-and-twenty, Osriel had mentioned sacrifice, and these two had muscles that looked like braided iron. No one was going to help me.

I bolted. I'd covered more than half the distance to the Sentinel Oak before one of them brought me down. Spitting grass and dirt, I slammed my elbow into the naked, wiry body on my back. He grunted, but did not let go. Writhing, twisting, I reached back in hopes of capturing the arm that was locked around my neck like an iron collar. I lifted my hip and bent my leg in unfortunate directions in an attempt to trap his feet. But my foot got tangled in my cloak, the Dané clung like a leech, and he caught my flailing arm with his free hand and pinned it to my side. His legs felt like steel ropes about my hips.

I wrestled my knees underneath my belly and prepared to lurch up and back, relishing the prospect of slamming him to the ground and crushing his balls. But as I rose, his friend pounced, and the two together flattened me again. Air escaped my chest in a painful whoosh.

While I fought to get a breath, the two Danae trussed my wrists and knees. Manhandling me as if I weighed no more than dandelion fluff, they dragged me toward the great oak on my back.

"Is this how the long-lived treat their kin?" I gasped as I bumped across the rocky meadow. The glowing pattern of oak leaves on one fellow's legs pulsed an angry purple in several spots. I hoped that meant they hurt.

"You're but a halfbreed," said the youth on my left as if I might have the intelligence of a stick. "Scarcely kin."

Entirely inappropriate laughter welled up from my depths. "Twice cursed!" Surely no man had ever been so afflicted with purulent family. Both branches of my ancestry grasped to hold on to a wretch that neither of them wanted.

When the dragging stopped, I assumed I'd be left until they were ready to take me wherever they thought to keep me. Did Danae have prisons? But the two uncoiled their loops of braided rope—vines, I thought—shoved me upright, and bound me to the massive trunk. I smothered a smile. No unspelled rope had held me for long since I learned how to make a voiding spell when I was eight. I just needed a little time and something to distract these two.

Yet as twilight dropped its mantle over this landscape, I could not focus on my spellmaking. Once they had secured my upper body to the tree, they spread my ankles apart and fixed them in place with loops of rope, a wooden block snugged firmly behind each knee.

"I would do this in thy stead, Kennet," said the taller of the youths, whose wheat-colored hair was braided with firethorn berries. "I'd not have thy gentle heart troubled by the deed."

The other youth, he of the bruised oak leaves, knotted the rope that fixed my thighs in place and looped it behind the trunk again. "I'd gladly give over the task," he said when he reappeared, "but I'd best not refuse Tuari. Give me leave to settle my spirit and strengthen my arm. I would make it fast and clean."

A third chunk of wood, long and narrow like a club—a very heavy-looking club—lay on the ground behind them.

A fluttering panic rose in my belly. "Great gods of mercy, what are you doing? I *can* be persuaded not to run again. Once sworn, I keep my word."

They wrenched the bindings tighter yet. I strained at the braided rope, but could shift neither legs nor torso so much as a quat. "What offense have I given? I've ever honored the Danae. I've left offerings even when I had naught for myself. Told your stories with reverence."

Their blue sigils glowed like traces of sapphire in the lowering dusk. A last tweak of my positioning and the Dané with the firethorn braid picked up the club and moved to one side.

"I did not make my father lie with one of you," I said, panic stretching my voice thin. "I've done naught but be born!"

The other youth, Kennet, extended his hand upward as if to grasp a fistful of leaves above his head, then coiled his body into a knot close to the ground. As I watched, breathless with fear, he unwound himself, spun once, and leaped into the air higher than my head, legs stretched fore and behind, as light and quick as a frighted doe leaps a fence.

My heart leaped with him. For a moment the sheer power of his body's feat overshadowed my foreboding. But as he sank to one knee, took a deep breath, and stood up again, terror came rushing back. No time for pride. "Please, I beg you—"

"No deed of thine has brought this trial on thee," said the one holding the club. "Only the Law. Halfbreeds cannot be allowed to corrupt the Canon again. Thou must never dance in Aeginea. Thou shalt not."

"Dance?" My eyes latched on to the brutish stick of wood as he passed it to the dancer Kennet. "I don't even want to *stay* with you! I've no intent to dance anywhere . . . don't know how . . . save in a tavern brawl . . . crude stomping to pipe and tabor . . . nothing like what you do. I'll swear it . . . swear obedience . . . kiss your archon's feet . . . whatever you want. If you cripple me . . . gods, what gives you the right? If you do this, I'm a dead man."

I'd seen what happened to cripples in famine times. For a man who could not read, the only labors that might keep him eating required legs that worked.

"We cannot take the chance. No argument will change that. But be assured, once thou'rt recovered, we'll help thee make a useful life." When I opened my mouth to beg and curse him, he shoved a strip of leather between my teeth. "Bite down hard."

Kennet stepped toward me, the club poised on a line with my left knee. I slammed the back of my head against the ridged oak bark, squeezed my eyes shut, and all at once the sky fell and lightning struck . . .

Chapter 12

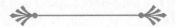

Stripes of lightning blazed on my breast. On the ground before me writhed a snarl of blue light . . . thumps, groans . . . quickly silenced. Beside me a dark shape yanked away ropes and my arms fell free. Dazed . . . confused . . . I spat out the strip of leather, but a hand clamped over my mouth, demanding silence before moving back to its other tasks. A whisk of cold steel sliced through the extra loops holding my thighs and knees, and I was free. My knees . . . intact. Of a sudden my every joint felt like mud.

My senses began to pick the truth out of the darkness. Blade strokes, not lightning strokes, had sliced through the braided rope across my breast. The spreading warmth dampening my shirt was my blood. And I had two rescuers . . .

Bright blue sigils faded to a dull glow, outlining my captors' sprawled bodies, then winked out. The third Dané, the one who had fallen . . . or jumped . . . out of the tree, fumbled at my arms. "How hast thou—?" Hissing enmity spewed through the night as if it were the glowing dragon on his face that spoke. "Who else walks here?"

"Stay away from him!" Saverian's brisk command whipped through the night as my ankles came free, the binding ropes hacked apart by her blade. "Run, Valen!"

Though I could not see the physician herself, her weapon—a dagger the length of my forearm—appeared to my right, reflecting the Dané's blue fire. I stumbled, weak-kneed, to join her.

"No!" Kol stretched out his leg and spun. The dagger went flying. He grappled with the shadowy figure, cutting off her growl of fury, and threw her to the turf. Then his iron hands clamped on to my arm and propelled me away from the oak. "Come with me,

Cartamandua-son, or count thyself captive of the archon once more and be broken. The remedy I've given thy captors will not quiet them long."

"Wait! What have you done? The woman . . ." Recovering some semblance of strength, I wrestled free of him and returned to Saverian, relieved to feel the beat of life in her neck. "I'll not leave her." She had thwarted the prince's will and jeopardized his bargain with the Danae, and I trusted neither Osriel's mercy nor his friendship.

"The human is no concern of mine." Kol's voice shivered my bones. "She interfered where she had no business."

So did you, I think, uncle. Though not for love of me. The memory of his grieving at Clyste's Well remained as vivid as on the day I'd witnessed it. Duty, not care, had brought him to my rescue.

The Dané moved away, the words trailing behind him. "Stay if thou willst. Gratefully will I be finished with thee."

I had only a moment to decide. Kol seemed honest at least, both in his dislike and in his grief. He held out some hope of evading Osriel, whose perfidy had sapped all faith. No vow, no pledged service for whatever cause, should require a man be crippled. I scooped the limp physician into my arms, heaved her over my shoulder, and hurried after the Dané, praying the gods to forgive my presumption of divine benevolence in the face of my oath breaking.

We moved west on undulating ground, the river a constant rush on our left, and the bulge of land and rock that formed the pinnacle of Fortress Groult a swelling blackness against the starry sky on our right. I fixed my eyes on the blue-limned shape ahead of me, while concentrating every other sense and instinct on my footing. The Dané acknowledged my presence with neither glance nor speech, but the distance between us did not vary, no matter that I flagged under Saverian's weight on every uphill pitch. He could have vanished in an instant. I had no choice but to trust him.

The night deepened. My shoulders ached. The wind grew into a constant buffeting, whipping my face with the hem of Saverian's cloak and the flaps of her leather skirt. The physical effort and the concentration required to avoid a fall made thinking impossible. So it was only when a sudden gust from my left staggered me that I noted the change in the air. The wind smelled vaguely of fish and felt odd—cold, yes, but heavy and sticky. A quick look around staggered me as well. Not three steps to my left, the earth plunged precipitously into the night. The far side of the river gorge had vanished. And beyond those black depths . . . the river's voice had changed into a rhythmic pounding crash. "Kol," I called. "Where are we?"

He did not respond. I repeated the call several times, especially once the path began a twisting descent that ofttimes seemed more vertical than not. Sand and gravel on the path set my boots skidding and my heart galloping. Immediately after one jolting slide, when only a nubbin of crumbling rock had saved me from skidding off the path and plummeting the rest of the distance to the bottom of the cliff, Saverian began to squirm, mumbling something about hands and castration. Her heavy cloak, leather overskirt, woolen riding breeches, and leggings were all in a bunch about her thighs, half obscuring my vision.

"For the love of the Mother, hold still," I shouted, planting my heel in a crack well suited to a cliff swallow's roost. "I've no place to set you down. And you don't want to see where we'll land if you throw me off balance."

If she spoke I didn't hear her, but she did settle. The roar of the sea grew louder, the scent of salt wrack affirming the evidence of my ears. At a slight leveling of the track, I risked another glance. A star-filled sky illumined the white curls of breaking waves.

Ardra touched the western sea just north of the tin mines and cliffside sea fortresses of Cymra. But to reach the shore one must cross the wilds of the Aponavi, painted clansmen who herded goats and crafted rugs and collected heads for sport. To consider how far we might have traveled stretched my tired mind beyond reason.

Below me, Kol's fiery sigils vanished, and I hurried onto the next downward pitch. My left boot slid sidewise toward the void . . . *Concentrate, fool!* But my right boot had no purchase on the skittering rocks, and I dared not trust it with our combined weight. Three quick steps at once brought me to another course reversal and an even steeper pitch. I dared not pause the entire last quarter of the descent, so that when I hurtled onto a shore of rippled sand I had difficulty persuading my feet to stop before they quickstepped right into the sea.

"Great Deunor's grandmother!" I said, dropping to my aching knees . . . my blessed, aching, unsplintered knees. A rush of gratitude led me to deposit Saverian onto the sand with far more care than my screaming shoulders would prefer. Then I sat back on my heels, gulping air. She sat up, pulled her half-unraveled braid out of her face, and gaped.

"You've infected me with your madness." Narrowing her eyes to slits, she rubbed her temples vigorously. "Else I've bumped my head, and all this"—she waved at the sea and sky and sand without looking at them—"is but my own mind's imagining. If you tell me it's neither, and that I've not just dreamed performing the single most appallingly stupid act of my life, I beg you snap my neck quickly."

"You saved my life, lady—you and he." I nodded a hundred quercae down the shore where Kol sat on a cluster of boulders, long arms wrapped around his bent knees, allowing the sea spray to shower him. "I could not leave you to reap Osriel's whirlwind for your kindness. But truth be told, I don't know as I've done you any favor. I've no idea where he's brought us . . ." . . . assuming Kol had *brought us* here at all. Just because I had managed to follow him didn't mean he wished us to be here.

She bent her head to her knees and beat her fists on her skull. Mumbled invective flowed from her like lava from a volcano. Her inventive mixture of human anatomy and unlikely violence altogether lifted my spirits.

The chill, damp wind flapped my cloak. Driftwood lay about the shore, tempting me to direct the prickly mage's attention to fire. But the luminous breakers, the wind-borne scent of unknown shores, and a heaven filled with brilliant stars of such profusion and arrangement as I had never witnessed reminded me that we were not in our own land, but lost in Aeginea.

I pushed up to my feet. "I must speak to him before anything. Find out where he's brought us and what he wants of me. You'll be all right for a bit?"

"On the day I require the protection of a lunatic, I'll snap my *own* neck. Yes, please go find out where we are, so I'll know whether I've a better choice to travel east to Estigure or west to Cymra to find a new employer." Her gaze, sparked with starlight, traveled up and down my height. "You're going to tell me we're in the realm of angels, aren't you? And that the naked man with the exceedingly odd skin that I've imagined seeing is some kin of yours?"

I grinned down at her. "My uncle. Though he's as loath as my every other kinsman to claim me. I'll be back as soon as I may, and I'd advise not burning anything right away."

I tramped the short distance down the broad tidal flats, finding it easier going than slogging through the dunes. Kol took no notice of my coming. Mustering every shred of graceful manners my tutors had beaten into me, I bowed and spoke the greeting Osriel had used. The Dané might not delight my eye, but my gratitude could not be measured. "*Envisia seru*, Kol. How may I serve thee in recompense for sound legs?"

"Be unborn." He continued to stare into the churning sea.

The rebellious ember that yet denied the story of my birth winked out of existence. Seeking shelter from the wind and spray, I squeezed between his waist-high perch and another slab, pressed my weary back to the damp stone, and sat.

"If wishing could accomplish such a thing, gods know it would have happened long before now," I said, twisting my aching shoulders. "My father's family wished it. Many's the time *I've* wished it— but that was before I learned that I had a kinswoman who could be spoken of as 'beloved of every Dané for her joyful spirit.' "

"Do not think to ingratiate thyself by speaking of her."

"I've no wish to ingratiate myself with any of your kind," I snapped, his arrogance a cold wash on my conciliatory sensibilities. "You have extended me favors I never asked of you and that are clearly at odds with your own inclinations. Thus I must assume it is your sister's desires you serve and that she wished us to treat each other with honor, if naught else. I offer no less than she would ask— and no more."

After a long moment, he jerked his head in agreement. "I retract my unworthy accusation."

Resisting the temptation to gasp in mock astonishment, I gestured at the desolate shore. "So, why would my mother want me here?"

"She chose me as thy vayar—thy teacher. The shores of Evaldamon provide a suitable place for teaching and are little traveled. Days pass slowly here. Yet were the days each the lingering of a season, the task is already impossible. I smell the remasti close upon thee. Once a body has passed the last remasti unchanged, naught can be done to alter it."

"The last remasti . . . my birthday."

He squeezed his eyes shut and ground his jaw. "Clyste trusted the Cartamandua to bring thee to me in the proper season—long ago. Despite what human lies tell, the long-lived do not steal human children away to Aeginea. Clyste's innocence burned as the stars; the Cartamandua's false promises stank as human dwellings do."

"So it was for one broken promise that you stole Janus's mind— stole his life." Kol's arrogance revolted me. "You mourn for my mother who broke your laws and sent me off with him. Yet for a failed human man, you alone issue a judgment that breaks all bounds of compassion. I've no desire for your lessons."

"Which is precisely why the teaching would be useless."

The Dané unfolded his legs, pressed the bottoms of his feet together, and drew his heels close to his groin. I squirmed as I watched, imagining the uncomfortable stretch. Clasping his hands together, he straightened his arms over his head, then slowly bent his body forward until his chest came near touching the surface of the flat rock. I hugged my knees tightly, as if someone might prod me to replicate his move.

The silence lagged. Already I rued my hasty retort. My life demanded answers. I needed to understand what I was and what I would be, come the winter solstice.

"You brought me here despite your belief that I could not learn what you would teach," I said. "She had some plan, didn't she . . . my mother? She mated with Janus because she—"

"I will not speak of that joining." He sprang to his feet, his sigils pulsing, posture and voice articulating bald humiliation. "It is enough that my sister's blood flows in thy veins. She believed the Everlasting had accounted a place for thee in the Canon. This I cannot and will not accept. And if ever such a disordered event were possible, the season of its accomplishment has long passed. Yet even so late in this waning season I know what she would ask of me."

"The Canon. A vayar is—" I pounced upon the absurdity, astonishment ruining my intent to curb my tongue. "You don't think to teach me to dance?"

His face, long, narrow, and perfectly formed, might have been cold marble beneath his sigils. "No. But if I gift thee the separation gard, as if thou wert a nestling new released from thy parents' side, the Law forbids Tuari to damage thee without informing thy *argai*—thy eldest kin, who is Stian, my sire. The custom provides only a delay, shouldst thou be taken captive again, for the archon's judgment of a halfbreed will never be other than breaking. But it might give trustworthy companions a chance to protect thee." He jumped down from the rock, landing on his bare feet with the weight of thistledown. "If I can convince Stian to agree and gift thee the walking gard as well, thou canst move through the world with certain skills of the long-lived, which will aid thee in eluding capture. Clyste would wish these protections for thee, though all other wishes fail."

"The gards . . . these markings . . . the sigils of Danae magic . . ." My hands crept inside my sleeves and rubbed my arms. Denial rose like bile in my throat. But a glance at the sea, churning a few paces from my boots where it had no business being, slowed my retort. The Danae could travel impossible distances . . . vanish as if they had wings . . . hide.

Twelve years I had hidden from the detestable life my pureblood birth prescribed for me. Lacking purpose beyond staying free, lacking skills beyond health and wits, I'd survived by embracing the chances Serena Fortuna had placed in my way. I had never turned my back on the divine damsel. And now matters were far more complicated.

I might be able to find a route out of Aeginea, but I could not imagine where I might be safe from Osriel's wrath *and* from these Danae who would maim me *and* from the Pureblood Registry, who yet believed me pureblood and would run me to ground without mercy did Osriel but hint that I had violated my contract. More important, a stolen child awaited rescue—so I prayed—and a murdered child awaited justice. I no longer had confidence that Prince Osriel would weigh their needs important beside this mysterious course he had chosen.

"So you could just . . . mark . . . me and I could travel as you do?"

"Not so simply as that. I would provide thee the necessary teaching."

"And the price? I understand that your . . . gifting . . . is to Clyste, not to me. But to gain these skills, surely I must be required to yield something. Janus warned me to stay away until I was eight-and-twenty . . . past this last change . . . ."

"The Cartamandua never understood the remasti or the gards." Kol's tone made it clear that folk held higher opinion of crawling snakes than he did of the man who'd fathered me. "Janus believed a vayar imposed some alteration upon the body at the remasti, thus making it something other than ordained by birth. Even while promising to do as Clyste asked, he confessed his fear that I would make thee more our kind than his. To him birth was blood, and blood was all. But the change is already trapped within thee. Necessary, even for one with a human parent. Thy own skills and talents and practices determine the partitioning of thy nature—entirely of humankind, entirely of the long-lived, or somewhere part of each."

"So my father was wrong, and you, who despise me and my kind, will generously share your Danae magic with me." Kol's assurances sounded promising, but I could not bar Janus's wild eyes and drooling mouth from my memory.

Exasperation broke through his chilly reserve. "I shall not harm thee. Many easier ways could I damage thee, if vengeance were my intent. I could have left thee for Tuari to be broken. Do thou pass the time of the last remasti entirely unchanged, thy skin will harden into a prison and thy spirit shall die captive within it. To change, thou must yield only the desire to remain ignorant and incapable and incomplete."

Ignorant and incapable and incomplete . . . my skin a prison. A pureblood diviner reading my cards could not have so captured the entirety of my existence. My gaze traveled the length of Kol's marked limbs. What did it feel like? Would my own human magic behave differently . . . be lost? Great gods, did Danae eat? Make love? Well, of course . . . I was evidence of that. But all I knew was fireside tales of beings forced to live as stone or trees, who died when trapped within walls. Different. Not human. I rubbed cheek and jaw, as if I might discover lines and sworls waiting beneath my skin.

Events were moving so rapidly. Gildas had taken Jullian to Sila Diaglou as a tool to manipulate me. Weeks it had been already. If she came to believe the boy of no use to her . . . I could not allow that, which meant my time was short. Yet Danae magic might make all the difference, enable me to get him away, to learn and do the things I needed to do. The lighthouse must endure, no matter what wickedness Osriel the Bastard thought to work with solstice magic.

I blinked and gazed up at Kol. "How long would this take?"

He threw up his hands. "How long, how many, how far, how much. Hast thou no questions of substance?" He pointed to the rock where he'd sat. "If thou art here when the sun wakes from the cliff, I will begin thy teaching, as my sister would desire."

He turned his back and waded into the sea. Once the slack water lapped his thighs he dived into the rolling waves. Lightning the color of lapis and indigo infused the churning surf and then faded.

Snugged between the two chunks of granite, wavelets creeping ever closer to my toes, I tried desperately to think of some reason *not* to be here in the morning. But I could command neither mind nor body to any useful purpose . . . what with the exertions of the day . . . with this unknowable path beneath my feet . . .

"You didn't ask him about a fire." Saverian's head popped up from the far side of Kol's rock, causing me to slam an elbow into the rock. My heart crashed into my ribs with the impact of the surf.

"Mother Samele's tits, do you forever sneak around and show up where you're not invited?"

"I've noted several nice-sized chunks of wood lying around. I can either set them afire so that you're not quaking like an Aurellian torturer on Judgment Night, or I can use them to turn your knees to powder as other relatives proposed. And then I'll politely ask the naked gentleman to tell me where in the Sky Lord's creation you've brought me. You forgot to discover that, as well."

I *was* trembling. Fear had its part, no question. But the damp had penetrated my sweat-soaked garments, as well, and though in no wise as frigid as in Evanore, the wind cut through the layered wool like

Ardran lances. "I'd say burn what you like. He's not going to be happy no matter what I do. Can you see where he's gone?"

Her gaze roved the enclosing night. "We should leave this place. Use your skills and get us away. Trusting a creature like that . . ." She shuddered. "His spirit is surely a glacier. He may have had feelings for his sister, but he has no feelings for you. He doesn't even hate. He exists."

"So speaks the woman who serves the Duc of Evanore."

She came round the rock and offered me her hand. "Osriel of Evanore is a human man of extraordinary discipline. His passions run very deep and sometimes lead him to ill choices. But I understand him."

"Explain the *ill choice* of crippling his friends." Weary to the bone, I accepted her hand—unusually cold on this night—and hauled myself up. We strolled down the shore, collecting the odd bits of wood thrown up on the sand. "Will he forgive what you did tonight?"

"Forgiveness is not Osriel's strength. He tolerates no weakness in himself, and while he does not expect the same of those who serve him, he *does* expect their trust. No matter how I argue with him, I've always given him that in the end."

"Even with whatever mystery lies beyond the rock gate at Dashon Ra?"

She halted in midstep. "If you ever whisper of that again, even in private, I'll unravel my spell and leave you gibbering until your mind is muck. Elene is a fool to have shown you." She snatched an arm-length branch from the sand. "*Never* misapprehend. I am Osriel of Evanore's loyal servant whether or not I dare stand in his presence again. As for tonight . . . in no way was I prepared to tend horses while you and Osriel strolled into heaven or hell or wherever we are. And when their intentions became clear . . . No worthy physician could stand by and see a healthy body damaged. But be assured I will always wonder what might have happened if I had let events play out as he planned. You would have survived without my intrusion."

So she knew at least somewhat of Osriel's plan for Dashon Ra. Unfortunately, as we wandered about the shore filling our arms, naught in her demeanor invited further discourse. At last we threw our bits and pieces into a pile, and I spread my arms so my cloak might block the wind as she arranged them and worked her magic. With her third snapped "*flagro,*" the center of the little pile began to smolder. She broke off splinters of the half-rotted wood to coax and nourish the little flame.

"I should have you teach me how to do that," I said, stretching my hands toward the growing flames. "Probably more use than what Kol will teach me."

"You're going to allow him to work his wiles on you? Have you heard no tale of the Danae? Great Mother, preserve my reason, you *are* a fool."

"So, my wise physician, come up with a better suggestion before tomorrow—something that does not include mutilation, chains, or removal of my eyes. An innocent child languishes in captivity, his days short unless I show up to claim him, and another lies dead, and I'm the only one who seems to care anymore. Indeed I've done nothing of worth in my life, and see little prospect of it. But everything in this world has a purpose: clouds, thorns, fleas. Perhaps I'll do better as a . . . whatever I am . . . than I've done thus far, pretending to be human."

We sat in uncomfortable silence. Saverian's stomach growled. My own had near gnawed itself through, and we'd not a scrap of food or drink between us. Though her flames grew and bathed my front side in warmth, I could not stop shaking.

A soft slapping sound from the darkness to my left sent me to my feet like a whipcrack. A dripping Kol stepped into the ring of firelight, tossed two fish the size of my boot soles onto the sand in front of us, then walked into the night without a word.

"So, are you mad or sane this morning?"

Saverian's bent must signal her when a person's awareness returned, for I'd not so much as lifted an eyelid or stirred a muscle in my nest of sand. I managed only a grunt in reply. Such early questioning left a body no time to enjoy those few moments of uncomplicated, irresponsible satiation that occur between sleep and waking. It didn't seem at all fair.

Of course, I *had* waked her with my screaming in the middle of the night, convinced the sea's crashing signaled the world's end and that hurricane-driven knives were flaying me. I vaguely recalled her yanking the gold disk from my neck and wrestling my thrashing limbs quiet as it sent forth its maggoty magic to quell the onslaught. Humiliating. I'd been so sure I could control her spell.

"You've likely an hour until the sun's above the cliff," she said. "There's fresh water in the rocks down that way where the cliff's collapsed."

I rolled to all fours, spitting sand, blinking away sand, shaking my head to speed the shower of sand from my hair. The stuff had crept into my boots and my ears and every pore and crevice in between.

As I stumbled through the cold gray dawn to relieve the pressure of food and drink, the grit abraded my feet, my eyes, my waist, and my groin.

I returned to our little camp clearer in the head at least. No matter what happened with Kol, if I thought to go anywhere and accomplish anything afterward, I needed Saverian's medallion back, along with better teaching as to how to use the thing.

The physician was cooking some eggs on the same flat stone I had used to cook Kol's fish. The lively fire and the replenished stock of wood testified she'd been awake much earlier than I.

"I hope you're not bruised," I said, squatting opposite her as she poked her eating knife at the eggs. "Thank you. Sorry for the fight."

"Having to deal with your illness was a good thing, I think. It made me forget what a puling coward I felt last night with all this . . . strangeness . . . and seeing Danae in the flesh and getting whacked in the head. I began thinking as a physician again."

Her admission startled me, but I detected no humility in her demeanor. She wrinkled her nose at the eggs as they quickly took on the color of dirt and the consistency of drying plaster.

"I considered what the Dané said about this 'change' being trapped inside you. Perhaps he holds the true remedy to your disease."

"I'd like to believe that. But clearly you've not met my mad patronn. Kol's work is not necessarily benevolent." I grimaced, as always, at the recollection.

"Osriel told me your history," she said. "I can't blame you whichever way you choose. But you can't go back to nivat, and I don't know how long the disk is going to help you."

"Your rock is a bit too hot." I offered her a flat piece of wood to use for a plate. If she didn't eat her eggs soon, she could use them to bandage wounds. My stomach growled and rumbled. "Were there more of those wherever you found them? Or did Kol bring them?"

"I've not seen him as yet this morning. And these were all I could find without climbing, so you might as well take half."

"I couldn't—"

"Would you stop being so polite? I've wiped up too much of your bodily fluids to like you, but I'm not prepared to let you starve or go mad, either one." She scraped the leathery mess onto the wood and ran her knife down the middle, dividing them precisely in half. "But I detest dirt and cold and sleeping on the ground, and as you see I'm worse than useless at cooking, so please just get this business over with and show me the way back to my own bed. I must get back to

Osriel. His illness does not wait. I can resolve my difficulties with him."

She pulled a spoon from her belt kit and began eating. A bruise on my hip, caused when the two Danae had thrown me to the ground, was the only remnant of my own kit. Her dagger lay wherever Kol had kicked it, and I had carried no weapon since Boreas stole my knife all those months ago. I scooped the ugly little mess with my fingers and stuffed my mouth full. A fine time for my uncle to walk out of the sea with his hands full of green stuff.

With only a cool observation, he dropped the soggy weeds onto the sand beside us and strolled down the shore to the clustered rocks where we were to meet. His gards gleamed silver, scarcely visible in the sunlight. Instead of climbing onto the rocks to wait, as he had the previous day, he propped one foot on the rock and bent forward, leg straight, stretching his arms to touch his toes, his chest flat along his thigh. He remained there, perfect in his stillness.

"Do you think he's praying?" I said, wiping my sticky hands on my chausses and imagining the ache of such posture. It made the abbey practices of kneeling and prostration seem benign.

"Did you not observe the way the other fellow moved . . . danced . . . before he set to crush your knees?" said Saverian. "Evidently even a Danae body must work to develop that kind of power and forestall damage. The sea is cold, which tightens the muscles. He's loosening them again. I suppose he means for us to eat this green mess."

"You're welcome to all of it," I said, not so hungry as I'd thought.

Kol shifted his stance to the other leg.

I pulled off my boots and dumped the sand from them. Examining the brightening sky above the cliff top, I judged I had time enough to wash the gritty egg taste from my mouth. Naught was like to wash away the taste of fear or loosen the tightness in *my* back.

Leaving my boots by the fire to warm, I headed up the shore barefoot. As I strode away from Saverian and her fire, and Kol and his rock, doubts crept forward, whispering that I was a fool to consider Kol's offer. Saverian's leathery eggs had reminded me of days when I'd had naught so fat and filling. I'd never been greedy of pleasure, wealth, or happiness. I'd enjoyed my life—eating what I scrounged, drinking, singing, dancing, albeit in my own crude fashion. I'd shared delights with women and left them laughing and satisfied; I'd worked hard and walked the length of Navronne beneath the skies of summer and winter. I'd seen marvels and talked of philosophy and nonsense with a variety of folk. What more did I want?

Education was truly a wicked thing. Ignorance had served me well for seven-and-twenty years, and now these monks, princes, and serious women and children had forced me to take note of the world's trouble, and got it all tangled up with honor and righteousness and good works. But I was no grand thinker. No mighty warrior. No martyr or hero or scholar. I had no plan for saving either Jullian or Navronne from Sila Diaglou, and no twisting of my brain since my recovery had devised one.

By the time I'd located the trickle of fresh water that burbled underneath a collapsed segment of the sea cliff, washed salt and sand from face and teeth, and swallowed a few mouthfuls, I'd half convinced myself to run away. I would persuade Saverian to return the gold medallion and teach me how to control my disease. Kol had offered no remedy to prevent me going mad from stinks and noises.

The Dané put himself through several more contortions, sitting, squatting, bending, and stretching. The fellow could not be built on bone. *Not human. Gods . . .*

I started back.

Kol positioned himself at the very brink of sea and shore. Facing the sea cliff, he raised his arms straight over his head, then allowed them to settle slightly lower, at an upward angle with his shoulders. He paused there, face lifted to the cliff top.

Without reason, my steps slowed. My breathing paused. At the moment the sun nudged its rim above the sea cliff, Kol ran five mighty steps forward and leaped into the air, knees bent—one forward, one behind—lifting my heart right out of my body. Music, some marvelous discourse of pipe and dulcian, burst forth when his feet touched earth and he began a series of impossible leaps and spins, linked with sweeps of arm and hand, with slow turns and long extensions of leg . . . skyward, seaward . . .

Great gods have mercy! As the rays of morning light touched my cheek, the earth shifted beneath my bare feet . . . breathing . . . rejoicing . . . grieving . . . alive. I felt the exuberant burst of its renewal, as I had felt my own upon waking in sunlight through Osriel's window. And this . . . the Dané's dance . . . had caused it to happen.

Down on one knee, chest heaving, Kol extended his muscled leg and back and touched his forehead. He held the position impossibly long until his breathing stilled, so that one might believe him transformed into the very stone statue I had seen in Osriel's garden. Perfect.

"Magnus Valentia!" Saverian called as I passed by her. "We need—"

"Can't," I yelled over my shoulder, for of a sudden I was running. Kol had risen, glanced at the barren rock, and was walking away.

"Kol, wait! I want . . ." Breathless, I came to the rocks and called after him, heedless of duty, fear, or pride. As if a sword had opened my breast to expose a wildcat in place of my heart, a lifetime's worth of dissatisfaction, of restless searching and unfocused longing made some kind of sense. I had never imagined such possibility as my uncle had just revealed. If I wanted to help my friends, I had to live. If I wanted to live, I had to take this chance. I could not let fear and caution make me run away—not this time. "Please. Teach me."

Chapter 13

"Season upon season does it require to learn the dance. The fullness of a gyre at the least to grasp the very beginning positions." Kol's hands flew up in empty offering, demonstrating the futility of what I begged. His every word and gesture spoke the extent of his scorn. "For a body half human, unpracticed, grown fixed in its working, for a mind distracted by human concerns and unprepared even by the remasti, the breadth and extent of the Everlasting would not be sufficient."

Not even such denial could discourage me. Could I but find the proper words to describe this revelation . . . this certainty that lived in my very breath and bone . . . I could convince him.

"I am not wholly unpracticed," I said, following as he strode along the shore, incoming wavelets lapping at his feet. His gards shimmered palest silver in the cold sunlight. "I've run since I could walk, danced since I first heard a flute in the marketplace. And I've vigor and endurance beyond other humans—I see that now." My pleas sounded weak and pitiful beside a hunger that left the doulon but a passing whimsy. All my life's desires and longings had come together in those moments of Kol's dancing. Could I but grasp this purpose, surely all other matters—duties and vows and promises—would fall into a pattern I could comprehend. I was meant for this.

"To master the correct line of a jeque—the simplest leap—and how to balance, how to approach, how to land, how to shift weight and control the strength required while bringing grace and smoothness, takes practice—every day, every night, season upon season, constant work to develop the flexibility of the hip and the power of the leg and the understanding of how these work together. A sequence of three eppires—spins on one foot—happens not in all the seasons before a wanderkin becomes a stripling. And these are only the movements. The wanderkin and stripling study the land and seasons, the growing things, the beasts. Even more difficult . . . the maturing student must learn to work with the music of the Everlasting, so he may devise sequences of steps to conjoin all these elements, else the dance is but exercise with no effect. And once these are mastered, even yet must one learn the lore of the Canon and how to work a sianou. Thou art far beyond teaching, even were I willing to take on such a task." He had drawn his brow so tight his dragon's upper wing curled into a knot.

"A lifetime of practice . . . yes, I can see that. Like a swordsman's training. I could not do what you do in any matter of months or years. Even the moves that appear simple are built on layers of strength and precision. But the other learning . . . Music lives in me; I hear it everywhere . . . even across the years, when I use my bent. And I've not spent my life without eyes or ears. Likely I picked up much of the worldly lore in all these years. It's just the movements . . ." My limbs and spine longed to stretch and spin and soar. My heart and lungs ached to fuel such power as I had seen.

We rounded the curving end of the shallow cove and came to a point where sand yielded to a cobbled shore, carved with tide pools. White-winged gulls flapped and rode the wind, while bearded ducks and thin-necked grebes pecked at sea wrack abandoned by the tides.

Kol took out across the cobble, and I followed, abruptly aware of my bare feet on the cold hard knobs. The Dané halted and pointed at a crescent-shaped pool near the water's edge. One could not mistake the challenge. "Share your knowledge, halfbreed. Tell me what lives here."

Having worked for a time in the ports of Morian, I knew something of shorebirds and fish and shelled creatures. But to recite them as for a schoolmaster . . . Kol's expression echoed my every childhood tutor's disbelief. *Ignorant* plebeiu. *Stubborn, ill-mannered whelp who refuses even to try. Have you some disease, Magnus, that you cannot pick out one simple word from a page, or is this but the incurable hardness of your spirit?*

I forced past failures aside. This was the dance, life that linked sunlight and sea and earth. Even the Cartamandua bent could never again bring me to this crossroads of possibility.

Kneeling on the hard cobbles, I peered into the clear water, the sunlight dazzling my eyes. I saw little but rocks and a few sea plants with long stalks and filmy red leaves. One tiny fish darted into the rocky shadows. The carnage the hunting birds had scattered on the cobble told me more. "There'll be crabs and mussels here," I said. "Those bunched green fronds are a snake plant stuck to the rock, I think. When the tide goes out, it withers."

"But does it live or die? Guesses and simplicities hardly suffice." Kol stood straight as a post. What did he want? Such creatures as lived in pools hid among the rocks and weeds. Who could know them all?

Irked by his contempt, I plunged my hands into the pool. Perhaps my bent might reveal what passed here in the same way it allowed me to distinguish footsteps. Elbow deep, the cold water wet my sleeves and crept upward toward my shoulders as I loosed magic to flow through my fingertips. I listened, smelled, tasted, stretched my mind into the crevices and crannies. Slowly, I began to comprehend what my senses uncovered: threads of color, of stillness and movement, of life and death.

"Fish live here," I said. "Shannies and bearded rocklings—and tiny shrimp, almost transparent, and the warty yellow lump that is a slug, not a pebble. And this"—I touched a dark, twisted knot of a shell—"is a dog whelk that Hansker milk for purple dye. The strawberry growing on that bulging rock is no plant, but a tentacled beast that stings its prey—the smaller creatures who hide in these forests of leaves, like the glass shrimp brought in by the tide and the mitelings of the dog whelk . . . ."

I told him of death and birth, of how the whelk's tongue scoops the flesh of the mussel between its closed shells, and how an entirely new creature can grow from the broken arm of the scarlet sea star that hid beneath a wave-smoothed rock. The pool was a world to itself, fed and ravaged by the god of the tide, as Navronne was fed and ravaged by our fickle gods.

When my hands grew numb from the cold, I had to stop. Bundling my fingers beneath my arms, I sat up, shivering and blinking in the watery light.

Kol sat on his haunches beside me, staring into the water. "As I have watched thee walk the land and sound the streams of the earth in company with humans, I assumed thy works a preening deception—the arrogance of the Cartamandua passed on in his seed. Again, I have erred." He shifted his gaze to my face as if he looked on me for the first time. "For a gyre—a full turn of the seasons—I studied this very pool, and only then did I understand so much. Thou hast a grace for seeing, *rejongai*. Did the gyres wheel backward, I would press thy sire earlier . . . convince him to bring thee to me for teaching, not wait, as I did, for him to fail."

He rose to his full height. "But no wishing can recapture lost chance. Clyste was wrong. Were all accomplished as she hoped, even then thou couldst *not* dance the Canon. Human blood flows in thy veins, and the archon forbids tainted blood nigh the dancing ground. Naught can change the lessons of the past. We will speak no more of the Canon. I can gift thee the gards of separation and exploration and the teaching of their use, as I said, and that only."

But the vehemence of his denial was no longer directed at me, but at himself. Pride had caused him to fail Clyste, a sister whom he loved. For the first time since I had seen him greet the morning, a spark of hope burned inside me. I would not push too hard. He would bend. Whatever the "lessons of the past," I believed as I believed naught else in this world that my mother had meant for me to dance.

"What must I do?" I shoved up my sleeves and stretched out my arms as if they were sword blanks to be heated, hammered, and shaped.

He motioned me to follow him back around the headland to the sandier shore. "As I said, each change lies buried within thy flesh already—the three suppressed and the great one yet to come."

"Then why didn't I change when the time was right? I suppose it's more difficult for ones like me. Halfbreeds. Which means this will likely be uncomfortable—" Memories of battle wounds came to mind, and those horrid birthdays when I'd gone half mad with pain and lashed out at anyone within reach, driven by an agonized restlessness that naught but violence or spelled perversion could still.

No matter my desires, dread shivered my marrow.

"It is neither fault in thee nor a factor of thy mixed birth that thou art unchanged. A remasti is impossible to accomplish alone. The vayar must guide the immature body to express its power, and the gards are the visible signs of its accomplishment. Other halfbreeds have taken the remasti without difficulty."

Kol motioned me to stand before him at the edge of the water, but I held my ground in the dry dunes. My nerves would not permit my mouth to be still. "What will I feel? What will change besides the . . . marks?"

As if even that alteration was a small thing! How would I walk the streets of Palinur again, with blue light glowing on my skin? "Surely it will be different for one who is part human."

"Certainly the result will differ." He visibly forced himself patient, closing his eyes, whose color had shifted from a deep sea green to aspen gold. "What hand or eye is entirely the same as any other? What walking step or standing posture is the same? The long-lived tread the path of perfection, but we each find our resting posture somewhere along the way, our own talents and our bodies' limits determining our place. Even tainted blood does not preclude one attempting the path. Now we must begin or even the slow days of Evaldamon will carry us to the Everlasting with thou yet unprotected."

I opened my mouth and then closed it again. Answers would come. With no more hesitation, I moved to the edge of the water. "Tell me what to do."

"We will begin by acknowledging our bond as vayar and tendé. Then, when I give thee a sign, thou must wash. Especially thy arms and legs. Sand is an excellent aid."

"Wash . . . here? In the sea?" Water and cold, my two least favorite aspects of nature, and not entirely because a diviner had once named them my doom.

"Yes."

The wind had risen, frosting the waves with foam. A haze paled the sky and sunlight, and a layer of deep gray banded the horizon. No chance Kol intended for me to stay clothed. Gods, I was damp to the skin, and now he wanted that skin bare. However Danae managed to stay warm as they ran about naked in winter weather, I had not inherited that gift. I glanced along the shore and over my shoulder. A trail of smoke rose from our fire, but I could not see where Saverian had got off to. "All right, then."

Kol bowed with all the formality of a pureblood head of family, then clasped his hands behind his back. He dipped his head in approval when I returned the bow without prompting. "The season has long passed for thee to leave thy parents' side, nes—"

His dragon gard drew up as he cut off this pronouncement. "What name dost thou prefer? Thou art very big for such address as *nestling* or *wanderkin.*"

This slight break in his formality nudged me toward an unlikely grin. Indeed, though he could likely break me over his knee, we were quite evenly matched in size. "I answer most to Valen. Is there some proper title I should use for you? I've no wish to be rude."

"Name me *relagai*—mother's brother—or *vayar*. To address an elder by name requires a harmony we shall never share."

I ignored his coldness and bowed to acknowledge his point. "*Relagai.*"

He took up where he'd left off. How much "elder" was he? Likely centuries. Gods . . . "Freed from thy parents' side, Valen, thou shalt have license to wander the world and learn of its wonders and its evils, to learn the names and natures of all its parts. I have accepted the duties of vayar given me by she who gave thee first breath and who nurtured thee for the long seasons of thy borning. I pledge with all honor and intent to provide thee truth and healthy guidance and to protect thee from harm to the limits of my being and the Law of the Everlasting. Come to me with thy questioning, with thy fears and troubles, with thy joys and discoveries, and I will hear thee . . . without judgment . . . and answer thee as far as I am able. Thy own part of this joining is but thy pledge to explore and learn and come to me if thou art troubled. If thou wilt accept my teaching, Valen, give me thy hands." He extended his own hands, palms upward.

I had not expected so solemn a swearing. The cost to his pride could not be small.

"Thy pledge honors me, *relagai*," I said, inclining my back in deference. "All the more for our disharmony."

At least my own part seemed uncomplicated—unlike the other oaths that bound me. I laid my palms over his, and the world—sunlight, colors, shapes, and outlines—dimmed and faded, as if reshaping themselves. Moments later, when he released my hands, the cast of the world returned to its normal state, as if I had but waked. He gestured toward the foaming sea. Time to wash.

I hesitated. It was not that I was shamed. Nakedness in the proper time and place was comfort and pleasure, not wicked. But somehow, when I glanced at Kol, I imagined myself as one of the transparent shrimp standing beside the scarlet sea star. And somewhere Saverian would be watching . . . ready, no doubt, to catalog my lacks.

My vayar raised his eyebrows and inclined his head toward the water. Waiting.

Reluctantly I shed my layers and tossed them onto the sand above the tide line. My bare feet had become something inured to the chilly sand, but the cold wind stung, my manhood retreated, and my first step into the water was a badger's bite. By the time I'd submerged to the knees, my teeth clattered like hailstones on a tin roof. If I were to be done with this before my blood congealed, I'd best move faster. I lunged a few steps farther into the oncoming waves and sat.

"G-g-great Iero's m-m-mercy!" Unfortunate if some ritual silence was required.

Once sure my heart had not stopped, I scooped sand from underneath me and hurriedly scrubbed at my flesh. The waves slammed into my back and lifted me from the sea bottom, threatening to tumble me over, but I splayed my legs and dug in my heels. For the most part I managed to stay upright and keep the salt water out of nose and mouth.

After the briefest service to every spot I could reach, I floundered and lurched toward the shore, only to discover what I should have expected. Emerging wet into the wind felt far, far colder than sitting in the water. "C-c-could we be quick about this?" I mumbled.

A scowling Kol moved to my side and cupped his hands about my right shoulder. Warmth flowed from his touch and again the world shifted. The sunlight dimmed, and the shore receded as if a great fog had settled over it. I no longer felt the buffeting wind or the gritty sand, but only Kol's warm hands and the sea that crashed and gurgled about my ankles, tugging at me . . . breaking the bounds of my skin . . . pouring into me . . . filling me. Drowning me . . .

Do not be afraid, Valen. Kol's sharp command interrupted my growing panic. *To make this passage, we must step outside the bounds of bodily form. This sea is myself and will not drown thee.*

I lost myself—limbs and torso, head and privy parts dissolved. His hands yet anchored me—one solid point of heat, a tether to the world, all that stood between me and blind terror. All else was embracing water, as if I were the immortal sea star tucked securely in the tide pool, knowing that any broken part of me would form another self, and that the tide would bring me all I needed to live. I trusted Kol, and so I drifted . . . tasting salt and fish and sand. I smelled green sea plants, felt the tickle of wind on the surface and the great heavy urging of the god of tides—everything a curiosity. I wondered at the endless play of daylight in the shallows and shied from the shadows of the boundless deeps. Fish in silver armor darted past me . . . through me . . .

For a nestling, such life as this is the greater part of what he knows— the safety and comfort of a parent's sianou, its myriad parts, its voice and texture, and the elements that make it live. Kol's voice existed everywhere around me and inside me, though I could not say I *heard* him. *The remasti of separation shifts a nestling from an existence sheltered and constrained by sire and dam into one shaped by his own body—a much greater change for most than for thee, one who has lived across a multitude of seasons constrained by flesh—however illfitting. Now, thou must choose to step beyond this place and allow thy true nature to reshape thy flesh. Let my hand guide thee.*

From the anchor point, warm strong fingers began to re-create my invisible arm, moving down its length as a sculptor's fingers might smooth his clay. Only *this* sculptor's fingers left traces of fire and blade in their wake. Cutting, burning, tearing . . .

Pain and panic bade me fight, but I could not locate the rest of my body. Nor could I find voice in the sea to scream or beg that he should stop before what flesh I yet owned was left in tatters.

Be easy, Valen, he said, as he released the fingers of one disembodied arm and shifted his touch to the place where another ought to be. *I but release what is bound in thee. It is so difficult, I believe, because thy true senses lie buried deeper than those of a nestling. Be easy and dream of the wide world. I shall not harm thee.*

Both arms now pulsed with agony. While the greater part of me yet floated insubstantial in the gray-blue water, I existed amid the frothing surf and freezing wind as well. Great gray masses of cloud boiled on the horizon, reaching for the sun.

Kol's hands left my fingers and began to sculpt a thigh. *Great gods among us . . .*

By the time his hands released my second foot, I existed wholly in the familiar world, sprawled on my face with my mouth full of sand. Though fire raged in my legs, my arms had fallen numb. I was afraid to move. I was afraid to look.

He relinquished my burning toes. "Stand now, Valen, that we may end this passage properly. Thou art free to wander Aeginea, and none may hold or hinder thee without our *argai*'s consent."

Entirely wrung out, I moved slowly to all fours. Every quat of my length felt something different from every other. Frozen or scorched or nothing. Worst . . . I could not feel my hands at all. "What's wrong with me?" I croaked.

He offered me his hand, but I was loath to touch him again. I stumbled to my feet and stared at my skin. My chest and abdomen and groin remained as they ever had been, cold pale flesh and dark hair caked with sand, but the now-hairless skin of fore and upper arms, of hands and fingers, of thigh and leg and foot, appeared an ugly mottled gray. Dead. No pattern was discernible, and certainly no beauty or power. And as the fire of Kol's touch died, every particle of that flesh lost all sensation. I shook my lumpish hands, kneaded them, slapped my arms and dying legs with no effect. "By Kemen Sky Lord, Dané, what have you done to me? I can't feel anything!"

Knitting his brow, he reached out to take my arm. I jerked away and stepped back, wincing from the fire in one foot, stumbling over the deadness in the other. "Stay back."

"Does not the world speak to thee?" he said, puzzled. "Thy gards will clear as thy senses waken, and take on their design as you walk the days. Touch the wind, *rejongai.*"

"I can't *feel* the wind, not with dead limbs! Is this your clever vengeance? What of Danae justice that punishes only the guilty?" I could not strangle his long straight neck, for my blighted arms could be used as naught but bludgeons.

"No, no. All was done as prescribed. Thou shouldst discern *more* than before. More intently. More delicately."

His conviction did naught but unravel me the more. My chest and stomach seemed stuffed with sodden wool that thickened and compacted with every breath. I dropped to my unfeeling knees and plowed my hands into the sand that might have been silken pillows or hot coals for all I could tell. Wrenching my focus tight, I sought magic, but no warmth flowed through my dead fingers. I sat back on my heels and roared in rage and frustration. "You've killed me, you cursed gatzé."

Kol crouched beside me, for once unwrit with scorn or anger. "This is not of my doing, *rejongai*. Why would I pledge thee care and teaching, and then set out to make my own words false? The remasti is a work of reverence for the vayar, a work that becomes a part of his kirani—the patterns he dances—as much as any jeque or eppire. No joy or use can be derived from such betrayal. It is why the long-lived fail in understanding of human ways."

"Then what's wrong?" I gasped, my chest laboring, my throat swelling shut as if a door had closed behind my words. I was suffocating.

He reached out again, and this time I had no strength to resist. I watched his fingers touch my arm and trace my sinews, but I could feel naught of it. "I experienced resistance as I released thy change," he said, puzzled, "but I assumed it to be thy years of restraint and thy intractable nature. It felt as if some other skin sheathed thee."

His surmise stung me as a slap on my cheek. "Get the woman," I whispered. "Hurry. Please."

The daylight blurred and wavered. I did not see Kol move, for I curled into a knot on the sand and concentrated all my strength on drawing air into my lungs.

"All right, all right, you can let go of me. Am I to be punished for watching?" Her dry voice rattled like a stick in a pail fifty quellae distant. "Egad, Magnus, you look even worse close by. Is this part—? Gracious Mother, what's happening to you?"

"Undo your spell," I croaked. "It's stopping the change. Can't breathe."

Praise be to all gods, she did not hesitate. She ripped the delicate chain from her leather pocket and pressed the gold medallion to my forehead. The maggots crept outward, only this time they left life, not deadness, in their wake.

With a great whoop, I inhaled half the sky, clearing throat and lungs and head. When she took the disk away, I stretched out on my back and flung my limbs wide, reveling in the delights of properly working heart and lungs. "Mother tend you in your need, good physician . . ."

No more had I begun to speak than the wind caressed my arms and legs. Of a sudden I drowned in sensation: the overwhelming scents of the salt and sea wrack, and the lingering aroma of our cook fire, last night's fish, and the morning's ill-favored eggs. I smelled a distant winter—rank furs and damp wool, the smokes of burning coal and pine logs, the damp earth and scat and piss of animal dens, the dust of empty grain barrels, the ripe sweat of lust beneath old blankets. And from other senses . . . Not only did I hear the crash of waves and the gurgle of the slops between the rocks, but I perceived the rustling of the red-leaved sea forest in the tide pools and the rippleless darting of the shannies. Not only did I feel the salt in the wind, but I knew that in its wanderings the air had once kissed a church, drawing away the scent of beeswax and marble dust, the sweet smokes of incense and oil of ephrain, the pungent perfume of ysomar, used to anoint the sick and dying . . . And still there was more.

"Holy Mother," I whispered, wrapping my arms about my head to prevent its bursting, "how can I ever sort it all out?"

"Are you well, Valen?" said Saverian, sitting on her heels at my side, the gold disk clutched in her hand. "What's happening to you? I can moderate the spell if need be and reimpose it."

Unlike the experiences I had named a disease, this barrage of scents and sounds neither seared my nostrils nor made my ears bleed. Nor did my eyes revolt at the daylight's complex textures of gray, blue, and silver or the impossible shapes of distant rocks that would have been a blur an hour before. I could make no sense of much that I perceived, but none of it drove me mad.

"For now, yes, I'm all right. Thank you. I think—" I swallowed hard, took a shaking breath, and stretched my arms skyward so I could see them. The gray mottling had brightened to the same pale silver as Kol's gards, though that could be but a trick of the shifting light. I could yet discern no pattern to the marks. My stomach hitched, and I folded my arms across it and stopped staring at myself. "There's just so much."

"So your disease is indeed of your own nature," said Saverian, kneeling in the sand, as matter-of-fact as if on every day she witnessed madmen transformed into Danae children. "As I predicted."

"Thy perception is quite limited as yet," said Kol, looking down at me. His handsome face expressed naught but tolerance—no more of concern or bewilderment. " 'Tis the task of wanderkins to learn the source and nature of what they perceive and to extend the boundaries of their skills. As they learn to walk in quiet, layers unexpected reveal themselves. Having lived in the world so long, thou shouldst have an easier task than most."

"You mean, there could be more?" How ever could a child manage all this?

"Always more. Subtleties. Grand things that might once have seemed whole display their sundry parts. The reach of thy experiencing shall widen from this small shore to distances and deeps. Wert thou a true wanderkin, destined to dance and live as one of us, such discrimination would be necessary to thy duties."

"And I'll perceive whatever exists in the human realm as well as Aeginea," I said, sitting up. Indeed, I was already experiencing many things far beyond this shore. No ale-sodden hunter lay snoring beneath fouled blankets anywhere near here, I'd guess. No wheezing practor in a freezing church anointed a woman dead in childbirth, unless . . . Perhaps those places existed as did Fortress Groult or the Sentinel Oak—visible in only one plane, though I could touch their very rooting place in the other.

His nostrils flared in distaste. "No. To experience the sensations of human works we must depart from the true lands and immerse ourselves entirely in the human world."

I glanced up sharply. "But I—" His certainty made me doubt. Perhaps my long-distorted senses were but remembering things I already knew. My finger crept up my ugly arms. The lack of hair was disconcerting, but I could not feel the marks themselves. I brushed at my skin, half expecting the pale mottling to fall away like dry flakes from a charred branch. Perhaps nothing at all had happened to me, save a blessed remission in my disease.

"A true wanderkin's primary tasks are exploration and the perfection of sensory knowledge." Kol took on his schoolmaster's aspect, as if I were indeed a new-changed Danae child. "I can teach thee closure . . . to silence one sense or the other . . . to quiet levels thou dost not wish to perceive. Control and discipline will ease thy confusion."

"Yes, I'd like that very much . . ."

Learning to manage this oversensitivity that had plagued me my whole life would be a grace indeed. But more awaited me. I was sure of it. My mother had believed that Kol could protect me from the Danae's crippling blows and instill in me what I needed to make sense of the world. If she knew Janus de Cartamandua at all, then she knew how unreliable his character. She would never have based her whole plan for me on his promises. I inhaled deeply, buried apprehension, and averted my eyes from my body.

". . . and then I'd like— How soon can we move on to the second remasti?"

"When we move on." Kol strolled away toward the water.

Saverian rolled her eyes as if I were a lunatic. The burgeoning clouds released their burden, binding sea and sky into a gray eternity of rain.

Chapter 14

Saverian pressed herself to the cliff to shelter from the rising storm. I grabbed my clothing from the sand and joined her. But the rain drove straight in from the sea, a cold sheeting deluge that soaked us to the skin—not all that far in my case—chilled us to the bone, and made it impossible to think too much about what I had just done. Certainly the ugly change to my arms and legs did naught to keep me warm or dry. Naught that I could see along the strand promised better cover, and a fire was out of the question. We could not stay here.

"We need shelter," I shouted at Kol over the hammering rain, the continuous rumble of thunder and surf, and the maelstrom of sounds and smells that filled my head with more images than I could possibly sort out. "Humans die of cold and wet."

I saw no benefit in pressing the point. The Dané would choose to help or not. I believed he would. He had squatted ankle deep in the surf and spread his fingers in the incoming wavelets, as if ensuring that their texture met his expectations. Rain sheened his long back like a cloak of transparent silk.

"Thou shouldst not have brought the woman," he called back without looking up. "I could have taken *thee* into the sea again."

"Did he do that?" I asked Saverian as we waited and shivered. "Take me under water? I mean, I experienced *something*. Naught I'd want to do again." My antipathy for water was too deep-rooted. The gray waves churned and frothed in nauseating rhythm. "I felt as if I were dreaming of the sea . . . of drowning . . . of his voice. I didn't think it was real."

"Nor did I. When you came out from your w-washing, he grabbed your shoulder and led you right back into the water." The shivering physician grimaced and wiped water from her eyes. "The waves boiled bright b-blue around you. You both vanished. I've seen nothing like it . . . nothing ever. How did you b-breathe, Valen? It was hours before he led you out again. Why aren't you d-dead?"

"Hours? That's not possible."

"I'm a good judge of time. I was beginning to think I would need to find m-my own way home."

I jabbed my fingers into my ribs. It hurt. "Well, I'm not dead. But I'm not going to try diving in on my own."

A reluctant smile teased at her mouth. "I'd planned to examine your new skin to see if you had scales or gills. But I've no paper or pens to record my findings. A poor practitioner to get caught without."

I could not but return her smile, grateful for her astringent practicality. Had she screamed or shrunk from me in disgust, the anxious knot lodged in my own breast might have unraveled into panicked frenzy.

Kol unfolded his limbs and struck out northward along the shore. His hand twitched in a gesture I interpreted as an invitation to follow. Saverian must have gotten the same notion. She sped after him like a constable after a thief. The physician might miss her bed or her books, but I couldn't imagine she would regret the absence of any *person*.

I used the moment's privacy to relieve myself and wrestle my ugly arms into my soaked wool shirt, hoping it might cut the wind and soften the impact of the driving rain. Then I set out after the others.

Saverian's time estimates could not be accurate. I could feel the sun hiding behind the storm. I could almost see it, in the way you see the rider in an approaching cloud of dust or envision a Syran woman's body within her cloud of drifting veils. And it had scarce moved from the cliff top since Kol's dance of greeting. As I marveled at this certainty, all out of nothing, a moment's flush left me warm and cold together. I tried to hold on to the sensation, but sounds and scents and images piled one up on the other like unruly children demanding my attention, and soon I was naught but cold and wet again. Strange.

Kol moved swiftly. Just past the slumped cliff where we'd found fresh water, the shoreline curved and took the two of them out of sight. I trotted a little faster and caught up with them just as the Dané started up a steep bank scored with rivulets of mud. The footing was tricky, and I was just as happy to be bootless, able to feel where rocks and rooted shrubs gave surer purchase.

Saverian climbed like a goat, but with far less grace. She was confident and fast, but grabbed on to every protruding rock and twig, and her boots slipped every other step. Her black braid had escaped its bonds and water cascaded from her straggling hair down her neck and the back of her cloak. When I came up behind her—by sheer virtue of my longer legs—she was mumbling through chattering teeth. "Wretched royal b-bastard. 'Leave your b-books and ride out with me,' you said. 'I need you.' Yes . . . to be trapped in a city full of torch-wielding madmen, chased by Harrowers, saddled with a d-doulon-raving lunatic, frostbit, saddle-sore, bashed in the head, d-drowned, and now abandoned in a monsoon in company with said madman and a cold-blooded dancing g-gatzé. Never again, Riel. Enough is enough." She stomped through the mud as if it might be Osriel's face.

I scrabbled upward, wondering if she'd find it amusing if I accused *her* of whining. Likely not. "You've not traveled with the prince all that much, then? On his visits to Gillarine? Or to . . . battlefields?"

Locked in her grumbling misery, she perhaps forgot what she considered my business and what not. "Stearc keeps him to his regimen when traveling. I give the thane spells and medicines enough to get Osriel home if he gets very bad. Of course, now Stearc's commanded to stay at the abbey, it's left to the dead man to see to Riel. The god-cursed fool oughtn't travel at all . . ."

The *dead man* . . . Voushanti? An extra chill raised my neck hairs. Her commentary flowed like the mud around our feet, and I didn't want to interrupt it, but someday I'd get her to explain.

". . . and certainly not in winter. The cold torments his joints, and swells his lungs and air passages. One day he'll fall off his horse and die, and *then* what of his grand plans? What of his father's wishes? What of his warriors and his subjects and his— The rest of them? Blasted, mite-brained, cold-blooded, soul-blind idiot."

The rest of *whom*, physician? Another question to save for a better time. "He told me that life is pain and only movement makes it bearable."

"Pssh." Saverian dispensed disdain as innkeepers dispense gossip. "His father spewed that drivel when Osriel was a boy and he was trying to coax the child out of bed on a day when every move Riel made was agony. He'd put Osriel on a horse or force him to run races with him. It wasn't fair. The child would do anything to please his father, though it caused his saccheria to flare and he suffered for days after, and King Eodward knew it. The king called this torment *love*."

"But Osriel got out of bed."

"He did. He does it every day. Honestly, I've no idea how. His father's *love* left his joints like broken glass and his soul a grinding stone." Saverian slipped again and only her grip on a pine sapling saved her from falling facedown in the mud. "The Mother spare me any such love."

I didn't think she had to worry. Loving the physician would be as rewarding as romancing the dunes we'd just left behind.

Mud squished between my toes as I climbed. I could well imagine robust, ruddy Eodward prodding his sickly child to be strong enough to survive in a brutal world. Yet I had received a privileged glimpse of the king's nature once when I was a young soldier under his command, and I surmised that the pain Osriel experienced on those hard days did not outstrip that his father felt at forcing him to it. Eodward had been rewarded by seeing his sickly child grow to manhood, an uncommon fate for a victim of saccheria. Saverian was right, too, though. Pain could change a man. Make him hard.

"Did you love the prince . . . when you were children?"

"No. We were friends. Playmates. My mother was his physician." As if she realized, of a sudden, the personal turn the conversation had taken, Saverian tightened her jaw and hauled herself upward even more forcefully. "Where *is* this creature taking us?"

That, too, was a most interesting question, for a glance back over my shoulder showed naught but rain and a valley of trees. No sea, no shore. Even more unsettling . . . the sun, yet buried deeply in the clouds, now lay behind us, what my instincts deemed west, though our path had not turned and scarce an hour had passed from my recovery. What daylight the storm had left us was rapidly failing.

I pressed my hand to Saverian's back, hoping to speed her steps. The Dané would likely welcome an excuse to abandon us. When we crested the steep slope, Kol's sapphire gards were just visible through a scattering of saplings that bordered a darkening wood.

"Come on." I took Saverian's hand, and we pelted after him through the trees. The gloom of the deeper woodland enveloped us.

Saverian slowed. "Valen, look."

"Best keep up. He's using no track I can travel on my own." I tightened my grip on her wrist. What with the rain, tired legs, a head packed with fears and nonsense, and Kol's disconcerting route finding, the shifting of north and south, of before and after and here and there, was twisting my instincts underside up and forepart behind. Our every step moved across time and distance in ways not even a Cartamandua could fathom.

But the willful physician snatched her hand away. "Stop! Look at yourself, Valen."

"We daren't lose—" *Iero's grace!* I stopped. Threads of pale lapis-hued light snaked about my fingers and bare legs. I shoved one sodden sleeve higher. The light—some threads fine, some thick—shifted and blurred beneath the raindrops. The knot in my breast burst. A cold shaft of terror pierced me head to feet. I had become . . . other.

"What's happening? Is it uncomfortable? Pleasurable?" She made her odd little open-palm gesture asking permission, but touched my arm before I could refuse it. The traces sparked silver and blue under her fingertips.

"I'm— No. It just itches. Stings." As if a swarm of ants had taken up residence on . . . or inside . . . my flesh and took it in mind to bite me every once in a while.

"Do you feel it atop the skin or deeper? Perhaps it's like a lizard's coloring that changes with its surroundings." She bent my arm at wrist and elbow, which caused the marks to squirm and blur. "Look at that! If I just had my lenses . . . better light . . ."

Queasy and embarrassed, I jerked my arm away. The shifting marks seem to be connected straight to my gut. "We'd best go. He's waiting for us."

I stumbled forward, clutching my bundle of clothes and boots, unable to keep my eyes from the unstable patterns on my bare legs and feet. Saverian grabbed my sleeve and guided me around trees and stumps.

A flare of white welcomed us into a rain-swept circle of trampled grass amid the trees. A starlike cluster of twigs, the source of the pale, magical light, dangled from an overhanging branch, unaffected by the rain. The light revealed several ramshackle sheds and lean-tos nestled beside a thatch-roofed hut. Kol stood at the open doorway of the hut, engaged in conversation with a man in a dirty white gown and a brown— I wiped the rain from my eyes. Not a brown cloak, but a *cowl,* and a well-delineated tonsure that bared half his scalp. I was speechless.

". . . Well, of course, I've been gi'en to welcome the stranger, and to hear a voice of home would put me out of mind in heavenly thanks, though I've renounced all such. But a woman born . . . Brave Kol, could ye not ask me please to slash my throat or draw down the poison of the hemlock, but ye must put me in the way of my sin? Half a century's turn must I have fasted and prayed by now—not to say, great God of all, that I've complaints or believe by any chance that I've full expiated my guilt, for certain not"—he raised a bony hand to address this side comment to the heavens—"but to come to this moment to find myself in the full occasion of repeating my defilement—more likely, e'en, being half mad as I am—'tis a sore deterrent to hospitality!"

The white light bathed his face as he stuck his head around Kol's rangy form and squinted into the rainy night. "Did ye not say ye'd brought two *human* folk? Or is it—?" As his examination took in my odd and soggy self, half dressed, legs flaring blue like miniature lightning, his own ruddy complexion lost all color, and he circled his breast with Iero's seal, completing the gesture by clutching his chest as if his heart might fly out of it. "Mighty saints protect me, Brother Kol, ye've brought me a halfbreed."

Assuredly his claim of fasting was no lie; the monk had scarce a citré's weight of spare flesh on him. But he had once been a robust man, perhaps a half head less than Kol or I, and his meatless bones were broad and thick. Gray-stubbled chin and tonsure appeared as ragged as his garb, and assuredly no cleaner. But despite his self-deprecation, his voice boomed clear and the pale eyes gleamed as sharp as a well-honed dagger.

"Is the woman also mixed blood?"

"Only the male," said Kol. "He is newly a wanderkin and cannot warm himself as yet. His companion has fallen afoul of Tuari, and the wanderkin would not leave her to the archon's retribution. She needs shelter."

"Ye've saved him from the breaking, have ye not, Kol? Put yourself in the way of burying, and if this girl aided ye in such an enterprise, then right and mercy it be to protect her. But how came ye to involve yourself with any human offspring, who've sworn never—?" The wide-eyed monk inhaled sharply. He stepped around Kol, and unheeding of the rain soaking his cowl and gown, grasped my arm and dragged me underneath the twiggy lamp. His fingers a manacle about my wrist, he swept my face as he might study his holy writs. "Merciful Iero, Liege of Heaven!"

"He is born of my sister," said Kol.

"The cartographer relinquished him at last?" The monk's fingers pinched my chin with the bite of a hungry dog on bloody meat and twisted my head side to side. "All count of human years has escaped me, but this one cannot have much time left before his maturing. Ne'er did I imagine your cruel penalty would budge the Cartamandua mule."

Kol stiffened. "Humans are not fit to judge cruelty."

"Strip off yer righteous skin, Brother Kol, and we'll argue it again," said the monk cheerfully, spinning about to face the Dané so quickly that his garb snapped my bare legs, causing a shower of blue and silver sparks. He tapped his own broad chest. "Would ye wrestle me to answer which of us has the One God's ear? I'm not what I was, but if blessed Iero doth keep this heart thuttering, a human sinner will yet crack your long-lived spine. Fasting and hard labor strengthens—"

"Janus did not send me," I interrupted, too curious to endure their jousting. "What, in Iero's glory, brings a Karish monk to Aeginea? You're not from Gillarine." The threadbare brown cowl and white gown were not the black garb of Saint Ophir's brotherhood. A century's turn, he'd said. Names and faces, plots and schemes flew through my overcrowded head—the abbey, the lighthouse, the succession, Luviar, Osriel, Janus, Kol, Eodward . . . "By heaven, are you Picus?"

Then I, too, drew Iero's sunburst upon my breast, for to see a man two centuries old and not dead drew truths of dread mystery and mortality all too near. Caedmon had sent a monk to the Danae with his infant son, a man charged to educate young Eodward as befit a human prince. But the fellow had vanished mysteriously some few years after Eodward's return to Navronne, and only rumors had ever said where he'd gone.

"Picus?" Saverian tilted her head to one side, looking him over. "Osriel has a set of journals written by a man of that name. He was King Eodward's— Mother save us!" Even the cool physician could not contain her astonishment.

The monk's pinched face blossomed into such a joyful alignment as coaxed my own spirit to a smile. "I'm not forgot, then?" He quickly raised his hands as if to stay a legion. "Nay, nay, don't tell me. Be it honorable memory or ill repute, I must not care. Penance is a narrow road. But here we bide in the deluge, and this lady's lips blue as a wanderkin herself! And the lad doth appear as he were a goat who's been witched into fasting. Prithee, come inside my cell and take what meager comforts I've to offer. Yes, the both of you. Should my weak character keep a drenched and freezing woman in the rain, 'twould be another sin to my account." Picus pulled back the hide curtain that served him as a door and waved us in.

"My gratitude, Brother," said Saverian as she hurried inside.

When I moved to follow the monk, Kol stayed me with a gesture. "Warm thyself, Cartamandua-son. I'll await thee, that we might advance thy teaching as the night settles in. If I can convince my sire of the need, I can gift thee the walking gard at next dawning, and so shall we be quit of each other the sooner."

"Tonight? Certainly . . . but . . ." I hadn't expected to go out again.

Yet it was really just morning down by the sea. The rain pounded Picus's thatched roof, the tumbledown sheds to either side of it, and the thick mat of leaves beneath the bedraggled maples and copper beeches. "Won't you come indoors with us, vayar? I've so many questions. We could talk where it's dry."

Kol reached for a sturdy branch above his head, and in one smooth motion lifted his shoulders above the branch until he supported his whole weight on his stretched arms and hands. A graceful swing of his legs, a twisting motion, and he sat on the branch, knees drawn up in his encircling arms, perched as easily as a cat. "Thou'lt not be long inside."

Whether this was a statement or a command, I wasn't sure. Kol's manner was a bit wearing. If my mother was beloved of all, then surely her brother must have something to recommend him. I just hadn't seen it . . . save, of course, the grace to protect my physical well-being against Danae spite. From the sheltering doorway I watched him turn his face up, allowing the cold rain to bathe his face and stream his long red hair down his back.

"He is beautiful, is he not?" Picus stood at my shoulder, the ripe aroma of unwashed flesh and a diet heavy with wild onions souring the autumn pungency of old leaves and wet pine bark. "No Ardran rose was ever so lovely, no Morian stag ever so regal, no Evanori boar ever so stubborn as Kol Stian-son. Had he a soul, the Creator would not know whether to name him Archangel or condemn him to eternal fire for daring rival Him."

"Kol is certainly hard, but even I would not call him soulless." Not one who danced as he did, who grieved as he did.

Picus held open the flap of leather behind me. "Nay, nay. It is not a matter of naming. Have you ne'er been taught the holy writs, lad? The Creator gave the spark of life only to human creatures. Danae have souls no more than red deer or ash trees or the wind."

"Then what of those like me? Am I half souled, part tree, part man, destined for half heaven or half hell?" I tossed this out in jest, thinking he but carried on his sparring with Kol. But his prattle stilled long enough to disturb me. I turned and found his pale eyes picking at my face as if to search the darkest nooks and crannies behind my heart and ribs.

"I know not," he said softly. "There was a time when I believed the One God could not be so cruel as to beget a soulless creature upon a human parent. But then I saw evidence . . ." He switched his gaze back to the Dané in the tree. "Perhaps it is one by one He chooses."

I swallowed hard and hid my mottled hands in my soggy bundle of clothes. No soul . . . that was not possible. I shifted my shoulders as if to prove I had will and sense of my own, and I remembered Gillarine Abbey church and how I had felt uplifted there, and reverent—surely the sign of gods speaking to a *person*, one capable of repentance and service, one possessing life beyond the body's limits. But then, I had also felt uplifted when I saw Kol dance, when I had looked on Elene silhouetted in sunlight, and when I'd sat in Gillarine's refectory eating stewed parsnips. How would one ever know if one lacked a soul? Even Danae had thoughts and will, emotions and, at least in Kol's case, some sense of honor—not the marks of soulless beasts.

"Was Kol so fierce before his sister—my mother—was imprisoned?" Cowardly, I asked no more of souls.

"Kol hath ever a sober cast of mind," said the monk, palpably relieved at my shift of subject. "More than most Danae, and of a certain, more than Clyste—not that she lacked intelligence to accompany her cheery nature. He ever seeks perfection in his being—a hard road for any of God's creatures. But Clyste made him laugh and softened his eye, and my dear lad challenged him to find delight in brotherly friendship as well as duty. Twixt them both, held so dear by their love, Kol reflected Iero's light upon us all. But I fear his joy has died with them."

My dear lad . . . It took me a moment to realize the monk spoke of Eodward.

"Come inside, lad, and relieve thy chill." The monk's hand gripped my shoulder kindly, even if his offer was wholly nonsensical. Naught could relieve the chill he had just laid on me. For a being without a soul, death became the end of all.

Moist heat slapped my face as I ducked and stepped into Picus's round hut—scarce eight paces across. Saverian knelt by a small fire pit in the center of the dark room, stretching her cloak to help the thick layers to dry. I needed no polite encouragement to sit on the hard-packed dirt beside her. Not only could I not stand upright without cracking my head on the low slanting ribs of the roof or poking my eye on wayward thatch, but I could scarce see or breathe at that height. If the monk had a hole in the roof to draw out his smoke, it was wholly inadequate to the task.

Picus let the door flap fall behind us. Quicker than blinking he had coaxed his fire brighter, set a clay pot of water over it, and snapped sprigs from a dry bundle dangling from his roof alongside a skinned rabbit, several woven nets bulging with pale, dusty vegetables, a variety of tools with leather-wrapped handles, and a pair of snowshoes. He settled cross-legged across the fire from me and Saverian and crushed the leaves into a clay mug and bowl. "We'll have a bracing tea anon. 'Tis such pleasure to have company, I scarce know up from down—not seen a human person in much longer than you'd want to account. I'm flummoxed that I can recall how to speak, so you must command me stopper my mouth when thy ears protest. Kol comes to check on me now and again. Tends my garden or brings me a fish or a bag of apples, and in return I deluge him with human words, poor fellow, the last thing he cares to hear. Which recalls . . ."

He sprang to his feet and poked his head through the door flap. "Kol, as thou'rt waiting . . . my turnips suffer black mold, and the onions pull up soft and slimed, scarce a layer fit to eat. I fret this rain will finish them. The spelt in the far mead has no ripe heads, and frost nips the dawn. I know it's been scarce a month since you've tended it, but if thou wouldst have mercy upon my poor plot, I'd be most grateful."

I tried to hear Kol's response, but I could not distinguish it from the sounds of snapping fire and rain rustling on the thatch, and the thousand other noises of storm-racked forest and distant sea vying for attention in my head. Overwhelmed with mystery, I could not even imagine what Picus required. I doubted Kol would set to work with rake and hoe. Another question to add to my growing tally.

I held my hands near the fire, but instantly withdrew them before my skin blackened like scorched paper. The shifting blue marks had faded to silver. I wrapped my arms around my unsettled middle and hoped the steam rising from my sodden shirt would suffice to calm my shivering.

Picus closed the flap again and lowered himself to the dirt floor, scratching his grizzled chin. " 'Tis a wonder Kol comes here. The land grows ill. Will not stay healthy no matter that he puts it right. And my company is no pleasure to him. Though, indeed, he's exiled himself from *their* company, save when he is summoned to the dance. Even his sire is near a stranger to him since Clyste's fall."

I believed I knew why. "None but you and he know that Janus fathered Clyste's child."

Picus nodded. "After Clyste's prisoning, I saw that Kol bore some weighty burden and seemed like to shatter with it. So I baited him into a fight—not so difficult to do, as you see—and goaded forth his secret. Took me a good trimonth to walk without those bruises squalling, and I've ne'er regrown the teeth."

He kneaded his unshaven left jaw for a moment, his attention suddenly far away. But then he scooted around and rummaged in the dark behind him, pulling out two irregularly woven blankets that might once have had some color. He gave one to each of us. "Come, thou'rt a soggy pair. Bundle up and get warm, mistress. I'll leave thee lone here in the house and take me to the shed when sleep time comes so ye can do what women must. And I'll not even think on it, I promise, or if I do, I'll perform my most rigorous spiritual exercises or even hike me down to the sea and douse my head, though I could wish for better weather or at the least Kol to take me down a shorter path. The determination to penance can take a man only so far until it falls into the sin called 'pride of mortification,' if thou'rt familiar with Karish vice and virtue."

"Good monk, you've no need to give up your bed," said Saverian. "I'm a daughter of Evanore and our customs see no wrong in stalwart women sheltering with honorable men." She was being exceptionally polite. She didn't correct his use of *mistress*.

Shaking his head sadly, Picus poured the simmering water over his herbs and handed the mug to Saverian and the bowl to me. "Ah, mistress, hope of heaven and true repentance bids me warn ye that I am no honorable man, but abjectly fallen. Though vowed chaste at fifteen, and gi'en naught to suffer in this life but a surfeit of adventure and the joy to serve the fairest prince the One God ever sent to humankind, I succumbed to the Adversary's assault and broke my vows and the most solemn responsibilities of a teacher to lie with a woman. None should trust me."

A long pull on the steaming tea seemed to restore the physician's ironical humor. She tilted her head and examined the monk, as he opened a flat wood chest he'd dragged from the same dark corner where he'd found the blanket. "So you what . . . consummated an attraction . . . kept a female companion . . . in two-hundred-some years . . . a healthy man who lives among beings who go about unclothed? I've little understanding of Karish ways, despite my association with Brother Valen here, but I hardly see the difficulty. If you are indeed this Picus . . . a man of such advanced years . . . I would think the continuation of a young man's animal urgencies would be more reassuring than problematical—mayhap a sign of your god's favor." She sounded little short of laughter, which I feared must surely wound a monk so determined to penance, no matter how foolish we judged his rigor.

"The structure of virtue was the last lesson of my novitiate, Saverian," I said, "though I scarce got beyond naming the seven great virtues and the twelve great vices. But pride of mortification made sense to me—the vice of those who aggrandize themselves by the extremity of their penance rites or humility. Clearly Brother Picus heeds the first duty of the sinner—to sincerely balance his reparations with his clearest assessment of the severity of his sin. We must honor his judgment, while welcoming his willingness to allow us to intrude upon his solitude."

Picus looked as though the portal to heaven had opened in front of him. His rounded mouth opened and closed like that of a fish. His hands, one holding a rank-smelling onion and the alter holding a leaf-wrapped bundle that smelled fishy, dropped into his lap. "Novitiate?" he stammered. "Thou art Karish, then, a monk vowed, as well as the Cartamandua's halfbreed son who has begun to take the Danae passages. How comes that—?" Pain etched his fleshless face. "Ah, great Iero's heart, I must not even ask. I have *renounced* the world."

"I did take novice vows, but my abbot sent me back into the world. The story is very long, Brother Picus, and not half so interesting as your own, which we would relish hearing."

This man had known King Eodward . . . and Caedmon himself. He could tell us of the Danae . . . of Kol and his disaffection from his own kind . . . of my mother and her plan . . . perhaps even something of the world's grief. A guilty fear gnawed at me that the archon would be so angered by my escape, he would refuse to tell Osriel what they knew of the failing world. If I could learn from Picus, perhaps I could make up for it. Once Kol set me free to go back to the human world in safety, I could send what I'd learned to the cabal, thus keeping my vow to Luviar. As for Osriel himself, I felt no pity. Likely they would not cripple him for their own failure to hold on to me.

"Thou must tell me thy names, at the least," said Picus, as he busied himself with his pot and his bundles, "and some small summary of thy purpose in Aeginea, lest I go mad and forget even my devotions. If the Cartamandua did not send thee to Kol, then how come ye here? Kol's pride would never allow him to fetch thee. Didst thou not know what breaking awaited a halfbreed, boy? I fought to convert the long-lived from all their heathenish ways, especially from such cruel abuse of their own children"—he clutched his hands to his chest for a moment, closing his eyes and looking as if he might choke—"but their terror of Llio's curse ever drives them. And you, lady, so wise and gentlewomanly . . . an Evanori warrior? Stalwart, I'll vow, but not half so ferocious as the warlords I remember, who painted their faces with blood and brought Hansker scalps to lay before King Caedmon. How come ye here with Janus's son?"

As his stream of words bounded and flowed like an exuberant watercourse, the monk dropped the leaf-wrapped bundle into the blackened clay pot and whipped a knife from the folds of his robe. Though the blade was worn near the slimness of a stiletto, he proceeded to slice the onion into the pot, as well, tossing the moldy outer skin out through the dripping door flap.

"My name is Valen," I said. "I've come here to learn of the world. Tell me, what is this Llio's cu—?"

Of a sudden, I was not sure I could sit still to hear the secrets of heaven, much less whatever tidbits the monk could reveal. Picus's pot belched steam, smelling strongly of fish and onion. The smoke filled my lungs, and the rank smell curdled my belly. My skin itched. My foot tapped the dirt floor uncontrollably. So little air.

I waved at the physician to take up the conversation, while I downed the lukewarm tea—mint and elderberry—and appreciated its spreading comfort. An unlikely sweat broke out beneath my wet, scratchy shirt.

"I am Saverian, physician and student of natural philosophy, house mage to Osriel, Duc of Evanore, Prince of Navronne. A daughter of warriors, not one myself."

Picus's expression blossomed with wonder. "You serve my king's son? What a fine man he must be. I had warned Eodward that the One God disapproved using holy marriage for wartime alliance, but the Moriangi grav and his men knew of ships, and when we drove the Aurellians to the sea, 'twas the grav who crushed them. And the grav's daughter produced such a robust babe. I knew him only as a motherless boy, of course, rough mannered and interested in naught but fighting. I tutored him in combat as I had his father. I tried to introduce book studies as well, but the fighting was heavy in those days, and we were constantly on the move, so we'd no time for it."

Saverian nodded. "You speak of Bayard, the eldest of Eodward's three sons. When times were more settled, another son, Perryn, was born to Eodward's second wife, an Ardran ducessa. My master is the third and youngest, born to his pureblood mistress. You *do* know of Eodward's fate, Brother?"

"Do I know he is dead? Aye. Even I, whose eyes remain steadfastly human, saw the sun dim on that day. Kol came to break the news and invite me to share his kiran, but I could not, though I knew it would be such a glory as I had not seen since he danced for Clyste. I sent him away, that a heathen creature would not witness a monk's blaspheming, for I had always believed merciful Iero must surely bring my lad home before the end. Whate'er his sins, as any king must commit in carrying his office, they could not be so dread as to forbid him one last glimpse of the Canon after so long away. Once thou hast seen it . . ." The monk dashed a hairy knuckle at his eyes, as he stirred his pot with a wooden spoon. "Three sons left. A mercy in that at the least."

A mercy only if we did not tell him of the princes and their war. Though Picus's talk touched on old mysteries, like the Canon, and new ones like this *Llio's curse* that caused the Danae to cripple half-breeds, and *kirani* that seemed something more than mere dancing, it was an effort to concentrate on the conversation. I hunched deeper into myself, cold and hot together, ravenous, yet unsure if I could choke down this mess he stirred. Something was definitely wrong with me. When had I ever found aught I would not eat? The light had gone completely from my gards, leaving my skin purplish gray and leprous in appearance.

"Why did you abandon King Eodward, Brother?" said Saverian, a physician setting out to diagnose the world's ills. "You vanished without a word to the king or anyone else. You were seen leaving Palinur, but no evidence of mishap or treason was ever found. Even the journals you left behind told Eodward nothing of your fate. The prince says his father died yet grieving for your loss, chastising himself for some unknown failure that drove you away. Surely your god would agree that service to Navronne's king supersedes any personal penance, especially for minor transgressions of the flesh."

Picus squeezed his broad brow tight as if to force aside the sentiments that had bubbled so near his surface. "One night's fall from grace drove me from my lord's side. I had long renounced the woman and thought I'd made amends. But when I was confronted with the lasting evidence of my wickedness and shown how it contravened everything I loved, everything *he* loved, I knew no man had ever so abjectly failed his god or his lord. Ronila said that to cleanse my sin I must bleed, suffer, and die by my own hand or hers. But the One God forbids self-murder, and I would not add to my soul's debt by allowing her to take my blood on her own hand. So I swore to her on Iero's name that I would die to the world—leave my prince and all my friends and holy brothers without apology or explanation, and live henceforth in solitude, penury, and repentance for as long as the streams of time might carry me forward. She knew me and believed I would keep any pledge so sworn. And so I have, save for these few untimely lapses, when I am out of measure surprised."

"Ronila?" said Saverian. "The woman you lay with . . . who must have been a student, if you betrayed a teacher's trust. But I thought your only student was Eodward himself."

I glanced up from my knees where I had focused my eyes to get control of my stomach. The dim smoky room swirled unpleasantly. "You mentioned Ronila in your journal—a disaffected halfbreed girl who left Aeginea after making her third change."

Picus wagged his head. "We witnessed her knee-breaking, my prince and I. A golden child of an age ye would judge fourteen summers. 'Tis after the child passes the second remasti they do it. She screamed and begged us to save her from crippling, but we could not. My prince was naught but a tender seven-year-old, and I God-sworn to protect him above all things, which meant honoring Danae customs. So much pain . . . After, I thought to give her something back to redeem her suffering, something the others would not have and could never take from her. The long-lived claim to bear no grudge against a broken halfbreed, but of course they do. They seek perfection in their arts—which are firstly their bodies and their use of them—and thus treated her with cruel disdain. She was clever at numbers and had such a vivid imagining that she devoured all I could teach her of Navronne, of natural philosophy, of human history and warfare, of moral philosophy and the teachings of Karus. Every afternoon when she had completed her tasks of the day—making baskets or weaving spidersilk or gathering apples or mushrooms— she would hobble to my canopy for teaching . . . Ah, I babble on too long. I sinned. I renounced that sin. But I will pay the price of it until my bones are dust."

He tightened his mouth and would not speak more for a while. He broke pinches of herbs from his dangling bundles and threw them in his pot, each breaking an explosion of fragrance. The scent of dried mushrooms, damp earth, and moldering leaves left the memory of nivat on my tongue. Sweat dribbled down my sides. My left thigh muscle cramped, and an ember burned in my gut . . .

No! Nivat no longer had power over me. I forced my thoughts away from my body. So the celibate monk, exiled far from home and holy brotherhood, had seduced a half-Danae girl. Or had she, a lonely outcast, enamored of a kind, virile young man, used her Danae wiles to tempt him? Yet more troubled me than such common failings as lust and seduction. Something in the telling of his story . . . something in the words . . . had touched off a bone-deep revulsion, but I could not capture it. Wit seemed to have drained out of me, along with the myriad telltales of my senses that had been with me since the remasti. This windowless room. So small. So close.

"Here, give me thy cup, good Valen, and we'll see thy belly filled."

I looked up and Picus's grimed face leered huge and grotesque in the garish firelight. The encircling walls of his hut bulged inward, threatening to squeeze the breath out of me. Heat seared and scoured my limbs. Of a sudden I was back in my bedchamber in Palinur, my skin on fire from my father's leather strap, panicked, cursing, screaming, beating on the door barricaded with sorcery as the walls closed in. The firelight wavered . . . darkened.

"Excuse . . . must go." Gasping for air, I scrambled to my feet, knocking my forehead on the roof beams, and escaped into the night.

Saverian burst through the door flaps while my hands were yet propped on the outer wall of a lean-to filled with wood, and I was gulping great lungfuls of cold air. "Do you need the medallion, Valen?"

"Just air. So hot." I fumbled at the laces on the scratchy shirt and ripped it over my head, allowing the cold rain to hammer and scour and revive every part of my skin. My senses quickly regained some balance. "Sorry. Rude of me."

From her shelter in the hut's doorway, she held out her cupped hand, overflowing with tangled gold chain. "Perhaps you should wear this."

Shaking my head, fighting to shed the oppression of panic and suffocation, I turned around and leaned my back against the woodshed. The sodden shirt wadded in my hands preserved a bit of propriety. "I'll be all right. You may write this in your notes: Danae halfbreeds sicken within walls."

Kol had known what would happen. The Dané no longer sat in the tree, but music had joined the clamor in my head, and I glimpsed blue flashes among the trees. "It must be time for my lessons. You'd best stay here, unless . . ."

I beckoned Saverian urgently. Without hesitation, she darted across a muddy strip and sheltered under the lip of the shed.

My finger on her lips silenced her question, and I dropped my own voice to a whisper. ". . . Unless you're afraid of the monk."

She yanked my hand away and took on such a look of scorn as would chill a salamander. "Afraid of the chance to converse with a man two hundred years old? I'd barter my maidenhead for the chance, and here it is laid in my—" Of a sudden the fireglow of her damp cheeks outshone the white light from the twiggy lantern. "What are you smirking at? That I happen to find many amusements more enticing than rutting like an overheated dog? Study the human body and its lamentable urges, and you'll see it is an altogether ridiculous object."

"Bless me, gods, that I remain an unstudious man!" Not even her sour expression could restrain my laughter.

But now that the rain had reawakened the chaotic information of my senses, I could give thought to the serious matters that had gathered with the deepening night. So I stifled amusement and quieted my voice. Despite her peculiarities, Saverian was a woman of sense and intelligence. I could not stay here to learn what I needed, but perhaps she could.

"Saverian, if you would, I beg you discover what you can of this Llio's curse—this Danae fear of halfbreeds. My mother conceived a halfbreed apurpose, knowing what her people would do to me if I was caught. Why would she do that? Kol says that she believed I belonged in the Canon, which makes no sense at all. The mere consideration appalls and disgusts him, and I've no faith that I can budge him to tell me more. And there's something else . . . something in the monk's story . . . that sets off warning trumps in my head. Truly I'm half knob-swattled with this day and cannot capture it, yet every bone in my body screams that all this is connected: Eodward's history, Danae intransigence, my birth, the wretched weather, and the sickness of the world, the Harrowers and their poisoning of the Danae."

A thought darted past like a firefly, before being swallowed in an assault of scents reminiscent of a town marketplace: baking pies, roasting meat, leather goods and perfumes, herbs, vegetables, and scented oils, horse manure, pigs. I prayed that Kol could teach me what to do with all of it.

"Even if you care naught for Navronne, you're Osriel's friend and servant," I said. "What we learn here could be the keys to his future."

"Osriel betrayed you. Why would you care about his future?"

"You've witnessed the havoc the Harrowers wreak in Navronne. And I promise the damage is much deeper than that you saw. Surely you saw, too, the hope he brought them, almost without trying. People wiser than me have entrusted Navronne's salvation to Prince Osriel's hand—but I fear that trust has been misplaced unless we can find out the truth of all this before he takes a path of desperation. This thing you will not speak of. This thing he hopes to fuel with Danae magic. I have this notion I can help him, but only if I learn enough."

What wastrel fool had ever made so pompous a statement? But I *did* feel it, however foolish. If I could only see the way.

Saverian nodded slowly, her clear eyes as lustrous as jade in the white light. I had never noticed their color. "I'll learn what I can." Then she lowered her lids halfway and snatched the wadded shirt from my hand. "Meanwhile, I'll dry this out. I doubt you'll need it for a while."

I grinned as she threw it over her shoulder and ducked into Picus's hut. Then I set off into the trees to find Kol. Amid the cascading telltales of hunting foxes, nervous deer, and mice and moles that burrowed through leaves and earth, I heard Picus greet Saverian with concerned questioning. She reassured him as to my health. "Ah, for certain," he said. "I'd forgot how the walls torment the odd creatures . . ."

Creatures . . . beings that had no souls. My smile faded.

Chapter 15

Kol crouched impossibly high in the limbs of a leaf-bare ash that bordered a swath of open meadow. The wind rustled knee-high grass and faded leaves, and the rain outlined odd dark shapes, barriers of timber and tied brush set at angles across the meadow. I blinked, astonished that I could see so much as that on a starless, moonless night. The air smelled of must and soured grain, of soggy earth and the small stream that bisected the gentle slope, and of a thousand other scents that had naught to do with this meadow. A wolf's howl sent chilly fingers up my bare spine, hinting that even the magics of Aeginea could not hold back this foul winter. Naked in the night wood . . . I'd never felt such an idiot.

As I opened my mouth to call him, the Dané rose from his crouch and brushed bits of bark and leaf from his skin. Angling his feet, as if for proper balance on the branch, he stretched his arms skyward. His gards brightened to the cold blue of a mountain winter sky. Somewhere—in my head, in my heart, in my imagining?—music swelled. The sweet clarity of a rebec's bowed strings twined my over-crowded thoughts in a single long note that stretched my nerves taut . . . and then Kol launched himself from the top of the ash.

My heart near stopped until his feet touched solidly to the grass, and he began to whirl and spin and leap through the meadow, a glory of power and strength, raising one and then another thread of melody to join in a driving gigue. Danae danced to the land's music—or made it.

Determined to understand what he did, I pushed aside the wet leaves and pine needles at the edge of the wood, pressed my fingers into the mud, and released magic. As if lightning illuminated the symbols on a fiché, I glimpsed rowed turnips, carrots, and onions slimed and rotting underground, a plot of stunted wheat across the stream, and hungry moles panting as they excavated tunnels underneath it all, their fur patched with disease. My spirit choked at the suffocating sickness. Kol's exuberant feet scribed silvered traces across the unhealthy landscape, his every bend, dip, and spin bringing new complexity to his insistent melodies.

I could have watched him dance until the end of days. Every note perfect . . . every step exquisite . . . exhilarating. Even when I knelt up, allowing the rain to rinse the mud from my hands, the magic he raised in Picus's garden meadow enfolded me in such beauty as would draw a stone's tears.

The music reached its whirling climax, and Kol stretched legs and arms to leap in one great arc across the stream, streaks of blue trailing behind him as if his gards were threads of silk, whipped to frenzy by the wind of his passing. Above and below and around me an explosion of color washed the landscape like watered ink. The healthier humors of a nearby forest glade flooded the diseased plots. Owl and hawk rose up from the wood, dark shapes diving and soaring to purge the pests, while other creeping creatures deep buried in the soil, too tiny for a human eye to see, woke to cleanse and nourish roots and stems. The waterlogged soil released its burden, riddling the undersoil with new channels to the stream. When the spinning Dané took a knee, aligning his back and outstretched leg in the position I'd come to know as completion, it seemed as if the earth gave a great sigh of contentment, while I was left roused and aching with unspent desire.

Kol held his position for a long while, and when at last he stood, his posture bespoke a man completely drained. His head came up, expression vague and lost, his sculpted features sharpening only slowly when he caught sight of me. He heaved a sigh, kneaded his neck, and started up the gentle slope, following the path of the stream. A slight sweep of his right hand commanded me to follow.

I joined him, padding through wet grass while he strode on a game trail that bordered the stream. "How do you do it?" I said, when it became clear he had no plan to initiate conversation. "Draw the music from plants and beasts and dirt clods? Use your body . . . your movements . . . to join all the parts together? Is the Canon something like this?"

"I am not here to teach thee of the dance. I'll not speak of the Canon. Nor will I guide thee through the remasti of regeneration. No use in developing skills . . . and hungers . . . thou canst neither use nor satisfy." He swept his dripping hair back from his face, squeezed water from it, and tied it into a heavy knot at the back of his neck.

"Regeneration," I repeated. Osriel had said the third remasti was the passage of regeneration, when Danae first experienced the hungers of fleshly love . . . when they became both capable and desirous of mating. "*That's* what you did to this field. Your dance healed its sickness as a human physician heals a body, diagnosing its ills and applying the proper remedy. You called forth creatures to cleanse and nourish it, changed its makeup in subtle ways to leave it healthier. But the way you accomplished it was more like mating than healing. The dance this morning touched my spirit, but this . . . I was honored . . . humbled . . . to witness it, *relagai*."

Kol cast me a sidewise glance. Suspicious. "Thy gards tell thee these things?"

I looked down at my mottled arms and legs, so pale and ill-defined beside the brilliant clarity of his dragons, reeds, and heron. My marks no longer flashed or swirled. I doubted a human eye would even notice them were I ten paces distant. Yet though the wind had picked up, and I felt its bitter edge, the cold no longer penetrated beyond my skin.

"No. Not the gards . . ." I stumbled a bit, as the truth of my change settled even deeper in my gut. "I saw, or well . . . rather, it's something like seeing. When I touch the earth and use my magic . . . my Cartamandua bent . . . an image of the surrounding land forms in my mind, in my senses, so I see and hear and smell what's there or has been there in the past—plants, beasts, humans, the paths they've left. And I can explore the image—look deeper, learn how it fits together, as I did with the tide pool. It's difficult to describe."

"Thy *senses* comprehend the particular changes I brought to this land?" Surprise and skepticism boiled out of him like seepage from a wound. "Without study or examination or practice?"

"The changes—the hunting birds you called forth, the water channels, the rest—yes. The paths of your movements that link them all together appear to me as threads of silver across the landscape. I can see the threads even as you draw them, and those of other Danae from earlier times."

He halted in midstep and glared at me, his aspen-gold eyes like flame in the darkness. "Thou canst see the *paths* of the kiran—the patterns left behind from the dance?" His tone dared me to affirm it.

"I could walk them as you do this track under your feet."

He clamped his mouth shut and stomped faster up the path. When a dead limb blocked his way, likely fallen from Picus's fence making, he snatched it up and threw it farther than even my improved eye-sight could make out in the middle of the night. Had it struck a fortification, even at such a distance, I would wager on the stick to penetrate the stone, so vicious was its launch. I'd thought he would approve my increased understanding. Perhaps I had trespassed some protocol by observing Danae mysteries or speaking of them. I trailed along behind him, my bare feet tormented with sticks and rocks, nar-rowly avoiding wrenching my ankle in some burrower's entry hole, and near giving up on comprehending my uncle.

As the vale sloped upward, the land grew rockier, so my battered feet could attest. The path soon vanished, as did the stream, replaced, almost before I could imagine it, by rills and rivulets that trickled across the hillside from thick forest on either side of us. The soil be-neath my feet thinned. At least the rain had slackened, holding somewhere between a drizzle and a mist. Kol's gards flared brighter.

Of a sudden, I realized that we had traveled farther from Picus's meadow than our steps could justify. Alert now, I began to feel a shifting when Kol invoked his magic—when the path took a sudden turning or broke dramatically uphill. When the scent of pine and spruce entirely supplanted the scent of oak and ash and hawthorn in the space of twenty paces. When the air grew sharply colder and very dry.

"Your gards carry power that enables you to move from one place to another," I said, pushing my steps to keep up with the fast-moving Dané.

"Aye. After the second remasti, the stripling's growing familiarity with the world becomes a part of the walking gards and can be called on as desired." The brisk walk seemed to have restored his calm. "The particular slope of a grass-covered hillside recalls that of a mountain meadow. The sound of one stream echoes another that happens to feed a mighty river. Just here"—he pointed to a stand of evergreens—"the odd shape of that tallest tree's crown recalls to me the outline of another tree against a different sky, thus forms a path from this place to the next. I can walk there if I will. It is all a matter of similarity and recollection, for all places are bound one to the other in ways a human—most humans—cannot perceive."

"Sometimes we do," I said. "We come to a new place, yet feel as if we've been there before. Or we meet a stranger and feel as if we know her already."

"Perhaps." A grudging admission.

By the time I wrenched my eyes from the fork-tipped fir, disap-pointed it had not belched fire or displayed some other obvious magic, we walked a slightly steeper path amid widely scattered trees. My breathing labored. Around another corner and we were traversing the shoulder of a conical peak outlined against a star-filled sky. Mist floated like a gray sea below us.

A half hour's hard climb and we had left the last stunted trees behind. We came to a rocky prominence—a thick slab of pale stone, some twenty quercae in height, that poked up in gloomy isolation from the mountainside. Kol propped one foot on a broad flat shard, long split off from the standing rock and toppled to the grass.

"We begin thy teaching here," he said. "Thy gards draw in the sights and sounds, tastes and smells from forest, vale, and shore, as well as the dust of Picus's foolish babbling and the stink of his dwelling place. No doubt rememberings of thy usual days intrude upon thy perceptions, as well. Likely it is some confusion of these impressions with the observation of my kiran that caused this *seeing* thou hast reported."

So he had not entirely dismissed his disturbance at my claim. "Yes, my eyes, nose, and ears are overwhelmed, but what I saw back there, the silver traces—"

"Thy task is not to think or speak," he snapped. "I'll give thee ample opportunity to question. 'Tis the deeps of the night here on Aesol Mount, the time when the world is quietest. Best for listening to voices that cannot be heard in the day. Best for learning control."

I shut my mouth, suppressed my resentful urge to kick him, and bowed. I needed to learn.

As before, the politeness seemed to take him a bit off guard. "I should not have taken the time to shape a kiran for Picus's plantings. Thou didst not linger within his walls as long as I thought a halfbreed might, thus my hurry opened the way for this misunderstanding. So, no matter." He waved as if his willing could dismiss my beliefs. "A wanderkin's task is learning of the world, thus the separation gards are the most sensitive and most subject to confusion. Thou must seek perfection in their use, as in all things. For now, I promised to teach thee closure and control. Sit before the rock"—he pointed to the featureless slab—"and listen. Stone speaks softly but with utmost authority. Seek its voice. Listen for it alone, and it will root thee firmly. Once thou canst hear the speech of stones, thou shalt begin to understand closure."

Were he anyone else, I might discount such instruction as lunacy. But the man who had made love to Picus's garden, tending it, infusing it with life, must be granted trust despite our other disagreements. The effects of his work yet fired my blood. Feeling exceedingly awkward, I sat cross-legged on the damp ground facing the rock and reached out.

"Do not touch the rock!"

I snatched my hand away.

"Our purpose is to develop and exercise thy control of the gards. Human tricks have no place here. Heed the stone. Work at it."

Balls of Karus, the man is difficult! The task seemed impossible with him standing not two paces behind me, with the riot of smells, sounds, and tastes from my senses swelling my skull to bursting. The traveling had, at least, reduced the uncomfortable involvement of my privy parts, but had presented its own myriad questions. And somehow in this clean and pungent air, my charge to Saverian kept repeating itself in my mind . . .

I needed to understand Llio's curse, which condemned halfbreeds to crippling. My sudden conviction that my own existence was intimately entwined with the fate of Navronne had surprised even myself. But surely my life had taken no random course—not from the day I was conceived, not from the day I happened upon the book of maps, not from the day three months past when I lay bleeding in a ditch, only to stagger, blind and ignorant, straight to my mother's sianou, where a Karish abbot had built his lighthouse. Clyste, a dancer so powerful that the earth itself had chosen her for a guardian, had laid the preservation of the lighthouse . . . of Navronne . . . at her son's feet. My feet. Of a sudden that seemed so obvious. And terrifying.

Listen for the stone. A hand clamped my bare shoulder as a dog's jaws grip a bone, infusing my body with my vayar's will. I had to learn before I could act. And so I shoved aside fear and looming destiny for the moment and set to work.

How would one recognize the voice of stone? First concentrate on hearing in preference to the other senses. Dismiss colors, images, tastes, and tactile sensations. *Soft*, Kol had described it, and so I dismissed the noisy, loud, and brightest sounds, the florid trumps and horns, the bawling of donkeys, the screams of prisoners, and cackles of madmen. *With utmost authority*, he'd said, and so I dismissed the quiet nattering of birds and insects, the trivial speech of gossips, and the soft mouthings of lovers, the pale colorings of everyday living. As if the entirety of my perceptions were bedcoverings, I peeled away layers, hunting a voice of solidity, of weight, of dense, slow changes . . .

Saints and angels, this is impossible! As if slogging through desert dunes hunting for one particular grain of sand, I would push one thought aside only to feel five thousand more cascade into its place. But in the end, when all else was stripped away, a soft word rumbled through my spirit like distant thunder, like the shudder of an avalanche halfway across the world. A burden settled on my shoulders . . . ponderous . . . immense. *Hold.* And some interminable time later came another. *Forever.*

This was no dialect a mouth could imitate. Truly I *heard* no speech at all—no sentient mind produced such words. Rather I experienced an expression of unyielding heaviness and stalwart density, stiffening my back and chest, forcing thigh and shoulder taut. Unmoving. Unshakable. Just as I was about to release my concentration and declare victory, for of a certain no entity but a mountain itself could speak with such weight, another word boomed from a wholly different direction. *Crush.* I held breathless, as if the massive boulder and its fellows were grinding *me* to powder. *Pound. Squeeze.* This voice drummed cold and harsh. Then came another voice—smaller, lost. *Deep. Tumbling. Diminished.* Dizzy, I imagined smooth rounded stones washed endlessly in a mountain river, their substance ground inevitably away.

Fascinated, I sorted through the slow-moving litany, seeking the voice of the particular rock before me, for the words came one and then the other with great gaps in between. Was this a conversation? I decided not. A foolish notion, and yet what would I have said a few days previous to anyone who told me I would hear words in the voices of stone?

Shattered. Waves of blazing heat rolled over me, and more of wet and brittle cold, an uneasy pressure culminating in explosive power and breaking—*this* rock, whose fractured shoulder lay prostrate beside it, whose enduring memory spoke destruction and ending.

I'm sorry, I answered. Not that I believed the slab could think or understand, only that its overwhelming desolation required some response.

Satisfied and weary, I released the sensory textures of the world to intrude once again. How small and weak they seemed. Not trivial. Not unimportant. But eminently controllable. This must be what Kol wished me to understand. Closure.

Excited, I nudged and poked at the clutter, recalling the depths to which I'd gone to hear the stone. The act cleared a small space where I could have a thought without intrusive clamor. Of course, my newfound order quickly collapsed into confusion again. This would take practice. I gave up and opened my eyes.

Mist had crept up the mountain and enfolded me, soft and damp.

The bulging moon hung in the sky, thinly veiled like a pureblood bride. A rush of air overhead marked a hunting eagle's quiet passage.

"This rock misliked its breaking, vayar," I said, grinning as I straightened my back and twisted my neck, stretching out muscles too long still. Had someone told me I'd sat before the confounded rock three nights in tandem, I could have believed it. I needed a piss so badly, I felt like to burst.

No one answered. And I felt no presence behind me. I peered first over my shoulder and then around the rock.

Kol stood slightly higher on the slope, conversing with another male of his kind, this one shorter and wider in the shoulder, though yet lean and tautly muscled. The moonlight-illumined moon-white hair, bound into a long tail tied every knuckle's length with scarlet. The gard on his broad back—a twisted pine as you might see on a mountain crag—gleamed a sharp and vibrant cerulean. The two of them were arguing and did not glance my way.

I shifted my position slightly, so that I could observe the two less obviously. Clearing away the clutter inside my head, I picked out Kol's voice.

". . . told the tale of my kiran as if he had himself designed it. He touches the earth to know these things. He *saw* my changes, Stian. He claims to see the kiran patterns themselves." Kol's voice rang tight. Anxious.

Stian . . . my Danae grandfather. The eldest of my family. Wonder held me speechless.

"And this is the same sorcerer who brought death to Aniiele's meadow? Who violated Clyste's sianou so that now thy sister, too, lies poisoned by the Scourge? How canst thou look upon a human without loathing? How canst thou ask me to approve a halfbreed as my charge?" The elder crouched beside a cracked slab of rock and picked at a tangle of vegetation, tossing aside dead leaves and stems. "The Cartamandua . . . healthy for them both thou didst hide this history from me. Humans are a breed of vipers."

I held my place behind the rock, excitement quenched. Fortunate that experience had given me no expectations of warm family welcomes.

Kol stood his ground above the older man. "Indeed, this Valen broached Clyste's sianou, but only his companion sullied the water that day. And I've told thee repeatedly that he *saved* Aniiele, though I did not understand how so at the time. The hands of the Scourge had struck down the victim and left him to bleed. But this sorcerer gave back the victim's choice as to the manner of his passing, and so, at the last, the victim's blood was freely given. Aniiele lives, Stian *sagai,* by virtue of this man's deeds."

Great Iero's heart . . . Kol had watched me murder Boreas! That terrible night had etched a vivid horror on my soul: the black, blood-smeared lips of Sila Diaglou and her henchmen; my old friend captive of agony and despair; the sweet meadow that had felt as a part of heaven stained in so vile a fashion by his blood and torment. *Blood freely given . . . Aniiele lives . . .* Though naught could cleanse the blood from my hands, Kol's words brought a measure of comfort I had never expected.

"I have tried to dismiss him," said Kol. "But he sticks to me like thorn. I have named him as insolent as his sire, yet he sounds the streams of earth with reverence and respect, using skills unknown to our kind. He hungers for learning and does not hold back. He led me to the poisoned Well, and I danced beside it. Had my kiran not been flawed with anger and grieving, I might even have reclaimed the Well. And Clyste . . . Thy daughter was no birdwit child, Stian, tricked into mating with a pithless fool. The Well chose her as its guardian, and she chose the Cartamandua as her child's sire. She never explained her choice even to me, but just this day I've wondered— Feel the waning season, *sagai.* The true lands are dying. Just this morning I've had to reclaim yon garden vale yet again. The Well and the Plain are lost, and my heart speaks what my mind can-not grasp—that the Canon is diminished by far more than we can remember. If this halfbreed's claim is true, if he can see the patterns, might he be—?"

The elder burst to his feet and shook his finger at his son. "*Thou* art our answer, Kol, not a halfbreed Cartamandua. Each season brings thee closer to perfection. All recognize it. Thou shouldst dance the Center this season. But thy petulant exile sours the archon and the circles, and as a storm wind among roses hath thine errant rescue of the halfbreed pricked Tuari's wrath. He would see thee bound and buried for the shame thou hast brought on our kind before Eod-ward's son. Only thy irreplaceable ability keeps thee free. Break the halfbreed. Give him over."

"Have I shamed *thee*, Stian *sagai*?" Kol's words cracked and snapped as does a frozen lake.

The white-haired Dané clasped his hands behind his neck and pressed his arms inward, as if to squeeze out the thoughts Kol had im-planted in his head. Only after long silence did he release his grip. Tenderly he drew his fingers along Kol's hard cheek and tucked stray red curls behind the younger man's ear. "Nay, *jongai*, never shame," he said softly. "It is only . . . for good or ill, the archon's word speaks our Law. My human son has met his mortal fate. My daughter ne'er will dance with me again. I would not lose thee, too."

"Then do not allow Tuari's blind hatred to speak for thee. This halfbreed is born of Clyste. *Her* choice. Grant him the walking gard to keep him safe."

Stian dropped his hand heavily, leaving three small flowers twined in Kol's hair. "Bring him."

The true lands are dying. So simple a phrase to leave my heart hollow. Did no one know the reasons? Were even the Danae, who could reshape the earth and command its creatures, confounded by it? What did that do to Osriel's hope? Navronne's hope?

Kol tramped and skidded down the slope toward me. Wary of this elder who spoke so casually of breaking halfbreeds, I chose not to let them know I'd overheard. I sprang to my feet and shouted louder than before, "I've heard the stones' voices, vayar. This one is most unhappy."

"Thou hast heard—" Kol stopped halfway down the slope and shook his head as if to clear it. "Come up, *rejongai*. We will talk of stones' voices later. Stian summons thee."

When I reached Kol's side, and we climbed slowly toward the waiting elder Dané, he spoke softly. "Thou hast shown reasonable manners thus far, Valen, and I would caution thee to continue. My sire hath only tonight learned of thy parentage . . ."

". . . and he is no happier than I was."

For the first time I glimpsed amusement twitch Kol's fine mouth. "Thou hast no measure of his unhappiness, wanderkin. And Stian's skills make my own appear but a nestling's tricks."

I doubted that, having heard how Stian spoke of his son's talents, having witnessed those talents summon the earth itself to his service.

"And mention *not* thy female companion or the monk."

No, Stian would likely have no kind feelings for Eodward's tutor or a human stranger, however unlikely that Saverian and Kol would repeat my parents' folly. Indeed, the consideration of a mating between Stian's son and the physician conjured a delightful image— something like the conjoining of a swan and a woodpecker. A virginal woodpecker.

I smothered a grin. "Aye, *relagai*. No mention of distracting humans."

The elder Dané awaited us where the rolling meadow formed a shallow bowl, choked with dead willows and matted vegetation.

His fingers stroked the blades of brittle grass that had once stood as tall as my hip.

"Stian *sagai*"—Kol bowed gracefully before his father—"I present a wanderkin of our blood-clan. I have accepted the charge of his dam to stand as his vayar. He hath pledged himself to explore and learn, and I judge that his talents and experience have given him knowledge sufficient to accept his walking gard. He answers to the name Valen."

Stian rose. A snarling cat graced the brow and cheek of the broad-shouldered Dané, its long tail twined about his neck. The gards that marked his flat belly, broad chest, and muscled limbs spoke of jungles and hot, languid pools. Despite his white hair, he appeared no older than Prior Nemesio. A man in his prime, with spring-green eyes that scoured me.

"Scrawny. Thick-boned. Weak." I might have been a cow. An ugly cow.

Kol answered coolly. "Valen followed me from the Sentinel Oak to Evaldamon without rest, *sagai*. Even so, his strength or endurance is no matter. I seek thy consent only for the walking gard, that Clyste's child may have skills to elude those who would break him . . . to our shame. His use of those skills shall be his own burden, not thine or mine. He is not to dance."

Stian's lean face resembled Kol's. The father's chin sat squarer. The son's eyes sat deeper. Stian reminded me of the first stone whose voice I'd heard. Unyielding heaviness. Stalwart density.

The elder's arched nose flared in contempt, and the creases about his eyes deepened. "The Cartamandua bragged that he sowed his seed across the lands and seasons and taunted his kin with his scattered offspring. That such a preening rooster laid hand to Clyste . . . that she chose prisoning to protect him . . . Pah!"

"When I was a boy, Janus named the Danae glorious, generous, and hospitable," I snapped, anger banishing caution. "I refused to believe him, madman that he was, preferring the common wisdom that the long-lived are spiteful, petty, and cruel. A child's insights can be astonishing, can they not? For even then, I did not know that a Dané had stolen Janus's wits over a broken promise. Nor had I been ensnared by Danae trickery designed to murder other humans. Nor had I yet experienced the Danae welcome for their imperfect kinsmen. Is your hammer ready?"

"*Rejongai!*" Kol barked.

I pivoted to face my uncle squarely and bowed. "Teach me, if I have erred, vayar. I assumed that frank speech must be expected between elders and wanderkins. Or perhaps it is believed that half-breeds do not hear when their lacks and parentage are so unkindly discussed, which, of course, must make it proper to cripple such a flawed being."

Stian's complexion darkened. He stepped forward, his fingers splayed in some fashion that caused sweat to bead on my brow and back.

I did not retreat.

"Stian *sagai!*" Taut as a maid on her virgin night, Kol stepped between us. "I am his vayar. Thou canst not touch him without first touching me."

"Give him passage, Kol," said Stian, snarling and pointing to the fractured rock. "I consent. But do it here. Without sparing. Then keep him forever from my sight."

Chapter 16

While Stian reclined on the fallen slab, glowering at us, Kol led me up the jagged southern face of the rock. Once we had left the ground behind, Kol's muttering never ceased. "Thou hast the thoughtfulness of a badger, Valen. Did I not warn thee of his temper? Did I fail to mention that this is the same Stian who must be consulted as the archon prepares to break thy knees? For a passing satisfaction, thou hast forfeited every benefit of his tolerance."

"What hope has any halfbreed of his tolerance?" I called up to my uncle, whose feet dislodged sharp slips of rock that peppered my face. My blood yet ran hot, as well, though it was cooling rapidly as the distance between my feet and the hard ground increased. Why did words bother me so?

The uneven steps, created by long-ago fracturing and smoothed by centuries of wind and rain, grew narrower and impossibly farther apart as we neared the top. I squeezed my fingers into a crevice, even as a fierce wind threatened to rip them out again. Praising Kemen Sky Lord for his moonlight, I gripped with toes curled as if they might hold me to the rock.

"Stian bears no inborn hatred for humankind," snapped Kol. "He nurtured Caedmon's son against all custom. Never did he fail in love for Eodward, even when my mortal brother broke his promise to return—a betrayal that cost my sire the archon's wreath and brought to power those who despise all humans and their works. Never did he fail in love for Clyste, though she tore his heart by refusing to explain who had fathered her child and who had taken the babe away, though it meant he watched her unmade and bound to earth."

With a last smooth effort Kol stood atop the rock looking down.

Wind gusts snatched his hair from out its knot and threatened to tear me from the wall. Every scrap of my will was required to loose my fingerhold and follow him.

"Nor did Stian fail in love for me when he saw I knew Clyste's secret and would not yield it. When my sire takes his season in this mountain, he feels the dying of the earth and believes some failing of his has left us helpless to change what comes. Thou knowest not of tolerance."

Of a sudden, my personal grievance seemed petty. Kol's passionate avowal touched the very heart of my purpose. Out of breath, heart galloping from the climb, I crawled over the rim of the rock. "Kol . . . *relagai* . . . why is the earth dying? In the human realms, matters are far worse than here. Our weather, our crops and herds—"

"Such matters weigh too grievously to be spoken of in passing, and we must begin the rite. I had planned more teaching, but Stian could withdraw his consent as sudden as he granted it. Get thee to the center spire."

The flattish summit of the rock encompassed only a few quercae around, and most of it comprised the jagged edges of great fractures, impossible to balance on. Even the more solid center was laced with cracks. Deep inside the rock, the rain froze and melted and froze, threatening to splinter it yet again—to its grief, as I had learned not an hour since. But as a spear thrust into a body's heart, a slender spike of harder stone protruded above the surface to the height of my shoulder.

Kol, of course, reached the spike in two easy leaps. Filled with misgivings about rites that took place atop such perilous perches, I stepped after him, only to wish fervently that I had remained on hands and knees. Every step across the gaping blackness of a crevice sent my stomach plummeting, no matter that most were narrower than my foot. Time and distance reshaped themselves in Aeginea, why not length and breadth as well? Had a crack yawned and swallowed me whole, I would not have been surprised.

Once I joined him, Kol whipped out the length of braided thong that tied up his hair and bound one of my wrists to the narrow column. "Hold up," I said. "What are you—?"

"The binding is to keep thee safe, *rejongai*, lest thou shouldst move untimely and fall. Stian insists we work thy remasti here, and not *solely* that the exposure might discomfort thee. This rock is called Stathero and plunges deep into the heart of this mountain, which is his sianou. Stathero hath a mighty presence, and wind is necessary for this passage as water was needed for the first. But thou needst not worry. I made my own remasti here and emerged unbroken."

Stian's sianou. I was not soothed. Stian *valued* Kol.

My uncle motioned me to stand straighter. "We must imagine that the rain hath sufficed to cleanse thee. I understand this passage comes hard upon thy first. Thy separation gards have not yet settled into their pattern, and thou hast much to learn as a wanderkin. Yet thou art full grown already and resilient, I believe, thus new changes should not daunt thee. Art thou willing to continue?"

I nodded, but kept my mouth closed lest my stuttering resolve declare this lunacy gone far enough.

He inhaled deeply and bowed. I returned the formality as best I could, tethered like a wayward goat. But then a blast of wind staggered me. My fingers closed around the black spire, and my free hand as well, and I wished heartily for a thicker leash.

Kol briefly touched his hands to my shoulders. Then, impossibly, he began to dance. His unbound hair billowing wildly in the wind, he spun on his toes about the perimeter of the rock. One misstep, one miscalculation, and he must crash to earth. No winged angel, he had *leaped* from the high branches of the ash tree, not flown, and Stathero reached more than three times the ash tree's height. In fascinated horror I watched the stars grow hazy and the moonlight dim, and I heard no music but the howl of the wind. "Kol, do have a care."

By the time a breathless *Do not be afraid* appeared in my head, I could not heed it. The bluster atop Stathero had grown to a shrieking gale, tearing at my hair and rippling my skin, lashing me with particles of ice and whips of cloud. Had I the benefit of clothes, they would have been torn away. My own gards pulsed a dull gray-blue, yet all perception fled as if the south wind blew straight through my head to empty it of thought, of prayer, of memory, of identity, and the north wind reached deep to snatch the very breath from my lungs. The world shrank to a roaring knot of black and gray, threaded with the blue lightning that was Kol. And then the lightning struck and set my back afire.

Somewhere Kol's voice called to me, but I could not heed it for the burning. The wind tore my free hand from the column and raised me in its giant's grip. Bound only by Kol's tether, I fought the wind, drew in my limbs, and crouched lower to find purchase on the rock. I touched my hand to the cold surface and released magic, but I could summon no thoughts save *Let me be somewhere else than this* and *Please don't let it blow me off the edge* and some fool's apology for causing such chaos atop the broken rock. Roaring, devouring, the lightning reached over my shoulder to fire my breast, and I closed my eyes and screamed . . .

"It is done, *rejongai*. Thou art—" The hands that had untied my wrist and now rested so gently on my scorched shoulders withdrew abruptly. "Stian! *Sagai!* Come up, quickly."

I was far too weary to heed unexplained urgency. My head rested on my arms. When had I last slept? The bitterly cold world whispered hints of rose-colored light around my eyelids. The wind had settled to a modest bluster, but something blocked it, so that it touched my face only now and then. My legs felt odd. Kneeling. Cold. Heavy. I didn't bother to look. Moving, thinking, choosing what to do next . . . those tasks waited far beyond me. I craved sleep.

Approaching voices. ". . . never seen such . . . not precisely a hole, but a niche . . . to fit . . ."

". . . some error in thy kiran . . ."

"My kiran intruded not upon this rock, *sagai.*" Kol stood over me as he pronounced this chilly conclusion.

I wished they would take their bickering elsewhere. A sunbeam touched my cheek, a lancet that pricked my veins, infusing warmth and light, as if I had drained the Bucket Knot's prize butt of mead. The fond memory of my favorite sop-house roused such a prodigious thirst as no man had ever suffered. The wind and lightning had surely burned out every dram of moisture in my body, and I would lick old Stian's toes did I imagine he had brought a wineskin with his grim company. As I had no wish to be subject to further insults, I kept my heavy head where it was.

"Didst thou sense a breach, Stian? What does it mean that he could do this?"

"No. And I cannot—" The elder Dané bit off his words. Did I not think it ludicrous, I would have called him frighted. "Get him beyond my boundaries, Kol. But let him not stray from thy sight until I come to thee."

The knots in my burning back did not relax as Stian's angry presence receded and vanished.

"Come, get up, Valen," said Kol, tugging on my arm. "Thou'lt have to extricate thyself."

I lifted my boulder of a head, stared at the Dané's toes, and realized my eyes were *below* the level of his feet. So the rest of me . . . I blinked, squinted, and peered downward.

I sat in a hole—actually more like a small, dark cave hollowed from the surface of the rock. My legs were tucked around a small protrusion, preventing Kol from pulling me straight out.

I looked up at my uncle, whose face was shadowed against a brightening sky. "This isn't usual, is it?"

"No. This is not usual," he said, dry as sunburned leaves. "Somehow your remasti has caused an unnatural change in Stian's sianou, one of the most stable locales in all the Canon."

"The wind," I said. "Never felt such a wind. And lightning."

He gave me his hand, and I untangled myself from the rock that appeared to have melted and hardened again in just such a tidy nest as to hold me. "The wind did not do this, *rejongai. Thou* hast done it—and if by accident rather than intent, that is perhaps worse. Assuredly were this known among the long-lived, knee breaking would be the kindliest remedy proffered thee."

I did not want to imagine consequences worse than crippling. Nor did I want to remember my prayers for shelter or think of what power might shape rock. Such wonders could have naught to do with Valen the Incompetent. I stepped out of the little bowl. Movement and the resulting sting front and back reminded me of the occasion for my presence atop this hellacious boulder. Apprehensively I glanced down. *Gods among us . . .*

A tangle of fading sapphire traces marked my breast and belly. Kol stepped back and cocked his head to one side, then walked around behind me.

"Stathero hath taken no offense at thy intrusion. Its likeness forms the gard on thy back, and here"—his finger traced an outline on my breast—"I have a thought we may find a sea star, a dog whelk, perhaps other beings from my own sianou." He sighed, and rueful resignation scribed his face as clearly as his dragon. "To carry so clearly the markings of the places thou hast touched . . . and so early . . . those things, too, are not usual."

Twisting my head in an attempt to see my back near broke my neck. That the marks faded into silver as the sun rose higher did not help. I closed my eyes and pretended I did not feel like some marketplace oddity come from savage lands to swallow fire and juggle hoops.

"Come, Valen. Thy tasks and lessons have scarce begun. And we must leave my sire's sianou that he may examine this night's work in peace. Thou'lt come to envision thine own gards, as their use becomes a part of thy nature. If thou art fortunate, their line and color will please thee."

We began the long climb down Stathero's jagged south face, a matter that consumed all my attention. *Down*, even in daylight, was at least as terrifying as *up* in the dark. Yet from the number of questions that tumbled out of me when my feet at last touched the ground, at least a bit of my mind had been working.

As we hiked down the mountain, away from Stathero and Stian, Kol responded to my barrage of queries with studied patience.

"The gards fade naturally in sunlight, save when we dance or otherwise focus our needs upon them. Once fixed in design, they do not change. Some believe they express a truth about the spirit who wears them . . .

"Wearing coverings, such as human garb, that hide the gards inhibits our use of them and the power they carry. Excessive covering and lack of use will weaken them. To travel the paths of linked remembrances requires full use of the gards . . .

"Males with maturing bodies oft bind their loins for dance training to ease soreness, but they cannot persist in it too long else they'll not progress as they should . . .

"Yes, we sleep and eat and drink, though not so frequently as humans. Of course we enjoy it. We do not understand why Picus's 'one god' prizes dirt and hunger. The sea doth not starve itself of rain to satisfy the requirements of the Everlasting . . .

"We do not understand human gods at all, though every human tries vigorously to explain them. The long-lived, as all things—sea and sky, humans and beasts—are both subject to the Everlasting and a part of it. The Law of the Everlasting has charged our kind to tend the land and sea. Thus in our work we seek beauty, balance, vigor and harmony to match that we see in the Everlasting. But even among the long-lived lie disagreements as to the exact nature of the perfection toward which we strive . . .

"No! As vayar I pledged to answer thy questions as far as I am able. But I cannot and will not discuss the Canon with a halfbreed stripling, though you were to stand twice my size or manifest talents to make your present ones seem small. Thy tasks are other and will never be concerned with the dance."

And this last answer drove me to distraction. "You've told me the world is dying," I said, as we trotted down the mountainside, "and I believe you. I've seen it. My prince, Eodward's son, a man who studies and reveres the Danae, has brought your archon news of those you call the Scourge—the Harrowers. We fear the Harrowers have some larger plan that threatens your kind. Ignorant as we are, we cannot guess what that might be or what must be done about it. That is what he hoped to learn from the archon . . . the reason he gave me up to them." I told myself that knowledge was Osriel's aim, not solely the power to aid in his unholy mystery, as Elene feared.

Kol listened carefully, gravely, his body poised in interest. But his response, when it came, remained unchanged. "Humans can do nothing. Nor can halfbreeds. I will *not* discuss this matter with thee." Which declaration, along with his troubled expression, told me that all of this most certainly had to do with the Canon, and that no matter my wheedling or pleading, he would not budge. All I could do was stay close and hope to change his mind. Perhaps Saverian would have more luck with the monk.

"Attend, stripling!" As we descended into the forest that wrapped the lower slopes of Aesol Mount, Kol broke his broody silence. "If thy walking gards are to be of use, thou must learn. Unless . . . Perhaps thy human half flags?"

His scorn grated, especially as it reminded me how long it had been since my restless night on the sand and Saverian's lusciously fat and gritty eggs. "I'm here to learn," I said.

He acknowledged my declaration with a jerk of his head. "Recall the crowned fir I showed thee. Dost thou see something like here in the daylight? Yes . . . there. Now consider the one that stood on the ascent from the meadow—the same in its shape against the sky, in its smell and taste, in its presence in the wood, though its location differed greatly . . ."

As dreams of food and sleep crept into my bones with the allure of nivat, Kol forced me to dredge up every recollection of the path we had been walking when I had asked about his mode of traveling— the slope of the land to either side as well as what had lain under our feet, the configuration of the stars, which I could not remember, and the taste of the air, which, to his surprise, I could. And then he bade me close my eyes and consider the new marks I wore, explaining that it was easier to begin this teaching while I yet could feel the burning of their newness.

"I've no expectation that thou'lt accomplish a shift so soon. Subtle moves give always the most difficulty to a stripling. The touch needed is not a grand jeque, but only a small leap from one manner of thinking to another. Haste leads to error. Thou must remember to—"

"Just so. I understand." Impatient with his tedious schooling, I glared at the treetop. I was accustomed to wielding magic, and the memory and instinct he described as bound into my new markings were but another form of it. My mind held to the recollections and reached into the faint blue aura that I envisioned near my heart, grasping the power I found there . . .

. . . and I was tumbling head over heels down a steep gully, snagging limbs and hair on rocks, wild raspberry thorns, and rotting timber. My sublimely graceful vayar, gards gleaming silver in the morning sunlight, stood on the path at the verge of the gully, one arm wrapped about a stately fir, laughing at me. It was worth the uncomfortable exercise to see him laugh. If his grieving made the mountains weep, Kol's merriment made the sunlight shimmer.

"Another lesson, my cocky stripling," he said, once on the near side of sober again. "One must remember to decide a position for one's feet, else one may topple from a mountaintop, step into a lake or tar pit, or slide . . . most wretchedly . . . into a ravine."

I struggled helplessly in my nest of raspberry thicket and rotted hawthorn, laughing, too, despite my humiliating display, the painful scrapes and bruises atop my already tender skin, and the long, steep climb awaiting me. Even beings of legend could not always get things right.

When at last I climbed onto the path, I stretched out my blood-scoured arms. "Tell me, vayar . . ."

"The gards survive all but the most violent wounding," he said, all seriousness again. "On our way, we shall practice closure. Clearly thou didst not find true closure at Stathero, if thine ears yet reported sound. Stone hath no voice."

"Nay, vayar, I heard them, even Stathero . . ."

Kol refused to believe my claim to have heard the speech of stones. Evidently the exercise was supposed to result in the silence I ultimately found. He set me other problems as we walked: to describe the scent of thistledown from one particular withered plant along the path, to isolate the feel of salt spray on the wind, carried from the northern sea. Some I managed, some I did not. But I felt more in control of my senses, and came to believe I could learn to pick and choose what I saw and heard.

"Control and discrimination must become as natural as breathing," said Kol. "With practice, it will."

He jumped from a steep hillside, where he'd had me examining the movement of the soil sifting ever so slowly downward, and landed softly on the path far below.

I flattened myself to the scrubby ground and crept downward, my tired feet skidding—speeding the hillside's centuries-long collapse.

When I joined my uncle on the path, pleased I had not slipped and broken my neck, he huffed scornfully. "Thou hast the capacity to jump as I do, if thou'lt but try. Drive thy spirit upward with the leap and hold it firm and soaring until thy feet touch solidly. It is will that counters the forces that draw us to earth." Without waiting for me to so much as catch my breath, he marched down the path. "Next task: Tell me which elements key our shifts on the way down. Be attentive."

After some half quellé of rocks and roots enough to make a goat stumble, Kol halted and asked me how many changes we had made since he had jumped from the hillside. The shifting exercise and the downward climb had sapped nearly the last of my endurance, and the wintry air had begun to penetrate the shield of warmth I had enjoyed since leaving Picus's house. Unable to summon words enough to describe or even count what I'd seen, I sat on my haunches, cleared away the leaves and debris from a square of earth, and sketched out a map in the soft dirt.

The exercise helped refresh my mind. I pointed to an angled square that signified a rock. "You shifted here, where that squarish boulder hung out over the path. Again here . . . I think . . . where the pond was choked with dead leaves. And here"—I pointed to a split in the path—"or just beyond . . . I'm not sure. Here, perhaps?"

Kol looked from my face to the sketch and back again. "Dost thou mock me?" he said stiffly. "Thinkest thou my object is to shame thee, that thou must attempt the same?"

I blinked, entirely confused. "No . . . I'm sorry . . . what is it? You asked how many shifts. My head is too tired to think. I drew the map so I could show you."

"Thou canst untangle such markings?" he said. "Like Janus's papers? Picus's books?"

"Read? Not words, no. I've never—" As the underlying sense of his question struck me, I understood his surprise . . . and his offense. I was *both and neither*, Osriel had said. "I cannot read words . . . books . . . the writing on pages as humans can. They appear naught but blotches and a jumble. However, the lines and patterns of a map, the pictures and symbols, those make sense to me. But you . . . and the others of your kind . . . can't sort out those, either?"

"We see what lives. What moves. We understand bulk and shape and eating and purpose. Scratchings on beast skins or wood chips or dirt have no meaning to us."

"And yet, your eyes can interpret these." I held out my arm where pale fronds of sea grass twined my fingers.

His eyebrows rose. "Thy gards live—a part of thee, as mine are a part of me."

I bowed to him in sincere apology. "Forgive me, vayar. I did not understand. Another lesson learned."

He jerked his head and walked ahead. "Attend, *rejongai . . .*"

Feeling as lively and attentive as a post, I stayed close enough to follow Kol's shifting paths the rest of the way, but was incapable of analyzing his moves or the terrain. When the woodland and Picus's little garden vale came into view at last, I had fallen considerably behind.

Kol halted a little upstream from the monk's tidy plots, and by the time I joined him, he had plunged his hand into a reed-shadowed backwater and pulled out a plump silver fish. As he stilled its flopping distress with a rock, I knelt beside the pool and plunged my head into the water. Though chilled already, I hoped the icy bath might set my sluggish thoughts moving again. I had so many questions I needed to ask, so many lessons to learn. I could not allow him to think me weak or foolish.

But when I sat up again, all I could think was how fine the sun felt on my back, and how soft the earth under my knees, and I could not help but sag into a formless heap on the stream bank, mumbling something to Kol about taking just one moment to consider all I'd learned.

Rosemary and basil. Fish. My stomach near caved in upon itself at the fragrant wood smoke. I blinked and stirred, grimacing at the twigs and pebbles embedded in my ribs. One numb hand prickled painfully as I raised my head. An odd coating of ash dirtied that hand, and I tried for a goodly while to brush it away before remembering that the livid marks were a part of me. I sat up quickly.

Thin blue smoke rose from a patch of sandy stream bank a few paces from my feet and dispersed slowly above a sea of yellow grass and the green islands of Picus's garden plots. A bundle wrapped in blackened leaves sizzled in the little fire—the source of the savory smells. Though steep-angled sunlight sculpted the nearby slopes, deepening the colors of the meadow to ocher and emerald and highlighting the splash of dark trees to either side, iron-gray clouds obscured Aesol Mount and all else to the east and south of us. I stretched and shivered, then stepped closer to the little fire and sat on my haunches.

Kol danced in the yellow grass, or rather practiced, I guessed, as he repeated a particular spinning leap for the fifth time. I felt no stirring in the earth or magic in the still, cold autumn afternoon. He stopped, stretched out first one leg behind him and then the other, bent himself in an impossible arc to one side and then another while clasping his hands at his back. Then he began again. Arms set in a graceful upward curve, now step, leap into the air higher than my head, spin with legs straight together, land like a settling leaf. Shake out the tight legs. Step back. Pause. Arms up, step, leap, spin. Step back . . . Whatever difference might exist between one exemplar and the next was far too subtle for *my* judgment. How could a man force his body into such feats?

I rose onto my toes, then bent my knees and jumped as high as I could, doing my best to turn but halfway round as I did so. My leap might have cleared the height of a small dog, and my feet struck earth so hard I rattled my teeth and came near falling in the fire. How could one even begin without music?

I squatted and touched the earth, not seeking, so much as wondering . . . and laughing a little . . . at what strange byways my thoughts traveled nowadays. Not so long ago my mentor was tidy Brother Sebastian, and my worst trouble the good brother's scolding me for a dirty cowl or discovering my inability to read. Danae did not read. Danae danced, healed, and moved, soundless and graceful, through the world like the bird that glided in circles high above the meadow.

"Hast thou failed in attentiveness and burnt my fish, *rejongai*?" Somehow Kol had come up behind me without my knowing.

I jumped up, my face blooming hotter than the coals. "I didn't know you intended me to—"

But the arch of his eyebrow and a particular compression of his lips gave me to believe, of a sudden, that I had no need to defend myself against his charge. And in the moment I comprehended that, I understood a number of other things.

"You have bested me, uncle, I'll confess it. All my claims of strength and endurance and learning crumbled at your assault. I suppose I'm fortunate that I didn't step off a cliff. I could neither have walked one more step nor imbibed one more lesson, which, I'm coming to think, is one of those very lessons you wish me to learn. And if you truly relied on me to heed your cooking, you're neither so wise a vayar as I'm coming to suspect nor so vigilant a guardian."

"To recognize a body's limits is surer protection than gards or human magic. I have pledged to ensure thy safety. The lesson had to be taught." He retrieved a stick and arranged the coals piled about his wrapped fish. "In truth thou didst surpass every boundary I foresaw. And I am not sure what to do about that."

My hopes, despite the tempering of truth, surged anew. His manner invited me to broach the most important topics again. "*Relagai . . .*"

The sunlight vanished. I shivered and searched for words sufficient to express my need. Snowflakes drifted from the overripe clouds. A red-tailed hawk circled lazily above the meadow. Kol turned his fish with a stick, frowned, and glanced upward. He sat up sharply.

"Valen," he said, eyes fixed on the bird. "Canst thou find Picus's house, by gard or eye or thy human magic?"

Of a sudden, the air thrummed with danger. My gaze swept the forest edge and the ash tree where he'd sat when I joined him in the night, then shot up to the bird, which had completed a loop and now arrowed toward Kol. I had walked here from the hut without any magic. "I believe so. What's wrong?"

"Kneel and bow thy head so the bird cannot note thy unmarked skin. Do it now." His command brooked no question. "When I leave the meadow, be off to Picus and await my return. Or Stian's. Do *not* walk the world unguarded."

I did as he said, extending my legs and bending over them in one of his stretching postures. The only reason to hide my unmarked face and groin would be to pass me off as a mature Dané. Which meant that someone—the bird's master?—must be watching. "Who's coming?"

"Hush." He tossed his stick into the fire and rose. Wings ruffled. "In the Canon, bird, and honor to thy master and mistress." I felt no presence save Kol and the bird. "Fortunately I've completed both work and practice this day, thus can answer their summons promptly."

No one responded. My uncle's chilly declarations seemed directed solely to the bird.

"I prefer to travel uncompanioned, as you know, but of course, I cannot prevent thee. Wait . . ."

Kol's hand rested lightly on my back for a moment. "It seems Tuari and Nysse require my presence, Jinte. Keep thy spine stretched and loose until the finger numbness subsides. 'Tis the surest method for relief."

I waved a hand and shifted my position slightly as if heeding his advice . . . as if the bird might remember my false name or how I had responded to the prompting. The evening's chill settled deeper.

The wings ruffled again and flapped, and after a moment, a sidewise glance showed Kol striding down the meadow and the hawk gliding in lazy circles above him. Once they had vanished into the evening, I jumped up and raced into the wood in search of Picus and Saverian. Kol's abandoned fish had charred to ash.

Chapter 17

"The messenger bird is like to be a friend of the archon, one who failed to make the fourth passage." By the light of the twig lantern, Picus picked bits of leaf and thorn from a sheep's skin. " 'Tis the common fate of those who cannot dance their Danae magic well enough or learn the skills required of them."

"They're forced to become *birds* if they fail to make the fourth passage?" Saverian paused in her frenetic pacing to gape at Picus as if he'd said Magrog himself would sit down with us to dine.

Saverian's relentless urgency had me gobbling much too fast. The woman had come near taking off my head with an oak limb when I refused to leave straightaway to take her home to Renna. The woman and the monk were bundled in cloaks and blankets, while I sat comfortably on the snow-dusted ground in shirt and braies, sopping up Picus's boiled turnips with a wad of doughy bread. Though I mourned Kol's fish, I would have relished far worse than the monk's meager fare by this time. Evidently two full days had passed since I'd gone off with Kol.

"None are *forced* into bird form," said Picus, scratching his arms thoughtfully before returning to his wool picking, "unless they've sore trespassed their Law, in which case their new form would more like be stone or snake. The alter choice for failure is to live on as a hunter, artisan, weaver, or some such like, and such is not a happy life for a Dané. While their fellows dance, their own bare faces wrinkle and their bodies fail near quick as us human folk. Without a sianou they will ever feel rootless and lost. Most prefer inhabiting bird or beast to such shame, though I've always been of a mind 'tis a perversion of the *ordo mundi* as if 'twere *I* had walked into Navronne as king instead of my good prince. But at the least, they choose it for themselves."

My hand paused twixt bowl and mouth, soup dripping from the bread onto my knees. "The hawk was a *person*, then, thinking and listening . . ." Which explained Kol's little deception. A person . . . trapped in that feathered body. And in Moth's owl, too. I had already decided that Moth, not Kol, had led me into murder in the bogs. I shuddered.

"Nay. No *person*. 'Tis said they lose most faculties, retaining only what wit their companions especially nurture." Which made sense if the person had no soul to begin with.

I stuffed the bread into my mouth, making sure to savor every morsel. I'd sworn not to think of souls. I'd plenty more worries closer to hand. "Why would Kol be summoned so abruptly? He seemed wary, but not afraid."

Picus shook his head. "Tuari hath neither favor nor use for Stian or his kin. If the archon has staunch witnesses to thy rescuing, he'll happily bury Kol."

"Bury . . ." Of course, that's why Kol had said Stian might come for me, if he could not. The gummy bread clogged my gullet. "Iero's grace, I must go after him . . . save him."

"Fie on that, lad. Ye'd make his good deed a waste and end up broken and prisoned alongside him. None's so clever as Kol, and he'll not be easily locked away. They need him."

I recalled Stian's words. "Because of his dancing."

"Because his line is fertile!" Saverian's declaration burst out like floodwaters through a breached dike. "Picus says the Danae have always been slow to reproduce—likely a matter of their long lives—but the problem has grown worse in the years since Llio's curse. Children have grown so rare among them that these Harrower poisonings are devastating. They can't replace those lost. For a Danae coupling to produce *two* offspring, as Kol and Clyste's parents did, is unheard of. That's why they were enraged when Clyste's child disappeared. To learn that she *wasted* her fertility on a human mate has surely infuriated them all the more."

"Aye," said Picus. "They're sore diminished from their greatest glory. Tuari blames humankind for all their ills." The monk's big hands fell still, and he closed his eyes as if praying. "Sin begets sin."

"Fear for survival will drive a species beyond custom and boundaries, Valen." The physician crouched at my side, her jade-colored eyes drilling holes in my skull. "Picus says that this Tuari's despite is so great that any bargain worked with a human—especially one of Eodward's kin—is surely devised to turn upon the human party . . ."

. . . and Elene believed that Osriel had come to Aeginea to bargain for power—a magical alliance to fuel the dread enchantment waiting at Dashon Ra. I could not imagine the magnitude of the working Osriel planned. But surely a backlash from its failure would be his ruin . . . and Navronne's. No wonder Saverian was agitated.

The monk filled my emptied bowl from the ale crock at his elbow, glancing from one of us to the other, his eyes sharply curious. "What troubles thee, friends?"

I took a swallow of thin ale. "Good Picus, I must get this lady home. She guards Prince Osriel's health and has been from his side too long. As Kol can care for himself, I'll see her safely back to her duty. We'll need a few provisions for the road, lest my poor skills delay us."

"But ye said Kol told ye to bide." His sheepskin dropped into the mud, and his broad brow knotted in concern.

Who knew how many human days had passed since Osriel had given me up to the Danae? Instinct told me that the winter solstice raced toward us with the speed Nemelez drove her chariot of ice through her demonic lover's fiery kingdom.

I drained the bowl and returned it to the monk. "We dare not wait. Tell Kol I'll return here as soon as may be."

We took our leave within the hour. Now I'd had a little rest and food, the cold did not bother me so much, but we bundled my thick hose, winter tunic, belt, boots, and pureblood cloak with Picus's dried fish, a skin of his ale, a clay bowl, and the remainder of his bread. Picus insisted Saverian keep the blanket he had lent her. "Best I not inhale the scent of a woman lest my dreams illustrate the sins I've banished from head and heart."

I bowed deeply, crossing my clenched fists over my heart— Gillarine Abbey's signing speech for farewell and a reminder to remain staunch in one's vows and devotions. Picus, eyes bright, returned the gesture solemnly. "I shall sincerely try to hold fast to my tottering virtue, Brother Halfbreed. But if a word as to the meaning of this haste should fall upon mine ear at thy return, I do not think Iero would grudge it."

"When I can, Brother. When I can." I grinned and waved as we headed into the chill autumn night.

At every step of those first hours, Saverian and I worked at cross purposes, my long gait unaccommodating to her quick, careful steps, my inclination to go over obstacles while she preferred under or around. And though I could not see well in the thick dark of the woodland, I could rely on my bent. She could see nothing at all. After she stumbled for a third time, near breaking her skull, I took her arm to steer her between the bare limbs and woody underbrush that snagged her cloak and skirts. That only made our disparities more awkward.

Before long, she sputtered and shook off my hand. Waving me to go on ahead, she snatched up a dry limb and set it gleaming with yellow light that had naught to do with fire. "I'll see to my own feet, thank you. By the Mother, how ever does a blind person manage without going mad?" She dogged my steps, tight-lipped save when urging me to go faster.

Happily, we soon emerged into the open, gently rolling country to the south. I knelt and sought a route to the Sentinel Oak, the only way I knew to get us back to the human plane. As in the garden meadow, the landscape took shape upon my mind's canvas in a single grand leap of understanding, rather than the slow building of the past. A confusion of tracks sprawled before us—migrations of great herds of elk and wild horses, footpaths of deer and Danae folk, and a great blight of blood in some past epoch—but no settled roads. And, unfortunately, the oak lay hundreds of quellae to the southwest, beyond expansive forests, a sizable rise in elevation, and at least two major river crossings. To travel the distance afoot would take us more than a month.

"But you've learned to journey as Kol does," said Saverian, when I announced this unhappy news. Like a fine hunting hound, she seemed poised to charge off in whatever direction I pointed.

"Only once," I said, sitting back on my heels and scratching my head. "And yes, I ended up in approximately the correct location. But I've too little familiarity with Aeginea to know many landmarks to use for shifting. Danae wanderkins are supposed to explore for years to learn the landforms and plants and trees and such."

Snowflakes flurried from overburdened clouds, melting quickly on our cloaks. A frost wind from the south had whipped the woman's deep-hued cheeks to a rosy brown. I'd been so sure I could get us home. *Cocky wanderkin*, Kol would say. *Recognize thy limits.*

Saverian was not so easily discouraged. "Osriel says that human lands and Aeginea are actually the same; we just experience different aspects of them in the two planes. You've traveled all over. You know *Navronne*."

"But no Navronne cities exist in Aeginea, no roads, no houses. The trees and forests are all grown up differently . . ."

Yet she was right. The terrain should be the same. Since I had walked into Aeginea, I had seen the chasm of the River Kay, the familiar climb from the valley of the Kay toward the mountains, and the rock of Fortress Groult, even though the fortress itself did not exist in this plane.

"Come on." I made for the top of a rocky little knob half a quellae ahead, stopping only when I reached its crest. Squinting and puzzling at the landforms, I reached up to clear the melted droplets from my lashes, only to see a sickly thread of pale blue snaking about my fingers and up my arm into my sleeve. Laughter welled up from deep inside.

"The humor in this situation entirely escapes me," said Saverian, heaving and gasping as she finished the sharp little climb and halted beside me. Her magelight had paled to the color of cream, and breath plumes wreathed her head. Her vehemence triggered a bout of coughing, aborted by a great sneeze.

"Are you all right?" I said. Her flushed cheeks flared brighter than her magical light.

"Well enough, considering I'm hiking into nowhere with a man whose walking pace is a modest gallop. Is *that* the joke?"

"I knew you'd wish no coddling," I said, shoving my bundle of clothes and provisions into her hands. "You should have yelled at me to slow down."

I unlaced my braies and shirt. She stared as if I were a lunatic. Which I believed I was. "Indeed, physician, *I* am the great joke. Here I've been so preoccupied with Danae secrets, princely deviltry, Kol, Elene, and what in Iero's name will happen to the lighthouse, not to mention this confounded route finding and the nature of Aeginea, that I've completely forgotten my lessons. If you'll pardon my boldness, I am going to remove my clothes just now and attempt to do as you suggest—see if I can make some use of this motley collection of strangeness that is my body. Yell at me if you see anyone coming."

She held out her hand to take my shirt, a smile tweaking the thin lips into something altogether more pleasant than their usual sardonic set. She waved her hand at my disrobing. "Please. Do whatever you must to get me home."

I grinned and left the rest of my garb in her custody. For certain she was no wilting ninny.

Sitting cross-legged atop the little knob, I listened for the voices of stone. It seemed to take quite a while—or rather I managed it only after setting aside all fretful sense of time. Once I had rediscovered that quiet place where only a few faint declarations of *Forever* and

Grind intruded, I allowed my Danae senses free rein and used the cascade of sensation to expand and deepen my Cartamandua seeing.

The cool dry air of summers past, along with the sharp blasts of past winters, teased my skin. The rich scents of soil and the buried roots filled my nostrils. I experienced not only the sounds and smells of wild Aeginea, but those of human habitation as well: sod houses, flocks of grazing sheep, the sharp bite of axes and tools. The blight of human blood and death near choked me. I explored deeper. Farther.

Were we walking the lands of Navronne, I would declare our location to be the upland moors of far northeastern Ardra, a long-settled expanse of sheeplands, grouse, and heather, whose streams and springs fed the riverlands of Morian. Indeed I had marched through those very moors with King Eodward's legions, camped and foraged on that land—this very land—fought a great bloody battle here with the Dasseur, the barbarians who had stripped the Aurellian Empire of its northwest territories. Eodward had triumphed in that battle, making his stand on a dimpled fell that was the highest point of the region. Even then the barren mound, shaped so like a young girl's breast, had reminded me of Mon Viel in the hills of southern Ardra, a region as familiar as my hand.

Carefully I shuffled through the cascade of impressions like a gem merchant through a bag of rocks, choosing only those that came through my eyes, while silencing all the rest. Then I stood up and peered again into the night.

As had happened on that strange night of my nivat madness, when Osriel and Voushanti and I had tracked Gildas's flight from Gillarine, the landscape gleamed of its own pale light. The route my Cartamandua bent had prescribed stretched south and west across this luminous terrain as if a giant had unrolled a spool of gray floss and left it behind to guide us. But it was the landforms I examined.

"There," I said, pointing to the gentle mound that sat in the center of the blood-tainted ground between us and the southern horizon . . . and, at the same time, far past it to that other swelling prominence some two hundred quellae to the south, known in the realm of humankind as Mon Viel. Reveling in the success of my combined Danae–human magic, I was already recalling the feel of the springy turf beneath my feet, the scents of wild lavender and lemon thyme, the calls of meadowlark and blackthrush that spoke freedom to a child run off from home in stinking, noisy Palinur. "We're going there."

*   *   *

Ignorance and inexperience put a quick damper on my satisfaction. Each leg of our journey took longer than it should. We had walked halfway to the horizon before I could join the knowledge of my senses with the power of my walking gards to make the shift southward to the slopes of Mon Viel. We were yet in Aeginea, of course, for the nearby heights where Caedmon's royal city ought to rise in all its glorious might sat dark and bare.

Next it required three false starts before I gave up trying to use a rocky little grotto to walk into a similar nook I remembered from my journey in Mellune Forest. Perhaps I recalled too little of the snow-drowned nook's scents or actual conformation to make the Danae enchantment work.

And then I discovered the risks of impatience when I tried to use a boggy spring surrounded by dry vineyards to plant us in the vastly different boglands of the River Kay. Saverian and I both spent two hours spewing our last month's meals from fore and aft into the muck and praying we would expire before we drained ourselves to raw husks. Human bodies—even those half Danae—were evidently not meant to move through the world so abruptly.

Subtle moves, Kol had told me. I now understood that he'd not meant subtle in distance, but in distinction. To shift from one steep, shaded mountain path to another so much like it was easy, even were they a hundred quellae apart. To shift from a puddle among barren hills to a forest-bounded bogland was possible, but would wring a body inside out. At least I had remembered to "place" my feet, so that we writhed and retched on mostly solid ground and not neck deep in mud.

"If you can find anything to burn, I can spark a fire," said Saverian in a croaking whisper. "Tea will get us on our feet again."

She sat halfway up the steep little bank, her head resting on our provision bundle nestled in her lap. A seep around the woody roots of a larch had induced her to crawl up the bank to clean her face and hands. That she could consider doing more stoked my admiration. I yet wallowed in my own stink half in the mud, half out, thoroughly humiliated, exhausted, and shivering. I wasn't sure anything could help.

"I'll find something," I said, dragging myself to my feet. This bog was the last place in the world I intended to die. Did I touch this muck with magic, I was certain I would hear the wails of drowned Harrowers, even across the barriers of the human plane and Aeginea.

I dragged handfuls of dry sedge and leatherweed and a few dead alder saplings from high on the bank to Saverian's feet, and tore open cattail pods to provide tinder. Half an hour more and we sipped lukewarm tea made from Picus's blessed herbs.

"I'm sorry," I said, clutching the bundle of clothes in my lap, my throbbing head propped on one hand. "I need a bit more schooling."

"You should put on those clothes," said Saverian, ever the physician, as she passed me the blackened clay bowl. "Your lips are blue, and not with Danae sigils, and I can walk not one quat farther tonight. Assuming this is night."

I gazed dully at the sky. Though it had gleamed azure in the wintry daylight at Mon Viel, it now glowered with the blue-black sheen of a magpie's wing. I could not sense the sun anywhere. Snow dusted the landscape, and wind moaned over the bog, rattling the leafless willows.

"We can't stay here," I said. "This is Moth's sianou. She hates humans—and has proved it. Would as soon drown us all as look at us. We can walk all the way to the oak if need be. Rest, get your legs back, and then we go."

I downed a swallow of the rapidly cooling tea and passed it back. The pulse and twitter of a curlew echoed through the morbid stillness, reminding me of the deserted mine above Renna. "When are you going to tell me what Osriel plans?"

"I will not. I cannot." She threw a rotting limb on the fire, and a veil of sparks spurted upward.

"Have you seen the place where he imprisons the souls? Have you felt them? It's wrong, Saverian. Evil. They are so angry, so terrified, filled with hate. I've never felt the like."

"Impossible. Those people are dead. Emotions are created by the living body and mind in response to changing circumstances. They are no more than the body's humors infusing the blood, like the tincture in an alchemist's vial. There is no such thing as a soul." Her utter conviction was tinged with a bleak and weary sadness that surprised and grieved me. What had happened to her to cause so sere a vision of life?

"Then what does Osriel capture when he seals a dead man's eyes in a calyx?"

"Waste. Dust. Echoes of life."

"So why not tell me what he thinks to do with his nasty treasury? Certainly it's not too dread to speak of, if he but plays tricks with dust and waste."

"He is my lord and my friend. I will not violate his trust."

I wished I had the wit to argue with her. So sharp and scholarly a mind as hers should not be burdened with so barren a philosophy. She was no alehouse philosopher, taking a position for the sake of argument. Yet having so recently examined my own state and come up with no conclusive evidence of a soul, I had no weapons to bring to a joust about the rest of humankind. And while I remained firm in my belief that the essence of a *human* person lived beyond the last breath, I certainly didn't want Saverian providing sensible evidence to crush my own hope for the same.

As the last of our pitiful lot of fuel fell to ash, I stood up, slung the bundle over my shoulder, and pointed south along the bank, where in the other realm so like to this, Thalassa had escorted me toward Gillarine. "Let's go."

Saverian wasted no breath on conversation along the way, so I amused myself imagining what various monks would say did I come striding through their gates clad only in blue fire. And then I thought of Thalassa, and, for the first time in my life, found myself wishing I could talk with my sister . . . half-sister . . . no, half-niece . . . now. A priestess of the Mother, she could tell me of souls. It might be easier to hear the truth from her than from Picus or Saverian.

We left the treacherous bogland and soon trudged across the river-looped valley floor where Gillarine ought to lie. Clumps of slender beeches dotted the grassland, their trunks split and peeling. The limbs of scattered oak scrub curled like the legs of a dead spider. And everywhere patches of blackened, slimy grass testified to the land's death—to my mother's death and Gerard's death—to poisoning by people who stole innocents like Jullian and slaughtered bold and noble spirits like Abbot Luviar.

I knelt and touched the damp earth, snowflakes melting on the back of my blue-scribed hand. The land's sickness coursed through me like a river of sewage, bearing the stink of betrayal, mindless ravaging, and death. I welcomed it, allowing it to fuel anger and temper the steel of my resolve. Whatever I had to do to stop this, I would do.

"We need to move," said Saverian, tapping a cold hand on my shoulder. "This place is too open. Someone . . . something . . . unfriendly lurks here."

"Did you not say such feelings are but a body's humors mingling?" I said, bitterness overflowing. "You are part alchemist, Mistress Mage, so repair them yourself." But I rose and led her southward.

Recovered equanimity told me when we passed beyond the boundaries of my mother's poisoned resting place. The gloom lightened a bit. I could sense the sun nearing the zenith behind the layered cloud. "I'm sorry," I said. "I was feeling a bit useless earlier and should not have taken it out on you."

"We could both use a real bed." Save for a fleeting smile, her expression was etched with determination. What drove her? Never had I known a woman so complicated. Strong, though. And honest. I could understand why Osriel trusted her with his life—and why he valued her prickly company.

"You never told me what you learned of Llio's curse."

She hitched her cloak about her shoulders. "It's difficult to know what to believe. Picus swallows every tale and grinds it in the mill of his faith. Simply stated, Llio broke the world. Somehow. Picus says that Danae speak of four sacred places, the first sianous where the first four of their kind were born of the Everlasting, brought to life and given bodily form. These four are the Mountain, the Plain, the Sea, and the Well."

As always, the mention of sianou joining made my skin creep. "My mother's Well."

"Exactly so. The guardians of the Four are always exceptional dancers. Llio, the halfbreed son of a Dané named Vento and a human woman, became the chosen of the Plain. Among his many couplings—it seems most Danae are not singular in such matters—Llio mated with a human woman named Calyna, and got her with child."

Saverian warmed to her storytelling, as we ascended the terraced foothills that would lead us to the Sentinel Oak. The snow swirled thicker, and the wind blustered as we came out of the valley.

"On the spring equinox, Llio attacked another Dané during the dancing of the Canon, and in the ensuing struggle, Llio died. From that hour the Plain was lost to the Canon. Picus does not know why or how—he babbled about human legends and the lost city of Askeron. But the Danae blame Llio's half-human temper for this great breaking and their decline in fertility that followed. They vowed that no halfbreed would ever dance the Canon."

"Thus they break our knees."

"That's only the beginning of the deviltry." Saverian double stepped to catch up with me again, and I tried to slow my pace to accommodate her. "Llio's father, Vento, held Calyna captive until the child was born, then drove the mother from Aeginea, while keeping the infant. But Calyna knew of the Danae's weakness—this bleeding rite they call the Scourge—and she bled some poor human to poison Vento's sianou when he took his sleeping season. As it happened, Vento also had a full-blooded Danae elder son, none other than Tuari, the present archon. Tuari used the child to trick Calyna to fall off a cliff! He claimed he did it to prevent Calyna telling other humans about the Scourge. But Stian, who was archon, believed Tuari did the murder from shame and vengeance, and he condemned Tuari to take beast form every summer until Llio's child reached maturity."

"So Llio and Tuari were half-brothers," I said, astonishment stopping me in my muddy tracks. "Saints and angels, no wonder Tuari has no use for human folk. Or for Stian's family either."

Saverian bobbed her head in a most satisfied manner. "Humans are not the only fools who cripple themselves with lust. Sin begets sin. And did you guess? The child of Llio the halfbreed and poor murdered Calyna was the same crippled halfbreed girl Ronila who stained Picus's virtue!"

"Gods!"

As all these threads raveled and unraveled, our urgency redoubled. We hurried through the chilly gloom, wondering what it meant that the Danae had now lost two of their four holiest places. And we speculated about Ronila's *evidence* that had driven Picus to such extremity as deserting Eodward and living out his life in penance. Saverian said the monk had refused to discuss the woman.

At last, weary beyond bearing, we dragged ourselves up the last steep rise. Across the rock-laced meadow stood the Sentinel Oak. Saverian leaned heavily on my arm, no longer reluctant to accept help. "Too much to hope that Osriel is camped at Caedmon's Bridge," I said.

"He told me he intended to return to Renna straightaway from Aeginea. But then again, he didn't mention he planned to leave you tied to a tree with broken knees. Damnable prick."

Smiling at her vehemence, I knelt and touched earth. I needed only my Cartamandua bent to find my way back to the human realm from here.

The patterns of the Danae were scribed everywhere upon this land—the fine sprays of silver, whorls and roundels, ovals, spirals, and multiple sets of straight lines that crossed to form gridlike shapes. What marvelous patterns must radiate from the four great sianous, the oldest, the first.

Though, for the first time, I felt close to answers, I'd no time to consider the earth's mysteries. We needed to find our prince and prevent him using whatever grant he had bargained from the Danae, lest the backlash of Tuari Archon's hatred make our problems worse. Magic flowed through my fingertips as I held in mind Caedmon's Bridge . . . the grim verges of Evanore . . . the snow-buried barrens we had left behind . . . every edge and sweep etched on my memory. And instinct led my eye to one bright track leading into a thicker night and deeper winter—into human lands.

"Valen!" Saverian's tense whisper brought my head up. She crouched beside me, pointing to the Sentinel Oak. From beneath its bare canopy three Danae moved deliberately toward us. Likely it was my imagination that told me two of them carried wooden clubs.

I grabbed Saverian's hand and bolted. The guide thread led us straight toward the spot where Caedmon's Bridge should span the Kay, and I dared not deviate from it in hopes I could take us to the human realm some other way.

The Danae changed course to intercept us. We had no hope of outracing them, and naught would prevent them following us into the human plane. I needed to shift us far from this place.

As we sped across the hillside, I focused on the great rocky pinnacle that overlooked this mead and recalled another rocky peak that overlooked a barren hillside. Both of them should house a fortress. "Physician," I said, breathless. "Pin your eyes straight ahead. Yell at me the instant you glimpse Caedmon's Bridge."

She jerked her head. The blood pounding in my ears near deafened me, as I concentrated on the fortress rock and the thick straight walls I knew existed atop it in the human realm. At the same time, I built the image of the second fortress: its rarefied air, its looming mountain neighbors, its thick, safe stone, the smell of warriors' piss along the inner walls, the welcoming fire of torches and the boom of the sonnivar, pitched to match no other in any world. Not at all a subtle leap.

The Danae cut a swath of sapphire through the snowy night. Moth wings gleamed upon a female's breast and brow. I gritted my teeth and dragged Saverian faster, gripping the dual images of the fortress. This *would* be enough. It had to be.

"The bridge!" gasped Saverian at the same time a killing frost enveloped us.

Trusting her word that we had entered the human plane, I shifted course abruptly, angling back across the hill toward the rocky summit of Fortress Groult, putting us directly on a course for the closing Danae. Then I reached into the blue fire that raged from my own breast and drew forth magic . . .

Harsh breath crackled and froze the hairs in my nose. My bare feet skidded on a patch of ice, and as Saverian and I crashed to earth, I whooped in exultation. We lay tangled in a heap at Renna's gates, and the Danae were nowhere to be seen.

Even the blinding pain in my head and the wrenching spasms in my empty gut could not damp my good humor. I had seen across the boundaries of Aeginea clearly enough to build the shift—a work of the senses that Kol had said was impossible for his kind. My every instinct insisted gleefully that I could have worked the shift directly, before we had even crossed the physical boundary between Aeginea and Navronne.

Arms and elbows dug in my gut. Boots scraped my legs. My throbbing head slammed abruptly into the frozen ground. "Gods, woman"—I pressed the back of my hand to my mouth to hold back the surging bile—"give me a moment's peace."

"Put on this cloak, fool." Even sick and frozen, Saverian could pierce a man's craw with her disdain. She threw something scratchy and wet over me. "You don't want anyone to see you . . . like *this*."

I thought at first she meant heaving, but when I drew my hand away and glimpsed the delicate outline of a dog whelk nestled in fronds of sea grass that twined my fingers, I understood—and blessed her practical wisdom. The brightness of my gards near cracked my skull. I closed my eyes and pulled the cloak around me. "Need to find my braies and hose."

By the time Saverian screamed out her name to the sentries, most of my gards were covered, and I had even donned the pureblood mask I'd found in the pocket of my cloak. Saverian and I stood in a delicate balance, supporting each other, but if someone didn't open the gates soon, they would have to drag us in by the heels.

The gates ground open with a soul-scraping cacophony. A torch flared the dark tunnel, searing my eyes, but I could not mistake Voushanti's bulk in company with the soldiers.

"We need to see Prince Osriel as soon as possible," said Saverian.

"Unfortunately His Grace is not in residence," said Voushanti. "Dreogan, prepare to close the gates. Muserre, Querz, wake Mistress Elene and tell the steward to prepare hot food and wine for the physician and the pureblood. I'll escort them in."

"Where in the name of all holy gods is he?" I said, unreasonably irritated, as my bowels churned.

Voushanti waited until the three warriors had left us. Then he turned his gaze our way, the red centers of his eyes flaring savagely. "Our master has been taken captive, sorcerer. He lies in the dungeons of Sila Diaglou."

PART THREE

Ever Longer Nights

Chapter 18

"How did this happen?" I said, rubbing my head to keep my sluggish blood flowing. I would need to sleep soon or I'd be gibbering. But not yet. Not until I understood the magnitude of this disaster. "You're sure the witch doesn't know his true identity?"

"We have no reason to believe she knows he is the prince," said Voushanti. The mardane stood stiffly at the door of Elene's retiring chamber. He had brought Saverian and me straight from the gates. "My lord's saccheria struck him hard just as we left the Danae. In the physician's absence, he chose to ride on to the monkhouse, where Thane Stearc would be able to care for him."

"Papa always keeps a supply of Osriel's medicines," said Elene, her circled eyes speaking raw grief and desperate worry. "Saverian sees to it that he knows what to do for every variant of the disease. He had to ride as Gram. No one remaining at the abbey knows him as anyone but Papa's secretary."

Saverian huddled by the hearth wrapped in a dry blanket. Barely controlled fury had sealed her lips since she'd heard that all her worst fears for Osriel had come true. She clearly blamed herself.

I perched on a window seat, pretending I was not within walls. As long as I could see the sky, my lungs did not feel quite so starved or my stomach quite so certain it was going to turn wrong way out.

Elene, flushed as summer dawn, sat in a padded armchair, a bright-colored shawl covering what her shift and hastily donned bliaut did not. Sleep had left half of her short bronze braids unraveled, the others matted or sticking every which way. Heat rose from her as from a smoldering bonfire. "Sila Diaglou and a small force lay in wait at Gillarine for Papa to return from the warmoot. Before the

priestess could remove Papa from the abbey, Osriel walked through
the gate and right into her arms."

Anger and resentment bulged Voushanti's fists and twisted his
scarred mouth. "My lord insisted I return to the bridge with my men
as soon as we sighted the monkhouse gates. He did not permit disobedience."

I squirmed at the remembrance of Voushanti's battles of will with
Osriel. Their hellish link of enchantment and submission still confounded me.

Elene beckoned me to her side and thrust a crumpled parchment
into my hand. "The witch dispatched two of the monks to carry this
message to Renna. Can you fathom her insolence?"

The precisely formed letters flowed into their usual incomprehensible blotches. My own cheeks hot, I shoved it back at her and
returned to my window. "So tell me, what does it say?"

Elene frowned for a moment before her expression cleared in
understanding. "Forgive me, Brother. Here, I'll read it . . ." She
smoothed the page and began, her voice swelling with repressed fury.

Osriel of Evanore,

*Believing our partnership holds more promise for Navronne's
future than our enmity, I extend to you my sisterly goodwill and
offer an exchange of benefits. Our purposes do not and cannot
coincide. I serve Powers beyond the ken of any mortal born,
while you serve your own secret pleasures of a diabolical odor.
Yet our interests may not conflict in every instance.*

*You hold an injured monk, the chancellor of Gillarine Abbey,
known to be involved in this Karish lighthouse foolishness. As
your deeds exemplify no maudlin sympathies for Navronne's
peasants, I cannot conceive that this errant project holds any innate value in your estimation.*

*On the other hand, your position as Evanore's lord makes
your defensive strength dependent on a handful of ancient families who demand certain strict loyalties and protocols. Unfortunately, one of your warlords seems to have connived with these
Karish librarians, and I have caught him at it. But he has convinced me he cannot work magic.*

*Perhaps you are strong enough to control your clansmen even
while abandoning one of them to your adversaries. But if you
prefer to avoid a disruption among your supporters, I can offer
you this bargain. I will return your errant Thane Stearc in
exchange for the monk Victor. To sweeten the offering, I will*

include your pureblood's catamite. I doubt your warlord's dis-
eased scribe could survive the journey, but if you prefer him to
the boy, you may have him instead. I believe we shall both be
well pleased with the outcome of the trade, and our relative
strengths will remain in balance.

I require this bargain be completed before the solstice. Do you
agree to it, take the monk to the crossroads at Gilat on the Ardran
High Road and send word to me at Fortress Torvo.

In the glory of the Gehoum,
Sila Diaglou

"Damnable . . . vile . . ." Rage threatened to cut off what remnants
of use remained in my exhausted brain. "Gods ship them all to the
netherworld!"

"Does anyone else find this letter's language odd?" asked Saverian, her fiery anger banked by curiosity. "I thought the woman
disdained learning."

"She didn't write it," I said. "Gildas did. Who else would slander
a child?" I pressed the heel of my hand to my forehead as if it might
prevent my skull's imminent disintegration. "Why would they trade
one for the other? Stearc can open the lighthouse as well as Brother
Victor, right?"

"No." Saverian returned to the hearth stool. "The opening requires *two* paired warders—one embodying the unlocking spell, one
with power to release it."

"And Gildas knows this?"

"Not unless they've tortured it out of someone," she said. "Until
this hour, I've been the only person outside the four warders themselves who knew. Luviar and Brother Victor were one pairing. Stearc
and Osriel the second. The priestess and her monk don't understand
what they have."

"Neither my abbot nor I revealed the secret." An ill-favored little
man wearing a black cowl and an eye patch shuffled through a side
door not three paces from me, leaning heavily on a cane.

"Brother Victor!" I popped up from the window seat. Only fear of
crushing his fragile bones kept me from embracing him. Which would
have been an entirely unseemly greeting for the chancellor of Gillarine, and an act I would never have contemplated when I lived there.
But I could not help the surge of pleasure as I bowed, cupping one
palm in the other and extending them in an offering of Iero's
blessings.

He smiled back, stuffing his cane under one arm long enough to return the blessing. "Dear Brother Valen, one of my three blessed saviors"—he nodded graciously to Voushanti and Saverian. "It is a grace to see you returned safely to our company. Though, as always, you present yourself at inconvenient times."

As I helped him settle gingerly into the chair beside Elene, he glanced curiously at my hands and then quickly to my face. I snatched my hands back under my cloak, hiding the marks that had paled to silver. I'd not told Elene or Voushanti of my own particular adventures in Aeginea as yet. Osriel's predicament preempted every other concern.

"These secret pairings . . ." I began, returning to the lighthouse secret. Elene could not work magic, but Brother Victor was a pure-blood sorcerer. The puzzle pieces shifted. "So, Mistress Elene, Osriel didn't send you back here to assume Brother Victor's burden, but to *partner* with him. To take Luviar's place."

She dipped her head, tears brightening her eyes. "We dare not leave my father and Osriel there together. Sila Diaglou will give them up only so long as she believes that only one warder is necessary. A pureblood warder. Dear, brave Brother Victor has agreed to the exchange."

"Brother!" Saverian looked up in shock. "You can't. You're scarcely walking!"

"And what of Jullian?" I snapped. "You don't think the priestess will notice you choosing to retrieve a sick man over a healthy, innocent boy?" That no one seemed concerned over the boy made me irrationally angry. I had yet to admit that Osriel's life was worth the saving.

"If there is the slightest hope to rescue our prince, I must do it," said Brother Victor. "I can transfer my wardship to another. And we must certainly do whatever we can to retrieve young Jullian as well. Perhaps I can speak to Gildas's conscience . . ."

Perhaps they hadn't told Victor about Gerard. "Gildas owns no conscience," I said.

"The priestess will never yield a living captive." Voushanti's opinion interrupted the discussion with the subtle grace of a crossbow bolt. "Go through with this exchange and you but confirm she has a prize in hand. Then she will redouble her efforts to extract the truth from Thane Stearc. Whether or not he tells her what she wants to know, Thane Stearc is a dead man. His endurance is all that stands between Prince Osriel and Sila Diaglou's questioning." He glared at Saverian as if it were her fault Osriel was taken.

Voushanti's reasoning—and its implication that Osriel was as good as dead, too—silenced us all. Elene closed her eyes and pressed folded hands to her mouth.

There had to be some other way to save three lives than to send this good man to certain death. I rolled the priestess's message over in my mind. With every skill of memory I had developed through the years, I reviewed the exact phrasing, my thoughts focused as if heeding the whispers of stone. "She wants to have it done before the solstice," I murmured.

Then truth struck home like a cudgel to the knees. "Of course!" I blurted out. "Max has settled her bargain with Prince Bayard!"

Saverian and Victor had not heard the details of Osriel's meeting with his two half-brothers at Gillarine. Thus I had to explain Osriel's agreement with Bayard to join him in confronting the Harrowers, and how my brother Max, as Bayard's negotiator, had been charged to drive a false bargain with the priestess over her demands for control of Evanore, the lighthouse, and me. ". . . and so Prince Osriel told them that either the joined might of Eodward's sons defeats Sila Diaglou on the winter solstice or the world we know will end."

"By the Mother, Riel!" Saverian's harsh whisper split the despairing silence.

The problem, of course, was that without Osriel, his plan, whatever it might have been, collapsed like an empty sack. What hope had we of preventing Sila Diaglou from doing whatever she wished on the solstice? She could make Bayard her puppet king or crown herself. As long as she possessed the book of maps and the traitor Gildas to use it, she could eventually find every Danae sianou and work her poisoning, further corrupting the Canon. Harrowers would lay waste to Ardra. The warlords might hold Evanore against the combined legions of Harrowers and Moriangi, but what light would ever draw them from their caves as night and chaos drowned Navronne? No more savior princes waited hidden in Aeginea.

"Osriel commanded the warmoot to muster at Angor Nav on the solstice," Elene said numbly. "He promised they would ride for Palinur the next day to enforce his claim to Navronne."

No need to remind us that Angor Nav lay more than eighty quellae from Caedmon's Bridge or to state the logical conclusion that Osriel had no intention of confronting Sila Diaglou with his Evanori legion. The prince had believed victory lay in the deserted gold mine of Dashon Ra, and if any knew what that dread solution entailed, it was Saverian. She looked as if she could snap bone with her teeth.

"Our first responsibility is to preserve the lighthouse," said

Brother Victor, always a man of practical reason. "Whatever plan Prince Osriel formulated and whatever he learned from the Danae that might aid him are imprisoned with him. So we must devise a new plan on our own."

"Unless *you've* learned what we need, Valen," said Elene, forcing her voice steady. "Perhaps he told you his intent before you were taken? Or perhaps you heard what he learned from the Danae?"

I heard her truer inquiry. Had I kept my promise to learn of Osriel's dire enchantment and dissuade him from it?

I met her gaze and shook my head, then spoke to all. "We learned nothing from the prince or his meeting. But Saverian and I did learn that the Canon has been broken for a very long time. The Danae themselves are in decline and have found no answer for it. With each Harrower poisoning—what they did with Gerard and tried to do by killing Brother Horach—another part of the Canon is lost."

Even as I spoke, many things seemed clearer in my own mind. On the day we retrieved Gerard's body at Clyste's Well, Kol, in his anger, had handed me the first clue. *You lead me here, cleanse the Well so I do not sicken, return it to my memory so I cannot escape knowing what is lost—though I must lose it all over again.* And Picus's failing garden had given me the second.

"Once a sianou is poisoned, they can't find their way there anymore," I said. "And the rest of the land, despite their care, keeps failing. I saw what they do, what they fight, and I would wager on my hope of heaven that this failure is the root of our plagues and pestilence, our weather disturbances, too, for all I know. Prince Osriel went to the Danae hoping to gain use of their magic on the solstice, and we've no way of knowing what answer they gave him. But what Saverian learned is that no matter what they promised the prince, the archon's enmity for humankind is so deep-rooted that trusting the Danae in any matter whatsoever *increases* our peril."

As I laid out these truths, I saw no hope for Osriel or Stearc. Even if the thane had endured Sila Diaglou's torments thus far, in the moment the priestess paraded her prisoners before Bayard, the game would be up and Osriel would die. It was only a matter of time.

"How long have we been gone?" I said. The confusions of Aeginea had destroyed my concept of time. Were we but a day or two from the solstice, I could see no course but to hide Elene and Victor and whatever monks we could salvage from Gillarine. Unbreached, the lighthouse might survive. But if those who could read the books and work the tools fell to Sila Diaglou's holocaust, what matter if the priestess took her time to find her way inside? On the other hand, had we a sevenday, something more might be done, though I had no idea what.

"Six days have passed since you were taken." Voushanti's harsh intrusion grated on my spirit. "His Highness was made captive that same night. I returned to Renna only two days since."

I spun to Saverian. "Only six! How could that be right?"

"Picus explained that it is not the days themselves, but the spending of human life that slows seven for one in Aeginea," she said, with only vague attention. "Though time itself is fluid there, as we saw, the years pass side by side in the two planes, the sun's passage marking the season's change at the same hour."

Saverian fell back into her own silence, distracted far beyond the matter of dirt and dishevelment and exhaustion. Her eyes flicked now and then toward Voushanti. But I accepted her word. Osriel had said something much the same.

Only six days . . . Perhaps we had a little time to work after all. "We've yet a fortnight until the solstice," I said. "When is the anniversary of Eodward's coronation? Has it passed? The prince was supposed to send to Bayard on that day to confirm their agreement."

"The anniversary is three days hence," said Brother Victor. "Mistress Saverian, did you say *Picus*?" She didn't look up.

"A small, fast force might be able to intercept the priestess between the monkhouse and Palinur," Voushanti broke in, his mailed bulk seeming to grow and fill the door. "One word and I can have the prince's elite guard riding."

"You will do nothing without my leave, Mardane," said Elene harshly. "Renna is the gateway to Evanore. I'll not leave it defenseless. As Prince Osriel's appointed castellan, I command you stay here until Thane Boedec and Thanea Zurina arrive."

"You cannot travel, Mardane," said Saverian. "You know it."

Voushanti folded his massive arms across his chest and looked away. I blinked, rubbed my own arms, and reached for better control of my wayward senses, for it seemed, just for a moment, that the edges of his flesh rippled like the surface of a wheat field. Though none acknowledged her comment, everyone looked as if a foul odor had wafted through the chamber.

"Sila Diaglou has several days' head start and can call up remounts and reinforcements throughout Ardra," I said, impatient with their secrets. "She's likely back at Fortress Torvo already. We'll have to take the prince from her there."

My vow to preserve the lighthouse demanded Osriel's rescue, no matter my grievances with him. And my vow to Jullian demanded my participation, for I could rely on no one else to protect him.

Brother Victor tapped his walking stick on the floor idly. "We would need to be sure Osriel and Stearc are inside the fortress. We've heard that Palinur is in confusion. Perhaps we could send in a small party, shielded with enchantment. Strike quickly."

Elene's head popped up. "*You* could locate them, right, Valen? Your magic . . ."

"Of course . . . yes." I knew Jullian and Osriel well enough that I could locate them if I had a clue where to start.

Yet a direct assault on their prison was out of the question; the ancient fortress where Luviar had bled out his life sat in the heart of Palinur. And negotiations of any kind could allow Sila Diaglou to discover the prize that lay in her hand. Our plan must use stealth. Something unexpected . . .

"As for getting inside the fortress . . ." A fearful, horrid idea began to take shape in my head. "There's a possibility I could do that, as well. Max has negotiated this solstice bargain between Bayard and Sila. If I were to go to Max . . . find out the terms agreed to . . . make sure they've no inkling of the prince's situation, I could likely get inside." As long as the priestess still wanted me. Getting four of us out would be another problem, unless my Danae skills could suffice.

Saverian threw off her blanket abruptly and kicked her hearth stool aside. "Your health is unstable, Valen. Someone should go with you."

"No choice," I said, shaking my head. "I can get to Max. But without a lot of awkward explanations, none of you would be admitted into the place I'll have to meet him. Once we've spoken, I'll return here, and we'll decide how to proceed. Unless someone has a better idea?"

I expected at least Voushanti to argue, but he merely stared at me, his hand caressing his battered sword hilt.

Elene looked bewildered. "But your brother is in Palinur with Bayard! That's weeks of traveling! We can't afford—"

"Our sorcerer has acquired new skills, lady," said the physician.

Brother Victor glanced between Saverian and me. "What's happened to you, Brother Valen? There's something very different about you tonight."

"Perhaps Saverian could tell you some of it tomorrow, Brother. Just now . . ." Somehow deciding a course of action had released my weariness to settle on my shoulders like the gods' yoke. And I would need all the wits I could muster where I was going. "I don't know about the ladies, but I can't promise one more sensible word until I find a bed. Mardane, if you could . . ."

"Excuse me, good Saverian," said Brother Victor, insistently, "did you say *Picus*?"

Voushanti, with as much curiosity as I had ever seen on his scarred visage, motioned me toward a side passage and a stair. When he showed me a small tower chamber, I almost wept at the sight of the plump pillows and folded blankets piled on a bed. Dané or not, world's end or not, walls or not, I had to sleep. "Four hours or morning, Mardane, whichever comes later."

Voushanti jerked his head and left. I drifted off still piecing together the puzzle of the Canon, the Danae, the Harrowers, the world's end—why had I not asked Kol about the damnable weather?

The ancient wall embedded in crumbling earth . . . pebbles and mud washed down to the road at its base, crusted and frozen in this early morning. A gentle rightward curve . . . dawn smells of roasting meat, of baking bread, of damp earth . . . And around the next corner the sound of dribbling water—here melting ice dripping into the cistern, there the font that never froze or dried. Scrawny trees grew sidewise from the bank, branches heavy with snow drooping over the road . . . in my face . . . tickling, scratching, freezing . . . the smell of burning from the lower city . . .

I walked around the corner, and in less time than it took to think it, the narrow alley that squeezed between Renna's kitchens and an ancient fortification built into an Evanori mountainside led me straight into the narrow lane in Palinur, more than two hundred quellae distant. The stare of an Evanori guardsman, flummoxed at the sight of an oddly naked man in the kitchen alley, now came from a ragged woman using water from the Aingerou's Font to wash vomit off her boy child.

The boy pointed at me and cried out weakly, "Mama, look! He's on fire . . . an angel . . ."

"Not so!" I whispered, embarrassed. "Sorry! Shhh!" But the lad's thready cry bounced through the lane like a child's ball, from one hushed voice to the next, for a beggars' city jammed the lane that ought to have been deserted.

In the past, this favored quarter of Palinur had escaped the untidy truths of hard living. Evidently that was no longer the case. A few small fires smoldered here and there among makeshift tents and crude lean-tos, built from branches cut from the overhanging trees. Fortunately most of the crowd still slept.

I jogged down the crowded roadway, jumping over pools of filth, bundled possessions, and sprawled bodies, then dived over the low wall into a crusted snowbank and scrambled well away from the lane. Thanks to half a night's rest and enough roast venison and jam tarts to breakfast a legion of halfbreed Danae, the cold did not bother me. All the same, best not dawdle. Fine houses, like those around here, would have pureblood guards and magical wards. Staying hidden in the straggling shrubbery, I donned my silk and satin finery.

Elene had somehow managed to get my pureblood cloak and mask cleaned by the time Voushanti woke me that morning. She had brought them herself, along with her thanks for my venture. "We all knew you were extraordinary, Valen, even when you were playing monk," she'd said, touching the gards on my hand. When I inquired about her health, her courage came near breaking. "He doesn't know," she'd whispered, crossing her arms on her breast. "He could die this very day, not knowing of his child."

I'd had little comfort to offer. The remembrance of her grief and the weight of her head on my chest ached like old wounds, as I slipped on my mask, hopped over the wall, and hurried up the lane. A cloud of yellow smoke and frost haze masked the lower city.

I had not expected ever to walk this particular lane again. But a pureblood head of family had the authority to summon each of his children to the family home without specifying a reason. If I worked matters right with Claudio de Cartamandua, he would arrange my meeting with Max.

"Best run, pureblood," snarled a woman who was skinning what appeared to be a cat. "Orange-heads drove out a number of your kind just yesterday. We'll see purebloods plowin' come spring. Your pretty fur cloaks'll ne'er keep ye warm in the mud."

A few others joined her taunts. For once I was happy to see armed warriors in Registry black and red patrolling the upper end of the lane. They rousted a few sleepers who had wandered too close, but did not challenge me as I strode past them to the iron gate with the bronze gryphon.

How truth can change everything. Unlike the last time Serena Fortuna had brought me to these gates, my gut did not seethe with fear and loathing, nor did my skin blanch at unwelcome memories. None of the past had been my fault. Claudio and Josefina de Cartamandua-Celestine were not my parents. As I touched the lock and assembled my favorite spell, it occurred to me for the first time that Claudio, not Max, was my brother—and only half a one at that. Laughing, I fed magic into my spell, and the familiar lock shattered in a fizz of gold sparks and twisted bronze. Then I yanked the bellpull to wake them up and walked in.

Chapter 19

F ive heavily armed guards met me in the entry court, blocking the gap between the iron lampposts and the lily-shaped brazier dedicated to Deunor Lightbringer. Their challenge died upon their lips as I removed my mask. They could not fail to recognize me or recall the dread prince who owned my contract.

"Announce me to Eqastré Cartamandua-Celestine," I said with true Aurellian arrogance, while gloating childishly inside at naming my erstwhile parent as an equal. Truly this pureblood lunacy brought out the worst in me.

I did not wait for their return. Rather I strolled into the columned reception room, where my family had sold me to Prince Osriel. Naught had changed there, from the richly colored floor mosaics that displayed the order of the planets to the marble statuary, gilt caskets, tapestries, and urns. For generations, pureblood families had profited from Navronne's hunger for sorcery. My family had been particularly successful at it until I'd come along.

". . . impossible! Where is this visitor?" Claudio strode into the room in the company of the guards, as well as two gentleman attendants of exceptionally sturdy physique. He halted when he caught sight of me. "Magrog's teeth!"

"Patronn." Maintaining protocol, I sank to one knee and touched my forehead with my gloved fingertips. His servants were present, and I was not yet ready to proclaim my true heritage. Proof of one member's tainted blood would call into question the lineal purity of every member of the family. I could ruin this house by removing one of my gloves.

For fifteen years this stocky, black-haired man adorned in red and green velvets and a fox-lined pelisse had been the bane of my life, unrelenting in his despite, deliberate in his cruelty. For twelve years more, I had struggled to survive in alleyways and battlefields, choosing poverty, abasement, and danger in preference to his sovereignty and the life it prescribed. Today, as I rose from my brief genuflection, I looked Claudio de Cartamandua-Celestine in the eye and smiled.

His glare of malice shifted to uncertainty. His eyes narrowed, and his powerful fists began to quiver. "Insolent . . ."

Protocol forbade him to touch me. My contract permitted only Osriel to do that. I longed to tell Claudio I knew his dirty secrets, but what I needed today was for him to summon Max. In no wise could I expect willing cooperation, and it was not yet time for threats, which meant I had to proceed very carefully.

"Please do not trouble yourself with the conventions of refreshment or pleasantries, Patronn. I am here strictly on business, and must make speedy work of it. My royal master bids me—" I twirled a finger to indicate his retinue. "Ah, I really must present his request in private."

Though he would clearly prefer to strangle me, Claudio motioned his attendants to the corners where they could not hear us, and then seated himself in a delicate armchair. He left me the choice to remain standing, drag another chair to his side, or sit on the floor—any one of which would be demeaning to a pureblood. As he intended. He was a bit discomfited when I chose to perch on a marble table a few steps away. My position only emphasized the difference in our height.

"You look well, Valen," he said. "Does submission to the Bastard suit you, then?" Curiosity poked through his studied calm like a kitten's sharp claws through silk.

"My master believes in strict discipline, as you warned me." I folded my gloved hands in my lap. "And he has schooled me quickly in his requirements. Fortunately, he is pleased with my talents. So much so that he is interested in pursuing a contract with another of our family. In short, he desires a cartographer to map the new bounds of his kingdom. My difficulties with written language preclude such service, of course. But what prince would consider other than a Cartamandua to make him maps?"

"His *kingdom*? You're saying Osriel the Bastard intends to claim the throne?" His dark eyes raked my face, hunting signs of the mockery and lies that had passed my lips far more often than serious discourse.

But thanks to this man, I was well practiced in deceit. I only smiled again and shrugged. "He has his plans. As you might imagine, I tried to divert his attention to other mapmakers, but he would have none. He bids me insist, and I do *not* disobey. I am to remind you that Evanore's gold could ensure our family's fortunes for decades to come."

My father sprang from his seat, walked away a few steps, then spun to face me, calculating. "You cannot be serious."

"I told him it must be Max or Phoebia, as Nilla and Thalassa have taken the Celestine bent instead of yours. Janus, of course, is out of the question. And you . . . well, you are head of family and could not possibly leave Palinur. My master will not be denied, Patronn."

There passed a long silence. He chewed on his lip and did not take his eyes from me. I strove to remain neutral in expression.

He lowered his brows, pursed his lips, and glanced at me sidewise. "Phoebia has decent skills. Max's are better, if he would only get off his horse and use them, but he is contracted to Prince Bayard."

I swallowed my disgust at his connivance. "I need to speak with each of them, of course, to form a better estimate of their experience with such work and their degree of willingness to cooperate with a demanding master. Once my lord has my report, he will send Mardane Voushanti to negotiate terms. He doesn't quite trust me to do that as yet."

Yes, that last point made him relax a bit. That any master would trust *me* was the most difficult of all these matters for him to believe.

"Phoebia is easily available," he said, "and Max . . . fortunately he is in the city just now. I can send an official summons as head of family, which requires no explanation to his master." He rubbed his chin in a mockery of indecision. "But, of course, to release him from Prince Bayard's contract . . . that would cost a great deal of money."

Somewhere in our family veins must run a river of lies. Had Max not complained to me of how our family's contract value had waned due to my rebellion and long disappearance, I would have believed his last concern.

"Understood," I said. "Now, I shall require privacy for the interviews. My master would not wish his business to become public prematurely. I've certainly no fear of anyone in the family speaking out of turn, but servants . . ." I shrugged again. "And you have frequently expressed your disinterest in anything from *my* lips. Unless that has changed?"

I thought his teeth might grind to powder. Mighty is the power of fear and gold to a pureblood. But Claudio's pride and hatred won out. He spread his arms. "Wherever you like."

Despicable gatzé! What kind of man would even consider pledging his young daughter to a master of Osriel's foul repute—a daughter who had amassed no history of violence or disobedience as I had? Even Max, though arrogant beyond bearing, had been the most dutiful of sons, deserving no such fate.

As I waited for Claudio to summon my young sister, I tried to think what to say to her. Bringing Max to the neutral ground of our family home, out of his master's hearing, had seemed a more reasonable course than tracking him down myself in war-ravaged Palinur. I had foolishly assumed Bia's father would wish to shield her from a monster, making this bit of playacting unnecessary. On the other hand, I wished again that I had some excuse for speaking with Thalassa, but this lie was elaborate enough without working Samele's high priestess into it.

Footsteps hurried through the tiled passages of the family wing. As I stood, the walls of the room wavered and bulged. I closed my eyes for a moment, breathed deep, and blessed the potion Saverian had offered me that morning to tame my nausea at sitting indoors. The insidious panic of collapsing walls, I had to manage for myself. The symptoms seemed much worse since taking on my Danae gards. Or perhaps it was only my approaching birthday.

"*Serena pauli*," I said, offering a shallow bow to the young woman who appeared at the door, her arm firmly in Claudio's grip. I motioned a servant to bring her a chair, and then waited as Claudio dismissed the servants and guardsmen. When he saw I was not going to begin until he'd followed them, the glowering Claudio whirled and withdrew.

My younger sister Phoebia, a plainer, less womanly version of her mother and elder sister, wore her heavy black hair wound about her head in tight braids like a warrior's helm and resentment about her shoulders like a mantle. She had been so young when I left home, I did not know her well enough to read beyond her sullen facade. The only time I'd seen her since my recapture, she'd spat on me.

"Our conversation will be private, Bia," I said, drawing my chair close so we would not be overheard. "Patronn told you why I've been sent here?"

She jerked her head in acknowledgment. Her knuckles were bloodless, and a thin film of sweat sheened her copper-colored skin.

"You've naught to fear from either me or my master," I said. "He is hard, and a man of fearsome mystery, but fair to his servants who carry out their duties . . ." We spoke for more than an hour of the tasks she performed for the family—coloring Claudio's maps, inking lists of place names and distances, using her Cartamandua bent to smooth curves and add in details he thought too unimportant for his particular attention. She did not travel, did not publish maps of her own, and had attracted neither a contract nor an offer of marriage. She blamed her sorry lot on me. I could not deny the responsibility. Despite my rehabilitation by the pureblood Registry, my years as a *recondeur* had made alliance with our family a risk for other purebloods. Petronilla's beauty had caught Bia's twin a lucky match, and Max and Thalassa had the talent and determination to gain them favored, if not excessively profitable, contracts. Which left Phoebia alone with a despicable father and a drunken mother.

Though she did not warm as we spoke, her fists unclenched. In the end, I felt sorry that I had no contract to offer her. When I heard the bustle of an arrival from the front of the house, I stood and, to her astonishment, kissed her hand. "I doubt my master will take you on this time, *serena pauli*. Right now he needs particular skills. But if this succession is settled favorably, he will have need of many services."

She touched her fingers to her forehead, then wriggled those I had kissed, examining them as if half expecting they might break out in a rash. "The city . . . out there . . . is very bad, is it not?"

"Yes."

"I've heard that Harrowers burn books, so I would guess that they'll have no use for maps. And they despise purebloods."

"All true."

She looked up at me, her dark eyes troubled. "What should I do, Valen? Matronn warns of this danger—a dark veil, she calls it—that is coming down on Navronne. She sees purebloods sent into the countryside to dig and plant . . . to labor in the fields like villeins. Patronn refuses to listen. He calls me stupid to worry."

I shivered. Josefina de Cartamandua-Celestine's divinations invariably made me shiver.

"You are *not* stupid to worry," I said, touching Bia's shoulders, wishing I could do more for her. "Go to Thalassa. Patronn can't stop you going to temple. Temples are little safer than anywhere else, as it happens, but Lassa understands what's happening in the world as well as anyone. She'll see to you."

Bia didn't question how I knew all this. I was no diviner. But she ducked her head and hurried out of the room a great deal livelier than she'd come. Then Max strode through the doorway, leather and steel gleaming from beneath his cloak, and I could think no more of frightened little sisters.

"What in the name of the blistering bawds do you think you're doing?" he said through clenched teeth, as he whipped off his mask. "If one word leaks out linking Bayard and Osriel, this little game is up. Are you as mad as your prince, or is this *his* imbecilic idea?"

"Sit down and speak normally," I said, as I bowed and touched my forehead. "Patronn believes I'm here to discuss a possible contract between you and Prince Osriel, and we would not wish him to learn differently. Hear me out, and all will become clear."

Though seething, he greeted me properly and lowered his compact bulk into the chair. "We are involved in no alleyway scrap, Valen. The witch has left Grav Hurd, her favorite ax man, here in the city. He's pushing Prince Bayard to close the temples and alehouses and ship any man, woman, or child convicted of crimes into the countryside where they can 'heed the voice of the Gehoum.' He threatens to bring down the Registry tower. We are drowning in madmen."

"I understand," I said, leaning back in my chair as if settling in for a long interview. "Prince Osriel has sent me to hear the terms of the solstice bargain you've worked out with her."

He leaned back, twisting the corner of his thick mustache where it tangled in his well-trimmed beard. The beard was Max's only true rebellion of his one-and-thirty years. Claudio hated it. "Why now?" he demanded. "It was your master who chose to confirm the agreement on Coronation Day."

I'd never seen Max so serious. His private face had always been a snigger, and he met every circumstance by boasting of some way to turn it to his advantage. Only a few short weeks ago, he had twiddled magical dust from his fingers and joked how sorcerers would be exempt from any harsh future by virtue of the awe in which we were held. Yet, in a way, his sobriety might make my task easier. I quickly rethought my approach.

"Prince Osriel is a hard master, Max, and more clever than you can imagine. He will do *anything* to accomplish his purposes. He's told me I need to prepare—" I leaned forward and dropped my voice even lower. "Great gods, Max, tell me that you've talked the priestess out of having me."

His black eyes sharpened. "Why would you care? I assumed from all he said that this bargain was but a feint as long as we got Sila into Evanore by the solstice."

"It is and it isn't. He wants her focused on the solstice and will do whatever is needed to convince her that she's won. Indeed that *is* the night that will prove who holds power in Navronne. But he also wishes—" I stopped. "Tell me the bargain, Max."

"One honest answer first. Did Osriel send you to me? Here?" He watched me unblinking, his every sinew like stretched wire.

I shook my head and felt him relax.

"All right, then. You'll be hearing the terms soon enough." He rested his thick forearms on his spread thighs and clasped his hands loosely. He was already gaining confidence . . . recognizing advantage to be won. "I met twice with this Grav Hurd—a smart devil, tough as a spire nut—and once with the priestess herself, to wring out the final changes. I tell you, Valen, these people make Patronn seem as charming as a courtesan. But we came to agreement, signed and sealed. It states that as of midnight on the winter solstice Sila Diaglou will reign sovereign in Evanore, subject only to Navronne's crown. She will administer Evanore's gold, but will pay the crown a twice-yearly tithe of no less than ten thousand solae—and don't ask me who will collect it. Prince Bayard will not release Prince Perryn into her custody, but agrees to parade him in chains through the streets of Palinur on the first day of the new year and allow the priestess to conduct a rite of purification for him. Perryn's life will *not* be forfeit—though I would not stand in his boots that day for all of Evanore's gold. As for the lighthouse . . . she dropped the demand for its location, indicating that it was no longer of immediate concern. But you, little brother . . ." He paused for a long moment in this impressive recital, gazing at his boots and shaking his head, near smiling when he raised his head and took up again. "On your contract she would budge not one quat. And no matter how I strutted or wheedled, the witch would not tell me why. So . . . Prince Bayard agreed that you are to be turned over to her on the solstice."

I should have been happy to hear this. My hope to get near Osriel and Stearc and Jullian relied on Sila Diaglou's intent to have me. It fit with my odd, unlikely belief that my personal mystery was fundamentally entangled with Navronne's doom. But all I could feel was hollow and clammy . . . the dread of being locked in a tomb while living . . . the dread of facing Judgment Night and seeing the One God point to the downward path. What did a priestess who found joy in bleeding miscreants and innocents want with me? I just had to believe she didn't want me dead.

I mustered a voice. "What of my master? What do they propose to do about him as they apportion his demesne?"

"Ah, yes . . ." He tapped his fingertips together for a moment, then shrugged. "If the priestess captures him on the night of the solstice, she may keep him, but he will neither be publicly punished nor publicly displayed. He will disappear."

"And if he were to end up in Prince Bayard's custody?"

Max shrugged and grinned. "Well, for the purposes of the agreement, we implied the result would be the same . . . Osriel would be neither seen nor heard from again . . . which *could,* of course, mean private retirement or exile. But, of course, Bayard believes that our joined might will defeat the witch and that Prince Osriel will come to an equitable and honorable agreement with his elder brother as to Navronne's ruling."

"Yes. That is certainly the intent." Though, after Osriel's betrayal in Aeginea, I had no more certainty of his true intent than I did of Bayard's.

Max leaned close again and his smile vanished. "Now, why are you and I discussing what must be laid out again three days hence for your master's messenger?"

"He desires for her to have me before solstice night, Max. She has a Karish monk in her party."

"Her pet monk . . . yes, I saw him. Smug kind of fellow, always whispering in her ear. I never trust a man who shaves off all his hair."

"That's him—Gildas. The monk owns some secret . . . gods, I don't know what." I rubbed my head and kneaded my neck. The wavering walls left me dizzy and sweating, like a prisoner awaiting the hangman. Did I appear as ill as I felt, Max would certainly believe me frightened—as I hoped for him to do. "So Osriel is sending me to Bayard. He's going to let you turn me over to the priestess as a pledge of good faith, as if you'd caught me by good fortune. And then . . . he's commanded me to kill Gildas. I've no qualms about that. We've no love between us, Gildas and I. That he serves the priestess is reason enough to condemn him. But my master's given me no way out. Just says that he'll *see to it* as he's no intention of forfeiting my contract. He says that all will be sorted out on the solstice. Max, I've seen what Sila Diaglou does to those who displease her. But if I disobey the Bastard . . ."

He settled back in his chair, tilting his head, saying nothing. It took no Danae senses to feel his mind racing.

I stood up abruptly. "All right, then. Thank you for sharing the information with me, *ancieno.* I'll figure out something." I hurried toward the entry court door, listening . . .

"Wait!"

Closing my eyes, I promised Serena Fortuna a grand libation. I swung around slowly.

Max waved me back to my chair, and when I was seated, leaned forward as if to hold me there with his authority. "I know exactly what solution you'll 'figure out,' little brother—the same as always. But running away will not save you this time. Despite Grav Hurd's best efforts to drive all purebloods out of the city, the Registry is like to be the only power that survives this war—and once they find you again, they'll bury you so deep, you'll remember this house as heaven and beg for Patronn's strap in preference to their gentle hands." He smoothed and straightened the front of my pourpoint as if he were a caring elder brother. "And, of course, you would destroy the family along the way, not to mention laying waste all this delicate negotiating—for which I have pledged every minim of my own future."

No matter that I had expected this response from him—no matter that I had come here rejoicing that I no longer accounted these people the whole of my kin—I could not stifle the rage his calculation roused in me. I let him see it. "And why would I be willing to suffer either Sila Diaglou's fury or Osriel the Bastard's to preserve this misbegotten family or this misbegotten kingdom?"

"Hold, little brother. I am not suggesting you sit back and accept your dismal lot." He smiled in the very same superior manner he claimed to detest in Gildas. "I owe you a debt. You gave me this chance for advancement when you stood up for my honor in front of your prince and mine. Even you know the importance of honor and trust to those of us who actually believe in pureblood contracts. So perhaps you and I can come to an accommodation . . . help each other . . ."

"Max will see no advantage to warning Gildas of my murderous intent. He'd much rather have Gildas's secrets." I dug into the platter of roast pork under Saverian's watchful eye. The two of us sat in the courtyard at Renna Syne two hours after my return from Palinur. "I'm not leaving Max personally at risk. He won't even know I was actually after Jullian, Stearc, and the prince until we're safely back here. All Sila's anger and Bayard's will fall on me and through me to Osriel. Bayard is conspiring against the priestess already, and I've hopes our prince will forgive me for saving his neck."

"But you trust Max enough that this weapon he promises to supply is your only sure defense and this escape route he gave you is your only way out?" Saverian's skepticism could have eroded Renna's cliffs, so it did no good at all for my fragile confidence.

"In the best case, I won't need to rely on either one. I've size, I've magic, and I've surprise to wield. Surely something in Fortress Torvo will remind me enough of something here that I can shift the four of us straight back here. And yes, before you ask again, I'll not let Max turn me over until I've made sure the prisoners are actually *in* the fortress."

The physician poked at the blaze in the fire pit. The serving man had thought she was mad to have wood hauled into the sunny court-yard of the window house. He was not present to note the greater oddity when I stripped off my cloak, tunic, and shirt as I ate, basking in the frigid air as if it were a river of mead, while Saverian huddled next to her blaze. Only a few hours remained until sundown, when Voushanti was to deliver me to Prince Bayard. Every time I thought of it, my gut tied itself in knots and my head got woozy.

"I won't argue that we've much choice in the matter," said the physician, "but your plan is madness. You've no idea what Sila Dia-glou thinks to do with you. Do you actually believe she'll allow you to roam free and abscond with her prisoners?"

"In the best case, I'll have the three of them out before she can get over the surprise. In the worst case, well . . ." The worst cases were innumerable, and I couldn't bear thinking about them. We'd no time to plan more intricate ploys. ". . . I'll just have to lie a bit more. It's still my finest talent."

I had exercised that skill in plenty since I'd returned from Palinur, pulled on the damp clothes I'd stashed behind a water cask in Renna's back alley, and rousted my fellow conspirators from their afternoon's business. I had told Elene I had no reason to fear Sila Diaglou's custody, as the priestess had made clear she wanted me alive. I had promised Brother Victor that no amount of intelligence and clever deceit could give Gildas the power to match a half-Danae half sorcerer. I'd assured all of them that my new skills could cer-tainly get me and the prisoners out of Sila Diaglou's house and back here in good order. I had even asked Elene to show me Renna's dun-geons so I could impress their complete image—the stink produced by the three drunkard prisoners, the chill, the taste and smell of iron and damp and enclosing walls—firmly on my mind. I had insisted that she needn't worry about my pallor as I followed her through those dank passages, and when we'd come out into the wintry sun-light, I distracted them all from my sick fear and sketchy plan by showing them the fronds of sea grass that marked my hand with pale blue and silver light.

Saverian knew better. I appreciated that she didn't contradict me until we were alone. While Elene, Brother Victor, and Voushanti pre-pared a letter in Osriel's name, confirming the solstice plan and offering me to Bayard as a "gift of good faith" to hand over to Sila Diaglou and close their bargain, the two of us had hiked over to Renna Syne. Along with some of the wardrobe Osriel had provided me, Saverian had supplied food, medicine, and her own astringent honesty.

"This Gildas will suspect you're there to take the boy and the others. He knows about your problem with nivat. That should worry you. One wrong word from Max and he'll pounce."

It *did* worry me. And then there was the matter of being staked bound and bleeding over some Danae sianou. Alone and dying slowly . . . great gods, what end could be worse than that? Especially when all assurance about what might come after my death had been upended. Saverian's marrow-deep scrutiny had surely uncovered this fear, too.

"Yes. Yes. And yes," I said. "It is a demented plan. A thousand things can go wrong. But from the beginning Sila has said she wants my *contract*, not just me. She has some use for me, Saverian. She's not going to kill me or let Gildas do it. And if she has some use for me, then I have leverage. I won't be shut up in a box. As for the nivat . . . I'll be wary. At the first whiff, I'll shut down my sense of smell—Kol taught me how to do that. Yes, I could be horribly wrong about all this, and if you think I am terrified, that's not even the half of it. Gods, I'm no strategist. This is all I can think to do."

I stuffed down more food, not knowing when I might get to eat again. I had to stay warm. I had to stay sensible. Saverian was too good at making me think, however uncomfortable. It was certainly possible that my connection with Osriel might lead Gildas to suspect that Osriel and Gram were the same man. In that case, the game would be up before it had even begun.

"You should get the others to prepare for the worst," I said. "They respect you, listen to you. They know about strategy and tactics and all those things I've no head for. They must know some way to call in Osriel's warlords. So use it and persuade the lords to defend Caedmon's Bridge on the solstice. Stash Gillarine's monks in the highest mountains of Evanore."

"What if you're wrong about bigger things, Valen?" said the physician softly. "What if your importance to the Danae is more critical than saving Osriel or Jullian or this lighthouse? Your mother had some plan for you."

That argument, of course, I had no possible way to rebut, so I tried to explain the course that spirit and instinct had chosen for me. "Jullian is my friend and my sworn responsibility. Stearc is an honorable man and beloved of my friends. Though Osriel betrayed me, though he terrifies me, he is my lord and rightful king. He wants to do right for Navronne, even beyond his own life and honor and future—I can see that much. My mother told no one her plan, so I can't see what would be so important that I must let my friends and my king die. And no one else has the skills to save them. I might. So, physician, steer me a better course."

"Kill Voushanti."

"Spirits of night!" I said, near choking. I dropped my eating knife into the platter as if it had given her the macabre idea. Had I not already closed down the rattling abundance of my senses, I would have been sure I had misheard. "Why, in the name of the Mother—?"

"He is already dead. Has been for over ten years. And if no one steps forward by tomorrow night, he'll die again, this time with no coming back. To continue breathing he must be blood-bound to another living person. Osriel and Stearc are not available. Elene will have naught to do with the business. The monk is too weak. I can't do it myself if I'm going to work the spell, not that *I'm* interested in having so close an attachment to him, either. He is brutish and bull-headed, frightens most of my patients, and has no respect for women, especially those who aspire to studies. I could perhaps persuade Philo or Melkire to the task—they respect him and are not so afraid as everyone else—but Osriel has given me no leave to tell anyone else of this."

I worked to take in so much information. "But you're telling *me*."

"I believe the prince would trust you with the knowledge. In the days ahead, you might need someone who is bound to your will and devoted to your service . . . at least until Osriel can take on the burden again. It won't improve your crazy plan, but it might give you and Riel a better chance of surviving it."

She spoke as seriously and reasonably as Brother Sebastian explaining the structure of virtue. But the little lines atop the bridge of her nose had deepened to little ravines. Slowly I wiped my greasy mouth on my shirttail, startled as always to see the silvery gards gleaming from my hand. I swallowed. "Are you planning to explain more or do you expect me just to agree to such a mystery at your suggestion? Which I won't."

She shoved the plate of meat back toward me and refilled my cup with Evanori ale that tasted as if it had been made from discarded boots. "Keep eating. You don't have much time, and if we're to do this, we'll need to do it soon."

I just looked at her with the kind of expression such a ridiculous suggestion deserved.

She sighed and rested the ale pitcher in her lap. "Voushanti was the third son of a minor Evanori family, a veteran, competent warrior. When King Eodward moved his mistress to Renna to get her away from your hateful purebloods, he sent Voushanti along as her bodyguard. Voushanti was arrogant and silent and not particularly happy at being shoved off to watch over a woman. Everyone here was a bit afraid of him. And then Lirene died."

The physician took on her most argumentative expression, but her eyes were focused on the past and not on me.

"You have to understand how Osriel adored his mother. She cared for him through so much pain and sickness, sang to him, bathed him, held him through long, dreadful nights. He was only seven when a sudden fever took her. He truly believed he would die without her. Evanori have stories . . . well, all warrior people have stories, I'm sure, about heroes that live beyond death. On the day of Lirene's funeral rites, Riel told me that his magic was going to bring her back. Voushanti heard him say it, and called Osriel a blasphemer to so question the laws of the gods and insult the memory of true warriors. Osriel hated Voushanti from that day."

"He planned to bring his mother back from the dead," I said numbly.

"Osriel read everything he could find about Aurellian sorcery, and he questioned my mother and his father's other purebloods until their ears blistered. He studied and followed my mother about as she worked with the sick. She said Riel could have been a healer himself were he not a king's bastard, required to study politics and war. Everyone believed Osriel sought a cure for saccheria, but I knew what he was looking for. At twelve, when his father took him to Ardra for the first time, he brought back a wagonload of Aurellian books, and in an old book of herb spells, he found the key."

Saverian's long, capable fingers were tangled in a knot, pressed to her chin, and she kept her eyes averted as people do when they tell stories they believe they should not.

"At fifteen, he showed me how he could smother a frog and set it breathing again. A few months later, he claimed to have touched the living soul of a villein who had been kicked by a horse, though the man's soul escaped him before he could catch it. By this time he had accepted that his mother was gone, but he could not stop." She paused, pressing her lips together.

"And Voushanti?" I said, urging her on.

"From the day Lirene died, wherever Osriel walked, sat, studied, or slept, Voushanti stood by. Riel hated it. He called the saccheria his prison, and Voushanti his warder. When he was small, he cast magical curses at Voushanti—little flaming, stinging things—and his father chastised him sorely for it. By the time he turned sixteen, he merely lived as if Voushanti did not exist.

"One winter afternoon, Osriel was sitting in the old library of this house, studying. He was feverish again, his joints so swollen that any movement was excruciating. He was practicing fire work, smothering the hearth fire and starting it up again with pure magic. Voushanti warned him repeatedly to stop, for the steward had reported the library chimney clogged. Voushanti stood directly in front of the hearth . . ."

I needed no more words to see what happened—a frustrated, angry, pain-racked youth flaunting his talent before his jailer, casting a great flaming spell toward the hearth.

Saverian stopped and drank from her ale cup. I was so caught up in the story, my own remained untouched. "Voushanti saved him from the fire," I said.

Saverian drained her cup. "The place burned like dry wheat. You can still see the ruin out behind the west wing. Voushanti took the full brunt of Osriel's fireburst and the eruption of the chimney, yet he carried Osriel out, completely shielding him from the flames. No one could have survived such injuries as the mardane bore. My mother pronounced him dead within the hour."

Like the tides of Evaldamon, cold dread swept over me again. "But Osriel . . ."

"He demanded servants carry the body into his private study. Almost a full day later, Riel summoned my mother to tend Voushanti's burns. Lungs, heart, all his organs were functioning, though his burns remained savage. Voushanti lived again."

"You say this has happened more than once . . . his dying . . ."

"Three that I know of. One that I saw, when Riel was too sick to complete the spell and called me in to help. Severe wounds can stop Voushanti's heart, but he can be brought back if the enchantment is renewed immediately. Time can stop his heart if the enchantment is not renewed at least once in a sevenday. But the one whose blood seals the enchantment on the mardane's lips is bound to him, able to command Voushanti to his service. Unless you force him elsewhere, Voushanti will not leave your side. He will sense your presence, know when you're in trouble, and he fights like a man who has nothing to lose. He could make the difference between your venture's success and failure."

"What of his soul?"

"I don't believe in souls."

"What does the prince say?"

She folded her arms tight across her breast and hardened her mouth as if expecting me to assault her. "He says that Voushanti's soul and body are fused, and that when his body dies at last—truly and forever—his soul will die with it. Osriel bears some dreadful guilt over the whole thing, which is ridiculous. The magic is truly remarkable."

I would have given my teeth to have more time to consider what Saverian had told me, for in her story of Osriel's bold sorcery lay the truth about dead men's eyes and votive vessels sealed with blood and what Osriel intended to do with them. I had assumed he planned some great enchantment, built with the substance and energies he had stolen from dying men. But now . . . It came to me that the Bastard thought to ensorcel himself an army.

Chapter 20

"Who gave you leave to speak of these matters?" The red centers of Voushanti's dark eyes gleamed with fury. "The prince will have you flogged."

Saverian stepped closer to my side, as if together we could withstand his wrath. I wished I was far from Saverian's meticulously ordered study.

"The prince commanded me to do what was necessary to give you a full span of life, Mardane," said Saverian. "You owe him your obedience, as I do."

"Him. Not you. Not this fey sorcerer."

"Then do as he would command you. If you have another partner in mind, perhaps Magnus could fetch him."

Cream-colored light streamed from a lamp of the magical variety that lit Renna Syne, illuminating shelf upon shelf filled with books, beakers, bottles, and jars. Two well-scrubbed tables laid out with brass implements, mortar and pestle, pans, and balances furnished one end of the room. A chair, side table, and footstool held the opposite end, with a variety of stools and benches in between. The physician had failed to mention the chamber's location in the bowels of Renna's fortress or its lack of windows. Evidently she disliked being bothered by household noise, outdoor views, or air as she worked.

When I had said I would consider doing as she suggested, Saverian had bustled me here immediately. "What of your scruples?" I'd asked her, as we traipsed across the dry hillside between Renna Syne and the fortress. "You once told me that 'no worthy physician could stand by and see a healthy body damaged.' "

"To cause death deliberately violates every principle of the healer's art," she had said. "And to keep a body alive by enchant-ment violates the good order of nature that stands before any god in my esteem. But if I refuse to perpetuate Osriel's ugly mistake, then I have destroyed Voushanti just as surely and far more permanently. He *will* die unless you and I do this." That was the point I could not argue.

Then we had arrived and Voushanti had been waiting for her. And before I could say yes or no, she had told Voushanti I would be his new partner in this macabre business. Since then he had been cir-cling the workroom like a trapped wolf.

Saverian continued to speak calmly. "It seems unlikely that the prince will return in time to perform this service for you himself. As you are accompanying Magnus to Palinur to effect our lord's rescue, it would be most inconvenient if you were to die in the midst of it. This seems a reasonable solution to your problem."

"*Reasonable?*" There ensued one of the most horrible sounds I had ever heard—a strident gargling bellow that might have emanated from one of the nearby dungeons. The accompanying jerk of Voushanti's shoulders and the spasm of emotion that crossed his scarred visage gave me the unlikely idea that he was laughing. "You cannot even tell me how this one's fey blood might affect the en-chantment. Would I had a tankard, physician, that I could raise it to your twisted notion of *reason.*"

Saverian, unfazed, pointed to a long low bench. Scuffed leather covered its thin padding. "I promise you will be no more dead using the sorcerer's blood than you will be without it. You've an appoint-ment in Palinur three hours hence, Mardane, which means you've little enough time for recovery. If we're to do this, we do it now."

Events swept past and over me like a flock of startled crows. Abandoning me at the door, where I held a drowning man's grip on a much too low lintel stone, Saverian dragged a stepstool to one of her shelves and retrieved a small enameled canister shaped like an angel. She set the canister on a knee-high table in company with a sil-ver lancet, a square stack of folded linen, and a bronze basin with an extended lip like that of a pitcher.

"Slitting your heart vein will be quickest, Lord Voushanti, though the blood loss will likely leave you weaker than you would prefer," she said. "But delivering Magnus to Prince Bayard should not entail a fight, and the journey . . . you will marvel at its ease and, in fact, de-cide that you have bound yourself to a fine racehorse. We'll hope he keeps his pace *reasonable* in deference to your recent demise."

Like dust motes floating on the light, her macabre humor failed to settle. Voushanti's pacing slowed. Perhaps he might refuse the enchantment . . . which seemed a vile and wicked hope.

Saverian paused in her preparations. "Do you wish a sleeping draught? I know Prince Osriel does not offer, but I could—"

"No!" None of his answers had approached the ferocity of this one.

Without further argument, the seething warrior removed his leather jupon, gray tunic, and wool shirt, exposing broad chest and shoulders mottled with ugly red burn scars, old battle wounds, and patches of black and gray hair. He laid his garments on Saverian's chair and reclined on the leather bench.

At Saverian's direction I moved to Voushanti's side. He averted his face, and neither twitched nor fidgeted.

With a flurry of brusque steps and clinking glass, Saverian added a few vials, tapers, and small dishes to her supplies. Then she doused the magical lamp and brought a lighted candle to her table. Drawing her stool beside mine, she thrust a stained but clean wadded sheet into my sweating hands. "Be ready with this," she said softly.

I could not think what she meant, but didn't ask. My eyes would not leave the wide flat handle of the lancet that lay snug in her hand.

"Mardane Voushanti, is it your will that I take you past the brink of unlife and work this magic to restore your breath and blood?"

He jerked his head in assent, but fixed his eyes on the far wall.

"*Speak* your will, or I'll have none of this," she snapped. "No man will say *I* chose this way."

Voushanti swiveled his head to glare redly at the both of us. "You've not bound me to this bench. Obey our master's will. Take this life and give it back."

He turned away again. Saverian probed his neck with two fingers and without hesitation jabbed her lancet in between.

Blood spewed from Voushanti's wound like the liquid fire Aurellians discharge from their warships to set their enemies ablaze. Only by fortunate reaction did I hold up the wadded linen to catch this monstrous volley. Voushanti jerked and gripped the edge of the bench, emitting only a grunt.

Saverian, her hands gloved in gore, snatched up one of her smaller folds of linen and held it to the surging flow, channeling it into the long lip of the tin basin, a river of red that threatened to overflow the vessel. The chamber fell silent, save for Voushanti's rapid, shallow breaths.

I rubbed my arms through the thin shirtsleeves, afraid to let myself feel anything. I had experienced a man's death once. Saverian must wear steel beneath her plain garb.

As the pulsing flow of blood dwindled, Voushanti's breath began to labor. The half of his face we could see was a morbid blue-white and sheened with sweat. His hands that had gripped the bench now lay flaccid on its cracked leather.

Saverian had me set the heavy basin aside while she wiped her hands clean. Then she turned the warrior's head to face us and slipped another square of folded linen under the wound to absorb the waning trickle of his life. His scarred face was slack, his stare dull, even as his chest strained and heaved to draw each breath.

I labored with him. The walls bulged and writhed around us. The flat iron stink of blood wakened reminders of battlefield nights, of wails and screams and dread visions. The physician dipped a finger into a small jar and dabbed a yellow ointment on Voushanti's eyelids, flooding the thickening air with the pungent perfume of ysomar that the Karish said would summon angels to carry the soul to heaven, and the Sinduri claimed would call the Ferryman to the earthly shore to transport the soul to the Kemen Sky Lord's feasting halls or Magrog's land of torment. But what if a man's soul was "fused to his body" and could not journey onward? What if a man had no soul?

I had stabbed Boreas for mercy, drowned a pack of Harrowers to save other lives, and slain Navronne's enemies for my king. None of these deaths rested easy in my mind, but at the least I had believed that those victims would be granted some existence beyond this life. Every god I knew promised a continuing for those who had a soul, so I'd never imagined I was sending them to endless nothing. But this . . . what was this we did here? A certain horror gripped my breath and bone. I could no longer sit still.

Grabbing Saverian's arm, I yanked her off her stool and dragged her away from the couch so Voushanti could not hear me. Scarlet cheeked, she wrestled to get free. "Are you mad?" she spat. "I need to watch him."

"Is there a chance this spell won't revive him?" I said, harsh and quiet. "Have you done it before . . . you yourself?"

"I've seen it done. I know what to do."

"But is there a chance? Could he not revive?" I shook her, unwilling to release her until I heard *yea* or *nay*.

"No spell is proof against failure," she said. "I'll do my best, which is better than most. Now let me go, lest his heart stop for too long, for then the magic *will* fail."

I let her go, and she hurried back to her work, examining the blood that dribbled slowly from Voushanti's neck. Briskly, she sprinkled herbs and powders from her vials into three glass dishes and used a thin brass spatula to dip blood from the basin and drip some on each dish. With thumb and forefinger she used one mixture to draw sigils on Voushanti's forehead and cheeks. With another, she marked spiked crescents under her own eyes.

Wiping her lancet clean on another folded square, she beckoned me back to my place. "The time approaches. Stop now, and *you* murder him."

Furious at myself for not questioning earlier, furious at Saverian, at Osriel, I returned to my stool. We might have already sent this man to his end. Alone. Before Saverian could stop me, I laid my hand on Voushanti's spasming breast.

"Valen! What are you doing?"

So near, linked by touch and his blood on my skin, I existed with and in him. I opened my senses.

The cold of Navronne's untimely winter was as nothing to the bitter hour of Voushanti's dying. One gouge of fire seared my neck . . . one grating burn marked agonized lungs . . . elsewise, waking mind hung suspended in a world of freezing black. Utterly alone. Anger rumbled faintly in the dark like retreating thunder. No fear, though. No grief. Not his, at least.

One more straining breath and the body could do no more. The candlelight retracted to a pinpoint, only bright enough to serve as a reminder of loss. And as light and pain flared and faded, Voushanti and I shared one silent cry of such piercing hunger as tore the fabric of the descending night . . .

"Valen! Give me your hand. Now!"

I gasped, blinked, and snatched my hand from the clammy, flaccid body. Shuddering, wagging my head, I tried to clear out the morbid darkness, but patterns of light and shadow, more than could be explained by one small candle, shifted and wavered on the walls and in the very air itself, overflowing that chamber as the mardane's blood did the tin vessel. Saverian's cheekbones, flushed under the blood marks, and her green eyes, fiery with purpose, supplied the only sparks of color. The angel canister stood open on the table, whatever enchantment it had contained now released.

Murmuring words I could not distinguish, Saverian scooped a fragrant green liquid from her third glass dish and traced patterns on my cheeks and forehead. Then her warm fingers clamped my wrist and pressed the back of my hand to a leather cushion that rested in her lap. Quick as lightning, her sharp little blade scored my thumb. Pain far beyond the wounding shot through my hand and up my arm as if traveling through my gards.

She pressed my bloody thumb to Voushanti's lips, crying out in Aurellian, "Rise and live, mortal man, all desire and worth bound to thy master's will until heart stops, bone crumbles, and breath fails." Her marks on my face grew hot, as if Kol were at his work again, and I felt the varied parts of the spell engage, as if they were the shafts and cogs of a mill wheel.

Shadows whirled over our heads, raising a wind that flapped book pages and rattled the shelves. Glassware tumbled to the stone floor and smashed alongside metal containers that clattered and bounced. The candle winked out. And still the physician held my bleeding thumb to those cold lips.

Then, of a sudden, Voushanti's head jerked beneath my hand, and a shaft of red lightning shot from his dead eyes straight into my own head. For one soul-searing moment, I could not look away . . . and then it was over. Darkness engulfed us again, the quivering excitement of air and life that signified enchantment vanished. Saverian released her grip.

Blind in the absolute blackness, I cradled my cut hand to my breast, hoping to ease the pain in my arm and in my soul. The marks on my face cooled quickly, and the rattles and clatters ceased as the whirlwind dissipated. A choking noise came from the bench in front of me.

"Come away," whispered Saverian in my ear, drawing me up and away from the muffled sounds. "Careful. Mind the lintel."

I shuffled my feet to keep from stumbling over the debris and extended one hand at head height. Just as my fingers encountered stone and I ducked my head to clear the doorway, a pale light burst out behind me, illuminating Saverian's face and hands. Two fingers of her right hand were pointed at a lamp in the room behind. I turned to look, but glimpsed only Voushanti's back as she pulled the heavy door closed.

"He prefers to be alone as he recovers," she said. "It takes him an hour or so to gather himself, somewhat longer to heal from whatever has brought him to the point of death. He likes it quiet."

Not quiet, I thought. *Private.* I could hear the groans of pain and despair that burst through his choking silence, only to be buried in his thick arms and in layers of bloody linen and leather.

"I need to get out of here," I said, as the torches that lit the long passage swelled into glaring banners of hell. The entire weight of the fortress pressed upon the back of my neck.

"You did well," said the physician, hurrying her steps and pointing to a stair that I knew led to light and air. "I was worried about your tolerating the chamber. But for me to attempt such a working anywhere else would have been—"

"Never again," I said, taking the steps three at a time, leaving her behind. "No matter who commands or who begs, I won't be part of that again." The enchantment clung to my spirit like dung to a boot. I had touched earth with magic and glimpsed its patterns of life and death and growing. Nowhere in that grand display was there a place for what I had just experienced.

Saverian rejoined me in the well yard where I sprawled on the dry grass inhaling great gulps of air and sky. Despite the hazy blue overhead, evening had already come to the little garth and the stone-bordered well, enclosed as they were in the heart of the fortress. "Osriel and his magics seem to have that effect on everyone."

"Are there others like Voushanti?" I said.

"Osriel says Voushanti is the only one."

"Is this what he plans for the solstice, Saverian?"

"That's impossible," she said, averting her eyes. "Osriel does not collect bodies. This enchantment cannot be worked on those dead more than a few hours."

But the weakness of her denial only made my conviction stronger. I rolled up to sitting. "I've little enough knowledge of sorcery or natural philosophy. But I know that such magic as we just aided will not repair what's wrong with the world. I won't let him do it."

Her color flamed like a bonfire. "You cannot leave Osriel with Sila Diaglou! The danger, if she identifies him . . ."

"I've said I'll do my best to get him out. But if none of you will explain what he plans, then he'll have to tell me himself, and I'll be his judge before I set him free to do it."

What if Sila wanted to bleed him? Osriel had said that sacrificing a body consecrated to Navronne might have consequences beyond the poisoning of one sianou. I needed to ask Kol if that was true.

Of a sudden my chest tightened with a longing that left me breathless, a wrenching ache I had known since childhood, never able to name its cause or its object. I had believed it only another symptom of the insatiable disease that drove me wild. But now images raced through my mind: of my uncle's grace and beauty as he strode through boundless vistas of earth and sky, forest and sea. Of the power he had brought to healing one small garden meadow.

Ah, gods, I wanted to be in Aeginea dancing and not setting out to war.

"Valen, are you ill?" Saverian seemed to speak from a vast distance, as if the few steps that separated us were the Caurean Sea. "What's wrong?"

"Naught," I said, blinking rapidly and stroking the blade of healthy winter-dry grass that grew in this little yard. Tears were surely but stray remnants of my long madness. "Naught."

From Renna's walls the watch called the second hour past noonday. So late in the year, sundown would follow in little more than two hours. Time to be traveling.

I left Elene's retiring room bearing a small case with my extra clothes, the vials of Saverian's potions—some for me, some for Osriel, some to use as weapons should the opportunity arise—and the fervent prayers and good wishes of Elene and Brother Victor.

The lady and the monk had read me the letter to Bayard they had composed while Saverian and I had been engaged in murder and resurrection. Had I not been so disturbed at my own part in Voushanti's ordeal and this entirely ludicrous bout of homesickness for Aeginea, a home I had known but a few hours, the scroll's contents might have given me a laugh.

> *I have enjoyed controlling Magnus's infamous streak of rebellion, but find him much less interesting without it. His myriad lacks—reading, writing, education, combat training, and even rudimentary sorcery—leave him somewhat bored and lacking purpose. As I cannot imagine what use the priestess has for him, I have decided that his best use might be to discover her intents.*

Though my life's purpose remained determinedly unclear, the past few weeks had been anything but boring. Elene and Brother Victor had sealed this missive with Osriel's signet. I wondered which of them had come up with the wording.

I hurried along the Great Hall gallery, where Saverian and I had spied on the warmoot. The hall sat dark and deserted, smelling of old smoke, old ale, and the old wood of the massive ceiling beams.

Our ragged little cabal of three had agreed that Elene and Brother Victor would send a long-planned alarm to Prior Nemesio at Gillarine. The coded message would bring the prior and his flock to shelter at Magora Syne—Osriel's most remote stronghold, deep in Evanore's mountains. A sevenday without word from me, and they would command Osriel's warlords to muster at Caedmon's Bridge on the winter solstice.

I had insisted that Elene and Brother Victor, as the last lighthouse warders, should not attend that solstice confrontation, but retreat to Magora Syne as well. "You guard Navronne's future in many ways," I said. "You must keep Saverian informed of all circumstances . . . see that she goes with you." I made sure Elene met my gaze and caught my double meaning. Should Osriel fall, she carried Eodward's rightful heir.

My footsteps clattered and echoed on the downward stair, and I emerged into late afternoon. Wind whined and blustered about the fortress arches and towers. Despite the hazy sunlight, the smell of the wind promised snow before morning. Halfway along the covered walk that led past the Great Hall to the kitchen alley, I switched the small, heavy case to my left hand, as it was irritating the cut on my thumb.

"I can carry that, sorcerer." Mardane Voushanti appeared at my left side, matching me step for step. Impeccably garbed in a spruce green cloak and a silver hauberk blazoned with Osriel's wolf, he kept his gaze straight ahead as he held out his hand for the case.

"That's not necessary."

I did not slow my pace and did not stare. I'd not quite believed he would meet me here as Saverian had promised when she left me in the well yard.

"You should take this, though." I passed him the scroll bearing Osriel's seal. "Max—Prince Bayard's pureblood—will meet us at my family's house with a small escort. If you sense anything amiss, we'll turn right around and come back here."

"And once you are in the custody of Sila Diaglou, I am to wait for some signal from you—a bonfire or magical explosion—at which time I am to charge into Fortress Torvo and pull you out. That is, unless you have burst from her dungeons with the prince and the thane or crawled out along some escape path given you by a generous not-brother who has always loathed you. That is a fool's plan . . . no plan at all."

If it *sounded* ridiculous, it *felt* impossible. "I believe I can do this," I said. "But I've no idea how long it might take to discover where Jullian is or to find the opportunity to get to the others. If I think of anything else between here and there, I'll be sure to tell you. Just stay close and be alert."

The mardane halted. I kept walking. "I'll give you two days," he called after me. "Mistress Elene has given me a well-filled purse.

Bring the prince out before midnight two days hence, or I'll buy me some fighters and come in after you."

I stopped and looked back at him. The scarlet centers of his eyes had heated in defiance, but I had not even asked Saverian how to call up the power I had over him. I had no desire to wield Osriel's red lightning. "*Three* days," I said. "But buy your fighters and have them ready beforehand."

"Done." He jerked his massive head and caught up with me. The unscarred half of his face was the color of chalk. We resumed our walk and rounded the corner into the alley that so resembled the lane in Palinur. "You *will* abandon me and get the prince straight back here if we cannot rendezvous," he said.

"I will. I assumed that's what his sworn protector would wish."

When we reached a certain dark little gap between two deserted storage buildings, I stopped and set down my case. "If you'll be so kind as to keep prying eyes away, I need to . . . uh . . . change my clothes."

Perhaps Saverian's summary description of my new talents had not included the required livery, for Voushanti's startled visage hinted that he'd not expected me to emerge from the gap lacking all accoutrement save light-drawn rocks and sea creatures.

"Strange, are they not?" I tossed the bundle of wool and velvet atop the case and stretched out my arms. With every passing moment in this shadowed alley, my gards brightened and their color deepened. Somehow the sight of them . . . or perhaps the gards themselves . . . left me feeling stronger, less battered by the wretched day, and if not exactly warm, somewhat warmer than my state of undress would promise. "Can't say I know what exactly they are. But they don't work if I keep them hidden."

His terrible eyes traveled up my body until they locked on my own. The red centers pulsed faintly, very like his blood as it had leaked out of him. "We are two of a kind," he said, his mouth twisting in his grotesque semblance of amusement. "Neither here nor there."

Squirming inside, I picked up my case and my clothes bundle. "We'd best move. Wouldn't want to be late." The ways in which I did *not* wish to resemble Voushanti were beyond numbering.

Shoving worries and plans aside, I stepped forward, my eyes on the stone walls and banks, on the overhanging trees, my ears on the dribbling conduit that piped water from the well yard. I inhaled the scents of the fortress cook fires and refuse heaps, and recalled the stink of fear as the ragged folk gathered on the hillside lane near the Cartamandua house. The air would be thicker in Palinur . . . and a wetter cold than here . . . with more snow on the ground—old, wet snow, freezing as the night approached.

We walked slowly along the alley. At a particular well-shadowed length of the wall, I threw my bundles over and climbed up the old stones . . .

. . . straight into the brushy, snow-clogged beech grove in Palinur where I had undressed on my way back to Renna earlier in the day. Voushanti topped the wall and immediately spun in his tracks, for the babble, clatter, and stink of the beggars' encampment fell on our heads like a bludgeon. Fires had driven more people into the pure-bloods' lane. Enchantments vibrated on every side of us, shielding the fine houses that stood back from the lane.

"I'll be ready to go in just a moment." As I bent down to retrieve my clothes, my foot broke through the crusted snow, scraping my ankle and shin. A youthful voice cried, "Mam, it's the angel come back again!" And Saverian climbed over the wall.

"Gods' teeth!" I said, as running feet crashed through the underbrush from farther down the lane, and bodies gathered just at the point we'd topped the wall—cutting off my return route. We had nowhere to run. This particular grove crowded between my family's garden wall and the lane. I shoved Voushanti and my case behind the largest tree, then grabbed my cloak and Saverian and dived into the underbrush. "What the devil are you doing here?"

Saverian crawled on top of me, spreading her own cloak wide and enfolding me in her arms. "Just be still," she whispered. "Your gards shine like a watch fire." I drew my legs up under her, while she proceeded to tuck all the straggling bits of me and my distinctively colored cloak out of sight.

"Over there in the trees," piped the child. "By the saints, I swear it. Knew he'd come back!"

" 'Tis a sign! The god's not forgotten us." Murmurs swelled from the lane beyond the grove. "He sends his holy legion to drive out these Harrowers!"

"Blue fire, ye say, child?" said a man with a voice like gravel. "My gammy told me of those who wear naught but blue fire . . ."

"And wings, boy, did ye see wings or no?" Boots and bodies crashed through the dry brush.

Saverian hissed. "Do something, sorcerer. Move, else they'll think we're dead and not just preoccupied."

The warm weight of her body pressed my bare backside into the twigs and snow. How like Saverian to lie close in a thorny bed . . .

which thought led me to remember *Elene* in my bed, sunlight bathing
her golden skin . . . which led me to recall Saverian's capable hands,
guiding me through my nivat madness . . . touching me everywhere . . .
Of a sudden, fear and strangeness and this ridiculous situation, lustful memory and a barrage of sensations—earth and snow and woman
and oncoming night—enveloped me in such a fever, I could not
control it.

"Deunor's mercy, mistress," I choked, "I dare not move."

But I did. Safely hidden beneath her cloak, I snaked my arm up
her back. Fingering her neck, I pressed her head gently downward,
until her face rested in the crook of my neck and shoulder. Her
breath so warm . . . so inviting. Her bones so firm and straight. My
alter hand stroked her rigid spine to yielding . . . then found its way
to her backside, while my knee drew up between her legs and nudged
them apart . . .

Her head popped up. "Villain madman!" A sharp blow stung my
cheek . . . and waked me from my fog of lust to shuffling bodies and
laughter all around our ungainly heap. "Get your hands off—"

I pulled her head downward, crushing her lips against mine. Her
hands scratched and gouged my arms and pulled my hair as she tried
to wrestle away. Scrabbling, wriggling, she drew her knee up sharply,
and I shifted to preclude disaster, praying her cloak would not fall
aside and display my glowing feet.

"No angel here, young Filp," said the gravel-voiced man. " 'Tis
only ones searching for a bit of heaven fallen in the midst of hell."

"Could ye not give a man a quat to 'imself?" I shouted, squeezing
Saverian's face to my shoulder before she bit my lips off. "Yea, laugh
as ye will . . . get ye all to Magrog's furnace and take all pinchy wives
with ye!"

The men shoved the pale-haired child behind the women. Ribald
comments all around and they decided the fun was over. Murmurs
and laughter faded into the evening noises of the lane.

"I'm sorry," I said, still muzzling the squirming physician. Torn
between annoyance that she had intruded her peculiar self into an
already precarious activity and a fear that I'd committed an unpar-
donable sin and forfeited her skillful and sensible aid, I couldn't stop
talking. "My head just went off . . . well, not my head exactly . . . but
it's been a long, weary autumn . . . yet I meant no ill to you. I would
never— Well, I don't think I would. I do appreciate your hiding me—
damnably awkward to light up like this when I can't afford attention.
Though one might say you invited this problem by coming along
where you were not expected—though certainly you did *not* invite

my inappropriate reaction—but I've no idea what we're going to do with you or how we're going to keep you safe when you cannot possibly go with us. What the devil were you thinking?" Hoping she had enough fodder for conversation beyond withering my manhood, I released her.

She climbed to her feet without the least care where her elbows, knees, and fists found purchase. Were her discomfiture a bit more intense, her complexion might have lit sigils of its own in purest scarlet.

"I *thought* that the people who were most likely to need my care happened to be in Palinur—three men with somewhat specialized needs that no hedgerow leech or back-alley surgeon is capable of tending. I *thought* that you and I had come to some kind of mutual respect, untainted, for the most part, by the brutish instincts of those who prefer action to reason."

"Well, of course, we—"

"As for my safety, you are most certainly *not* responsible for me. Nor is anyone but myself. After a discussion with Brother Victor, I decided that I might better be close by as you attempt this rescue, and that as long as I was here, I could bring news of these ventures to your sister, the Sinduria, who seems to care what becomes of you, though she's not yet been informed that she is *not* your sister. And I brought these." She pulled a vial and a scrap of stained canvas from her pocket and shoved them into my hand. "Elene told me that touching blood enabled you to track a person more easily—a detail that you failed to mention to me. While you and Mistress Moonhead exchanged your overwrought farewells, I was retrieving a sample of Prince Osriel's blood, which I keep on hand to formulate his medicines. I also managed to acquire this scrap cut from one of Thane Stearc's old jupons, though I don't know that dried blood has the same useful properties for pureblood magic."

"Blood . . . gods, yes. It makes tracking much easier. I just never imagined anyone would have any." Thickheaded and embarrassed, I brushed twigs and ice crystals from my skin. "And, yes, Thalassa should be told. All right . . . yes, that would be kind of you . . ."

Happily for me, Voushanti joined us before I could get too tangled up in words or recollections of the sensation of Saverian's breath on my skin. The sun was sinking. I turned my back to her and donned my finery as quickly as I could. Nothing like the luxurious restriction of buttons and laces for taming lustful mania. Gods, Saverian . . . of all women in the world . . .

So do as she says, fool. Attempt to reason, instead of acting blindly.
I fastened my cloak with the ivory-and-gold wolf brooch.

"You can't traipse alone through Palinur, mistress physician," I
said, tugging the mask from my pocket. "No matter how easily you
can ensorcel those who aim to harm you, it's too dangerous. I
wouldn't let *any* friend of mine do so. I'll come up with some explanation for Max, so Voushanti can deliver you to Thalassa."

Voushanti, his own attire impeccable despite his sojourn in the
shrubbery, glared at me as if I were a particularly stupid infant. "To
change your arrangements this late risks the entire plan, such as it is.
And I must follow you to the Harrower priestess, so we'll know
where you and the prince are held. I've no time to coddle foolish
women."

"I'm not an idiot," said Saverian, her dignity regained though her
skin retained a rosy hue. "I'll wait here until Magnus is delivered and
transferred. Once you know his location, Mardane, you can return
here for me. I would welcome your escort on my brief visit to the
Mother's temple."

"Leaving the scene will jeopardize the prince's rescue," snapped
Voushanti. "You have blood-bound me to this man, but I cannot read
his thoughts. With no means of contact between us, I must be available at whatever time he chooses."

"No means of contact?" Saverian raised her eyebrows, quite smug.
"You gentlemen really should have said something earlier. I can, of
course, work a small enchantment . . ."

Stupid not to think of it. My sister Thalassa had once worked a
word trigger with her favorite insults, so that anywhere within ten
quellae, I could hear her address me as *fiend heart* or *iron skull* did
she but feed magic to the words.

Voushanti and I left the beech grove tight bound with the names
of *dead man* and *bluejay* and a few specific signals for special circumstances. If he didn't hear from me in three days, he would force
his way inside Fortress Torvo. As we picked our way through the
crowded lane to our meeting with Max, my hearing picked Saverian's laughter out of the noise. I smiled as I remembered the warmth
of her breath and the feel of her firm flesh and slender bones crushed
against my skin. What an extraordinary woman.

Chapter 21

"See the iron grate over the drainage canal? That's where you'll come out. You *can* still quicken a spell, yes?" Max spoke using only the half of his mouth beneath his mask. As protocol required refraining from conversation in the presence of ordinaries, every pureblood youth developed the skill early on.

"Yes." I mimicked his trick. Though I stood slightly behind him, I was enough taller that I could easily be observed by either the spear-wielding Harrowers guarding Sila Diaglou's gates, the bowmen on the barbican above the gate tunnel, or the five of Bayard's warriors who surrounded us protectively, while their captain identified our party to the gate commander.

The knee-high grate to which Max referred blocked the only breach in the thick, ugly walls of Fortress Torvo. The canal had once drained water and sewage from the fortress, but that function had likely been relocated as the city grew up around the place. Weeds, dirty snow, and broken paving choked the old ditch, which disappeared into the squalid houses and snow-clogged ruins that crowded this miserable square. Riie Doloure. Last time I had been here, Harrowers had been throwing severed heads from the battlements down to their rioting fellows and fire had raged in the tenements. On that vile morning, men and women had been screaming from behind those walls, one of them Abbot Luviar, as his executioner exposed his bowels and set them afire.

Another wave of the sweats dampened my skin, my hands trembled in their bonds of silk and steel, and my own bowels threatened to betray me. What kind of idiot would broach Sila Diaglou's fortress in shackles? And Gildas would be here. Gildas, who knew all my weaknesses.

The plan we had made over the past day had gone smoothly thus far. Max, Voushanti, and I had made a show of my resistance in front of Prince Bayard, enough to make Bayard think me cowardly and not worth keeping for himself. Sila Diaglou had accepted Bayard's request for a meeting. Now it was up to Max to convince her of our story, and it was up to Max's spy within Sila's entourage to provide me a blade. With a weapon and a smattering of luck, I could get out of a warded cell. Outside of a cell, I could use magic to free the others. Somehow. That was the plan. As with most plans, it seemed far less plausible in daylight.

"Forward," ordered Bayard's captain upon his return from the gate. "Lower arms."

He pivoted smartly. We marched briskly past the gate guards, under the raised portcullis, and into the gate tunnel. I resisted the urge to look back at the burned-out tenements where Voushanti and Saverian were to have set up their watchpost by now. Rather I gave thanks that my hands were silkbound and that Max's hand gripped my arm to prevent my stumbling in the dark. I did not want to touch earth and sense the horrors that had gone on here.

The dark-stained gallows, the judges' platform, and the prisoners' cage stood vacant in the outer bailey, like the bones of some vicious monster left to rot in the weak sunlight. As we were hurried across the yard and through the inner gate, I noted the rubble-filled drainage channel. Another grate barred its passage through the inner wall. If I could find no promising venue to key my Danae shifting, I might be forced to use Max's route to the outside. Naught of this executioner's yard recalled enough of Renna's baileys that I could take us from one to the other by Danae magic.

Sweat dribbled down my back. I could not retreat now. They were here—Stearc and Osriel at least. One touch of the blood samples that Saverian had brought had told me that much. But I could get no better sense of their exact location until I was inside.

We proceeded up a narrow ramp, overlooked by the inner wall walk, two flanking towers, and the arrow loops of the blocklike keep. What remained of Fortress Torvo's conical roofs stated that this small fortress had been here long before the Aurellian invasion, long before Palinur had grown into a great city.

A barren courtyard awaited us, and more Harrower troops—some in the shabby cottes and braies of townsmen or the shapeless tunics of villeins, some in sturdier padded leather jaques with metal plates sewn on arms and breast. But all of them wore orange rags tied about their necks or arms or trailing from their hats. At the head of a wooden stair, two Harrowers opened the iron-bound doors of the keep.

Max released my arm and smoothed the wrinkles his fingers had made in my velvet sleeve. His dark eyes glittered. "Well done, little brother. I doubted you'd balls enough to make it so far without bolting. Are you ready?"

Who could be ready for the things Sila did? I ducked my head, rather than embarrassing myself by choking within his hearing. The priestess wanted me alive. She had some use for me. I had to believe that.

Max grinned and flicked a finger at one of his men, who quickly knelt in front of me with a weighty set of shackles. I lashed out at the soldier's head with my bound hands and twisted away as if to bolt. But as Max and I had planned, a few wrenched muscles, bruising holds, and snarled curses later, I was well subdued and stumbling up the steps in chains.

Max gripped my arm with one hand. "After you." Then he added so that none but I could hear, "May Serena Fortuna smile on our first fraternal venture. My spy will use the password *brethren*."

Inhaling a last breath of the open air, I stepped inside.

No dais or grand chair marked Sila Diaglou's barren hall. No tapestries covered the smoke-blackened walls. The old fortress was well suited to a temporary military headquarters—the best-fortified position in the city outside the royal compound itself, plenty of space for bedding down men and animals. Splintered remnants marked where wooden walls had once divided the long chamber into three. Where the roof had leaked at one end of the hall, the rotting roof beams sagged ominously. Harrower fighters drifted in and out of the hall, warming themselves at the cookfires scattered across the cracked stone floor. I doubted the drafty ruin ever got warm.

Leaving our escort at the door, Max led me confidently through the busy chamber, past five or six warriors arguing across a broad table propped up at one corner with stones. A troop of perhaps twenty—a mix of poorly turned out swordsmen, ragged townsmen, and several sturdy women—stood attentively as an officer gave them orders to raze a mill outside the city's southern gates. Women and boys served out the steaming contents of copper cauldrons to the milling fighters.

At the far end of the hall, a group of ten or fifteen split and moved aside at our approach. Sila Diaglou stood in the center. Warrior's garb of steel-reinforced leather rested as comfortably on her tall, slender frame as on any man's, while her flaxen hair, cut short since I had seen her preside over Luviar's execution, now curled about her pale, imperious face like the fair locks of painted cherubs. Here in the ruddy light of cook fires and torches, the murderous witch appeared little older than Elene.

A tall, elderly woman in shapeless brown leaned on Sila's right arm. Though the wisps of white hair escaped from her wimple seemed oddly out of place in such a company, the old woman's narrow eyes gleamed as sharp as an Aurellian poniard. Beside her stood a beardless man with a needle-sharp chin, a small, copper-skinned young woman with great brown eyes, and a soft-looking man with oiled black curls and an ear that was split, gnarled, and bulging like a chestnut canker—Sila's accomplices in slaughter.

But it was the youngish man on Sila Diaglou's left who spurred my deepest revulsion. Though he had traded the black gown and cowl of Saint Ophir for gray tunic and black braies and hose, his hairless skull, the solid line of black eyebrows, raised in surprise, and the deep-set eyes and well-drawn mouth, so quick to take on a grin, marked him as Gildas—child stealer, liar, and traitor to all he professed.

"Holy one," said Max to the priestess, touching his fingers to his forehead in respect, "I bring greetings from His Highness Prince Bayard and a gift to serve as proof of his sincerity and good favor. Have I your leave to tell the tale?"

"Speak, pureblood." Sky-blue eyes stared coldly from beneath Sila Diaglou's intelligent brow. Her face, square cut like a faceted gem, was flawed only by the diagonal seams on her cheeks, carved by her own hand on the day she had publicly abjured Arrosa and the rest of the elder gods. As a girl she had pledged service to the goddess of love, so I'd heard, but only a year out of her novitiate, she had claimed Arrosa's temple corrupted, its priestesses little more than whores for wealthy donors, its rites a mockery rather than a celebration of fertility and renewal. How her indignation had translated to leveling civilization I had yet to comprehend.

Max inclined his head. "Early this morning, I was summoned to my father's house on urgent family business. Unlikely as it seemed, my brother had arrived, ostensibly to seek my young sister's contract for a mapping project desired by his master, Prince Osriel. Further questioning revealed that he had, in fact, approached us without the knowledge or permission of his fearsome lord and sought our aid to escape his burdensome contract on the grounds that his master had threatened his immortal soul. Of course, revoking a contract is impossible without the Registry's consent, which will never be granted in Valen's case. But I, ever mindful of the gifts that fate lays before us, agreed to allow my foolish brother to plead his case before Prince Bayard."

The priestess scrutinized Max as if she were a gem cutter examining the facets laid bare by her work. Her attention did not waver, even as Gildas murmured into her ear.

"Speaking frankly, holy one, this put my lord in a difficult position." Max, the consummate performer, stood with his hands clasped behind his back, well away from weapons, his feet widespread, back straight, and voice casual and confident—postures taught us early to put ordinaries at ease. "Until the day he assumes his rightful crown, Prince Bayard must obey the law of the land, which demands he return a *recondeur* to his contracted master within a day. But my master, also ever mindful of the gifts that fate lays before us, understands that *you* do not recognize the authority of the Registry, and that this brother of mine is the very pureblood whose submission you desire. In short, lady, Magnus Valentia de Cartamandua-Celestine is yours to do with as you please."

Max sounded altogether too pleased with himself for my comfort, though I had devised this story and put it in his mouth. He stood to gain in everyone's favor. We had ensured that he remained entirely within pureblood discipline. The only untruths he told were those he had agreed upon with Bayard for the purposes of his bargain with Osriel.

"And what change does Prince Bayard seek in the terms of our agreement?" asked the priestess.

"My master concedes that you have been most generous in our negotiation, holy one, and asks only your continued assurance that once you and he have subdued the Bastard of Evanore, you will take a knee at my lord's coronation on the first day of the new year, then sit at his right hand as his most valued friend and ally."

An old comrade of mine, a veteran of the Hansker wars, had once pointed out that only the most assured of commanders would approach a subordinate or prisoner of greater height while in the presence of other subordinates. I had observed the rule proven time and again, and this occasion was no different. Despite my topping her by a dozen quattae, Sila gave her elderly companion's arm to the doe-eyed woman and came forward to take a closer look. She appeared supremely confident, as only those who hold the leash of heaven can.

She touched the ivory-and-gold wolf brooch on my breast, then lifted the front laps of my cloak and tossed them over my shoulders. Folding her arms, she walked around me, her face unexpressive as she examined the fine embroidery and ivory buttons on my doublet, my gold-link belt, and the pearl trilliots sewn on my green satin sleeves. She even crouched down to examine my shackles and ran her fingers over my fine leather boots.

At such close proximity, I expected to see lines and weathering in her cheeks, signs of her age that I knew to be past forty. Yet save for the dual scars, her skin shone as flawless as that of a healthy child. Cold, though. Great gods, the air around her felt colder than the winter sky, so cold I could neither smell nor taste her scent. I could sense nothing of her at all. Perhaps I'd worn clothes for too long.

She straightened up again. "No weapons save these," she said, touching my silkbound hands. "I had understood his poor skills warranted no such restriction."

I had persuaded Max to allow me to keep my gloves on beneath the cord bindings, as the weather was so bitter. Though my sweating palms had dampened both gloves and silk, my gards remained hidden. The longer I could conceal them, the better. I had few enough surprises to spring on Gildas.

"The binding is merely a formality, holy one," said Max. "My brother is adept at lock breaking and crude illusions, but little else of sorcery. But what gentleman would lay an unsheathed knife in an ally's hand, though the blade be dull as lead? The shackles . . . alas, I must warn you that it is only with great . . . firmness . . . that my lord and I have persuaded him of his limited choices. He will likely walk gingerly for a few days. He has a nasty habit of bolting his responsibilities."

"Indeed, he shall serve for much more than lock breaking." The priestess's blue gaze met mine . . . turning my bones to ice. With a firm finger, she traced the line of my mask down my brow and nose, coming to rest on my lips, her touch so charged with heat and light, it sent waves of urgency straight to my groin.

"I accept the gift," she said, breaking away briskly. "Tell your prince that I find it most pleasing. If all falls out on the solstice as he has promised, he need have no fear of my defection." Which sounded no firm assurance to *me*, though, in truth, my head had emptied of all save an ill-defined dread that fell far outside the bounds of my expectations.

"Then I shall take my leave of you, holy one. May your life and health prosper." Max signaled one of his men to hand over my case and left the key to my shackles with one of Sila's guards. Then he stood at my shoulder, straightened his back, and touched fingers to brow. As he spun around to go, his cloak flared. Under its cover, where Sila Diaglou could not see it, his hand squeezed my arm.

Still dazed, I met his gaze and caught a quick wink. Then he was gone. I had not wits enough to decide if his gesture was reassurance or apology or merely Max's usual self-indulgent humor, combining the concern of a proper brother with a taunt. All I wanted to do was run.

"Falderrene, Jakome, take him to the chamber we have prepared for this day." As she issued this unsettling command, the Harrower priestess had already turned her back to me.

She spread her arms as if to embrace the rest of the company. "My beloved companions, have I not assured you that our dedication and righteous service will force the world into its proper order? Destiny has laid a treasure in our hands—one I have long sought. The future proceeds as I have spoken!"

Addressing such a multitude did not coarsen the priestess's voice. Though speaking in such a cavernous space, her tone maintained a certain intimacy, as if she spoke to each of us alone. Every conversation ceased. Every face turned toward the woman, as if she were the divine prophet Karus, come back to life clothed in the sun.

"The last walls shall crumble!" Triumph . . . exultation . . . joy . . . her song without music rang from the rotting rafters. "The mighty shall be brought low, no being that breathes the air of this world set above another. No cache or hoard shall remain unopened; no treasure be locked away whether in vault, veins, or marrow. Burn, harrow, and level this blighted land! Let all who stand in our way feel our knives, our spears, our claws that in the future we shape, all may be one in awe and service before the mighty Gehoum!"

Cheers shook Torvo's foundation. Ferocious. Wild. Terrifying. As if there were seven hundred partisans in the hall and not seventy. The only one who did not cheer was the old woman in brown.

As the cheering throng swarmed Sila Diaglou, Falderrene, the murderous minor noble with the malformed ear, and a bony pale-haired young man she had named Jakome led me briskly toward the corner where the rectangular hall butted into one of Torvo's massive towers. A third man followed with my case. To my surprise, once we passed through a low arch into the tower, they shoved me onto the *upward* stair.

My escorts did not speak, save for whispered watchwords for the guard at each landing. Shaken by the intimate intensity of Sila's touch, appalled at the power of her conviction, and alarmed at the mysterious connection of such ferocity with me, I felt what small confidence I had brought with me seep away. As well I did not know what to think, for getting my shackled feet up the tight, narrow stair without hands to grip or balance proved a challenge. I listened for any hint of my friends or the prince along the way, but the fortress walls were so thick that a hundred muted conversations sounded no different from scuttling rats.

Our destination lay at the very summit of the stair, where the tower roof of layered wood, earth, and lead pressed so low I could not stand straight, where the steps were so impossibly shallow, only the toe of my boots could fit, where the only light was an arrow loop. No matter Saverian's potion, I pressed my bound hands to my mouth to keep from heaving as I waited for my escorts to unfasten the latches of a solid iron door. Surely I would die in such a prison.

The door swung open with a metallic screech. Blessed cold air bathed my feverish face, and the last rays of sunset, arrowing beneath a thick pall of clouds, near blinded me. All gods be praised, the chamber was open to the sky.

"In with you." Falderrene motioned me forward.

I ducked my head lower and stepped in, astonished to discover I could stand straight without touching the ragged timbers of the ceiling as it swooped upward to its conical peak. Not one, but five tall windows opened onto the settling night. Though defensive iron grillwork yet guarded the window openings, only rusted hinges remained of their wooden shutters. A laugh bubbled up inside me, withheld only by my silk mask. Did they think to torment me with exposure to the elements?

Falderrene unhooked a jangling ring from his belt and dangled it in the air. "Shall we toss a coin for who plays nursemaid tonight, friend?"

The pale-haired Jakome snatched the keys and twisted his whey-colored face into a bitter snarl. "I've a personal interest tonight. The holy one forbids me interfere, but I'd stay close. He is an animal."

Falderrene grinned unpleasantly and swept an oily lock behind his malformed ear. "As you wish. Might as well remove his shackles. Not even his gatzé master can retrieve him here. He'll not escape lest he can fly. I'll wait on the stair lest he give you any trouble."

As the pale-haired Jakome bent to unlock my ankles, a survey of the chamber's furnishings revealed comforts not usual for a common prisoner. A small cabinet held a painted washing bowl, night jar, and neatly stacked towels. The bed, piled with thick quilts, was a rarity—built long enough to accommodate a person of my size. And though the crumbling hole in the center of the stone floor had not held a watchfire for many years, a lamp with a glass wind shield sat on a small round table beside a bowl of apples.

The chains clanked and rattled as my bony jailer stood up again. I shook out my legs, relishing the lightness.

"A meal will be brought shortly," said Jakome. "The same as we all eat. Though the chamber's open to the weather, you've been left blankets enough. This is no pureblood palace, but Sila Diaglou has no wish to starve or freeze you."

His wish, though . . . His face told me that his wish was different and had a great deal to do with sharp knives and stakes through the gut. Would that I could shove the man and all his fellows down the stairs and burn this maniac-infested den until the lead roofs fell in on them all.

The ragged guardsman had carried in my case and set it beside a plain wood chest. Jakome yanked open the case and threw my silks, velvets, damasks, and linens onto the stone floor, searching them briskly. Looking me straight in the eye, he hawked and spat on my spare mask, wadded it up, and threw it atop the pile of clothes. "We'll see you get proper clothes. When all are brought low, such pureblood fripperies will have no use."

No use mentioning that I'd done my best to forgo pureblood frippery for most of my life.

He turned the emptied case upside down and shook it. Naught fell out. "That's it, then," he said as he stood up again. Tossing the case onto the pile, he waved the guardsman toward the stair. "Get on. Tell Falderrene I'll set the locks and meet him below."

Once we were alone, Jakome's colorless lips curled into a toothy grin. He pulled out his knife and twirled it in his fingers. "I've heard you have need of a knife. Heard it from my *brethren.*"

"Saints and angels!" Surprise and relief turned my spine to jelly. "Do you ever need a recommendation for an acting troupe, say the word! Can you get me out of these?" I held out my bound hands.

"Aye, I can and will. But you must kneel first, pureblood." His bony chin indicated the floor.

"Why so?" I was already spying out places to hide the weapon.

"Because I'm still thinking whether or not to give you what was promised. Matters have changed." Venom laced his tongue. "Do your knees bend? I've ne'er seen a pureblood kneel."

I knelt, my spirits plummeting. I knew this kind of man. Give him the deference he wanted and he might relent. He couldn't have much time until he was missed. "Come," I said, wheedling, "you were trusted . . . well paid . . ."

"Shhh." He pressed the knifepoint to my lips, unmasked rage and bloodthirst reddening his white skin. I held my tongue and gave up hope of the knife. Keeping blood and breath would be enough. "The thing is, I was paid to give you a knife if I could manage it without being caught. But if I've decided I can't manage it, who's going to hear your complaint?"

He spun the weapon in the air and snatched the hilt, then waved the weapon slowly side to side as one might try to mesmerize a dog. "You're being given what you don't deserve, as pureblood pups are always given what they don't deserve. It would please me to carve your throat out."

I maintained discipline, keeping my shoulders relaxed, my mouth shut, and my gaze somewhere neutral, even when tiny flames rippled along the edges of his blade. The fellow must have a trace of sorcerer's blood, at the least.

After a few uncomfortable moments, he exhaled in disgust and let the flames die, then began to cut away the silken cords that bound my hands. "Fortunately, you've worse to come than I could do to you."

"Ouch! Careful!" I snatched my hands away and shook off the remnants of the bindings. His last cut had slashed through cords and glove alike, leaving an ugly red smear on his dagger and a fiery laceration at the base of my thumb. "Are you wholly an idiot as well as a scoundrel?"

"Not I, pureblood. Not I." Sneering, Jakome left the chamber, slammed the iron door shut behind him, and shot the noisy bolt.

Breathing raggedly, I sagged back onto my heels, bent my head to my knees, and tried to slow my hammering heart. When my refocused senses told me that no one remained outside the door or on the stair, I pulled off mask, cloak, and gloves and got to work. Without a weapon I would have to find another way out of this prison. And if Jakome was going to report Max's bribe to Sila Diaglou, I'd best get out of here fast.

First, test the door. I structured a voiding spell. Releasing magic into the spell, I traced an arc at the bottom of the iron door. The iron remained cold and inert. Neither did the locks respond to my best probing with so much as a spark. Disappointing, but no surprise. I had assumed Sila would have my prison warded to preclude all common spellwork. Jakome had worked his little fire magic with the door open.

I retrieved my leather case and ripped out the false bottom Saverian had cleverly disguised so that I needed no magic to open it. I pulled out her three vials of medicines—blue for me, amber for the prince, clear for the tincture of yellow broom—a useful common remedy that could ream a man's guts. I had intended to carry these in my pocket once I had been searched, but after Jakome's words about new clothes, decided I'd best find a place in my cell to stash them. With the open windows, perhaps I wouldn't need my own remedy.

The clothes chest had no pockets or drawers, but a wooden tray, half its length, had been crafted to sit in the top of it to hold buckles or belts or other oddments. Several objects sat in the tray already: a dice box, a canvas bag of knucklebones, a long narrow board pocked with egg-shaped hollows for playing armaments, and a set of ivory and jet pebblelike game pieces. I emptied the canvas bag, dropped the vials into it, then replaced the bones. I had always been luckier at knucklebones than dice.

Games. From the look of it, they intended to keep me here a while. Which made no sense at all. If Sila and Gildas didn't want my bent to lead them into Aeginea . . . or anywhere else . . . then what, in Iero's heaven, did they want with me?

Now to test the greater magic. Common wards laid to prevent spellworking could not disrupt the bent—the inborn talents of a pureblood. Most talents prescribed by a pureblood bent had naught to offer in the way of escape routes or weaponry and posed little risk to a jailer.

I loosened my belt and fumbled beneath layers of pourpoint, shirt, and tunic to find the upper hem of my chausses. Two scraps of stained fabric lay hidden next to my skin—one, the bloodstained canvas from Stearc's jupon, the other a square of linen Saverian had dipped in the vial of Osriel's blood.

Best not think too much of what I had to do. I laid the scraps on the floor, pressed my hands atop them, and closing my eyes, poured out magic enough to search Fortress Torvo. Indeed, naught prevented me . . . though I came to wish it had.

I cursed. Swore. Eventually I crawled away, buried my face in the bedclothes, and screamed out a monumental rage. Had any other edifice this side of hell seen so much of torment? The Harrowers' self-righteous slaughter was only the most recent depredation. For decades this ruin had been a secret prison, used by nobles who took pleasure in meting out punishments in cruel excess of those mandated by Eodward's ideals of justice. Men, women, children, noble or common . . . none were exempt. Before that, the fortress was used similarly by the Aurellians, a race whose delight in torture reached levels of depravity that counterbalanced every glory of their arts and every marvel of their building. And in ancient Ardra, before the rise of the enlightened Caedmon, Ardran nobles had lived in constant war with one another, as well as with the Moriangi Gravs to the north—and they had locked their rivals and their families here to starve. Every wail and scream and bloodletting had left its mark upon this stone. Despair had become its mortar.

But my uncomfortable exercise had repaid me. Osriel and Stearc were held straight down below me, six levels, at the least. Both men lived—that the magic had worked told me that much—but I could discern naught of their condition. I fixed their guide threads in my mind, the route of steps and passages through layer upon layer of blood-woven history, a trail that would lead me to them as soon as I could manage it. Some of the blood and pain I felt was surely theirs.

But what of Jullian? I had no blood to trace him. Of all the prisoners who had trod these vile halls, far too many had been boys. Three days . . . most of this one gone already.

The sun had gone, leaving the night beyond the windows black as pitch. The wind whistled through the window grates, as I yanked and twisted each one. Many of the bars were loose in the weathered stone facings; some were rusted through, some missing altogether. A little brutish work would allow me to crawl out. But one glance down into the blackness showed the pinpricks of light that would be torches at the gates. As far as I had learned, Danae did not fly, and surely even Kol could not survive so great a leap. Damn the cowardly Jakome to the nethermost regions of hell!

Of a sudden I heard murmurings outside my door, and the bolts and latches scraped. By the time the door swung open, I was seated in one of my two chairs, feet propped on the table, and my gloves covering the blue telltales on my hands. I snatched up an apple and started munching. The taste of the fruit and the scents of porridge and wine waked an appetite I'd thought ruined by my searching.

"Good evening, Magnus Valentia." A small woman hurried past me and set a loaded tray on my table, as an invisible companion closed and locked the door behind her. "A simple meal, but nourishing. And hot, if we partake right away."

The soft-voiced visitor, barefoot and clothed in a plain white shift, was Sila Diaglou's young devotee, the copper-skinned young woman with the earth-brown eyes. Thick hair the color of walnuts hung over her shoulder in a single plait, as if she were on her way to bed. Any man would find her alluring did she not have a habit of smearing her victims' blood on her full lips.

"I do not sit down with murderers."

She wrinkled her brow as if pondering the course of the universe. "But you've broken bread with other warriors, have you not—your comrades-in-arms in Prince Perryn's service? War is dreadful, but when the world's need demands it, all must serve. Some by killing. Some by dying."

"My comrades took no pleasure in their deeds. They did not slaughter innocents or lick their blood." Yet Boreas had notched his spear whenever he skewered a beardless Moriangi, saying he'd "keep the river dogs from growing up another warrior from a whelp." And Boreas was not near the worst of those I'd called comrade.

"Some kinds of killing cannot be justified by war," I said. "Unclean killing. Children."

"If the war itself be noble, then I can't see how one death be different from another. Please, let us not argue this evening. You should eat." She had set out two deep bowls of porridge, a small plate of butter and bread, two spoons, and a steaming pitcher, and now poured wine into two waiting cups, sloshing a bit onto the table. The stout fragrance of wine and cloves filled the room, swirled by the chill breeze, setting up a raging thirst in me. Of a sudden I was sweating.

The girl perched on the second chair, tucked her bare feet under her robe, and dipped her spoon. "Will you not tell me more of yourself, Magnus?" she said between bites. "Then I'll do the same. My mistress would not have us enemies." Her great eyes gleamed in the lamplight, no hint of guile. Indeed they were empty of anything save eager curiosity and a certain sincere . . . appreciation.

I looked away. I did need to eat. Even more, I longed for the wine. It was a mercy that only this girl had been sent here. I was much too tired to spar with Gildas or Sila herself. Yet I would need to have a care. This girl was little more than a child herself—sixteen, seventeen—but a child who collaborated in murder. I dared not forget that.

I swirled the wine in the wooden cup, inhaling. Bless all gods, no lurking scent of nivat or anything else untoward wafted from it. Cloves certainly . . . a touch of cinnamon. Sweet Erdru, the aroma itself could get me drunk. All the better to sleep and forget what my bent had shown me.

I touched my tongue to one drop left hanging on the rim. Warmth spread from toes to eyebrows in less time than a flicker's peck. No nivat. No lurking trace of herbs or potions. But the wine itself was disappointing, heavy on the tongue and tasting as if it had been kept in a cask of iron instead of oak. No use risking a muddled head for spoilt wine.

Unable to stomach sitting with the girl, I left the wine cup on the table and perched on a window ledge with bowl and spoon. Perhaps I could induce her to tell me where Jullian was kept or discover a way to get out of this room. The cursed Jakome's treachery had been a sore blow.

"You speak first," I said. "You likely know a few things about me already. What is your name?"

"Malena."

An Aurellian word. *"Goddess's treasure."*

A pleasured flush deepened her already richly colored skin. "That's right. I was a third daughter of a third daughter, so my parents gave me to the temple in Avenus when I turned five. They'd no coin for the fee, so I was put to work in the temple baths—scrubbing tiles, fetching water or towels or candles, waiting in corners till I was needed." She popped a bite of buttered bread in her mouth.

"Arrosa's temple, then." Only the goddess of love required baths in her temple.

"Mmm." She nodded and swallowed her bread. "I was lucky to serve and not take vows, though I didn't know it then. I didn't understand what I saw—the wickedness what took place in the baths." She licked the butter off her small, delicate fingers.

"Copulation . . . mating . . . is no corruption," I said. "Arrosa blesses earthly love, makes it divine, if pleasure is shared freely." The qualifier was not widely preached, of course, but its truth had become apparent to me early on, and no woman I'd had since had ever disagreed.

"Well, of course we're meant to join and make more of us, and if we can take comfort in it, all the better." A sprightly smile illuminated her round cheeks and pointed chin, then faded as she knit her brow. "But in the temple, pleasure was *not* offered freely. Novices younger than me were used by whatever great lords and warriors took a fancy. I heard them screaming from the bath, saw them thrashing in the water when the lords forced them down on their . . . laps. And I had to bring towels to wipe the girls' blood, and oils to anoint their skin, so they could be sent into the bedchambers to *glorify Arrosa* through the night."

I well knew such crimes happened. I had warned Jullian of them, sworn to protect him. I wished she would speak of something else. All manner of unseemly urges seemed waked in me this night.

"One night when I was ten, a lord tired of the priestess who serviced him in the bath. He bellowed that he preferred a younger body. He saw me hiding in the corner and demanded me. And he got me.

For a sevenday. Even though I could offer him no temple blessing. Even though I could not read to him from the temple writs or recite the lays of love."

Her simple statement of evil gave weight to her story that indignant diatribes could not. I believed her.

"Afterward, I ran away. If I had taken vows, like Sila, they would have come after me, and I would have had to cut myself as she did to undo the swearing. But I was just a bath girl . . ."

". . . Yet your parents refused to take you back—their gift to the goddess." No need to ask what had happened to her after. I had been fifteen when I ran away, and the ways to feed oneself so young were very few. "I'm sorry for what happened to you, but it does not . . . cannot . . . justify—"

"But I am *not* sorry! Don't you see?" She twiddled with the lamp, retracting the wick so its fire dimmed, confining the pool of light to the table and her red-gold complexion. "Had I stayed a bath girl at the temple I'd not have met Sila. I'd not have learned of the Gehoum, and how we must make ourselves humble before them. I'd not understand the need for cleansing and repentance or to tear down the false structures of learning and privilege that make one man's will more powerful than the purity of a girl."

I had learned long before that when a certain note crept into an otherwise reasonable argument, it paid a man naught to continue. The fanatic's gleam shone in Malena's soft brown eyes, and she was never going to agree that her slaughtering children in the name of her uncaring Gehoum was no holier than a lord's raping children in the name of his own pleasure.

"I've eaten all I can bear," I said, setting down the tasteless porridge. I wanted this woman out of here. Long-buried memories of drunken soldiers and their rough, fumbling hands, of filthy alleyways and painful humiliations, had gotten tangled with images of bath girls and swimming brown eyes and soft copper-hued limbs. "Tell your mistress and her monk that sad stories and beds with quilts will not make me their willing captive. Let them come and tell me what they want of me."

I saw no use in pretending cooperation. Gildas knew me too well. I just needed to keep their eyes on me and away from the captives down below. But what if I found a way to get Osriel out of here, yet had not secured Jullian? I shoved the thought away as soon as it appeared. I had two more days.

Malena set down her spoon, picked up my wine cup, and joined me at the window. Her round cheeks bloomed with health. "Dear

Magnus," she said, pressing the cup into my hand. "The holy one has sent *me* to tell you what she wants of you."

Her lips parted slightly. Soft. Waiting. I drained the cup in one gulp, and her smile blossomed in fragrant sweetness like moonflowers. A gust of wind whistled through the iron grate, and she shivered.

"And what is that?" I said, relishing the potent richness of the wine. Malena was so small . . . so fragile in the thin white shift that fluttered in the wind, giving shape to the ripened form beneath. I wrapped my arms about the trembling girl to shield her from the cold.

She wrapped her arms about my neck and pulled my head down so she could whisper in my ear. "I am your chosen mate."

Chapter 22

"Chosen mate?" Increasingly thickheaded, as if I'd drunk a vat of wine, I could not seem to grasp her meaning.

"Mmm. The world shall be renewed." Her fingers stroked my neck and teased at my ears.

My body swam with lust. My mind swam with the wine and unfocused danger, and I knew I should stop what I was doing. I just could not remember why. Even as I voiced the question that might elaborate the risk, my gloved fingers found the ties that held her flimsy shift closed, and I pulled.

Goddess Mother . . . Her breast tasted of ginger and honey.

"I am the holy one's gift to you . . . prepared . . . purified . . . ah . . ." The soft catch in her throat as I pushed the gossamer fabric downward and shifted my mouth from one sweet curve to another drove me out of my senses. I drew her to the bed and lay beside her. As she unfastened my buttons and laces, I imagined vaguely that I should stay her hand. But instead I loosed her hair, inhaled her rising scent, and traced the line of neck and jaw and mouth with kisses, inhaling her sweetness as a starving man devours the first spoonful of sustenance.

"Why would the goddess send a gift to me now?" I whispered, my words buried in Malena's smooth belly, as somewhere above my head her trembling hands unbuttoned my gloves. "I've failed to honor blessed Arrosa for far too long, though I am ever her servant in mind."

The girl's laugh echoed the song of larks, until she freed my hands and gasped again. I took full advantage. My fingers explored silken breasts, smooth flanks, and swollen lips, while my mouth continued its downward trek. "Careful, lady," I mumbled, as her quest to strip away my layered garb grew insistent enough to tear skin along with fabric. But I was as eager as she. More.

"Ah, Magnus, they told me you might— But I never—" Her voice quivered . . . caught in a sob . . . as her fingers traced a path on my naked back. "They are so beautiful. *You* are so beautiful . . ."

Of a sudden my back bloomed in exquisite fire. Her fingernails had transformed to steel blades that slashed a path of agony across my skin. The pain drove me into frenzy.

I buried myself in her. Heedless . . . mindless . . . I strove and thrust and drowned in sensation that sent coils and spirals of lightning to every quat of my skin. Were the dissolution of the world appointed for the culmination of my act, I could not have stopped. And the explosion, when it came, had naught to do with sweetness or shared pleasure. Only need.

Laughter eddied about my head, swirling, dipping . . . changing pitch from low to high and back again. Sluggish, sated, incapable of movement, I sat with my fire-scoured back against the curved wall of my tower prison, my head on my knees. Wine lay sour on my tongue, though I could remember only one cup.

"Well done, child." The higher-pitched voice. Sila Diaglou. She had said this three times. I couldn't understand it. Why weren't they angry?

The two of them—priestess and monk—had burst through the door and pulled me off the girl. Was it Malena's strangled cries and strident weeping had brought them or was it my bellow of completion? They were gentle enough, supporting me stumbling toward a window and lowering me to the floor. But since then, my head had grown so heavy I could not lift it. Nor could I persuade my tongue to speak such apology as I wished. *Sorry . . . sorry . . . sorry. Never do I take without giving . . . or so I intend . . . never, never would I take pleasure in forcing . . . in injury . . .*

The tide of shame drenched me yet again, swirling my meager thoughts into confusion. The girl had screamed and wept and begged. How could she not be injured? Why did they laugh? Gildas's robust chortle was unmistakable. Even Malena's moans and whimpers had yielded to girlish giggles.

A bitterly cold wind raked my naked skin. Sapphire light danced beneath the flutter of my eyelashes. My gards entirely visible . . . I tried to draw in my limbs . . . hating to be so exposed . . . hating for them to see. But I could scarcely twitch my fingers.

I had felt washed clean in Aeginea—the gards a sign of renewed purpose, a hint of a joy that I had not believed existed in this life. No more of that! I had proved myself an animal, a damnable, brutish thug who had so pompously called judgment on men who corrupted children. What had come over me?

Someone new arrived, cursing under his breath, his malevolence hammering at me.

"Get her up," the priestess commanded. "Carefully, Jakome! Do not drop her on the stair. Stay abed and still until I come to you, child."

Feet shuffled and scrambled. "*Kasiya Gehoum*, mistress. *Sanguiera, orongia, vazte, kevrana.*" Bleed, suffer, die, purify. Malena's cheerful invocation of blood and suffering only worsened my confusion. *Your chosen mate . . .* not chosen by Arrosa, but by Sila Diaglou. They had used the girl—a willing girl. And used my cursed weakness for pleasuring, for wine . . .

"Did I not tell you that his appetites would be his leash?" said the monk, as if in echo of my self-condemnation. The syllables grated on my ear like steel on glass. "A little wine, a fair young body . . . and so much easier than reasoning with him or putting him to the question. He will be everything you wish. Pliable. Controllable. One taste of decadent pain and pleasure, and he is yours."

How did the priestess bear his patronizing manner? How had I ever mistaken it for brotherly mentoring and friendship?

A finger began tracing the patterns on my back. The priestess's, I knew, from the heat. At least her touch did not sap my wits this time, as I had so little remaining. Her exploration, though not purposefully brutal, did not avoid the lacerations that dribbled warm blood down my flanks. That I flinched each time she encountered one did not deter her. The blade had been no lust-fueled imagining. They must have hidden it beneath the palliasse.

"What does it mean that he displays Danae markings, Gildas? You said he did not know what he was."

"It would appear he's found out. We can ask him, as soon as he recovers enough to speak, but I would not count any report he gives as reliable. Not yet. He has no fond feelings for either of us, and you've heard his history of lies."

Recovers . . . Like a sleeping lion, mortal dread raised its head and set me screaming inside. *Wake up, fool. Wake up.* But I had smelled the wine, sampled a drop before drinking. And porridge could not mask poison.

"We must ask the old one what the marks signify and what powers they give him."

Unnamed panic threatened logic. How was it possible they knew of my mixed birth? And what *old one* could they ask? Not Stearc or Osriel. The image of Picus flew through my head, but he had no intercourse with Navronne. Why could I not lift my head and ask them?

This leaden indolence, this sodden paralysis that left me near incapable of reason . . . I had not felt the like since the morning Luviar died, the last time Gildas and I had spoken, when I yet believed him my friend . . .

And then as words and events settled like a silken shroud, giving shape to those things beneath, the simple truth came clear. Fear robbed me of breath. *Pain and pleasure . . .* Gildas knew all my vices.

Of course, I'd not smelled nivat in the wine. The heat of enchantment burned away the scent of blood-spelled nivat. They had laced the wine with doulon paste. Never had that possibility crossed my mind. Gildas was no sorcerer; he would need my blood. And now, too late, I remembered Jakome's knife and his smirk as he had slashed my hand. I had been lost the moment the first droplet of tainted wine had touched my tongue. Saverian had warned me. *A fool should know what his stupidity has cost him.*

Sila Diaglou knelt on the floor beside me. Her breath smelled of anise, and her hand stroked my hair and the back of my neck as if I were a favored hound. I would have given an arm not to shiver at her touch. I would have given both legs to believe they had not infected me with my old sin.

The woman gently blotted the blood dribbling down my back, and in a flutter of panic, I wondered if she licked it from her fingers. "They truly find pleasure in the wounding . . . during the carnal act? I'd never heard that. It seems depraved."

"Dear Sila, in these few matters . . . especially in regard to the male response . . . how could you know . . . how could even the old one know? The journals of Picus recount the Danae male's need for pain during copulation."

For one brief instant, the world grew quiet, as if I had closed off my senses to heed a stone's cry. Gildas lied. Saverian had told me the journals did not speak of nivat. And in this lie did I sound a gulf between the monk and the priestess. *Great Iero, mighty Kemen, give me strength and wit to fill that gap with liquid fire and shatter their unholy collaboration!*

"Your plan is sound, mistress. The pureblood stranglehold will be broken. The long-lived will infuse your people with strength and endurance beyond human understanding. Navronne will be brought to its knees, groveling before the Gehoum for generation upon generation." His passion sounded convincing . . . except to one who had heard this same passion for the lighthouse and its learning, for friendship and holy brotherhood.

"I must see to Malena," said the priestess, rising from my side. "That we could have a catch at first mating is presumptuous, but failure shall not be accounted to any lack of diligence on my part."

Infuse your people . . . a catch? They wanted me to breed a child on the girl . . . Harrowers and Danae and Aurellian sorcery. My spinning head came near flying off.

Gildas chuckled. "I yield to the students of Arrosa's temple. We were not taught of such women's matters at Gillarine. I'll put this one to bed. I doubt my old friend will be lucid before morning. To get him drunk loosed his true nature."

"Bring him to me as soon as he wakes tomorrow. As yet we've had no response from Prince Osriel on our offer to trade these useless prisoners for the monk. The Bastard is the last obstacle on our road. If Magnus can unlock his plots and mysteries, our war is won."

"As you command, priestess. A peaceful night to you."

"And you, Gildas. Well done."

Osriel the Bastard . . . the King of Navronne. The lord's secretary who lay ill in their dungeon. They didn't know! This reminder of my purpose gave me an anchor. They must not find out.

The door opened and closed. Someone set the lock. The wind howled and swirled, rattling the loose bars. In the lulls, I heard Gildas's breathing as he waited, and I smelled the taint of nivat on him. Had I thought it would do any good, I would have stuck a finger down my throat to purge the poison I had downed so blithely. Naught could purge the evil if I had planted a part-Danae child in Sila Diaglou's hands this night.

"So, friend Valen, do you appreciate your lovely open chamber? What captive in all Navronne has a cell so suited to his nature? You can thank me for that. I'll confess I did not at all expect to see you marked, but then, Stearc and his tidy Gram were always parsimonious with details from old Picus's journals. Did the Bastard whip these sigils out of you, or is it something like a boy's night spew that comes upon one like you at the proper time and season? And you ran away from Osriel—no surprise that—but to your family? That is perhaps the most difficult of all these manifold mysteries to comprehend." Gildas's questions were like a sea creature's tentacles, touching me lightly on every side, exploring, distracting, any one of them capable of stinging me to death.

"So am I to be kept here like a stallion until I breed true?" I said, summoning control enough to lift my head. Gildas sat across the chamber, his feet propped on the clothes chest. The faint azure glow from my gards, our only illumination, kept him a dark outline.

"I suspected you were more wakeful than you showed," he said, white teeth gleaming. "It saves me a deal of explaining. And the answer is yes, at least until the balance of power shifts on the winter solstice. The lady thinks to create a new world, where the boundaries between purebloods, ordinaries, Ardran, Moriangi, and even your dancing kinsmen are erased. You are to be—excuse the crude expression—the seed and root of that new world. Half pureblood sorcerer, half Danae. My reports of you had already intrigued her, but when I informed her of your unique bloodlines she came near rapture. We have no evidence of another Danae–pureblood mating in the history of the world."

My mind stuttered over the simple immensity of what he described. Somehow I had always dismissed Harrower rants as ploys to attract the gullible. I'd never imagined the priestess *believed* what she preached. "She would destroy pureblood sorcery?"

"Certainly the end of pureblood breeding laws will dilute the Aurellian bent. But it will take on a new life and character by the infusion of Danae blood—so Sila imagines. From the long night of the great Harrowing shall rise a new race of men and women—robust in health, what remains of the world's magic held captive in their veins, with no need for books or gods or kings or anything else that might elevate one above another. A seductive vision, is it not? She sees you, the Danae-bred Cartamandua *recondeur,* as the exemplar of her new world."

Seductive . . . deeply, intelligently seductive. Magnificent. Surely it was my addled state that came up with no answer to it. How could I argue against breaking down barriers of birth, a man who had rebelled against the strictures of breeding my entire life, son of two people who had done the same?

"How did you guess what I was? How could you possibly have known?" I had more pressing questions, but I needed time to think. Gildas lived by his cleverness. If he kept secrets from Sila Diaglou, then he likely had no confidant among her company and might enjoy a bit of boasting.

"I put it all together when you refused to walk into the Well grotto. The place profoundly affected you—as if you could feel the myrtle and hyssop that bound its guardian—and yet you had taken on the search eagerly and actually found the Well when no one else could do it. You could not have used the maps, for I had long discovered your inability to read. But the possibility that you were a Cartamandua simply did not occur to me. You are so unlike the rest of them."

"I'll thank you for that, at least." I pressed the heels of my hands into my eye sockets, trying to squeeze out the muzziness. Beyond Sila Diaglou's seductive vision lay her murderous war to implement it. I needed some way to free my friends.

Gildas continued eagerly, as I had known he would. "You'd had me curious from the night I submitted to Sila's whip—proofs of devotion are a dreadful bother. You located me despite a barricade of magic, and our companions told odd tales of ghostly apparitions that night. As I asked myself why visiting the Well would affect you so strangely, I recalled your collapse on that very first day I took you into the cloister garth—the residue of the Scourge clearly affects you, whether the rite succeeds or no. And, of course, I had witnessed your uncontrollable aversion to captivity. I could find only one explanation to encompass all these things. Days later, when Gram told me of your emotional response to seeing a Dané, I was sure of you. Truly you had me coming and going when you were exposed as a pureblood."

I blurted one cheerless guffaw. "And then I begged you to bring me nivat. You must have been beside yourself." I had handed him the very leash that would bring me to heel.

His white teeth gleamed in the dark. "The tainted water was the final test. By that time I could see that your Danae characteristics were tempered by your human heritage, so I trusted you wouldn't die from a few drops of blood in the water."

Damnable savage to so callously dismiss a boy's torment! "Do you long for hell, child murderer? For I swear by every god and demon, you will meet the Tormentor himself before another season passes."

"You will do nothing to me." He jumped up from his chair, his playful drawl abandoned. "Claudio de Cartamandua did me a great service when he made your childhood a misery. He left you weak. A penchant for unsavory pleasure rules your flesh, and this maudlin sentiment with regard to children rules your wit."

My loathing for Gildas eclipsed every hatred of my life. "If you've touched him, Gildas—"

"I've kept young Jullian safe. Intact. Healthy. He begins to understand that men of exceptional mind must lead the world out of its morass. If I choose to complete his education, he will serve as a fine acolyte in the new order. Indeed, friend Valen, I hold *everything* you want and need."

A soft clicking sound came from his direction, almost like a shower of raindrops . . . or nutshells shaken in a bag . . . or seeds . . . The earth-ripe scent that accompanied the sound constricted my lungs and clenched my gut. With every breath the craving spread its spiked tentacles through flesh and bone. The same paralyzed incapacity that prevented me from shoving Gerard's murderer through the iron bars into eternal night was all that held me back from snatching away his hoard. His soft chuckle said he knew that.

My hands trembled like a palsied beggar's. I needed to drag my mind away from nivat and the hellish cost of deeper enslavement. Saverian . . . great heaven grant that she would help me again. For now, I had to live with it and find a way to damn Gildas to eternal fire.

Somehow thoughts of my astringent angel affected me as might an icy plunge, for it occurred to me that Gildas's lie about a Danae predilection for pain meant that he had not told Sila Diaglou of my problem with the doulon. Harrowers despised twist-minds, and burnt or bled them. They did not use us to breed favorites. Which meant that Gildas intended to hide his deepest hold on me. Which meant that he had plans beyond those of Sila Diaglou, and it would best serve my interests if I learned of them. So let the arrogant gatzé believe he owned me.

"Indeed, it seems I am your thrall." It took no effort to mime a doulon slave with an aching head and resentful soul. "How much did you give me that morning you betrayed Luviar? I lost the rest of my supply on that day's adventure, and you've no concept of wrath until you try telling Osriel of Evanore that you're no good to him unless he feeds you nivat every five days."

"Every *five* days?" Gildas chortled. "I'll confess I gave you most of what you had in hopes you would lose track of the day's events. And I knew it would accelerate your cravings, a matter I thought might be useful. But I'd no idea it would compromise you so sorely. I am *sorry* for that. Truly I bear you no ill will. Tell me, what use did Osriel have for you?"

This casual inquiry bore all the power of his considerable intellect and will. The answer would take some care.

"What do you think? The Bastard wanted entry to Aeginea." Summoning every reserve of will, I reached a hand behind me to the window facing, hauled myself to my feet, and rested my ponderous head on the iron grate. "I refused to take him, and he did exactly what you will do. I held out for three days from the onset of my hunger. Remind me not to do that again, Brother."

"So you took Osriel the Bastard to Aeginea." Gildas hated that thought. "What did he learn? Who did he see? What was it like?"

"I've no idea. He waited until I was near my time again. I led him past the Sentinel Oak and promptly lost my mind. But somewhere along the way, he sold me to a clutch of the blue-marked gatzi. One of them did this"—I swept my hand across my pulsing sigils—"which makes the entire world into a madhouse. Then someone tied me to a tree and said he was going to break my knees. Gods . . . I went crazy. Broke the bindings and ran. I hope they killed the Bastard. I hope they died doing it."

"And you ran to your family. Astonishing . . . and yet your family is a strange mix. What could exemplify it better than your brother's clumsy attempt to bribe a weapon into your hand after serving you up to Sila Diaglou?"

I sputtered in disgust. "I needed money. I needed nivat. I needed a roof and walls to protect me from this rabble you've joined. That Max betrayed me to Bayard Slugwit was no surprise. And only a doulon-crazed fool would believe he'd help me out of this madhouse. He likely paid your whey-faced lout to taunt me with the knife, not give it." And more clearly than ever, Jakome was *Gildas's* whey-faced lout, not Sila Diaglou's. Jakome had taken my blood for the doulon.

"So, tell me, Brother Gildas, if the mad priestess plans to create a new world from mingling my blood with that of her mad followers, what is to be your place in it? Chief Corrupter? The Baron of Books?" And here I took the dangerous leap. "Or are your aims, perhaps, different than the lady's?"

He strolled across the room and halted just behind me. I gripped the iron window grate, straining every sense to decide if cold steel was aimed at my back. But instead, he spoke softly over my shoulder. "You know I cannot trust you, dear fellow. You have made clear that you have no use for practical, unsentimental men. Know, too, that I have given the priestess everything she has demanded of me. She is fiercely loyal and will believe no slander—especially from a renowned liar. And she relishes bleeding doulon slaves to poison Danae sianous. But I will also tell you this, my friend: Heed my direction, and one day soon, before these cretins wreak heaven's wrath on the winter solstice, you and I will exchange favors. You would like to keep your mind and be free of this madhouse and a future impreg-nating Harrower broodmares. I would like to spend the next few hundred years in Aeginea. I believe I've knowledge enough that I can buy the archon's good will, but alas, your book of maps does not suffice to get me beyond their borders."

Inside, I smiled with grim satisfaction and chose to take one more risky step. "Give me Jullian along with the nivat, and all my skills will be at your service, Brother Treacher. The boy stays with me until we go, and I breathe no word of your plan to him, to Sila, or to anyone. Sentiment and pragmatism will walk hand in hand."

His breath moved on my back, fast and hot. My own breath held still as my mind raced over everything I'd told him—where I might have yielded too easily or pushed too hard.

"Done," he said at last, clapping a hand on my bare shoulder, his forced joviality reopening one of Malena's lacerations. He snatched up the bloody rag from the floor and blotted the wound.

I did not allow him to see my fierce hope. If I could truly persuade the blackguard to give me Jullian, I would tear down these walls with my toes if need be to get us out.

"The diviners have foreseen the fall of humankind, Valen. It is up to each of us to find our way through it. Follow my lead, and you will survive as you have all these years." He dropped something onto the table and tapped on the door. The door guard let him out and set the lock.

His parting gift comprised a small canvas bag holding a silver needle, a linen thread, a finger-length rectangle of mirror glass, and three nivat seeds—far too few for one doulon spell, but sufficient to rouse my hunger. I clutched the bag to my chest and told myself that I dared not risk my pretense of cooperation by tossing the seeds from the window.

If I were actually planning to deliver Gildas to Max, I could save my brother the work of interrogation and tell him Gildas's secrets, writ as plain as my own on this night. Instead of serving as the lighthouse Scholar, vowed to teach the world what might be forgotten in the Great Harrowing, Gildas planned to keep his treasury of knowledge all to himself. Instead of watching magic that he himself could never possess become every man's birthright, he could astonish the ignorant by fashioning a spindle, by predicting the sunrise or the change of seasons, by working the magic of fire by striking flint to steel or the magic of life by suturing a wound. Gildas fancied himself a prophet, an alchemist, a sorcerer. The weary survivors of the world's chaos would name him a god.

Chapter 23

Lust and nivat plagued my dreams. I was out of bed and pacing my tower cage well before what passed for sunrise. I donned my shirt and chausses, unable to bear the thought of my captors gawking at the mystery of my gards, and hoping that clothing might quench the dual fires that plagued me with fits of the shakes.

Trying to recapture some use of my senses, I examined the inner side of the door locks, peering through the seams of the door, tapping, shaking, rattling. The exercise revealed little. I needed to be out of here.

When Malena brought ale and bread, I could not eat. I could not speak. I could not look at her without wanting to tear away her gown—stitched of common russet, buttoned tight across her breasts to reveal everything of softness and curves. I hated myself for it. I hated those who tempted me to it. I didn't understand it. In the past, the doulon had quenched all fleshly desires, not driven them. I donned my pourpoint, thinking to put another layer between my skin and temptation.

The girl played the good wife, commenting upon the weather and the food and did I wish for a heavier cloak to wear over my garments. She folded the clothes still scattered on the floor and laid them in the clothes chest. She even began some apology for serving me wine laced with "vigger's salt," which was the common name for saffron that alley witches swore could inflame a man's flagging prick.

I choked on a miserable laugh, closed off my hearing, and clung to the window bars. Saffron was more expensive than nivat.

Though I did not suffer from the cold, the morning was bitter. Ice crystals whipped through the barred windows, swirling on the floor and settling like dust in the cracks and crevices on either side of the door. In the mottled gray of storm and smoke, Palinur spread below my tower like a battlefield, its streets and houses like fallen soldiers— some of them charred ruins, half buried in mud and blackened snow, a few still displaying life and movement. Somewhere out there, Voushanti and Saverian awaited my call.

Considering the two of them gave me extraordinary comfort. That a dead man with a mote of hell in his eye and a physician with a desert for a heart seemed like the world's finest companions told me what a nest of lunatics I'd come to. And I was as bad as any of them. The moment I had Jullian at my side, we would find a way through this damnable door, down to the prison level, and out of this cursed place.

"Dear Magnus, the day is so very cold." A weight pressed softly against my back and Malena reached her arms about my waist. She was shivering, and my arms ached to enfold her. "Could we not begin again? If we learned more of each other, we could be friends." Her fingernails were chewed and broken, ridged with black dirt and a rusty residue that could so easily be old blood. *Saints and angels!*

I grasped one of her hands as it snaked toward my groin and twisted her arm as I turned, using it to force her back toward the door. "Let us learn more of each other, Malena. Shall I tell you stories of my friend Gerard, of how he loved to watch the wall of light move across the refectory or how he named all the abbey's goats after holy saints or how this boy, who blanched at butchering a chicken, sat bravely on a wounded soldier, singing of hearth and home, as our infirmarian sawed off the man's leg? Tell me, Malena, did you cut Gerard at the Well? Did you drive the spikes that held his hands to the rock or taste his blood? You will need more than vigger's salt to make me lie with you of my own will."

Even as I spoke these things, my body craved her. Revolted, I shoved her against the wall and returned to my window. I would bind my hands to the bars before touching her again.

"You speak bravely in the light, Magnus," she said, all sweetness foregone. "But when I come in the night, you shall bend as the earth must bend before the power of the Gehoum. They care naught for one boy, naught for you, naught for me, but only that the land and people be subdued and humble and made clean. Your body speaks their will. Look at your hands." Indeed my shaking dwarfed her shivers.

She rapped on the door and was released. I wondered if the unhappy Jakome was forced to deliver her to me. I hoped so. I wondered if she had "caught," and near screamed at the thought of a child given life from a doulon-fed frenzy and in such a creature as Malena.

The morning was quiet so high in the tower. I fidgeted and paced. I sipped Saverian's potion, hoping it might quench these other uneasy sensations as effectively as it controlled my stomach. After my outburst at Malena, I might find myself in the dungeons by midday. I touched the stone floor and, for the tenth time that morning, verified that the guide threads I had established the previous night were still intact. Somewhere far below me, Osriel and Stearc yet breathed.

I had just emptied the ale pitcher out the window without tasting its contents, when the bolts and latches rattled again. This time I heeded every snick of pins and levers in the locks. My visitor was Gildas.

"You've distressed our little wench this morning, Valen."

"As long as I've a mind to choose with, I choose not to dance to Sila Diaglou's music," I said. "Which leaves me perhaps two days until I succumb." I prayed I was misleading him. The more preoccupied I seemed to be with my cravings, the less cautious he might be.

"I am to take you to the priestess. Alas, good Jakome is required to bind your hands against the chance of some magical escape. Do I need to call for shackles, as well, or ruffians with blades?"

Lifting the hems of pourpoint and shirt, I showed him his little bag tied at my waist. "Your leash is quite strong enough, though it's mostly promises as yet; three seeds get me nowhere but sick. Nor have I seen my young friend this morning. And all bargains are moot, if the priestess thinks to bleed me."

Gildas grinned. "Sila much prefers you alive . . . as do I. I discussed Jullian with her last night, suggesting we entrust the boy to your care. I proposed that he could relieve Malena of serving your meals. Thus reassured that we mean well, you might be more attentive to the young woman's charms." Sila seemed receptive. Perhaps you could set her remaining doubts at rest during this morning's interview. Each hour you behave well will add weight to your nivat bag."

Gildas admitted Jakome, who carried a grimy wad of silken cord. The silkbinding took an extraordinarily long time, for Jakome wasn't particularly good at it. He bound the cords tight, but uneven. And unlike pureblood guards, whose skilled binding left no bit of flesh exposed and not the least possibility of movement, Jakome failed to keep my fingers properly clasped and tucked as he worked. With a little time, I might be able to wriggle my thumbs loose and poke them through the coils of cord. The bony man completed the tedious task by spitting on the already filthy wrappings, evidently his idea of a proper torment.

Gildas led the way down the tight coil of worn and broken steps. Jakome followed behind me.

Once free of the wards on my door, I snatched the opportunity for spellwork. *Dead man. Fallow.* I closed my eyes and fed a bit of magic into the words. *Fallow* would inform Saverian and Voushanti that I was alive and safe enough for the moment. I strained my inner ear until I heard the echo. *Bluejay. Fallow.* In heart and head I thanked Saverian for her cleverness and skill.

How different from this doulon-fed frenzy had been the forces that heated me as I lay with Saverian in the shrubbery. I needed to hold fast to that memory . . . which made me smile at what Saverian might say to my using carnal thoughts of *her* to shield me from unsavory lust.

Three landings down, a doorway opened into a long, wide passage. Embrasures along the left-hand wall admitted smoke and dusty light. A purposeful stumble allowed me to sneak a glimpse through one of them. The passage was actually an enclosed gallery that overlooked the long hall where I had been delivered the previous afternoon. Observers or bowmen could lurk here, completely hidden from below.

Opposite the embrasure wall, dim chambers opened off the gallery, appearing, for the most part, to be but habitat for spiders. But Gildas stopped at one doorway hung with a blanket. He held back the dingy wool, and Jakome shoved me into a cavelike chamber.

No windows graced this room. Arrow loops on the outer wall admitted bitter air and threads of wan daylight that scarce sufficed to keep me from colliding with Gildas. The now-familiar pressure of walls grew as I stood in the close quarters, but my stomach stayed in place, and again I blessed Saverian for her potion.

"Sila should be here by now." Gildas's voice dripped annoyance.

The sullen Jakome fed and stirred coals that smoldered in a rusty brazier. The rising flames pushed the darkness back a little.

The long, narrow chamber appeared to be a soldier's billet, or more properly, a commander's billet, as I saw no sign that more than one person slept here. Wool blankets were folded neatly atop a rolled-up palliasse. A folding table and several stools leaned against one wall, alongside a pile of leather saddle packs. For the most part the accumulated dust, dried mud clots, ancient straw, stone flakes, wood chips, bark, and ash that grimed the chamber and hearth had been left where they lay. But the end wall closest to me, where the firelight shone brightest, had been swept and scrubbed clean before someone mounted a map of Navronne. Only in my family's home had I ever seen a map so large—fully twice the width of my arm span and almost as high. Janus de Cartamandua had drawn both of them.

Jakome took up a guard stance at the door. Gildas had begun to pace, glancing constantly into the shadows as if expecting gatzi to pop out at us.

I could not take my eyes from the map, noting the bold arcs of Janus's roads, each drawn in one stroke of his favorite pen, the particular feathery gray foliage of his trees that no artist had ever been able to duplicate, the oddly individual faces he gave to the birds that inhabited the map borders. Heaven's mercy, had he known what happened to failed Danae?

Gildas glanced from me to Jakome. "Something's off. Don't let him out of here."

The monk pushed through the hanging blanket and disappeared. Jakome drew his sword and blocked the doorway behind him. His mouth twisted upward and his sharp eyes fixed on me, as if he hoped I would challenge him.

But it was the map that drew me, not the prospect of being skewered trying to escape while my hands were bound. Jakome made no move to stop me as I strolled across the room to an arrow loop and peered down at an inner ward littered with broken masonry and fine rubble. Several corbeled privies had collapsed, tearing down half of a sewage-stained wall. After a short time, I drifted idly toward the map.

Something struck me as odd beyond its grand scale, but I couldn't decide what it was. The borders and compass rose were grandly decorated. The firelight sparkled from flecks of gold that had been mixed with some of the inks. It was certainly very old. A Cartamandua map never yellowed or cracked, but rather took on a certain luster, as if the lines and colors, the drawing and the magic had blended and transformed it into something richer and deeper than its parts. This one seemed near as deep as it was wide. The ink washes were curious—only two colors, green and ocher, spread across irregularly shaped areas that corresponded to no other boundaries. Yet there was something more . . .

Uneasy, I glanced over my shoulder at the bored Jakome and at the far end of the chamber where the darkness hung so deep, unpenetrated by flame or thready daylight. Then I peered a little closer at the map.

Increasingly frustrated, I tapped my silkbound hands on my mouth and chin, rested them on my head, and dropped them down again. My fingers itched to trace the web of paths, like those through Mellune Forest, where I had misled the pursuing Harrowers. They ached to touch the fine details, such as the cairn that marked the split in the track leading to Caedmon's Bridge and Fortress Groult. In satisfaction I noted the vast distances Saverian and I had frog-leaped from the rounded hills of northeastern Ardra to the hills of Palinur, to the bogs, to the cairn, to the Sentinel Oak—

I blinked. I would have sworn I had seen the faint shape of the Sentinel Oak depicted beside the cairn near Caedmon's Bridge, but now I stared at the spot directly, I saw only the cairn. I angled my head to the side, and again glimpsed the tree.

Shifting my examination westward, I scanned past the limits of civilized lands, across the wilds of the Aponavi, to the shores of the western sea that separated Navronne and Cymra from the uncharted lands beyond. Under a wash of green, the coastline jagged and curved, and I wondered which curve might be the shore of Evaldamon—Kol's sianou, where the days passed more slowly than elsewhere in Aeginea. Somehow I felt that if I could touch the map, I would know such truths—as if I were a blind man touching his lover's face.

Of a sudden, I caught my breath—that's what it was. This map had no words! Not one anywhere.

"Wait outside, Jakome." Sila Diaglou's cool voice spun me away from the map. "And you, dear Gildas, I wish you to take our provisioning in hand. Hurd's fifth legion, the last of our assault force, marches for Evanore this afternoon, and Falderrene has not the cleverness to see it done properly. The Grav has been so busy rousting purebloods, he's had no time to see to it himself."

Sila swept through the door curtain. Gildas followed close behind, protesting. "But, holy one, I was to be here—"

"I prefer to interview Magnus alone. Remind Jakome that no one interrupts me. And take the book—I want another site before tomorrow."

"Of course, holy one." Gildas, flushed the hue of poppies, rummaged in the piled baggage and pulled out a thick square of brown leather, then inclined his back and left.

I stared after him, ready to bash my head against the wall in frustration. Perhaps Sila knew Gildas was not entirely committed to her purposes. Perhaps not. But she had just sent him away with my book of Cartamandua maps. I had not been certain it yet existed.

Once we were alone, the priestess moved briskly to retrieve a soiled cloak from the piled baggage. She fastened it about her shoulders and drew it close, giving an exaggerated shiver as she moved to the hearth. The action made her seem almost human.

"The cusp of autumn arrives untimely." She gazed into the leaping flames and spoke in a dreamy singsong voice. "Dun haze. Tarnished gold. Leaves . . . glory dulled . . . whipped from their branches. Wolves gather, howling, gnawing the light. No more the culmination of summer, but harbinger of bitter blue days and ever longer nights. The dance is finished, and my heart aches for the waning season."

She looked over her shoulder at me, her eyes narrowed, judging. "My grandmother taught me that when I was very small. It's supposed to be sung. Have you heard it?"

"No," I said, mystified, wary.

"She called it 'The Canticle of the Autumn.' I'm sure there once was a canticle for each season, but she never sang any but this one. Autumn is a sorrowful season. A dying season."

Somehow such flat pronouncement raised my dander. "This autumn, yes. But a rightful autumn is golden and fruitful, a worthy celebration of summer's labors."

"And so you would say, too, that winter is not death."

Who could argue that the winter that held Navronne in its grip was not death? Not I, who had always envisioned the netherworld as a dungeon of ice.

Turning back to the fire, she drew a greasy packet from her cloak, unwrapped it, and pulled out two flat strips of dried meat. She tore off a bite and closed her eyes in the way of a soldier who has been too long in the field and savors his meat as a sign he yet lives. Wordless, she offered me the second piece. I shook my head, and she devoured it, while I repeatedly rolled one thumb against the other in an attempt to free them from their bindings. I hated feeling so helpless in her presence.

When she had finished the meat and wiped her hands on her breeches, she drained a small flask rifled from the depths of her cloak. Then she sighed and tossed another stick on the fire. "I apologize for your hand bindings, for your confinement, and for last night's . . . coercion. You showed up at my door so unexpectedly. Though I believe you will eventually grant me your willing cooperation, events leave me little leeway for chance, and I must seize opportunity. Malena happens to be fertile just now."

"I await your explanations, madam." Though expert at lies, I had never been very successful at feigning cooperation with those who restrained me and pretended they were doing it for some greater good. Yet I neither spat at her nor cursed her soul to everlasting fire as I would like to have done. If I were to save my friends, I needed to find some common ground with this woman.

"You were examining my map," she said, ignoring my abruptness. "It's a Cartamandua map, as I'm sure you can tell—an unusual one."

"I've seen only a few so large." Perhaps she would tell me what *she* thought was unusual. No words . . . I'd never seen a finished map lacking written names and keys. Janus had not made it for me; it was far too old. Yet naught gave me indication that it was incomplete. His own gryphon mark was scribed at the lower right corner. The cartographer's mark was always the last thing added.

"You may study it sometime, if you wish, before I destroy it." No gloating or cruelty or irony accompanied this offer. With the same casual sincerity that Picus spoke of forsaking the human world to live in penitence, she spoke of destroying a work of incomparable magic, artistry, and breadth of knowledge. It must have taken Janus more than a year just to render it, and untold years of travel and study to gather the material for the early sketches. Saints and angels, the vellum itself was priceless without accounting for the map. Only a few sorcerers in the history of Navronne had been able to transform sewn vellum into so large and seamless a whole.

"Why would you destroy such a marvel?" I said, the tantalizing mystery overwhelming my wish to let her lead the conversation. "What god could possibly wish it? Surely to know the size and variety of the world can but glorify whatever powers rule it."

Sila nodded, as if expecting that very question. "The map, like those things hidden in the Gillarine lighthouse, is an artifact of corruption. Until we have lived through the age of breaking and repentance, we have no need for such knowledge. Until we have destroyed the barriers that separate those who can make such a thing from those who cannot, we have no right to it. We shall drive the purebloods from their comfortable walls and squeeze the long-lived from their hiding places, breaking down the boundaries of birth and blood that hoard their gifts from humankind. When my use for this map is done, I'll burn it. I don't expect you to grasp everything right away."

Right away . . . So she expected me to live beyond the moment, at least. "Do you truly believe that mating me with your illiterate handmaiden will enable every man and woman to create such a work as this?"

"If not, then we have no need of such works." Always simple

answers. Of all the things I had learned in my life, nothing was so simple as fanatics imagined.

"I don't understand any of this," I said. "I very much dislike being used for *anyone's* breeding projects."

Even from the side, I could see her smile blossom. The curve of her lips dimpled her left cheek just below the terrible scar, completely transforming her. She would never be a transcendent beauty like Elene, but when Sila Diaglou turned her smile on me, it felt as if Navronne's winter had yielded to such a glory of summer as I could scarce remember. The world and all its troubles receded into dim anxiety beside an urgent need to touch her cheek. *Great merciful Mother!* Was my entire being reduced to naught but my treacherous prick?

"I fully expected such rebellious sentiment from you, Magnus. Your indignation but confirms that you are meant to stand at my side and lead our people into a new age."

"*Lead?* At your side?" No beggar presented with a crown of rubies could be more astonished or more skeptical.

She rose and joined me at the map, smiled again, and with one finger gently closed my mouth. "Who else could I trust to see both the wisdom of the future I propose and its dangers? Your life will stretch long enough to ensure we move past our time of suffering and penitence and into the new order"—she touched my wrist, setting my skin afire where a streak of pale blue peeked out between the silk-binding and my sleeve—"longer than I first imagined, longer than my own. Your unique magic will grow in these stretched years, serving to keep you safe and strong enough to lead. And your moral stature will shield the remnants of the old races from oppression as they die away."

I had expected to find Sila Diaglou evil incarnate, a leering devil who relished blood, or perhaps a drooling madwoman who saw macabre visions. What was beginning to disturb me most were these times that she seemed halfway reasonable. She shivered in the chilly fortress, relished her supper, had a grandmother who taught her songs. She worried about moral stature and oppression . . . which made her act of stabbing a spear through Boreas's gut to pin his bleeding body to the earth all the more horrific. I would not allow myself to become one of her besotted sheep.

I wrenched my attention from her face before I was completely undone. Behind her, the hanging blanket that covered the door to the gallery swayed, as if just dropped back into place. Despite Jakome's wards, someone had been standing there, listening to what she had just said. Or perhaps I was merely twitchy because Gildas's danger loomed so large. The last place on earth I dared stand was on some pedestal Gildas desired for himself.

I stepped away from Sila. If she viewed the move as a retreat, so be it. "Madam, I claim no unique magic and no moral stature. Indeed I think you mistake me for someone entirely different. But even if I were as you say, and even if I espoused your goals—which seem so grand as to be impossible—how could a person of any 'moral stature' countenance your tactics? These rites of blood, these burnings, and spreading fear . . ." I dared not mention the Danae. Not until I understood more. "I don't believe in your Gehoum."

"Your feelings are but confirmation of my judgment," she said without the least trace of rancor. "They do you credit. But you must abandon your childish views, these notions of benevolent mother goddesses, compassionate father gods, and nurturing Danae guardians. No one tends this world. The universe is not benevolent. Look upon the stars—equal in their clarity, undivided in their brilliance—and the harsh truth of the universe becomes clear. I name this truth *Gehoum* that my followers might grasp it. It prescribes simplicity and demands order, and we who see the rancorous division and greed our ancestors have wrought upon the world, the corruption, this hoarding of talent, wealth, and privilege, the cruelties of war and servitude, must accomplish its return to purity. To me falls the dread task of cleansing, to you the task of regeneration. Our destinies track side by side, but shall never . . . *marry*." Her apologetic smile ravished my wits.

Of a sudden, wood rapped on stone from the gloom at the far end of the chamber. "*Regeneration*? Fool of a girl! Didst thou think I would not learn of this connivance?"

"Grandam! Why are you hiding here?" Sila grabbed an unlit torch from the sconce by the door and shoved it into the brazier. Once it flared, she raised it high.

The shadows fled to reveal a person sitting in the room's farthest corner. Shapeless robes and wimple hid all but her face and the walking stick she rapped angrily against the floor.

"I seek to understand why my dearest girl has not brought me this perverse creature fallen into her grasp. As she does not see fit to confide in me, I must resort to devious means."

The pale-complected woman who voiced this harsh complaint was the ancient I had seen with Sila in the hall the previous day.

"Have you learned no lesson I've taught you, girl? The long-lived are a wound, festering with pride and corruption. They serve no purpose and cannot be made clean. And these Aurellian magicians dare set themselves above the rest of us. The world must be purged of them both, along with Caedmon's prideful get. This halfbreed is abomination, yet you think to breed him and make more?"

"I will not bend just because you and I disagree, Grandam." Exhibiting her coldest self again, Sila set the blazing torch in its sconce and knelt beside the old woman to kiss her cheek. "You would chastise me did I betray my convictions for sentiment, would you not? Thus I chose not to distress you with my decision."

"But what is this breeding plan but sentimental attachment to corruption?" No excess affection displayed itself between Sila and her elder as they argued the merits of the world's ruin.

Momentarily abandoned, I shook off my fascination with Sila Diaglou's family disagreements, and stooped down as if using my bundled hands to adjust my boot. A little more wriggling and my thumbs poked through the layered cords and touched the floor. I poured out magic, searching for the threads of life I had created the previous night. Gods, I was halfway to the prince and Stearc.

"Magnus?" Sila's hand touched my shoulder.

I blinked and looked up. "My boot . . ."

The lady's laugh bit flesh as fiercely as Malena's blade. "Do you think I don't know what you do when you touch the ground? Gildas has told me of your Aurellian bent—and of your fondness for the Karish boy. Truly I have no wish to do him harm."

This gentle declaration appalled me. She did not see what she had done to Gerard and Jullian as harm. How could a flesh-and-blood woman feel *nothing*?

One by one my secrets had fallen open to her, but anger hardened my resolve that she would *not* learn the rest. "You are most gracious, madam," I said, bowing my head and climbing to my feet with as much dignity as bound hands allowed. "This child . . . I'll confess I am preoccupied. He saved my life. Such a debt must be repaid, else a man's life never comes into balance. With my own fate so little in my control, my concern for *his* rules both head and heart."

"You must tame such weakness that your mind may be devoted to the greater good, Magnus. So my grandmother taught me." She beckoned me to follow. "Come, she asks to meet you."

Dutifully I stood before the old woman—older than I had thought from a distance. Framed by veil and wimple, her brow was high and her cheeks taut over square-cut bones like Sila's, her dry skin finely checkered, like linen washed too many times and shriveled in the sun. Yet her turquoise eyes were astonishingly unclouded by time.

They could have looked out at me from the face of a maid of one-and-twenty, save for the layer upon layer of despite in them. No few decades could have accumulated the depth of malice written in this woman's face.

"Tell me of your parentage, abomination," she said, wasting no time on pleasantries.

More than Gildas, more even than Sila, this woman incited me to caution. Her intelligence and festered grievance were so closely twined, opening anything of myself to her felt akin to spreading the lips of a wound and asking for salt. "I believe your granddaughter thinks bloodlines important only in their purposeful unraveling."

She leaned forward, her invisible hands propped on her stick, her body formless beneath the heavy robes that draped her head and spilled from her shoulders. "Call it an old woman's curiosity."

Years . . . malevolence . . . somehow the pressure of her scrutiny squeezed an answer out of me. "My father is Janus de Cartamandua-Magistoria, a pureblood who languishes in drooling mania for his sins. I did not know my mother, and he did not tell me of her. I was raised as human, only learning of my dual heritage these past weeks."

"Son of the pureblood who returned Caedmon's spawn to Navronne." Hatred poured out of the old woman in a poison spew. "That itself is enough reason to drain thy blood. Who told you of your unnatural birthing if not the animal who caused it?"

No difficulty in framing this answer. Truth would suffice. "My master, Prince Osriel, is an uncommon mage. He suspected the truth—using much the same evidence as Gildas, I suppose. Once his theory proved correct, he discarded me in some bargain with the Danae. Osriel explains neither his methods nor reasons."

"And now you have passed two of the remasti while out of your head. How is that possible? The dam directs such matters. Yet she has clearly been uninterested all these years, and who else of the long-lived would bother to force a human-raised halfbreed through the passages? And why?"

The old woman held me paralyzed with her attention—a much more fearsome scrutiny than Sila's. I dared not answer. I dared not meet her gaze. Surely she could read my flesh and bone. Sila saw people as clay to be molded to her will. This woman viewed us as prey.

"I desire to look upon his gards." The old woman's crackling voice rose a note. "Perhaps they are but pureblood enchantment designed to deceive, some play of this cursed Osriel. Have him show me, Sila."

"This serves no purpose, Grandam. His marks are not spell-worked." Sila's impatience scraped my nerves, creating noise and distraction when some insight waited just beyond my grasp. How did the old woman know so much of Danae?

As much to quiet the argument as anything else, I stuck my bundled hands in front of the old woman's nose. "Look as you please, gammy. The god-cursed Danae did this thing to me. For all I know, they were trying to drive me as mad as my father."

With a sigh of exasperation, Sila yanked my sleeve upward as far as it would go, exposing my right wrist and half my forearm. The gards had paled to silver, faintly tinted with blue. The old woman bent her head over my arm. Her breath seared my skin, as if hellfire burned within her withered body.

She slumped back into her chair. "The gards are true," she said, her venom muted.

"As long as you confess their validity, then tell me what skills they give him, Grandam."

The old woman averted her face. Had I not been cranked tight as a crossbow, I might not have noted the alteration in her expression— a closing, as if she had determined not to share what she had seen. "After taking the two remasti so short a time ago? Nothing of import. He experiences the world as unending noise and confusion. If you want to keep him living, lock him away where he can touch the wind and breathe. I am surprised he is not slamming his head against these walls. I am *not* surprised you find him pliable to breeding lust. He has completed only two changes. The third awaits."

The third remasti—the maturing of fleshly desire—was that what was happening to me? How did she know?

Frigid as the coming night, Sila glanced from her grandmother to me. "And one more question . . . Gildas says that Danae males need pain to quicken their seed. You never told me that."

The old woman snorted, an amusement that sounded like cracking wood. "I'm sure he must be correct," she said. "Gildas knows everything. My small experience is of *human* males, and that is quite revolting enough. Do not fear, granddaughter, this one shall become everything you wish."

"Who are you?" I whispered.

The old woman merely bobbed her head while staring until I felt naked.

Sila grabbed two of the folding stools and beckoned me to the brazier, leaving the old woman hunched in her dim corner like a mother spider. Relief warmed me more than the flames.

"Do not expect me to apologize for my grandmother's plain speech. Grandam has a gift for seeing through all the world's masks, and she has taught me to do the same. We speak as we find. But my experience out in the field, seeing the cleansing as we accomplish it, has caused my vision to expand beyond hers. Once the harrowing is done, something will grow; it can be weeds or it can be wheat. I have great hopes for you."

She beamed, and I began to understand why men and women destroyed themselves for her. Her beliefs permeated her being—flesh and spirit indistinct one from the other and exposed for all to view. She stood as an exemplar of truth, naught hidden, naught sly or deceitful. She wore no mantle of ambition or greed. No petty grievance sullied her mission. No wonder the battered poor overlooked her ruthless strikes against their own interests. They *believed* her.

I could not succumb to fascination. For every answer I gleaned, two more questions arose. "To learn more of this vile"—I gestured toward my body—"*state* I have been left in would be a boon. *Noisy* is a mild description of what they've done to me. How does your grandmother know these things?"

"She has lived a long time. And now, dear Magnus"—she leaned forward, hands folded—"I must know about Prince Osriel."

For near an hour, she questioned me, precisely and specifically, about Osriel's magic, his fortresses, his legions, and his gold. The intriguing map loomed over us, yet I could spare no thoughts for it. The interrogation justified the prince's close grip on his secrets, for I had scant need to lie or hide anything. I spoke of his cruel and varying humors, of his disdain for friends and confidants, and his callous use of Jullian as hostage. Without mentioning gold mines or walking dead men, I spoke of my certainty that Osriel dabbled in vile and wicked sorcery, developed through long study. I described in gruesome detail the scene in Gillarine's kitchen when he took the dead messenger's eyes, while disclaiming any knowledge of what he did with them. When she asked me what I could tell of his military aide, Mardane Voushanti, rumored to be under diabolical influence, I said only that the man was a formidable warrior and shared his master's scorn for unskillful pureblood vagabonds. And I could certainly tell her nothing of Osriel's bargain with the Danae.

When she questioned me of Evanori military strength, I gave her modest estimates of the warmoot and vouched the warlords' loyalty was for Caedmon's kin and no love for Osriel himself. And when she probed to discover his plans, I said only that I had been discovered and tossed out before I could hear the prince's charge to his warriors. The Bastard believed his brothers weak and untrustworthy, I said, and Sila herself to be his only worthy rival. All his machinations were to defeat her—but I swore I could not tell her what those strategies were. "He never trusted me."

While displaying reluctance to aid her cause, I let her tease out this information. And I focused my answers through the prism of Osriel's betrayal, allowing my rage to surface and taint every detail of my experiences with the worst possible interpretation. And as I spoke, I gave full rein to my body's certainty that the arrow slits in her walls were closing and I would soon be dead of suffocation. Sweat beaded on my forehead, and I twitched and fidgeted. Her grandam should be well pleased that I was half a lunatic.

"What of this Stearc of Erasku?" she said, after I repeated my claim that Osriel favored no Evanori lord above another. "Your friend from the cabal? And his secretary and his charming *squire*? How does Osriel view their activities?"

I croaked a laugh. "Friend? The thane damned me as a coward from our first meeting. And I don't believe he changes his mind. The only time I saw Stearc at Renna was on the night of the warmoot, amid the other lords. I glimpsed Gram—the secretary—only briefly on that visit, but was not allowed to speak with him. I doubt the prince takes notice of secretaries. As for the girl, she near fainted from fright when I once mentioned Osriel's name. I gathered she believed he would flay them for their activities."

"Why did you help the cabal? Gildas could not explain why you would endanger yourself for those who want to preserve their superiority over common men."

"I was looking for advantage," I said. "If they had found out I could not read, they would have thrown me out of Gillarine. I had no intention of starving." As I said this, it came to me that this crass rendering was naught but truth. Yet even if I had dared explain to Sila Diaglou how my motives had changed, she would not have understood. *Faith* was not a word she had use for.

"So what of the monk you saved from my hangman—the chancellor Victor—what happened to him?"

"Osriel never permitted me to see him. He claimed that his house mage had put Brother Victor into a healing sleep to recover from his wounds. I didn't particularly care. Save for Jullian, the Tormentor can take the whole lot of the cursed cabal—including your pet monk, Gildas. They thought to use me, just like every other person in my life has sought to use me, and when they had squeezed the use from me, they threw me to the dogs. The boy was the only one of the lot who tried to teach me how to read their fine books."

"Loyalty is a great virtue and should be rewarded." She stood and motioned me toward the door. I prayed I had not given her anything of value, nor condemned myself with some contradiction of Stearc's testimony.

"Jakome!" The guard came running. "Return Magnus to his chamber and unbind his hands. Then inform Gildas that, at his convenience, he may release the boy to our guest's protection."

She held my wrists and smiled, sending spiders' feet creeping up my back. "Sleep well, and do not think to deny Malena again. She is strong and faithful, and it is my will that she catch your seed."

Chapter 24

Leaving Sila's chamber felt like crawling out of a grave. Jakome led me to the tower stair, only to have Sila call him back to her door for one more message—a summons for Gildas to join her for the evening meal.

As I awaited my jailer's return, the downward stair gaped dark in front of me. I wished an apology to those who languished below. *One more day, Lord Prince,* I said. *One more day, Stearc. Let me get Jullian and then I'll find a way down to you.* More than any bloodline, book, or tool, this world needed something of innocence preserved.

"Come, Grandam. I will take you back to your room." As Jakome sauntered back toward me, Sila led her grandmother down the gallery. The old woman moved in a halting, rolling gait, leaning heavily on Sila's arm and a walking stick. Surely some cruelty had blighted her life to nurture such malevolence.

Of a sudden, the world held its breath . . . as bits and pieces of our strange interview peppered my thoughts like wind-driven sand. "What's wrong with the old woman?" I whispered, not expecting an answer.

"Move along or I'll see you walk the same as she," said Jakome, snarling and shoving me roughly toward the stair. "Even crippled, you can still service a quenyt."

I balked, staring at the two receding backs. "Sila's grandam . . . her legs are crippled . . . or is it her knees?"

"What of it?" he said. "Now get on with you."

The *old one,* they called her, the venomous old woman who knew the lore of Danae. A woman bitter at humankind and the Danae and Caedmon's line alike, whose shapeless garments hid hands and feet, arms and crippled knees . . . and what else?

"What do you name the old woman?" I said, as I stumbled numbly up the stairs and through the door of my tower chamber.

"She gives no one her name," said my jailer, unbinding my hands. "She says we're to call her the Scourge."

Surely breaking a girl's knees at fourteen would sow hatred enough for a lifetime of bitter harvesting—especially in a girl whose half-Danae father had broken the Canon and whose human mother had murdered her kin. Especially in a child who had been taunted and shunned and used to trick her own mother to her death. Ronila.

The one person who had ever been kind to her—a human man vowed to chastity—had tormented himself with guilt after lying with her. And even Picus had turned away from her, choosing to hold to his monk's vows and stay with his young prince while Ronila fled to the human world, bringing with her knowledge of the Scourge— the Danae vulnerability to tormented death.

Wind howled through the window bars. I had neither eaten nor drunk since the previous night, and the hunger and chill crept into my bones. I wasn't sure whether I needed to crawl under the quilts or take off my clothes.

Jakome slammed the door and shot the bolts. I sank to my bed and imagined what might have gone through Ronila's mind when Eodward and Picus had returned to Navronne. An old woman by then, she would have seen Picus still in his prime, reflecting his prince's glory. Five short years after their return, Picus had vanished—after Ronila had shown him evidence that the offspring of Danae–human mating had no souls, a grandchild, perhaps, nurtured and tutored in the ways of hate, a granddaughter who saw no crime in slaughter, who believed that art and beauty, learning and faith were corruption and that the earth must be wiped clean of gods and Danae, monks and kings—everything Picus valued. Even in his despair, he could not have imagined what she would grow up to be.

Now I knew what had nagged at my head when Picus recounted Ronila's accusations. The halfbreed girl's condemnation had reflected the words of the Harrower blood rite—*sanguiera, orongia, vazte*. Bleed, suffer, die. Ronila, the Scourge. Sila Diaglou, a mixed-blood Dané.

No wonder Sila used a wordless map. She could read words no better than I could. No gards marked her hands—not even the pale silver of gards too long hidden. So she had not passed even the first remasti. My experience was so different—being half-Aurellian sorcerer already—I had no idea what power Sila might have. Was it her Danae blood that enabled her to mesmerize a crowd, to make women weep when they saw her scarred cheeks, to make men believe that they should tear down their cities and burn their fields? She had said her grandmother had taught her to control her heart and her body, so she must be unmatched in discipline . . . but then, the world knew that already. And she would not be easy to kill. Gods, the others . . . the cabal . . . Osriel . . . needed to know this great secret.

I crouched beside the door and ran my fingers over the lock. The warded iron was no more yielding of its secrets than earlier. Nonetheless, I pulled one of the pebblelike armaments game pieces from the clothes chest, examined it carefully, and used its likeness along with my experience and estimates of this type of lock to lay the rough groundwork for a spell.

Once I had done what I could—without a better idea of the lock or magic to feed the spell, that was not so much—I shed my outer layers of pourpoint and boots, hiked up my shirtsleeves and unlaced the neck, and sat against the wall under the middle window. As sheltered from the wind as I could manage, I hoped the bit of exposure might strengthen my gards without giving me frostbite. I practiced closure and control, listening only for footsteps on the stair. Ready.

Next time the door latches rattled, I was able to visualize the snap of the bronze levers and the draw of the lock pins. By the time the door opened to Gildas, I had refined my internal image of the lock.

"Whoa, a dismal, blustery afternoon," he said, standing in the doorway and holding a small lamp. "Is the coming storm too stout even for a halfbreed Dané?"

"Where is Jullian?" I said, without moving. "The priestess gave her permission for him to stay here."

"Jakome brings him. I wanted to make a few things clear before his arrival."

Gildas wrenched a balky handle on the outside of the door and shut the door firmly behind him. The pins and levers moved—slight differences this time with the latch already set. I refined the lock's image yet again.

Suppressing a smile, I opened my palms in invitation. My gards wreathed my fingers in sapphire light.

He used his small lamp to light the larger one on my table. Then he squatted beside me and reached for my right arm, hesitating only at the last moment. "May I?"

In the interest of our partnership, I suppressed my revulsion and allowed him to take my arm. He peered at my wrist and turned it over. "It seems you have powerful kin, Valen, and we don't quite believe your claim that these marks happened by chance."

I followed his gaze. The grass outlined so delicately on my forearm and fingers might have been sea grass as I assumed. But among the fronds that curved along the inside of my wrist, where I had not seen it before, stretched a long, lean cat with a snarling face. I thumped the back of my head against the wall. Ronila would surely know Stian's mark.

His long brow drawn tight in consideration, Gildas released my arm and returned to the vicinity of the door. "Something is not right about your presence here, friend. I am told that you may have acquired certain . . . capabilities . . . along with these Danae markings, skills that might contribute to an escape. We can't have that."

"Did you forget your leash?" I said bitterly. "You own me now."

"I've not forgotten." Leaning in deceptive ease against the door, he tossed a fist-sized pouch across the room. It landed heavily in my lap. The smell near set me howling. "Because you lied to me, I think we must restructure our agreement slightly. I want you to work your nasty little enchantment this afternoon."

A stray wind gust snapped my hair, stinging against my cheek. "But it's not time yet. If I do it between times . . ."

". . . your need will grow stronger and demand to be serviced more often. Alas, that's true." He cocked his head. "But it only accelerates a condition that exists in you already. Do it now, or Jakome will introduce our young friend to the doulon."

I stared at him in disbelief. "Iero's holy name, Gildas. You would not . . ."

But whyever would I imagine that he would balk at this depravity? No one would ever fault Gildas de Pontia for failure of insight. His very posture, so like a strutting rooster, told me he knew that of all the torments he might promise, this one I could not abide.

Rage and hatred only fueled the need lurking in my veins. I struggled to form a plan. To attack him. To delay. To run. But each solution would forfeit lives more important than mine. One more doulon would not kill me, only embed the craving deeper. What did he plan that called for so strong a control of me?

"You lied to me, as well. You've Ronila to take you into Aeginea. Why do you need me?"

"So the clever sorcerer has guessed the crone's name," he said. For one moment I glimpsed the true man—greedy, prideful, jealous— the man who had grown up shamed by his poor and ignorant family. Then he slipped on his smiling mask again. "Let's say I enjoy watching you grovel. Do it now, Valen. And don't think to throttle me or toss the bag through the windows. Without my password, Jakome will not open this door. When he informs Sila, you will bleed out your remaining life in ways most unpleasant. And then he'll see that Jullian loses his soul to this perversion." He shrugged and screwed up his mouth in distaste. "You must understand, I intend to live in this world on my own terms or none, and you are necessary to my plan. Do as I say, and Sila will not know the ugly truth about the abomination she has chosen to . . . plow her fields. We shall merely proceed with our bargain as before."

I knew well the determination to find something better than the life one was born to. Not even Voushanti would be so dangerous a foe as Gildas. I wanted to tear out the blackguard's heart.

Hands shaking, I set out the needle, mirror, and thread and spilled out a pile of hard black seeds beside them. I was a doulon slave already. Gildas and Jakome had but fed tinder to the coals that Saverian had warned would ever burn in me. To do it once more . . . truly it could not make ridding myself of the doulon's yoke worse than what I'd gone through after twelve years' enslavement. I just needed to retain as much sense as possible. Control it. And before they could force me to do this a third time, Jullian and I would be away from here.

Gildas watched from the doorway. Using my arm to shield the work from the wind, I crushed the seeds with the bottom of the wooden cup. I tried not to inhale as I worked, but by the time they were powder, my heart was galloping. I dragged the lamp close.

"Wait," he said. "Before you begin, double that amount."

I stared at the pile of seeds in horror. Double . . . never had I known any doulon slave who used so much at once. "Fires of Deunor, Gildas, you'll leave me no mind! I've told you I'll do as you wish."

"I want this leash secure." Why would he doubt? Unless Ronila had told him something . . .

I recalled his anxious glances into the corner when he took me to Sila's room . . . his annoyance that Sila was late for the meeting. He had known Ronila was there. The old woman had not contradicted his pronouncement about Danae males and their need for pain, though she had grown up in Aeginea and knew better.

I poured out more seeds, crushed them, imagining each as one of Gildas's bones.

Ronila had no use for Sila's vision of regeneration and neither did Gildas. At least for the moment, they were allies.

I pricked my finger with the silver needle. It was not so insulting a discomfort as Jakome's knife, but the pain of this exercise ran much deeper than my skin. I would give much to believe that the remasti had given me a higher tolerance for the perverse enchantment.

My blood dripped into the crushed nivat, the scents mingling. Desire crept upward from my toes, inward from my fingers. "Gildas, please . . ." My voice was already hoarse with need.

"Remember, I've watched you do this. I'll know if you don't complete it correctly."

I held the little mirror glass upright, angled so that I could see the fumes rise. Between two fingers of the alter hand, I gripped the length of linen thread, dangling the end into the sodden little heap. Gildas would expect that. But he didn't know why I used the thread. Thus he didn't stop me when my last two fingers made contact with the mound. To touch the paste as it heated drew off some of its potency, spreading the infusion over the preparation time. A small difference only, but perhaps enough to keep me sane. I released magic to flow through my fingers and down the thread.

My gaze fixed on the ensorcelled mirror, as the otherwise invisible fumes rose from the bubbling black paste. Wind doused Gildas's lamp and threatened the shielded table lamp. Sweat dribbled down my cheeks, down my spine, as dark fire prickled my hidden fingers and surged up my arm. The locks snapped on the door.

Ought to look. Ought to listen . . . to refine the lock spell. Ought to stop . . . But I had gone too far. Even when the damnable mirror glass reflected the ruddy young face and the widening eyes of Ardran blue, I could not stop.

"Your protector is occupied for the moment, lad," said Gildas. "Did you not know of his little problem?"

"What does he, Brother? Is it some pureblood magic?" Innocent still.

Had I owned a mind or conscience just then, I would have wept at Jullian's wondering stare. As it was, my arm quivered with the doulon's burning, and all I could think was, *Please, gods, make it hurt more.*

Gildas chuckled. "I'm sure he'll explain when he's done. Tell him that Malena's forked blade can seal the spell, if he can but wait till nightfall to soothe all his lusts together. Then the priestess and I will both be happy."

His voice swelled in my ear. "You will be *my* slave, halfbreed, and I will not be a kind master."

Whispers and laughs faded. Friends . . . concerns . . . dangers faded. The world faded. Eventually the fumes ceased their rising, and

I let the mirror glass fall. As my fingers scooped the hot paste onto my greedy tongue, my other hand groped about the table as if it had a mind of its own. *Glass will cut . . . hot oil will burn.* I needed pain.

The doulon itself carved paths of agony from eyes to heart to limbs. My vision blurred. My back spasmed as if an Aurellian torturer had hung me from his hook and dragged me behind his chariot. Every nerve stretched taut and snapped like drawn bowstrings, launching nets that encompassed every part and portion of my body. *Not enough. Not enough.* Gods . . . I did not want to be this thing.

I swept my arm across the table. The lamp crashed to the floor; the oil pooled and flared. The black paste clogged my gullet, slid downward, and seared my empty stomach. Still the enchantment would not resolve, but kept building . . . waiting. I choked and gasped and shook, hammered my fists on the table, then gripped its edge as if to snap the oaken plank in twain. I needed more.

"Brother Valen? What's wrong? Why do you look like that?"

"Strike me . . . please . . . use anything!" Lest I be driven to roll in burning lamp oil or gash my hands with shards of glass, damaging myself beyond recovery.

Wind tearing at his hair, Jullian backed away and pressed himself to the door.

"Do it now, boy! Make it hurt!" My heart rattled my ribs, threatening to burst. My lungs strained for air enough to feed the raging power of enchantment. I screamed at him. "By holy Iero's hand, strike me! I beg you!"

His twelve-year-old limbs had done their share of labor around the abbey. He broke the second chair over my head. It was enough.

A bolt of joyless ecstasy shot through my head and heart and gut, wiping clean the canvas of agony, settling the shards of life and mind into their proper places. I roared in release and rapture.

As ever, the sensation abandoned me as quickly as it had come, and I collapsed across the table, dull, lead-limbed, sick. Only this time my head and shoulders felt as if I had rammed into a tree. And this time it was Jullian weeping.

Though I could not lift my head from the table, I clung to conscious thought, heeded the crackle of dying flames, the smoky stink of cheap lamp oil, the blessedly cold wind—anything to keep me sensible for one moment. The two gatzi had left the boy and me to enjoy this vileness alone.

I stretched out my hand across the table, palm up, and beckoned him nearer. "It's all right, Archangel," I croaked, near weeping myself when I felt him step closer. I did not deserve such trust. "You did well. Thank you. Just . . . give me a little time."

He tiptoed across to the bed and sat, and I fell into blackness.

"Brother Valen." The whisper came from a thousand quellae distant. From another world. I turned my back on it and slipped again into my sinful dreams.

"Brother Valen." The whisper touched me again, like the soft pecking of a chick.

I reached for my wits, caution nagging that I had been unconscious much too long. Mud clogged my veins. Every pore and sinew begged for sleep, and I longed to drag my leaden limbs into a badger's burrow and hide. From what?

"Brother Valen." Quiet. Patient. Terrified.

Like a rain of sewage, the abasement of the day fell on my head. I located my hand and raised it, hoping he would see I was something awake. Then I turned my face to the windows, inhaling wind and cloud and winter to sweep away the detritus of sin. The sun, fallen far into the west, hid deep behind Navronne's shroud of storm. I willed it to sear away these aches and guilts as if it were a cautery iron.

I had no more time for sleep. Soon would come nightfall and Malena. Goddess mother, even after all this, the passing thought of the hateful wench . . . so ripe and willing . . . heated my core. I had no time for that either.

I raised my head a quat or two. Blotted my mouth on the back of my hand so as not to drool before the boy. Which seemed a silly matter now he'd seen my worst. "Are you well, lad?"

"None's harmed me." The terse declaration spoke more description than a warmoot's worth of tales. Jullian, the scholarly boy who read books I would never comprehend, had no words to explain what his captors *had* done. What *I* had just done. *So, Valen Lackwit, let anger banish lust and shame.*

"Sorry I took so long to find you," I said, shuddering as a howling gust billowed the shirt on my back. "Not much of a rescuer, eh?"

"I knew you'd come."

Needing to be still before my skull cracked, I lowered my head onto my hand, where a sea star nestled in the grass. "A few matters came up along the way. Some ugly . . . like what you just saw. Some wondrous . . . unexpected."

"Guessed that." The bed creaked. His sandals scuffed a step or two in my direction. I felt his eyes on my glowing arms and feet. "Are you a demon?" he said softly.

"Great gods, no. Or . . . I believe not." I grinned into my hand. "I'll show you later. Just now"—I opened my ears; no one on the stair as yet—"we need to prepare for visitors. In the chest, there's a bag of knucklebones."

He scrambled to the task. Before I could lift my head up again, the canvas bag sat in front of my nose, alongside Gildas's small lamp, relit from the dying flames of the spilled oil. "Do you know about the others held captive here—Thane Stearc and Gram?" he whispered over my bent back. "They need rescuing more than me. When I heard you'd come, I thought . . ."

"Aye, I know of them. We're all getting out."

"I don't think—" His breathing came heavy and fast. "I don't think they could possibly— I've heard Thane Stearc since they brought him here. Why would they do that to anyone? They've kept me just down the passage from his cell. They wake me so I can hear. I pray . . ." His voice quivered. "I pray for him to die."

"The pr— Gram. Have you heard him, as well?" Jullian did not know Gram's true identity.

"Coughing. Crying out. Mumbling madness like with a fever. Gildas complains he's dying and can't tell them what they want." Good to hear the boy's touch of anger. He *should* be angry. "Gildas says Stearc will open the lighthouse or they'll burn off his—"

"Doesn't matter what the gatzé says, Jullian. We'll get them home." I ignored the way the room sloshed like the waves of Evaldamon and lifted my head higher where I could look at the boy, so he might believe. His aspirant's gown had been replaced by scraggly leggings and a thin yellow tunic, belted with rope. Dirt and grease matted his red-gold hair, and his ruddy cheeks were pinched with cold and fear. But his hands held steadier than mine, and his slender jaw jutted firm, willing to work with a demon to free his friends.

"Father Abbot would be proud of you, Jullian. There's naught you could have done to help Stearc. Stearc himself would tell you that. The god knows it, too."

I had once imagined Jullian to be Eodward's youngest bastard, a Pretender to the Navron throne, hidden at Gillarine until his majority. Though I knew better now, he was well worthy of it—likely more so than any of the three men who stood in line.

"Gildas said I would stay here with you from now on, save when your . . . woman . . . came."

"We've a thing or two to teach Brother Gildas."

I fumbled Saverian's vials from the knucklebone bag, wishing one of her medicines might help what was most wrong with me. I drained the blue vial. If we were going to be rousting dungeons, my stomach would need calming. The prince's vial I stuck in the pouch at my waist, along with the vial of yellow broom. On the floor the silver needle gleamed in the lamplight, and beside it lay the little mirror, cracked through the middle. The nivat bag lay soaking up the unburned lamp oil. Even shamed and sickened, I dared not touch them.

"Those things I was using . . . toss them through the window bars. Quickly, before I tell you different."

"What are they?" he said, retrieving them gingerly. "I thought you were working some powerful sorcery. Or dying."

"Something of both."

"While I waited . . . I touched you . . . to make sure you were breathing." Gods, he was apologizing.

"The enchantment is called the doulon, Jullian. It is a sinful weakness, a poison that enslaves the mind and body. When I was scarce older than you, I used it to run away from terrible things. But the doulon itself is more terrible than any of the things I ran from. Someone may tempt you to it some day. Gildas may. But don't allow it. Not ever."

I did not watch as he disposed of the implements of sin, lest I grab them away. Instead I pressed my eyeballs back into their sockets and tried to think how to go about what we needed to do. Last time Gildas had given me an excess of nivat, I had experienced recurring attacks of thickheaded confusion for most of a day. Abbot Luviar had died because of it. I could not allow that to happen again.

"Gildas says you're to be his slave," said the boy. "I didn't see how he could force you."

I shoved myself to my feet. "He won't. Help me with this palliasse."

Using the lamp flame to burn through the rope webbing, we unstrung half the bed and ended up with several moderate lengths of rope. I had Jullian pile the palliasse and quilts back over the half-strung frame, using the broken chair to create a hollow like a badger's burrow at one end, while I rested my woozy head between my knees. Great gods how was I ever going to accomplish anything?

"Can you tell me what guards watch Stearc and Gram?" I asked from my odd position.

"There's always one or two in the passage except when they all go down to beat Thane Stearc in the morning and when they . . . hurt . . .

him in the evening. Nikred or Crado mostly. Both of them in the day. At night they take turns for rounds, changing at Matins and Lauds and again at Prime." Matins—morning at midnight. Lauds was third hour, Prime sixth—the dawn hour in summer. "I try to keep the Hours here. I thought . . . I hoped I might help him."

"And this torturing happens the same time every night?"

"Between Vespers and Compline . . . when they call the last watch but one before Matins. Crado says they like him to know when it's coming."

"All right." Slowly I sat back onto my heels. The boy perched on the rumpled bed, two or three steps away, his body a wiry knot. "So tell me how the cells are laid out, if you can."

In moments he had sketched an outline of the prison block in the sooty remnants of my lamp. I planted the image in my head, then had him rub it out with his boot. "Clearly you're a good observer. So did you happen to note the guards when they brought you up the stair earlier?"

Though his eyes flicked between my face and my glowing hands, he did not falter with his answers. "One at each level. Sometimes when Gildas brought me to walk in the inner ward or to study the map, I'd see two at the hall level."

I popped my head up, blinking until the windows took their proper places instead of whirling one atop the other. "To study the map—the big one in Sila's sleeping chamber?"

"Aye, that's it. Gildas doesn't understand what she does with it, so he studies it when she's not there, and he has me study it, too, so I can remind him of details he might forget. It maddens him that no paper or pens are allowed here, save the map, your grandfather's book, and the Aurellian book he uses to interpret the maps."

The great map . . . its luster of age and art and magic . . . its shifting images . . . had captured my imagination. I closed my eyes and envisioned the green and ocher washes over the wordless fiché. Made for those who could not read words—Danae, then, or halfbreeds like me and Sila. Just as in the book of maps, Janus's secrets lay exposed for all to see, if only I knew how to look at it. "Does Gildas say what he suspects about the map?"

Jullian shook his shaggy head. "Only that the features change over time. He thinks the old woman knows a secret about it that even Sila doesn't know, and that bites him sorely."

A map made for the Danae . . . but Kol had shown me they could not interpret maps, even ones without words. What would prompt

Janus to make them a map—a map that Sila found use for and that held place in the gap of secrets between Sila and Gildas and Ronila?

I felt the sun slipping lower. Both enlightenment and vengeance must wait, for I'd yet to come up with a route out of Fortress Torvo. "Where did they take you to walk?"

"Gildas would walk me in the inner ward—"

"—where half the north end wall has collapsed? Piles of rubble all around?"

"Aye." Wind rattled the window bars. Jullian scrambled back onto the bed, shivering, burrowing slowly into the quilts.

I pushed myself up to a squat, summoned all my resolve, and stood up. In hopes that movement might shift the clay in my limbs and rouse some insight, I crossed the room, raking fingers through my hair, trying to reconstruct the scene I'd glimpsed through Sila Diaglou's arrow loops. "The broken wall once supported a row of privies hanging out over the court. Do you recall seeing a drainage canal on that end of the yard? It would only make sense . . . the sewage draining out of the privies into the canal." Unless the privies had been put in after the canal was rerouted, or no one had considered draining the muck from an inner court that was naught but a well in which to trap one's enemies and pour down death on them.

"A cistern sits in the middle of the court, but I didn't see a canal. If it's there, it's full of rock."

I grabbed my heaviest wool shirt from the clothes chest, convinced my leaden feet to carry me back to the bed, and dropped the shirt over Jullian's head. Then I took myself to the window, bathing my skin in the cold afternoon. "Did you notice any grates around the walls? Something as tall as my knees?"

His head popped through the shirt's neck hole, his eyes curious. "Aye, I saw a rat squeezing through a grate . . . just south of the broken wall . . . at the ground where a canal *might* run . . ."

I grinned as he wrestled his arms into the warm gray shirt and retied his rope belt to tame its bulk. "I know going inward seems an unlikely route to the outside, but it might serve if we can find no better. You *can* find the way to this yard in a hurry?"

He gave me his most scathing look. It was all I could do to keep from ruffling his filthy hair.

Footsteps echoed on the stair. I knelt in front of Jullian and took his cold hands in mine. "A woman is going to come here soon. You must hide in the burrow you made, and make not a sound, not a sneeze, not a prayer, no matter what you hear or think you hear. You'll come out only when I tell you."

He nodded, solemn faced, curious, but not so frightened anymore.

"Gildas thinks to torment me by prisoning us together, knowing you'll see what this vile enchantment does to me and what Sila Diaglou intends for me to do here every night. But then, he doesn't believe in angels or aingerou or any other blessing that a god might send to sinful men. We're going to show him different."

Chapter 25

Malena arrived with the early nightfall. I waited behind the door. In the instant the door opened, breaking the barrier ward that bound the room, I touched the lock and quickened the spell I had built throughout the day. Anticipation held my bones rigid . . . with so much depending on a blindworked spell in an unfamiliar lock . . . and every alternative sure to draw blood.

As the girl crossed the room with a supper tray, I buried my face in my hands, listening for the latch. The guard on the stair pulled the door shut. The pins and levers moved . . . and stopped short, as if a small clot of dirt, oil, and bronze shavings, about the size of an armaments game piece, had slipped into the works and prevented them seating properly. I smiled into my fists.

Again Malena wore naught but flimsy shift and braided hair. Again she set out warmed wine. I had eaten nothing since the previous night, and even the prospect of maggoty bread would have set me ravening had I not spent the last half hour practicing what Kol named *closure*, attempting to subdue every sense to my will. Three times in the past hour echoes of the doulon had threatened to unhinge me, wreaking havoc in my head and shooting spasms of pain and desire through breath and bone. But I had cut them off like rotted limbs. No matter desire, no matter temptation, no matter perversion, neither Gildas nor Sila Diaglou would control my deeds this night.

"Where is the boy?" said my chosen mate, forgoing all pretense of holy ardor. "I was told he would be here. We're to send him out to Jakome when the time comes, unless you wish him to watch."

"Gildas took him," I said. "They fed me extra vigger's salt this afternoon and I got a bit . . . tightwound . . . waiting for you."

I shrugged and pointed out the broken lamp, the rumpled bed and scattered cups.

She pouted a bit, as if she had been looking forward to the extra company, then watched in puzzlement as I tied my spare hose over my feet like soft slippers, hiding my gards. The hose would be easier than boots to remove if I had to bare my gards in a hurry. "Cold feet," I said.

She retrieved the wooden cups from under the clothes chest where I'd thrown them. "Do you wish to sup first or shall we do our mistress's bidding so I can be away from here the sooner?"

"Our mistress has explained her remarkable . . . glorious . . . vision," I said. "And I understand a great deal more about what we must sacrifice than I did this morning. But I've not eaten all day, and I'd not wish to fail in strength or endurance tonight." I smiled and tugged at the lace that bound up her braid.

I did not want to tip my hand by rushing. The call of fifth watch had not long passed and Stearc's punishment would not begin until sixth.

Malena did not seem mollified. She dragged a quilt from the bed and wrapped it around her shoulders. Blessings to Serena Fortuna, Jullian's hideaway was not exposed.

I took possession of the remaining chair, poured the wine, and offered her a cup. As she drained her cup, I swirled my own and sniffed it. Though I doubted Malena was a doulon slave, and I didn't think Gildas would risk a second doulon for me in the same day, not after the pile of seeds he'd had me use, I dared not taste it. I did devour the porridge and bread, and when Malena said she had already eaten, I ate hers as well, praying with every bite that nourishment might put some bone in my knees and wit in my skull.

I was not halfway through the second bowl when my body spasmed with a burst of heat that shot me to the verge of ecstasy only to send me earthward again, as if I plummeted from Stian's rock Stathero. Breathing hard, trying not to lose what I had already eaten, I pushed the porridge away and told myself this was but an echo of the doulon as I had experienced before when I had used too much nivat. *Keep moving. Hold fast. Men will not die today because of your weakness.*

"What's wrong?" said Malena, from her perch on my clothes chest.

"Naught," I said. "I just— Birthing a new race is a great responsibility."

I beckoned the girl to my lap. She had refilled her cup, and a droplet of red hung at the corner of her mouth. It sickened me.

"A cup of wine can smooth over many a grievance," I said, and traced my fingers about her face. Her body softened in my arms. When I touched her lips, she nipped my finger and smirked. A few kisses and I set her cup aside, gathered her in my arms, and carried her to the bed. She did not protest at its sagging middle nor did she argue when I took both her wrists in my left hand and drew them up over her head, kissing her neck.

"Shhh," I said, as I pulled out one of the lengths of rope from the side of the bed and tied her wrists. "There are many variants of pleasuring, Malena."

Her eyes grew very wide. She licked her lips and attempted a smile. Only when I snatched my mask out from the same hiding place and stuffed it in her mouth did she understand. She growled and struggled, drumming her feet on the palliasse, squirming and writhing to get out from under me or at least get a knee where she could do some damage. But I had very long legs and arms and the memory of Gerard to force her still.

Once the rope was snug around her ankles, I tucked quilts around her. "We're going to have a very quiet evening tonight, chosen one," I said, using spare laces to snug the mask in her mouth. "I do not sit down with murderers. I do not lie with them. Holy Mother Samele grant that you *never* carry a child—mine or any other man's."

Malena's glare could have poisoned the world ocean itself.

I detached a little bag from my waist, made sure the three lonely seeds remained intact, and tucked the bag between her breasts. "I am returning the holy one's gift. Gildas gave them to me and told me that Sila wished me to be a slave as well as a whore. Tell her I prefer not." I trusted her to report my words exactly. I hoped Gildas would be in Sila's presence as she did so.

And then I peered around the end of the bed, met Jullian's very large eyes peeking out from his burrow, and grinned. "Time to go."

Regrettably we dared not take my pureblood cloak with its thick fur lining, so I pinned a plain gray blanket around Jullian's shoulders. The boy gaped at the writhing Malena as I handed him our remaining lengths of rope and grabbed the bag of knucklebones from the clothes chest. I dropped the dice and the armaments game pieces into the bag, as well, tied it at my waist, and pulled on my gloves to hide the last of my gards. Jullian, looking puzzled, pointed at my discarded boots. I shook my head, pressed a finger to my lips, and doused the lamp. At the last moment, I snatched one of the oaken legs of the chair the boy had broken over my head.

I held the door handle for a moment, listening. Only one person stood beyond the door. I hoped it was Jakome. A shudder of warmth raced up my spine, threatening my concentration, but I held tight to my focus. Making sure Jullian stood behind me, I pulled open the door.

"Malena?" growled the man on the dark landing.

Grinning in unseemly pleasure, I triggered the second piece of the lock spell. The lock burst in a shower of yellow sparks, illuminating Jakome's shocked face. Backhand, I slammed my arm into the join of his neck and shoulder. He slumped to his knees, retching, and I whacked the chair leg behind his ear to put him out of his misery for the moment.

Before very long, Jakome was bound as tight as I could draw rope, rolled up in a quilt, and deposited alongside Malena. I tied his orange scarf about my head and his dagger sheath about my thigh. His greasy brown cloak hung from my shoulders. As we pulled the iron door shut behind us, I triggered the last piece of the lock spell, unraveling the obstruction and fusing the broken pins in place. Someone would have to ram the door from its hinges to release the two.

Jullian started down the steps, but I snagged the neck of his shirt and forced him to sit on the step beside me. "What?" he spluttered.

"We need to listen for a bit to learn the exact time." Given the early nightfall, and the span I'd used to eat and secure the two upstairs, the hour should be very close to sixth watch—poor Stearc's wretched hour. The fortress was filled with muted sounds—barked commands . . . roaring fires . . . the boots and grunts of departing patrols . . . grim laughter. I listened carefully for sounds from Sila's bedchamber. If the map was left unguarded . . .

The mystery of Sila's map grew on me like a boil. What use did Sila find in it? She already had my book and Gildas to take her to Danae sianous. Osriel must come first; to go after the map before securing the prince would be sheer lunacy. I wanted it, though. If I got the chance, I'd take it.

Of a sudden, fire ravished my limbs yet again, then abandoned me chilled and dizzy. The dark stair gaped and deepened in front of me like the maw of hell . . .

"Brother! Wake up!" Hands tapped my cheek and shook my shoulders in company with this anxious whisper.

I blinked. My heart sank. Jullian's scrawny limbs were knotted about my arms and shoulders, preventing me from sliding farther down the stair. My head was jammed uncomfortably against the curved wall and seemed to be several steps lower than my feet. "Ow!" I sat up, untwisting my neck and getting my legs below me.

"You fell . . . just rolled forward off the step."

"Dizzy," I said. "Part of that ugly business earlier. I'll try not to let it happen again. But if I should, just slap me. Kick me. Call me a gatzi spawn and get me moving."

There was no going back. I shook off the worry, took myself back into quiet, and focused on the plan. "I wasn't out for long, was I? They didn't call the watch?"

"Nay. Not yet."

"Sixth watch. All hail the mighty Gehoum!" When it came at last, the call rippled through the fortress, passed from one voice to another, advancing and receding around each level according to the caller's distance from our stair.

"I'm going to treat you like a prisoner," I said, prodding both of us to our feet. "When we reach the prison level, call for your mam to let me know."

When the watch cry circled the level just below us and came round again to the stair, I bellowed my own, "Sixth watch. All hail the mighty Gehoum!" I grabbed the neck of Jullian's borrowed shirt and whispered in his ear, "Fight me." Then I dragged him down the stair as fast as I could, right past the guardsmen changing their posts. "Filthy little beggar," I grumbled. "Ye'll sleep in yer cell again tonight, and every night, if I have my way of it. Don't think to get out of it by whimpering to no one."

I was afraid at first Jullian hadn't understood my instruction, but then he set to pummeling my ribs with such ferocity, I had to wrestle him under my arm, and still he would squirm loose. One of the guards we passed on the downward stair laughed and called after us, "Got a feisty one there!"

No one bothered us as we descended into the depths of the fortress, and Jullian had no need to call for his long-dead mother. The stair ended in a circular pit. Torches burned in sconces on the wall, but their light did not illuminate much past three dark openings in the wall. *Mighty gods . . .*

Two of the openings were blocked by collapsed walls or ceilings. The third opened into a passage, and from it issued a low keening I could scarce define as human, as if all the pain and despair this place had known had been drawn together into one terrible voice. Stearc's voice.

I set Jullian on his feet, but I did not release my hold on him.

To Gram, I mouthed, and urged him forward, my hand on his shoulder, ready to sweep him out of the way if we encountered trouble.

The passage appeared to be deserted as the boy had said. And as his sketch had shown, his own cell was first inside the doorway. Its position near the exit and its door of open bars had left him better air, if the thick, unwholesome vapors of this place could be named *air*. Torchlight revealed straw and blankets and a rusty lamp mounted on the wall unlit. Perhaps it had been a guardroom at one time.

But the cells farther down the passage—all but two empty, according to Jullian—had no such amenities. I held my arm over my mouth and nose and worked as hard as I knew how to keep focused. My king lay dying in this fetid darkness.

We arrived at a thick iron door similar to the one on my tower room, only with a slot at the bottom for passing food and slops, and an eye-level grate for observing the inmate. A lung-stripping cough and fevered mumbling from inside the cell were sufficient to set me working on the lock.

Crude, warded by only the simplest magic, it succumbed more easily than the one on my tower door. I dragged the heavy door open, hoping the scrape of hinges would not bring guards running. The stench of sickness and rot escaped the cell in a flood, clogging my throat with bile. Torchlight from the passage revealed a dark form curled on the floor of dirt, rubble, and a scattering of moldy straw.

"Close the door all but a crack," I whispered to the boy. "Keep watch."

I ducked through the low door, stepped over a tin cup and an untouched bowl of something manifestly inedible, and dropped to my knees beside the prisoner. He clutched a threadbare blanket around his racked shoulders. The cramped cell felt cold as a tomb.

A cough broke into words. "Milkmaids merry 'neath a cherry blossom tree. Spring comes anon and they're beckonin' me." The chatter of teeth punctuated this rasping singsong.

"Quietly now," I said, and touched his shoulder. He jerked as if I'd stabbed him. The heat of his fever near blistered my hand, even through blanket and glove. "Can you sit up?"

From the far end of the passage, Stearc's formless wail sharpened into a bellow of agony. A shudder rippled Osriel's slender body. "Master's crying in the hall. Kenty's never got the ball. All fall. All fall. All fall . . ."

"He's been that way since they brought him," offered Jullian in a whisper. "Out of his head."

Great gods have mercy. Trying not to twist or strain his joints—

Saverian had warned me to be careful—I rolled him onto his back. Osriel was almost unrecognizable in the poor light . . . more than being grimy and unshaven. His eyes were sunken, his neck swollen, his skin cracked and peeling. I fumbled at my waist for Saverian's amber vial and broke the wax seal.

Though the prince's eyes were closed, his unmusical croaking continued. "Grapes die in the fields. Warriors die on their shields. Angels dance in the trees. Gatzi dance—"

"Gram, listen to me." I lifted him up and cradled his lolling head, shook his chin, tugged at his hair. "I've brought you medicine from an old friend of yours. She says you must drink it all, even if it tastes like the dead man's boots."

His fevered mumbling ceased abruptly, and his eyes flicked open as if I'd dropped ice in his trews. He squinted in the feeble light, his gaze running from my fingers to my head. "Valen!"

I almost dropped him from the surprise.

His mind, it appeared, was not so sorely affected by his illness as his body. His hoarse expulsion of my name sent him into a fit of coughing, and his body tried to roll to the side and curl into a knot, as if to escape the force of the spasms. Every movement wrenched an agonized grunt from him. I would have sworn he was laughing, too, or sobbing. Or more likely both at once, as Stearc was screaming again.

Trying to cushion his pain, I held Osriel tight until his paroxysm ceased and his shallow, gasping breaths had slowed. "Let's get the good physician's potion down you." I emptied the vial down his throat, stuffed it back in my pocket, and used my teeth to yank the glove from my free hand. Whispering the words Saverian had said would speed the healing effects of the medicament, I touched his forehead and released magic in a tickling flood. Unfortunately we'd have to move him before the remedy could do its work.

"The boy," he croaked. "He's in this pit, too. And Stearc . . ."

"Jullian's here with us. We're going to take you out of here first. I'll come back for Stearc." Even if the thane had no torturers working on him at the present, I could not carry two injured men at once.

"He can't last much longer. You won't leave him here . . . no matter what . . ." This was as close to a command as a man in Osriel's state could give.

"I'll do everything I can."

He squeezed his eyes shut and his mouth tight as I helped him to sitting. Shoulders, elbows . . . his every joint felt hot and swollen.

"He has held all these wretched days . . . giving them some story. They haven't touched me."

Once he was sitting up on his own, I scraped together what straw and rubble lay within reach.

"Sorry, I need your blanket." I snatched it away, near ripping the worn fabric in half, and tucked it around the pile. With a poorly structured inflation spell, the mound somewhat resembled a body.

As I picked up the glove I'd pulled off to work the magic, Osriel grabbed my wrist and held my glowing hand where he could see. His face tilted up toward mine, unreadable in the blue glow. "Two wonders in a single day," he whispered. "A Harrower gives me a blanket out of mercy, and you appear at my side like Iero's angel. Did I die when I was not paying attention, or have you come to see to that?"

I bent down and spoke in his ear. "*My* grievances will be reckoned later, lord."

Jullian dragged the door open as I lifted Osriel to his feet and pulled his arm over my shoulder. After only a few agonizing steps, it became clear that this was much too slow. His joints could not bear weight.

"Wait," he said, "I can—"

But with one hand holding Osriel's arm, I bent down, caught him behind the knee, and drew his weight across my shoulders. He didn't scream, but the heat of his fever burnt through my clothes. "Is this our reckoning?" he gasped.

"No."

Jullian sped down the passage toward the stair. I hurried after him as quickly as I could, ducking to avoid the stone spans that supported the fortress floors above us. I tried not to jolt, as I could feel Osriel's muffled groans rumbling down my spine.

Stearc's cries had reverted from the rhythmic, escalating madness of a man under the lash to a constant drone. Even if his body survived until I could get back to him, what of his mind?

"Gildas and Grav Radulf are his questioners," said Osriel as we ascended the prison stair. "I hear them pass every day. They laugh." Hearing his bated fury, no promise of heaven would make me step between Osriel and Gildas, should such a meeting ever come to pass. Nor would I be so inclined did Iero himself command me.

I halted Jullian just below the main level, listening for movement both above and below, and trying to recall possible routes across the main hall to the outer wards. Sila's great hall surged with people and noise. We hadn't a chance of making it across to the exit doors. But according to Jullian's description, we had but to slip behind the guards on the landing and through an alley to the left to reach the inner court.

A heated shudder arrowed through my limbs, and the curved walls began to melt like frost wraiths at sunrise. I planted my hand on the grimed stone and forced the walls back into their proper shape. I would *not* falter.

"Two guards at the landing," I whispered to Jullian. "When I poke you, run for the inner court as quietly as you can. I'll follow."

"*I'll* distract the guards," said Osriel through clenched jaw. "Just signal me when."

I jerked my head. Remembering several instances of his unsettling magics, I didn't bother to ask him what he intended. So we crept upward to the juncture of the tower and the keep.

The smoky hall was a patchwork of cook fires and torchlight. The two orange-heads stood on either side of the arch that led into the noisy vastness. But no one guarded the path to the alley. Indeed, no intruder in his right mind would head into such a trap. But a torch blazed on the flanking piers, and the two men stood at such an angle they would surely spot any movement from our position on the stair. They carried bill hooks.

I tapped the prince on the hand and made sure he could see our problem, even from his awkward angle. He squeezed my hand in answer. He emitted a long sigh and the weight of him sagged even heavier on my back. I thought for a moment he'd passed out. Then I felt a low rumbling under my feet . . . or perhaps in my bones. Just enough to make me want to crawl into bed and pull the bedclothes over my head. The two guards, no disciplined warriors, shifted their stance uneasily, glancing over their shoulders. When a shadow darted past them into the hall, they pointed. A second one flew past, and they shouted, but no one paid any attention. The third set them charging into the crowd, yelling warnings, weapons leveled.

"Saints and angels," I hissed. "Could you not have done something a bit more subtle?" Every blighted Harrower in the place was on the alert.

Jullian and I sped through the junction and into the alley, which was not an alley at all, but a short passage that opened into the undercroft of the keep. The cavernous vaults were long emptied, and only broken chimneys and masonry foundations remained of the kitchens and barracks that had once adjoined the bays on the outside walls. Some halfway along, Jullian angled sharply toward the inside walls and up a few steps into the rubble-strewn interior yard—the heart of Fortress Torvo. The place was as dark as a well of pitch.

"Where—?"

I hushed Jullian. Anyone could be watching from the walls that rose starkly on all sides. We crept along the wall that stretched to our left, disturbing several scuttling creatures on our way toward the collapsed privies. I set Jullian feeling along the lower spans of the wall for a grating that might indicate the outlet of a drainage canal. We reached the corner without finding it. The mounds of rubble would disguise any remnant of the canal itself.

I squatted and set Osriel on his feet. Jullian lent his shoulder, while I touched earth and hunted the way with magic.

My bent did not serve well to examine layers of human-built works. Only the passages of people and their purposes made sense of structures. But after sorting through two centuries of death and ugliness in the courtyard, I found an old streambed that coursed this dry slope in the direction that I wanted, and I surmised that the original drainage canal had channeled the stream. We should be standing right on top of it.

Holding tight to my fading hope that I'd not stuck us in a trap, I reached for Osriel. He stayed my hand when I moved to heft him across my back again, but accepted my arm under his shoulders. Jullian held close on the other side of him. The three of us proceeded slowly across the court to the far end wall, at the spot where the buried canal should pierce the foundation of the great hall. And indeed, set into the wall was a grate identical to those Max had shown me on the outer walls of the fortress—an iron-barred rectangle as high as my knees and twice that wide, and only halfway blocked by stones and dead thornbushes.

I lowered Osriel to the ground and pulled him and Jullian close, draping Jakome's cloak over us to muffle the sound. "I'm going back for Stearc. Max—Prince Bayard's pureblood—told me that this drainage canal tunnels under the fortress and exits outside the walls. But he's got the grates warded, and the moment we breach them, he'll know. I'd like to postpone that as long as possible, as I'd rather not end up in Bayard's hands after getting out of Sila's, so I'm going to leave you here. A certain touch on opposing corners will unlock the grates, if you need to get out before I return. Do you understand, Gram? Can you manage that much?"

The prince nodded. His magic would suffice.

"Good. Voushanti will be waiting for us outside the walls, off to the right. Give me an hour past seventh watch. No more. And mind your voices. These upper walls open into occupied chambers."

"Iero's grace," whispered Jullian. "I'll keep watch so Gram can rest."

I smiled and ruffled his hair. He hated that.

A hand squeezed my aching shoulder, then three fingers touched my cheek in the manner of a king to his knight. Osriel's hand seemed steadier and less fevered than earlier. My hopes crept higher. As I slunk away, I let magic flow into three whispered words, charging them with power to reach beyond the fortress. *Dead man. Parley.*

Moments later, I heard the response. *Bluejay. Parley.* Voushanti and his bought fighters would not attack the fortress, but would watch for us to emerge from the drainage canal.

The return across the courtyard seemed interminable. I dared not hurry, lest some scuffing or stumble alert a watcher in one of the chambers that overlooked the yard. It was easier to walk quietly without boots, though the hose tied over my feet were getting a bit ragged. But eventually I reached the passage and the undercroft, and I raced back to the tower.

The hall remained in an uproar. A crowd of orange-heads, many with torches, centered on a few men arguing. Only one guard had returned to the tower stair. He shifted nervously, starting at every shout from the conflict in the hall, frequently spinning around to stare behind him, approximately in my direction. From the bag at my waist, I pulled one of the knucklebones and lofted it into the hall behind his back. He darted forward a few steps, and I slipped behind him and took the downward stairs three at a time.

I flattened my back to the wall beside the doorway to the prison passage. The torture session was ended, and the slow pacing of a single guard echoed in the passage. Praise be to Serena Fortuna, they seemed not to have discovered their missing prisoner.

The guard's footsteps paused. Soft fumbling noises came from just beyond the doorway, and then a trickle of water that grew into a stream. An opportunity not to be missed.

I took him from behind with angled blows to his neck. He dropped to his knees. Reaching around, I slammed a sidearm blow to his chest. My forearm glanced up to his throat, sending him to the floor clutching his throat and wheezing like a bellows. An elbow to the back of his neck stopped his clutching and wheezing.

Only after I had the scraggly fellow unconscious in his pool of piss did I remember Jakome's dagger strapped to my thigh. It had been a very long time since I'd possessed a weapon.

Had I been sure he'd caused Stearc's screams, I might have slit his throat and thought it justice. But it occurred to me that this might be the very guard who had shown a sick prisoner the mercy of a blanket. I was no judge. So I tied his hands with his orange scarf, emptied Saverian's vial of yellow broom into him, and tucked him under the blanket in Osriel's cell. Whenever he woke he would be so busy puking, he'd not be able to raise the alarm. I snatched up his ragged cloak and flop-brimmed hat, grabbed one of the torches, and ran for Stearc.

They hadn't bothered to lock the door at the end of the passage. The chamber was no cell, but a charnel house. Yet neither the implements on the walls nor the grotesque evidence of horrors held my gaze. In chains suspended from the roof beam hung the remnants of a man. The once powerful body of the Thane of Erasku had been purposefully destroyed by whips, murderously precise knife and ax work, and cautery irons. He had no feet. No nose. No ears. No fingers on his right hand, and only three remaining on his left. Had I not known who was held here, I could never have identified him as the proud warrior who believed in the honor of learning as much as he believed in the honor of his sword. The low despairing moan that seeped from his slack mouth might have been a threnody for the world's reason.

"Stearc, it's Valen come to help you," I said, throttling my rage. Using a length of timber, I scraped away the filth underneath him and spread out the guard's cloak.

"Valen?"

"I'm going to get you down."

"No . . . no . . . no . . . no," he rasped. "Must not falter. Will not." Blood bubbled from his lips.

"You've held long enough, Thane. They've not touched him." With my brutish lock spell, I burst his manacles and lowered him to the floor.

He cried out, little more than an animal's bleat. The bloody claw that was his left hand gripped my arm with desperate strength. "He is safe?"

"He will be with Voushanti and Saverian within the hour." Avoiding his dreadful wounds as best I could, I took Stearc's face in my hands, making sure his eyes met mine. "I'm going to take you to him, Stearc. You will not die in this vile place, but in the shelter of your lord."

Die he would. The instinct that had ever spoken to me of death and life told me clearly. But anyone with eyes must understand that will alone drove Stearc's heart and lungs.

"No!" His hand pawed at me, and he came near rising from the ground. "Don't let him— I honor him above all men. My king. But I would not meet the Ferryman blind." Terror radiated from him like fever. "I would not be Voushanti."

How could I console such fear? I saw no means for Osriel to work his dreadful rites in Torvo's inner courtyard. But that was poor assurance for a man who had spent his last reserves of courage fifty times over. The prince might have other means to capture souls.

"All right, then." Which set me a dilemma. I could not leave Stearc living. "I would do you a last service, Thane. Tell me what you want."

"A blade." He opened his bloody palm, rock steady. In the command I heard a trace of his old accusations. He had ever believed me a coward.

I gave him Jakome's dagger and wrapped his bloody fingers around the hilt. Then I spoke clearly so he could not mistake. "I will tell your king and your daughter only of courage, lord, not of horror. The lighthouse will stand. *Teneamus.*"

He jerked his head. "For House Erasku," he whispered. "For Evanore, for Navronne . . . *teneamus.*"

I took off my glove and laid my hand on his forehead, determined Stearc would not die alone. His existence comprised naught but shadings of mortal agony . . . a map in which every road led but to another shock or scouring, and every border marked but new violation. My part in his pain, shared through my bent and the gards on my hand, ended mercifully fast.

Gripping the dagger with the remaining fingers of his left hand, he used the palm of his mutilated right hand to plunge the blade into his throat. Blood spurted from the wound. His hands dropped away.

I stayed with him, and when the face of the world had faded to naught but cold and gray, I whispered in his ear, "Know this, too, warrior of Evanore; the blood of noble Caedmon mingles even now with the blood of House Erasku. Your beloved daughter carries Caedmon's heir. And I vow upon the soul of our holy abbot that I will see them both safe until the end of days."

The revelation did not violate my vow to Elene, for I told her secret only to a dead man. But I believed Stearc heard me, for his eyes grew fierce and bright just before the life went out of them.

I hung him from his chains again and removed all evidence of my coming. Let the butchers believe Iero's angels had released him from his pain.

Chapter 26

"Seventh watch! All honor to the Gehoum!"

As the call caromed through the fortress, I crouched on the prison stair at the verge of the main level. This was taking much too long. At any moment a replacement would be coming down to relieve the guard who lay vomiting in Osriel's cell. But a pair of cursed orange-heads stood just in front of me, one blocking the doorway to the great hall, one blocking the doorway of the alley to the inner court. Neither clattering knucklebones nor a shower of armament pebbles had distracted them. I had been hoping they would just go away. To get up to the gallery and Sila's chamber, I would have to run between them.

Forced to stillness, I had grown even more determined to take the map. I tottered on the verge of understanding. My glimpse of the Sentinel Oak had told me the map held two layers of information—perhaps that was what Gildas could not see. Sila was using the map in her campaign to squeeze the long-lived from their hiding places so that she could mingle Danae blood with Aurellian and Navron bloodlines. Something in the map would tell me her next move or which boundaries she thought to break. Though I regretted every moment's delay in getting Osriel free, I had to take the chance. The map could be the key to everything, and I had no intention of ever returning to this fortress of horrors.

The echoed call of the watch was slowing. Replacements had arrived for the two guards. I had to move. I seated the guard's flop-brimmed hat on my head. Then I pelted up the stair as if newly come from the depths, sweeping Jakome's brown cloak about my shoulders and calling to the two guards, "Tell Nikred I couldn't wait for his lazy ass to show. I'm to relieve Jakome at the tower for the night."

The two grunted assent and turned back to their replacements, while I raced up the stair to the gallery. One torch burned outside Sila Diaglou's chamber, but no guard was posted. Soft light leaked around the door curtain. I held my breath and listened. One person inside, breathing softly.

I drew the knife, pulled back the edge of the curtain, and peered inside. Torches blazed on either side of the map. Ronila sat in front of it, her chin propped on her walking stick. Nothing for it but to slip inside, keeping my back against the wall.

"You might as well come in, abomination," she said, not even shifting her gaze from the map.

Of course, Ronila would have skills like mine. Once I had confirmed that no one else was in the room, I strolled over to the map, keeping the knife under my cloak. "Did you know my father, Ronila?"

"I suppose you deem yourself wise." Never had I heard amusement that tasted so much of gall and rancid life. She cocked her head at the map. "The answer is no. Cartamandua first came to Aeginea long after I had left. He is talented, I hear—talented at finding places he should not. As you are."

"He *was*," I said, staring at the map, trying to gauge its secret. Knotted cords looped from bolts in the wall through three bound eyelets sewn into the map's upper edge. Three strokes of the knife would take it down. "The Danae took his mind for a failed promise."

"Pah!" She blew a note of disgust. "The long-lived cannot admit they are as crippled as I am. Mixed blood will be *your* doom as it has been mine, abomination."

"You know not even the half of it, Lady Scourge." Though, in truth, I'd always thought the *blood* of my erstwhile mother's prophecy meant I'd die in battle or at least in a fight. I'd never considered it might signify heritage . . . bloodlines . . . family. Even queasier than usual at recalling the divination, I shoved the annoying hat backward and scratched my head. "Do *our* kind see the future? I've not been taught that skill."

"*I* see the future," she said. "In the hour he broke me, I told Stian what I planned. He didn't believe a crippled halfbreed girl could bring them down. But when he feels the world die, he will confess it at last. When he sees Tuari Archon himself lapping from my hand, he will admit my power, and I will see Stian Human-friend stand alone in the ruin of his making. Was it the proud son—the most arrogant of an arrogant race—who marked you or the old cat himself?"

"You made Sila a perfect tool for your vengeance," I said,

unwilling to yield even so small an answer. "You hate the Danae because they did not allow you to be one of them; you especially hate the archon because Tuari killed your mother. You hate Stian because, out of fear for the Canon, he crippled you, and because he allowed Eodward and Picus to live in Aeginea, so that a human man became your temptation. You loathe humankind because it was humans who sullied your blood, and you hate both Eodward and the Karish god, because they stole Picus's affections that you believed should be yours alone. But I don't understand your particular antipathy for purebloods. That mystifies me."

She snickered at that. "My daughter, Sila's mother, was more Dané than human. Such grace . . . such beauty . . . When she danced in my kitchen, she made Stian's daughter, Clyste, look as a stick. The Aurellians ruled this benighted land . . . and one of their knights rode through my village when Tresila was but thirteen. He dragged her to their pleasure house, forced her to service his common soldiers and Navron slaveys. Not the purebloods, though. She was not perfect enough to break their bloodlines. Thirty years they kept her a slave."

"But she birthed a child . . ."

"You've yet much to learn of your Danae kin. Even halfbreed females can choose to conceive or not. One of Eodward's soldiers rescued Tresila from the Aurellian pleasure house. In gratitude . . . in *gratitude* . . . she gave him a child." Her tongue near curled with her bile. "The slut died bearing Sila. That's as well, as I would have killed her for it, as I did the cur who plowed her. You cannot measure my hatred for this world. Sila merely wishes no blot of green to remain on this map, but *my* vengeance will be sated only in the hour humankind reaps eternal desolation and no Danae gard lights the world's darkness."

No blot of green . . . I caught my breath and spun to look at the map again. This map was no ordinary fiché, where the significance lay in written symbols and proportionate distances, nor was it a grousherre, where disproportionately sized features demonstrated the mapmaker's judgment of relative importance. In this map the shifting colors told the story. My eyes raced across the expanse. The lands about Gillarine gleamed ocher. The meadow near Elanus yet green. The bogs—Moth's sianou—green. Kol's western sea and its bordering shores green. The tangled waste of Mellune Forest ocher. Sianous—living or dead.

When a sianou was lost, the Danae could no longer remember it. Sila wanted to force them out of their hiding places, out of their sianous and into human lands. She wanted them to forget Aeginea completely and merge with humankind. What if Janus had made this map to show the Danae the lands they had forgotten, so that Kol and the others could dance and reclaim those lands . . . repair the broken Canon . . . repair the broken world? Gods, I was looking at the answer!

Excitement surged through flesh and bone as I reached up and sliced through the first cord holding the map. "I'm sorry for all that happened to you, Ronila. Sorrier for what you did to your granddaughter, a child who did not deserve to be warped for your vengeance. But Sila's rapine cannot be allowed to succeed—nor can yours."

The second supporting rope at the opposite corner split like dry wood at the touch of the knife. Rolling up the bottom edge of the map with my left hand, I reached for the third cord.

Ronila lunged from her chair, grabbed one of the torches, and flung it at me. As the old woman toppled to the floor, bellowing with spiteful laughter, the ancient parchment exploded into fire like nitre powder.

"No!" I bellowed. I dropped the rolled map, and it crashed to the floor. Using hands . . . feet . . . cloak . . . I tried to smother the spreading fire. But sparks set my cloak ablaze, and searing heat drove me backward. The flames chased charring blackness across the lustrous colors with the speed of shooting stars.

The woven curtain behind me roared into flame. Shouts and footsteps rang from the gallery. Ronila lay in a rumpled heap. "You'd best go quickly, abomination," she said, waving me off with a hand streaked with azure. "My granddaughter will flay you."

Blazing ash floated in the air. Acrid smoke billowed from blackened, smoldering curls of vellum, my hope vaporizing with it. With every breath I wanted to crush the cackling crone, but I dared not compromise those awaiting me. I had no such strength as Stearc. I ran.

Whether it was only the smoke from the gallery or someone had discovered the missing prisoners or the fused lock on my tower cell, the stair was swarming with Harrowers. "The gallery chamber's afire!" I shouted when someone barred my way. And when a rough hand detained me and its owner snarled, "Who are you? I saw you go up . . ." I shoved him against the wall and said, "I'm Jakome's brother. Where is he?" Then I grabbed a woman warrior and another man and dispatched them to the "east tower," hoping such a thing existed, and the hunt for strangers quickly became the hunt for Jakome.

My hands were scorched and blistered, my gards peeking through the charred tatters of my gloves. I tucked my hands beneath my half-burnt cloak.

"Grandam!" Sila Diaglou raced past me, Gildas close on her heels. I pressed my back to the wall and ducked my head so that the flop-brimmed hat shadowed my face. Only the tether of Osriel's illness kept me from plunging my knife into one or the other of them; he might need me to get free. I galloped downward just as Sila screamed, "That was Magnus! The one in the hat! Take him!"

I dodged down the prison-level stair, just far enough to discard the hat. Then I raced upward again, tossing two knucklebones over my shoulder, and commanded two men to check on the clattering noise. The moment the two were out of sight, I bolted for the alley. The hose covering my feet, soggy with the guard's piss and Stearc's blood, disintegrated as I sped through the voluminous undercrofts. When I reached the arch into the inner courtyard, I paused long enough to rip them off before they tripped me. I draped the scorched remnants of the cloak over my head, so that at least my pale face would not be visible to those above. I had to hope it would suffice to block any view of my blue-streaked feet as well. Then I moved.

The temptation to dash through the yard straight to Jullian and Osriel nearly overwhelmed me. But the arrow loops on the second level were bright with firelight, and the fortress exploding with shouts. I crept softly, silently through the rubble.

I was halfway across the yard, angling toward the corner, when footsteps and voices echoed in the undercroft behind me. "I'm sure I saw a fellow run this way. Same one as came up the stair."

I dropped to the ground and held still under the ragged cloak, not even daring to look around to see if they followed me. Face buried in the dirt, I scrabbled for some spell that might give us time to get away, but I had naught in my bags of tricks that might deter a determined pursuit. *Stupid . . . cocky . . . arrogant . . .* Thinking I could get away with this. Allowing myself to be distracted and beaten by a bitter hag. Disappointment gnawed at my gut like rats.

"None would come in here. There's no way out but this." Though the sharp-voiced woman kept her excitement tight-reined, the close walls amplified her every word and footstep. I scarce breathed.

"Sila said to search everywhere."

"She'll tear every stone down before he gets away."

At least three of them . . . curse the luck. Light danced on the broken paving that pressed my cheek. I could smell the hot resin of the torches. One step in my direction and I would have to run.

"Over there, Braut! Summat's at the wall!" The three raced past me toward the north wall and the canal and my friends.

I leaped up, shouting, "Here, you damnable fools!"

They stopped, and turned my way, then looked back to the wall, where a shadow mimed a running man—though none of us were running.

"What is it?" They were pointing at me, and I realized the burnt cloak remained on the ground and the gards on my arms and feet glowed the hue of summer midnight. "Where's the other?"

As their resolution wavered, a great explosive crack shot dust and rubble from the wall, and in a roaring avalanche the remainder of the privies crashed down, pulling much of the standing north wall down with it. Osriel . . .

The three Harrowers retreated screaming—more in fear than pain. Had they paused two steps closer to the wall, the masonry would lie atop their heads. And I was no more than ten paces farther away. I leaped and dodged the debris, grateful my half-Danae eyes could penetrate the clouds of dust that fogged the yard.

"Glad I didn't choose to hug the wall," I said, as I skidded into the corner where Jullian and Osriel waited. "Now we move. Even *that* display won't hold Sila for long."

Jullian quaked like a spring leaf, his mouth opening and closing soundlessly as he gaped at the man he knew as quiet, studious Gram.

Osriel huddled in the blanket Jullian had given him, his head resting heavy against the grate, as if he had expended every remaining portion of his strength. But his dark eyes blinked open when I knelt beside him. "Stearc?" he said.

My elation at the moment's reprieve sank quickly under the burden of rage and disappointment. "I'm sorry, lord. He gave everything."

Jullian choked back a cry.

We had no time for grief. The two of them had wisely cleared the rocks and weeds away from the grate. I touched its opposing corners, as Max had instructed, and fed magic to the spell that vibrated in the iron bars. A pop and hiss and the grate flopped forward into a very dark hole.

"Jullian first, then me, so I can help you through," I said to Osriel, who had rolled forward onto all fours. He nodded without speaking, his head drooping between his quivering shoulders.

I reached out to the boy, but he scrambled backward. "*Aegis Ieri,*" he whispered, his head shifting frantically between Osriel and my glowing hand.

"You've no need of Iero's shield, Jullian," I said, as calmly as I could, considering my own heart clattered like hailstones on a slate roof. "This was but magic—considerable magic, to be sure. Gram has hidden skills—inherited from his mother, as my talents and my strange appearance are inherited from my parents. Whatever else he may be, he is still the good man you know as Gram." It was the argument I used with myself every hour.

"I thought I knew *Gildas*," said the boy.

"Indeed Gildas fooled us all," I said. "But you know me, and I promised to protect you and get you out of here. We must go *now*."

Had any man or woman I knew committed such a feat of bravery as Jullian when he crawled into that blackness under Fortress Torvo with Osriel and me? I felt humbled. And very anxious. This was Max's route. Once I'd crawled into the hole myself and helped Osriel through, I set the grate back into the hole. It seated with a satisfying *snick*. I wondered if the unlocking spell worked from the back. In any case, I dared not leave it open.

After a brief attempt to confirm the route with my own skills—straight on, from what I could tell—I took the lead. Osriel tried to conjure us a light, but his hands were shaking with exhaustion. "Perhaps later," he whispered hoarsely.

Sighing with inevitability, I removed the rest of my clothes, allowing my gards to provide us soft illumination approximately the hue of cornflowers.

Osriel's eyes traveled my gards; then he turned away, unable to mask the beginnings of a smile.

Jullian needed a bit more reassurance after that. I pointed out Stian's mark on my arm and the sea creatures that seemed to have taken up residence on my chest, and asked if any demon he could imagine would have cats and fish among their markings.

He heaved a great breath and pronounced his rueful verdict. "I suppose no immortal demon would have bothered eating Harrower porridge either."

Even Osriel chuckled at that, though it set him coughing again.

We all needed something to take our mind off the place we traveled. The only thing worse than seeing the soured black slime we had to crawl through was smelling it. Osriel retched after every coughing fit. I tried not to inhale at all. Jullian vomited when he encountered a more solid lump that had at some time been a hound . . . or perhaps a pig. None of us complained that it was winter. To make this passage in the heat would have been insupportable.

"My mother was not who I thought," I said to Jullian, hoping to mask the sounds of scuttering rats and the ominous creaks and groans from the masonry above us. Max must have enjoyed the thought of me enduring this place. "Nor was my father, as it happens, but it is my mother's race who display such marks as these. Her kind must go through four changes as they grow . . ."

By the time I had told them a bit about my uncle and tide pools and distressed rocks, a whiff of fresher air floated amid the fetid murk. I quickly hushed Jullian's assault of questions and handed him my bundle of filthy clothes.

I crept forward the few quercae to the grate. Voices carried clearly through the frosty night, issuing crisp orders. Clanks and creaks were weapons being shifted in their owners' grasp. Sila kept more experienced men on the gates than on the interior watch. I hoped their eyes were focused outward.

As far as I could tell, the bailey itself was deserted. The drainage canal was blocked by rubble, which left us either the more exposed route straight across the bailey to the grate in the outer wall or a series of shorter jaunts between gallows and stocks and prison cages. For the time, Osriel's magic was spent. We could not depend on his power to hide us.

Still undecided, I touched the corners of the warded grate and quickened its unlocking spell. The grate fell smoothly into my hands. So far, Max's route had worked perfectly. But he would never trust me to show up with Gildas at our rendezvous three streets away. Warned by his wards that we were coming out, he would be waiting, and he would insist on knowing everything about my companions. Best go for speed.

"Only two bits still to go," I said when I returned to my companions. "Straight across the bailey and through another grate will take us under the outer wall. Do you need me to carry you, Gram? This is no time for pride. We must be quick."

"Saverian is very good at potion making," said the prince, already sounding stronger than he had earlier. "Just don't ask me to conjure a rat's squeak along the way. Hadn't you best take this and cover up? My attire is less . . . conspicuous . . . than yours."

I stayed his hand before he could shed the filthy blanket. "I—uh—hear better when I'm like this," I said. "The blanket's not big enough to hide all of me anyway. When you see I'm across with no disturbance, come after. Once we're outside the walls, the nearest cover will be to the right. Go as fast as you can and stay low. I'm hoping that only friends will be waiting, but . . ." I shrugged.

We moved to the hole. One careful listening revealed no change;

a careful observation revealed no eyes turned inward from the walls. I crawled through and dashed across the bailey. My bare feet made no sound, and I caught the third grate as it toppled inward, lowering it carefully into the hollow under the wall. I scuttered through and across the blessedly short distance to the outermost grate, then quickened its spell. A glance beyond the wall showed me naught but night in Riie Doloure. I left the grate leaning against its hole and crawled back the way I'd come.

The two hunched forms moved steadily across the bailey in my direction, not invisible but dark and quiet. They had crossed three quarters of the distance when the doors of the great hall burst open, and torchlight flooded the steps. A patrol of ten Harrowers emerged and ran for the gates. More men took positions on the steps and spread slowly outward, approaching the gallows platform, searching on and underneath it.

Osriel and Jullian had flattened themselves to the ground at the first disturbance and blended well into the mottled landscape of rubble and refuse. But if they remained where they were, the searchers would surely find them. I considered ten different plans and discarded them as quickly. If I set one foot out of the hole to distract the hunters, every eye would be on me. Osriel and Jullian might reach the tunnel, but I never would.

Under, through, or over a wall, thieves and lovers learn them all. The tavern reel's chorus defined my dilemma. There would be no way *through* a gate so well guarded, and no way to get back to the tunnel and *under* the wall faster than Harrowers could be outside it waiting for me. Which left *over . . .*

My stomach lurched. I closed my eyes and recalled the layout of the bailey as I'd seen it from the inside. The stair to the wall walk was some halfway between my position and the gates. No time to think. No time to doubt. *Holy Erdru, god of drunkards and madmen, preserve your faithful servant.*

I crawled out of the hole and darted up and over the wooden platform where Sila's judges had mandated death and mayhem, crouching low and putting as much distance as possible between me and the open grate in the corner. I was halfway to the gallows when they spotted me.

"Look!" Twenty voices at once screamed out. Everything seemed to stop for that moment, just as on the day Voushanti and I had stormed this same gallows under the shield of Osriel's enchantment to rescue Brother Victor. I spun in place. Searchers backed away. Some weapons clanked to the ground—not all, sadly.

Murmurings rose through the hush. *Sorcery! Ghost! Spirit!*

Stubbing my toes on broken planks and mounds of crusted snow, ignoring splinters that pierced my blistered hands, I climbed up onto the gallows. I quickened my simplest, crudest lock spell and touched the chains on the bloodstained drawing frame, where Luviar had been splayed and gutted like a boar. The iron shattered in a shower of red sparks. And then I did the same to the hinges on the gallows traps.

Angel! Guardian!

I dared not look to the corner. How long would it take for Osriel and Jullian to understand and move?

Somewhere behind the glaring torches, a snapped order imposed discipline. Boots crept toward me from the direction of the gates. I gripped a post, swung around it, and leaped off the platform, mustering what grace I could so as not to eternally sully all legends of the Danae. I landed on the balls of my feet with only moderate jarring of spine and limbs. Then I sprinted for the stair to the walls.

"Magnus!" Sila cried from the doors. "You will not escape! Your destiny lies with me!"

I had no breath to answer as I took the stairs three at a time. No wit to create some memorable farewell. I was too busy trying to remember what Kol had told me. *Drive thy spirit upward with the leap. Hold it firm and soaring. It is will that counters the forces that draw us to earth.*

For my king and my friend, I thought as I topped the stair and bounded across the wall walk with ten Harrowers charging from each flank. *Stearc died to keep Osriel safe.*

But it was not such noble thoughts that drove my spirit upward as I leaped from the wall of Fortress Torvo, or held it firm and soaring as I fell toward earth, but the remembrance of my uncle's healing grace as he danced, and a stubborn will that Ronila's malignancy would not destroy the beauty he had wrought.

Chapter 27

I landed on one foot and one knee. Breathless. Not with fear, though I would have sworn I'd left my stomach on Torvo's wall. Not with pain, though grit and gravel and all manner of foulness had most uncomfortably embedded themselves in my knee. Exhilaration starved my lungs. I felt as if angels had borne me on their wings, as if I had lived my life in a cave and only now had glimpsed my first sunrise.

But four men with swords pelted toward me from the gates, Torvo's portcullis ground upward with a troop of Harrowers ready to burst from behind it, and five well-armed riders in Registry colors blockaded Riie Doloure. Their commander sat astride a very large bay, perhaps ten paces from me. Only my conviction that he would be waiting kept my eyes from sliding away from him. Max was a master at obscuré spells.

I could not but grin when I saw his face illumined by Torvo's torches. Not even when we were boys had I seen Max completely unmasked—which had naught to do with the pureblood silk that clung to half his face.

"Balls enough?" I called across the distance between us, opening my arms.

A slow grin broke through his awe. "Balls enough, little— Little bastard. Did you accomplish whatever you came here for?"

"Beware of Jakome," I said, grinning back at him. I would not take his bait. "He's false. But I've left you clean, do you but go now. If these Harrowers identify you . . . take my word, they *will* be out of humor."

Whether or not he believed me, he must have decided he could work no more advantage from the situation. Laughing robustly, he wheeled his mount and rejoined his men. With a snapped command of dismissal, they vanished into the city. I sprinted back toward the hole in Torvo's wall.

"Dead man!" I bellowed, quite unnecessarily, for Voushanti and a handful of leather-clad irregulars were already swarming out of the charred ruin of a tenement and inserting themselves between me and the oncoming Harrowers. Jullian was helping Osriel away from the wall. Between the two of us, we half carried, half dragged him toward the ruin where Voushanti had been waiting.

My back itched. I prayed that Sila had made it clear she wanted me alive. Bowmen on fortress walls in a night action could get twitchy fingers, and a glowing blue rock on a man's back would make a fine target.

Battle erupted behind us. Weapons clanged and shouts of bravado warped quickly into cries of anguish as we ducked under a fallen beam and into the blackened skeleton of a house.

Half of a blackened wall leaned crazily against a snow-clogged hearth. With my gards and the faint wash of torchlight from the fortress the only light, the mottled floor was tricky going. Pools of sooty slush made it difficult to distinguish pits where foundation stones had been carted away. Bundles of unburnt straw lay around the place, as if someone was trying to blot up the slush. The ruin reeked of lamp oil.

"This way!" A pale light bloomed at the back of the ruin, where a stone stair led downward. "Mother of Night, Riel! And Thane Stearc?" She must have read our faces. "Ah, a pestilence on these vermin."

Before we could blink, Saverian had Osriel seated on a bit of broken wall, draining vials of two different potions, Jullian wrapping the prince and himself in dry cloaks, and me dispatched to find us a way out. The physician's practical fury seemed to cleanse the air of Ronila's madness like a taste of fresh limes cleanses the palate. "Make it fast, Valen."

I hurried down the broken steps into the ancient lane that had been uncovered two months ago by the raging fires of a Harrower mob. The noise of the fighting fell away quickly. The lane cut across a hillside, and its builders had installed high stone walls to hold back the dirt. But the stone houses that had lined the lane had vanished long before I was born, and the fires had burned off the vegetation that held the hill stable. Now mud had slumped down from the hillside, and I couldn't find the place I was looking for . . . a courtyard . . . a way out . . .

The intoxication of my leap from the walls deserted me, leaving a profound uneasiness in its wake. I felt cold, light-headed. The place, the night . . . everything felt wrong. I needed to get back. Voushanti and his men were sorely outnumbered.

In desperation, I knelt and touched the frozen mud, pushing magic through exhaustion and confusion. And there in front of me lay a silver path. A Dané had once walked here. More than one, perhaps, for just ahead lay a knot of silver—not an unruly tangle, but layer upon layer of loops and windings as Kol laid down when he danced. In the center of the knot grew a winter-bare apple tree, vibrant with life and health here in the midst of a city gone mad. I should have guessed this was a Dané sianou when I'd first found it, but I'd not known how to look.

Racing back toward the others, I gave the final signal. *Dead man. Harvest.* Voushanti would retreat to the ruined tenement to join us. *Bluejay. Harvest.*

The physician, the prince, and the boy crouched in the lane behind a fallen beam. Osriel held a decrepit sword, while Saverian hefted a rusty ax—perhaps better were hard to come by in the city. Jullian seemed to be their rear guard and sagged in relief at the sight of me, lowering a dagger half the length of his arm. The combat was deafening and very close.

Voushanti's bellow thundered through the din. "Fall back! To me! To me!"

"I've found the way out," I said, "or would you three prefer to stay here and fight?"

Osriel conceded me only a glance. "Saverian has propped me up to scare off Harrower crows," he said with a hint of laughter. "But altogether, I'd prefer a bed."

"As soon as Voushanti steps under the beam, we can go," said Saverian, dropping her ax. "Wait here and be ready." She ran up the steps into the ruined house.

"Hold on!" I bolted after her. "Are you mad?"

She ignored me as first one and then another of Voushanti's exhausted fighters yelled *haven* and stumbled through the crossed beams. Four . . . five . . . six of them . . . and then Voushanti himself burst through. "Now, mage!" snapped the warrior.

As Voushanti twisted and skewered the Harrower who tried to follow him inside, Saverian touched the bundles of straw nearest the opening. Green flames exploded from the bundles, consuming another attacker, who stumbled screaming over his dead comrade. The physician ran from one bundle to the next until the entire front of the ruin was walled in flame taller than my head. Only one of Voushanti's goggle-eyed mercenaries stood his ground long enough to catch the bag Saverian tossed him. Payment in hand, he followed his comrades straight up the steep hillside behind the ruined house and into the night.

"Time to go," said Saverian, as Voushanti hacked at another man who braved the flames. "The fire won't hold them long."

Voushanti held the doorway until we were down the steps, lining the opening with dead and screaming wounded.

"Now, dead man!" I yelled over the roar of the flames. "Stay with me!"

As I led them down the ancient lane, I had a vague impression of Voushanti descending the steps in one jump and green flames exploding behind him. Shoving the roused fear and anxieties of battle aside, I sought clarity and memory enough to make the shift. A small courtyard . . . healthy growth bared by winter . . . high walls and the knee-high ring of stones in the center . . . a pool of sustaining life— here an apple tree rooted deep in the hillside, there a well rooted deep in a mountain . . . air touched with winter and smoke, here from straw burning to preserve valuable lives, there from hearth fires and kitchens . . .

One by one, my charges hurried into the apple court, as I had named the strange little lane in Palinur—Jullian, fiercely determined; Osriel, flushed and wheezing; Saverian batting sparks from her jupon; and then Voushanti, blood-splattered and facing backward. From the smoke behind us burst another figure, a giant-sized warrior wearing a ragged cloak, dented helm, and orange badge.

When Voushanti took him down with an ax to his thigh, the Harrower bled his life onto the winter grass of the well yard at Renna, some two hundred quellae south of Fortress Torvo. It was snowing.

Jullian, who had spun around to watch Voushanti dispatch the Harrower, bumped into me when I halted at the stone circle of the well. I caught his arm before he stumbled over my feet and stuck me or himself with his dagger. "Easy, lad. I don't think any others can follow us here."

The mud-drowned lane, eerie flames, and rampaging Harrowers had vanished. Behind Voushanti stretched a colonnade fronting the cold inner wall of Renna's keep. The boy heaved a quivering sigh as he looked up at me. "Magic again?"

I squatted beside him and held out my arm in parallel with my glowing thighs. "Aye. It's one thing these are good for. You'll note that Gram is fairly well astonished, too."

Osriel spun so quickly with his neck craned up at Renna's heights that Saverian stood ready to catch him should he topple. "Well done," said the prince. "Oh, very well done, Valen."

Jullian leaned his head to my ear. "He's not just *Gram*, is he? All three of you call him lord. And he brought down that wall."

"He *is* Gram, but no, not *just* Gram. By now you've surely guessed his true name."

The boy acknowledged without words, his face a pale blur in the night.

"You've no need to be afraid, Jullian." I made no effort to keep my voice down. "Prince Osriel has found it necessary to keep people fearful of him . . . to protect himself and our cabal and his people here in Evanore. Abbot Luviar was once his tutor."

But, of course, there *was* ample reason to be afraid of Osriel, not for Jullian alone, but for all of us together. Grateful as I was to stand in Renna's shelter instead of Sila Diaglou's tower, much as my legs felt like clay, my back wrenched, and my feet battered, my night's work could not be declared finished.

"And Voushanti"—Osriel gripped the mardane's shoulder and inspected him as if seeking the source of the blood that stained Voushanti's hauberk and leathers—"a magnificently executed retrieval. Your valor and your skill in arms are unmatched." His voice dropped a little. "You are well, Mardane? Saverian took care of you?"

"I am whole for now, my lord. The physician did as you commanded. I am bound to the sorcerer."

"To *Valen*?" On any other night, I might have missed the hint of dismay in Osriel's voice. He masked it quickly by a gallant bow in Saverian's direction. "And *your* skills, physician . . . and friend . . . remain unmatched and irreplaceable. What greater wonder can I demonstrate to these present than walking up yonder stair without reclining on Valen's shoulders or weighting my noble companion Jullian's arm?"

"Your physician prescribes food, wine, bath, and bed," said Saverian with no hint of sentiment, as she shoved her straggling hair away from her soot-smudged face.

"I must see Elene first," said Osriel, his momentary lightness shed like an unwanted cloak. "Perhaps you would accompany me, Valen, and tell us what you can of Stearc's end."

Ah, Mother Samele embrace Elene, who must soon be torn asunder by sorrow and relief . . . and all the questions and fears this prince held for her. Her plight only hardened the resolution grown solid in my gut.

"I will, of course, lord," I said, standing up, while keeping a hand on Jullian's shoulder. "But I might suggest we not wake her to such ill news before I've had a chance to discuss the matter with you. Saverian, as the prince has downed multiple vials of your marvelous elixirs, would it compromise him too severely to speak with me for a little?"

She raised her eyebrows and twisted her mouth in her ironical fashion that illumined her awkward features with life and wit. "As Lord Osriel will tell you himself, I am *not* his keeper. He knows my recommendations and will likely do with them as he always has."

She rummaged in a pouch at her waist and tossed me another vial. Then she held out her hand to the boy at my side, let her magelight swell to a soft ivory where he could see it glowing from her fingers, and smiled in a way that instantly dispatched his awe. "Come, noble Jullian. You, at least, will enjoy what I have to offer in the way of food and bed. Prince Osriel has told me a great deal about you these past few years. He lives in awe of your scholarship . . ."

As the woman and boy headed for the stair at the corner of the colonnade, Osriel glanced my way and dipped his head, then addressed Voushanti. "Mardane, perhaps you would notify the watch that we have returned, and that Mistress Elene is not to be disturbed until I wait upon her."

Voushanti shifted his attention to me. Pinpoints of red centered his dark gaze. Only after I had given an uneasy nod did he bow to Osriel. "As you command, my lord prince." He pivoted and followed Saverian and Jullian out of the well yard, leaving Osriel and me alone.

"So we are to have our reckoning before even we get warm." Osriel spread his arms as if to welcome whatever I might bring, then seemed to think better of it. Shivering, he drew Saverian's heavy cloak tight. "It hardly seems fair to ask me to take you on when I've just seen you leap to earth from a height no man should survive, clad in naught but mythlight, and you've carried me out of hell to my own house in less time than it would take me to walk my own walls."

"Let us walk a bit, my lord. I'd not wish some lurking guard to hear what we might say." I pointed to the colonnade. Rather than taking the upper stair to the Great Hall and bedchambers or the lower stair to the passages where Saverian's workroom lay, we strolled along the covered walk so like those surrounding the cloister garth at Gillarine—the three-petaled lily of Navronne embedded in its stonework, the cherubic aingerou carved into the slender pillars, the square of grass alongside our path, centered by a spring-fed font. We rounded the corner in truth and memory . . .

. . . and we were there, staring up at the shattered tower of the abbey church, at the gutted remnants of the library and scriptorium, at the darkness of the deserted dorter. At the burnt and broken shell of a place once holy.

Osriel halted and stepped away from me, whipping his head from one side of the cloister to the other. "What have you done? Why have you brought me here?"

"I needed us to be in a neutral place," I said. "Away from devoted warriors, away from swords and dungeons and magic—or, at least, magic that is outside of ourselves. I thought at first to take you into the wild, to some place where you could not find your way back if this discussion goes for naught. But I've no wish to harm you, lord. This place . . . I think we both care for it and will think twice before bringing any further evil to it. I thought perhaps to find my friend Gram waiting here."

In the azure light of my gards, his gaunt face appeared carved in ice. "I am your king and your bound master. I need discuss nothing with you."

He thrust this harsh rhetoric between us like the first feint in a dual. I didn't think I needed to remind him of his promise that once I took him into Aeginea I would be free to go my own way. Nor did I mention that to abandon him here in his present state without Saverian's medicine would likely mean his death. Instead I strolled down the west cloister walk away from the church. After a moment he joined me.

"I wish we were not so tired," I said, offering him my arm. He shook his head. "I wish you were not ill. I wish we had more time to debate and reason."

We rounded the south end of the cloister and walked past the refectory to the calefactory—an open room lined with stone benches and centered by a great hearth and a neat wood stack. "You need warmth, and I need open air. I doubt Nemesio would mind if we use his warming room. The brothers have taken refuge at Magora Syne."

In normal times the brothers kept the calefactory fire burning through the winter for the monks to stop in and warm their hands as they went about their work and prayer. Once I had laid the fire, Osriel summoned a spell to set it ablaze. He sat cross-legged beside it, hunched forward as if hoping to draw strength and nourishment from the flames as well as warmth. I sat on the stone bench where I could breathe cold air and see his face.

Even the bright flames could not push back the shadows of Gillarine. Too much death and sorrow lingered just beyond the light.
Stearc's presence loomed very large. And I held the memory of the
thane's last fear as a shield before my own.

"So speak," said the prince, once his shivering had eased. "You've
not brought me here to play monk."

"I will ask you to hear me out before argument or comment," I
said. "I've never laid all this out at once."

He did not respond, so I plunged ahead. "You are my rightful king,
son of a man I honored and vowed to follow to the death. You are a
man I have been astonished and pleased to name my friend, for one
of the things I've learned since first I came to Gillarine is that I never
before owned a true friend—one who would hold me fast as I fell
into hell and strive to pull me out again, one who would trust me in
matters of importance, one who would *know* me, for I believed I
could not allow anyone to *know* me."

He propped his elbows on his knees and rested his chin on his
clasped hands. Waiting for me to go on. Yielding nothing. A wall
stood between us, and my purpose was to shatter it and expose what
lay beyond—marvelous or terrible as it might be.

"I've not brought you here to explain why you betrayed me to
those who would destroy me. I've convinced myself that you saw no
other choices open to you." His unguarded smile when he first
looked full on my gards had but confirmed my growing suspicion. "I
believe you held a hope that my uncle would do exactly as he did.
I believe you brought Saverian apurpose on that journey, knowing
that her nature would prompt her to do exactly as she did, or if the
worst came to pass, to amend matters as she could."

That surprised him. His head jerked up and his dark eyes met
mine. Though he made no acknowledgment, I took his silence as confirmation.

I pushed on. "Rather I want to tell you what I've learned these
past days, in hopes we can make some sense of it together before we
fall off the edge of the world. Some you surely know, some you surely
don't. I told you and Jullian some of what Kol taught me, but I didn't
tell you about Picus."

"Picus?" Another surprise that shocked him rigid. "Where? How
did—?"

"Please, lord, hear me out. Picus lives in Aeginea . . ."

I told him of the monk and his sin, of Ronila and her web of hate,
of Gildas and Sila, of the lost map and my conviction that it had depicted the tale of the world's ruin. I laid out the evidence of Tuari's

humiliation at the actions of his half-human brother, his retribution on Llio's wife, and his punishment by Stian. And I told how Saverian and I had both realized that Osriel's quest for power from the Danae could backlash and make matters worse.

"... and so we are left with Sila Diaglou, entirely sane, entirely ruthless, and determined to purify Navronne and reshape it according to her peculiar vision, with Gildas, who schemes to become the lord of chaos, and with Ronila, who intends to destroy us all. They will cross Caedmon's Bridge in little more than a sevenday. I don't completely understand my skills, lord, but I have bound them to your father's service, to Abbot Luviar's vision, to Jullian's protection and the protection of two others whose names I cannot reveal. I would use them in the service of Navronne ... in your service, too, if those two are the same. Tell me what is to happen at the mine called Dashon Ra on the winter solstice."

Osriel's eyes were closed, so that for a moment I thought he had fallen asleep. But he shifted and straightened and met my gaze unflinching, though his dark eyes held the bleakness of Navronne's winter. "I will position a small force at the Bridge, commanding them to lure the Harrowers into the hills behind Renna. Thanks to preparations I have made over the years, Sila will find the vale of Dashon Ra harder to escape than to enter—now I know she is half Dané, I'll have to consider more carefully how to deal with her own person, and her gammy's, I suppose. With enough magic entirely channeled into the gold veins at Dashon Ra, I can free the souls I have imprisoned. Bound by blood to my will, they must and shall do my bidding. I plan to give them the Harrower legions."

Cold horror struck me like a demon's hand. "Instill the dead souls in living hosts?"

He shot to his feet at my first word, gripping one column of the great hearth as if it were all that stood between him and dissolution. "Do *not* preach to me of the evil of this course until you have seen the future your sister, the diviner, has shown me. Were I to send a *living* army down upon Sila Diaglou's trapped legions to save this kingdom from such a future, no man or woman would fault me. Kings *must* command their people to die for them. Had I the slightest hope of an alternative, I would welcome it with all my heart. But I cannot condemn Navronne to centuries of starvation, disease, and enslavement for my lack of will to use what knowledge and skill I possess."

"But what becomes of such an army?" An army of revenants ... living bodies possessed by the angry dead.

"Under my command, they will turn on my brother's troops. If my brother is wise, he will lay down his arms and come to terms with me. We must consummate the bargain quickly. Without an infusion of my blood, my warriors will have but seven days of life, perhaps twice that if the Danae keep their word. But those will be days they would not own had I left their corpses undisturbed on Perryn's and Bayard's battlegrounds. Perhaps they can make some peace with that."

I shook my head. "Not peace, my lord. And you well know it. Their souls' future will be forfeit. You will force them to trade seven days of breathing for the fullness of whatever life lies beyond this one. They'll not have even the time to seek out their families. And what of the Harrowers' souls displaced? Are they rightfully dead or are they lost to heaven as well? Or are they, in turn, prisoned in your veins of gold? Three days ago, I shared Voushanti's dying, lord, and such despair as I felt cannot heal what ails Navronne. If you win your throne by such means, how ever will you govern?"

"My warlords will protect me in the beginning. From there my own deeds must tell. I'll do what I can to hold back the night. And we must hope that the Danae, left alone and undisturbed, can heal the things I cannot." He braced his back against the graceful column, as unyielding as the stone. "I have pondered this course for three years, Valen. Could I see but a glimmer of hope in some other plan, I would leap at it. Luviar knew about Voushanti. He knew of my work with the dead, and why I donned terror as a pureblood dons his mask. Indeed, he knew better than I of all my strengths and weaknesses, and to the very end he counseled me that his god would show me the path of right. Yet even Luviar, in all his wisdom, could not tell me another way."

I stepped out of the calefactory enclosure full into the wind, for it felt as if the heat muddied my thoughts. "And what if Tuari Archon betrays you?" For, of course, Osriel intended the magic of the Canon to be channeled into the veins of gold to empower his army of souls. "Ronila spoke as if Tuari was already her tool."

The prince riffled his hair with his slender fingers, truly puzzled. "Spite would be his only reason. I yielded every point, gave him everything he asked for. To demonstrate trust and buy the parley, I pledged him fair recompense for my father's failure to return to Aeginea. To prove my faith, I returned the treasure that was stolen— and it is his own people who lost you again, after all. Our joined power on the solstice will end the sianou poisonings. But in the event you are right and Tuari upends the bargain, I do have an alternative. Certain rites can release the power bound in my blood as Caedmon's heir. It should be enough to do as I want. Perhaps that is the only just solution after all."

And then I put together the clues and understood what he had planned all along. No wonder Saverian would not speak of it. Sila Diaglou had once demanded a scion of Caedmon's house to bleed in her penitential rites, and Osriel had told me that blood consecrated to Navronne would be supremely potent. He had told Elene that his plan would end his last hope of heaven, but he had not meant that merely as an acknowledgment of a monstrous crime.

"You think to have Saverian bleed you as Sila would," I said, appalled at what I envisioned. "You die in torment to release this power in your veins, and she returns you to life to use it. You would yield your own soul to win this battle."

He let his head fall back against the pillar and closed his eyes. "Actually I intend Voushanti to do the bleeding part. I'll need him back from you before we begin."

To spend one's entire life dependent on the blood of others—whom would he choose? Saverian herself . . . his loyal childhood friend coerced into this macabre partnership? Not Elene. He had pushed her away, for love must surely wither in such a feeding. Voushanti . . . their survival linked one to the other like conjoined twins?

"I'll not put Voushanti through another death to change guardianship, lord. Though I know he will obey you, even in this, it is cruel and inhuman and unworthy of you to ask it of him."

"We must all heed cruel necessity—whether prince, warrior, or halfblood Dané, whether man or woman."

And then did another consideration chill me. "Ah, lord, what did you promise Tuari to redeem your father's betrayal?"

"Only that which I shall make sure never to have—a firstborn child for them to nurture in my father's place."

"Spirits of night, but you—" I bit my tongue. I was sworn to secrecy on the matter. Of course the Danae would require balance in such a bargain, and if Osriel's firstborn was the price of the parley itself, this bargain would stand . . . no matter what happened on the solstice. I was sworn to protect Elene and the child, whatever that might mean in the future. Osriel could not know. "Could you find naught else, lord?"

He dropped his head between his stiff shoulders and laughed—a sad, despairing humor. "How far you've come, friend Valen, from the rogue who tried to steal my nivat offering. You lack even a sprout of wings, yet I feel as if the judgment of heaven rests in your word.

Can you not see? My father left his beloved kingdom—his people—in my protection. Do I wait another season, I'll have naught left to save. How can I ask of others what I would not give myself?"

I stared into the broken, snow-drenched cloisters of Gillarine and sought answers. Ruin lay in every direction that I could see. To stop Osriel left Navronne at the mercy of Sila Diaglou. But I had no confidence that even so determined a warrior as Sila could outfox the witch who had made her—and that made our end far worse. No wheat would grow from an earth of Ronila's harrowing. And Gildas, the monk who aspired to godhood, was the blind bargain in the game. At some point he would strike out on a separate course from his malignant partner. He intended me to be a part of it, and the hunger lurking even now in my blood gave me the unsettling feeling that my escape from Fortress Torvo had not concerned him as much as it should have. Though even a victory would tally an unsupportable cost, who else but Osriel had the remotest chance of stopping these three?

Not I. If I had a part in this conflict . . . in this world . . . it yet remained hidden from me. My mother's purposes were unfathomable. The impossible yearnings waked by my contact with my Danae kin seemed selfish and trivial beside the magnitude of the ruin we faced. And so I was left only with tangled vows and awe for those who would give so much for naught but sheerest love. I felt in sore need of counsel.

I wiped the sweat from my forehead and approached the drooping shape braced upright by the pillar. "Come, my lord, let me take you home to bed."

He cocked his head. "No argument? No fiery sword?"

I gave him Saverian's vial. When he had drained it and some of the rigidity had left his stance, I offered him my arm. He relinquished his pillar and allowed me to slip my arm under his shoulders. As we moved slowly through the cloisters, a flurry of bats flew out from the burnt undercrofts.

"Just . . . wait for me, lord," I said as I walked us back to Renna. "Don't tell anyone about your plan, and don't do anything irretrievable until I get back. I doubt I've the wit to find you another way, but perhaps my uncle does."

PART FOUR

Canon

Chapter 28

I crouched in the lee of a limestone scarp—the only shelter in the storm-blasted wilderness—and vomited up nothing for the fiftieth time in an hour. Had my throat not already taken on the character of raw meat, I would have screamed into the earth as my limbs seized with cramps, my gut twisted into knots, and my skin felt like the vellum of Sila's map as it charred into ash. Instead, I writhed and moaned and cursed, ready to devour the frozen mud or my own flesh did I have the least imagining it would taste of nivat.

The hunger had come upon me as I had traveled the first shift from Osriel's gates, as if my body knew that my responsibility for others' safety had ended for the present and it could now indulge itself. Determined to seek my uncle's counsel, I had ignored its warning and traveled the meadows beyond Caedmon's Bridge to the Sentinel Oak. Once in Aeginea, I shifted straightaway into the terraced land where, in the human plane, Ardra's prized vineyards lay dying. I had no notion of how to find Kol, even assuming the archon had not turned him into a beast or locked him out of his body. But if I could just find my way back to Picus, surely he could tell me how to locate my uncle or Stian.

Over the hours my craving had deepened, and the blizzard that had struck with the sunless dawn grew so violent I could not see. The onset of familiar cramps and tremors banished all my suppositions that relinquishing this renewed craving would somehow be easier than what I had undergone before. I could have torn through steel with my teeth to find the makings for a doulon. And this time I had no Osriel or Saverian to hold me together.

Miserably lost and dreadfully sick, I had wandered in circles for more than a day. And when my strength failed, I had crawled to this meager shelter to escape the storm. So much for great vows and resolutions.

A bout of coughing and sneezing felt like to push my eyes from my head. Somewhere in my mindless wandering, I had lost my bundle of clothes and provisions, which left me naught for wiping my streaming nose or eyes and naught to keep me warm now my gards could not. My shivering could have rattled even Renna's stout walls.

I tried to muster the sense for a seeking. Grateful that the sky did not shatter with my first movement, I rested my forehead on the snowy ground, pressed my palms to the earth on either side of my head, and forced magic through my fingertips. Instead of a nicely measured flow, power gushed through my wretched body in one enormous surge.

What felt like a hard-launched stone struck the center of my already tender forehead . . . which made no sense at all as my forehead yet rested on the snowy earth. But the image of the landscape struck me clearly: rolling meadows . . . not barrens, as they seemed in this grim weather. Dormant, yes, with the waning season, but in summer, thick with hazel and dogwood, grouse and falcons, roe deer, and myriad other creatures. The undersoil smelled rich with life and health. Well tended.

As I lifted my head a little and pressed the heel of my hand onto the unbroken flesh centering my forehead, a rush of warmth flowed up and around and over my back, flooding me with scents of clover and meadowsweet. Azure lightning threaded the snow all around.

"What thinkest thou to do here, *ongai?*" A woman's words peppered my skin like wind-driven needles. "To break my sleep without greeting . . . to broach so deeply. Such blatant rudeness requires explanation before I report thee for sanction." And then a bare foot struck me in the chin.

I fell back on my heels, clutching my rebellious stomach as a trickle of blood tickled my raw throat. *Sanction . . . captivity . . . breaking . . .* Panic near shredded my wits. I scrambled backward . . . and then I saw her.

Long arms wrapped about her knees, she sat in the snow—no, perched atop the snow like a bird, so weightless did she appear. Tousled curls the silvered rose of winter sunrise framed her round face. A butterfly, its lace wings tinted every hue of sunlit sky, hovered on her ivory cheek and trailed threads of dewy cobwebs down her shoulders and arms. What scraps of wit I had left escaped me.

"Thou'rt but initiate!" Her face blossomed in surprise as she looked on mine. She tilted her head, and her eyes traveled downward. "I could have thee sanctioned for—" Her examination halted in the region of my groin, wrinkling her glowing face into a knot. "No initiate, but a *stripling* male of full growth. You're failed, then. Hast thou no shame to come poking around my sianou like a mole in the heath? Unless thou'rt but some odd dream come to warm me this winter . . ." Her pique trailed off in whimsy. "I've a fondness for dream lovers."

"You are . . . so . . . lovely." As I stammered this inanity, the surge of blood that spoke the goddess Arrosa's will seemed to flush the sickness from my veins. Though my state was no more sensible, at least I might not vomit on the small, pale feet that glimmered not a quercé from my knees. I inhaled deeply, dabbed the back of my hand against my bleeding lip, and tried to remember the polite address for an unrelated Dané female. "Shamed . . . yes, *engai*. Forgive my rudeness. I've been wandering. Ate something I should not. I seek my vayar to discuss my future and, in my confused state, mistook the place."

"Ah, I once mistook mustard seeds for nivé, and they roused such a storm inside me, I could not dance the moonrise." Her smile set my gards afire. She touched my knee, releasing sparks of silver and blue. Did all Danae have moods that switched from storm to sun faster than flickers' pecks?

I leaned forward. Inhaled again. The afternoon smelled ripe as an autumn orchard. "Surely the moon wept on that sad night."

Pleasure rippled the brightness of her gards. "Sweetly spoken, stripling! Perhaps I should feed thee belly-soothing tansy before I sleep again. Thou'rt lovely, as well, and bring a powerful presence and a lusty vigor to my meadow." As she brushed her finger over my bruised lip, a veil of disturbance dimmed her starry brightness. "How is it possible thou art failed? More important, how is it possible a failed stripling can broach my sianou?"

"His blundering feet but sounded a dream, Thokki." Kol's voice cleaved the thickening air as the bells of Matins shatter a monk's wistful dreams. "*Envisia seru*, sweet guardian."

The female jumped gracefully to her feet, a move that did nothing to calm my urgent admiration. Woven spidersilk draped from one shoulder front and back. A girdle of strung pearls, wound thrice about her, caught it loosely at her hips, whence it fell to her knees. The veil hid naught of importance.

"Too long since the sight of thee hath delighted my eye, Kol Stianson! Why are—?" A catch in her throat signaled alarm and wonder as her gaze switched back to me. She stepped away, arms crossed on her breast. "This is the Cartamandua halfbreed. The violator."

Kol spoke up before I could protest. "He is no violator, Thokki. Tuari's long-soured spirit speaks blight upon my *rejongai*. Blight upon my sister for her choice to bear him. Blight upon me for choosing to spare him the pain of breaking. Yet I have released his true being and found him reverent and gifted, though indeed clumsy as a bear in spring."

"Willing, then, I yield to thy judgment." Brow darkening, she touched Kol's arm. "Is it true they have passed over thee, Kol? That Nysse is the Chosen for the Winter Canon?"

He nodded stiffly. "But I am neither locked away nor beast-captive. I need not be at the Center to dance my part fully. And come spring"—he shrugged—"perhaps eyes will be clearer."

"Winter already bites deep, thus I have bedded early." She hunched her shoulders and wrapped her arms about herself, allowing her gaze to travel the gray dome of the sky and the wilderness of snow. "But I shall wake for the Canon and make my voice heard to argue this decision. I'll not be alone in it. Thou shouldst challenge Nysse, Kol. The world is injured, and any who keep thee from dancing the Center tear at its wounds. Thou'lt have a care with this halfbreed?"

Kol stepped close, took Thokki's head gently between his hands, and kissed her hair. "I shall chastise my tendé for blundering so crudely into thy dreams, and then commend him for his choice of beauty to admire. Wilt thou partner me for a round this Canon, Thokki?"

She flushed cheek to toe—a fetching glory, to be sure. I near swallowed my tongue.

"I—" She tilted her head and looked askance at my uncle. "Thou needst not offer such a gift to keep me silent about this encounter."

Kol bristled. "I do not use a Canon partnering for bribe or payment."

"Of course," she said quickly. "I never meant insult. That thou wouldst mark my dancing in anywise near thy level humbles me. Honored and joyful would I be to partner thee."

"We shall be on our way. Come, *rejongai*." My uncle's curt command brought me to my feet and into a respectful bow, determined not to shame him further in front of Thokki. I sincerely hoped that he had not compromised his honor to prevent her telling tales of me. I wasn't sure he could forgive such a necessity.

I bowed to Thokki, as well, but deemed it best to keep my mouth shut. The language my body spoke was boorish enough.

"In the Canon, Thokki," said Kol.

"In the Canon, Kol," she called after us.

My uncle struck out across the fields without any word to me. Outside of Thokki's warm presence, his tension was as palpable as the bitter wind. He set a blistering pace. I struggled to keep up, doing my best to ignore the returning symptoms of my craving. We made two magical shifts, and though I felt the moves clearly, I could not have repeated them.

After the second shift, the snow yielded to a cold, pounding rain. The land stretched flat and gray as far as I could see. The air weighed heavy on my shoulders and smelled of river wrack. Sweat poured from my brow, and my knees quivered.

"Vayar," I called hoarsely as Kol began to move even faster. "We must talk. Matters of grave import. Please . . ."

My legs slowed on their own, threatening to give way completely as cramps and shakes racked my back and limbs. At first I thought he might abandon me in the rainy desolation, but as I willed myself a few more steps along his path, he spun and waited for me.

"What ails thee, Valen?" His speech pierced like shards of bronze. "I expected thee stronger, faster, and more attentive on thy return. I expected thee careful. Had I not kept my ears open in readiness, only cracked bones wouldst thou have to walk on this night. Thy coming rattled the Everlasting as crashing boulders, so that any who heed the movements of the air could feel it."

He rested his hands on his hips. "That thou dost dawdle and moon along the way is my responsibility; I should have taught thee better how to curb the rising heat of a stripling till thou shouldst encounter a proper companion. But it is naught but madness to risk thy safety by broaching the sianou of a sleeping guardian—a deed no stripling of any maturing shouldst be able to accomplish. Only by fair chance didst thou choose Thokki, a merry spirit who trusts her friends. Has sense left thee entire?"

I summoned control and stood straight, determined my ragged condition would not interfere with the world's fate. "Vayar, I bring news of the doom of the long-lived. These wild folk that poison the guardians are led by one who once lived in Aeginea. She means to destroy the Canon . . . destroy you all."

"We spoke of this before, and I told thee—"

"Her name is Ronila."

"Ronila!" His shocked echo split the air.

At the same time, pain lanced my middle, causing me to double over. He caught my arms just before my knees buckled. "Art thou injured? Broken? Come . . ." In a blur of pain and dark rain, he sat me

on a muddy hummock, filled his hands, and poured rainwater down
my throat. To my shame, it stayed down no better than any other
contents of my stomach.

"I'm just sick," I said, wiping my mouth on my arm. Not even the
fires of shame could quiet my shivering. "It's nivat—"

"Fool of a stripling! Thou art completely witless! Complain not to
me of nivé, if thou wouldst ever have my ear." He grabbed my arm
and, without another word, dragged me through a series of nauseating shifts. The world dissolved in churning gray and I completely lost
track of body and mind . . .

"So, are you more sensible now?"

Sand in my mouth. In my eyes. Everywhere underneath me. Rain
drummed on my back and cascaded over my head. I squinted into
the murk. The pounding in my head was not just blood but waves, out
there beyond the veils of rain that merged sea, air, cliffs, and sky into
one mass of gray. Evaldamon. The salty residue in my mouth
evidenced Kol had dunked me in the sea at the very least.

"Yes, *rejongai*. Better." I sat up, feeling scoured inside and reasonably clear-headed. Recollection of his warning postponed my
questions about nivat and what he'd done to aid me.

"Tell me of Ronila," he said.

"The priestess who destroys your sianous is Ronila's granddaughter, raised to be Ronila's vengeance on humans and Danae
alike. But it is Ronila and her toady that I fear most. They have some
scheme . . ."

I told him all I knew of the old woman and Sila and Gildas.
Though I did not describe Osriel's particular plan, I revealed how
Tuari had pledged to spend the power of the Winter Canon into the
golden veins of Dashon Ra and fuel the prince's dangerous enchantment.

". . . but once Picus told me of Tuari's hatred for humankind, I
could not believe the archon would keep the bargain. I had to warn
Osriel of the potential treachery. That's why I left Aeginea so
abruptly."

Kol sat on his haunches, his mouth buried in his hands as he listened to my story. Through a sheen of raindrops, his dragon suffused
his lean face with a sapphire glow. "Though my sire and I disagree
with the archon on many matters, Tuari has always attended his responsibilities faithfully. He does not make bargains he has no intent
to keep; nor would he ever compromise the Canon. When he failed to
name me Chosen—the one of us who dances at the Center—none

could understand it. My dancing is unmatched in this season." Honesty, not pride, birthed his claim.

"As Picus told thee, Tuari is least likely of all of us to join a human—especially Eodward's son—in any endeavor. Yet Dashon Ra *is* the Center of the Winter Canon, and he *has* named his consort Chosen. She could do this thing—divert the wholeness of the dance into the veins and not the land itself . . ." The words faded. His thoughts drifted deeper.

This was not what I wanted to hear. "Janus said the Chosen dances at the Center to 'bring all life to joining.' All life—human, Danae, birds, beasts . . . everything?"

"The dance of the Chosen joins *all* that is brought to the Canon by the long-lived—trees and rivers, mountains, stones, sea and shore, earth and all that grows, as well as all thou hast named."

"But only the lands you remember. You can't include the parts of the earth that are corrupt."

Kol straightened abruptly. "I have told thee, I will *not*—"

"I know that you and your kind forget places that have been poisoned, Kol. Janus once created a great map, hoping to show you the places you had lost. But he didn't understand that Danae could not make sense of such patterning. Somehow Sila Diaglou got hold of that map and was using it to judge her success in forcing your kind out of Aeginea." I could not let him avoid the subject any longer. "Vayar, you vowed to provide me truth and healthy guidance. As you see I need both of those now more than I have ever done, else we have no hope of untangling this mess. My mother intended me to help. You know that. I've just no idea how. Permit me to do so. Please, uncle, teach me."

Kol scooped a handful of sand, allowing the rain to wash it through his fingers. Only when his palm was clean did he respond. "Janus said he would help us reclaim the Plain. It is only a name in our tales of the Beginnings, yet we believe its importance equal to the Sea, the Mountain, and the Well. Thou hast judged rightly; we cannot bring it back into the Canon if we cannot find it. We cannot find it if we cannot remember. In the same way each of the sianous lost to the Scourge falls out of our memory and thus out of the Canon. Only the names linger to remind us of our loss."

Sorrow, grief, and shame clothed him as new gards. "Clyste traveled with Janus as he marked his papers," he continued, "returning joyful, for her eyes had seen these dead places. For one or two she was able to work a kiran to bring to the Spring Canon. With Janus's magics we would be able to find these places again and reclaim them all. But when at last the Cartamandua returned and unrolled his great skin, we could see naught but scrawling that twisted our eyes and turned our heads wrong way out."

"Ronila could read it," I said. "But in her spite, she told no one. She must have taken the map from Janus then, or perhaps Picus gave it to her when he came back to Navronne. The hag burnt your only hope to find the dead lands. Sila wants you to forget Aeginea and interbreed with humans. Ronila wants to ensure you never remember. Ronila wants you dead."

Kol scratched his head. "Neither of those could have taken it. Ronila was long away from Aeginea when Janus brought the great map. Picus too. I know that because the Cartamandua brought the skin map on his last visit, the same visit that Clyste lay with—"

He whirled about sharply, his golden eyes as bright as small moons in the gloom. Before I could ask what insight had struck him so forcefully, he yanked me to my feet. "Come, *rejongai*, we must resume your lessons. Take me to the Well."

"We've no time. And I cannot—"

"The long-lived do not grasp humans' constant invocation of time. *Before* and *after*, *soon* and *how long* seem to us but walls built to imprison you. But indeed, the change of season bites the air, and I see such danger and such possibility as tell me I have lived blind until inhaling this very breath that leaves my body." His hands near burnt their image into my shoulders. "If thou wouldst justify Clyste's fate, Valen Cartamandua-son, then do as I say, without thought, without distraction, without artifice, living only in the embrace of the Everlasting."

His urgency made my heart race. And as dearly as I desired to determine my own course, the past months had taught me faith and trust. I trusted Kol in the same way I had trusted Luviar, when every mote of common wisdom said to distance myself from plots and conspiracies. In the same way as I trusted Osriel when the accumulated witness of my eyes and ears clamored for me to slay, not save him. But I hungered for answers as I hungered for spelled nivat. "I will obey, vayar, but I beg you answer one question: What have you guessed?"

"Many things, but only one sure. *Tuari* has given Ronila the map."

No matter how I pestered, Kol was adamant. He would explain no more until I led him to Clyste's Well. I had no capacity to judge what it might mean for the Canon if Tuari had been duped by his half-brother's daughter. *Duped*, to be sure, for if the archon was a person who attended his responsibilities faithfully, and who would never compromise the Canon, then he could not possibly have read Ronila's true intent. Yet no warning from Kol or from me could stop whatever scheme Tuari had devised. The archon had no use for either of us.

I had come to Kol for guidance. Thus, over the next hours, I indeed left everything behind and gave myself into the embrace of the Everlasting. We traveled the length of Navronne. Again and again I sank to my knees, placed head and palms on the mud, snow, or rocky ground, and released careful dollops of magic to seek a route to the Well. Though Kol's dunking had eased my immediate sickness, the yearning for nivat dogged my heels like an unwanted hound, as I sought out landmarks . . . rivers, seas, mountains . . . anything that might tell me where we stood and where we must go next. Subtle steps on this journey; I needed naught else to make me heave.

When storm and night and weariness left me too confused to continue, I attempted what I had never done before, seeking through the wind-whipped clouds above me to find the guide star. Fixed and firm, Escalor took its place in the landscape of my mind with the brilliance of my uncle's gards. Using its anchor, I knew which way to go next. *Thou shalt map the very bounds of heaven*, Janus had told me, and wonder and gratitude swelled within me.

Happily, the harder I worked to juggle the fruits of senses and memory with the direction of magic and instinct, the less my nivat cravings troubled me. Not just in the way focused attention masks a nagging distraction, but in truth. My gards grew brighter as night closed in.

When my steps flagged, Kol taught me how to sniff out a Danae cache—a small stone vault filled with provisions and marked with an aromatic cluster of horsemint seed heads. I devoured every morsel of the dried apples and walnuts we found in the store. Kol watched me eat and eased my concern when my full stomach at last waked my conscience. "Replenish the cache next time thou dost walk these hills, and it will serve another who lacks time to hunt," he said. Beyond that he refused to speak, save for an occasional, "Attention, stripling. Thy mind doth wander."

My first shift after the cache took us from one ledge of rock to another and into calmer weather. The strip of blackness west of the ledge was the valley of the Kay. Only a few steps more and I led Kol down the slotlike passage through the cliff and into the high-walled corrie of my mother's sianou.

Saints and angels . . . it felt as if we plumbed the very heart of winter. Ice as thick as my thigh sheathed the walls of the Well, glinting eerily with the reflected lightning of our gards. The pool had shrunk. Crumpled, broken ice hid its sunken surface. The wind moaned softly through the heights, swirling dry snow from the crevices.

"Inerrant thou hast come here, just as on the morn we met," said Kol, who remained in the dark mouth of the passage. "The Well has not faded from thy memory."

"No," I said, hoping he would now explain. "Its location is as clear to me as on the night I first walked here."

"Canst thou see . . . ?" His voice trailed away as he walked toward the pool. After only a few steps, he sank to one knee and touched the ice-slicked rock. "Follow one of her paths. Prove it."

I knelt and yielded magic, and it was as if the hidden stars came streaking into the corrie, embroidering trails of silver light upon the dark stone. Everywhere, circles and twining loops, layer upon layer of threads, as deep as I dared plunge, all quivering with light, each one that I touched with my inner eye thrumming with stretched music.

The uppermost image was bolder than those that lay immediately below, the steps larger. This was Kol's own path, when he had danced his grief on the day we had retrieved Gerard's body from the pool. Carefully I studied the interlaced threads of his steps, comparing it to the images that his movements had etched on my memory. And then I peeled away that layer—as one could with the thin transparent layers of the stones that men called angels' glass—and examined the next.

My mother's feet had laid down a more intricate pattern than Kol's. I began to walk the silver thread. "She began here," I said, touching the place at the far side of the pool. "Here a small leap." A faint thread between a hard push and the landing. "Then a spin. A step and then another spin. The pattern repeated three more times . . ." As I walked I could almost feel her movements. "Here she paused, bending I think because the thread is uneven . . . another sequence of five steps and spins, and then here she made that twisting move as you do, on one foot, lowering her heel to mark each turn, again, and again . . . ten . . . twelve times . . ."

"Eppires," he said, suffused with awe. "Thou canst truly see her steps. I recognize this kiran."

"There are hundreds of paths here, layer upon layer. I could walk each one if you wished."

"Do this one again," he commanded, resolute. "And this time, shadow her moves."

"I cannot—"

"Do *not* say *I cannot.* I do not expect thee to dance, only to move in the manner of the kiran, to *feel* that I may also feel."

And so I began again. I pivoted and jumped in my own limited fashion. Wobbling. Awkward. I spun a quarter turn and tripped over my own foot, where Clyste had made three full rounds and landed on her toes. Filled with the remembrance of Kol's grace, I knew I must appear a lumbering pig with feet of lead.

I balanced on one foot for a moment at the first spot where Clyste had paused . . . and felt a feather's touch along my spine. At the next step I touched more softly on the ball of my bare foot and when I leaped to her next landing place, I recalled my leap from Torvo's wall and drove my spirit upward with the imagining of my mother's gift. I landed gently on my left foot, my knee and ankle bent. No wobble.

My skin flushed. Alive. Awake. As if the air spoke to me. As if a lover's hand touched my lips. The color of my gards deepened. Eyes fixed to the silver thread, I brushed my right foot forward and shifted weight, as the pattern told me . . .

I finished the kiran on one knee, the alter leg stretched out behind me in line with my straight back, my fingertips touching my forehead. Only when I became aware of Kol's gaze did I break into a sweat of embarrassment. "I got caught up in it," I said, drawing into a huddle, wrapping my arms about my knee. I could not look at him. My crude miming must surely have appalled him.

"The ending position is called an *allavé*," he said dryly. "Wert thou to stretch the spine longer, round the arms as if embracing a tree, and lower the hips, while aligning the back foot and hip properly with the correctly curved shoulder, I might call thy position . . . minimal. Now, touch the stone beneath thy feet."

The ice had melted along the silvered path. The stone, warm beneath my fingertips, swelled as if with living breath. "This is not usual," I said, half in terror, half in question, "for one of my poor skills."

"No. Not usual." Kol knelt beside me as my fingers traced the silver thread in awe and wonder. "In these few steps . . . a youngling's raw beginning . . . thou hast summoned life where none dwelt when we stepped through into this place. Think, Valen, is it possible thou couldst find other kiran shadows like these, without knowing their location beforehand or their makers? Without maps or books?

Couldst thou walk the world, seeking with thy hands and thy Cartamandua magic these patterns scribed in seasons past?"

"Yes, I believe—" And then did my thick head begin to comprehend what he was asking me. Janus's map had failed to tell the Danae what they had forgotten, because they could not read the language of lines and symbols. But Clyste had seen my father's truer magic. He had taken her into places she could not find on her own . . . and she had been able to coax dead lands back to life with her dancing. Danae could see only living things, and so Clyste had chosen to create a living map—a child who could find what was forgotten and dance it back into the pattern of the world.

"Thou art the answer, Valen," said Kol softly. "Thou are the healing for the breaking of the world."

Chapter 29

As a red tide departs a once-healthy shore, leaving behind a plague of tainted fish, so did my moment's exhilaration rush out to leave me aghast, aching, and empty. "How can this fall to me? I've so few skills . . . scarcely begun . . . God's bones, years . . . lifetimes . . . it would take me to seek out such places without the guidance of the map."

Not soon enough to tilt the world's balance on the solstice. Not soon enough to shield Osriel or Elene from dreadful choices, or save anyone, Danae or human, from coming treachery and chaos. And I was not fool enough to believe that this glimmer of life evoked by my awkward capering meant I could ever reclaim a sianou for the Canon.

"Best begin, then. Attend, stripling." Kol laid his hand on the crumpled surface of the pool. Around his spread fingers the blue-cast ice began to melt, until an oval hole penetrated the thick layer all the way to the dark water. He stood up, towering over me, his dragon etched sharp against the night. "Wash thy skin. Snow and ice would be excellent aids."

I glanced up sharply, fear and excitement prickling every hair I had left. "I'm to go on? The third passage?"

"No matter what else comes at the Winter Canon, thou must be a part of it. Only then wilt thou be long-lived and free to undertake this task of healing. Even a halfbreed is made new by the Canon, so that none can hinder thee without new cause. Once thou art past this change, we will speak of Tuari's blundering and thy prince's need, and how we might make answer to them. Those will be simple enough beside the matter of intruding thee into the Canon without dooming us both." He blinked and softened his stern aspect for a moment. "Thou art *willing, rejongai*? To take on the fullness of thy being? The responsibility it entails? To accept my teaching?"

My hands took a notion to rub my knees, even while my innermost heart told me that this was what I had come to Kol for. My answer had been given when I woke at Gillarine and saw a child had preserved my life, and in Gillarine's garden, when Luviar had deemed me worthy of trust, and again on Kol's own shore, when I understood that it was not disease or perversion or mindless rebellion that drove me. "I trust thee with my life, vayar. Yes."

A skim of ice had already formed inside the hole. I broke through the brittle layer, scooped out a handful of water, and splashed it on my face. The cold took my breath. Another handful on my head. *Gods in all reaches of heaven!* I scraped up shards of ice from the pond surface, and the coarse-grained snow caught in the crevices, and scoured the mud and sickness and dried sweat from my skin, rinsing with more of the damnably frigid water. Sea bathing. Wind scouring. What shape would this passage take?

I was soon ready to declare myself clean enough for any enchantments, but the direction of Kol's unsatisfied inspection reminded me of the exact nature of the third *remasti*—the passage of regeneration. *Sweet Arrosa, preserve and protect!*

Steeling myself, I doused my shrunken nether parts. I thought my skull might split from the shock of it. Surely I must be sprawled in some dark alley, my body gone doulon-mad, my mind locked into these perverse dreams.

"We shall attempt this passage here," he said, when satisfied with my ablutions. "In the usual course for a stripling, thou wouldst encounter groves or streams, fields or hillocks whose guardian is fading or ready to move on to a new place. Across the seasons thou wouldst learn and study these places, speaking with their guardians, weaving their patterns of life into your own. And on the day of thy third remasti, thou wouldst choose one of these places to partner in thy change. But at the tide pool on mine own shore didst thou show me another way of learning." He gestured toward the frozen pool. "So, learn of the Well."

Sitting on my heels, I laid one hand upon the stone bared by my crude echo of Clyste's dancing. The other hand I dangled in the dark water through the hole Kol had made. I closed my eyes and released magic, and the story of the Well unfolded.

Unlike the tide pool, or Picus's garden, or the meadows near Caedmon's Bridge, each of which teemed with layered life and growth, the grotto of the Well was a barren place. A few astelas roots lay shriveled in the cracked walls. Tucked into the rock near the top of the crags sat an abandoned aerie. But flowers and eagles had been intruders here. The Well was visited by rain, wind, and snow, but few creatures of any sort. A cold, lonely place, even in summer. The patterned music of the Danae, buried so deep in other places, lay very near the surface, as in a temple where gods and angels hover close to us. I breathed deep, exhaled slowly, and learned.

Stars lived here, even hidden above the clouds as they were. Cold and sharp as the rock and ice, their exposed light would arrow into the pool. I scooped water in my cupped hand, and it teased my tongue and palate with bubbles like sharp cider. But a sour second taste bloomed when my tongue touched a ragged black string that lay in my palm.

I shook the slimy thing off my hand, bent closer to the pool, and again plunged my arm into the cold water to the elbow. No fish, no creatures, no plants had ever lived here. But the stringy black growths slimed the smooth pale curves of the Well and even the disturbance of my touch broke off more feathery tendrils to taint the water. I reached deeper yet, toward the spring's source, through layer upon layer of porous stone. The deeper I probed, the warmer the water, as if the Well's source were the fires of the netherworld. I widened my exploration into the channeled rock, which spread the Well's bounty through a vast area of the surrounding lands.

Black slime clogged every watercourse. The channels lay barren and dry, and beyond them I found the withered roots of the forest across the vale, the starved confluence with the River Kay, sluggish and teeming with pestilence, Gillarine's soured barley fields, disease-ridden orchards, and cloister font—it, too, slimed with black.

Sick at heart I withdrew, sat up, and told Kol all I had found. Poison, death, blood-fed corruption throughout the lands where my mother's gift had once spread health and life.

"Thy learning surpasses my understanding, *rejongai*. Now I, too, know the Well." Though his finger touched my cheek gently, Kol's stern visage did not soften. "Breathe in the essence of all thou hast learned—good and ill, sweet and bitter—and weave it into thy spirit. Open thyself, as to a lover, yielding thy boundaries. Give and receive, reserving nothing."

Yielding thy boundaries . . . My heart near stopped its rattling, and every terror of confinement and suffocation rose into my throat to strangle me. I knew what he meant for me to do. Now the moment had come, my instincts screamed of danger, of entrapment, of choking death and failure. But memories of Stearc's monumental sacrifice, of Jullian's courage, and of Elene holding life and love so dear, put me to shame. If I could not face my own small terrors, how could I take on Osriel and those he planned?

Near paralyzed with cold and fear, I crept gingerly onto the frozen pool. Facedown, limbs spread, I tried to imagine how to accomplish what Kol described. The bit of warmth I had engendered in the stone lay well out of reach, and the expanse of broken ice beneath me was hardly a lover's body. Saverian's bony substance might come close, but she was at least warm. The thought of the acerbic physician made me smile through my fear. *Naked again,* she would say to this. *Feeling grandiose, Magnus?*

Behind me the air shifted, and I heard a quick breath and the soft impact of a landing. Kol was dancing. Like Saverian's gifted fingers waking my skin, so did the wind of his spins brush my back and flanks, riffle my hair, and tickle my bare feet. His leaps and turns drew forth a stately drone of invisible pipes, and the countering rhythms of sawing strings filtered through ears, through skin, through the cold air I drew in with every tremulous breath. Music thrummed in my bones, and its harmonies played out in the air above me . . . in the ice beneath . . . in the tainted water below, and the earth that cupped this pool in its arms. My blood heated . . . and I became aware of every quat of skin where it touched ice . . . melting . . . dissolving one into the other . . .

To yield. To become nothing, trapped in stone. I wriggled a little, flexing fingers and toes to make sure I still had them. In the movement, a shard of ice gashed my belly. *Merciful gods . . . blood . . . water . . . ice.* A cold sweat drenched my body . . .

. . . and then I laughed. I rocked to and fro and rapped my head on the ice, chortling to think what Josefina and Claudio de Cartamandua-Celestine would say to this unlikely version of my doom. Never in Josefina's wildest divinations could she have seen me like this. *Facedown in a cesspool.* Great gods, I would *not* go back to that life. I would trade not one moment of this fear and doom and terrifying beauty for anything those two had offered me or any fate I had imagined for myself. Let it come!

Kol's music pulsed and drove, and a hunger deeper and more profound than nivat welled from my depths. Groaning . . . laughing . . . I let go of thought and reached out with my spread limbs to embrace the world of the Well . . . water and stone, forest and barley fields, streams and orchards, river and valley . . . reserving nothing . . .

. . . and I plunged through the ice and into the cold, wet blackness. Spears of ice pierced my skin. I dared not scream, because I could not breathe in the water. Yet the scream leaked out of my dissolving flesh, and the cold and the water passed through me as I fell . . . blind, for not even my gards lit this darkness.

Softly, rejongai, *settle. Do not fight. Do not fear. Feel. Touch this place and allow it to touch thee in return. Thy laughter is surely the heart of thy magic . . .*

Kol's breathless voice faded as hearing followed sight into the void. But I clung to his assurance that this was as it was meant to be. Thus I did not go mad when I fell through cold stone and gritty soil, and my thoughts disintegrated like a snowball striking a brick wall. All that remained was raging desire, as I plummeted deep into the molten fires of the earth and was reborn as the guardian of the Well.

I could not breathe. Could not move. Could not see. Sated, conjoined with flame and left hollow as a burnt-out stump, I could but exist for a while. Thus I did not panic when waking mind insisted I no longer had a body.

First, I knew the water. I flowed in stately rounds, cooling as I rose from steaming depths to surface ice, brushing against rocks and clumps like a purring cat's tail, and then sinking again to dissolve and dance in the fire. Starlight bubbled in my shallows—not so much as I would prefer—but tart and sweet, as intoxicating as the laughter of angels.

The black tendrils, on the other hand, tasted of decay, sapping my pleasure. My solid faces, cracks, and crevices—the curving walls that existed in and of myself—burned with the painful gnawing of the invasive slime. I grieved for the tormented dead whose blood had fed this poison, even as I swirled around it, prying it from my bones and dragging it down to the fire.

My veins were dry, clogged with the foulness, so that my fair limbs—my fields and groves and waterways that lived in the light—withered and languished. With rising anger I slammed against the barriers of corruption, shifting them enough that I could slip through—a few droplets, then a trickle to begin the healing. I had always been a quick healer.

Valen! Draw in thy sense and spirit. Reach for my hand. Already, I do feel thy life in the land . . . a glory, rejongai, *but we must go forward . . .*

The summoning waked tales and memories that had been scorched away in my passage: the tale of the world's end, the waiting legion of the dead, the friends depending on me. I could not rest here to scour and clean and repair my wounds. I could not sleep. Other duties called. Regretfully, I retreated from earth and bone. With what my mind insisted was a hand, I reached upward . . .

My uncle dragged me, coughing and gagging, from the frigid water. I collapsed on a skid of ice, kicking, writhing, and scraping at my skin. My groin was tangled in strings that stung like the tentacles of a bladderfish. "Get them off," I cried hoarsely. "Holy gods, get them off!"

"Easy, easy, *rejongai*." Kol held my arms as I writhed and flailed, coughing up water and trying to breathe. " 'Tis only thy new gards. Breathe. Be patient. The soreness will ease."

"*Soreness?*" I croaked, as I clutched my knees and curled into a quivering ball around my wounded parts. "It feels as if I've been whipped. And drowned before that. And before that . . ."

I could not fathom what had happened to me. Remembrances of overpowering need, of raging fire, of immeasurable release lurked somewhere below my present thoughts, too immense to bring into the light. And then I recalled my bizarre impersonation of water and stone, more vivid than doulon dreams.

"The Well has chosen thee, *rejongai*. Marked thee. I have danced here, and it lives in my memory as it has not since Clyste faded."

My uncle sat beside me, waves of heat radiating from his sweating body, as if he had danced the night through . . . perhaps several nights, judging by the starved hollow of my belly. For certain we had come here in the night. Now weak and cloud-riven sunlight glinted on the ice walls.

"If thou but knew all those of the long-lived who have attempted the Well only to emerge bruised and bleeding, weeping for their failure. Not only brash initiates, but mature dancers, worthy to take on great sianous. Valen"—I looked up at the severe pronouncement of my name to see my uncle's eyes bright as summer and his brows raised high—"this is not at all usual."

Weariness set me laughing this time. I tucked my head into my arms and longed for food and sleep and one of Saverian's balms to ease the vibrant sting in my flesh.

"And now we must speak of more lessons," I said, "and of the Canon and Tuari and those who wish to murder the long-lived, and I must learn what to do to save my king's soul and his"—no, even to Kol I could not mention the child—"and his subjects and my friends."

Kol sighed and offered me an insistent hand. "Lessons, yes, but

I've brought thee sustenance, lest thy strength or attention should waver."

Ever a slave of my flesh, the prospect of food cheered me greatly. As I accepted Kol's hand and proceeded gingerly to the almost sunny, almost dry spot where he had laid out his provisions, I kept glancing downward, afraid to look too closely.

"Feathers, I think," said Kol, inspecting me as I lowered myself carefully to the ground. "And braided . . . something."

Unable to imagine what such decorations might mean, I shook off the oddity and devoured his small feast: two knotted carrots, four chewy figs, and three round, sticky cakes made of hazelnuts, dried blueberries, and honey. Every delicious bite warmed and strengthened me. I could have eaten ten times the amount.

As I ate, Kol taught. "When I danced in Picus's garden, my steps were not random. I designed a kiran, a pattern of movements to encompass a living landscape—the beasts, plants, trees, earth, stone, and water that comprise it, the air, the light, and the storms that shape it. I, and the others of our kind, dance many kirani throughout a season, not just at our own sianous, for many small places in Aeginea have no guardian of their own."

"So the silver threads I see are the evidence of a kiran—not just any dancing," I said, licking the honey from my fingers.

He acknowledged the point. "We bring these kirani to the Canon, dancing them in the various rounds throughout the day or night. The Chosen, the one named to dance at the Center, takes in all that is brought to the Canon in each dancer's kiran and joins them together as I told thee, building the power that thy prince desires to feed on. At the moment of season's change, the Chosen yields this power to the land through the Center, whence it spreads throughout Aeginea and into human realms through the connections that bind our two realms into one whole—"

"—the Well, the Mountain, the Sea, and the Plain, the sianous where the first of your kind were born of the Everlasting and took bodily form." My hands fell still.

He nodded. "It is also the duty of the Chosen to strip away those kirani that are incomplete or poorly effected, any that might violate the harmony of the dance and reduce its power. This stripping removes the kiran-hai—the affected land—from the Canon for the season. Though an embarrassment to the dancer who shaped the defective kiran, one season's removal does not poison the land or wreak irreversible harm. In the usual way, the kiran is repaired or improved and brought to the following season's Canon."

Kol braided his hair as he spoke, his wrenching twists and yanks speaking eloquently of his agitation. He tied off the thick braid with a solid knot, then pushed aside the strands of hair that had escaped his control.

"When I was but a nestling, the halfbreed Llio, Ronila's sire and guardian of the Plain, brought an unusual kiran into the Spring Canon. Tuari was Chosen—his first naming—and he removed Llio's kiran as flawed, tainted with too much of human influence. Llio argued that his steps were not flawed, but only new. When Tuari refused to reconsider, Llio—impetuous, foolish, driven to rage unnatural to the long-lived—tried to take Tuari's place at the Center by force, a forbidden act that threatened the entirety of the Canon. In the ensuing struggle, Llio fell and broke his skull. Before the dancing ended, he had returned to the Everlasting. It was as if Llio had been poisoned of our ancient Scourge while joined with his sianou, for we could not find the Plain again, and it quickly faded from our memories in all but name. So was the Canon sorely broken."

"The long-lived blamed it on the fact that he was a halfbreed," I said. *Llio's curse.*

"Aye. My sire and others have come to admit that the nature of the Plain as a channel to the human realm, and the nature of the Canon when we are wholly at one with our sianous, must have caused the breaking in some part, and not entirely Llio's human violence. Tuari does not agree. But those events and those that followed—the unstable storms, our own failure to regenerate, the weakening of the bond between our kirani and the land, the increasing incidents of the Scourge—have ever preyed on Tuari, plaguing him with doubts and leading him on a wavering course."

Kol's silence was the quiet between rainstorms as a line of squalls moves in from the sea. And so I waited.

Eventually he sighed and began again. "When Tuari summoned me from Picus's garden, he said he had been searching every channel of wisdom to learn how to restore the Plain and the Well, but all had failed. He had come to the conclusion that the human realm weighs too heavily upon the Canon, causing this imbalance in the world that we all see. He asked that my father and I consider abandoning our sianous for the Winter Canon to see if such removal might correct the imbalance. We refused, both Stian and I, for our kind emerged from the Everlasting in the beginnings apurpose to hold the four great sianous that join Aeginea and the human realm. Stian believes that to yield the remaining two would surely rend the world. Tuari appeared to yield to our misgivings. Now, hearing your tale, I surmise that he has reconciled with his kin-brother's child, Ronila, and given her Janus's map, hoping that Picus's teaching and her life in the human world would reveal to her its meaning, thinking she might show us a way to recover the Plain and the Well and these other lost sianous. If, instead, Ronila has spoken smooth lies and convinced Tuari that such recovery is forever impossible . . ."

". . . the archon might instruct his consort to repair this imbalance," I said. "And the Chosen can forcibly remove the kirani of the Mountain and the Sea from the Canon."

"I believe this is why he names Nysse Chosen. He hopes to repair the Canon by sheering it in twain." After speaking this grim verdict, Kol stretched his legs straight in front of him, linked his hands behind his back, and bent his forehead to his knees, raising his linked hands skyward.

I leaped to my feet, appalled, certain that Kol's theory was correct. Ronila had purposely destroyed the map in front of me, knowing that my news of it would be a torment to Kol and Stian. "Tuari may have yielded to your argument, uncle, but Ronila will find a way to kill you . . . you and Stian . . . and me, too, if she learns what's happened here. She wants to ensure the Mountain and the Sea are lost forever along with the Plain and the Well."

"I shall warn my sire," said my uncle, his voice muffled by his knees and the effort of his stretching. "We shall need his help to get thee into the Canon."

This made no sense at all. "I cannot pass for one of you, no matter my gards. I cannot dance. I've no idea what to do."

He released his arms, drew in his legs, and bounced to his feet. "Return here at high sun on the solstice, and Stian will instruct thee. There will be sufficient distraction in the Canon for him to slip thee into his round."

"Distraction?"

Kol raised his arms and bent wholly to one side and then the other, holding each for longer than my sympathizing muscles could bear. Then he stood upright and bent forward from the waist. Supporting his weight on his arms, he slid his feet in opposite directions until it seemed he must rip himself in two. He settled his groin to the ice, then stretched his arms forward, flattening his chest to the ground as well. After a very long time, breathing slow and deep, he rose again.

"I shall issue challenge to the archon, asserting my right to dance the Center," he said. "If I prepare sufficiently, my kiran of challenge shall be of such a nature that none shall question my right, and for certain none shall pay any mind to a new-marked dancer in a minor circle of Stian's Round. *I* shall dance thy sianou, *rejongai.* Unusual—but then, all that touches thee is unusual. That the Well is reclaimed will ripple through the senses of the long-lived as a spring zephyr. And on solstice night when the season shifts, I shall infuse the gold veins of Dashon Ra with the power of the Canon and trust *thee* to put the world right again."

His confidence . . . his courage . . . left me breathless. "And if you fail, uncle? Or if Stian is caught bringing a halfbreed into the Canon? Or if Ronila—?"

"Be off, Valen *rejongai.* I've work to do."

Chapter 30

The few-quellae walk took me from the Well into the ruin of Gillarine, and only twenty or thirty steps more transported me from the cloisters into Renna's well yard. The high walls left the yard in gray-blue shadows. A leaden afternoon—a proper reflection of my spirits. Flicks of sensation—a taste of moisture in the air, the feel of damp earth beneath my feet, the spongy moss between the stones—afflicted me with a yearning like that of a traveler on an evening road, hoping to see a warm and well-lit house over the next rise. And my gut felt uneasy.

I sighed and strolled toward the stair. I dared not hope that this third passage had somehow cured my doulon craving. I must speak with Saverian. I needed clothes. I needed sleep. I needed to know what day it was.

"Who's down there?" The gruff challenge came from high atop the wall that separated the well yard from the inner bailey. Someone had spotted me. "Gatzi's thumb! What's that?"

"There you are!" This shout, emitted in the squawking timbre of a young male, came from much closer. "Did you fall out of your head just because you spilt a bit of dye on you? You'll freeze out here, and His Grace won't like you tainting the well with dye!"

Confused, I glanced over my shoulder just in time to see a great bat flying across the yard, only I realized, as the dark mantle of wool fell over my head, that it was but a boy carrying a very large cloak. No sooner had I twisted the heavy folds so that my face poked out of the hood rather than into it, than Jullian shoved me into the deeper shadows of the colonnade.

"I've been waiting for you, Brother Valen," he whispered, as the guards on the wall speculated quietly on the likely parentage of a fool who'd walk naked in the freezing well yard after spilling dye on himself, and wasn't it an odd kind of dye to shine so brightly. "I didn't think you'd want to be seen . . . this way." He sounded disapproving, but then, he persisted in calling me *Brother*.

"I'm grateful," I said, fastening the clip at my neck. "It feels right to wear only the gards when I'm in the wild, just as wearing a cowl feels right in an abbey. But when I'm back amongst the rest of you, it's damned awkward. Tell me . . . how long was I gone?"

"A sevenday, it's been."

"Seven days!" Dismay erased what smattering of confidence I'd held on to. The solstice was but two days hence. Sila Diaglou would likely be crossing Caedmon's Bridge this very night.

"Everyone's worried, but no one will speak what's on his mind, especially to me. There's going to be a battle here, isn't there? A magical battle that will mean the dark age is come?"

"Yes." Jullian was no longer a child to be sheltered with sweet lies.

He straightened his back. "I knew it. They keep saying I need to be hidden in some fortress along with Mistress Elene and Brother Victor, but Mistress Elene vows she will ride out to war tomorrow. Mistress Saverian insists Brother Victor is too weak to travel anywhere, but he winks at me when she says it. We believe—Brother Victor and I—that there's only one place we ought to be when this battle comes. Prince Osriel told us how you took him there so quickly, and if you were to take us that same way, then Brother Victor wouldn't have to ride out in the cold. We've no other Scholar."

His boldness stilled my churning thoughts. "You want to go to the lighthouse."

He bobbed his head.

Simple logic and the boy's stalwart stance testified to the rightness of such a course. Brave Jullian, the brightest student the abbey had ever nurtured, with the wise and capable Victor to mentor him, could become a Scholar well worthy of those who had died to give the world hope. To deny these two the chance to honor their vows to their god and their brotherhood would be to forswear my own.

I bowed to him with sincere solemnity. "In the name of the lighthouse cabal, I would be honored to transport the Scholar and his mentor to their duties. *Teneamus.*"

Jullian released a deep-held breath, no doubt erasing the pent arguments he'd held ready to hand, and squared his shoulders for the next challenge. "I suppose we'd best tell the others."

I grinned and started up the stair. "I'll tell them. But I'd give a good deal for a shirt and a mug of ale first."

"I've tunic, braies, hose, and all over here. The physician gave them to me to hold for you."

"Just tunic and leggings, I think. No braies today." The walk from the Well had kept my new gards stinging.

Osriel, Elene, Saverian, and Brother Victor were taking supper in a small dining chamber. The sight of my friends tucked away in the homely warmth of the firelit room struck me with a terrible sadness, poised as we were at the verge of the abyss.

Word of my arrival had preceded us. The prince had abandoned his meal and stood stiffly by the hearth. "Welcome, Valen," he said, gesturing to the table where two fresh bowls, spoons, and cups had been set. "Refresh yourself. You, too, young watchman. We've sent for more."

"Thank you, lord." I took a knee, hoping to reassure the prince that I wasn't planning to abduct him again. "It is fine to see you recovered from your ordeal." Though he was gray-skinned and gaunt as always, naught of weakness marred his posture, nor any outward sign of his saccheria.

As soon as he gestured me up, I turned to Elene. Her skin bloomed a much healthier hue than his. Even from across the room, I felt the robust life in her. Only her great eyes betrayed knowledge and grief beyond bearing. "Dearest mistress, forgive my not coming to you on our return from Palinur. Anything . . . anything . . . you need of me, please ask."

She lifted her chin. "Later this evening, after you have paid your service to His Grace, I would appreciate a private word. I wish to hear of my father's death."

"Of course, Thanea." I bowed deeply. Osriel would have a deal of trouble preventing his newest warlord from riding out to face her father's murderers.

Beside Elene sat Brother Victor, resting his diminutive chin on folded hands. I smiled and cupped my palms together. "Iero's grace, Brother."

He smiled and returned the gesture. "Good Valen. Well met."

I had saved Saverian for last. As I'd pulled on the clothes she'd left me, I had imagined her ironical smirk as she attempted to pry out what I'd been up to by inspection alone, and I had prepared a properly humorous and mystifying retort.

But her dark eyes smoldered, and she seemed on the verge of explosion. "Gratifying to see you've rejoined us, Magnus."

"Saverian," I said, swallowing my jests unspoken. How had I offended this time?

I took the vacant stool between her and Jullian. The boy was already laying a fine-smelling portion of meat over a thick slab of bread in his bowl. Timely and agreeable as Kol's provender had been, my stomach yearned for the hot and savory. I dug in and rejoiced when a serving woman brought in another tureen. Perhaps the uneasiness in my gut was just this and no warning of perversion.

The small room vibrated with unspoken questions. Yet, though they had already finished their meal, the company gave me time to eat by sharing news. Elene reported that Prior Nemesio and his monks were safely bedded at Osriel's remote hold at Magora Syne, that Thane Boedec and Thanea Zurina had arrived with their house warriors three nights previous, and that scouts had reported Harrower troops on the approaches to Caedmon's Bridge.

"I'm glad to hear the brothers are safe," I said as I refilled my bowl. "I presume Prince Bayard's legion accompanies the Harrowers."

"They follow," said Osriel, "but they appear to answer only to my brother, not the priestess."

"Thanea Zurina and her men rode out yesterday to meet the Harrowers at the Bridge," said Elene, a simmering anger scarce contained. "But Boedec's force is ordered to remain here along with Renna's garrison. His Grace seems to believe such a strategy does *not* condemn Zurina's house to annihilation. Though my liege forbids me, I've sworn to ride after her come the dawn and lend her my household's support."

I glanced up at Osriel, whose dark eyes had not left me, and at Saverian, who brooded and bristled, mouth tight as a pinchfist's heart. Then I blotted my mouth and decided I'd best forgo a third portion of the well-seasoned mutton, lest the tensions in the room crack Renna's thick walls.

"I've had a strange journey," I said. "I'd like to think I bring some small hope for this confrontation, but I'd best let His Grace judge. However"—I stood, raising my cup that brimmed with its third filling of Renna's best ale—"as this might be the last feasting night of the lighthouse cabal for a goodly while, I would like to wish godspeed and all good hopes to our new lighthouse Scholar and his mentor. Luviar himself could not have chosen better or braver."

No honorable Evanori may refuse to join a toast to a fellow warrior. Nor may he interject his own contravening opinions before the drinking's done. Monk, prince, physician, and thanea raised their cups and drank. As I was likely thirstier than any of them, I drained my cup first and got the upper hand in the ensuing remarks.

"Abbot Luviar would not have us forget our vows on this night," I said. "I understand the urgency of getting these two securely housed before the solstice. Thus I've offered my newfound talents to escort them to Gillarine. Yet, were I to attempt more Danae shifting before I've slept, I would likely deposit them in Aurellia or in the middle of the sea. Which means, Mistress Elene, that I must prevail upon you to delay riding out to war on the morrow, as you and Brother Victor will *both* be required to open the lighthouse. Am I correct in that?" I did my best to appear guileless.

It was Brother Victor who started laughing first. Jullian appeared to have acquired a healthy sunburn, but soon ducked his head and snorted into his sleeve. The prince blurted a modest chuckle that soon erupted into Gram's best humor, and even the two women, one beset by indignant grief and the other by gods knew what, soon joined in. Elene knew very well that her intent to ride off to the bridge was rash and futile.

Naught was fundamentally changed by our laughter. Grievance and worry held their grip on each of us. But no one argued with my pronouncement. Osriel returned to his chair, and we talked for a while of how the lighthouse had come to be. Brother Victor recounted the story of my novice punishment when he first showed me the astonishing library, and we spoke of what might be needed to keep the two scholars safe in a future that was naught but hope.

As Brother Victor and Jullian withdrew to their night prayers, Osriel saluted the monk with a hand on his heart, then turned to Jullian and bowed. "Brave Scholar, wisdom, courage, and honor must ever be our beacon through this storm. I can think of no one better suited to light our lighthouse."

Elene touched my hand as she made to follow them from the room. "I want to be angry with you, Valen, but you make it difficult."

"I must keep practicing, then. No one has ever noted such a difficulty."

"When you've done with Osriel . . ."

"I'll come."

Saverian had slipped out without a word to anyone. Her anger afflicted me like a saddle sore. Every passing moment seemed to aggravate it. Only duty kept me from running after her to settle matters. Osriel was waiting.

"As always, you tread the verge of treason, friend Valen." Cup refilled and in hand, he stretched his feet toward the fire. "But I do thank you for reminding us of our common purpose. And most especially— Elene will *not* hear logic from me."

Without waiting for an invitation I dragged my stool closer and perched. "And it is entirely *logic* that forces you to hold her back from danger?"

His color rose. "*Logic* is all I can afford. Believe it or not, Elene is her father's worthy heir, a dauntless and skilled warrior, and a leader warriors will respect. Anger makes her even more formidable. But for this mission, courage must take on a different face. Zurina knows exactly what I'm asking of her."

"To run. To let the Harrowers believe that her sex makes her weak and afraid, so they will think nothing of chasing her all the way to Renna and the world's end."

He drank and then swirled his cup idly. "So must I die on the solstice or not?"

"If Kol succeeds at what he plans, no . . ."

I told him all. And as I feared, neither Kol's intentions nor the chance that I could heal the world's wounds changed his determination.

"If you bring me word that Kol has won his challenge, I will joyfully accept the personal reprieve," he said, after reviewing every nuance of my story. "And that you could be destined to heal these plagues and storms leaves me in awe and inspires hope for our future. My faith in you is immeasurable. But I must and will raise the revenant legion. Tales of hope and faith will not persuade Sila's fighters to lay down their arms, even if you were to stand before the hosts in all your glory to deliver them. Do I not fight the battle two days hence at Dashon Ra, then it must be fought another day in Ardra or Morian. Here I can set the terms. If you've brought me an alternative, Valen, then tell me."

And I could not. Though I believed Osriel's enslavement of dead souls would carry him down a path of wickedness no honorable intent could redeem, I had no argument to stay his hand. Sila Diaglou and her grandmother would leave Navronne in ashes and Aeginea desolate.

My conversation with Elene was little easier. We sat stiffly in her chilly retiring room. The hearth fire had already been banked. I spoke of her father's courage, but gave no details of his horrific end. And I confessed that I had not been able to redeem my promise to turn Osriel from his path. "I've brought him hope, though," I said, but did not reveal how slim. "How goes it with"—I waved vaguely at her belly—"you? You seem well."

"I could not hide it longer from Saverian. She says all seems to be as it should be. A hundred times I've thought to tell Osriel, but then I say: If he did not change his plans for me, why would he change them for a child he does not even know?" She did not weep or plead this time. Nor did she invite an embrace or comfort.

"Hold your secret close, mistress. Even so important a matter, from one who is dearer to him than all others . . . I doubt it could sway him just now. He is too locked into this course, and at the least, we need him clearheaded. But there will come a time when it's right." I hoped.

We agreed to leave for Gillarine at midmorning.

I returned to the tower room assigned to me, threw open the window, and sat on the bed to unlace my boots, imagining each of my friends doing the same. Each of us alone, anticipating the trial to come. Of a sudden I could not bear solitude. I relaced my boots and hurried down.

I gulped great breaths of air before descending the stair to Saverian's den. *You're being wholly irrational,* I told myself. *What difference does it make what she thinks of you?* No answer made itself known, and would have made no difference anyway. I needed to see her.

"Saverian?" I tapped on the open door.

"I'm here." The rattling and banging going on inside the low-ceilinged chamber where we had revived Voushanti served as evidence enough of that.

It was impossible to tell what she was doing, beyond removing every bottle, box, and packet from her well-ordered shelves and putting them back again. I stood awkwardly in the middle of the room, waiting for her to turn around to see who had come.

I cleared my throat. "I thought you might be interested . . . as my physician . . . as a matter of your studies . . ." Weak. Insipid. "As you weren't with me this time, and I found myself thinking about you right when something most astonishing happened. I fell out of my body—"

She spun about, a nasty-looking pair of sprung forceps in her hand. "You damnable, god-cursed, splotch-skinned toad. How can you let him do this? I'm to *bleed* him? Watch him suffer? Watch him die? And then perform this despicable enchantment to bring him back to lead an army of dead men?"

I felt unreasonably stung. "I tried to talk him out of it. I thought you knew what he planned."

"About the dead men's eyes, and giving the Harrowers to the dead, yes. That's vile enough. But not the other. Not murdering *him*. And of course Riel chooses to explain my part in his villainous little scheme after you *vanished* without saying anything to anyone. No one knew where you were going or when or if you might come back, and then the boy told us what Gildas did to you, and I can't conceive of how your mind or body can deal with the doulon again so soon. And every moment I thought we'd have to take Voushanti through another death ritual. He must either taste your blood soon or die again—it's surely some marvel of your damnable blood that he has survived this long. So comes tonight, and after worrying myself half sick, you stroll through the door all politeness and deference to Riel, and offering such kindness to poor, half-crazed Elene, and such honor to that brave child—able to work this magic of yours, twisting them all inside out for love of you. But I won't do any of it. Not for you, not for him, not for anyone. By this unmerciful, coldhearted, god-forsaken universe, I won't."

But, of course, she would, because she loved Osriel and believed in him, though it ripped her asunder. And somehow hearing that concern for me had some small part in her fury scratched the itch that had driven me down into her pit of a workplace to stand in the way of this outpouring.

"Please believe me, Kol is doing all he can to see that Danae magic will carry Osriel through what he needs to do. If all goes well, you'll not need to retrieve him from death. And I yet hope that somewhere in the great mystery that's to happen on that night, we'll find him an alternative to his legion of revenants. As for Voushanti . . . I've already told the prince that the mardane will *not* die again. I'll let the man suck my marrow if that prevents it." I stepped close enough I could feel the heated air quivering about her, and I could smell the salt in the tears she would never shed. "You know why Osriel's chosen you for these hard things—because he knows of no one more clever or sensible, no one more skilled. Because he knows you will do it only if you are convinced it's right, and we have no choices left. I'm sorry I didn't tell you where I was going. I was already half out of my head when I left. But I'd like to tell you what's happened, because you were with me through the other, and I need— I think you might understand the parts I've not told anyone . . ."

I told her all of it—about my doulon sickness, about my guilt over Luviar and my shameful liaison with Malena, and my horror that she might carry a child of my loins. I told of exploring the Well, and how awkward and ungainly I had felt tripping over my feet in my mother's footsteps, and how quiet and lonely it had been to *be* the Well, and how terrified I was of losing myself, and how it was the memory of her touch and her good humor that had soothed my fear, so that I had been able to yield my boundaries when I had to . . .

When I began to sweat and hold up her ceiling for fear of it crushing me, we moved outdoors—and still I babbled as I had never done in all my life. She asked sensible questions, and gifted me with thoroughly unsentimental encouragement when I confessed my doubts that Valen de Cartamandua could possibly be destined to heal plagues and pestilences, and she laughed when I told her of stinging tentacles and blue-scribed feathers in unlikely places.

When the stars had spun out their rounds, and she sat pinched and shivering in the well yard, no matter that I had given her the heavy cloak and wrapped her in my arms, I bent down and laid my forehead on her hair, inhaling its clean scent. "I thank you for this," I said. "I don't know what came over me. Next time, *you* must do the talking."

She pushed me away, quirked her mouth, and stuffed the cloak in my lap. "Perhaps I'll conjure myself into a tree, and you can dance around me—or I'll come to you when you are living as the Well and can't talk back."

I slept long and deep that night, and I dreamed of dancing around her and of hearing her speak in the rustling of leaves and bubbles of starlight and the silence of stones.

"I presume the lighthouse is still at the abbey," I said when Brother Victor joined Jullian, Elene, and me in Renna's well yard on the morning before the solstice. "Never thought to ask."

"It is," he said through the windings of scarves and cowl and the extra cloak Saverian had insisted he wear for our short journey. Jullian carried a leather case filled with medicines, each labeled with uses and doses. Saverian must have been awake preparing them all night after I'd left her in the well yard.

I glanced up and all three of them were staring at me expectantly. I tried to take on a properly sober expression. "Well, we should be off, then. I— You must excuse me, mistress . . . Brother."

Embarrassment quickly heated the still and bitter morning, as I wore naught but my gards beneath my cloak. I removed the cloak and draped it over Jullian's shoulders. Trying to concentrate, I motioned for them to follow me down the colonnade.

Once we walked Gillarine's cloisters, I held the others still for a moment, while I ensured no Harrowers lurked nearby. Jullian grinned as if he had invented me. I snatched my cloak from the boy, while Elene and Brother Victor gaped at the abbey ruins.

The little monk clenched his fist at his breast, his odd features lit from within. "Great Iero's wonders! Who could imagine that it might take us longer to reach the lighthouse from the west cloister, than to reach the west cloister from Renna?"

Victor led us around the north end of the cloister, past the church and the carrels where the monks had pursued their studies in the open air and around the corner by the half-ruined chapter house. He stopped short of the worst of the blackened rubble and turned down the alley that had once marked the ground-level separation of chapter house and scriptorium.

Just beyond a mountain of fallen masonry and charred timbers, a perfectly intact arch supported what remained of the upper-level passage that had connected the two buildings. Set into the wall beneath the arch was a niche where a soot-stained mosaic depicted a saint reading a book.

"Now, mistress," said Brother Victor, "I need you to lay your hands in the niche as we discussed." The monk placed his own small hands atop Elene's and closed his eyes.

A rainbow of light reived the day with magic, scalding my gards and near blinding me. The air crackled like burning sap and tasted of lightning. Neither Elene nor Jullian seemed to notice anything beyond the door that now stood open in the wall and the lamp that hung just inside, ready to show us the way downward.

"Brother, I am happier than ever that I never crossed you in my novice days," I said, shaking my head clear of sparks and glare.

He smiled and motioned us into the doorway. "You had naught to fear. Only in the service of the lighthouse am I exempted from Saint Ophir's proscription of sorcery."

While Jullian and the chancellor inventoried pallets and lamps, blankets and pots, to see what extra supplies they might need brought from Renna, Elene and I explored the two great domed rooms. Though her father had been one of the lighthouse founders, she had never been inside.

The walls of one room were devoted to thousands of books, while the storage cases that lined the narrow walkways held the collected tools of physicians, masons, tailors, and every other craftsman. The second room held the collections of seeds, as well as plows, looms, lathes, and every other kind of implement the human mind could invent.

"Ah, Mother of Light," whispered Elene as she gazed at the searing glory of Osriel's domed ceilings—the overlaid wedges of jeweled glass that shone as if the sun itself hid behind them. "These are the very image of his soul . . ."

She expressed a wish to be alone; thus I wandered back to the other room. The books were useless to me, but I found the tools fascinating. Beside a case that held a collection of pens and inks, measuring sticks, compasses, and the like, stood a tall shelf holding a collection of scrolls and flat maps. Many bore the Cartamandua gryphon. On the lowest shelf sat a number of books.

I squatted beside the shelf and ran my fingers idly over the spines. I pulled out one book, but it was all text, not maps. The age and the decoration of its thin leather cover named it Aurellian . . . which reminded me of a small puzzle.

"Jullian, back at Fortress Torvo you told me that Gildas used an Aurellian book to interpret my grandfather's maps. Why did he need such a thing? What did it tell him that the maps could not?"

The boy unrolled a palliasse, releasing a cloud of dust. "He didn't use the Aurellian book so much to *interpret* the maps, as to tell him what to look for. It was a book of legends of the Danae. He said the stories told him where the holy places . . . the guardians . . . might be. And then he would know which maps to use to locate them."

The world held its breath. "Did he ever mention something called the Plain? Or the legend of Askeron?"

Jullian's brow wrinkled. "Not that I heard. But he'd not even worked a tenth of the way through the book. The Aurellian script was an ancient kind, written by some adventurer long before the invasion."

My brief hope sagged. Surely bringing some news of the Plain to the Canon might bolster Kol's challenge.

"Narvidius," said Brother Victor, poking his head from the storage room. "*Narvidius, Viator.* I know that book." He craned his neck to scan the vast shelves. "We have a copy here somewhere. That's how Gildas knew of it."

"Find it," I said, my excitement rising. "By Iero's hand, Brothers, find it before tomorrow."

Chapter 31

Vermilion streaks scored the ragged black scud whipped from the peaks of Evanore. The mountains themselves stood black, still, and immense, untouched as yet by the fire to come. Despite the livid ground fog that seeped through the iron gate of Dashon Ra to twine my feet, the air between the wakening mountains and this rocky perch snapped clear and brisk on this solstice morning.

My fists drummed softly on the rocks at my back. My stomach had surely shrunk to the size of a nivat seed. Every untimely bird squawk came near sending me crawling up the cliff. I tried to concentrate. I sensed the plodding hoofbeats and harsh breathing of thousands of men and horses advancing relentlessly from the north. Only light, dry snow had fallen in the past weeks—crystalline fluff that you could blow off surfaces as if it were dust. Sila's troops would experience no delays on the road to Renna.

I deemed myself fortunate to be in command of my senses and in control of this fiendish restlessness. Today was my birthday. The day I was to become one of the long-lived. The day the world could plummet into the abyss.

Firm, heavy footsteps approached from the direction of the stair behind Renna's Great Hall, and moments later, Voushanti strode past the outcrop where I stood waiting for him. Not an hour since, Osriel had passed through the gate and vanished into the fog-choked gully behind it. Before Voushanti could do the same, I stepped out of my hiding place and called after him. "Mardane, do you endure well?"

The warrior whirled around, sword in hand. "You're not supposed to be here, sorcerer."

"I searched for you half the night, Mardane. More than ten days have gone since our blood-bond was created." Saverian suspected Voushanti did not want to be found. "The prince told me that you are to lead his personal defense tonight, while he works his great magic."

"But this morning I am to bleed him. That *is* what you command me, is it not—to aid him in this madness and then save him from it?" If words could slash skin, so his would have done. "I need naught else from you."

"I would not have you weaken, no matter what the day demands. I may not be available to succor you later."

He turned as if to continue on his way, but his feet did not move. Though his broad shoulders held rigid beneath his mail shirt, his neck bent forward. "Indeed, I flag," he said at last. "Do you know what to do?"

"Saverian gave me the words."

Voushanti pivoted smartly and waited for me, the unscarred half of his face gray and sagging in the half-light. His knife's fiery kiss on my thumb burnt like the solstice sunrise.

"Live, mortal man," I whispered, frost pluming from my mouth, "all desire and worth bound to my will until heart stops, bone crumbles, and breath fails." A sour odor crept through the air as I fed magic to Saverian's spell and pressed my bleeding thumb to Voushanti's cold lips.

His eyes locked with mine, resentment and shame flaring scarlet in his depths. Though every instinct prompted me, I did not turn away.

The moment passed. The enchantment resolved. I removed my hand.

Voushanti wiped the last traces of blood from his mouth with his sleeve, averting his gaze. "May I go now? His Grace awaits his torturer."

"Heed this command, Mardane: Obey Prince Osriel exactly in this dread matter. In all else protect him unto the limits of your life . . . no matter his orders."

The warrior bowed curtly, stepped past, and vanished into the gully.

I did not follow. Osriel did not wish any to witness what he was to endure at Voushanti's hands. No matter Kol's intent to yield the power Osriel needed, the prince could not be certain of it. Only a long, slow bleeding into the earth would generate magic enough to raise his revenants, and so he must initiate his grotesque alternative early on this still, cold morning, hoping that I would bring him news of Kol's aid before he was too weak to pull back.

Did Kol's challenge fail, Osriel would use the word trigger *blood-witch* to summon Saverian to carry out her grim assignment. He had refused her plea to set up a second trigger in case he changed his mind. Furious, she had disobeyed his command to stay away, hiding herself and a supply of medicines, surgical instruments, and blankets in one of the stone sheds left by those who had mined Dashon Ra. From there she could observe Osriel throughout the day and ensure he did not fail too quickly.

Osriel's first scream rent the brightening morning. I shuddered. What faith he must have in the mardane. Voushanti had to take the prince to the precise juncture of torment without death, to induce him to forget hope, that Osriel's despair might create power for redemption. Faith and honor, love and duty . . . I could not deny the virtues that drove the prince and his servants. But with every breath, in every bone, I knew this horror was wrong.

So I did not go to Saverian, though I hated the thought of her lonely vigil. And I did not drag Osriel away from his torment or Voushanti from his cruel task. The only way I could prevent the dread conclusion of this harsh beginning was to take up my own part in the day's events. By midday I must be back to the Well, where Stian would be waiting to take me into the Canon. The situation of Dashon Ra, the silhouette of its rocky parapet against the sky, the thinness of its air, and the gouged and damaged bowl carved from its heart already lived in my memory, ready to bring me back here again.

"Who's there?" Two warriors stood watch at the bottom of the rock-gate stair. They whirled and presented arms as I descended, clearly surprised to see anyone approaching from the direction of the heights. It was ginger-bearded Philo who challenged me, along with Voushanti's other faithful lieutenant, the dark-haired Melkire.

I lowered my hood. "At ease, friends. It's just Valen."

The two men lowered their swords. "Should have known you would be a part of all this strangeness, pureblood," said Philo. "Perhaps you can tell us why we're posted here behind the hall and kitchens, instead of in the field."

"We've heard reports that the Ardran prince and Sila Diaglou herself are but half a day out in hard pursuit of Thanea Zurina," intruded Melkire.

"The *Ardran* prince . . . *Perryn* rides with the priestess? Does

Bayard, too?" It could be disastrous if Bayard brought a Moriangi legion here.

"The messenger said no Moriangi regulars rode with Sila yestereve," said Philo. "Only Prince Perryn and a handful of Ardrans. It was their route worried him the most. Zurina is leading them straight for the eastern approaches, showing them the secret ways not even the Aurellians could find. If they come upon Renna from the backside, they'll drop these rocks right on our heads."

This bursting unease from two well-disciplined warriors but reinforced my beliefs about this day's battle. Naught would be held back today—no secret, no life, no soul. Ronila and Gildas would unravel their plots, too, and like these two, I didn't know whence the attack would come.

"Zurina is no fool," I said. "She's surely got her reasons—and her orders. And certainly Thane Boedec and his warhost will be ready to meet whatever comes. Does Voushanti know that Perryn rides with Sila?"

"Aye," said Melkire. "He received the report."

"Good. Stand fast and have faith in your prince and your commander," I said. "Guard them well, warriors. And may your gods do the same for you."

"Godspeed, pureblood," said Philo. "It gives us heart to know you are with us."

I wished I had more reason to be optimistic. And this matter of Bayard . . .

A few steps took me to a patch of bare ground behind the bakehouse. Though lacking a sample of Max's own blood, I squeezed a few drops from the fresh cut on my thumb and used it to touch earth with magic. Whether it was the half-Cartamandua blood or merely the heightened alertness of this day that fed my skill, I located him quickly.

Spirits and demons . . . Max had crossed Caedmon's Bridge into Evanore. Bayard's legions could not be allowed to join Sila's. So great a host could overwhelm Osriel's fragile trap, or break too quickly through the defense Voushanti would mount for Osriel. Osriel must not be forced to take action before Kol's release of power at the change of season.

I pelted through the halls and passages of Renna. In a great show of noise and sparks I burst a bar on the wicket gate, then promised the quaking gate guards dogs' faces if they failed to let me out. Bayard wouldn't listen to me. I needed to see Max.

Out on the open hillside, I stripped and bundled my clothes, tying them over one shoulder, and touched earth again. Carefully I recalled the landscape of the southern bridge approaches—a steep descent from the mountains over treeless slopes, leveling out only within the last quellé. As certain as I could be of Max's position along that road, I headed northward along Renna's rutted road to the point where it began its steep descent. Holding the two landscapes in my head for similarity, I worked the shift . . .

Two riders pulled up sharply when I stumbled through a washed-out rut ten paces in front of them. Unfortunately, they were but the first of a sizable vanguard and neither of them was Max.

One sidewise glance and I dived off the road, tumbling farther than I liked down a precipitous slope of rocks and scrub into what appeared to be a snow-choked gully. I landed facedown and skidded farther yet, digging in my toes as my head and shoulders crashed through brittle branches and crusted snow. When I came to a stop, my head hung out over a precipice of at least a thousand quercae. My stomach plummeted the entire depth; thankfully, my body did not.

I held still, stifling my gasping breaths, while fifty other horsemen passed by and the two riders argued with each other about exactly what they had seen, and whether the slope was too dangerous to explore. As my legs began to cramp from my desperate hold, another man joined them.

"A naked *demon* glowing with light, you say?" said the newcomer, snorting in sarcasm after their lengthy description. "More likely a boulder tumbled off the cliff. Speak such foolishness again, and I'll conjure tails on your backsides."

"Aye, master." The clank of harness and whuffling of horses was followed by departing hoofbeats. But only two beasts had gone.

"Are you falling out of the sky now, Valen? Pardon if I don't come down to join you."

I crept backward crabwise. Once I found a firmly rooted branch to rest my foot on, I turned around and scrambled upward. "I need to talk to you, Max."

He dismounted and sat on the verge of the shelf road, waiting, examining me carefully as I crouched just below him so as to remain out of sight of the road.

"First you must tell me what you are," he said in as soft a voice as ever I'd heard from him. "And who you are."

I extended my arm so he could see. "I'm still kin—of Cartamandua blood. It just happens my father was not Claudio, and my mother was not human."

"Not human . . ." He stared at the sapphire sea grass and the snarling cat, but did not touch them.

"You're not half so surprised as I was. But much as I would love to share the tale—one could say I'm the younger brother of a map—we've far more important business. Bayard was supposed to wait at the bridge."

Max tore his gaze from my hand. All wariness now, he scanned the cliffs and the upward road, as if hordes of my kind might be lying in wait. "Bayard released Perryn to ride with him, believing him chastened by his tongue-tied captivity. Then the little fair-haired weasel rode ahead with the priestess. It makes Prince Bayard exceeding nervous—the idea of Sila, Perryn, and Osriel working some compromise without him."

"Listen to me, Max, and believe. There will be no compromises at Renna. The only way Bayard comes out of this with even a portion of what he wants is to honor his agreement with Osriel. You must persuade him. My master will not be denied this day."

Max leaned forward—all business—worried and angry. "You lied to me about Fortress Torvo. Used me. And yes, it seems you left me clean of blame. But it left my master chary of Osriel's schemes and *me* chary of persuading him to trust the Bastard. Why should I believe you now?"

"Have you touched earth since you crossed the bridge, Max? Have you allowed yourself to feel what haunts Evanore?" Even lacking Danae blood, Cartamandua talents should detect the sickness lurking in the veins of Dashon Ra.

"Osriel's wards." His voice dismissed the fears he named, but his pureblood mask could not hide those written on his face and in his eyes. He had felt the anger of the dead.

"Exactly so. Whatever you perceive, it is only the beginning for those who challenge Renna. Do your master and his men march on Osriel, they will curse the day they were born, and they will curse the day they died here. Do you understand me?"

"I'll think on it." He averted his eyes, shuttering fear behind perfect pureblood indifference.

Such feeble assurance did nothing for my confidence. Too many pieces of the day's puzzle remained tenuous. "I'll tell you a secret—*you*, Max, not your master. Perhaps if you understand why I could trust no one in Palinur, you'll give credence to my word today."

"Perhaps."

I prayed that I revealed only what no longer held importance.

"Sila held three prisoners on the day I came to you. My master was one of them. Does that justify my deception?"

Dismissive laughter burbled from inside him and made it so far as his throat. But then his eyes met mine, and laughter died. "By the night lords . . . the sickly secretary."

His gaze traveled my length as I climbed back onto the road. "Believe, Max. You must find some way to persuade your master to hold back. If not, then in the name of heaven, look to your own soul and ride away."

I prayed my vanishing trick would leave him convinced.

The sun had traveled much too far from its fiery birth by the time I returned to Renna's well yard and shifted back to Gillarine. That such a journey should by rights have taken me three days did naught for my growing fever. I needed to be at the Well. I would spare only a few moments to learn if Victor and Jullian had discovered word of the Plain.

Once sure the abbey hosted no unexpected visitors, I hurried to the lighthouse door and invoked the trigger word *archangel*. The lighthouse door burst open. Jullian must have been sitting on the other side.

"We've found it!" The boy bounded down the stair ahead of me.

Brother Victor sat at a worktable half buried in books and scrolls. "Iero's grace, Valen!" he said. "Read him the passage, lad. I'm determined to find him a map."

Jullian proudly showed me the pristine copy of the book Victor had named *Narvidius, Traveler*. My restless feet had me circling the room as the boy read the Aurellian text.

> To discover the lost country, the seeker must divide the riverlands in twain, and the eastern half in twain again. In the innermost of these two last divisions, known as the Barrowlands or the Haunted Plain by the local peoples, travel the winding thread of the River Massivius, called in ancient times Qazar or the "Twin," as it crosses a series of rocky berms and parts itself into two waterways. On a fertile isle between, enriched by the water's flow, once stood the garden city of Askeron. Here did great sorcerers raise the river water to their uppermost towers and channel it through the lanes and terraces, so that water flowed through every man's hold, the streets were ever clean of dung and waste, and the air was ever sweet with the roses and honeysuckle that grew in wild cascades from the walls.

The lost city of Askeron figured in numerous legends. Narvidius speculated that the sorcerers had grown cocky and cultivated all of Askeron's terraces, forgetting to leave a wild place for the guardian Dané to enter and leave. Thus had the crops and gardens failed one dreadful summer. In that autumn, the river grew to a mighty flood and washed away every trace of Askeron and left the ground dead so that the eye of humankind could not see its remains.

"There's no other reference to a *plain* in the book?" The link seemed tenuous.

"None. But we found no mention of the other particular names you said either—the Mountain, the Well, or the Sea," said the boy. "Though he writes of many mountains and seas. Surely holy Picus would not have told you of the story did he believe it false."

I wasn't at all sure of that. Holy Picus enjoyed his storytelling.

"We've few good maps of eastern Morian," said Brother Victor, beckoning me to his table. "No Cartamandua map. But I've found one that shows a divided river."

The monk showed me the sketchy rendering of a river that split into two only to rejoin itself on its way to the northern sea. A different, later map purported to show the River Massivius and its relation to several other rivers and the Trimori Road, the Aurellian trade route that led to the great port city, only this map showed no division in the river.

"Tell me the names of these towns and cities, and these other places," I said, tapping my finger on the words around the divided river. I had marched with Eodward to the defense of Trimori, along that very road, and it seemed as if we'd crossed a thousand rivers. "If I could but find some place I can remember well enough, I could transport myself there." I had no time for long expeditions.

Jullian began reading the names: Armentor, Vencicar, Pavillium . . . None was familiar. For each map, Victor and Jullian read me the marked distances and interpreted the key, but the Barrowlands were marshy and had a reputation for ill luck, thus Eodward's legions had avoided it.

Out in the cloister garth, I touched earth, bringing to mind all I had learned of the divided river, but a path failed to resolve. It would take me weeks of traveling to approach the Barrowlands and the River Massivius from anywhere I knew.

A crestfallen Jullian trotted alongside me. "Is there naught else we can do to help? Another map? Some question that needs answering? I want to fight in this battle beside you and Gram, but I know my best use is here and not behind a sword."

His earnest innocence, as always, made me regret the flaws and failures that left me unworthy of such admiration. "Here's a question: Find out what use Danae have for nivat. My uncle gets testy when I mention it. And I suppose I'm ashamed to press him. Perhaps if I knew what they do with it, I'd know how to prevent the vile things it does to me."

His face brightened. "I'll do it. I swear—"

"Be careful with oaths, lad," I said, smiling. "They'll take you where you never thought to go."

When I delivered Jullian back to him, I clasped hands with Brother Victor and thanked him for his help. "Lock your door, Brother. Stay safe. I'll come when I can to tell you what transpires."

"No one will find us." Brother Victor touched my bare shoulder. Somewhere in all the taking off and putting on, I had lost my bundle of clothes. I hadn't even noticed. "You shall be Iero's finger of grace this day, Valen. Do not doubt."

The silver-white disk of the sun had slipped past the zenith, and I was yet climbing the last steep hill toward the Well and my waiting grandsire. The day had grown oppressive—the air so cold and thick it was an effort to breathe. Not a whisper of wind stirred the dead grass that poked from the rocks in stiff clumps. The light was flat, a gray-white haze dulling the faint blue of the sky. I felt screams on the air. The taste of blood filled my mouth, no matter how often I spat or grabbed a handful of dry snow to wash it out. Was it that this land's king lay bleeding, or had Sila and her allies already reached Renna and bent their minds to slaughter and corruption?

I jogged lightly across the ledge and down the narrow passage through the cliff that led to the Well. A white-haired Dané squatted beside the dark, still surface of the pool.

"With all respect, grandsi—*argai*." He looked up sharply and I bowed. "Duties prevented—"

"Thy duty lies here and only here."

Stian's greeting halted my apology in the way of an avalanche—rock and ice and inarguable finality. Which, on this day when my turbulent insides already seemed to be digesting briars and knives, drove me to bursting. "My duty lies wherever I choose to pledge my service. Here at the Well. With my king. With my human friends. And with my Danae kin."

"This is impossible," he roared, shaking the ice-clad granite. "Kol is mistaken in thee." He jumped to his feet and strode across the corrie. In moments he would vanish.

"Wait, please, *argai*. Permit me . . ." Damnable touchy bastard. I dropped to my knees and laid hands on the stone, and felt a welcoming warmth flow up my arms. But it was a pattern I sought, the newest one—of course he would have danced here.

It began and ended at the spot where he had been kneeling. First a powerful spin. More turns than Kol's, but a heavier landing. I brushed one foot to the side. Shifted weight. Brushed the other. And then a leap—*drive your spirit upward, Valen*—scarcely landing before another, and then another, circling the pool. *Do not think of your loutish, graceless bumbling. Only of the steps . . . feel them . . . show him . . .*

Such twisted grief I felt as I moved through his steps, such wrenching guilt for blindness and stubborn pride, for anger and righteous belief. Stian's grief and guilt. Clyste, the brightest spirit ever gifted to the long-lived, had died here unforgiven. She had not dared tell her own sire of her hopes, and this shadow of his kiran told me she had been right to keep her secret. That was the worst. He would have woven her bonds of myrtle and hyssop himself. Pain drove Stian's dancing, relentless, unending self-condemnation for beliefs he could not recant.

I stumbled to the end of the silver thread. Trying to stretch my spine longer, lower my hips, and round my arms as to embrace a tree, I made my imitation of the *allavé*. I closed my eyes, determined to hold the position as long as possible, more afraid to hear Stian's scorn than to exhibit my incapacity. But, at the least, I understood him better.

To my astonishment, a hand grasped my back foot, shifted it slightly toward the center of my body, stretched it out farther, and left only my great toe touching the ground.

My forward thigh heated. My supporting ankle wobbled. But I squeezed my eyes shut and willed myself still.

The hands grasped my waist and pressed me down and forward, and then pushed my shoulders down to realign them with back, hip, and leg. I thought my burning thigh would rip. But I held.

"Remember," he said as he pulled my elbows wider and lower, twisted and kneaded my wrists until they felt like softened clay, and riffled my fingers until they rested light as ash on my forehead. Cradling my head in his palms, he drew his thumbs across my eyelids and forehead, smoothing away my frown of concentration. "Thou'rt a stick. Pounding will break thee . . . or leave thee pliable. Now stand up."

I drew in my back leg and pushed up, resisting the urge to groan or knead the muscles of my aching thigh.

"I could not believe what Kol spoke of thee," he said, his granite cheeks unsoftened. "Come. We must prepare. Nightfall opens the Canon."

Chapter 32

I held my tongue and followed Stian through the cliff passage. My actions seemed to please him better than my words.

We emerged from the passage into a wholly different landscape—a valley of tall pines decked with frost. Then Stian transported me through a series of breathtakingly fast shifts that demonstrated how rudimentary Kol had been with his teaching. No shift left me nauseated until the last, when we strolled onto a grassy hilltop, the high point of a ridge that protruded from the mountains. The oppression of the day, the anguish on the air, the blood and pain and unyielding winter came together here, leaving every movement an effort.

With only a gesture, Stian bade me stay where I was, while he wandered about the hillside. Every once in a while he would execute a breathtaking leap or a jump and spin that denied the god's firm hand that holds our bodies to the earth. At last he seemed to find what he wanted. He knelt and began to clear a spot of rocks and grass.

The view from the hilltop was magnificent. A little to the north, a small lake reflected the flat light, its outflow several small streams that shone like steel and gouged the hillsides. East of the ridge, the land dropped into a tangle of rock spires and knobbed hills that stretched to the horizon and the deepening blue of winter afternoon. The shortest day of the year. I was eight-and-twenty, and I was not mad. Not yet.

I turned to the west and caught my breath. A parapet of red-and-orange-streaked stone edged the ridge, dropping precipitously to a broad slope—the apron of the greater mountains to the south. The jagged rim reflected the very shape I had etched into my memory that morning.

"This is the Center," I murmured. "Dashon Ra." Only we stood in Aeginea, where no human had gouged and scraped and hollowed out this hilltop in search for gold. I knelt, and though I dared not touch the earth of such a place with magic, I believed I heard Osriel's harsh breathing and felt the seeping of his blood. "Be strong, my king," I whispered as if he might hear me across the distance. "Do not yield your soul too quickly. I *will* find you a way."

"Come here." Stian sat back on his heels and motioned me to do the same on the opposite side of the barren patch he had created. "Do not move. Do not interfere."

With the same powerful fingers he had used to correct my *allavé*, he scooped up the damp soil and spread it over every finger's breadth of my face and neck. "Do not touch it," he said as he closed my eyes and packed the soft soil over them as well. "Do not remove it until I tell thee."

My skin heated. Itched. Burned. Panic welled up from my depths. "Iero's grace! Please—"

He gripped my wrists firmly until my breathing settled. "When I lay a hand on thy breast, follow me. Move as I do, as best thou art able, and attend carefully the earth beneath thy feet. *Remember.*"

I could not imagine what he meant until he packed my ears with dirt, causing another bout of terror. He gripped my wrists until I understood he was not going to fill my nose or mouth.

A touch under my arms brought me to my feet. Thin cold air cleansed my lungs and whispered over my skin. Over my gards. I wriggled my feet and noted the surface of sere grass and thin soil, shards of rock and pricks of ice.

His hand touched my breast for one brief moment. Then the air moved. I panicked. This was impossible. But somewhere inside, the part of me that was coming to understand the language of the gards knew that he had spun in place and taken one step to the right. I did the same and managed not to fall. This time a shard of rock pricked my left great toe and a sprig of tansy tickled my heel.

The air moved again. Another spin. Another step right. Five more. A small leap from one foot to the other. Left, then right, then left again. Repeat. At the end of the sequence, I would have wagered my left arm that I stood exactly on the same spot where I had begun. Without sight or hearing, I had to focus on the gards, the shifting of the air, and the feel of the earth.

Hands touched my arms, extending them straight from my shoulders, kneaded my wrists, and riffled my fingers to ease their stiffness. Then he touched my chest, and we began again.

By the fifth time through, I heard the music, a stately rondeau. By the tenth, I knew every pebble and sprig of the ground, and I was able to concentrate on the spinning, sensing every twitch of Stian's muscles and striving to emulate him until I could sustain an entire revolution without wobbling.

When we completed yet another repetition—the fourteenth or fifteenth—Stian changed the pattern. He clapped his hands and stomped his foot at the same time, then clapped three more times rapidly. A step to his right. So odd not to hear the sound, but only to feel it. I mimed his moves. He repeated the pattern. Again and again, until my heart stuttered in the same rhythm. This one was much easier. Simple. Boring. One more and then he walked away. I waited for him to jump or spin, but he didn't. Fear nibbled at my mind, but I focused on his movements and did not rush. I executed the last repetition and walked after him. He would not lead me off a cliff.

The surface changed from grass and stony earth to sheer rock. Then to ice. He was shifting as he walked. When the rushing movement of a stream confused me, I hesitated briefly, then stepped forward. My foot found no purchase and I toppled . . .

Hands grabbed my arms and dragged me backward, holding me tight until I regained balance and firm footing, and longer yet until my senses calmed and I could feel subtleties again. I inhaled deeply. Just beyond my feet the rush of water drew its own wind and shed a fine spray. The hands released me and touched my chest lightly.

More careful this time, I swiveled right and followed him down a short, steep path and into fast-flowing water. Treacherous rocks underfoot, round and slick. Water so cold it stole my breath. But I did not fall or step into a waterfall.

When I stood ankle deep in the stream, Stian halted. A startling application of freezing water cleared my ears. "Holy Mother!"

"Discipline and obedience serve thee well. Wash now. Then we will speak."

I rinsed the dirt from my eyes. The stream that froze my feet was the outflow from the small waterfall and the deep pool at its foot. I dived into the pool and washed away the residue of the afternoon. When I climbed out again, shaking off the freezing water like a pup, my waiting grandsire inspected me, giving particular attention to my face.

"Did I get it all off?" I said, a bit impatient. My skin yet burned from the grit.

"The soil . . . yes." His middle finger traced an outline about my left eye, around my cheek and ear, and down my neck. "Fitting, I suppose, that it should be the Cartamandua beast."

"The Cartamandua—?" I slapped my hand to my cheek. "A gryphon? That means you— But I thought the remasti didn't happen until the Canon. I assumed you were testing me."

"The remasti must be *sealed* in the Canon. Wander away from Aeginea just now and this gard will fade, and thou shalt be no more than before. And indeed I used preparation for this night's deception to distract thee from thy fears. I would not have thee damage the dancing ground as thou didst gouge Stathero. Kol spoke to me of thy peculiar nature, and I did not dismiss *all* of it as foolery."

I could not help but grin. A gryphon. Great Mother . . . that would explain the feathers and braids down below—eagle's feathers and lion's hair. I stretched out my left arm and found that my gards had shifted. Talons wrapped my shoulder, draped by an eagle's wing. The breast and legs of the lion scribed the left side of my chest.

I bowed to Stian. "My thanks for your care, *argai*. I will strive to learn all you teach."

He seemed satisfied, if not pleased, as he beckoned me to follow. "As thou art prepared, we retrace our steps. Here is my plan for the Canon . . ."

The daylight was failing.

.

"So if all goes well, if Kol takes the Center and holds the magic of the season's change, how long will I have to inform my prince?"

Even in its fifth variation, Stian could not seem to grasp my question. "The power of the joined kirani shall flow through his hands and feet. He does not hold it. *How long* has no meaning."

Stian and I crouched in the gully that penetrated the rocky rim of Dashon Ra. No iron gate barred the gully's western end. No fortress pressed its back to these vermillion cliffs. Not in *this* realm. Did the same steep-angled sunlight that bathed these cliffs shine on my dying king?

"How will Kol know the moment of the season's change? Will he do something so I'll know he's ready? Or just before?" I knew the dancing would not stop. He'd said they danced till dawn.

I felt confident that I could get to Osriel's side in the space of a few steps. After the afternoon's exercise, this hillside felt a part of me, and I would never shed the image of the ravaged mine . . . and the souls that dwelt there. I just wasn't sure *when* I would need to go. At what point could I tell Osriel that Danae power was his for the taking?

"Thou shalt know the season's change as well as Kol. Dost thou not know when the wind shifts or the sun rises?"

"Yes, yes, of course I do." Faith came very hard on this evening, when every moment threatened disaster, when so much was new to me.

I peered out from our seclusion, and my breath caught as it had repeatedly over the last hour. How could I respond to the sights before me but with aching wonder? Danae, hundreds of them—male and female—roamed the hillside, greeting one another. Some practiced dance steps; some stretched out their limbs. Many wore veils of spidersilk that floated in the breeze, echoing or elaborating their movements. Others wore flowers in their hair—hair long and red like Kol's or white like Stian's, or palest gold, silver as moonbeams, or green as the sea. None black as mine. Stian had threaded my hair with vines to disguise it.

More Danae arrived, appearing in a wink of light here and there across the landscape. Age did not mar their ravishing beauty. Stian pointed out those who were eldest—recognizable by a luminous aura that left them almost transparent. And I noted Tuari, his rust-colored hair wreathed with autumn leaves, his haughty face marked with a roe deer, and his consort, Nysse the Chosen, with her cap of scarlet curls and a swan scribed on cheek and breast.

These two walked an arced path through the crowd, greeting the others, drawing them into ordered ranks behind them like a ship's wake. By the time Tuari and Nysse reached the apex of the hill, the other Danae encircled the hill in spiraled bands of light. Three initiates stood at the lower end of the spiral, their full complement of gards pulsing a dull gray like my own. A few immature initiates—young males and females lacking facial gards as yet—scrambled onto the rocks south of my position, where they could watch.

Here and there a latecomer winked into view and hurried up the hill. As Stian moved to join them, he glanced over his shoulder. "Our fate lies with thee, Clyste-son. Have care with it."

I bowed. "With all my heart and skill, Stian-*argai*."

He nodded and ran up the slope to join one of the ranks, greeting those on either side of him.

Great gods, please grant that I do not fail them. Breathing deep to calm my jittery gut, I hugged the rock and waited.

The last rays of the sun were swallowed by the horizon. From the hilltop, one of the eldest Danae began to sing a simple wordless melody, eerie, haunting, marvelous, wrenching, for it touched all the yearnings and confusions that had marked my life from my earliest days: the pain that had dragged me into perversion, the fury that had lashed out at confinement and tawdry concerns, the truth that had teased at me in temples and taverns, in drink and in lovemaking. The song called me to the dance.

Tuari spun on one foot, straight and powerful, then came to rest and touched Nysse's hand. She stretched one foot skyward, impossibly vertical. Tuari held her hand and walked a circle around her, turning her as she balanced on her toes. When he released her, she touched the next in line, a luminous elder who jumped and scissored his straight legs so fast they became invisible. He landed and touched the next . . .

And so the connection of movement and grace passed down the spiral around the hill until it reached the three initiates at the end. Their gards pulsed a faint azure. But not mine. My breath came short and painful, as I withheld my answer to the call. I had to wait. This was but the first round, the Round of Greeting, so Stian had schooled me.

A livelier song began the Round of Celebration. The ranks of dancers broke into smaller circles or duets or solo dancers, each following the music as they would. Soon other songs drowned out the voices—the songs of trees and wandering waterways, a pavane as stately as an oak, a gigue, light and joyous like the water. Or perhaps only I heard those particular harmonies, and others heard songs drawn from their own senses.

I climbed the gully wall and found a perch whence I could see farther down the hill to the lake, where the reflections of the dancers grew brighter as the afterglow faded from the west. Danae everywhere. An hour, they must have danced that second round.

The third round began with the Archon's Dance, a courtesy to his position. All others sat wherever they had finished the last round and watched attentively. Tuari was a powerful dancer. His jumps were almost as high as Kol's, his eppires charged with life, his positions held to the point of breaking. Though glorious in themselves, his movements spoke more of vigor than of grace. Yet at his *allavé*, the watchers all over the hillside offered their approval, slapping one hand against a thigh—the sound of hailstones rapping on a slate roof.

The next to dance was Nysse, for this third was the Round of the Chosen, where the archon charged the one judged finest among all Danae to demonstrate her skills and invited any who wished to challenge her naming to do so.

Indeed Nysse was lovely. She could weigh no more than cloud, for though her jumps were not so high as those of the males, she seemed to hang suspended in the air for an eternity and land without disturbing the grass beneath. Her willowy grace evoked the image of a pond where swans glided in the moonlight and once a year white lilies bloomed. Yet the dance affected me with a wrenching sadness, as it told how early snow had blighted the lilies and sent the swans southward over the mountains.

To feel Nysse's movements was to understand that every passing season weakened the bonds between the kirani and the land. When even so beloved a sianou as the Pond of the White Lilies suffered, the world must change or be lost. Her *allavé* drew a sigh of wonder and grief from the Danae host. Without a word, she had made a strong argument for the unlinking Kol feared.

As the slapping noise and cries of approval grew, Tuari spread his arms, inviting any to challenge his consort for the Center. I could not imagine who would attempt it. Even Kol must doubt. I crushed that thought before it could blossom. Three dancers tried, each one better than the last, though none were a match for Nysse. Few from the crowd voiced support for any of them.

An expectant murmur traversed the crowd as a fourth challenger strode up the hill and nodded to the archon—Kol, unmatched in his pride.

He began slowly, a simple series of steps and blindingly sharp triple spins, one and then another, scribing a circle on the hilltop, so that those on every side could see—every movement precise, composed, and very large. His body spoke that this was to be a monumental kiran, for he did not stop or slow or hesitate or miss the next . . . or the next . . . or the next . . . And when he had drawn us tight enough, when I could not believe that he could possibly execute one more movement without flaw, he coiled and leaped into the air like the explosion of a geyser, soaring twice the height of a man, his legs split wide and straight. No sooner landed than he bent gracefully to earth as if to work a summoning, then rose and with his powerful leg drew himself into one eppire and then another, driving his body until my heart felt like to burst. The music he drew from earth and sky began with the grieving strings of vielles and the cool flowing sorrows of a dulcian—my lost mother—with hints of mysteries and secrets, and moved with driving purpose to trumps and songs of triumph.

I could not have said that those who watched held breath as I did. They could not know how much depended on this kiran. But when Kol had built the image of the Well, so true that I could feel my own deep-buried fires, my veins of stone, my bed of earth and wounded walls, wonder and memory surged through the host. One and then another of the Danae stood as if they could not believe what they perceived. Some spread their arms as if to bask in their awe.

By the time Kol stretched leg and back and bowed his head in his *allavé*, every Dané in Dashon Ra was standing. And when he rose to his feet, a great cry of joy and triumph shattered the night.

"He said to prepare for a surprise, but who could have guessed this marvel?"

I almost fell off my perch. Kol's friend Thokki stood just below me, looking up with eyes the same color as her gards—the hue of morning sky in spring.

"In the Canon, Thokki." I jumped down and kept my distance, wary, ready to pounce if she cried out warning.

"Thou hast naught to fear from me, initiate," she said, raising her hands as if to ward a blow. "Kol asked my help—a matter of such astonishment that all else he babbled was but chaff tickling my ear, save for his promise that his challenge kiran would vouch for his actions—as indeed it has. He asked me in his sire's name to partner thee in Stian's Round and disguise thy . . . limitations."

"I promise you that—"

"*Thy* promises carry no vigor with me, initiate. Kol's and Stian's serve well enough." Her ready smile dismissed whatever offense I might have taken. "Ah, see? Tuari has no choice now."

I looked back to the hilltop where Nysse herself took Kol's hand and presented him to the exultant Danae. Another cheer broke out as Tuari followed her lead. Then the two of them backed away, leaving Kol alone at the Center.

Kol stomped one foot on the ground, then clapped his hands together over his head. He set up a steady rhythm that subsumed the random slaps and cheers and drew them into unison. Soon every Dané kept his pace, so that the earth thundered with it. They continued all together until Kol nodded, and a group broke off and set up a counterpoint of three quick claps in between Kol's steady marks. My blood pulsed in time with them. Simple. Powerful.

"Dost thou feel the call?" asked Thokki, tight with excitement. "This is Stian's Round."

My foot hammered the beat—the same rhythm Stian had driven into my head that afternoon. How had I ever judged it boring? All across Dashon Ra, the Danae formed circles large and small, wheels within wheels. Circles of light. "Aye," I said. "I feel it."

Thokki clasped my hand and grinned. "Then let us join in."

She paused, watching, as one great wheel expanded to catch up more dancers, burgeoning in our direction, and then shrank again, spinning off minor circles like sparks from a fire. "Now!"

We ran across the small dark gap and joined three others—two males, one female—in a minor circle. I stumbled at first, my heart in my throat.

"Welcome the initiate!" called Thokki as she stomped and clapped.

The others shouted, "In the Canon, initiate!"

"In the Canon," I croaked. Then I stomped and clapped, kept the rhythm and moved in the circle, and within three beats felt like crowing with the joy of it. I could have continued a lifetime with naught but this.

But the dance was not static, and Thokki leaned close. "Thy feet, initiate. Do not lose the pace. *Remember.*"

She stepped back, and I felt sere grass and thin soil, shards of rock and pricks of ice underneath my feet. I spun in place and stepped to the right. Gods cherish all . . . a rock pricked my left great toe and a sprig of tansy tickled my heel. And so we moved into the patterns Stian had drilled into me. Simple steps and spins and short leaps about our small wheel. The music of pipes and tabors swelled from the earth and stars. My gards took fire with the deepest blues of lapis, sapphire, and summer midnight in the frostlands, and I thought I must be raised into heaven. And when Stian's Round came to its end in a great crescendo, I thought the hands that reached under my arms as if to embrace me must surely be my grandsire come to welcome me. Kol had won, and I was Danae.

The arms squeezed upward, crushing my shoulders. "Take the halfbreed to the pond. And remove that one." Thokki stumbled forward and fell, her head slamming into the turf. "I'll have Tuari break her for this trespass."

No mistaking the crone's voice that gave the orders, or the stick that fell so brutally on Thokki's shoulder, or the shapeless form that moved into our circle from the night. Underneath her hood, golden eyes smoldered with hate, and her thin lips broke into a smile that none but I could see. Ronila.

Chapter 33

"No!" I yelled as a Dané with an unmarked face hefted a dazed Thokki to his shoulder and disappeared into the night beyond the circles. "Don't harm her. Please, you don't understand!"

The glare of sigils and starlight became a blur as I tried to wrestle free. But the owner of the well-muscled arms that gripped my shoulders locked his hands behind my neck. No matter my kicking and writhing, another Dané bound my ankles. If I could not walk, I could not escape.

The youth glanced up at me and wrenched his knots tighter. My heart sank as I recognized him as Kennet, the initiate whose legs were twined with oak leaves, Tuari's attendant who had bound me to a tree intending to break my knees. His tall, strong companion with the wheat-colored hair was likely the person crushing my neck.

The other three dancers of our circle gawked in disbelief as the two young Danae bound my wrists behind my back. "My kin-father, the archon, has charged me to root out the causes of our failing life," Ronila said to them. "What more cause could we discover than a halfbreed flaunting illicit gards in the Canon?"

"Don't let her do this," I said. "She wants to destroy us all!"

Ronila touched each of the three dancers on the shoulder. "Human interference has corrupted the long-lived, even he who is Chosen. *I* have paid the just price to preserve the Canon, and so must every violator. Go. Dance Freja's Round and restore innocence to the change of season."

The three glanced back uncertainly as they moved off to join Freja's Round or the Round of Learning, where one dancer would move about the inside of a wheel of light, striving to match every other dancer's most difficult steps.

"This is no violation!" I shouted after them. "Kol brought back the Well. It lives in your memory again."

Kennet's comrade hefted me onto his shoulders and carried me down the hill, past circles and spirals that twisted and turned like jewels of heaven strung on silken threads. Ronila hobbled alongside.

"I am made new by the Canon," I said, recalling Kol's teaching. "You cannot hinder me."

"The archon will render that judgment," said Kennet. "We but ensure thy attendance."

With only a few hundred steps we traveled far from the dancing ground and the Center. This pond lay in a nest of meadowlands in the lee of a gentle hilltop, very like the lake at Dashon Ra. But here spike-thin pines and dark spruce mantled the surrounding hillsides. Snow lay deep upon these meadows, frosting every twig and needle of the trees. And the new-risen moon set the crystals sparkling and laid a path of silver light across the rippling lake. The splendor of the scene pierced my heart.

Two Danae walked out of a rainbow flare and joined us at the lakeshore. "What urgency demands our absence from the Canon, Llio-daughter?" said Tuari. "The change approaches. The dance beckons."

My captors threw me to the ground at Tuari's and Nysse's feet. I rolled to the side, spitting out snow and dirt that filled my mouth. My cheekbone stung, sliced by a protruding rock.

"Behold, Tuari Archon," said Ronila, "all has come about as I warned thee. You asked me, as your kin, as one who has paid the just price of imperfection, to uncover evidence of the corruption that cracks the world. Here is the halfbreed Cartamandua found preening and prancing in Stian's Round. Canst thou mistake whose work this is?" Ronila's stick poked my back, where the second remasti had etched Stian's rock, and my arm, where the cat lurked amid Kol's sea grass.

"Thou dost accuse the Chosen and his sire of willful violation?" Sounding truly shocked, Tuari stooped to examine me closer. "How can this be the Cartamandua halfbreed? He wore no gards when I saw him."

"Clearly they have forced his body through some corrupt remasti," said Ronila. "Canst thou not feel the storm wind rising in the human realm? Look out upon the beauty of Aeginea, Tuari Archon, and tell me that human violence and filth do not threaten its annihilation."

"Good archon, gracious Nysse, I bring you hope of healing," I said, struggling to my knees. "Your kind were given guardianship of both Aeginea and the human realms. Surely no mere chance caused the first four Danae guardians to arise at the points of our joining. I beg you heed what you have felt this night. Kol has given you back the Well, where my mother was poisoned by this harpy and her minions."

"Who can say what deceptions Stian and his brood have wrought in our minds?" said Ronila, sneering. "The daughter who gave a child of our blood to a human. The son who steals the Center, as he stole this halfbreed from your just breaking. The father who once condemned you—Tuari Archon—to live as a crawling beast. They have brought a halfbreed to the dance, as your own proclamation of the Law forbids."

Tuari looked from Ronila to me, his rust-colored eyes flaring with anger and mistrust. "Did Kol and Stian bring thee to the Canon, halfbreed?" he asked.

"Ask him about Thokki, as well, *resagai*," said Ronila eagerly. "She who has lusted after Kol since he was nestling. Corrupted, as are all those touched by Stian's get."

"More pain and vengeance will not repair what's done," I said. "But I can help you heal the Canon without breaking it further. All I ask is your hear—"

"Thou art halfbreed, Cartamandua-son," said Tuari sternly, interrupting. "Thou hast reached maturing this night, thus the Law forbids me to break thee. However, those who brought thee illicitly to the Canon are forfeit. Answer truth, if thou wouldst have me hear another word from thy lips. I will judge silence as agreement. Did Kol and Stian bring thee to the Canon, using Thokki to shield thee?"

How could I weigh the consequences of my answer? I, who was a master of lies, could likely devise a reasonable story. But Ronila had built her life on lies, corrupted Sila with lies. We stood at the brink of the abyss, and I needed this man to believe what I told him. Surely it was the time for truth. Kol and Stian . . . and Thokki, too . . . had known the risks they took.

"Yes," I said, "because they believed—"

"There, you see?" crowed Ronila.

"Silence, Llio-daughter." Tuari held up a warning finger to the old woman. "I have sought thy forgiveness for the wrongs I've done thee and thy dam, and thou hast offered me generous service in return.

But I am archon and would hear what healing this Cartamandua-son believes he can bring to the Canon. Despite our hard experience of him, Stian is no mindless actor."

Ronila pressed her hands together and bowed. "It is but sincerest concern for the Canon that drives my crone's tongue, *resagai*. Thou art most generous to allow thy flawed kin to be of use."

"Speak, Cartamandua-son."

"I am born of a line of cartographers—human sorcerers who can find their way through the world with magic . . ." With cautious hope and urgency, I told the archon of my bent. Of finding the Well before I knew of my parentage. Of my ability to follow the paths of kirani laid down on this day or those long past. Though I dared not mention that the Well had chosen me as guardian—not with Ronila present, not when I was captive—I told him how I had walked my mother's kiran to build Kol's memory and understanding of the Well, and what Kol believed about my talents.

"I know not what to believe," said Tuari, throwing up his hands. "How can I accept that a human-tainted abomination, one ignorant of the Canon, can accomplish what our finest dancers cannot? We feel the chaos of humankind; we suffer these poisonings and betrayals, and blind though we are, we know our lands diminished. To hear thy claim that *we* are responsible for this great imbalance drives me to fury."

"Allow me to show you, good Tuari," I said. "I can help you restore what is lost."

"This halfbreed is poison, Archon," snapped Ronila, growling with hate. "Stian has set him to bring you down in—"

Tuari silenced her with a gesture, then turned to Nysse, who had been quietly attentive throughout all. "Kol's and Stian's violation—deliberate and well considered—risks the very survival of Aeginea . . . of our kind," he said in anguished indecision. "How can I allow it? And yet this halfbreed's sincerity rings true, and Kol's kiran hath bespoke a marvel this night. I must consider: What if his claims be true, and I refuse to heed?"

Before Ronila could burst or Tuari shatter with his vacillation, Nysse laid her hand on Tuari's shoulder. "The season's change is upon us, my love, yet clearly these matters cannot be settled in haste." Her clear voice rippled with light, just as the pond did. "Stian and Kol have certainly trespassed the Law. Thokki to a lesser guilt. Yet unless we can prove, without doubt, that their violations have done damage, Kol must dance the Center. To force him out on uncertain grounds could be judged an equal risk to the Canon. Nor will I have it said that private jealousy spurred me to take his place. His kiran was flawless, and none other can approach our level. Only in the dance and its consequences can we judge truth."

As a snarling Ronila clutched her walking stick and muttered indecipherable venom, Tuari kissed Nysse's forehead and gazed adoringly on his consort. "Nysse's wisdom frees my own thoughts, good Ronila," he said, his relief blinding him to the old woman's burgeoning malice.

But the archon immediately quenched my own surging hope. "By the halfbreed's own word are Kol and Stian guilty," he said. "We shall hold the Cartamandua-son as surety for their guilt until the dance is finished. If they value him sincerely, they will step forward to accept the consequences of their violations—myrtle and hyssop and forever unbinding. Then shall we give the halfbreed an opportunity to prove his promise of restoration. If they do not step forward, we shall judge their violations frivolous and force them to their punishment, proceeding with whatever is necessary to rend our unwholesome bond to the human realms."

"Whatever is *necessary*?" I cried. "You mean you would lock the guardians of the Mountain and the Sea in their sianous, and allow them to be slaughtered as was my mother. But, of course, Ronila will see them dead in any case. Tuari Archon, Ronila despises human and long-lived alike. In the human world, she names herself the Scourge. She has corrupted her granddaughter and taught her to poison sianous. She wants to destroy all possibility of recovery for the Canon, condemning the world to chaos."

But the weak-livered fool would hear none of it. "None shall be slaughtered," he said, insufferably condescending. "If you are what you say, we shall discover it. Ronila has long suffered the consequences of her mixed blood and aspires to naught beyond her place. I sought her aid to recognize human-tainted corruption, and by your own word, she has done so." He took Nysse's arm. "Kennet, Ulfin, secure the halfbreed until we are ready for him, and see that Thokki is returned to the Canon undamaged." The two regal Danae strolled toward the lake . . . fading . . .

"Archon," I called in desperation, "I can restore the Plain!"

Tuari paused and looked back, shaking his head in disbelief. "Bring us to the Plain in the hour of Kol's trial, halfbreed, and I shall deem all transgression worthy." He and his consort vanished in a streak of light.

Despite my futile struggles and impotent pleas, the two young Danae seated me on a jumble of rock so that I had a place to rest my back for the long night to come. Ulfin left to find out where their third companion had taken Thokki, while Kennet gathered a handful of reeds from the lakeshore and spread them on the rocks as if to sort them. Ronila crouched in the lee of a pine tree, watching us and jabbing her stick repeatedly into the crusted snow.

Urgency near drove me wild. Kol danced the Center and would do as he promised, but all would go for naught did I fail to let Osriel know. And even then, I must persuade the prince that allowing dead souls to devour the Harrowers must surely violate the Canon we were trying to heal. Then must I bend my thoughts to finding the Plain before Kol could be imprisoned. I twisted my hands in their bindings of braided vines until warm blood welled from the raw scraping.

As I tore my wrists, Ronila drew a bundle from her voluminous robes. "Those of us half human can suffer from the cold," she said. "The gards are never quite enough. I would lend the Cartamandua-son my spare cloak. No ill in that, eh, lad?"

"Come ahead," said Kennet, who perched cross-legged beside me, head bent, braiding his reeds into a mat.

"I need naught from you, Scourge," I said, cursing the bindings that would not stretch.

"Oh, you need this." As the old woman approached our rocky perch, she juggled her bundle of brown wool and stumbled awkwardly over her walking stick.

Kennet reached out to catch her, and she fell forward into his lap, a shapeless heap. Startled, he looked down at her and grunted wordlessly. Ronila wrenched and twisted as if to free herself of his grasp, but his hands had fallen limp. She stepped back, and the young Dané shuddered and slumped sideways, his lifeblood gushing from the ragged hole just below his breastbone, his gards fading. His head rested on my thigh.

"Murdering witch!" I cried, horrified. Twisting my shoulders half out of their sockets, I slid my bound hands under me and around my legs to the front. Too late for Kennet. I pressed my shaking hands to his face and felt the surety of death.

Ronila backed away, laughing at my contortions. Dark stains covered her brown robes. "The long-lived take exception to those who slay their young. As you do. My faithful monk sends word that he plans to shred thy archangel before he bleeds him. He has only to choose which sianou to poison."

She turned her back and hobbled away.

I bellowed in wordless rage. The knife lay on the rock in a pool of

Kennet's blood, and I fumbled it into my grasp. I sawed at the ropes on my ankles until they fell slack. Heedless of the blade's lethal edge, I cut my hands free. Some of the blood that slathered them was certainly my own. Weapon in hand, I sped after the retreating demoness . . .

. . . only to have the old witch shift and lead me past a different lake . . .

. . . and again, so that I pursued her alongside a broad, sluggish loop of a river . . .

. . . and again, to find my feet on a rutted cart road, skirting a river bend. Inside the river's loop, a jagged ruin loomed darkly through a driving snow, and in the moment I spun, blinking, to confirm that we had come to Gillarine, Ronila vanished in a burst of red light. Hand of Magrog!

Hate and fear driving me, I pelted toward the ruin, leaping the jagged foundation walls that were all that remained of the infirmary. I cut across the buried herb garden, and sped past the great chimney of the bakehouse and around the corner between the refectory building and the dorter. Then caution slowed my feet, and I crept through the ruined east cloister. I could not hide myself in the dark, but at the least I didn't have to announce my coming like a maddened bull. What better way for these demon gatzi to gain entry to the lighthouse than to prick Valen Blunderer into a mindless rage and send me charging forth to rescue Jullian?

Breathing deep, I called on my finest senses. The air tasted of fear and torment, and reeked of blood and nivat, so strong it came near choking me. No surprise that Gildas would wield my weakness as a weapon. Reawakened hunger ground my gut. But I would not run away.

I crept around the ruined scriptorium and down the alley toward the sounds of tight breathing and rapid heartbeats, grabbing up an iron torch bracket to supplement the bloody knife. The lighthouse door stood open, a soft light emanating from inside, illuminating a vision of horror in this once-holy precinct. Brother Victor's body dangled from the arch that bridged the alleyway. The pool of blood underneath him had long clotted and frozen.

Ah, merciful Iero, cherish your faithful servant. Yielding time only for this one prayer, I pressed my back to the broken stone, and crushed both deep-welling grief and an explosive lust for vengeance. Gildas and Ronila must have planned this damnable sight to send me further into frenzy. But my best honor to a man of reason would be to hold on to my own. My rage froze as cold as the night. I acknowledged no fear, as I considered spells . . .

"Right on time, friend Valen!" Black cloak, hood, and boots made it difficult to identify the man who stood behind the shadowed arch. But Gildas's condescending humor was unmistakable. "We've not even gotten too cold awaiting you." He jerked one shoulder, and Jullian stumbled up the stair and into the light spilling from the lighthouse doorway. The boy's hands were bound behind his back, and a rope encircled his neck. "Did I not tell you that an archangel would be my shield when the last darkness fell?"

"The Tormentor readies a special pit for you, murderer," I said, tightening my limbs to pounce.

"Oh, I would not risk a move just yet," said Gildas. The monk waved a small knife, smeared with black, at Jullian's face. The boy tried to pull away, but the taut leash held him close. "Throw away your weapons, Valen, then proceed down the stairs and seat yourself on the stool beside the worktable. I expect to see your palms flat on the table when I bring our young friend down. One move of disobedience and I prick him with this blade. Doulon paste prepared from your blood would be a nasty balm for a wound, would it not?"

"Don't do it! He plans to—" A jerk of the rope silenced Jullian's anguished warning.

No curse seemed sufficient to the occasion. I tossed Ronila's knife and the iron bar into the rubble and did as he had instructed. The lower doors were thrown open, so that a table sat in plain view of the stair. In the center of it sat a bowl of nivat seeds. The scent near caved in my skull. Beside the bowl sat a leather pouch, a rushlight in a small iron holder, and a lidded calyx of silver, the size of my fist. No doubt the pouch contained linen threads and silver needles and enchanted mirror glass.

As I sat on the backless stool and laid my palms on the table, I summoned images of Victor and Kennet to divert my cravings into anger and purpose. I recalled the collections of tools and mapped out where knives, axes, or any other sharp implements could be found and estimated how long it would take me to reach them. Always too far and too long.

Though reason told me that one exposure to the doulon would not enslave the boy, even an hour of such craving for pain must scar a tender soul, no matter that soul's courage or resilience. I had been fourteen and far from innocent, and I would never be free of it.

Jullian descended the stair, Gildas behind him, clutching the short neck rope. Great gods, what I would have given for the ability to touch minds. If I could but induce the boy to dive or duck, yanking Gildas off balance, I could leap the table and take the villain before he could strike. But Jullian's face shone pale as quicklime, and Gildas maintained distance enough that I could not possibly reach him soon enough. The monk settled on a bench and forced Jullian to his knees in front of him, the knife poised at the boy's cheek.

"And so we have come to this day, Valen. The day the world ends." He tilted his head. "The gryphon gives you a rakish air."

I would not trade quips with him.

As ever, he grinned, reading me like one of his books. "So well disciplined. You've learned much since you first came here. You seethe and plot, seeing naught but obstacles as of yet, and so also you must know what I intend for you to do now."

One more doulon would not end me. I would control it. Wait for him to let his guard down. Kill him. I reached for the leather pouch.

"Not the pouch. Not just yet. Open the calyx."

I did and almost choked. The silver vessel held doulon paste—more than I had ever seen at once. It must have been made with two hundred seeds. "Just stick a knife in me," I said. "I'll do you better service as a corpse than what this will leave of me." I would be one twisted scab, a gibbering cripple.

"Made with your own blood. You've no need to use it all. Scoop out double your usual amount. Remember, I'll know."

I did as he said. Taking tight grip of my senses, I licked the tasteless mess from my fingers. "Iero have mercy," I whispered as the vile paste ignited the fire in my belly.

Every muscle spasmed at once, every quat of my skin screamed as if I had fallen into the everlasting fire. Yet even such pain as constricted my lungs and shredded my spine was not half enough to resolve the doulon spell.

In mounting frenzy, I slipped from the stool, ground my head into the floor, and clawed my skin, tearing at the cut in my cheek. All foolish notions of control, of retaining sense and purpose vanished. All I could think of was my need for pain.

"Go on now, boy, draw us a pitcher of mead, while I tend him. With a regular diet of nivat, Valen will become quite docile. Rely upon it, a slave who can shelter us in Aeginea shall make all the difference over the next few years as we await the deepening dark. Perhaps we'll teach him magic."

Gildas bent to whisper in my ear, his scorn mingling with the shrieking of my blood. "I'm going to let this build for a while, Valen.

But don't lose hope. Just implant the lesson in your head. Relief comes only when I say."

The fire grew, and my mind broke. I writhed and moaned. I begged him to strike me. But only when my body seized into one unending cramp, and my heart balked and swelled into an agonized knot, did Gildas lay my left hand on the seat of the stool and slam a knife through it.

I screamed at the moment's blinding rapture, blessing Gildas for the divine release, though I had danced in heaven on this night and knew this was not at all the same. He yanked out the dagger, and I curled into a knot around my throbbing hand and my shame.

Time slumped into a formless mass, even as I struggled to retain some grip on it. *Stupid, vile, perverse fool, your king awaits you.* How many hours had passed since I had been carried from the Canon? My heart cracked to think that Danae were yet dancing without me.

From Stian's naming of the dance rounds, I had estimated the change of season would come some two hours past midnight. I would know, he'd said. But then, he had not thought I would be wallowing in a stupor, clutching a pierced hand and working not to empty my guts onto the lighthouse floor.

Gildas had returned to his bench. He cleaned his knife and coiled the rope he had used to hold Jullian. "Come, sit up, Valen," he said when he'd finished these tasks. "We'll share a pitcher of mead. Very good mead, I would imagine, as it was laid down in the early days of the lighthouse."

Behind him, Jullian was twisting his face like a mischievous aingerou, and one of his hands kept making sharp jerking movements. Something about the pitcher in his hand. About Gildas. *Distract him . . .*

Gildas narrowed his eyes and glanced over his shoulder. Jullian stepped around us, and I heard him set pitcher and cups on the table behind me. I uncurled, pushed up with my arms, and vomited into Gildas's lap. That he then kicked me in the face with his slimed boot didn't matter. Nothing could hurt me.

"Disgusting filth," snapped Gildas. "Find a rag and clean this up, boy. My boots, too."

Jullian trotted off and soon returned with a ragged towel. Once the mess was dealt with, Gildas ordered Jullian to pour the mead. "Remember what I told you, boy. Whatever I eat or drink, your protector eats or drinks, as well."

"Aye, I remember." So much for my muddled hope that Jullian had poisoned the damnable monk.

Gildas watched as Jullian poured, then prodded me with his boot. "Get up and get something in your stomach, Valen, or I'll have to drag you to your cell. You remember Gillarine's little prison? You've chains and silkbindings waiting."

Gildas and I drained our cups in perfect unison. And in perfect unison, we gasped. The bone-cracking spasms came hard and fast; the light splintered.

"J-Jullian," I croaked, aghast, "what have you done?"

Gildas paled and clutched his belly. Shudders racked his limbs. "The wretched little beast . . . poisoned us both."

Not poison. The doulon. I wanted to weep and laugh all together. So bright a mind, but the boy didn't understand. This would hurt Gildas for a while. But me . . . two massive doses in the space of an hour . . . The colored ceiling plummeted toward me, and I threw my arms over my head. My skin felt as if it were peeling away from my bones. Gildas screamed and collapsed on the floor.

"I'm sorry, Brother Valen. So sorry. I know it's awful." Jullian kicked Gildas's knife away and shoved stools and table out of the monk's reach. With the coiled rope that had bound his own neck, he tied the weeping, writhing Gildas's hands behind him. Then, grabbing me under my arms, he dragged me, quat by quat, toward the stair. "I had to pour from the same pitcher—give it to you both—else he'd never drink it."

Trumpets blared inside my skull and would not stop, no matter how I tried to crush them, and always the pain grew, squeezing harsh bleats from my ragged throat. In all my life I had never hurt so wickedly—and my body seized and begged for more. "Kill me. Please, god . . ."

Images flashed before my eyes and fractured before I could identify them. The world was crumbling, and even Gildas's groans could not put it to rights.

"Come on, Brother Valen. We've got to get you up the stair. I know what to do. I found out about nivat in a book. As you asked me to."

He forced me to crawl . . . nudging, shoving, yelling unintelligible words . . . into the night . . . into the cold that sent spears of ice into my lungs and my heart that hammered to bursting. Through the snow that seared my raw flesh. More steps. More stone. Endless misery. Endless agony . . .

At last he propped me against a ring of stone, grasped my head, and forced me to look at his face. He was so ragged . . . weeping . . . but he did not falter. "This is Saint Gillare's font, Brother. It's a part of the Well—your sianou. Nivat is like spirits for the Danae. When they have too much of it, they go into their sianous and it puts them right. You've got to go into the font. Back to the Well."

Snow drifted through the strips of stone above his head. I could not comprehend what he asked of me. "Sorry. Sorry. I can't . . ."

"You must let go of your body, Brother. Then it will be all right again."

He threw water in my face—bitterly cold and tasting of starlight— and my body understood. He shoved. I crawled. Once my aching belly rested on the font's marble rim, he tipped me forward, and I rolled into the burbling water. With a sigh, I yielded my boundaries and plummeted, and with water, stone, and the deep-buried fires of the Well, I purged spirit and flesh of my old sin.

"Just implant the lesson in your head, Gildas. Relief comes only when I say. Food and water come only when Jullian says."

Pain-ravaged, slimed with vomit and worse, the man who had once been my friend slumped against the stone wall of the abbey prison cell. The manacle that held his ankle to the wall gleamed bright in the light of Jullian's lamp. The mark on his cheek, where I had struck him to resolve his first doulon and teach him of perverse pleasure, was already swelling and would make a lovely bruise.

Jullian swore that no more than half an hour had passed from the moment I rolled into the font a madman until I climbed out again, refreshed and clearheaded. I would have believed it if he'd said days or weeks, for I'd had no sense of time at all. Yet I had carried with me the urgent understanding that I must return to physical form as soon as possible. Even so, we had gone to Gildas's relief only after we had buried Brother Victor in the herb garden.

Our prisoner croaked a laugh. "One doulon does not enslave me, Valen. I'll walk free and never look back." He spoke bravely now I had refused to soil my hands with his blood.

"Very true. So let me show you magic, friend Gildas. A talented physician taught me how to enhance the effect of medicines fivefold." I crouched beside him, placed my fingers on his brow, and triggered the spell. "The doulon is but a potion after all, which means— assuming a normal cycle of eight-and-twenty days, shortened by the extra-potent paste you prepared—you have perhaps two days until you feel the hunger ready to devour you. Perhaps only one. By that time, either the world will have fallen into the chaos you desire and no one will ever come to succor you, or Osriel of Evanore will be King of Navronne, and I will bring you to his justice for the murder of Brother Horach, Brother Victor, Thane Stearc of Erasku, Gerard of Elanus, and Clyste Stian-daughter. He will not be merciful."

Gildas lunged toward my ankles as I headed for the door. "Wait, Valen, I can tell you secrets—"

I slammed the prison cell door and locked it. "Never step within his arm's reach, Jullian," I said, as Gildas yelled after us. "Never open the door, but just shove a water flask through the slot. He will beg and wheedle and play on your conscience, but this is no sin to confine him."

"He didn't listen to Brother Victor," said the boy as we climbed the three short flights of steps back to the alley and the lighthouse door, trailed by Gildas's hoarse curses and a last despairing wail. "I'll vow he didn't listen to Gerard or Horach either. This is justice, not sin. Not at all what he did to Thane Stearc."

"Exactly so. Now, I must go. You're all right with being alone, lad?" I hated abandoning him. "You'll not go out again?" Victor and Jullian had stepped out to retrieve what was left of the abbey service books and stores when Gildas took them.

The boy shook his head and hung the magical lamp on its hook just inside the door. "Brother Victor showed me how to lock and unlock the door wards without magic. I'll be sorry he's not here to teach me more, but I'm not afraid and not alone. Iero and his angels are with me. *Teneamus*, Brother Valen."

"Indeed, I'm sure they are. *Teneamus*, brave Scholar."

I jumped lightly up and over the fallen masonry that I had scarce been able to crawl over two hours previous and sprinted for the cloister. As I worked the shift, the boy closed the lighthouse door and the ivory light from across the garth winked out, plunging the ruined abbey and the world into a sea of night and winter.

Chapter 34

The battle had been joined at Dashon Ra. The earth itself had told me of the assault while I had purged myself of nivat in my sianou. And now my senses perceived the dread results. A cacophony of drums, trampling boots, and rage-filled cries blared about the ancient mine and its rugged approaches, and I smelled battle sweat and loosened bowels and warm blood dripping on consecrated ground.

The Harrowers threw themselves against Thane Boedec's warriors like the raging sea against the cliffs of Cymra, only these cliffs were not formed of granite, but of five hundred brave men who knew they were outnumbered ten to one. Strung out in a long crescent about the rim of the vast bowl, they had bent at the first wave. Torches and magelights flared bright in the driving snow, lighting the way for the frenzied mob that raced steadily upward from the east. Gods preserve my erstwhile brother, I saw no sign of Bayard's Moriangi. But the banner of Perryn of Ardra flew alongside the orange pennant of Sila Diaglou at the solid center of the assault. Their wedge had already driven Boedec over the rim and onto the downward slope to the mine's dark heart where Osriel lay bleeding—preparing to become a blood-addicted shell like Voushanti in order to preserve Navronne.

"We'll get you down there," said Philo. With his faithful comrade Melkire, the ginger-bearded warrior crouched beside me atop the west rim of the ridge, where Renna lay below the rock-gate stair. "But we'd best be quick. Old Boedec is as strong as lords are made, but none were made to withstand such odds as this."

Of course they weren't. Such was Osriel's plan. When Boedec's line broke, the Harrower legions would rush down into the bowl of the mine—and into Osriel's trap. Only Voushanti and a handful of soldiers would stand between the mob and our prince. At that point Osriel would have to act—to summon power for enchantment—whether the Canon had reached its climax or not. It would be a race to determine which happened first. My blood thrummed with the imminent change of season, and my stomach throbbed with the pounding of Harrower drums. And Osriel did not yet know that Kol could give him the power he needed.

I snugged the dark cloak Voushanti had left for me and raised the hood to hide my facial gards. Then the three of us scrambled down from our perch and slipped and slid downward between spoil heaps and broken slabs, through snarls of iron and rope, and under rotted sluiceways. After Melkire twisted his ankle in a trench, I led the way with my better night vision, while the two warriors guarded my flanks. Voushanti had pledged their lives to protect mine.

The oppressive horror of the souls' prison had not waned. The music of this ravaged landscape was as frigid as the frost wind that pierced flesh and bone, and as dissonant as the clangor of weaponry from the approaching combat. Yet something *had* changed here since the morning. On my every visit, these prisoned souls' pervasive, virulent enmity for all that lived had left me shaking and ill. But on this night, I felt only confused anger and an overpowering grief. What had happened to their hate?

The wind whined and swirled powdery snow into our faces. Philo crept under a dry sluiceway, peering around the rotting supports to ensure no Harrower flankers had sneaked so far around the pitted vale. He waved us through. After a long, shallow descent, we encountered Voushanti and his sentries posted about the rim of the pit, a steep-sided grotto the size of Renna's Great Hall, ripped out of the core of the mine. The Center of Dashon Ra matched the Center of the Danae dancing ground.

"Merciful Mother," I whispered when I gazed down into the pit, for surely this place was the inverted mockery of the Canon's heart. Where, in Aeginea, wheels of light turned to the earth's music, here a thousand calyxes sat upon the layered rocks and ledges that lined the walls of the grotto, each giving off a bilious glow. And with the stench of leprous decay speeded a thousandfold, a monstrous, corrupt magic shaped of human torment and royal blood poisoned the air and earth. Its source lay in the center of the pit, where a dark-haired man had been stretched and suspended facedown across the black, gaping mouth of some deep shaft or sinkhole. His wrists and ankles were bound to iron stakes driven into the rock. Wide bands of gold encircled his upper arms, smeared with the blood that ribboned his shredded back. Only slight jerking movements of his shoulders told me that he lived.

Recklessly, I galloped and slid down a crumbled, near-vertical stair, unwilling to take the long way around to the sloping cart track that led into the deeps at the north end of the pit. "My lord, I'm here," I yelled. "You need not suffer this. Voushanti, get him out! Saverian!"

The mardane followed on my heels. By the time we skidded to the bottom and dashed to the sinkhole, Saverian was pelting down the cart path, arms laden with blankets and medicine bags.

Strips of cloth bound Osriel's eyes. Tufts of wool stopped his ears.

I touched his hand. He jerked, the binding ropes squeezing blood from the raw wounds about his wrist. "Valen?" he whispered. "Tell me."

Stretching my arm across the empty blackness, I yanked the tuft of wool from his ear. "Kol dances the Center," I said softly. "The change of season is not yet."

A quiet noise that might have been a sob caught in his throat. I did not release his cold hand. "Hurry!" I called to the others. "Get him out of this."

Deep walls and howling wind muted the noise of the approaching battle. The mardane and his men slipped a wide plank under the prince's torso and another the length of his body, supporting him as they unbound his limbs. Carefully they lifted him away from the gaping shaft and onto Saverian's blankets, where he lay quivering, gasping for breath. I could not imagine the agony of his fevered joints.

As I slipped off Osriel's blindfold, Saverian unstoppered a vial and pressed it to his lips. "Mother of life, Valen, I thought you'd never come," she said.

"Get me up," Osriel murmured into the blanket. "Help me into my armor."

"You're mad, Riel," said Saverian, near tears as she sponged some potion on his lacerated back and peeled away his shredded shirt. "You must stay down until I stop this bleeding."

"If I am not to share their fate, then I must *lead* them, at the least," he said, drawing his hands underneath his shoulders as if to rise.

Their fate . . . He spoke of his prisoners. He had spent this day of torment listening to the dead.

Voushanti squatted beside us. "I'll send down your arms, Lord Prince. Then I'll deploy my line farther up the hill, as you commanded." Osriel jerked his head, but Voushanti looked to me for confirmation. I nodded, and the warriors left Saverian, the prince, and me alone.

"Valen, would you give him—?" Saverian's stopped breath made me look up. I had thrown back my hood, and she stared at me, blue sigils reflected in her dark eyes. I'd near forgotten my newest gards. Smiling and rolling my eyes, I took the proffered flask. But she quickly averted her gaze, and even amid these matters of far more import, I selfishly wished she had not. I hated that she might think me some freakish creature.

While she prepared another potion, I helped Osriel sit up. I knew he needed to be on his feet to get his blood moving, to feel alive. Strength would come. He had reserves I could not imagine, and a physician unparalleled in any kingdom.

"Breathe a bit, get warm, and drink this nasty stuff," I said. "Then I'll help you stand. God's bones, you look a wreck." Gingerly I bundled blankets about his torn shoulders and helped him drink. His face was the color of ash, save for the bruises and blood.

He drained the flask and opened his eyes. A faint smile tweaked his bloodless face. "You're not so handsome as you might think, Dané. Looks as if Grossartius let fly his mighty hammer at your fine gryphon."

"And why is your hand bandaged?" said Saverian, the moment's crack in her brittle shell quite well sealed. "I'll vow you've not cleaned that wound any more than the one on your cheek."

"It's a reminder from Ronila and Gildas," I said, brushing dirt from Jullian's bloodstained linen wrapping my pierced hand.

One of Voushanti's men arrived with Osriel's shirt, jupon, and hauberk, greaves, and gauntlets. Another dropped chausses, boots, and swordbelt at the prince's side. Osriel dispatched the two men with his demand for a scouting report. "Now I would have your report, Valen," he said, once they'd gone.

"Brother Victor is murdered," I said, grieving again that the chancellor's passing must be slighted amidst these dread events. "But Jullian is safely locked in the lighthouse, and Gildas is secured until his king can judge him. So we've only the priestess, her gammy, your brothers, and their soldiers to worry with. And Ronila is by far the most dangerous . . ."

While Osriel downed two flasks of ale and another of Saverian's potions, I sketched out the day's events. "You can't imagine how fast Ronila can shift. Keep someone at your back at all times. And don't take one step toward her, or you'll find yourself somewhere else altogether."

"You've already taught me that lesson." Osriel reached for my hands for help to get up, and I hauled him to his feet. He grimaced and gripped his shoulders. "Would that I had a sianou where I could be taken apart and put back together again without this cursed sickness."

"Perhaps, as the land heals . . ."

As I sensed the change that had come about in this haunted place, I recalled Luviar's words: *The lack of a righteous king speeds the ruin of the land.* The king and the land were so intimately bound, that his blood could charge it with power. They lived and died together. Osriel's great enchantment would be a terrible wrong, even if wrought with the Canon's magic and not his own soul's death. What could be less righteous than stripping the dead of eternity?

"Something happened with you as you suffered here today, didn't it, my lord? Something's changed here."

His gaunt face hardened. "Nothing's changed. Do you hear what's coming down on us from the east? Have you brought me an alternative?"

"Only this hope that we can restore the land. Lord, you must not sacrifice these souls." My conviction grew with every passing moment.

"Hope will not save us, Val—"

A thunderous blast shook the earth. As votive vessels rocked and toppled from their perches with a clatter, Saverian and I jammed Osriel between us and hunched to the ground.

A bloodstained young warrior, wearing the green of Evanore, raced down the cart path, Voushanti, Philo, and Melkire on his heels. "Boedec's broken!" cried the youth, chest heaving, looking wildly from one to the other of us. When Osriel stood up, half naked and scarred with blood, the boy went white.

"What is your name, warrior?" said the prince as calmly as if he wore ermine robes and crown.

"P-Prac of Noviart, Your Grace." The boy trembled so wildly his empty scabbard rattled.

"Report, Prac of Noviart. You've naught to fear from your duc, no matter how ill your news."

The young soldier straightened his back. "Prince Perryn's cadre split us in two, lord. Harrowers have engaged our reserves. Thanea Zurina has fallen. Her house—what's left of them—yet holds the left, but not for long." The left was the easiest approach to Dashon Ra. "The priestess d-demands parley."

"Philo, find this brave messenger a sword to fill his scabbard and a drink to ease his thirst, then bring him back here for my reply. Melkire, I want a report from Renna. We must have no interference from our backs."

As the three soldiers did his bidding, Osriel spun to me. "How long, Valen? I must be *here* when Kol grants us the power of the Canon."

My sense felt the night yet rising, a bowstring stretching its last quat. "Not yet, lord. Soon, but not yet."

"We'll not be able to hold the mob off you for three heartbeats, Lord Prince," said Voushanti, his jaw pulsing—his only sign of agitation. "We should move you into the fortress."

Shaking his head, Osriel folded his arms and summoned Philo and the messenger. "Prac, tell the priestess I will meet her here or nowhere. I guarantee her personal safety, but offer no bond of truce with those who have tortured and murdered my warlords. Can you say that exactly?"

"Aye, Your Grace." The youth, become a man again with a weapon at his side and the trust of his lord, bowed. Philo escorted him back the way he'd come.

"She'll never come down here herself!" said Voushanti, near exploding. "She'll expect sorcery."

"She's attacked because we've told her my power is weak on this night. My warriors are in disarray. Will she not believe in a demonic prince brought low?" He spread his arms to display his wretched state. "All we need is to slow down the assault until Valen signals I've power to act. Return to your post, prepared to escort the priestess here when she arrives. And, Mardane"—Osriel glanced from Voushanti to me and back again—"I issue this command as your sovereign king. Valen has no say in it, no matter the bond between you. Is that understood?"

Voushanti bowed stiffly and hurried away.

"We need to put these aside for the moment," he said with a sigh, nudging his padded leathers and mail. "I'll keep the cloak, at least, lest I be too frozen to speak. And, Saverian, if you have more of the samarth, I would be grateful."

"Your purveyor of potions obeys, as always," said Saverian harshly, shoving a vial into his hand. "I don't know if I'll ever forgive you for this day."

Osriel drank and tossed her the empty vial. "I would regret that, whether or not you continue to keep me living. Now you'd best return to your hiding place. You, too, Valen. Sila mustn't know you've escaped her trap."

"Lord Prince, you must not—"

"Stay or go, Valen. I'll do what I must to preserve this kingdom." I had no answer.

We upended a half-rotted cart to hide Osriel's armor. The prince himself settled in the lee of the upturned cart. Bundled in blankets, he quickly lost himself in contemplation, the air about him fraught with spellwork.

Saverian gathered her flasks and jars and packed them away. I offered to carry her bags up to her hiding place.

"Stay with Riel," she said. "Another time, though, I want to hear about the Canon. You said so little, but your face—it's not only the gards that have left you . . . radiant."

"I'd like to tell you," I said, wishing I could erase the wistfulness that poked through her frayed emotions. My fingers twitched, as I fancied that I might touch the furrow between her brows and make it vanish. "As a part of your studies, of course."

"Of course." She started up the path, and I already missed her— so real, so human, our odd companionship grown as if by magic into a sweet tether, binding me to this human realm.

A hacking cough caused me to turn. Osriel's head rested on his arms. So alone in his harsh resolution . . .

Of a sudden I charged after Saverian, instinct pushing me where I'd no thought to go. "We need Elene here tonight," I said, breathless. "Something about his experience here today has made Osriel doubt his course. She, of anyone in the world, might be able to sway him when the time comes. I know it's a great deal to ask. And risky. Holy Mother, I've sworn to keep her and the child safe . . ."

Saverian agreed without hesitation. "Elene is a warrior of Evanore. She belongs where she can fight the battle given to her. I'll see to it." And then my friend, the physician, smiled in a most enigmatic fashion. "I think all your instincts are reliable."

I stared after as she hurried away. My blood warmed, bringing a smile to my own lips, while the wind erased her footsteps as if she had never been.

Melkire brought Osriel the news that Bayard's legion had camped on the slopes before Renna's gates. The Moriangi seemed in no hurry either to engage Osriel's garrison or to join forces with the Harrowers at Dashon Ra.

A clever solution, Max, I thought, as I perched on the rim of the grotto at the end opposite the cart track. *Be ready to make a quick assault in case Sila gains the upper hand, but don't jeopardize the alliance with Osriel by overt action.*

The rising blizzard hid the battle and muffled its clamor. Below me, Osriel had returned to his spellmaking. Fires popped up here and there about the pit—garish green and yellow flames that enhanced the vile colors of the luminous vessels and gave off a nasty odor. Shadows of unseen movement danced on the rocks, and the air filled with sighs and moans that were not the skirling wind. I didn't think such tricks would frighten Sila Diaglou or her vile grandam.

My fingers tracing spirals in the dry snow, I strained to hear the music from the other plane that existed here. A few steps and I could likely be on that hillside where the dance was reaching its climax. Sky Lord save me, how I wanted to be there. I rubbed out my idle markings and listened for Ronila. We could guess Sila's plans. The crone was the real danger.

Footsteps crunched beyond the veils of snow, and I heard Voushanti's gruff challenge.

"They're coming, lord," I called down softly. "I'll be close. The gods hold you."

Osriel threw off his blankets and glanced up. "Thank you for your care, Valen." He cocked his head with a quiet amusement that reminded me very much of Gram. "Tomorrow, remember, we renegotiate the terms of your submission."

I could not but laugh at such a bold pronouncement in the face of the world's end. "I doubt I'll ever be free of you, lord."

I ran lightly up a steep rib of rock that had once supported a wooden sluice. Lying flat on the ground beside the splintered trough, I could both get a superior view of the proceedings in the grotto and be in the midst of them with only two long strides and a stomach-lurching jump. Not that there was much I could do to help. Matters had moved beyond my talents.

Voushanti, Philo, and Melkire led the small party out of the storm and down the cart track. Sila's orange cloak floated in the wind, revealing the steel rings of a habergeon rusty with blood. Beside the priestess walked a tall, gray warrior, whose baldric of woad bore the steel house emblems of a Moriangi grav. This was Hurd, I guessed, the military mind behind Sila's legions. He might have walked straight from his arming room. Only his boots, caked in filth that blackened the snow, gave evidence of his day's activities. Behind Sila and Hurd stood her faithful henchmen, the scurrilous Falderrene and the needle-chinned Radulf, both carrying spears. No Perryn on this day. Most worrisome, no Ronila. Where was the poisonous spider who had woven this web? My back itched. Every nerve end quivered as I stretched my senses, but discovered no trace of her.

"Is my brother not bold enough to face me even under truce?" said Osriel, hunched and shivering. His wet hair straggled over his face, and his cloak flapped, revealing his battered state.

"Prince Perryn is destroying the remnants of your warriors, Bastard," said Sila, all serenity. The steel helm hung from her belt had molded her fair hair to her battle-flushed cheeks. "He saw no need to gloat. Though your tongue-block halts his speech, he channels his fury into his sword. Is it not time to call a halt to this slaughter?"

"Few dare challenge me on my own ground," said Osriel, waving a hand that trembled far too much. His scattered magefires snapped and billowed erratically.

Sila knelt and examined one of the votive vessels, passing her hand across its bilious gleam. A disturbance rippled through the earth under my knees. Her companions, even the formidable Hurd, squirmed uncomfortably and backed away. "I was warned that you dabbled in unwholesome arts," she said. "Tell me, has your halfbreed servant visited this place?"

"Pious Valen? Pssh." Osriel sneered. "True magic frightens him. He pretends he is an angel in a world that has no use for childish legends."

"He was to be mine tonight . . . so your brothers promised me. No matter what other terms we agree to, I will hold you to that. Are you not well, Prince?"

Osriel gathered his cloak tight, shaking violently. Three of his magefires flared and winked out. The dancing shadows slowed. "I've had my use of Valen and much good has it bought me," he croaked. "Have him if you will. I assumed you *already* had him. My spy reported his meeting with your monk yesterday."

Sila looked up sharply. "Valen is with Gildas?" *Nicely planted, lord. Make her doubt.*

Osriel shrugged. "These cabalist lunatics are inseparable. As to terms: I retain Renna. You cannot care; no gold remains here. And I'd keep Magora Syne; I've a fondness for the high mountains. I'll be neither *your* prisoner nor my brothers'. My warlords"—the prince began coughing, deep, racking coughs—"must be paroled—"

Sila watched dispassionately. "I think you are in no condition to make demands, Lord Prince."

Falderrene and Radulf stepped out from behind her. *Holy Mother . . .*

Osriel stayed Voushanti with a gesture and held his palm straight out. Green light flared for a moment from his fingers. But another coughing spasm soon had him clutching his chest, and the light winked out—as did the rest of his magefires. As Osriel's foolery collapsed, the livid gleams of the votive vessels paled as well, and one by one, faded into nothing. What did that mean?

I peered anxiously through the murk across the side hill, willing Saverian to stay hidden, worried about Ronila. When would the crone make her move? When I looked back to the pit, Falderrene had raised a yellow magelight to stave off the night.

"The remaining gold—we divide—" Osriel's breaths came harsh and strained between his bouts of coughing. He sagged against the cart that hid his armor.

"Soon, lord," I whispered. "Hold on. Stand up, or she'll pounce."

"I think we've heard enough," said Sila, turning her back on Osriel. Weapons bristled around her. "Falderrene, prepare your silk-bindings. A sick man is no more trustworthy than a healthy one. Hurd, signal—"

Voushanti moved. He embedded his ax in Hurd's arm before the grav could bring his horn from his belt to his lips. Radulf reared back, aiming his spear for Osriel's breast, but Voushanti's sword sliced the devil's neck just below his needle chin. Philo bellowed, *"Avant! Avant!"* and placed his bulk between Osriel and Sila, while Melkire gave chase to Falderrene, cutting him down before he could reach the cart track.

Osriel, unruffled, retreated to the verge of the sinkhole.

Sila, protected by Osriel's bond, watched the brief skirmish calmly. "That was foolish, warrior," she said, picking up Grav Hurd's dropped instrument. "Do you think you can hold back what is to come?" The horn blast pierced the darkened pit.

Of Voushanti's sentries, only three answered Philo's summons, and ten yelling Harrowers raced hard on their heels. The pursuers cut down one of the three survivors before he reached the cart track.

In the distance, torches and magelights and screaming hordes broke through the last defenses of Dashon Ra and flooded the lower slopes. As earth and sky and past and future muddied one another like great rivers joining the sea, I burst from my hiding place, ready to snatch Osriel to safety . . .

The stretched string of the world snapped inside my chest. As Earth itself heaved a great sigh, I stumbled to my knees, shaken by the power of a blood surge more potent than heaven's own wine, more passionate than the drive to love's release. "Now, lord!" I cried, throwing off my cloak so he could see me on the verge above him. "The change!"

Osriel raised his fists. In the space of a thought, midnight boiled from the bowels of Dashon Ra—plumes of purple and green and black that hissed in the snow. Warriors the size of Renna's towers, steeds built to carry them, howling wolves with maws like caverns, and all with eyes of scarlet flame raced across the sky to surround the massed legions of Sila Diaglou and Perryn of Ardra, creating a barrier of terror that no man with half a mind would challenge. From the farthest reaches of Dashon Ra the shouts of battle lust and triumphant carnage transformed into wails of soul-deep terror. Yet these were but Osriel's long-set illusions, designed to trap the Harrowers in the bowl of the mine; the truer horror yet waited.

"Smoke and puffery," said Sila Diaglou, drawing her sword.

Standing at the verge of the black sinkhole, the prince touched the blood leaking from his torn wrists and drew circles around his eyes and sigils on his cheeks and brow. And then he touched his gold armrings and set his fingers glowing, and he knelt and touched the gold-veined earth, gleaming with the Canon's magic. My gards turned to ice. *Mother of night!*

Sila's new-arrived warriors gaped and moaned and let their arms fall slack.

"Grayfin, Harlod, Danc, Skay . . ." From the prince's lips fell a litany of names—Ardran, Evanori, Moriangi—summoning those he had bound to him until the world's end. With each name a splotch of gray slipped out of the pit intermingled with the purple and black clouds, and a shudder ran up my spine. The pall of illusion fell away from the votive vessels, unmasking their livid gleam.

The Harrower soldiers collapsed and buried their faces in their arms. While Voushanti's sword held Sila and a bleeding Hurd at bay, the mardane harangued his own four men to ignore the roiling heavens and to maintain their protective line in front of Osriel. Sila lifted her eyes to the vague gray faces that appeared among the towering phantoms, and for the first time, appeared uneasy. "What have you done here, Prince?"

"He is a bold sorcerer. I like that." A shapeless figure in brown hobbled away from a flash of scarlet light toward Osriel.

"Grandam!" Sila's shock raised the hairs on my neck. She did not expect Ronila here. Which meant the old woman was making her move . . .

"No!" Cursing my distance, I leaped from my high perch, driving my body forward to clear the rock ledges below. I jolted to earth some fifty quercae from the prince and raced toward them across the grotto, yelling, "Take Ronila! Keep her away!"

"And our Bastard is a fine liar." Ronila waved her walking stick.

"Even now the Cartamandua abomination comes to shepherd his prince onto your throne, granddaughter. I think it is time to be quit of this nuisance."

Osriel's men did not understand threats from old women. Ronila nudged an astonished Philo with her stick. Melkire merely shoved her back with the flat of his sword.

The old woman tottered and growled. But then she stepped deftly to one side, raised her walking stick again, and poked one of the surviving sentries so hard he staggered backward. I arrived in time to grab his arm before he toppled Osriel into the sinkhole.

"You will *not* touch my king," I yelled, spreading my arms wide to keep her away from the others, keeping a wary eye on her empty hand. "You will *not* do murder here."

Cackling, Ronila poked her stick at me—only this time, a blade protruded from the end of it, aimed straight at my gut. Voushanti launched himself into me, staggering me sidewise. Fire blossomed deep in my side. The witch growled and yanked the stick away. And then I was falling . . .

Crushed between Voushanti's prone bulk and iron-footed Melkire, I sagged only as far as my knees. Fear and instinct and every urgency of life demanded I stand up again. The old woman's leering face loomed in front of me as huge as the Reaper's Moon, her wild white hair a corona, her bloody blade aimed at my heart. A din of screams and wailing seemed to fill the universe.

Yet Ronila's blade did not strike. Her gleeful cackle twisted into such a wrenching intake of breath as comes only with pain. Shock dulled the feral hatred that glinted in her eyes. And even as I clutched my middle and stumbled to my feet, sure that my stomach and liver must fall out the hole in my side, the old woman wobbled and crumpled. Sila Diaglou stood calmly behind her, her pale hands drenched in blood.

"Child?" the old woman whimpered.

The priestess knelt and touched the blood bubbling from her grandmother's lips as if it were a great curiosity. "Could you not see, old woman?" she said. "I value the sorcerer far more than I value you. He is the new world. You are but the dregs of the old." Then she reached around Ronila's back and yanked out her dagger, wiped the blade on the stained brown robes, and stuck it in the empty sheath at her waist.

All the air in my lungs might have escaped through my punctured flesh.

The priestess proffered me a smile worthy of an angel. "There, my beautiful Dané sorcerer, the hag shall not threaten you again. It is not too late to join me. Malena awaits. Are you not curious—? Ah, the witch has wounded you!" Her smile quickly faded as Hurd, a belt wrapped around his bloody arm, gave her a hand up. "Do you need help?"

"Keep away from me, priestess," I croaked, stepping back. I could not allow thoughts of Malena and what she might or might not carry to distract me. "Your kindness is as bloodstained as your hate."

"And I choose to keep my annoying servant." Osriel stepped from between two of his guards. "This war is ended, priestess. The lighthouse stands. The Canon shall be healed. Command this traitorous grav of Morian, my brother, and the rest to lay down their arms."

"Because you play with corpses?" Sila said scornfully, glancing up at the towering phantoms. "Once I speak to my troops, they will fight—no matter how frightened they are of your ghosts. You have no kingdom, Bastard of Evanore, and no subjects but the dead. My legions will follow me to the netherworld."

"They shall long for the netherworld, lady, when I am done," said Osriel, in such tone as would shudder the most jaded soul. "I give you fair warning. Lay down your arms, or curse the hour you first saw daylight."

"Your threats do not frighten me." And yet, they should. Was that the difference? Was it only those with souls who felt the fear of losing them?

"Then our parley is ended," said Osriel, and turned his back on her.

The prince hissed a command, and scarlet streams of light flowed from the sinkhole. From the gray faces in the clouds erupted a howl that only one who had experienced the doulon hunger would recognize. Or perhaps one who had tasted blood and despair. Of all in that grotto, only Voushanti and I did not stare upward. Terror was written on the faces around us . . . and pity, too.

Melkire pointed to the sky. "Skay," he said. "By the holy angels, it's Skay. And Bergrond. Merciful Iero, what's happening to them?"

"Hurd, form up these whiners," snapped Sila. "I will have Renna by dawn. We shall dismantle this prince limb from limb as we dismantle his house stone from stone."

The gray-faced commander bellowed orders to the ragged Harrowers, kicked and slapped them and got them moving up the cart track. Sila followed. A shoulder touch here, an encouraging word there, an admonishment not to heed the Bastard's illusions, and they moved faster.

Halfway up the sloping track, she looked back and smiled down at me. She waved her hand at Osriel, hunched over the gaping hole. "How can you bear this ghoulish prince, Valen? We need not be rivals. You are the essence of magic; I have rejected and forsworn all such power. You honor all gods; I acknowledge none. You care for humankind and the long-lived; I despise them all. You yearn for decadent pleasure; I need none of it. I am death, as is this prince of yours, while you, Valen, are life itself—more than any cold Danae. Come with me, and I will give you a world cleansed and purified. You can change its face forever, giving every man and woman the chance to wear silk or work spells or dance on the solstice." No matter her smile, her eyes chilled even so bitter a night.

"I do not argue with your vision, lady," I called up to her, "but that you slaughter children and destroy all that is holy and good to create it. There must be another way. I'll have no part of you."

"So be it." She shrugged and ran after her troops.

"Voushanti, you'll see to Valen?" said the prince. His voice sounded hollow, as if he walked yet another plane, or as if he had fallen into the sinkhole after his blood. He knelt beside the dark shaft, the scarlet streams of enchantment giving his pale skin a ruddy cast to match the blood marks he'd drawn. Yet Sila's words prodded me to move. Osriel was not at all like her.

"Lord Prince, don't do this," I said, limping across the drifted snow to his side. "Not before you tell me what you felt here this day. Not until you tell me why I sense no more hatred from these lost souls that only one day ago cried out for vengeance."

Despair and grief stared out at me from my king's bleak face. "Because I bled with them. Because I remembered them, as I promised when I took them captive. Because I knew their names." He dropped his eyes to the roiling pit. "And now I must command them to go forth and live and die an eternal death for me."

"Your very nature rebels at this crime," I said softly. "Let them go."

"I cannot."

I knelt beside the bottomless hole that stank of death and corruption. "Think of the day we rode down from Renna, when you walked among your people who had been burnt out by the Harrowers. They had nothing before you arrived, and no more when you left save your care and your promise of hope. With but those few words from you, they stood straight and were able to do for themselves. You have given everything for love of these people and this land, and a lover does not torment his beloved. Use the power that has been given you. Let them go."

"You have brought me no other answer, Valen."

"Because it has lived inside you all this time, lord. Behind a mask. Hope is enough."

He raked his fingers through his dark hair. "I would condemn us all."

"Then we will die with love," said a soft voice behind us. "And honor. And faithfulness. But I don't believe we will die. I watched these Harrowers just now, and they are frightened, too, misled by a glamor—despair masquerading as hope. You are their king, Osriel of Evanore. Save them."

When Elene knelt beside him, it was almost as if I heard the earth heave another great sigh. Or perhaps that was only me, watching surprise and weariness unmask his love at last.

Chapter 35

Osriel stood beside the sinkhole and called on those he had named to attend him. And so did every one of the gray phantoms in the cloud turn their empty eyes toward him. How he bore the cold weight of their attention, I could not imagine, for when I, by chance, met the gaze of only one, it placed a burden of lead and earth upon my shoulders.

The prince removed his gold armrings and held them in the scarlet light, and the phantoms' eyes burned red and gold, so one could believe they listened. "Hear my commands and obey," he cried. "I charge you, by the bond I hold, find all who bear arms on this field of woe—your brothers in war, whole or wounded—and speak to each soul what you know of death and life. And at the ending, give this message: A new reign of law and justice shall come to Navronne with this new year. Do this, and I count your service to me ended. Duty done, make your way through the world as you will and find those whom you would comfort at your parting from earthly life, and when the sun touches the sky, be gone to your proper fate. *Perficiimus.*"

The gray phantoms vanished from behind the cloud warriors, and an unsettling energy infused the air and land, like the building tensions of a thunderstorm. All the anger and confusion I had felt here was turned to eagerness. To hunting. Never had I been so glad I did not bear a blade. I did not want to hear what they would speak. I'd seen and heard enough of death and life.

Voushanti knelt at Osriel's feet and spoke what none of us could hear. Osriel held out his hand. Voushanti kissed it, then handed over his sword and ax. And then the mardane turned to me, expressionless. I nodded, and he walked out of the pit and into the night. I did not think we would see him ever again.

Osriel knelt at the pit, his eyes closed as if he could hear his messengers. Elene kept vigil with him, her hand upon his shoulder. Philo formed up his three comrades at the foot of the cart track, weapons laid on the ground at their feet. The light of the votive vessels dimmed and faded. And so we awaited the end of the world.

Accounts differ about what happened on that winter solstice. Some say Iero's angels visited the homes of the dead all over the kingdom and brought them heaven's solace, while the Adversary himself visited wrath upon Sila Diaglou's legions, showing them the paths of hell and sending them home repentant.

Some say the Danae brought forth Eodward's Pretender, another young prince fostered in Danae realms. The guardians left him in the place of Osriel the Bastard, who had made one too many bargains with Magrog the Tormentor and was carried off to the netherworld. That this Pretender named himself *Osriel* was only to avoid the tricky business of Eodward's will. Two copies of that document came to light with the new year, both proclaiming Eodward's youngest son King of Navronne. All agreed that the first day of that winter dawned with a hope Navronne had not felt in living memory.

I know only what I saw.

When Osriel turned away from his enchantments, exhausted and at peace, Elene placed his hand upon her belly and whispered in his ear. It was the right time, when life displayed its truest mingling of joy and grief. For, of course, he had promised his firstborn to the Danae, and he could not break such fragile alliance as might come from this night's work. They clung to each other for a while; then he donned his armor and became Navronne's king, and Elene donned her fairest courage and became Navronne's queen.

I saw no more than that. Saverian found me slumped in the corner of the grotto, trying to find my way back to Aeginea, and offered to sew up the great hole in me instead. Once assured that the blood soaking her garments was soldiers' blood, not hers, I mumbled that my wound would surely heal of itself, and that her stitches would make my fine sea grass look like brambles, and that I had urgent matters to attend if I could just remember what they were. But indeed I came near collapsing on her boots from the great gouts of blood that would not stop oozing, though I felt shamed when I considered how Osriel had bled near a sun's turning and was yet spinning out enchantments and traipsing off to meet with his brother Bayard.

Evidently the prince persuaded Bayard to round up the hardened elements of the Harrower legions and Perryn's men, while Renna's household garrison and the survivors of Boedec's and Zurina's legions gathered the Evanori dead for proper rites on the next day. After what Bayard's men had seen happening in the sky over Dashon Ra that night, they were quite compliant. Many had been visited by the spirits of friends or brothers and had come to believe that Osriel had sent these spirits as a warning and a mercy to keep faith—as, indeed, he had. But I didn't see any of that. Saverian had taken me in hand.

"I must go back," I said thickly. It was very awkward after the physician had just spent most of an hour with her hands in my blood and flesh, and had given me some lovely potion to dull the wicked fire in my side.

"I suppose the ceilings are coming down on you again," she said, emptying yet another basin of bloody water down her drainpipe.

"Not too awful as yet. No, it's Kol." As sense returned, the remembrance of Tuari's impending judgment had me frantic.

She set her basin carefully on her table, as I slid my feet to the floor and put some weight on them to see if my legs would hold me up. "They're still dancing, aren't they?" she said.

"Until dawn. I doubt I'll be allowed anywhere close. Kol and Stian are already at risk of ruin for bringing me to the Canon." There was also the matter of Kennet. For all the Danae knew, I had killed him. I had to explain. Fear more than blood loss threatened to buckle my knees.

"Go, then," she said. "I'll be here if ever you choose to return to Renna."

As I touched her narrow face, drawing her worry into a rueful smile, a cheerful determination captured my soul. "None shall keep me away. There are things that even Renna's powerful house mage has yet to learn," I said, grinning at the thought. "I do think the gods intend me to see to her instruction."

I slogged back up the rock gate stair to Dashon Ra as fast as I could, holding my bandaged side. Saverian had come up with another cloak—I seemed to be shedding them like snakeskins—and chausses, so I was able to walk unremarked through the grisly business of battle's aftermath. The snow fell gently now, laying a soft blanket on the cold faces of the dead. The waning night yet squirmed and wriggled uncomfortably, and I imagined souls passing on their missions of warning and mercy.

Once out on the hillside, I thought to shift, but my steps were halted by two weary veterans hauling a bloodstained cart loaded with weapons and armor. "I've heard Boedec had her, then lost her," said one. "She can slip through a man's fingers."

My ears pricked, and I turned to listen.

"Harrowers turned on her," said the other man. "Ran her off. I'd love to get my hands on her—slaughtered my whole village, she did."

Gods, Sila was still loose! I pushed past them and ran down the slope, touched earth, and poured in magic. Only one other halfbreed Dané walked Dashon Ra.

She was hiding in the dry bed of the leat. I rested my forearms on the rim of the great trough and peered over the side. "Ah, priestess, what are we to do with you?"

"These whisperings are like to drive me mad," she said, sitting up and shuddering as she glanced into the unsettled sky. "I'm glad for human company. Or at least mostly human. You can kill me if you want. Better you than one who holds grudges, which seems to be everyone. Perhaps before you do it, you could explain to me what went wrong. I was ready to take him down. We would have taken Renna by midday. Then, all of a sudden, my warriors began weeping and mumbling. Even the commanders. No one would listen to me."

"Osriel held a more powerful weapon." I climbed up the great sluiceway and perched on the rim. "I don't want to kill you. I think I've given up killing altogether. Never was very good at it. Neither can I allow you to go free. I'd like you to understand what you've done . . . and what was done to you . . . and why Osriel is nothing like you . . . but I don't know enough words to explain it."

She sighed and brushed dirt from her face. "I'm too tired to listen. Besides, you'll not change my beliefs. This world is corrupt beyond saving. The universe cares naught for our human politics. It demands purity. Plague and pestilence will accomplish the cleansing I could not. Just more slowly and with more pain."

"You're wrong," I said. From our vantage I could see the fields of wounded and dead and those who tended them. "But clearly you must be judged by wiser heads than mine. Two realms have claim to your punishment, and I think . . . Will you come with me?" I jumped down from the trough and offered my hand.

She took it and jumped down beside me. "Nothing better to do at present."

I threw off my garments and gathered my thoughts and memories. We walked back toward the gully. I listened for music as we climbed the rocky parapet . . . .

... and by the time we reached the top, the cries of wounded soldiers had become the music of a single vielle, its strings picking out a pavane. The dancers were paired, one lifting the other or lowering, closing or separating but always touching, entwining their bodies in a single expression of grace, never stopping, as the music never stopped in its round. As far as we could see across the grassy hillside, the lines of sapphire, azure, and lapis flowed and swirled and bent, but never broke. Kol and Thokki danced the Center, and if grace and strength could speak of heaven, then their partnering was divine.

Sila's face grew still. Stunned. "What is this?" she whispered.

The music swelled as it began another round, and slowly, one by one around the circles, the partners held their last position, then settled to the ground until only Kol and Thokki danced. He lifted her above his head, her arms and back and legs one smooth curve. Then Kol settled into an *allavé* with his own back straight and his leg a perfect line with it, and Thokki held above him. And then did the first light of dawn fall on them and the music fade.

"This is what you would destroy," I said, tears pricking my eyes.

She did not respond. Did not speak at all, as the Danae embraced and bowed and vanished, one by one, into the morning. "Come," I said. "We can go back now."

But a small knot of Danae gathered atop the hill, and as I suspected would happen, several more were waiting for us by the time we climbed down the rocks. Sila was strong but not strong enough to resist three determined Danae. I did not run. "It is time for judgment," I said.

Tuari and Nysse and ten more of the long-lived stood at the Center. Kol, Stian, and Thokki stood before them. They paused in their discussion, and all heads turned as we were brought up the hill.

"In the Canon, Tuari Archon," I said, bowing. "I have brought you the hand of the Scourge. She is of our kind, but was nurtured in Ronila's bitterness . . ."

The trial was long and required much discussion and argument. Such punishments as were to be meted out could not be Tuari's decision alone.

I was cleared of Kennet's murder. Ulfin knew that neither Kennet nor I had possessed a knife, and he had seen Ronila throw herself on Kennet as he himself brought Thokki to the pond.

For their part in bringing me to the Canon, Stian and Thokki were condemned to beast form for a gyre—a full term of the seasons. It was a bitter punishment and dangerous, lest some accident befall or some rash hunter fail to recognize them, but mild for the offense. The judges said they were brought into the conspiracy by their love for Kol and not of their own part, and indeed a marvel and no harm had come of my presence at the Canon.

But Kol was judged to have given long thought to his misdeed. He had begun my training and had failed to bring the issue of my talents to the archon. He had defied every precept of the Law and had taken fully on himself the risk of breaking the Canon. At noontide on the following day, he would be prisoned in his sianou, bound forever to slow fading with myrtle and hyssop. They accepted no plea from Stian to trade punishments with his son, no argument that Kol's dancing was unmatched in any season. And the marvel of the Well's recovery could not mitigate both Stian's punishment and Kol's.

Kol accepted the judgment without argument. "I did as was necessary," he said. "I saw no other way. I would do it again." Though many of the ten were uncomfortable with his sentencing, his own words condemned him.

"I can find your lost sianous, Tuari Archon," I pleaded. "I can find the Plain. I just need time." But they believed in swift judgment and would not yield. One look from Kol closed off further protests. He would not have me prisoned as well.

Sila Diaglou they condemned to beast form for as long as she might live. She said nothing. I did not know if she was yet mesmerized by the Canon or believed she was lost in dream. When they asked her what form she would prefer, she asked only that it not be vermin and that it be done right away.

Tuari took her. As she stood waiting to hear what they would do, he wrapped his arms about her from behind and whispered, "Do not be afraid." Before I could blink, both bodies had vanished, and a sparrow fluttered along the ground as if its wings were broken. Moments later and Tuari was back, kneeling beside the bird. He nudged it with his finger, and startled, it flew to a nearby rock. I wanted to watch her as she tried her wings, but a flurry of birds rose from the ground, wheeled, and vanished into the morning, leaving none behind.

The Danae dispersed, one and then the other. As a courtesy to Stian, they would not execute Stian and Thokki's punishments until Kol's was done. The three of them were taken away and I was left alone at the Center, weary and sick at heart.

At nightfall, I took Philo and a cadre of men to Gillarine to take custody of Gildas. Evidently the doulon hunger already burned his flesh. I did not stay to hear his pained sobbing and curses as they shackled him for the short journey to Renna's dungeon, but hurried to the lighthouse door. "Archangel!" I said, infusing the word with magic.

In three heartbeats, the door flew open. "Brother!" The boy peered outside as if to see if the moon had fallen or the earth cracked. The sheer joy that dawned on his young face warmed even such a cold night.

As I told him briefly of Osriel's great magic, and how we had hopes that my peculiar combination of talents might help set the weather back to rights, he served me a small cup of ale, taking as much pride in his hospitality as a new householder. He offered me cheese and dried figs, as well, which reminded me how dreadfully long it had been since I had eaten anything. My aching side and pierced hand had stolen my appetite.

"Do you think the brothers will come back to Gillarine now?" he asked, hesitant. "I can do very well here for as long as needed. But if they were to come . . . there would be singing . . . and they might raise the bells again. The quiet . . . I don't mind it, but . . ."

"I'm sure they'll come back. But you will always be the Scholar. The king will have it no other way." I stood to go. "Iero's grace, Scholar."

"Iero's grace . . . Valen. I don't suppose you'll be coming back here to take vows."

I laughed and looked askance at my gards. "I think I've vows enough for three lifetimes. But if you've matters to discuss with me, you can always go to the font, yes? See if I'm at home?"

He giggled like a boy again and thought that was very fine, and said he would read more in the book of Danae lore and discuss it with me to see if it was accurate. "If not, then I might write a new book that will tell the truth of Danae."

I left him then and jogged across the cloister garth to meet Philo and his prisoner.

"Brother Valen!" Jullian's call turned me around when I was scarcely past the font.

The breathless young scholar stood atop the alley rubble. "I forgot. Do you want to take the book?"

"It served me well, Jullian, and bless you forever for finding it, but you know it's of no use—"

"Not the book about the doulon, but your grandfather's book— the book of maps." He held out a square volume, bound in brown leather, the very book that had gained me admittance into the lighthouse cabal. "I thought you might have use for it."

"Saints and angels! Gildas brought it!" I had no way to carry it with me or keep it safe, but to use it . . . "Quickly, let's get back to the light."

Gildas sweated and his guards cooled their heels while I sat in the lighthouse doorway and paged through the book to find what I needed—a wholly unremarkable fiché, little more than a line drawing without colors or gold leaf or any other elaboration. One smiling aingerou lurked in a corner. Janus had scattered five rosettes across the rough outline of Navronne. Touch a finger to one of the rosettes and a symbol appeared beside it—one displayed the symbol for a mountain, one for a sea, one for a water feature such as a well, and one showed a spiral that Janus had called the Center, before I understood what that meant.

I touched the fifth rosette, the one drawn in the northern half of the map between the arms of a divided river, unmasking a symbol I had not recognized until now. Surely the tiny prongbuck marked the Plain.

Heart swelling with excitement, I touched the aingerou, drew my finger from the Well to the Plain, and poured magic into the enchanted page. In my mind appeared a certain route—a path of roads and fields, hills and valleys, images so vivid that I could use them to find a destination for a shift—a birthday gift from my Cartamandua father.

"The gods ease your pain, madman," I whispered as I closed the book and gave it to the boy for safekeeping. "I'll tell you all about it when this is over."

At noontide on the next day, when they brought Kol to Evaldamon for prisoning, I was waiting for them. Nysse, as always, stood at the archon's side, and ten other Danae had come to stand as witnesses. Kol, hands and feet bound with braided vines, gazed out onto the sea—deep green on this day beneath the winter sun. My uncle's proud face displayed no fear, though a Dané dropped a pile of fragrant green myrtle boughs and arm-length stems of dried hyssop only a few steps away. Stian and Thokki sat atop the cliffs under guard.

"Tuari Archon, I beg hearing," I called. "I have brought you that which must reverse this judgment."

When Kol glanced my way, I bowed. He nodded without expression and returned his eyes to the sea.

"What evidence can change what is confessed?" said Tuari.

"On the solstice, you said that if I could return the Plain to the Canon, you would judge these transgressions worthy, did you not, Archon? And worthy deeds merit no punishment."

Tuari's rust-colored hair was wreathed on this day with holly leaves. "I said this, but thou wert incapable."

"On this day, I am capable. Send whomever you will to judge me."

After some discussion, it was decided that Nysse and Ulfin would verify my claim, and that Kol's imprisonment would be delayed until our return. To the fascination of the Danae, I knelt and laid my palms on the earth. The route unrolled in my mind like a scroll of parchment, and I recalled the shore of the small lake until I could smell the marshland and hear the birds and the lap of the wavelets. "This way," I said, and we made the first shift into Morian, retracing the route I had worked out from Janus's map over a very long night.

In a matter of an hour, we stood in a thick winter fog on an island between the forks of a mighty river. I stepped along a long-faded silver trace and described the dancer's astonishing leaps and his intricate footwork. And soon Nysse herself danced a kiran, echoing Llio's last.

"It is the Plain, Tuari Archon," she said when we returned to Evaldamon. "I can return there at any time. With work, it shall live in our memory as clearly as the Well." Ulfin vouched for all she claimed.

And so were my uncle and grandsire and merry Thokki set free to dance again in Aeginea.

"So why art thou heartsore, *rejongai*?" said Kol, as the two of us strolled down the strand that evening at sunset. "Didst thou expect some other marvel than these thou hast described to me? The world is changing. And thou art fully of the long-lived and fully of the human kind. That is not at all usual. In the coming seasons thou shalt restore the Canon."

"I feel knob-swattled," I said, rubbing the wound in my side that ached more than it should. "Neither here nor there. The prince needs a pureblood adviser and has asked me to stay with him . . . and I desire greatly to do what I can to help him and teach him . . . but I want to be here and learn . . . and I need to travel and begin to reclaim what we've lost . . . and then, there is a woman . . . human . . . very human . . ."

Kol halted and put a hand on my shoulder. "Sleep, Valen. When thou art . . . knob-swattled . . . it is the call to sleep. Take thy season, and thou shalt wake clear and purposeful. It is our way. Necessary. No lesson is more worth the teaching. Renew thyself, that thy work shall be worthy."

"Thank you, vayar."

"Address me as Kol, *rejongai*. We get on well."

PART FIVE

God's Holy Book

Chapter 36

The drips and splats, dribbles and trickles have annoyed me for days. Pesky noises. I want to hear words, not plops and spatters. So easy to forget words when I nestle in the deeps close to the fire or flow through my clean and healing channels to mind the roots. Words land on my surface like pebbles and sink down to where I sleep, nudging me to wakefulness. I curl around them, cherish them, and comprehend matters that have naught to do with seeds or roots or beasts.

It is the woman comes most to bring me words. "The king has taken up residence in Palinur. Prince Bayard swore allegiance in the Temple District, and Osriel named him Defender of Navronne. He left immediately and is to live on his ships. Prince Perryn is branded a traitor on his forehead and is exiled in Bayard's service. The people do not know that Bayard is forbidden to set foot on Navron soil again. But his children shall be fostered in Evanore, while Perryn's are married off to foreign lords. Bayard is satisfied. Riel says he might find use for this onetime brother of yours—Max—who negotiated all these matters.

"The change in Riel is astounding. In these few short weeks, he has had no flare of the saccheria. No cough. No limp. No fever. Whether his pain is truly gone or just so much lessened that his dead nerves cannot feel it, I find myself weeping like a sentimental granny to see him ruddy-cheeked and able to ride and work and love his mooning wife. You will think me entirely changed.

"Those people not touched by the solstice magic are coming slowly to understand that he is not as they believed. It will take time and work, but Riel's peace—in the kingdom and within himself—are his best heralds."

I laughed to hear this and dived down to the earth fires and embraced them. My instincts had told me true: The land heals the righteous king.

Comes another day: "The queen blossoms, though not without sadness. The child will arrive with the summer. Two years Nysse Archon will give them together. But kings' children are often fostered, and unlike Caedmon, Riel and Elene will get to see their little one often as he grows. And yes, I know it is *he*, though I've not told them. And another secret, only for you, the child is also a she . . . for it seems our king got twins upon his beloved. Which will be firstborn and have to go, and which will dawdle and get to stay at home? Perhaps you can persuade Nysse to allow them to trade places from time to time! With Jullian as their tutor, they will learn. With you as their sworn guardian, they will laugh and thrive."

Joy and grief forever mingled. Ever will I give my friends what they need of me.

"Gildas was hanged yesterday . . ."

Justice. But I do not rejoice in ending life.

Did I make a child with Sila's handmaid? I will have to know before it breathes. No child of mine will suckle on hate.

"Bright news this day, dear Valen: The monks have come home to Gillarine. Brother Sebastian is named abbot. They send their prayers for you. They don't seem to realize what an unlikely messenger I am, who puts no faith in gods or prayers. I am helping Brother Anselm set up his new infirmary, and so they allow me to stay in the guesthouse despite my sex. They would like it better were I a married woman. And I would like—

"You must understand, Valen, I'm neither ashamed of my virgin state *nor* overprotective of it. Can you truly hear me? I must not believe it, for I would never say such a thing in front of you. In truth, I've never understood what men and women found together. My parents . . ." She spoke of a pureblood mother who came to regret the life she had given up for love, and a warlord father who resented that his wife held power he could not master. They grew apart and disliked the reminder of their connection in their daughter. A harsh and loveless lesson they taught. ". . . but at least I was clever enough to bury myself in books, not the doulon!

"Ah, friend, sometimes I think I hear you laughing as the ice melt dribbles into your pool—into you. Even if you are truly here, I suppose you sleep. Rest well, Valen. Riel needs you. The world needs you. And I . . . I will be pleased to see you and argue about gods and prayers, souls and immortal life."

She touched me that day—dipped her hand in the pool, and I burned with such fire at the remembrance of her hands that the trees on the ridge will be full green well before the spring change.

The dancer comes, too. He does not speak to me with words, but with leaps and spins and everlasting grace. He charges my dreams with glory, and my lands with the health and nurturing that I can only begin to provide. I feel the shifting of the air as he drives his spirit upward, and I yearn for my body that I can begin to learn how he does it.

The sun warms me on this day, and I feel lazy and still. And lonely. Yet, though the snows lie deep upon the mountains, the sap rises in the trees. I will sleep again another night or three or seven, but spring shall soon fill my loins and call me to the dance, and I shall have my way with living. *Teneo!*